SAINTS AND SINNERS

BOOKS 1-3

JOHN BROUGHTON

Copyright (C) 2024 John Broughton

Layout design and Copyright (C) 2024 by Next Chapter

Published 2024 by Next Chapter

This book is a work of fiction. Names, characters, places, and incidents are the product of the author's imagination or are used fictitiously. Any resemblance to actual events, locales, or persons, living or dead, is purely coincidental.

All rights reserved. No part of this book may be reproduced or transmitted in any form or by any means, electronic or mechanical, including photocopying, recording, or by any information storage and retrieval system, without the author's permission.

SAINTS AND SINNERS

SAINTS AND SINNERS BOOK 1

GLOSSARY

Anglo-Saxon names and their modern equivalents in order of appearance:

Bryn Alyn: Iron Age hill fort, Denbighshire, North Wales
Mierce: Mercia, Anglo-Saxon kingdom centring on the Trent valley (Midlands of England)
Powys: Welsh kingdom
Tame Weorth: Tamworth, capital of Mercia
Pengwern: Capital of 7thC. Powys, exact location unknown today
Gwylog ap Beli: King of Powys (born ?655, died 725)
Wealisc: The Welsh
Trente: River Trent
Lindisfarona: The folk of Lindsey
Lindissi: Lindsey
Northanhymbra: Northumbria
Estseaxna: East Saxons
Bretwaldas: King of all Angle-land, supreme ruler over all the Anglo-Saxon kingdoms
Beardan: Bardney, Lincolnshire
Hwicca: Anglo-Saxon kingdom, covering Gloucestershire, Worcestershire, part of Warwickshire
Gegnesburh: Gainsborough, Lincolnshire
Lindcolne: Lincoln, Lincolnshire
Withma: River Witham
Suthanhymbra: Southumbria, the easterly part of North Mercia
Newerche: Newark, Nottinghamshire
Snotingham: Nottingham
Northworthig: Derby
Woercs-worth: Wirksworth, South Yorkshire
Hymbre: River Humber
Loidis: Leeds, Yorkshire
Elmet: Brittonic kingdom, modern Peak District and parts of Yorkshire
Elmetsaete: The folk of Elmet
Saefern: River Severn
Scheth: River Sheaf
Hreapandune: Repton, Derbyshire
Heyholand: High Hoyland, Yorkshire
Cezeburgh: Kexbrough, Yorkshire
Wacanfeld: Wakefield, Yorkshire
Estdeping: Market Deeping, Lincolnshire Fens
Weolud: River Welland
Norðsae: North Sea
Cruwland: Crowland, Lincolnshire Fens

Nen: River Nene
Witentreu: West Shropshire area. In disuse, a name continuing to this day in Whittery Wood
Cyricbyrig: Chirbury, Shropshire
Wealas: Wales
Waelheal: Anglo-Saxon version of Valhalla
Lunden: London
Weala-denu: Saffron Walden
Licidfelth: Lichfield, Staffordshire, site of the most important see in Mercia
Akeman: Street A major Roman road linking Watling Street with the Fosse Way
Medeshamstede: Peterborough, Cambridgeshire
Wockingas: Woking, Surrey
Cantwaraburh: Canterbury, Kent
Hludoham: Lowdham, Nottinghamshire
Dummoc: Walton Castle, Suffolk, seat of the Est Anglia Church
Deope: River Deben
Grantebrycge: Cambridge
Holbece: Holbeach, Lincolnshire Fens
Wintan-ceastre: Winchester, Hampshire
Fyrdmen: Anglo-Saxon freemen mobilized for the army
Hlydanford: Lydford, Devon
Tamur: River Tamar
Tantun: Taunton, Somerset
Langeberga: Langport, Somerset
Sumorsaete: Somerset
Perryt: River Parrett
Hamwic: Southampton
Salwic: Droitwich Spa, Worcs.
Stanford: Stamford, Lincolnshire
Sunnendaeg: Sunday
Saeterdaeg: Saturday
Couentre: Coventry, Warwickshire
scir: shire
Castra: Weogernensis Worcester

KINGDOM OF MERCIA
ca. 700AD

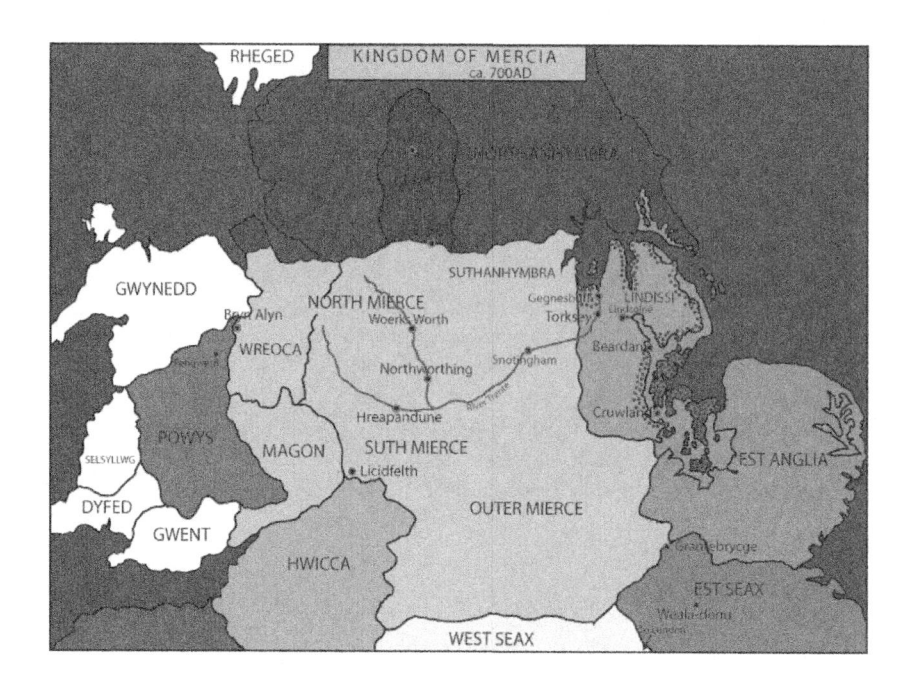

ONE

Bryn Alyn, North-west Mierce, 697AD

Lit by the thinning arc of the sinking sun, Aethelbald prowled the ramparts of Bryn Alyn. To his fancy, the last red sliver resembled a mouth turned down, bathing him in melancholic light. The feeble glow suited his sombre mood and that of his comrade, Guthlac, pacing at his side. Weeks of enforced idleness and futile vigilance stoked their despondency, monotony gnawing at their youthful exuberance. Another two months of this torture to endure – if only Wealisc insurgents would resume their raids on Mierce! Silent in bored comradeship, they paused to lounge against the wooden parapet, until, heartbeat quickening, Aethelbald seized the arm of his companion: the blare of a horn!

Had the men of Powys summoned the courage to start an assault? At twilight? Sheer folly! The mysterious folk who had built this fortress at the dawn of Time had chosen the west-facing limestone cliff of Caer Alyn as a buttress to repel invaders. It meant a daylight attack was daunting, but only extreme foolhardiness might account for an onslaught in the gloom. In any case, as Guthlac pointed out, the strident note had resounded from the east.

Hurtling down from the parapet, Aethelbald halted, planting feet apart and arms folded, while the guards swung open the huge oak gates. In seconds, Guthlac joined him to witness the scouting party, out since noon, canter into the enclosure. Their leader, a half-blinded thegn who had fought with Guthlac's father at the Battle of the Trente, dismounted and fixed his sighted eye on the commander.

"Lord, we came upon a rider in the forest watering his horse at the brook by Rhydtalog. He sought not to flee but asked to be led to you and Lord Guthlac. He spoke your names and claims to bring a message."

An imperious wave of the hand made the horsemen part their animals to reveal a dark-haired, swarthy individual astride a bay mare. The features of Aethelbald clouded, "A Briton! Am I surrounded by dolts? A spy of Gwylog ap Beli spins a tale for witless fools to swallow…seize him! Haul him down and flay the truth out of him!"

Six of the party, prepared to haul the stranger from his mount, leapt off their horses.

"Stay!" Guthlac glared around the men, stilled at his command. Raising his hands in a gesture of apology to Aethelbald, his leader and closest friend, he said, "Let us hear what the Briton has to say for himself."

Heedless of the hostile scowls and muttered threats directed at him, unruffled, the newcomer addressed them in their own Anglian tongue.

"Lord, I am indeed a Briton, my forefathers are of the Lindisfarona not of the Wealisc. I travel from Lindissi bearing a message."

"Out with it then!" Aethelbald's patience, eroded by inactivity, creaked like thin ice.

The messenger shook his head. He reached for his sword and the warriors surrounding him did likewise, only for the Briton to unhook the weapon and drop it, his seax followed.

"The message is for your ears only," he indicated Aethelbald and Guthlac, lifted his chin in defiance and added, "and for none other."

Within the storeroom adapted to plan sallies from the stronghold, hands flat on the chart-covered table, Aethelbald leant forward, curiosity aroused.

"What's so urgent to make a man ride two score leagues and more?"

The messenger delved deep inside his tunic and pulled forth a heavy ring, handing it to the Miercian ealdorman. Aethelbald turned the band in his palm and stared at the roundel wrought with a fine-scrolled edge. The raised circle contained alternate strips of red and yellow gold – eight red and yellow stripes: the emblem of Northanhymbra. Overlaying them, embossed in white gold, shone the letter *O*.

"I'm sure this ring graced our former queen, Osthryth. How came you by it?" asked Aethelbald, passing it to Guthlac whose whistle betrayed awe and admiration for the lustrous jewel.

"Entrusted to me in secrecy by her hand, Lord, that you should know this message reaches you in good faith from the Lady herself."

The news-bearer held up his hand in refusal when Guthlac tried to give back the ring, "My instructions are to leave it in your safe-keeping, Lord."

Guthlac passed it back to his leader who turned it in his hand once more admiring how the light caught its facets and played across the different coloured gold.

'I'll keep it willingly. One day, beautiful objects like this will be mine by rights.'

Back to matters in hand. The puzzled expression of Guthlac mirrored his own.

"What of your message?"

"Nought but a summons, Lord. Make all haste to Beardan!"

"Is all?"

"Ay, Lord."

"Will you accompany us there?"

The messenger shook his head, "I fear not, for I have another aerende. I leave at dawn."

"Whither are you bound?"

"...I must not say!"

"Sup with us tonight, friend," Aethelbald said. "Go, tend your horse, rest before joining us in the hall at table."

When the door closed, Aethelbald took the ring and contemplating it, said, "I loathe riddles! At board, we'll ply the Briton with ale and loosen his tongue. By the gods, Guthlac, there's mischief afoot! I may yet skin the cur alive for I swear I'll get the truth out of him!"

When Guthlac was a princeling of Miercian royal descent he

upped and left home, tired of studying, to form a war band. He paid for their arms from his own purse. He led them to Mierce's troubled borderlands where he slaughtered, plundered and raped without mercy until King Aethelred ordered him to form a garrison at Bryn Alyn under the command of the teenaged Aethelbald, a kinsman also of royal descent. The leonine head and tall well-muscled build of Æthelbald belied his youthfulness. Yet, he proved more ruthless in battle than Guthlac. Away from fighting, the two young men shared a love of heavy drinking and wenching, thus they forged a deep friendship that would endure a lifetime.

An hour later, a serving woman ladled steaming white carrot and onion stew into bowls set before the ealdormen. The chair beside Aethelbald stood empty.

"What do you mean, he left?"

His bellow caused the servant to start and slop scalding liquid over her lord's hand.

"Whore! Get out of my sight!"

The warrior struck out sending the ladle clattering to the floor and leaving a red weal on the skin of the offending arm.

"Hold!" Guthlac leapt up and caught the weeping serving maid, stroking her wet cheek before bending to pick up the utensil. "Our commander meant no harm, he is overwrought," he said, grinning into her face and handing back the implement, "come! I beseech you, my stomach is that of a ravening wolf!"

She rewarded his good looks and gentle mock howl close to her ear with a feeble smile and a brimming bowl of stew.

The wench forgotten, Aethelbald stared at the warrior who had failed to fetch the messenger to table.

"Left?" he repeated.

"Ay, Lord. The men at the gate say he came straight from your quarters after delivering his message, gathered up his weapons, took his horse and rode out into the night."

"Wolves devour him! Wights snatch his soul and carry it to Hell!"

The ealdorman dismissed the man and turned to Guthlac. "He'd leave at dawn, the cur said. He played us for a fool! It will be well for the Briton our paths never cross. What do you make of it?"

Guthlac tore at a piece of bread and dipped it in his stew,

"The message is vouched by the ring," his next words came muffled by food, "the messenger doubted our intentions…and he was right!"

Aethelbald frowned, considering their situation, "You're right, of course. Our thegns can hold the fortress with Gwylog holed up in his den at Pengwern–"

"But what of our King?" Guthlac asked. "Should the Wealisc shrug off their lethargy and reave the farmsteads of Mierce, Aethelred will skewer our heads on stakes for leaving our post."

"Powys, our spies inform us, turns its eyes westward where the men of Gwynedd play them at their own game of plunder and rape, of skirmish and ravages. That is why, my dull-witted friend, these eastern borderlands are as still as a graveyard."

Guthlac laughed, "A mournful place befitting a headless ealdorman seems excuse enough to leave!"

"Agreed then, *we* set off at dawn!" Aethelbald clapped his comrade on the back and poured more ale for them both, adding half under his breath, so only Guthlac caught his words, "though no-one must know whitherward."

At daybreak, with care for their horses legs, they picked their way down over the rutted, slippery limestone pavement fringing the summit of Bryn Alyn. Aethelbald gazed around, pleased to be leaving the joyless outpost behind but at the same time overawed by its wild beauty. To the north, the Irish Sea reflected the rosy hue of the rising sun while overhead, the towering song of the skylark accompanied them. His eyes roved to the west to the Clwydian Hills where he could almost imagine the bald pate of Moel Fama nodding a sullen farewell.

Deep along a forest trail, riding side by side, Guthlac glanced at the fierce countenance of his comrade, and was startled to meet an intense stare.

"What?"

"Here, we can talk. There are no ears to seize on careless words."

"Well?"

"The loyalty of our queen lay ever with her homeland and not with Aethelred. Too much blood spilt between Northanhymbra and Mierce to hope their wedding might heal old wounds."

"Ay, added to her father's defeat at the Trente with her brother slain…"

A jay, in a pink and blue flash, burst from a blackthorn bush and startled their horses. Aethelbald cursed and soothed his skittery beast before continuing.

"We must be wary, Guthlac, I sense a plot. At the centre is Beardan and the nun, our erstwhile queen."

"A plot?"

The face of Guthlac, troubled now, brought a wry smile to Aethelbald's lips. His friend's childlike sincerity bordered on ingenuity. He would trust him with his life but not if any threat involved deceit.

"It might not be a coincidence," he flicked a hand at a bothersome horsefly, "the kingdom of the Hwicca preoccupies Aethelred. Remember, their King Oshere is kinsman to Osthryth."

Wordless, they rode on but not in silence, the air laden with buzzing insects and birdsong until Guthlac asked, "Ay, but where do we fit into this *supposed* plot?"

"What do we have in common apart from bedding comely wenches and supping ale?"

"We're both warriors?"

Aethelbald snorted, "Ay, and each has two arms and two legs for that matter! Think on, we're both sons of two of the mightiest men in the north of our kingdom!"

"So?"

"So? *So!* By Thunor's anvil, Guthlac! Is there not a grain of guile in yon pretty maid's head of yours? If Osthryth wishes to weaken Aethelred in favour of Northanhymbra will she not seek to detach the underkings from their Miercian overlord? Might she not desire to dethrone the king and put her son in his place?"

"And you think this is her game?"

Aethelbald brushed his long blond hair back from his brow, "Of one thing I'm sure, we'll find out when we get to Beardan."

They dismounted by a brook fringed by lush grass where they filled their leather flasks after leading their horses to drink and to graze. Over a frugal meal of bread and cheese, Guthlac resumed their earlier conversation, "We ought to go back to Bryn Alyn. Why risk being drawn into a secret scheme against the King?"

Aethelbald sat up, eyes blazing with an ardour Guthlac had rarely seen. Taking Osthryth's ring from inside his tunic, he stared at it long and hard as though drawing inspiration from the jewel. Fist closing over the ornate band, he thrust it back out of sight.

"My father's father shared the throne with his brother Penda, to rule over North Mierce. There was no love lost between the brothers and when Oswald of Northanhymbra took up arms against Penda, my grandsire fought beside him and was slain at the battle of Maserfield. By Thunor's hammer, are you following me, Guthlac?"

The younger man met the steely gaze of his companion and looked down at the ground. In truth, the harshness and passion in his comrade's voice disconcerted him.

"Ay, go on!"

Aethelbald drew up his knees to his chest and leaned his forearms on them. This concentrated Guthlac's attention on the piercing blue-grey eyes blazing amid the coarse beard and long hair.

"Since his death, Penda's offspring rule over Mierce. My father was never king." The warrior sprang to his feet and his powerful frame towered over his friend, "but I have my dreams. Our King Aethelred is old. He is loosening the grip of Mierce on the south, making concessions to Kent and the Estseaxna whilst he fails to crush the Wealisc. The court is rife with would-be successors each weaker than the other. What we need is a *Bretwaldas* – a 'Britain-ruler' – someone to sweep aside the underkings and take control, one brave and ruthless – of the ilk of Raedwald – now *he* was a great king!" He held out his hand and seizing Guthlac's, hauled him to his feet. Thrusting his face into his friend's, he said, "*I* am that man! Not Aethelred or any other! That is why we go to Beardan. One day, I shall rule from the coast in the south to the land of the Picts. I swear it to you. Remember these words!"

TWO

Beardan, Kingdom of Lindissi, 697AD

A Princess of Northanhymbra and Queen of Mierce, of late a nun in the abbey of Beardan, every day Sister Osthryth rose before Lauds and sunrise. Shaded by her hand, a flame flickered in the breeze off the river. Her steps, guided by familiarity, needed little light for the short trip from her cell to St Oswald's church. Therein lay the mortal remains of her sainted uncle.

She slipped through the heavy oak door and, grateful now for the candlelight, pattered down the stone stairs into the bitter chill of the crypt. Her frosted breath mingled in a rising wreath with the faint smoke from her candle. An involuntary shiver shook her slender frame, making the shadows cast by her taper leap like a band of villains assailing a vulnerable nocturnal prey.

The thin weave of her woollen dress offered no protection from the ice-cold paving as she knelt before the tomb of the martyred king. Used to the harshness of the fenland winter, Osthryth ignored the numbing surroundings and set about her devotions. She spoke aloud, certain the nuns, deep in sleep, would not rouse until the abbey bell summoned them.

"Uncle, I beg you, intercede on my behalf with the Lord! Beseech His help to sup, regardless, from the bitter chalice of scorn placed to my lips…and to bear this cross. How my heart aches to think of Aethelred lying with his new wife and, I, reviled, tossed aside like a worn shoe! O my dear King, be my guide, assist me that I accept my lot and lead me to the light!"

On the last word, the candle guttered and she gasped, fearful of being left in complete darkness among the dead. She and Aethelred had founded the monastery and its doors had opened less than a year past. Six months ago, the same entry, she recalled, had remained resolutely barred to the ox-cart carrying the earthly remains of her beloved uncle, leaving her party to pitch a tent on the isthmus connecting the isle to the mainland.

"Dear heart," she whispered to her departed relative, "forgive me when I spit out my bitterness. I ought to be grateful, to be here beside your shrine," a wry laugh escaped her, "remember how hostile were the monks who shut us out? They knew you were a saint but would not accept you. Oh, the folly and weakness of men! They pursued you dead, with ancient enmities, for you from a distant kingdom had taken rule over them, my dear." Osthryth groaned altering her position by leaning backwards to take some weight off her frozen knees. "But then came the miracle!" she continued, "the beam of light from your coffin shining into the sky all the night. The sinners no longer defied God's will and let us enter!"

A rhythmic tolling, faint here below the earth, urged her to curtail her prayers.

"Hark! The bell! Uncle, I wish grace to you and peace from God our Father and the Lord Jesus Christ. I must away to join my brothers and sisters at Lauds. Until the next time, dear heart."

She rose, her joints protesting at the mortification they had endured, knowing not that her poor body would ere long suffer no more.

Sister Osthryth climbed the crypt steps and emerged from the church to be greeted by the first feeble rays of the rising sun. The nun stamped her feet to revive them before setting off towards the Church of Saints Peter and Paul in the wake of several of her confraternity.

At the same moment, two cowled figures tugged together on a rope rigged around a pulley. The splashing of water breaking against the bows of the ferryboat as the hooded men hauled it across the River Withma was the only sound to disturb the silence preceding the dawn chorus. The whole island formed the abbey. When the two men stepped ashore they found no obstacle to their entry. The only gate was the one in the palisade across the isthmus at the opposite end of the isle. The taller of the two men pulled his cowl farther down over his face and said to his companion, "The ringing carries in the air from over the rise. It's there we must go." Receiving only a grunt by way of reply, he added, "There's plenty of time before they come out. Hark, the chiming stops! The priest begins the Dawn Prayer."

Under a lightening sky, they made their way past the dew-beaded thatch of the nuns quarters and beyond the dormitory of the monks. They passed the dorter used for guests, aware of it as the only building where careless noise might wake someone. On they went, leaving behind the refectory and two churches with no sign of life. Off to their left, a cock began to crow setting geese honking – a greeting to the new day. Unperturbed, the men walked on before halting in front of the largest of the places of worship whence shone light through the scraped pigskin windows. Muffled voices rose and fell in praise of the Lord. The men stood side by side and waited without exchanging a word.

At last, the recital of the final psalm reached them: '...*laudate eum in cymbalis tinnientibus omne quod spirat laudet Dominum alleluia...* and the voices ended the chant. A single voice dismissed the congregation and the church door opened to allow the nuns to file out.

The two men stiffened and from under their hoods scanned the faces of the women, seeking a refined lady of two-score years and more. Their task, no simple one, was made worse by the modesty of the sisters walking with their wimpled heads lowered. Except for one! Her upright, self-assured gait born of inbred haughtiness set her apart and betrayed her.

The taller of the men approached her, "Lady Osthryth?" he asked, loud enough for her to catch the words but insufficient to draw the attention of the departing sisters. Behind her, the first of the monks emerged from the church.

The nun turned and, unsuspecting, paused to face her questioner with a half-smile, curiosity creasing her brow.

"What is it, Brother?"

"Lady, I have a gift for you from the nobles of Mierce," and he reached inside his tunic.

At those words, quick as she was of wit, Osthryth understood her doom. She had but time to widen her eyes and gasp before the sharp steel sliced into her stomach. Another blade wielded by a different hand pierced her heart to stop its beating. Regal in life, crumpled in death, the body of Osthryth sagged to the earth. Nuns screamed and monks shouted, some began to start forward but halted, cowed by the brandished seaxes.

"Make haste, Guthlac!" the taller man called, "away to the gate and into the forest!"

"I hear you, Aethelbald!" yelled the other and clutching their cowls close over their heads they raced down the slope to the palisade and nobody dared stop them.

Monks and nuns crowded aghast around the contorted body on the ground, appalled at how much blood could flow forth from one so slight of build. Last to leave the church, and oblivious of what had happened, the priest pushed his way to the front of the crowd.

"Murder!" he exclaimed, "Where is our Abbot?"

"Here, Father!" a stern voice replied, "I arrived a second before you. I am apprised the Lady Osthryth is slain and on consecrated ground. Vile sacrilege! Who would commit such a deed?"

The priest knelt and making the sign of the cross over the body, began to pray for the soul of the deceased.

"Brother Brynstan," the severe voice continued, "take a horse and hie away to Lindcolne to King Aldfrith for he must raise the hue and cry." The abbot, pensive, paused. "Wait a moment, Brother!" He peered from under bushy silver eyebrows at the dismayed throng. "Whatever aid we can give to the King, we must, for he will inform the lady's family who will seek justice. Can anyone describe to us Sister Osthryth's assailants?"

A shuffling of feet, shrugging of shoulders and shaking of heads made him shout in exasperation, "How can it be you all saw nothing!"

"Father Abbot, begging your pardon," the monk entrusted with the message spoke, "but the fiends were cowled and did not show their faces. No-one can describe them except they were tall and built like warriors…not like us!"

"We have their names, Father Abbot," said an elderly nun. "They were foolish enough to say them in front of us. One is named Guthlac and the other Aethelbald if I do not err."

"You do not, sister!" another nun confirmed.

"Ay, those were the names!" a monk concurred.

Everyone nodded and murmured in agreement.

"Well," said the Abbot of Beardan, "Sisters, see that the body of poor Lady Osthryth is bathed, wrapped in a winding sheet and taken into the church. Brothers prepare a coffin. Brother Brynstan that is what you must tell our King and may God grant these foul murderers and defilers hang for their crime!"

THREE

Kingdom of Lindissi, 697AD

A silver ribbon under the gaze of the two horsemen, the River Trente sparkled and shimmered in the afternoon sun. The illusion vanished before their mounts clattered over the bridge leading into the royal burgh of Gegnesburh. A beehive came to Aethelbald's mind, the crowd the insects buzzing about their various labours. They threaded past carriers of flour sacks, a hide bearer jostled one who cursed while two women left off weaving crayfish baskets to add bawdy remarks to his overripe words. Hammers clanged from a nearby forge and the din mingled with the chime of church bells, the shouts of street traders and boatmen from the river. Yelps and growls of squabbling dogs, the clatter and creaking of wooden cart wheels over uneven cobbles and the ringing of iron-shod hooves added to the clamour.

The boredom of Bryn Alyn receded into dim memory for the two ealdormen caught up in this tumult of activity. A vibrant town offered the prospect of decent ale and shameless wenches – the gist of Aethelbald's bellow to Guthlac as they searched for a tavern.

A hostelry found, they stabled their horses, paid for a room and ordered food.

"What's the best thing about this inn?" Aethelbald asked his comrade as he emptied his beaker.

Guthlac scanned the cobwebs dangling from the oak beams in dust-laden black strands, his gaze passing to the stained rickety wooden tables.

"The ale, I suppose," he frowned, "at least it's not watered down."

"Not the drink. Don't pretend you're not interested!"

"In what?" the younger man's brow creased.

"Who…not what…"

Guthlac stared at the rowdy locals, some arguing over dice, others sharing laughter – nobody out of the ordinary. He shrugged.

His friend grinned, "You don't fool me with your innocent expression. I know you too well! Right, it's a straight fight then! May the best man win!"

Exasperated, Guthlac slammed down his beaker, "What are you on about?"

"Let battle commence! I'll call her over for more ale. I can tell when a maid is game for a little sport, by the roguish glint in her eye. She boasts the chest of a proud dove—"

"Get the drink in! I'll go and check on the horses. I need a piss anyhow."

Aethelbald scowled at his companion. What ails him? Fair of face and quick-witted, Guthlac never failed to seduce a maid when he set about it. No time to dwell on the imponderable, the object of his lust was bending over the table dabbing at an invented spill with a cloth and displaying her alluring wares. What better opportunity?

"What name do you go by, maid?"

"Goda, Lord," she opened wide her eyes and tilted her head in a pretty smile.

He used his charm and wit ordering two bowls of hare stew and more ale, but caught her arm and dragged her close to whisper in her ear.

"When you finish for the night, come up to my room, you'll find me a generous lover!"

As expected, the wench did not blush or protest but gave him a shameless smile and gratified him with a nod. He kept his voice down. "Wait! Do you have a friend comely as yourself? There's my companion to think about."

She put a finger to her lips and hurried off to fetch the beer. When Guthlac returned, Aethelbald said nothing of his encounter. This would be a night-time surprise.

A short while after midnight, a gentle knock came on their door. As an exception, the ealdorman had left it unlocked. He lay awake, no need, in his state of anticipation, to fight off the tiredness that had led to the steady breathing of his comrade. What a thrill awaited Guthlac! By the light of his single candle, Aethelbald watched the door open and two young women slip inside the room.

"I've brought my cousin, Luba," the maid said in a low voice and they both giggled.

"Make haste! Take off your clothes," Aethelbald said, "get in with me and you, Luba, slide in with my friend!"

The girls hurried to oblige but as Luba pulled back the bedding to lie beside the warrior, Guthlac woke and pushed her to the floor.

"What the...let me be!" he exclaimed, "I'm tired, I want none of this!"

He tugged the blanket over his head.

Aethelbald gaped at the hunched form of his comrade. What a shock! The Guthlac he knew never spurned a maid. What ailed him? The ealdorman recovered his poise at once. He shuffled, drawing his conquest to one side of the bed, "Come, Luba, there is room for another and I have the energy of two men!"

Guthlac slept untroubled through the lewd and torrid cavorting of his leader. At first light, as he dressed, he bestowed a wry smile at the entangled figures and left them undisturbed. He preferred to seek water and to check his mount. The innkeeper, one who sported a straggling beard and a bald pate, told him of an ancient pathway. At this end, its course led on from the Trente between a break in the marshes to a bygone army camp at Herwik. Thence a league would take them to the Roman road, straight as a spear to Lindcolne, whence Beardan lay but three leagues to the east.

Taking the route suggested by their host, accompanied by the receding chime of church bells from the town, the friends rode without speaking. The early morn induced this in Aethelbald after his nocturnal exertions whereas for the refreshed Guthlac, his muteness was naught but a preference. Curiosity, at last, overcame Aethelbald.

"What got into you, last night?"

"I don't know what you mean."

"By Thunor's black forge, Guthlac, I've never seen you turn your back on a sultry wench!"

"Not in the mood, is all."

True, Guthlac was a thinker more than a talker, but the shortness of Guthlac's tone irked him. They cantered on, Aethelbald pondering this rather than what he had said. After a while, he asked, "What ails you? Are you ill?"

"Not in body, in mind. As a child, I was pure and clean of disposition but as my strength waxed and I grew to manhood, I changed."

The ealdorman waited, sure from his friend's expression of a struggle to express his thoughts and unsure he liked their drift.

Slowing his mount to a walk, Guthlac added, "Strong deeds of the heroes and men of yore captured my imagination. It's why I took up weapons and wreaked grudges on our enemies. I met you and we burnt villages, ravaged towns, slew men and took their goods. We gave ourselves to ale and wen—"

Drawing his horse closer, Aethelbald laid a hand on his arm and interrupted, "It's a good life you describe. What's wrong with bedding wenches and supping beer? And don't warriors slay their foe?"

"There must be more to life. That's my point. I feel my spirit wilting like a faded flower—"

But he had no time to develop his discourse. Aethelbald had drawn his sword — not a reasoned decision. Galloping toward them was a group of ten mail-shirted riders armed with spears and swords. They fanned around the Miercians to form a ring of steel and force them to halt.

Aethelbald slid his sword back through the loop in his belt. In spite of the gesture of submission, he shouted, "What is the meaning of this?"

A warrior of rugged aspect, unsmiling and cold-eyed, said, "*I* ask the questions. Give your names!"

The ealdorman studied the crooked nose, likely broken in a fight and the accompanying scar from mouth to jawbone. The rude manner irked him but it was senseless to disoblige the leader of nine well-armed men. Eking out time as a sop to his pride, he delayed until the man's expression hardened before conceding, "I am Aethelbald, son of Alweo of North Mierce." He stretched out a hand, "And this is Guthlac, son of Penwalh of Suthanhymbra."

The glint of elation and exchange of glances among the horsemen left no room for doubt in Aethelbald's mind that they were the quarry. But why? Who had sent these louts? The answer came at once.

"We will escort you to Lindcolne where you will account for your crimes to King Aldfrith."

"Crimes! What crimes?" Guthlac exclaimed.

"Ah! the pretty boy has a tongue, after all!" sneered the thegn. "Enough! We ride for Lindcolne."

They suffered the indignity of yielding their weapons but Aethelbald consoled himself by muttering, "We were going that way, anyhow." He considered bright conversation with his comrade to show they were undaunted but dismissed it as futile. Their captors, taciturn to a fault, by their wordlessness, heightened the sense of oppression and frustration gripping him. He took his pent-up rage out on Guthlac when the younger man spoke.

"Do you think our arrest has anything to do with—"

"Shut up, you fucking dimwit!"

"Silence!" bellowed the scarred thegn at the same instant.

The vehemence of his friend's reaction startled Guthlac. Aethelbald was given to occasional moments of ire and insults but never directed at him. Cold fury, not unchecked wrath, was the ealdorman's way. Hurt, he relapsed into the gloom that appeared to be his closest companion since they had left the Gates of Bryn Alyn. Aethelbald studied him from the tail of his eye, displeased to have upset his friend but satisfied he had prevented him from betraying the purpose of their journey. Until they knew the charges levelled against them better to keep their own counsel. He would soothe his ruffled feathers later.

Scattered pebbles, holes and ruts along the once well-surfaced road brought them in a straight line to a dramatic hill, rising from the surrounding marsh. Once, as a youngster, Aethelbald had listened to a scop chant the tale of a great battle fought hereabouts. The stone-built walls with turrets and gates dominating the land around must be those of the song, built long ago by the legions from overseas. His gaze swept down to where a river widened into a huge pool busier, noisier and more bustling than the waterfront at Gegnesburh. No time to survey the scene, their captors rode on, through the mean hovels and past the stone rubble of three part-demolished buildings. Nearby, a wooden church and its cemetery stood at the foot of the hill. Aethelbald stared aghast at the winding steepness of this road before which the stoutest steed might quail. Yet they rode on, horses snorting and sweating with effort till the oaken gate under its brick arch swung back until, relieved, they reached level ground. Inside the walls, rose an impressive stone basilica, whose squat form Aethelbald had never seen the like.

At last, they stopped by a foul, stinking cesspit humming with flies. The ealdorman wrinkled his nose at the stench but this dump served the stable and here they surrendered their mounts to youths scurrying to tend the animals.

Rough hands pushed the captives toward a squat thatched building remarkable for the carving in the uprights and lintel of the doorframe. There, ran a repetitive design of two outer rings of decoration enclosing a circular field dominated by an equal-armed cross. Triplet leaves occupied the spaces between the arms of the rood and the whole pattern sparkled in crimson, myrtle green and gold. Three steps down to the sunken floor of the gloomy interior explained the stocky aspect of the exterior. Inside, the white-daubed walls gave a surprising sense of space, but the air hung heavy with the reek of charred ash from the spent fire in a central hearth.

The scarred thegn bowed to a group of four men seated in bowl-shaped chairs contrasting in their incised elegance with the rude benches otherwise providing the seating in the hall.

"Lord, we caught them on the road near Herwik. They claim to be Aethelbald, son of Alweo of North Mierce and Guthlac, son of Penwalh of Suthanhymbra."

"They confessed to such of their own free will?" asked a tall thin man, the long grey hair of nobility falling straight over his shoulders, his shrewd pale eyes boring into Aethelbald's. The King of the Lindisfarona? He stared from Aethelbald to Guthlac and back again. "What brings you to Lindissi?"

Aethelbald opted for as much of the truth as suited their plight, "We were on our way to the Abbey at Beardan."

The broad high brow furrowed and, hesitating, the man turned to a younger fellow on his right and raised an eyebrow. The merest flicker of assent spurred on Aethelbald's questioner.

"How so?"

"On a visit."

"Ay? And in that religious house who would be honoured to receive two noblemen from Mierce?"

Several lies flashed through the ealdorman's mind but discounting each as perilous, once more, he chose an honest answer. Reaching inside his tunic, he brought forth the jewel consigned to them at Bryn Alyn – the reason for their journey. For a moment, he admired the fine craftsmanship before, with some reluctance, dropping it into the palm of his interrogator. With no more than a cursory glance, the greybeard gave it, in turn, to the same yellow-haired man by his side. With a start, Aethelbald realised his error. This was King Aldfrith! Of course, he ought to have known. The bright intelligence in the sharp reactions, the fine lineaments of a noble–

A cold voice interrupted his considerations, "How come you have the ring of Osthryth of Northanhymbra?"

What gain would be reaped from falsehood? As an excuse to check on the resolve of his comrade, Aethelbald involved him in the confirmation of his account. When he ended, in the silence that followed, the King stared at the gold band in his hand as if it might speak and reveal some underlying unspoken truth. The ealdorman feared they were in mortal danger. As yet, they faced no charge, but the certainty of its imminence chilled his veins. Sure enough, it came.

"Men do not travel half the breadth of the land to an abbey in the fens to exchange pleasantries with an estranged queen." Through half-closed eyes, the King spoke his thoughts, "A lady whose origins are hostile to her former husband might well choose to discuss affairs of state in remote marshlands." Directing a piercing gaze at Aethelbald, he mocked, "The taint of treason cannot be rinsed like soil from the hands. The price of the said crime is death…"

Aethelbald blanched but held the King's eyes with his own unwavering stare.

"Lord, we travel on a direct summons. My comrade," he swept his hand toward Guthlac, "indeed, feared a plot and wished to turn back but as his leader, I ordered him onward."

"How so?"

Ever quick-witted, Aethelbald's reply rolled off his tongue, "We swore fealty to King Aethelred and it behoved us to delve into this matter to denounce intrigue. But as to any plotting, on my oath, we have no part!"

"And you say the messenger who brought the ring pressed it upon you and vanished when invited to sup?"

"Ay!"

"That is something *you* will not do."

There was no mistaking the menace in his tone. What fate did the King of the Lindisfarona have in store for them? Aethelbald feared the worst.

Leaning back in his chair, he stroked his beard, a faraway look in his eye, then taking a decision, said to Aethelbald, "You will eat with us this evening. Move where you will but I ask you not to set foot outside the upper town for there is much yet to discuss and…" he waved a hand at his counsellors, "…for us to ponder."

Aldfrith handed back the jewel and Aethelbald held it close to his breast. Addressing the thegn who had brought the Miercians, the King said, "Restore the weapons to our guests and find them a bed for the night."

Aethelbald bowed in acknowledgement and above all relief, Guthlac did the same, "I thank you, Lord, we are pleased to accept your gracious invitation." He kissed the tips of two fingers and placed them over his heart, "On my word, we shall not try to leave."

They were quartered in a spartan room furnished with two pallets, a bench and two square-headed nails hammered in the wall, they presumed, as hangers for a cloak or sword. A brief exploration revealed the place was empty for the moment, but three similar lodgings gave off the main dormitory. A few belongings scattered on beds told them they were to spend the night among the king's warriors. Back behind the closed door, Guthlac sat on the bench and shook his head.

"For a moment, I thought we would be imprisoned for treason," he said, "why the sudden change of mind?"

"Strange! I wish I knew. By Thunor, King Aldfrith is no fool. You heard what he said… *'there's much yet to discuss.'* "

"Well, if they were going to accuse us of a crime, they'd have done it by now, wouldn't they?"

"Till he makes his decision, we are guests in name only. Our lives hang in the balance. To flee would be a confession of guilt and talk of free movement is not worth a breath of air." The ealdorman laughed, "This place has few comforts, imagine what they reserve for criminals!"

As a relief from the cramped confines of their billet, they strolled into the upper town, past the ancient construction of the west gate through which they had entered earlier. A warrior stared down at them from the first-floor guardroom, a reminder they were here on sufferance.

The sound of sawing came through an open door. Aethelbald glanced inside where a man was cutting off a length of antler. Piled on his workbench were heaps of bone and the more sought after ivory from walrus tusk, likely traded with Northern hunters. The man looked up and greeted them so Guthlac hauled the ealdorman within. Among the spindles and whorls, pins and counters he had spotted an ivory comb. A short haggle and exchange of coin and it was his.

"You can use it too, Aethelbald. Our best clothes are back in Bryn Alyn but at least our hair can look the part at the King's table!"

Three children dashing headlong and their frisking dog needed sidestepping before dodging the smoke from the smouldering ash covering a potter's pit. They dawdled to watch his skilled hands raise a sausage of clay into a pot shape on his wheel, doubtless made by the wheelwright next door. There, buckets, tool handles, boxes and chests spilt out on the street. Inside the cavernous workshop among carts and wheels, a man worked a foot pedal to turn a lathe. Not stopping for idle chatter, they moved on past a woman casting powdered madder into a vat to dye her yarn red.

"Look! An alehouse, that's more like it!" Aethelbald nudged his comrade.

"Don't be getting ideas about serving wenches, that's all!"

"Ay, we never did finish our conversation—"

"Nor will we. Else you'll drink alone!"

Aethelbald scowled, he'd let him be for now, but swore to get to the bottom of the matter sooner rather than later. The woman waiting on them, judging by her loss of shape, had given birth to many a babe and her charmless gap-toothed smile did nothing to improve her appearance. Nor did her matted hair and filthy apron. She hurried off to fetch their drinks and Guthlac said, "I wouldn't put it past you!" earning himself a jocular cuff around the ear.

The imminent arrival of beer meant Aethelbald took banter in good part and the aspect of their hostess prevented the ealdorman from staying to overindulge.

"She doesn't know what a comb is. Better we keep clear heads," Guthlac said, "we might need our wits at the King's board."

At table, ushered directly opposite the King, Aethelbald admired the fern green twisted glass, another product of a Lindcolne craftsman, he suspected. Servants began to pour ale and others to place bowls of soup before them.

"Delicious!" Guthlac said.

King Aldfrith crooked a finger, questioned a servant and said, "Kale and chestnut with pieces of ham." He smiled but Aethelbald noticed that his eyes were hard and calculating. As he suspected, they did not have to wait long for more serious matters to be mooted.

In a casual tone, the grey-haired ealdorman said to the Miercians, "So, son of Alweo, you knew nothing of the murder?"

Aethelbald and Guthlac exchanged puzzled glances and the former shrugged, "Murder?" Was this the crime they had been coerced here for?

The eyes of the King never left their faces for a second, scrutinising their every reaction.

"Ay," went on the greybeard, hand hovering over the steaming bowl, "murder! At Beardan Abbey."

A frown and silent shake of the head was Aethelbald's reply. His pulse began to pound at his throat.

"The Lady Osthryth, stabbed through the heart as she left the Dawn Service by two men built like warriors but disguised as monks…one named Aethelbald and the other Guthlac–"

Aethelbald dropped his spoon and leapt to his feet, pale, on the brink of a strident denial.

"Be seated, friend!" commanded Aldfrith. "No-one here is fool enough to believe you committed the foul deed."

The muscles in his face taut, Aethelbald lowered himself to the bench. Was the danger over?

"Murderers do not bandy their names to the four winds," the King said, "nor with witting complicity do they ride *toward* the scene of their crime. Sooner, in furtive flight, they leave it behind." He resumed sipping at his soup, his disconcerting eyes never leaving the ealdorman's face. "The questions to be asked are others," he went on, "Who wanted the Lady dead? Wherefore lure the two of you to Lindissi hoping to implicate you in the deed? What is to be gained by the slaying? And…" he paused for effect, his words cut as sharp as a well-honed seax, "…what is to become of our Miercian lordlings? Come, drink your soup while it is hot!"

In truth, Aethelbald imagined his stomach might be less knotted fighting with famished wolves for a leg of lamb. The King appeared in no haste to reassure them of their blamelessness and consequent deliverance. Was he enjoying his power over them? For the moment, he seemed more to be appreciating his soup.

The greybeard counsellor spoke, "As to the first question, Lord, there was no love lost between Queen Osthryth and her Miercian subjects. The pagan Penda killed her devout and beloved uncle, Oswald, and ritually dismembered him." His voice lingered on the last three words and he stared around the table relishing their effect. His smooth voice went on, "Penda's son converted to marry Osthryth's sister, but his new wife's loyalty lay with Northanhymbra and her father, the king of that land. Through her treachery, her husband, Paeda, died. Unavenged, his death still rankles with the Miercian lords. The wedding of Aethelred and Osthryth did nothing to impede the frequent outbreaks of war between the two kingdoms and the victory of Mierce at the Trente…" here he waited to add weight to his words, "…involved the slaughter of the Queen's favourite brother–"

"Which means, of course," cut in King Aldfrith, laying his spoon with care in his empty bowl, "the Lady had more cause to hate Mierce and to *plot* against her estranged husband. Reason enough for the Miercian lords to want her dead and at the same time avenge Paeda's death caused by her sister's deceit two-score years before. Long memories are the mark of a blood feud."

Aethelbald nodded in silent accord. All this was more than plausible, but the riddle tormenting him was why he and Guthlac were embroiled in this affair at all. The arrival of platters of eel cooked in celery, parsley, carrots and crab apples and flavoured with horseradish distracted him for a moment, but it did not distract the elderly ealdorman.

"As for the reason for trying to implicate you two in the murder of Queen Osthryth, we can do no more than guess. You come from different under-kingships in the north of Mierce. Might it not be a bid to topple those who enjoy Aethelred's favour in those parts?"

Setting aside his bowl and taking a draught of ale, Aethelbald said, "Or simply to suggest the Lady was fomenting unrest among his sworn underkings in outlying areas of Mierce."

"More likely," King Aldfrith assented, "but of course this is secondary to what murderers gain from her death. Why kill a lady who is paying harmless devotions on a remote isle in the fens?"

"Unless she were indeed plotting, Lord. She dared not contact you so as not to risk her safe haven. But assume she contacted the King of the Hwicca, a kinsman of hers, and, say, the King of the Est Angles?" Frowning, the ealdorman tugged at his grey beard, "But to what end?"

To general surprise, Guthlac spoke, for hitherto he had sat in silence, "Queen Osthryth has a son, Coelwald. By detaching the underkings with promises of independence to weaken Mierce, might she not have planned to call in her relatives from Northanhymbra? They would depose Aethelred and enthrone Coelwald, at last bringing their hated rivals under their dominion?"

Aethelbald gaped at Guthlac. He had supposed him incapable of such contorted thinking, but the more he thought about it the more likely it seemed. Not wishing to give his comrade too much credit, he murmured, "By Thunor's wrathful bolt, you should eat eel more often."

The King drained his glass to wash down his food, called for more ale and said, "You are in danger, young men. The accusation has been made and the kin of Osthryth will seek you out for revenge. But here's the thing, your enemy in Mierce, whoever he is, has been sly. Linking you to a possible plot of Osthryth's means that King Aethelred and his loyal nobles will be after your blood." The King's expression changed to one of sorrow, "I cannot give you refuge here as my fealty is to Aethelred. I can say we searched for you in vain but you must leave without delay."

The tall ealdorman nodded his grey head, "Ay, depart at dawn. Bear in mind, by now the King of Mierce will know you are no longer at Bryn Alyn."

Guthlac looked appalled at his comrade. "Where shall we go? Nowhere is safe."

"It's best our hosts know not…there is one place…I'll tell you as we ride."

FOUR

From Lindcolne to Northworthig, 697AD

Relieved to reach the foot of the steep hill in Lindcolne, Aethelbald relaxed amid the first shimmering rays of the sun. The sky changed from an indistinct grey to a soothing cornflower blue with wisps of blushing clouds. Not one to notice the beauty of Nature, unless in the form of a shapely wench, after the threat to their lives the ealdorman revelled in his surroundings. With uplifted spirit, he watched the leaden water of the River Withma brighten to silver tinged with pink.

"The dawn," he said to Guthlac, "is like an invisible hand lifting a veil from the world to reveal its colours."

His friend's horse snorted but it might as well have been its rider, judging by his tone, "So you realise there's more to life than wenching and slaughter! Since you did not wish to mention it in the King's hall, tell me the one place you believe to be safe."

"In truth, the arm of King Aethelred is long and nowhere is beyond his reach. One thing is sure, while our families may not be able to protect us, they will not betray us. Suthanhymbra is nearer than North Mierce, I say we seek out your father and his counsel. An older, wiser head will know what to advise—"

"Ay, and maybe he will suggest the identity of the skulking

adversary tainting our names. But if we are going to my father's estates why are we riding north?"

"We return to Gegnesburh to set a false trail."

"Or to tumble with the maid! By all the saints, a two-day-and-a-half's ride separate Lindcolne from my father's land! Would you add a day to our journey to sport with a wench?"

Aethelbald glared, "I gave you my reason and there's an end to it!"

They rode on in silence following the straight road and reached Caenby by noon, breaking for an hour to water and restore their horses. Provisions begged from the royal kitchen served to reinvigorate them in the face of the remaining two leagues separating them from Gegnesburh where Aethelbald intended to spend the night. By mid-afternoon, Guthlac's natural good humour returned and they rode into the town in companionable conversation before making for the inn where they had stayed before.

After more than an hour, in which they chatted and supped ale, the serving woman, Goda, came to their table once more. Before Aethelbald could order again, she bent to his ear and whispered fast so Guthlac did not catch a word. A wry smile made it clear to anyone who might be interested that the wench was propositioning his friend. But nothing could have been farther from the truth.

"Lord, do not look round, she breathed, "in the corner sits one in a green cloak. A few minutes ago, he arrived and gave coins to the landlord to seal his mouth but I overheard everything from the scullery door. Whence were you bound? At what hour? What names go you by, he asked all that and more—"

"Is he alone?" the ealdorman murmured.

"Ay."

"Another two ales and a wedge of your best cheese!" he said in a loud voice and slapped her bottom to aid the pretence but also because he found it enticing.

"Do you think of nothing else?" Guthlac sighed and shook his head. "Keep the noise down when you go at it tonight. I need my sleep!"

"By Thunor, like wasps to ripe fruit, maids are drawn to me! How can I turn them away?" Aethelbald made no attempt to lower his voice and from the corner of his eye was gratified to see the spy curl his lip in a sneer. This situation changed everything. Guthlac erred, there would be no amorous cavorting with Goda tonight since he would need to be fresh and have his wits about him on the morrow. With the utmost discretion, he ensured his companion noted the features of the spy.

Upstairs in their room, Aethelbald explained their changed circumstances and his plan for the next day.

"I agree we have to clear our names," the younger man said, "but how? Oughtn't we to go to King Aethelred and declare our innocence?"

"Are you mad? Walk into the bear's den? Whoever murdered Osthryth and lured us to Lindissi will not rest till we are dead. Nay, we keep to my plan. Time to sleep."

In spite of the early hour, labourers scurried and scrambled along the wharves below the bridge over the Trente. The populace of the wakening town outdid one another in their contribution to the infernal din: the bell ringers, the smiths, the traders, the drovers and their dogs. Glad to leave the chaos behind, once over the river, Aethelbald said, "Stop looking back! The cur is unaware of our suspicions. Do you want to alert him?"

There was little movement but for two carts and a ceorl driving spindle-legged swine into the woods, to grub for acorns, toads and worms. The companions followed the valley toward Torksey coming to where the road passed through woodland on either side.

"It's here we separate," Aethelbald said, "stick to our plan!"

"*Our* plan, is it?" Guthlac muttered so his leader did not hear him.

He urged his horse among the trees and Aethelbald did likewise on the opposite side of the thoroughfare. The ealdorman unslung his shield from his back, drew his sword and waited. A short while later, at the thud of approaching hooves, he kicked with his heels and his mount plunged out of the woodland. At the same time, Guthlac and his horse burst from the forest. The startled beast of the unsuspecting rider reared and all but threw him. Reining in with difficulty he glared in rage at his assailants, laid his hand on the hilt of his seax, but what use was it against two swordsmen? He released his grip.

Drawing close to the fellow, Aethelbald scrutinised the face of the spy from the inn, "Why are you following us?"

"I am not. The road leads to Newerche where I have family."

"You lie!" Guthlac said, "You paid the innkeeper for news of us."

The eyes of the man, a poor ceorl judging by his close-cropped yellow hair, darted from Aethelbald to Guthlac and back again when the latter spoke anew.

"A fine mount for a fellow without coin! If you value your life, you will tell us who set you on our trail."

The breathing of the villain came faster and beads of sweat appeared on his brow, "It's more than it's worth, I cannot!"

Quick as an adder, Aethelbald struck the side of the man's head with the boss of his shield knocking him from his horse and leaving him stunned. The animal bolted.

"Catch the beast and bring it back!" the ealdorman shouted as he dismounted, throwing down his weapons. Obedient, Guthlac galloped his mount after the frightened steed.

Kneeling on the man's arms, Aethelbald drew the ceorl's seax and, remorseless, drove the point through his palm pinning the hand to the ground. Drawing his own seax, he did the same to the other hand so the screaming man lay spread-eagled before him.

Riderless horse in tow, Guthlac rode up and stared dispassionately at their victim.

"It ill behoves you to withhold what we seek," he said, dismounting and tethering the two horses to nearby trees.

The agonised man rolled his head from side to side in refusal, "Kill me and be done!" he groaned.

"Give me your seax!" Aethelbald ordered his comrade, who in growing realisation, looked on in dismay. Drawing the blade across the flesh of the forearm, in a trail of crimson beads, he etched a rectangle, pitiless, flaying the skin, indifferent to the screams of his victim.

"The name," he said, "and I'll stop."

Sickened, Guthlac turned away and wandered over to the horses, consoling himself by comforting the beasts. True, his and Aethelbald's lives were in danger, but he had no stomach for this. He loved him as a brother, but this side to his character tested his affection.

In spite of his suffering, the man did not utter a word. Aethelbald proceeded until Guthlac raced across and pushed his friend to the ground, "For pity's sake, stop!

To free the bleeding man, he pulled out the seaxes. The wretch sat up and rocked backwards and forwards clutching his wounds in agony.

"We'll find out who our foe is sooner or later. There's no need for this!" Guthlac said.

"There's every need. By Thunor, our lives are threatened and you behave like a faint-hearted maid!"

Aethelbald picked up his sword and shield and with one swift lunge ran the weapon through the ceorl's throat.

"And don't tell me there was no necessity for that!" He wiped the blood off the blade on the grass. "Help me drag the body out of sight before wayfarers chance upon us."

Another hour and they rode through the village of Torksey close to the Trente, stopping to buy fresh-baked bread and water the horses. To rest his animal, Aethelbald mounted the bay mare they had taken from the ceorl.

"This is a fine beast," he said, a few hundred yards down the road, "no more than a four-year-old. No ceorl owns one of these. Whoever set that wretch to stalk us, I swear the steed is but the smallest forfeit the cur-dog will pay when I unmask him."

For all his bluster, Aethelbald was worried. Their nameless adversary, to challenge for power, must be formidable, potent, a danger not only to them but also to their King. The unexpected behaviour of Guthlac concerned him too. What caused one of the deadliest warriors he had ever had the pleasure of fighting beside to change into a weakling overnight? Determined to find the source of this disquiet, once he had, he would destroy it before the day was out and it harmed them again.

They pressed on down the Roman road to Newerche, ate on the riverbank, swapped horses so Guthlac rode Aethelbald's and reached Snotingham by early evening. After their meal and two hours of drinking, they retired to their room. In Aethelbald's experience, ale had little effect on Guthlac's mood but tonight it made him querulous. To the ealdorman's annoyance, Guthlac grumbled, "It is but four leagues to my father's hall. The decision to go to Gegnesburh means we are stuck here, not there. Nobody travels at night. What a waste—"

Aethelbald kept a tight rein on his temper but interrupted, "As well we went *there*! Thanks to the goodwill of Goda, the stalker lies dead and no-one knows where we are. By midmorning on the morrow, you will embrace your family."

The sullen expression of his friend as he tossed himself down on his pallet made him shake his head. Better not tax him about his change of spirit until his mood improved, which was sure to happen when he reunited with his family. Opting to bide his time, Aethelbald knew a few days at his homestead might restore to him the comrade he cherished.

The sun would have shone directly overhead the next day, had it not been cloaked by cloud when the bear of a man hauled Guthlac into a formidable hug. Fearing for his companion's backbone, Aethelbald supposed whatever brightness the day lacked, the expressions of father and son made up for it. To be sure, he had not bothered to ask himself what appearance Penwalh might have. The iron-coloured locks were no surprise in a man of two score and ten springs but the knotted muscles of arms and calves bespoke huge strength. A warrior to be feared in spite of his years.

"Come, I must greet your comrade!" roared the ealdorman as a middle-aged woman came out of the hall wearing a splendorous gold necklace and at her waist, an amber and amethyst girdle.

"Mother!" Guthlac hastened toward her, leaving his fellow traveller and Penwalh to clasp forearms in greeting.

Pleasantries over, the lord of the estate led his two guests into the building. A youth scampered off with instructions to fetch… Aethelbald paid no heed to the names…two thegns, and the lady head of the household gave orders to slave girls to bring refreshments.

They drank beer made sweet with honey and ate oatcakes also prepared with honey and a precious spice Aethelbald had never tasted. It pleased him so much, he asked Guthlac's mother about it.

"These cakes are delicious, Lady. But what is this strange taste?"

The sweetness of her smile reminded him at once of her son, who shared her delicate features,

"It is a spice hard to come by and known as cinnamon," she

said. "In a distant land to the east giant cinnamon birds collect the sticks and use them to build their nests."

At that moment, two men entered the hall speaking in hushed tones. An almost imperceptible eye movement from the lady was sufficient for a slave girl to whisk away the cakes and for another to replace them with a bowl of sweet curd cheese and hunks of bread. The lady, appreciated Aethelbald, did not reserve her spiced treats for thegns. Two more drinking horns appeared. Hospitality in Suthanhymbra, as throughout Mierce, was never wanting in an ealdorman's hall. The newcomers bowed to their Lord and upon a gesture took their place at table.

"Welcome, Lord Guthlac," said the older of the two, "more than a year away, is it not?"

"Ay, Allwald, fretting on the confines of Powys of late, waiting in vain for Wealisc to show–"

Penwalh cut in, "Tell them what happened yesterday." The lord lent back resting an elbow on the back of his seat better to face and explain to Aethelbald, "Allwald has a village a league hence to the southeast..." he waved a hand, "tell them!"

An apologetic glance at Guthlac and the thegn shifted his attention to the other guest, in recognition of his rank. "Lord, my ceorls were toiling in the South Field, before noon, when a band of armed men rode up to press them for the whereabouts of two – *er* – lawbreakers. On pain of death...they fair scared them witless...they made them swear that Lord Guthlac and another – we know now is you, Lord Aethelbald – had not set foot in or around Northworthig..."

Aethelbald frowned and exchanged looks with his comrade, "Yesterday, before noon?"

"Ay."

The Lord of Northworthig, slammed down a fist, "Lawbreakers! The cravens minded to come nowhere near my sword arm with their false accusations."

Gratitude and love shone in Guthlac's eyes at his father's words. The ealdorman knew not of what they stood accused, nor did he care, sure of his son's innocence. He addressed the other thegn, "Tell them, Wulfric!"

The thegn placed his elbows on the table and cupped one hand over the other, leaning forward. "The same thing, Lord," he said to Aethelbald, "my ceorls were driving sheep from the *ofer* – the flat-topped ridge above our village – a while before dusk–"

"Where is your holding?" Aethelbald interrupted.

"A mile more than a league to the west, Lord…" he waited for reassurance to continue, "…they asked the same questions as of Allwald's men and when they were satisfied you had not ventured thereabouts, they left. But not before one of my men heard them say…" unease showed in his lowered head, "…forgive me Lord, their word…the *criminals* must have gone to the village of the iron mines. My shepherds knew not of the place but of course, it is Woercs-worth. They were sure they would find you there at your father's hall."

Nobody spoke as they reflected on these words. Through the open door came the high-pitched whining of a demanding puppy over the constant chitter of nestlings from the eaves. Supping a draught of mead then setting down his drinking horn, Aethelbald recounted the tale of the mischance that led to their arrest by King Aldfrith in Lindcolne.

The broad brow of Penwalh furrowed, "I knew naught of the murder of Osthryth. And you say the messenger insisted you kept her ring?" He drummed the tips of his fingers on the table, "Proof of your contact with the Lady. A deft ploy, but Aldfrith is no fool and has no reason to throw in his lot with a plot to overthrow Aethelred. The Miercian yoke over Lindissi is made of light wood." The drumming grew more insistent, "What's more, the Lindisfarona smart at the memory of the Northanhymbrian invasions. Mierce keeps the northern wolves at bay." A pause for a drink, and refreshed, he resumed, "Ay, Northanhymbra. The heart of the problem. There are those who would use the ambition of the men from north of the Hymbre to their own ends–"

"Who, father? And to what gain?"

"As to who, there are many pretenders to the throne. How are we to know who among them sullied your reputations? The reason is much clearer. Urge the underkings to break free from Mierce, encourage the Northanhymbrians to invade. Show Aethelred is unfit to rule and seize the kingship."

Aethelbald followed Penwalh's reasoning with close interest. In an unconscious movement his hand slipped into his tunic and closed over Osthryth's ring.

"But if we don't know who blighted us, how can we clear our names?" Guthlac frowned.

At last, the rhythmic beating ceased and with it vanished the wrinkled brow as though all the ealdorman's cares, of a sudden, had flown out the door.

"Well," Penwalh smiled, "you cannot stay here. The king's men will soon realise you are not in Woercs-worth and like baying hounds they will not cease their hunting. You must confound their plans."

"But how?" Aethelbald asked.

The ealdorman raised his drinking horn but held it in mid-air as he spoke, "By showing the world you are no friends of Northanhymbra." A smile, impenetrable, curled his lip before he drank.

"Lord, you speak in riddles," Aethelbald shrugged, staring at the other men and noting in their faces bafflement to match his own.

Penwalh gazed at the puzzled faces and chortled, "Ride north steer clear of Woercs-worth and make for Dore."

Aethelbald scratched his head as his perplexity deepened, "North? Into the land of the Britons?"

"Elmet Saetna, where Miercians seeking new land strive to repel the Northanhymbrians and Elmetians. The leader of the settlers is an old friend, Ealdorman Wigstan. What better way to prove you are not scheming with them than to fight them? Two snipes with one stone! You will be out of the reach of Aethelred and at the same time disproving those who wish to besmirch you."

"There! I told you father would know what to do!" Guthlac cried and raised his mead to Aethelbald.

"Lord, it is a fine plan," Aethelbald acknowledged, "with the merit that we are tired of idleness on the western borders. Our sinews grow weak with inactivity!"

"The scheme offers further prospects," their host cast a fond glance at his son, "Wigstan is a widower and boasts a daughter of rare beauty, Faryn. Beware, they say he's a wrathful and jealous guardian. Now alas, away! It saddens me you must leave my hearth. Know you are ever welcome but make haste lest the hounds of Aethelred pick up your scent and come snapping at your heels!"

FIVE

Elmet 698 AD

"Gone! Gone? Impossible!"

The son of the underking of Elmet, awake now, threw aside his sheepskin bedcovering. Unconvinced, he pulled open the flap of his tent and stared uphill. The moorland, streaked with long shadows, stretched bleak and empty to the prominent ridge forming the not too distant skyline.

"We caught them like a grouse in a trap. How can this be? Sound the horn! Rouse the men!"

Dressed and armed, the fretful young lord, forced to wait for the readiness of his warriors, incredulous, stared once more up the steep approach to the head of the valley. Turning to the Northanhymbrian ealdorman who served in name as his war counsellor or, he suspected, as his overseer, he could not contain his frustration.

"By God's blood! How can a host vanish in the night?"

"I close-questioned the lookouts, Lord. They swear they stayed alert and saw no lights, heard no sound of–"

"Then Satan sent his demons pluck them away."

The ealdorman made the sign of the cross, spat on the coarse grass at his feet and grumbled, "They *were* trapped. Enclosed on three sides. And we, twice their number...the onset of night saved them…" he hesitated, stared into the distance, "…now there's a thing…

"What? Out with it, speak!"

The Northanhymbrian gazed up the slope and shook his head, "When night cast its shroud, they lit no fires or torches as though they wished to disappear into the blackness. Our camp was alive with bustle, shouting, and leaping flames." He pointed uphill, "They slithered away over the ridge on their bellies like vipers. Pah! Even snakes keep to their burrows in the darkness."

"They will not escape us. Make haste! Order the thegns to harry the men."

The oxen, they decided to leave at the foot of the incline owing to the unsuitable terrain for baggage carts. Gruelling enough for warriors carrying packs and spears, the ascent became more arduous as their commanders urged them on to greater pace. Neither did the coarse grasses and bracken underfoot aid progress up the limestone outcrop. The hardier ones pushed ahead and the host strung out. But this did not perturb their leaders in this wilderness devoid of life. What risk of attack was there? Once surmounted the ridge, they would halt for stragglers while gaining the first sighting of the fleeing enemy below.

The war cries and the hail of javelins that rent the air stated otherwise. Caught unawares and hampered by their burdens, the Elmetians and their Northanhymbrian mercenaries succumbed to the full onslaught of the foe. Splitting into three bands, the Miercians made light of their fewer numbers. In the face of relentless slaughter, their adversaries sought to free themselves of any encumbrance to make use of their spears.

At the head of the leading band of Miercians, Guthlac reached the cluster of warriors around the commanders shouting orders – those he wished above all to slay. Nimble and seasoned in battle, he sidestepped the first iron tip levelled at him and clove the arm bearing it. These weapons were no longer a threat once past the outer rank, the poles too awkward to wield in the confined space. Instead, three warriors brandishing swords rushed at him. One, eyes fixed on the advancing Miercian, tripped over a pack dropped in haste and clutching the man next to him to break his fall, pulled him off balance. Linden shields offered insufficient resistance to the might of Guthlac's battleaxe and neither strength nor courage could prevail against his skill in the face of such mishap. Hard behind him, Aethelbald hewed and hacked towards Guthlac fearing the numbers ranged against his implacable comrade would overwhelm him. His misgivings proved ill-founded.

At last, the remorseless blood-spattered Miercian stood, chest heaving with exertion, facing the commanders of the enemy force. To his astonishment, a rough grasp from behind checked his advance to finish the foe. His commander took charge.

"Look about you!" Aethelbald roared at their adversaries, "See, the day is lost! Lay down your arms! As our hostages, you will be treated with respect until negotiations are concluded."

Guthlac relaxed, understanding at once the good sense behind Aethelbald's decision. These two beaten enemies would be more use to them alive than dead.

The wiser head of the ealdorman overcame the rashness of youth. Seizing the raised sword arm of the underking's son to prevent further foolhardiness, he murmured close urgent words and gestured to the bodies scattered over the moor. The few men left standing were disarmed and captive destined to slavery.

Defeated, the young Briton planted the point of his weapon into the earth and his shoulders sagged, the Northanhymbrian did likewise.

(Three months later).

The sun rose due east, marking the end of summer when a warrior rode into Dore with four companions. The delicate weave of his cloak and the refinement of his features indicated the newcomer as one of noble birth. Servants hastened to stable the horses and others to lead them into the hall of Ealdorman Wigstan, the leader of the Miercian settlers in the south of Elmet. The ealdorman, discussing an offer for the hostages with his counsellors, broke off to greet the newcomers. A cry of recognition from Aethelbald thwarted him.

"Coelwald! Well met! What wyrd leads you to cross our path?"

The countenance of the Miercian nobleman shone with

unfeigned pleasure, "Lord Wigstan, Aethelbald, Guthlac!" The slightest tilt of the head conceded, "Why, to lend my arm to your cause...but more of that ere long. The dust from the road torments our throats!"

At these words, the demure, slender young woman standing to one side, her beauty hidden by her bowed head under a thin head-dress of cream-hued silk, clapped her hands. A servant dashed to provide beakers and flagons of ale. Her eyes the colour of spring-time mint, met with those of Coelwald but she flushed and lowered her head.

"Welcome to my hall. What is mine is yours, but for my daughter," the grey-haired ealdorman said, with more than a hint of menace in his tone.

The hour of affable companionship that followed belied this unpromising start. In that time, Coelwald learnt about the situation in Elmet but those at table were no clearer as to the reason for his arrival. Aethelbald decided to be direct, "What brings you here? We, to clear our names. But you have no such problem."

Taking the nearest ewer, Coelwald sighed and gained time for reflection by refilling each vessel within reach. At last, he said, "The King is at war with Powys, a dispute over Hwiccan lands—"

"The Wealisc rouse themselves too late for us," Guthlac cut in, "Had the wildlings moved sooner, we were never lured to Lindissi." He raised a hand in apology, "Go on!"

"My words will be plain. The same person who drove you here seeks my death. In the confusion of warfare, he made three attempts on my life." The handsome features of the Miercian aetheling took on a troubled faraway expression.

"We hoisted the shieldwall to fend off the hail of weapons from the invaders of Powys. The man at my flank...fell...pierced by a dart...slain."

A moment's silence followed.

"It happens in battle," Aethelbald voiced the thoughts of the others.

Coelwald shook his head, "Not in such a way. My thegn perished not at the hands of the Wealisc. True, he parried one of their javelins with his shield. The force of the weapon forced him backwards to keep his footing and that is when the iron spike impaled him…" he paused and stared at Aethelbald, "…from *behind*!"

"Behind?" Guthlac frowned.

"Ay, it was meant for me. If he hadn't stepped back—"

"The fiend!" Wigstan exclaimed, "With all eyes on the foe, whoever launched it knew he'd be seen by those conniving with him and no other."

Looks of consternation exchanged, they waited in vain for the nobleman to continue.

"By Thunor's bolt, thrice, you said? Three attempts?" Aethelbald urged him on and stroking his beard, with the other hand reached for his ale.

"The battle won, we set up camp for the night near the Saefern." Reliving events, Coelwald stared into his cup as though the amber liquid might reveal some hidden truth. "More often than not, yon valley blows windy and a good breeze fans the campfires. In the darkest hour, I lie awake full of rancour, thinking about yon javelin and grieving for my friend slain by his own. Of a sudden, a red and yellow light flickers and the smell smoke fills my nostrils. My tent flares like a torch. The flames leap with such ardour – I'll never make it out! I slash at the canvas with my seax like a man possessed by a demon and all the time the stench of oil—"

"Yet, you live to tell the tale!" Guthlac said, his voice awed.

"What you should know is…" Coelwald tapped the table with his forefinger, "…someone doused the linen in oil beforehand to feed the fire."

"Did no-one else suspect it?" Wigstan asked.

The distant gaze returned to his face, "There's a clamour of half awake men, one voice rises above all others, *'the wind carried a spark to the cloth,'* shouts he. Men beat out and quench the blaze and the matter ends in confusion."

"And might it have been so?" Aethelbald said.

"But for the javelin, the smell of oil and the third bid to end my life. Poison! I'd quaffed it too if it hadn't been for the King's lolloping gellgi—"

"The King's *what*?" Guthlac laughed.

"Gellgi! Great wolfhounds the Wealisc use in battle. After the fight, we netted several and bought their trust with raw flesh for them to devour. Curious to see them close by, King Aethelred ordered two of them brought to his tent."

The young nobleman closed his eyes, to visualise better the scene.

"These are strange red-gold beasts, wild, savage…my…how their eyes bulge and roll white. Those fangs bared, dripping slaver from the corner of their mouths. Look at this one, why does its nose twitch? The ham shank in the ealdorman's hand! Oh my God! It flashes like an arrow. My mead, dashed to the floor! It's nigh taken the poor man's hand along with the meat…see how he recoils in fear. What's this? The other brute laps up my drink. Oh, how it staggers! Drunk? But, nay, it shudders, whines, foams at the mouth. Dead? Can this be? Poison! Meant for me…"

"What did King Aethelred do?" Guthlac asked.

Narrowing his eyes, Coelwald's spoke in a calmer more measured tone. "The King commanded all the fare be tested on slaves for a few days. None of it poisoned of course. The one who passed me the horn, denied any blame. But let me tell you: a thegn of Coelred gave that vessel to me. Again, another of his closest thegns suggested a spark set my tent afire and the javelin meant for me came from the direction of his men."

"Coelred?" Aethelbald asked, "Why would he wish you dead?"

"Why wouldn't he?" came the sharp reply. "Aethelred is not a young man and since childhood, Coelred has watched his uncle reign in his stead. There are obstacles to him being chosen by the witan as the next King of Mierce, above all his own weak nature. There are others more worthy."

Aethelbald and Guthlac exchanged glances.

As if reading their thoughts, Coelwald went on, "Ay, now you see why Coelred arranged my mother's end at Beardan and tried to settle the blame on you. Thus, he rids himself of two renowned combatants of noble blood, possible contenders to the throne, and involves me in your so-called plot." Wrinkles creased the smooth brow, "I decided not to trust in my luck lasting. We may aid our wyrd, so I chose to distance myself and throw in my lot with those who Coelred seeks to destroy. True, there is no proof against him to lay before you, but the circumstances hint as much." A grim smile curled his lip, "You baulked him by fighting the Northanhymbrians.

Had his scheme succeeded and we three been slain, my half-brother remained to contest him. But he, as the whole kingdom knows, is a weakling, the one person weaker than himself. The witan would never choose either of them in the stead of any of us—"

"True!" Wigstan cried, "I, for one, would not raise my hand in favour of Coelred. Could he have slaughtered the host of Elmet as Aethelbald did? They outnumbered us two to one! What cunning and strength!"

A broad grin lit up Coelwald's face and his deep blue eyes shone, "Come, fill the cups! This is a tale that bears the hearing. Aethelbald, tell me how you bested the foe."

"The situation looked grim for us. Their host, as Lord Wigstan said, far greater than ours and the valley rose to a head enclosed on three sides, with them sealing the fourth."

"Caught in a trap, then."

Guthlac laughed, "Ay, but they reckoned without the cunning of our leader!"

Aethelbald raised his beaker to his friend in acknowledgement, "But it all served for naught were it not for chance. Darkness fell at the right moment, else all was lost."

"So, you attacked in the night, like wolves on the drove?" the aetheling enthused.

The broad features of the warrior needed little incitement to take on an aspect of wolf-like ferocity, "We did not. The rough ground and the blackness made surprise a feat beyond our means. Still, the land around yon valley befriended us."

A frown furrowed the brow of Coelwald, "A riddle is it?"

Wigstan, Guthlac and Aethelbald joined together in hearty laughter.

"The rock is limestone and *riddled* with caves," Aethelbald said, "at the head of the vale to one side is a huge cavern called the Devil's Arse—"

"Why so named?"

"Deep inside, water drains away and makes a noise like a giant's fart! Once within, for the space is vast, it took all our men with room for more, I threatened death to anyone who roared in merriment at the sound." The ealdorman smiled at the memory, "The oafs grew red in the face with the effort not to bellow their mirth at the farting.

We slept in silence and at dawn, like a bear roused from its slumber, we prepared for battle."

"Were you not a-feared to be trapped in yon dank hole?"

"Lost for lost, we risked all. At worst, an attack on a narrower shieldwall, at best – as it turned out – they gave no thought to the hillside but stared ahead, intent on pursuit–"

Guthlac cut in, unable to contain his glee, "They stretched out like a herd of deer and we hit them from the side–"

"Ay, and we seized the lead stag as hostage!" Wigstan's leathery features creased in a huge smile. "We were discussing that when you arrived, Lord Coelwald." He clapped his hands once more and ordered food and more drink.

He set about explaining how Miercian settlers, respecting the land of the local Britons and clearing new acreage from the forest, managed to trade with their neighbours. In this, Guthlac helped, with his gift for understanding the Brittonic tongue. "How these people of South Elmet hate their King, naught but an underking, a Northanhymbrian puppet. One who places them under the heel of the foreign invader. Even so, this wretch still has dreams of driving the Miercians out of his *territory*," he concluded.

All this, Coelwald followed with interest, "Hence the Battle of the Devil's Arse," he said with relish. He raised an eyebrow and looked confused, "so why then, do the Britons not turn to their overlords for help? They pay tribute in cattle, corn and gold, do they not?"

"True," Wigstan said, "it would concern us. Were the Northanhymbrians to raise a host, they could drive us out of Elmet since our own King is occupied in war with Powys, but fate has it that the Northanhymbrians are also thus engaged to the north. In fact, they are hard pressed. News came of their defeat to the Picts less than two moons past."

"We hold the son of the underking of Elmet," Guthlac intervened, "their messenger awaits our reply to their offer."

"Which is?"

"An exchange. The firstborn for younger twin brothers who are but children and a promise of peace for settlers in the south as far as the River Scheth but not beyond."

Resting his chin on his fist, Coelwald said, "Reasonable enough, on the face of it, but can you trust them?"

"Lord Guthlac suggested meeting at the crossing of the Scheth. From the near bank, there will be clear sight of their party with no chance of betrayal. What say you?"

"The plan is sound," the aetheling nodded toward Guthlac, "I shall ride with you for the exchange of hostages."

"By Thunor's anvil, I do not trust the Britons," Aethelbald growled, "here is what we will do…"

SIX

Elmet 698 AD

From the steep wooded hillside of the Limb valley, the Miercians gazed down beyond where the stream merged with the River Scheth to the designated meeting place. For the moment, out of sight to any observer, they surveyed the forest behind the approaching group for the slightest glint of metal. Nothing untoward caught the eye and the party below of six horsemen, escorting the two children on ponies, appeared in accord with the agreement struck. The lead rider nudged his mount into the river, shallow where the Scheth flowed over impervious shale and grit.

Cautious, for each man feared betrayal, Ealdorman Wigstan leant toward Guthlac and said, "On the face of it, we can proceed."

"What say you, Coelwald?" Guthlac asked.

"The ford is our friend. Once they are across and in the open, there is no chance of a treacherous attack. Hidden in the forest, Aethelbald and his men by now will be sure no foe lurks. I say we go down to meet them."

The sneer on the face of their British hostage at their wariness annoyed Guthlac, "your people," he patted the haft of his axe, "are known for perfidy. At the slightest hint of deceit, you will be the first to pay!"

Under a domed canopy of ash trees, they urged their reluctant horses down the slope until they came to level ground where they veered toward the crossing point. A rough voice, with a heavy accent, hailed them in their own tongue. "We have the hostages to exchange! Let's get it over so we can be on our way!"

A curt nod from Wigstan to the others and he ordered the two captives to dismount.

"What, why!" the Elmetian lordling cried.

Gratified to pay back the Briton's smirk with mockery, Guthlac said, "Don't imagine we'd waste a good horse on you! Whelps like you are more suited to a pony."

The hate-laden glare directed at him pleased Guthlac. An unwise retort from the hostage might have been punished. As it was, he revelled in taunting him with laughter as he walked towards his own people. Passing the two children, the King of Elmet's son did not deign them with so much as a glance. Guthlac frowned and edged his horse on a few paces. Strange a brother should not look at, never mind comfort, his younger siblings on consigning them to the enemy! The skinny, pinched faces of the children lacked nobility contrasting with their fine clothing. Unwary and knowing not the foe spoke their language, Guthlac heard one of the escorts snigger, "The fools will believe anything!"

In a rush of blood, he kicked his horse to a gallop. "Betrayal!" he yelled as he bore down on the two men drawing nigh unto the awaiting group. A sword flew through the air and the Northanhymbrian seized it in time to turn and parry a shuddering blow from the axe of the enraged Miercian. The other hostage dragged a rider from his horse and mounted it while his five warriors drew their weapons. Over the shock of these events, Wigstan, Coelwald and the other three men charged forward to prevent their brave comrade from being overwhelmed.

Out from the trees, on the far side of the Scheth, emerged the enemy host bristling with spears and javelins. In response, a war cry echoed across the valley as Aethelbald and his warriors poured out from the undergrowth. The sight of their swollen numbers halted the men of Elmet in their tracks. But by the river, the skirmish raged. The Northanhymbrian, clutching a gaping wound at his throat fell dying, his blood soaking into the earth. At the same time,

Wigstan crashed to the ground in the throes of death. In turn, Coelwald's sword impaled the warrior who had dealt the ealdorman the mortal blow.

To the fore of his running men, Aethelbald seized Wigstan's frightened horse, calmed and mounted it, grabbed a javelin from one of his men and headed for the fray. At the same moment, the son of the King of Elmet wheeled his steed and galloped for the ford. Leaving his comrades to finish off the two remaining warriors, Aethelbald sped past in pursuit of the Briton, heedless of the enemy horde on the opposite bank. The fleeing man's beast had entered the river in a cascade of silver sunlit spray. The rider rose and fell four steps with the motion of the jolting animal as Aethelbald, slowed his own mount. Entering the water, he gripped the creature with his knees, steadied his aim and hurled the weapon. The spiteful iron tip pierced the Briton between the shoulder blades and the howl of fury from the onlooking Elmetians bade their toppled Lord farewell to this world. A hail of javelins darkened the sky above the river in swift retribution as Aethelbald struggled to turn his horse and scramble up the bank. Three of the darts found their mark, two in the flesh of the bucking, squealing, animal and one in the shoulder of the Miercian, sending him crashing to the turf.

Unmolested, the Elmetians retrieved the body of their King's son while the Miercians tended to Aethelbald. In the time needed to ease the spike out of the wound, the men of Elmet vanished into the forest. The ealdorman refused to have a litter made for him, "By Thunor's hairy forearm, it's naught but a scratch," he muttered, clutching a cloth to the gash to staunch the flow of blood. "Give me a horse and make the stretcher instead for the body of our brave comrade."

"Ay," said Coelwald, his expression grave, "we must console his daughter and consider her prospects. She is without protection."

"Poor Faryn," Guthlac said, "she will be heart-broken. We must do what we can for her."

"Whatever is needed," said Aethelbald, masking the curl of his lip with a groan.

The two horsemen who had accompanied the four ealdormen each hoisted a child hostage on his mount. On the ride back, the comrades discussed the implications of the skirmish at the river.

"I told you, Britons are not to be trusted," Aethelbald said.

"Pity I didn't realise the deceit sooner…" Guthlac said, in idle recrimination. Gone, the safeguard for their settlements. The implacable enmity of the King of Elmet would be stoked further by a desire for retribution for the loss of his firstborn.

"Nobody plays us for fools," Aethelbald said, teeth gritted against the pain, "I slew him and I'd do it a thousand times over."

They agreed there would be no immediate consequences following the slaying. Elmet reeled from defeat high on the moors and Northanhymbra struggled with graver problems of her own.

Behind Guthlac's horse, the birch poles of the litter carrying the corpse of Wigstan bounced over the rough ground and stirred up a plume of dust. Thus did the bedraggled group enter the stronghold of Dore.

At the sight of Lord Wigstan's body, women wailed and small children buried their heads into the folds of their mother's dress. Faryn knelt, pale and drawn, in dignified silence beside the stretcher, where she brushed the dust from the brow of her sire.

"Come, let us take him to the church," Guthlac said, "the priest will pray for his soul."

Graceful and slow, the daughter rose, clasped her hands in front of her lap and walked head bowed next to the horse. Still no tear ran down her face.

Speaking with urgency among themselves, a group of thegns watched as Coelwald helped Aethelbald down from his steed.

"We must find a healer—" he began but broke off as the first of the thegns addressed the wounded ealdorman.

"Heed me, Lord, if you will."

Aethelbald winced and nodded, "What is it?"

The remaining five men hastened over to stand at the other's back.

"We are of one mind, Lord. With the sad passing of our leader, there is but one man fit to take his place," the weather-beaten scarred face dared to express hope, "I pledge my service, Lord."

"Ay, me too!" gruff voices echoed each other.

Settlers not occupied in the fields set down their tools and gathered to witness the scene. A cheer burst from them at these words.

Coelwald grinned into his comrade's face, thought better of

clapping him on the back, given the gash on his shoulder, and said, "What say you, Lord Aethelbald?"

"I declare ten days' mourning for Lord Wigstan. Everyone to attend Mass each one to pray for his soul. At the end of that time, I will give my reply…if I don't bleed to death first."

The clamour of voices, the din of shouted advice, the bustling away to a healer, all served to conceal the ealdorman's true feelings.

When he lay on his pallet alone, his wound cleansed and treated with salve, he allowed himself a grim smile. Reaching across to his tunic, he pulled out the beauteous ring and contemplated its exquisite craftsmanship. If the jewel could speak, he fancied, would it not relate that his wyrd bore the guise of a setback? At the end of the allotted period, with some feigned reluctance, he would accept the settlers' offer. Unbeknown to them, they would be the first stone paving his way to his ultimate end: 'Britain-ruler' – *'Bretwaldas, by Thunor!'*

Three days after her father's death, Faryn knelt alone before the mound of fresh compacted earth of his grave. The tears she had held back from the scrutiny of others coursed down her cheeks. Head bowed, she felt his presence beside her and murmured her despair to his spirit.

"Father, what is to become of me without you? Wherever you are, gaze down upon your daughter, bereft and unshielded. I pray protect and guide me, as ever you did." She offered up a *Pater Noster*, as he had taught her, for his soul before wiping her face with her sleeve. Then she stood and with determined step made her way to the healer's hut.

The unmarried woman with a squint from birth, well-loved in the burh for her gentle nature, opened the door to Faryn's knock. Surprised to see the daughter of her Lord, her mouth dropped open, giving her the ill-deserved expression of a simpleton.

"Lady," she said, "what brings you to my poor home?"

Unsettled by the spinster's cross-eye, used as she was to meeting the gaze of other women and not knowing where to look, she covered her confusion by blurting, "May I come in?"

Inside, she revealed the reason for her visit: to relieve the woman of her duty to tend Aethelbald.

She left the cluttered cavern of herbs, petals and vials of garish liquids with her head full of instructions and a woven basket on her arm. The trug contained a salve and a solution of crushed plantain to bathe the wound to keep it free of infection. She hurried away with a spring in her step for the first time since losing her father.

"Well met! Where are you off to in such a hurry?"

Startled then flustered, caught dwelling amid her thoughts, Faryn stared into the beaming face of Coelwald. Regaining her composure, she greeted him and replied, "On my way to treat Lord Aethelbald's wound."

The young nobleman, elegant in utterance as in garb, said, "Let me carry your basket, Lady, for I crave your forbearance."

In spite of herself, her deep green eyes widened and her cheeks flamed but she surrendered the trug, asking, "Lord Coelwald, what is it you wish to tell me?"

They strolled past the low thatched eave of the forge, whence a blast of hot air accompanied a youth bearing tongs outside, a red-hot horseshoe in their jaws. He plunged the ardent metal, hissing steam, into a barrel of water standing by the door.

Not sparing the ceorl a glance, the aetheling sought the right words. In truth, he had practised this in his head countless times, but his sincere admiration for the maid, to his own surprise, stilted his tongue. His speech seemed clumsy to his own ears, "Lady, the – *er* – unfortunate circumstances you find yourself in…I mean without a protector…fill me with dismay…" he paused with a sideways glance to gauge her reaction. Apart from a tightening of the lips, it was impossible to tell. Heartbeat quickening, he struggled on, "…you are a woman of ten and seven years and most comely. Were your father with us, I am sure he would agree the time is ripe for you to wed."

The colour rose in the young woman's cheeks but she said nothing. Taking her silence as consent, Coelwald strove to make his case. Turning to stand in front of her, staring submerged in the depths of her eyes, conviction in the rightness of his decision grew.

"We are what our parents made us," pride in his forebears evident, "wed with me Faryn and you will lack for naught. Who knows, one day you may be Queen of Mierce. What say you, will you take me for your husband?"

Where before she stood with heightened colour, now her visage was pale and she no longer met his eyes. The torment of her silence ended at last, "Lord Coelwald, you do me great honour beyond the wildest hopes of any maid. I cannot give you the answer you seek. Three days separate me from my father's loving embrace and my heart overflows with sorrow—"

"Dear Lady, forgive me. Driven by love and concern, I meant no thoughtlessness—"

"Why do we not each take time? I should not wish to be wed out of pity and, at present, grief veils all thoughts in a grey mist."

Aware impetuousness had clouded his judgment, Coelwald sought to remedy the error, "Give no consideration to the former, Lady, you shall be betrothed for your beauty and charm. As for the rest, I am content to wait for the pain to ease."

They came upon two small girls sitting in the shade of an oak growing but a score and ten paces from the house where Aethelbald lay. They broke off their activity to greet Lady Faryn who, with great seriousness, inspected their handiwork. Twigs dressed in a rag formed the body and a turnip top, the head of a doll.

"What a lovely creature you have made!" the noblewoman exclaimed. "Now you must collect daisies to make a chain to go round her pretty neck."

Bursting with excitement, the infants dashed off to begin the adventure of picking the flowers.

Coelwald laughed, "You have a way with little ones, Lady," he handed the basket to her. "here you are arrived."

He took his leave, elegant as ever, and she watched his back as he strode with purpose past her father's...*her* home. Fighting back a tear, she reflected that she had lied to the ealdorman. If there was but sadness in her heart, why then did it skip and flutter at the thought of treating Aethelbald's wound? She hurried to his door, knocked and entered at his call.

The patient crossed himself in mock horror, "Swear by all the saints you will not change back into the cross-eyed witch who seeks to frighten my shoulder back to health."

Setting her basket down by the bed, the young woman laughed, "Let me raise you to sit against yon bolster. It will be easier to unbind and see the cut."

When she placed her hands under his arms, he made to kiss her on the lips, in an instant she turned her face away and took it on her cheek. She hauled him up with excessive force, marvelling at his solid weight. For his part, he winced and complained, "Ah, vixen, I meant no harm!"

"Behave in a seemly manner," she warned, hiding her true emotions, "else I shall send straight back the poor healer it pleases you to scoff at."

She removed his shirt and her pulse pounded at the sight of his broad shoulders and muscled chest. Their eyes met and the roguish glint she found there did nothing to calm her. Ruffled, she leant him forward, relieved not to see his face and took off the binding. The ragged gash, bright red and grainy startled her but she unstopped the vial and rinsed the raw flesh. The liquid must have stung but he did not flinch nor utter a word as she applied the salve. Bandage tied and shirt laced, he seized her by the wrist, but let her go at once.

"Pray Lady, sit here with me a while," he patted the bedcover, "the hag says I must stay abed for two more days that the cut may heal the better. But I am bored and lonesome."

"I will. But see your hands do not stray and recount what happened by the river," his brow furrowed as her voice caught, "I-I must learn how my father died."

Gentle in the telling, he embellished her father's role in saving the brave Guthlac and played down his own role in the skirmish.

The next two days, she came and sat with him, part nurse, part companion. In particular, she questioned him about life in the King's hall at Tame Weorth and listened to his descriptions with rapt attention. The quirks of his expressions, the creases in his face, the ready smile and the dangerous glister in those eyes that reminded her of the blue of harebells grew familiar and irresistible. At night, before she fell asleep, by day as she went about her household tasks, she thought of naught else.

On the third visit, as Faryn bound his gashed shoulder, he let his head loll close to hers. A wily hunter too experienced to startle the doe, he made no move other than to gaze into her eyes. The longing dwelling there told him she was his for the taking, but shrewd and guileful, he made the drawing of his lips toward hers imperceptible. They met. Shy, she pulled away and he let her. Scrutinising his face, she saw what she believed to be love and gentleness. It brought her back and their kisses became long and sensuous.

When his strength returned, Aethelbald began to walk outdoors and, to Coelwald's vexation, Faryn accompanied him. Harvest time nigh, the wheat swayed in the breeze and coated the land in a golden mantle stretching out before the burh. The stalks stood as tall as Faryn as they approached the edge of the field.

"Give me your hand," he took it and led the virgin in among the corn.

"What are you doing?" she asked, but she knew full well.

They lay down together out of sight and their kisses became more passionate. After their coupling, he took a cloth from within his tunic and used it to wipe the blood from the inside of her thighs.

"We cannot have you staining your dress for all to see, my love," he whispered and helped her to lower the garment back down to her ankles.

She gazed wide-eyed with a mixture of love and shock into his face before burying her head in shame against his chest. Knowledgeable in these matters, Aethelbald stroked her hair and murmured the sweet lies he knew she wished to hear. When she lifted her head, as he expected, her visage was radiant with adoration.

The days passed in delight as they entwined until Faryn knew every feature of his body from the smallest scar to the curious crescent-shaped mole at his hip. Under his deft touch, instead, the folds and crannies of her entrancing form revealed their secrets.

The first morn of reaping arrived and Aethelbald vanished. Faryn sought him throughout the burh but did not find him. In the evening, she sat under the spreading branches of the oak. When he appeared, an inane question escaped her, "Where have you been?" while he stood with a hooded falcon on a wrist and six quail dangling from a cane.

"What does it look like?" he said, passing her the game birds, "Find a woman able to pluck them without tearing the skin. They will make a decent supper. Now I must rest until dinner."

Dismayed at his coldness, she watched him turn his back on her and disappear indoors. Blinking back tears, she shook her head as if to shake away her doubts. Tiredness might account for his manner toward her after being out so long in the fresh air. Convinced of this now, she went off to attend to the quail.

Early the next morning, no reply came to her knock at his door.

On asking one of her father's thegns, she discovered the three ealdormen had ridden into the forest to stalk deer. Indeed, they returned blithe but weary with a hind slung across Aethelbald's horse. Pleased to see him this cheerful, she told herself there was no harm in his going hunting with Guthlac and Coelwald. But why hadn't he told her beforehand?

Courteous as ever, Coelwald begged her to arrange a dinner in the hall that they might enjoy their prize together. Having obliged them in this, at last, she found Aethelbald alone resting on his bed.

"Why did you not tell me you would be away to the forest?" She tried to keep her voice light and carefree.

"Must I account for my every movement?"

"Indeed not. Rest. I will see you at dinner."

A dignified exit might undo the mischief of her question, she hoped but she had no need of instinct to tell her all was not well. Had she done something to upset him? Was she suffocating him with her presence? Hadn't he said he loved her? She loved him, what then was the problem? At dinner, as of custom, she sat with the other noblewomen at the far end of the hall and her gaze kept straying to Aethelbald. Not once did she catch him looking her way. Instead, the banter and mirth of his comrades held his attention. And where was the harm in that? She had little appetite and excused herself with the ladies. If he saw her leave, might he not come to her out of concern? When she awoke after a restless night, she had the answer to this fancy.

The pattern of evasion and coldness continued for days with Aethelbald supplying one plausible excuse after another until she was forced to face the truth: he had cast her aside. First, her father's death, now this – she gave in to her tears. Guthlac came upon her sobbing on a bench near her house, in the shade of damsons vying with nearby greengages to boast the heaviest laden tree.

"Lady, what ails you?"

He sat next to her and took her hand and though he squeezed it, she remained in silence, head hunched over her knees. The ealdorman waited but she was not forthcoming.

"The pain of your loss will ease, Faryn, as the memory of your father grows warmer in your heart."

At last, she looked up at him, wet-faced with red-rimmed eyes, her beauty striking in her grief.

"It is Aethelbald…" she quavered.

"What of him?"

"He told me he loved me but now he uses me ill."

"Aethelbald adores nobody more than himself. Why waste your attentions on him, when there is one better than he despairing for love of you?"

She sniffed and rubbed her cheeks with her sleeve, never letting go of his other hand.

"Who?"

"Lord Coelwald wanders the burh like a wraith bemoaning his bitter fate. Were you to give him the slightest hope, he would betroth to you in a trice. Upon my oath."

She began to weep again, "I am not worthy of him."

Guthlac wiped the wetness from her face with his free hand. "Come, you are a fine lady and one of great beauty. What nonsense is this?"

"I am blighted," she hung her head in shame, "and I love another. If I cannot have Aethelbald, I will hie me to a nunnery."

"A nun? That is a serious decision, not to be taken out of anger or self-disdain."

"Often have I thought about it in these days. My mind is made up!"

"How strange!"

"Strange?"

"Ay," Guthlac smiled, "odd we should set the same course at the same time."

Faryn frowned, confused till realisation dawned, "You? You will become a monk?"

The ealdorman nodded, "I leave for Hreapandune within the week. There is a double house there," he noted her confusion, "I mean nuns and monks worship in the same abbey. Will you travel with me, Lady Faryn?"

She questioned him at length about his choice and discovered a man she did not know existed. Satisfied, she said, "There is much to learn about the faith but I shall be a willing novice. My heart is a hollow vessel. At least, I shall try to make amends for my sins and hope God will give meaning to my life."

He left her more uplifted, agreeing to break their separate decisions and shared destiny to Aethelbald since the noblewoman could not bear to look her seducer in the face.

Guthlac chose to impart the news of Lady Faryn first.

The fleeting relief smothered by false incredulity on the part of Aethelbald did not deceive his friend, who knew him too well.

"A nun! Well, if that's what she wants. The poor child must miss her father."

Guthlac snorted, "You, of course, have nothing to do with her choice! But hark, I did not come to judge or condemn. I came to tell you, I too shall enter the monastery at Hreapandune."

A slap across the face could not have left Aethelbald more shocked. The stunned silence lasted the time it took for the ealdorman's face to register a range of emotions. The one that prevailed was disbelief.

"It's not true!" he cried. "You cannot become a monk!" His stare probed his comrade's face searching for any trace of insincerity. Failing in this, he began what he supposed might be an appeal, "But you cannot, I love you like a brother. Don't leave me here alone after all we have been through together!" Guthlac stood unmoved and wordless. Aethelbald bunched his fists, "I need you to help me conquer Elmet and by Thunor's—"

"I told you before, I'm tired of this life."

"It's because of what I did to Faryn isn't it? I can make that right. If you agree to—"

"Make no promises you will fail to keep. My decision has nothing to do with the maid. I believe, though I knew it not at the time, at Bryn Alyn the resolution matured."

While Aethelbald, pale and tense, digested this, Coelwald arrived. Fury distorted his visage, his natural grace replaced by a rude accusation levelled at Guthlac.

"What have you done to Faryn?"

Aethelbald and the accused exchanged glances: one man's guilty, the other's confused, "I, nothing!"

"Don't lie! You poisoned her mind."

"How so?"

The colour rose in the aetheling's face, "You are going to be a monk and you persuaded her to become a bride of Christ. I would wed her. Will you snatch her from me?"

Guthlac tried to place a hand on his comrade's arm but Coelwald shook him off, his anger mounting.

"The decision of Faryn has naught to do with me. I told her of my choice *after* she informed me of hers. Mine was a long time in the making and I kept it to myself."

A sneer curled Aethelbald's lips. "It was not *you* she wished to wed but me. Since I will not oblige, she looks beyond this world for another to take my place," he ended with a harsh laugh.

The hand of Coelwald flew to his sword but Guthlac moved in front of him.

"Be not rash, there is nothing to be gained. The Lady is lost to you. No need to add to your losses. I wish to leave Dore secure in the knowledge my dearest friends remain boon companions."

"Friends is a strong word, but in any case not in Dore for I too will depart. Neither is this a sudden decision," Coelwald said, "I must return to Tame Weorth to the King. He must be warned against treason and set on his guard. In spite of our differences, I will speak up for you Aethelbald, rest assured." Turning to Guthlac, he added, "On your account, there is no need for my intercession. A monk is no danger to anyone." A step forward and he embraced the ealdorman.

"Is this wise? After three attempts on your life?" Guthlac asked.

"It must be done."

He turned to Aethelbald, "We shall meet, I hope, in happier times. Come, Guthlac!"

Aethelbald watched them walk away and disconsolate, fingering Osthryth's ring, muttered, "By Thunor's hammer, how will I take Elmet without the two of you?"

SEVEN

Hreapandune 699 AD

Moonless the night, on his way back to the dormitory from the refectory after Vespers but nearer Compline, Guthlac stared up at the starlit sky.

'As if God, the Illuminator, took a paintbrush, charged it with blue-white paint and flicked it at a black canvas.'

The bright pinpoints scintillated but afforded little light. The two and a half months of his time at the Abbey had taught Guthlac to find his way around the abbey in the dark but this night proved blacker than most. A chilling breeze wafted against his cheek from the River Trente flowing adjacent to the monastery walls.

A sound made him start, setting the warrior in him on his guard, "Who's there?" he called, feeling foolish.

'Who will be here if not a fellow monk?'

The rustling again, the slap of a sandal and he turned only to take a mighty blow to the side of the head.

"Brother Hethor, have you brought the ewer?"

"Ay."

"What yer waitin' for? Pour it over his tunic."

"Waste of good wine if you ask me."

"No-one's askin' ye. Do it! Ay, that's right. Now ye two, drag him over to the well."

The band of six, the worse for drink, struggled to haul the dead weight to the waterhole. Hethor, unsteady on his feet and stupid in his cups, cackling, flung the earthenware pitcher down the shaft and rejoiced in the resonant splash his action provoked.

"Let's drop him down after it," he said and he belched.

The youngest of the brothers protested, voice slurred, "We're supposed to teach him a lesson," he tugged at Hethor's sleeve, "not kill him and lose our souls to the Devil."

"Ay, yer right Brother. Yon's a bad enough cut to his head, oozin' blood. Wyard, yer a bit too handy wi' yon cudgel. Hie away to the stables, hide it be'ind the bales of straw. Don't want no-one findin' it an' askin' awkerd questions."

The aggressor dashed off to do his bidding.

"Hethor, make yersen useful and get some of yon blood on the stonework round the well. Go on, don't be a shrinkin' wench! Ah, get away! If yer want summat doin' best do it yersen." Thus saying, he wiped his hand across the wound and smeared the sharp edge of the low wall surrounding the well. Till he was satisfied, he repeated the action, not that he could be too sure, given the darkness of the night.

"That should do it. Makes it look like he fell and hit his head in a drunken stupor…"

The monks joined him in his foolish laughter heedless of their own befuddled state.

"Shush!" he hissed, "Lest anyone hear or see us. Come on let's get away."

The brothers staggered towards their sleeping quarters and spun round alarmed at the sound of running.

"Wyard! Ye idiot, ye had us worried!"

"Good and proper," the monk whispered, short of breath, "it'll learn him to play the high and mighty and preach to us. We'll drink what we want, eh, brothers?"

"Ay," they chorused as they barged into each other in their oafish clumsiness trying to enter the doorway to the dormitory.

"Wait! No-one breathe a word o' this. Keep yer mouths shut. Ye all saw how much *Brother La-di-da* quaffed from the cellars, didn't ye? Now *that* ye can talk about."

A short while before Compline, a commotion broke out in the enclosed courtyard of the abbey. A monk on his way to the church for the service went over to the well to slake his thirst and found the body.

"Help, help! Here's a disgrace! Quick!" He pressed his fingers to the monk's neck. "Fetch a torch! Get Brother Infirmarian! This man's barely alive, his pulse is weak." Straightening up, he rose, "Here, by the well!" he called to the one with a flaring brand, who hurried over, trailing three companions. By the light of the flickering flame, he gasped, "Why, it's Brother Guthlac. See! he must have fallen, there's blood here on this stone where he fell and struck his head. He reeks of wine!"

"But Brother Guthlac is abstinent–"

"He must have given in to temptation…"

"Strange!–"

They broke off as the infirmarian, bearing another torch, and in the company of curious monks, hastened over to them.

"Stand back, stand back! Hold the flame steady. Let me see…"

A brief inspection, a series of orders and soon, brothers returned carrying a stretcher to carry the victim to the infirmary.

The next morning, his head throbbing and eyes two narrow slits, Guthlac tried to focus on the blurred face of Abbess Aelfthryde and the infirmarian. When he heard the Mother Superior state his actions were out of character, he wanted to protest his innocence but he lapsed into unconsciousness. Thus, he failed to hear the monk tell her to return in two days when the patient ought to be in condition to respond to her questions.

This proved to be right. Bound head still pounding, his vision of the stern and disapproving expression of the abbess did nothing to raise his spirits.

"What in Heaven's name drove you to abuse the wine the Cellarer never begrudges? I expect better conduct from a man of your upbringing."

"Mother, I do not drink–"

"Silence! Do not test my patience! There are witnesses to your sinful excesses. Six brothers describe how you indulged in one ewer after another until, like a sot, you staggered out of the refectory into the night. Thence, though no-one saw you, you fell and broke your head against the well. Divine Providence led one of the brethren to draw water and find you lying senseless." The Mother Superior paused to let her words take effect, she pursed her lips, then added, "Are you ready to answer my question? Or do you need a confessor? What made you yield to the wiles of the Devil?"

"I did not! They are liars—"

"*Six* monks lie?" The abbess shook her head, "Brother Infirmarian when this sinner is well enough to leave his bed, have him taken to confinement. Three days alone without food and only water ought to be time enough to reflect on his misdeeds."

Guthlac tried to sit up to plead his innocence but his body betrayed him. Falling back to his bolster with a groan, he managed to utter, "Wait!…" in a feeble voice. In vain. The head of the abbey had more important matters to attend to and her determined stride had taken her beyond earshot and out of the infirmary.

Within the barred room, two days later, Guthlac knelt and sought the grace to forgive his lying assailants. In one corner of his bare cell stood a bucket for his bodily ease and on a bench, a pitcher of water. A stone shelf, without blanket or pillow, made a comfortless bed. Regret served for naught, but he chided himself for having remonstrated with the drunkards. His attacker must be one of them. Acting like his brother's keeper had brought him here – foolish presumption. What authority had he? Those sinners would answer like everyone for their conduct on the day of judgement.

Prayer and contemplation did not weigh on him. Indeed, he welcomed the chance to reflect in peace and solitude. There was so much he did not understand about the course his life had taken and of his relationship with God. Thus, he regarded his release, when it came, as an unwelcome intrusion. A monk unlocked the door and gave orders to follow to the quarters of the abbess.

A surprise awaited him there. The six inebriates stood in a line, heads bowed. Abbess Aelfthryde faced them, a nun at either side of her and, behind, a threesome of laymen. Upon his arrival, her stern expression if possible grew graver. Guthlac's heart sank. Were the false accusations to worsen? Was he to be expelled from the abbey?

"Brother Guthlac," the Mother Superior said, "we owe you a

deep and sincere apology. The Holy Spirit has moved the youngest of these miscreants to a full confession. The Devil sets snares for the weak and ignorant and plays on their vices. Pope Gregory taught that *gula* is a deadly sin and the intemperate consumption of wine is, indeed, gluttony." The abbess pointed to the group of monks, their abject attitude, Guthlac felt sure, owing more to being unmasked than to real contrition, she paused and closed her eyes. Standing in this way for a time, the silence weighed like a millstone. At last, she looked up her stare piercing the malefactors. "Wyard, step forward!"

The cudgel-wielding rogue moved two paces towards his abbess.

"Thank God every day your sinfulness did not end in murder. In His mercy, he spared you the noose. Reeve, this man is no longer a monk. Take him and punish him as the king's law obliges." The oldest of the laymen gestured to the two stout men by his side. They seized his arms and dragged him away.

"Osulf, you instigated the attack and for this reason you are unworthy of the Order of St Benedict. You will leave this abbey forthwith!"

"My Lady," he knelt, "I beg yer, it wuz the drink as did it. It clouded me thinkin'. I promise ye, I'll n'er touch another drop–"

The Abbess turned to the Reeve and nodded, "Ensure this wretch is escorted out of Hreapandune and sent on his way."

"Ye'll pay fer this–" the villain snarled, glaring at Guthlac but his voice was strangled as the huge hand of the Reeve encircled his throat and forced him out of the room.

"As for you three," the Mother Superior indicated the three abashed monks one at a time with her forefinger, "no wine or ale for a year and a day. You will linger after every office and recite the *Pater Noster* five times for the same period. At the next delivery of wine, *you* will haul the waggon from the wharf to the abbey in place of the ox. Now go!"

The last monk, a youth of but a score of winters, sank to his knees and begged permission to speak.

"Granted."

"Brother Guthlac, I beg pardon for your poor head…and for you – *er* – being shut away and all…how can I ever forgive myself?"

"Brother Bernulf, the Abbess' voice cut like a seax, "forgiveness is not yours to bestow. You must prostrate yourself before the Lord and, He, witnessing true repentance will ease your pain."

"Come, Brother," Guthlac raised him from his knees, "Let's embrace and bear no grudges. I had no right to chastise you. I shall pray to learn humility."

The two men embraced and Guthlac clapped the younger man on the back.

"It is well done, brothers," Abbess Aelfthryde said, "but there remains the matter of your penitence, Bernulf. It shall be thus: for a year and a day, you will serve Brother Guthlac. Whatever task he gives unto you will be performed to the best of your ability. Eschew the company of the other three offenders and drink no more than one cup of wine or ale a day. Go now, ask the Lord for absolution."

The monk bowed out of the chamber and Guthlac made to follow.

"Wait, Brother! I would speak with you." The Abbess gestured to one of the nuns, "Remind me to talk with the Cellarer, Sister, for he must mend his profligate ways." She faced Guthlac, "When the Prior admitted you into our community, he assured me of your calling and his judgment is sound. Since you are here, I admit to the sin of curiosity. Why would a famed warrior, of a sudden despise the world, turning his back on his parents' wealth and home and his companions?"

Guthlac, who had thought of little else during his confinement, began an explanation. Of how, abandoning his youthful virtues for love of tales of yore, he had gained his fearsome reputation. But in Bryn Alyn, admiring the beauty of Nature created by God, in a moment, he had changed. Pondering on kings forsaking this world through miserable death in a wretched end to a sinful existence, he understood their great wealth held no worth for them in their graves. And he mused on his own vain life daily hastening to an end. Face alight with joy, he smiled at the Abbess, and said, "Inspired by godly fear, I vowed to the Father I would be His servant."

Before leaving the presence of the Mother Superior, Guthlac declared his desire to learn the Psalms, canticles, hymns and prayers.

Abbess Aelfthryde, struck by his words, watched the handsome novice leave her room. She looked at the elderly nun by her side,

"Sister, what think you? Have we not stood in the presence of a mild and modest…an exceptional…young man?"

The three nuns discussed Guthlac for a while and concluded that God had sent the abbey a convert out of the ordinary, one with remarkable purity of mind.

After lunch each day, Guthlac went to the library, using his free time to study the psalms. For afternoon work before Vespers, he was allocated to the scriptorium, where he would learn the skills of bookbinding. A week after meeting the Abbess, he was concentrating on splitting an oak log lengthways into four wedged-shaped pieces under the supervision of a skilled monk. The boards acquired would serve when covered in leather as fine covers for bound illuminated manuscripts.

"Perfect," the brother praised him, "now, tip it on its point and saw the board along here–"

The door to the workshop flew back with a crash.

"What in Heaven's name–"

"Sorry, Brother! Brother Guthlac, come as fast as you can! There's been a horrible mishap!" Brother Bernulf, red in the face and breathless, blurted his message. "Go to the Werburgh chapel at once. The Abbess awaits you there!"

Guthlac hastened out of the scriptorium with his young servant beside him.

"What is the nature of this *mishap*, Bernulf?

"I know naught, Brother, a nun charged me with finding you and told me: *'There's been a horrible mishap. Send Brother Guthlac to the Werburgh chapel where the abbess awaits him.'* That's what she said, word for word."

They hurried into the abbey church where Guthlac gestured to Bernulf to sit and wait in the nave. Light flickered from the aisle to the left of the raised platform where the altar stood and whence came subdued voices. There he knew, was the small shrine dedicated to Saint Werburgh, the first abbess of Hreapandune. Genuflecting before the tabernacle, he made the sign of the cross before striding to the small side chapel.

"It's Faryn, poor child!" the Abbess greeted him, "I fear she committed a mortal sin." The nun stood aside to let Guthlac pass. Lying on a board supported by two trestles, beautiful in death as in life, so natural did she seem he half-expected the young woman to open her eyes. Guthlac's heart sank. Was it possible that this splendid creature would laugh and sing no more?

"How?" he managed in a choked voice.

In an act of uncommon kindness, Abbess Aelfthryde rested a hand on his arm and murmured, "Strength, Brother!"

An elderly nun, one he recognised from the Abbess' room, answered.

"Our sister cannot have been in the river long as you can see from her flesh, not bloated or spoilt in any way…"

The dispassionate tone of the woman did not please him but she continued, "…the Brother Infirmarian says he found her lungs filled with water – death by drowning."

Guthlac turned to the Abbess, "Why did you say she committed a mortal sin?"

Aelfthryde frowned and stared glassy-eyed at the pilaster behind Guthlac, "Only God knows how much we love Him and how responsible we are for our actions. We must leave judgment to Him alone."

"Are you saying she took her own life? It cannot be!"

The lips of the older nun tightened into a thin line, "Sister Faryn spent her days weeping. No-one could console her. Nor would she tell us what ailed her. At first, we thought she wished to return home but when I suggested this, it worsened her anguish." The nun put her hand over her mouth for a moment as though wishing to halt her flow of words. At last, she added, "We sent her to our father confessor but she refused to tell the priest of her woes–"

The Abbess intervened, "Hers is a grave sin. Not only did she end her life but the Infirmarian is sure that she was with child."

The words stung and Guthlac gazed upon the fair features in anguish.

"Why, oh why did she not come to me. I know the father and I might…" his voice broke and he fought back a sob, instead, moving to the side of the trestle table to stroke the dead woman's hair, still damp from the river. "…Ah, Faryn, Faryn, what have you done?"

"We should not despair of the eternal salvation of those who commit this act," the Mother Superior said, "but Faryn cannot be buried in consecrated ground, in the abbey. That is why I sent for you. Shall we send the body back to Dore? Is there family?"

"Nay, My Lady," his reply was near to vehement and the abbess widened her eyes, "Faryn would not wish to return. Let her be interred by the Trente where she chose to end her suffering."

"I feel sad this poor troubled child faced the gift of a new life as something so unbearable, so insurmountable she opted to withdraw from the love of God and of her sisters," Aelfthryde murmured, "we must all pray for her."

"My Lady, may I be excused my afternoon work? I need to be alone, beyond the gates."

"Of course."

In the nave, Guthlac waved away Bernulf, "I wish to be on my own."

Outside the confines of the abbey, Guthlac strode the short distance to the river. There he stared at the grey water sliding past on this dull winter's morning. Tears ran down his cheeks and he fought back the urge to curse his friend. Why ill use the maid and cause her despair? Coelwald had loved the girl. Did Aethelbald even know the meaning of love? Would he care that two souls had been lost?

'I must pray every day he mends his ways and like me finds God. I must pray for Faryn and for her unborn babe and I must pray for myself for the absolution of the terrible deeds that haunt my dreams.'

EIGHT

Elmet, 704 AD

Six oxen yoked in pairs to each of nine carts laden with beech trunks lumbered along the ridgeway to the fortress of Heyholand. To the eyes of onlookers off to the east, the procession, men leading the beasts, the animals and the waggons appeared in black outline against the evening sun. Below them, the clouds dappled the brightly lit moorland with scudding patches of darkness. Pointing to the stronghold from the vantage of the rampart in Cezeburh, Aethelbald said to his visitor, "The ancients chose their hill top with a shrewd eye. The ditches follow the shape of the slope and, with the defences of this burh finished, my men are erecting walls there on the innermost embankment." He lowered the hand shading his face from the strong light and added, "It's my guess they who dug those earthworks did the same. We found remains of rotten wood in the soil but Time, unlike the raven, is of small but endless appetite."

Impressed, Coelwald imagined the situation a leader of a hostile host would face, caught betwixt hammer and anvil, should ever he dare pass this way.

"These past five years you spent strengthening the approaches to the south, you said?"

"With the invaluable help of Meriet," he jerked a thumb at a greybeard standing a little apart, also peering at the progress of the ceorls on the ridge. "One of my father's most loyal thegns and now my right arm, in the absence of other true friends." He watched the point drive home with bitter satisfaction as Coelwald looked abashed. "Meriet's a great warrior. Forsook his lands to follow me and as a reward for his faithfulness has gained threefold – the soil is less fertile, but he manages all the farming and harvesting, the stock rearing and settles disputes when they flare up." Of a sudden aware of Aethelbald's gaze upon him, the thegn nodded. "What were we saying? oh, ay, strengthening the approaches, right, when not fighting off raids from the Elmetsaete. But their feeble efforts bother me not. The day will come when Northanhymbra, unshackled, turns its bloody thoughts towards Mierce. When the moment arrives, we shall be well prepared to repel them."

"Mierce owes you a debt. Where else–"

"Straight as geese fly eastwards, at Wacanfeld on a hill above the river where dense forest lies to the north, with its own springs and becks. And beyond, at Castleford, another ancient fortress with commanding views. At worst, I trust we can hold any foe long enough for Mierce to raise a host and hasten to the fray. But tell me, what brings you to seek me out after five long years?"

"I come to warn you. I have told you Mierce is in your debt but not all men think alike. At court there are murmurings Lord Aethelbald waxes mighty and there are those who have the ear of the new King–"

"New King?"

"Ay. Aethelred upped and hied him to a monastery. The one he founded at Beardan in Lindissi. Before he renounced the throne, he named his brother's son as successor and the witan confirmed it."

"By Thunor, Cenred! The runt! Why not one of his sons? You or your half-brother?"

"In the absence of yourself or Guthlac, the choice fell on Cenred or his cousin, Coelred. They chose the better of two evils. Can you imagine Coelred, yon coward, as King?" the aetheling's laugh came bitter and harsh, "Who knows his nature better than his own father? As for me, I'm tainted. Do you think the Miercian ealdormen would spare me the fate of my mother if I showed the slightest desire for the throne? The wraith of Northanhymbra stalks their nights. As it is, in the weeks leading up to the abdication, rumours of Aethelred's intentions were rife. The day before the proclamation, Coelred – my own half-brother – once more tried to murder me for fear I, not he, might succeed to the–"

"Again? Then you possess more lives than a wildcat in the Elmet Wood! Tell all!"

"Market day in Tame Weorth. All those stallholders, as you know well, come from the surrounding villages and the town itself. I do not bother with markets," he sniffed, "but on my way to the smithy, for I wished my sword to be honed to slaughterous sharpness–"

"Fit to cleave a helm in two!" Aethelbald grinned.

"…my way took me past a bread stall. How strange the weaving of wyrd! A skinny, filthy, half-starved urchin thieved a bun and the baker made to chase him. Thus, I sprung to seize the trader, meaning to pay for his loss, so the wretch didn't end up in the stocks…" he paused and gave Aethelbald a meaningful stare, "…an arrow pierced a loaf and embedded in the wooden board beneath. It came from amid the throng milling around the stalls. The baker blessed me for saving his life," he laughed at the irony, "but the dart was meant for me."

"How do you know sent Coelred the rogue whose bow loosed the shaft?"

"Who else? There are no others who mean me harm. That same morning, two days ago now, I decided to come here for my own safety and to warn you. Upon hearing the announcement of the abdication, one of my thegns rode with all haste to overtake me to give me the news of Cenred's kingship. Yesterday. But enough of me. Tell me, what of Guthlac?"

"Guthlac? Last I heard, he left his monastery after two years to become a hermit. Went off to the fenlands…" Aethelbald grew thoughtful and his expression mournful, "…what made a fine warrior like Guthlac lose his mind?"

"The Church would have it the Holy Spirit filled him with grace–"

"By Thunor's black forge, only a madman would choose to live alone among toads and biting bugs. He left me when I needed him most. As did *you*."

Coelwald scowled at the ealdorman, "Need I remind you why I went away?"

"To warn the King of the plotting and clear our names?"

"Which I did. And the fact Aethelred allowed you the peace to secure Miercian settlement in the south of Elmet is witness to my good faith. I meant my leaving on account of Lady Faryn."

"Why let a foolish wench–"

The countenance of Coelwald darkened, "Have a care with your words," he growled.

Aethelbald sneered, "She went to be a nun these five years past. Another one who lost her reason."

"If she did, the fault is yours. Faryn took her own life, did you know that? I sought out Guthlac some months after he entered the abbey and he told me. Not only that, but she ended the life of *your* child."

Teeth clenched, face of a sudden paler, Aethelbald replied, "I have no child and the witch lied!"

Flushed with rage, the aetheling drew his sword and, stepping back, the ealdorman did likewise.

Neither man made the first lunge but as the shoulders of Coelwald sagged and his blade lowered so did that of Aethelbald.

They glared at each other in silent wrath for long moments.

"I'm sorry about Faryn," Aethelbald said at last, "I meant her no harm. She came willingly to my bed. What man turns away a fair maid? How was I to know–"

Sheathing his weapon, Coelwald frowned, "Whether it be so or not, quarrelling over what cannot be undone is pointless. In part, I came out of friendship to warn you but also to put many leagues between myself and Coelred…"

"Then let us be friends," Aethelbald replaced his blade and stretched out a hand, "let bygones rest in the past. We'll begin afresh."

Coelwald strode forward and clasped the proffered hand.

Across the moor, the last of the carts creaked and groaned out of their view. Satisfied, Aethelbald placed a hand on his comrade's shoulder, "Come, let us away down to my hall. there we can best decide what's to be done about the viper, Coelred. A beaker of mead might clear our thoughts."

Aethelbald stood in front of the largest central building in the settlement and said, "Those laden waggons you saw, covered the same leagues you rode from the Elmet Wood. Doubtless you passed them on the road. On this windswept moorland there are no trees," he swung a hand to take in the huts around the hall, "to haul timber so far for homes makes little sense." With pride, the ealdorman explained the settlement had grown three times bigger than when he first came. The place lacked its menfolk since they were out either shepherding the flocks that made their livelihood or unloading the huge trunks from the carts. At this hour, the women were indoors preparing food or suckling the babes.

"I see the roofs are turfed," Coelwald said.

"Ay, and the walls are of stacked turf and cob."

"Cob?"

"Come inside and I'll explain."

There followed a long explanation of construction with straw, clay, gravel and sand and Coelwald soon lost interest. In truth, he was more taken by the banner nailed to the wall over a dais with a bowl-shaped throne. Aethelbald accompanied his gaze, "What do you think?"

A helm and in turn a boar's head topped the central shield emblazoned with an oak tree. "The emblem of Miercian Elmet," he added without waiting for an answer.

"Or the standard of underking Aethelbald," came the aetheling's biting response.

Unfathomable, the expression of the ealdorman but, astute as ever, Coelwald caught the fleeting glint in the other man's eye.

"We cannot go into battle without colours. I do not pretend to bear the golden cross on the blue of Mierce. This, I sketched myself, see the oak for the Great Elmet Wood and the boar, a beast that therein dwells. The helm – *Elm*et," he smirked at his own joke.

'By Thunor, one day the emblem of Mierce will be mine as of right.'

His hand slipped inside his shirt to where Osthryth's ring dangled from a gold chain. He squeezed it into his palm.

'Thank Heaven he knows nothing of my thoughts nor that I hold his mother's jewel.'

He poured mead from a pitcher into two beakers, "Here," he said, passing one full to the brim to his companion, "be seated and tell me if it's good, it's made from heather honey and has a special taste."

Complimenting his host, Coelwald savoured it on his palate before putting his mind to the matter in hand. An explanation followed of how the incursions, pillaging and devastation of the Wealisc needed urgent attention. King Cenred faced the problem of the western borderland before he could turn his attention elsewhere, always assuming he could be swayed by Coelred to set upon Aethelbald. The ealdorman filled their cups once more and pondered the situation. After a few moments, he said, "Cenred will welcome the aid of two warriors like us in his war with Powys. The Elmetsaete are weakened and cannot attack alone whilst the King of Northanhymbra lies ill, some say dying, and his sons begin to dispute the succession." His self-satisfied laugh made Coelwald raise an eyebrow, "What better time to take a third of my thegns and their sworn men south to succour our King? With our new fortifications, it leaves men enough to repel the puny raids from the north."

Coelwald rolled the mead on his tongue and considered Aethelbald's proposal.

"I see the worth in what you suggest. But do you not fear the conniving of Coelred?"

Aethelbald's smile unsettled his companion, wolf-like if he must describe it, neither did his words reassure him. "Sure, but now is the time to lure him into the open as he concentrates on the kingship he failed to gain."

"There may be attempts on both our lives."

Aethelbald scrutinised the face of his friend but saw consideration, not fear.

"The error will be of staying and waiting for a call to arms. If we seek the goodwill of Cenred, we seize it by forestalling his summons."

Coelwald conceded the wisdom of this ploy and accepted the less time they allowed Coelred to poison the mind of their King against them, the better. As an afterthought, he added Cenred ruled Suthanhymbra for two years as underking before taking the throne of Mierce. Guthlac's father, Penwalh, having been one of his trusted counsellors ought to mean the King for the moment viewed Aethelbald in a good light. The decision was taken. A last beaker of mead to seal the pact and Aethelbald led his friend out to a dwelling used for guests. A rest before supper would precede a meeting between the two of them and Aethelbald's thegns.

The ealdorman made haste to organise the meal before throwing himself down on his bed in a warm glow induced by mead and satisfaction. As was his wont in such circumstances, he toyed with Osthryth's ring.

'A good day, I'd say. A friendship is sealed. When I am enthroned as Bretwaldas, Coelwald shall be underking of Northanhymbra.' A smug laugh escaped him, *'The time is not yet ripe for him to learn of my plans. We leave for Mierce two dawns hence.'* His fist clamped around the golden band, *"Then we'll see whose wiles are the craftiest, Coelred, dear second cousin!"*

NINE

(five years before)
Abbey of Hreapandune 699 AD

Respecting the silence imposed by his Order and the abbey library, Guthlac gestured to Bernulf to approach. The young monk bent over to peer at the parchment indicated by his learned brother's forefinger. The silent movement of his mouth as he struggled to form the words betrayed his difficulty with reading.

Outside, in front of the scriptorium, hazel eyes bright with eagerness, Guthlac whispered in Brother Bernulf's ear.

"Do you understand? St Antony survived alone in the desert in an abandoned Roman fort on Mount Pispir and he didn't come out for twenty years."

"I wondered about that," the novice said, "what did he live on?"

Guthlac laughed, "For shame! Your thoughts are ever for your stomach. The folk nearest the area brought him bread and passed it through a crevice in the wall. Apart from thanks, he uttered not a word."

Bernulf scratched his tonsured pate, "All that time alone. A man could go mad."

The reply came sharp and scolding, "Alone! What better companion than the Holy Spirit?" Guthlac looked around, conscious he had raised his voice, "I read another book about St Cuthbert," he murmured so low the other strained to hear. "He lived on his own on Inner Farne, blasted by the wind of the North Sea."

"Well, I'd rather be safe and warm in the abbey, a meal every day and in the company of my brethren, wouldn't you Brother Guthlac?"

" '*To every thing there is a season, and a time to every purpose under the heaven,*' " Guthlac quoted Leviticus, baffling his servant.

Later the same day, Guthlac obtained an audience with Abbess Aelfthryde. Before mooting the matter close to his heart, he began a preamble regarding the fruitfulness of his two years at the abbey. After a deep study of the psalms, canticles, hymns and prayers, he said, he had applied himself to good observance of the virtues. Gentleness, obedience, patience, long suffering and abstinence of the body, all acquired as his armoury, he assured her.

"Mother, I learnt of the anchorites and the Lord stirs in me a yearning for the wilderness and a hermitage. Therefore, I beg leave to depart the abbey in search of such a place."

Surprised at his words, the Abbess probed at length the motives of the one-time warrior kneeling before her. Satisfying herself of the soundness of his calling and of his spiritual readiness, she promised to meet with the elders and let him know their decision. The next morning, Aelfthryde summoned Guthlac and gave him permission to leave.

The monk, whose studies embraced charts not only of Britain but of the wider world, knew whither he was bound. Weeks before, he had drawn a map showing the trackways to follow and the monasteries where he might eat and sleep. Such a longing for the wilds filled him, so in his haste, he forgot to bid farewell to his brethren, remembering only after crossing the Trente at Twyford. Too late to turn back, marching, he chanted hymns to the glory of God.

On his journey, he thanked the Lord he had renounced earthly possessions such as his horse. The blisters on his soles meant he shared in Christ's suffering and thus he sang Psalm 148 as he bathed his feet in a cool stream.

Praise him, sun and moon; praise him, all you shining stars.
Praise him, you highest heavens and you waters above the skies.

One week after setting off, Guthlac came to the small settlement of Baston on the edge of the fens. Heart filled with joy, he pulled out his sketched map, worn, creased and torn with use, knowing his journey neared its end. The immense marshes, black pools and foul running streams he sought lay to the east. Drawing near the village, on its confines, he hailed a goatherd.

"Well met, fellow! What road must I take to reach Estdeping?"

Never having encountered a monk, the man gawped and gathered his wits only when Guthlac repeated the question. Even so, Guthlac struggled to understand the rude, thick speech assailing his ears, "Who in his right mind would want to go there?" being the gist. Patience and long suffering, the brother reminded himself. Seeking in vain the beauty of God's image in the rotten-toothed ceorl of the close set eyes, he tried again. Piecing together what he grasped, Guthlac interpreted, "The old road… gravelly ridge…yon side of the village…deep, low place…league east…" among the torrent of other words he failed to understand. Thanking the goatherd, blessing him and his seven skinny beasts, in relief, he left the miserable creature. In spite of his wariness regarding the ceorl's directions, the ill-kept road revealing an occasional ancient paving stone, at last, brought him to the settlement by the River Weolud. In doubt as to what he must do after tramping thirty leagues, Guthlac sank to his knees and prayed.

The sensation of being stared at made him open his eyes. A round-faced ceorl, swarthy skin offset by a shaggy blond beard, viewed him with suspicion and an expression that meant, *'what are you doing here?'*

"Call me Brother Guthlac," he said, rising and gesturing a benediction for the reed cutter. The bound and bulky sheaf over the man's shoulder bespoke his occupation.

The fellow's speech though strange to Guthlac's ears for its cadence, bore no likeness to the guttural grunting of the goatherd.

"So, what ye doin' 'ereabouts, Brother? We don't get many outsiders comin' to these God forsaken wastes. *Er* – beggin' yer pardon."

"Wrong, my friend, no place under the sky or above it, for that matter, is cast aside by the Almighty. What am I doing? Seeking so obscure a plot of land men never set foot upon it. Know you of such a place?"

The reedman adjusted the weight on his shoulder, "Might. Come wi' me for my burden's growin' 'eavy an' ye look as if ye could do wi' summat to eat."

They walked to the edge of the small settlement where four shabby women and a child gathered to stare at the newcomer. Guthlac raised his hand in blessing, curtailed by his guide who seized his arm and steered him toward a makeshift barn. Depositing his bundle among many other sheaves, the ceorl smiled, "Let's put summat b'tween our teeth—" He broke off with a grin when Guthlac stared around the outbuilding in surprise, "Not 'ere! Follow me!"

The fellow led the way to a small conical hut. The roof of sedge covered the wattle and daub walls and stretched down almost to touch the ground. Without a window, the light entered through the door held open by a wooden wedge. Inside, a narrow bed, a table with bench, a board on trestles laden with pots, pans and utensils, flasks and boxes, made up the chattels. Crab apples, pears and haws hung in string sacks on nails in the wall. Beside them dangled bunches of sloes, burdock root and mint. The charred remains of a fire gave a pungent odour to the room, making Guthlac wrinkle his nose. In vain, he sought an outlet for the smoke other than the door.

'I hope he does not mean to cook.'

Indeed, he did not, opening a wooden box, he took out two oatcakes and laid them on the table.

"On'y spring water ter offer ye," he said pouring from a leathern bottle.

Grateful for the simple fare and above all to sit and take the weight off his poor feet, Guthlac blessed the food and murmured a short prayer of thanksgiving. Before biting into the coarse offering, he asked, "What name do you go by?"

"Tatwine," came the reply, indistinct, through a mouthful of half-chewed biscuit.

"Well, Tatwine, what of the place I seek?"

The reed cutter swallowed and sipped his water, frowned and ignoring the question, said, "Tonight, ye can sleep in the barn, ought ter be cosy." He made to take another bite of his oatcake. Instead, he set it back down on the table and stared hard at Guthlac.

"Never met a monk before. Not sure one like ye got the pluck to live where I'm thinkin' of."

Interest pricked, Guthlac smiled, "Cutting down reeds is your work. Until not long past, hacking down men was mine – may God forgive me! So, Tatwine, speak out! Where is this place?"

The gaze of the fen-lander, of a sudden more respectful, lingered on the muscular arms of the brother. Tone more subservient, he said, "Yon marsh stretches from the Weolud, wide and long wi' many windin's as far as the Norðsae. Countless isles wi' 'illocks an' thickets," adding a smirk of self-approval, "full o' reeds." A pause for a gulp of water before he continued, "There's an island known ter few men. Them as tried ter live on yon…all fled."

"How so?" the attentive and eager monk asked.

"On account o' the accurs'd spirits dwellin' there."

"Can you take me, Tatwine?"

"Yer don't want ter be goin' ter yon isle, Brother."

A long discussion followed but in the end, Guthlac prevailed, wresting a promise from his host to take him by boat on the morrow. The ceorl prepared a bed of reeds and after his devotions, the monk fell into a dreamless sleep.

Stale hard bread eaten by moistening with spring water, cheese harder still, gnawed not bitten, served to start their day. The reed cutter led Guthlac to the bank of the Weolud where his boat, moored to a stake, was one of a dozen swaying with the gentle current. As they strolled towards it, the brother marvelled at the vastness of the sky in this flat land of water. The heavens tinted by the sunrise pressed down in swathes of jay pink and lilac. Without mountains or hills, he mused, with no trees but only the swaying reeds to measure the wind. As Tatwine rowed, his words revealed his love for the fens.

"This 'ere's a place as ne'er changes. Oh, ay, it's allus in movement all right, the water against the land an' the land against the water. But it ne'er changes. Perfect balance, see? Water makes the silt and yon blocks the water an' causes the floodin'." Tatwine warmed to his argument, "O'er yonder's a silt bank, see? Yon's where a river ran. Don't no more. Silt, makes us the meres. An' the meres throw up dank clouds as chills yer ter the marrow."

The ceorl fell silent with a faraway look. In his silence, Guthlac wondered at the sense of remoteness of his surroundings, at the stable co-existence of land and water created by his Father in Heaven. The gentle plash of the oars, the croaking of frogs, the plop of ducking smeath and coot soothed his soul and made him ever more convinced of his decision. Tatwine broke across his reflections, pointing out three bowed grey shapes, cranes feeding amid the swampy grasses of an islet. As if in response to being watched, one straightened and protested with a harsh clanging call.

"I'm pullin' o'er ter yon ait a moment Brother. Set some traps yest'day mornin' before I met ye."

The prow shifted to head to the north side of the island where two oak traps more than a foot long floated under a bank. From each of them hung a dead otter, necks broken in a rectangular opening by a valve snapped shut by a stout ash bow.

"See, the creecher comes up from unnerneath an' goes fer the fish. Sticks its 'ead through yon 'ole an' the jaws trap it. Skin 'em we gets back."

During the hour it took Tatwine to row them to their destination, he delighted in showing off his knowledge of the wildlife. They glimpsed a fen beaver and the waterfowl he named as godwits and teal, dotterel and ruff, widgeon and coot.

"Yer'll not go short fer fish, Brother, these waters are full o' eels an' sturgeon an' lamprey."

At last, the reed cutter jerked his head over his shoulder, "This 'ere's the place, Cruwland it goes by."

"Cruwland?"

"Ay, see? Yon's the south bank o' the Weolud we're comin' in on an' the channel o'er yonder goes by Catswater. Yon's as old as the 'ills. That is if there were any!" He chortled at his own joke, "Catswater leads to the Nen as runs the other side o' the isle."

Keen, Guthlac's eyes roved over the form of the land. To his left, lay marshland, full of pools and meres stretching away as far as he could see. To his right, the isle, and he pointed to the rounded hump above the reed bed Tatwine was pulling past.

"Can we stop here? I'd like to stand on the hillock and look at the view."

"Ay, I know a spot ter run in o'er yonder. An' yon's not an 'illock, yon' an' three o' its ilk are why no man can stay fer long."

"How so."

"Mounds. Lost in time when they lay the dead in yon. Evil spirits come out at night an' a-shriekin' an' a-fearin' anyun as dares linger a'ter dark."

The reedman ran the bows into a muddy hollow in the river bank, "Ye'd best take yer shoes off, Brother, bit messy 'ere."

Seeing the good sense in the suggestion, Guthlac obeyed and was glad he'd undone his sandals when he sank mid-calf into the slime. Unpractised, he needed Tatwine's strong hand to haul him up to the springy turf.

An irregular ditched enclosure ran around the tumulus. Guthlac climbed to the top of the round barrow and from there eyed the outline of the ditch: man-made without a doubt. On the inland side of the hump, someone had dug into the earth.

"Looks like a cist here," Guthlac called down to his reluctant companion.

"Ay, raiders, I reckon. A'ter gold, 'appen."

"Perfect!" the monk cried and he set off to explore the rest of the isle. Passing vegetation rotting in the sunshine and teeming with insects, he disturbed them and a cloud of whining gnats, mosquitos and midges flew around his head and into his face. Two bites caused Guthlac to rub his arm. When he returned, he found Tatwine sitting in his boat. "Perfect," he said again seizing the proffered hand to be hauled from the sucking ooze into the small vessel.

Back in Tatwine's home, outside of the abbey, he forgot the rules of his Order. The eagerness of the monk for *his* isle waxed to excess. Unlike the fervent brother, Tatwine neither practised the virtue of patience nor of long-suffering. With a knife, starting at the tail, he skinned around the back legs of one of the trapped otters.

"Enough o' yon chatter, Brother, here take this knife an' follow me! Mind, it's sharp."

Picking up the dead creature, he carried it outdoors to a pole sunk into the ground. Above head height, it had a hook and Tatwine hung the animal from it. Taking the blade, he made a few more incisions before saying, "Brother Guthlac, make yersen useful. Take 'old his tail now an' pull. Them strong arms'll do the job."

As Guthlac pulled, with great skill, Tatwine cut back the skin and before long the monk held the best part of the creature's pelt.

"Ease off," the reedman said, "I'll slice round the front legs and the 'ead."

"What does otter taste like?" the brother asked.

"Fatty an' fishy. Nowt yer'd want ter be eatin', Brother."

Tatwine pulled the rest of the skin free and marched indoors to begin the second skinning. Following, Guthlac said, "I'll stay one more night and at dawn, I'm away back to the abbey."

The reedman looked up.

"Them spirits scared yer off, then Brother?"

"Not in the least. I shall come back and if you will be good enough to take me to Cruwland, there I'll make my home."

The reed cutter shook his head, "Yer a braver man than me, Brother. It'll take more 'an pluck ter stay on yon cursed isle, mark my words."

The monk laughed, "You forget, I'll be wearing the chain mail of the Holy Spirit. No demons can pierce it!"

A week and a day later, weary and footsore, Guthlac stood in front of Abbess Aelfthryde. Ending the long description of his future hermitage, he begged permission to take Brother Bernulf and another novice with him if they were willing. They would live in Estdeping, where they would serve him as well as the spiritual needs of the settlement. The abbess considered the request and acceded.

"I shall time my leaving so I reach Cruwland on St Bartholomew's Day, Mother.

"Why that date, Brother and why in particular Bartholomew?"

Guthlac smiled and his handsome features lit up, captivating the nun, "Mine is a devotion to the apostle, Mother; besides, the otters told me…"

The Abbess gazed at him with puzzled eyes, "Otters?"

"Ay, we skin otters for their pelt and the heathen flayed Bartholomew alive."

TEN

Tame Weorth 704 AD

Aethelbald paced to and fro in front of the tents. Ranged around him on pastureland outside the walls of Tame Weorth were the canvas dwellings of twelve thegns and the sixty men at his disposal.

"What ails you friend?" called Coelwald, head appearing around the entry flap of his temporary shelter. "You'll wear a trench in yon grass before long."

Waving him over, Aethelbald wrinkled his brow, "What troubles me is Cenred. When last I clapped eyes on him…*er*…what, seven years past, he struck me as a carefree youth in spite of two score and two winters on his shoulders,–"

"Ay, I catch your drift. At that age, both of us were hardened warriors. In truth, our King is not famed for his prowess in battle. But you must form your own judgment. Pay no heed to my blathering."

The chance for appraisal came after noon when in response to the King's summons, Aethelbald and Coelwald stood before a Council of the noblemen of the kingdom. In their midst sat the ruler of Mierce. A shaft of sunlight through one of the high windows of the hall struck the reddish-golden hair of Cenred. Unswayed by this effulgence, Aethelbald noted the weak chin, hidden by artful combing and greasing of the beard to a point and the vacuous shifting pale grey eyes. What he saw did not reassure him. Quelling an inopportune impulse to turn and leave, Aethelbald knelt before the throne.

"Lord, I pledge my loyalty to you. My sword and three score men encamped outside the walls await your command. A word from you and the number will swell."

A fleeting look of pleasure crossed the countenance of the King and one of sourness the visage of Coelred standing behind him. In an instant, Aethelbald caught them both.

"Reports tell of the admirable work you undertook to safeguard our northern border, welcome cousin."

Even as the ealdorman bowed his head at these gracious words, Coelred spoke.

"I beg your forbearance Lord if I speak out of turn. Knowing your trusting and kind nature and since I am truthful and sincere, I pray you hear me out."

Cenred's brow tightened in a troubled frown and he twisted in his seat to look up at his counsellor and kinsman.

"The undoubted honesty of your counsel is ever my guide, speak!"

"Lord, you point out our cousin's praiseworthy strengthening of the confines with Elmet. But consider, a man's hand is formed of two sides. When we look upon the back, we cannot inspect the palm."

Aethelbald glowered.

'What is the glib-tongued louse hinting at?'

Coelred paused for effect and looked round his fellow noblemen before continuing, "Nor can we view what is held therein." He tapped the high table with his fingers, "Elmet is strengthened but against whom?"

Ill faith imputed to him in front of the whole council, Aethelbald stifled the wrath urging him to spring to his feet and strike the coward.

'I must bear his insults, by Thunor's hammer, but there will come a time...'

Aware all eyes were on him, Aethelbald drew a deep breath, "Lord, I beg leave to stand to reply to my *upright* kinsman."

The King gestured to rise but the ealdorman noted a hardness of expression lacking before in his countenance.

Unblinking, he met Coelred's ironic stare, "Against Northanhymbra, of course."

'Why is the cur so gleeful?'

The answer was swift in coming.

"There's the thing. Northanhymbra! Do you deny you bear the seal of Osthryth? The word is, you and the jewel are inseparable."

'So that's it! If they search me, they'll find it at once.'

Glaring at his accuser, Aethelbald reached into his tunic and pulled out the ring on its chain, letting it dangle in full sight on his chest.

A grating laugh greeted the gesture. Elated, Coelred addressed the murmuring counsellors, "What more proof is needed?" King Cenred leant forward and peered at the gold band. Behind him, a sneer curling his lip, his denouncer pressed on, "Is it mere chance our *dear cousin* keeps company with the son of Osthryth? Is it not common knowledge the late Queen strove to bring Mierce under her family's rule?" A growl of agreement from the gathered noblemen met these words. "Why–" but an impatient wave of the King's hand stemmed the flow.

Gaze still fixed on the ring, the Lord of Mierce said to Aethelbald, "The charges are grave and put forward by my most trusted counsellor. In the face of them, let us hear what you have to say."

The ealdorman looked around at the hostile faces of his peers. Swayed by their hatred of Northanhymbria and the persuasiveness of Coelred, he did not doubt they had decided his guilt.

"Grave and groundless, Lord. We have heard much of the frankness and sincerity of our cousin and I too believe him to be an honest man... *'The cur-dog is false and plays on the King's trust.'* ... and yet, a worthy man, for a greater love than he bears for the truth, may err." Aethelbald lifted his chin and looked around the counsellors, he made his tone solemn and dignified, "Our cousin's devotion to his King and to Mierce... *'The rabid fox would slay him in a trice.'* ... leads him into misjudgement. Pray recall, I, who stand before you slew a Northanhymbrian ealdorman by my own hand. Did I not act out of loyalty to Aethelred? As to this jewel," he grasped the ring, "I wear it to remind me of the falsehood spread against my name and that of Guthlac." He stared straight at Coelred, "When I uncover the defamer, I will cut out his tongue and ram it down his throat." Uncertainty showed in the frowns and mutterings of the counsellors. Aethelbald needed to drive home his ascendancy, "River slime is clearer than the death of Osthryth. Am I supposed to have slain her? Yet, am I accused of aiding Northanhymbra too? Where is the sense? Either I am one thing or the other." The nodding heads and mumbled accord spurred him on. "*Dear* cousin," he smiled at Coelred, "you are mistaken but in good faith… *'as much good faith as the serpent in the Garden'*… "Would I have come with Coelwald to pledge my arm in the King's service if we were against him?"

The noblemen cheered and beat their fists on the table. Coelred tried to change his scowl into a smile and the King rose from his throne.

"Aethelbald, Coelwald, welcome to Tame Weorth. We embrace you as kinsmen and bid you join our Council."

That night, lying stripped to the waist on a sheepskin in his tent, Aethelbald toyed with Osthryth's ring. In his mind, he relived the events of the day. The Council's decision to appoint him commander of the Miercian forces heading for the western marches at the end of the wet season, pleased him. As did the choice of Coelwald to flank him. One campaign against the Wealisc would not imperil his work in Elmet. The death of Osthryth's step-brother, the King of Northanhymbra had left the kingdom fighting a civil war.

'Eadwulf and young Osred dispute the succession – a usurper and a brat.' Bringing the gold band to his lips, he kissed it and smiled, *'The Picts will be ready to pounce. Shame, the moment was ripe for me to take the rest of Elmet. As it is, Cenred has not the stuff of kings – too weak to last. With the Miercian host at my back…win their affection…a good campaign…then, by Thunor, cousin Coelred, time to pay for your guiles.'*

The month's wait until the gathering of the Miercian warriors did not pass without incident. First, Meriet brought an unknown ceorl to Aethelbald's tent with a message from his Lord. Were he and the Aetheling Coelwald disposed to meet with his master in the White Horse Tavern? They were.

On the day arranged, the two ealdormen, curious, waited at a corner table. When the man joined them, Aethelbald scrutinised the scarred and weather-beaten face suggestive of a warrior. He seemed familiar. The open, honest face of a middle-aged man stared back, his wariness betrayed by his constant glances around the crowded inn. From his speech, the comrades gathered he came from the western border area of Mierce. This deduction was confirmed from his rounded, drawled vowels.

"My name is Beorhtric, ealdorman of the hundred of Witentreu in the Wealisc marches. My home town is Cyricbyrig and I'm sworn to Coelred."

At this name, Aethelbald tensed and the newcomer noted the reaction.

"Ay, the same as sought to discredit ye afore the King."

'Seen that face…ay, at the moot! And he says Oi when he means I!'

"What makes a man of Coelred's seek a meeting with us?" Coelwald wondered.

The eyes of the ealdorman once more darted glances around the room. Satisfied, he leaned forward and breathed, "I come to warn ye. Coelred plans to slay ye. Our King Cenred," his words uttered so low both men struggled to catch them amid the hubbub of the tavern, "is a weak ruler. To sweep him aside, Coelred first must remove more awkward obstacles if ye take my meaning."

"Why risk meeting us? Why warn us, Beorhtric?" Aethelbald asked.

The ealdorman frowned, "A feeble king is better than a wicked un. I watched the boy Coelred grow into a man and I don't like what I see. I'll play no part in his baleful scheming."

"I told you not to come to Tame Weorth," Coelwald hissed at Aethelbald before looking at Beorhtric and informing him, "your master tried to murder me three times. He's bound to strike again."

"Ay. Mierce needs a strong king, not an evil one. Down my way, Gwylog ap Beli smacks his lips at the thought of Miercian noblemen at strife among themselves. He waits on the slightest excuse to raid–"

Of a sudden, Beorhtric appeared fretful. Placing an elbow on the table, he covered his face with his hand, lowering his head to one side.

"What is it?" Coelwald queried.

"Thingfrith!" came the muffled reply. "Coelred's horse thegn. I swear he saw me. Pray God I'm wrong! Any case I must leave."

A fortnight passed before, one drizzly morning, Coelwald pushed back the flap of Aethelbald's tent and, uninvited, entered.

"Thought I might catch you with a maid!" he laughed.

Aethelbald, running a whetstone down his sword blade, looked up, "No-one catches me by surprise. You only got in because Meriet let you past! Anyway, wenching's best done in pairs. My wenching companion's gone and made himself a monk. Can't interest you in an assault on the maids of Tame Weorth, I suppose?"

His friend chortled, "Why? Want to make a monk of me too? No thank you! But it's of incursions I wish to speak. One of my thegns back from the town brings news of Coelred. Seems he rode off with a force of his sworn men to the borderlands, to the marches."

"He did?"

"Ay, and he took Beorhtric and two other ealdormen with him."

"How so?"

Coelwald wrinkled his brow, "It's odd. Do you believe in chance happenings? I don't."

Aethelbald snorted, "Stop talking in riddles, man."

"By all accounts, the Wealisc crossed the border and razed three villages in the Witentreu hundred. They slaughtered the menfolk and seized the women and children for slaves. Coelred rode off to right this wrong."

Aethelbald stopped his whetting, "The Witentreu hundred, isn't that where—"

"—ay, where Beorhtric's from! I hope I'm mistaken but…"

Two days passed and Aethelbald, the idea of wenching sown in his mind, left the encampment in search of a willing maid. The finding of one to match his desire proved taxing. After an hour of searching, followed by another of rampant coupling, he stayed in the inn where the whore transacted her custom, to slake his thirst.

When he exchanged the dim tavern for the gloom of the narrow street, in spite of the ale, his wits were sharp enough to alert him to three louts with cudgels lurking in wait. Sword drawn in a flash, he spun and feinted to avoid a huge metal-spiked club before driving his blade into the brute's throat. Swerving to one side, he took a glancing blow to his other arm. In spite of the bruising ache sustained, the cruel point had not bitten into his flesh. Skipping over the body of his fallen assailant, Aethelbald backed away from the pair of advancing villains.

A glance over his shoulder to ensure there were no other attackers, he crouched ready for the next assault. Not warriors but ne'er-do-wells, Aethelbald decided and convinced by this, considered the fight would end in his favour. Making light of his throbbing arm, he drew his seax. Used to facing two or more opponents in battle, he waited as the clubmen advanced, weapons uplifted. Knowing they must not strike first, he surveyed his surroundings. To his right was a wooden water trough for draft animals. Raised a yard from the ground, it rested on sections of a tree trunk. Two seconds hesitation, two breaths and he jumped on the rim of the trough. His assailants came on in a rush but with the advantage of height, he kicked one full in the chest before the bludgeon swung down. In an instant, he leapt between them, his momentum crashing him into the off-balance oaf. With a backhanded blow, as he fell, his seax flashed up and out into the shoulder of the other, who screamed and dropped his cudgel. On the ground, Aethelbald sprawled over the brute he had kicked.

Clamped around his sword wrist, the huge fist of the dolt began twisting to force him to release his weapon. The warrior raised his seax to finish his opponent but the mace of the other came down. The blow pierced the outer flesh of his upper arm and a searing pain replaced the throbbing ache, making him drop his knife. Unlucky arm! The same impaled by the javelin at the Scheth. He rolled, butting the man under him with all the force he could muster, breaking his nose and causing him to release his grip. Aethelbald needed to get back on his feet, the second clubman was above him now, poised to deliver the fatal strike with the heavy mass.

Rage pounded through Aethelbald's veins. He, a warrior, refused to die at the hands of half-witted clods. A twisting kick caught the villain at the side of the knee, tripping him as he advanced for the kill. Blood running hot down his wounded arm, Aethelbald raised himself upright. The clubman recovered his balance and the one with the crimson-stained face rose to a crawling position.

The other with the club, hampered by having to use his 'wrong' hand, attempted a clumsy swing. Dodging the blow with ease, Aethelbald stepped in at a crouch and thrust his blade beneath the man's flailing arm. The upward lunge drove the steel into his armpit and on through his heart. One gasp and a gurgle in the throat and the eyes of his attacker dulled. The ealdorman freed his weapon from the body and spun to face the other lout. But he was gone. The empty narrow street stretched lifeless except for three faces peering around the frame of the tavern door.

One belonged to the slut he had sported with earlier.

"Woman," he called as the three emerged from the inn, "run and fetch the Reeve. Let's get to the bottom of this affray."

The face of the whore set in a stubborn expression, "I bain't 'aving ought ter do wi' the likes o' 'im."

"I'll go, Lord," said the younger of the two men, judging by his wispy beard, aged no more than six and ten years.

"Wait!" Aethelbald said, taking a coin from his purse and pressing it into the youth's hand, "Run as fast as you can."

A grin and the fellow ran off.

He returned with a stocky, officious-looking individual with grey whiskers covering his face except for one suspicious eye, the other obscured by a patch. Behind them, two other men kept pace. At their appearance, the whore vanished inside the tavern.

Aethelbald, with the natural authority of his rank, took charge of the situation, ignoring the Reeve's injured protests. Stating his name proved enough to restore humility to the official's demeanour.

"I knows them well enough, Lord. A pair of good-for-noughts. Done Tame Weorth proud, you have, ridding the place of those layabouts." He bent over the nearest corpse and frisked his hands over the clothing. A metallic clinking stopped him. "What's this?" He patted the tunic again to more jingling. Sliding his hand inside the man's shirt, he pulled a handful of silver coins out. Counting them with a finger, he cried, "Ten penings! Why yon's a fortune for a rogue like him." He waved to his men, "Check his mate for what he has on him."

"Ten penings an' all!" came the reply.

"Who would have paid them to slay me?" Aethelbald knew full well.

The Official shrugged, "Who can say? These are nobody's men and at the same time, everybody's."

"Well, dead men tell no tales, Master Reeve, but a third huge lout attacked me and I've left him with a fresh-broken snout. Set up a hue and cry! You ought to have no trouble finding him and when you do, be sure to fetch me. By Thunor's wrath, I have ways of making men squeal, no matter how hulking they are. I await your man in the encampment."

The vicious glint in Aethelbald's eye brooked no argument and the Reeve thanked the stars he hadn't crossed the ealdorman.

Later, when the Reeve's man arrived at his tent, he was unlucky enough to experience the full extent of Aethelbald's daunting fury. He found himself seized by the throat and shaken, feet off the ground.

"Stay! The messenger has no fault," the aetheling said, in a calm voice, "Let the poor fellow be!"

Frustrated, Aethelbald released his hold, "Ay, you're right. I beg your pardon," he said to the white-faced ceorl. "Here, take this and buy yourself a drink. Away with you!" Only too eager to oblige, the man fled the tent.

"A pox on Coelred!" the ealdorman exclaimed, "The cur covers his tracks by having a man's throat slit and stilling his tongue forever. No way to lay the blame on him now." Aethelbald turned to face Coelwald, "See the cunning of the cur-dog. Too wise to use his own men, he unleashed those mangy stray hounds on me when far from Tame Weorth. Smart, I'll give him that! How can he be at fault when he's on his way to Cyricbyrig?"

"I warned you not to come to Tame Weorth."

"From now on, I shall be more prudent. No wandering the streets alone. With Meriet by my side, between the two of us, twenty attackers won't suffice."

Another side to Coelred's character was revealed to Aethelbald on his return to the town. At the Moot held to discuss the impending war with Powys, given the imminent departure of the Miercian host, Coelred expressed regret for the absence of Beorhtric from the Moot. He was pleased to report the razing of the Wealisc settlement of Rhandir and two nearby villages as redress for the raid on the hundred of Witentreu. Out of revenge, they had slaughtered the menfolk and enslaved the rest of the villagers.

"Just as well you are off to quell Powys," he smirked at Aethelbald, matters are getting out of hand on the borders of Mierce.

Take care, down there, cousin. I see you are hurt," his eyes sparkled with mirth as he waved at the ealdorman's arm in a sling. I'd hate anything *worse* to happen to you." Forcing his narrow visage into an attempt at sadness, he added, "with sorrow, I must relate the untimely death of our beloved Ealdorman Beorhtric during the Wealas campaign. An arrow pierced the great vein in his neck. Nothing to be done," he said with a slow shake of his head, "A sore loss, indeed."

In his tent, Aethelbald, seething, paced backwards and forwards. "May demons rip off his bollocks and roast them over hellfire!"

Tiring of these outbursts, Coelwald sought to calm his comrade. "Tomorrow, we leave Tame Weorth and with it, Coelred, for the present. We can give our attention to the Wealisc—"

"Don't you see the slyness of the cur. He couldn't wait to destroy their villages, to stir up Powys. Thus doing, he's shorn us of our best weapon: surprise. Do you suppose he wants us to quell Gwylog ap Beli? He yearns for us to fail! A rout of our host is what he longs for, I'm telling you. Better still if we die in shameful defeat. Look what he did to Beorhtric. Shows you what he's capable of!"

An incident occurred two weeks later, which revealed the thoroughness of Coelred in attaining his designs. Determined to visit the birthplace of Beorhtric, Aethelbald encamped his host by a small river in the vale with an unobstructed view into Wealas. A pungent odour hung in the air from the charred remains of nearby Cyricbyrig.

Aethelbald, Coelwald and Meriet strolled in the late afternoon sunshine into the blackened skeleton of the town. From the burnt-out shell of a building in what must have been the main street came a crash.

'Not even a dog, would go in there.'

The ealdorman drew his sword and his companion did likewise. They approached in silence and discovered a youth picking through the wreckage of a house.

Sheathing his weapon, Aethelbald asked the soot-smeared ceorl, "Found anything useful?"

The stripling stared wide-eyed and trembling, replied, "Nay, Lord."

"The Wealisc will have plundered ought of use or value before they torched the place…" Meriet said.

"Not Wealisc, Lord," the youngster said. "Them was our own as done this. Angles them was, Miercians!"

Speechless, the warriors stared at each other. First to recover, Aethelbald said, "Did you see them?"

"Ay, Lord. I was out fishing in the river. When thems rode up I hid among the trees and spied. I saw it all." The frail body shook and tears traced white rivulets down the grimy cheeks. "Horrible!" he said, "Slaughtered them, the children, my little brother and raped the womenfolk and…" He sank to his knees and bowed his head, giving in to the anguish racking his bony frame.

When the sobbing ended, Aethelbald asked, "What is your name, boy?"

"Ordric, Lord."

"Well, Ordric, this is no place for a young man. Come with us. I am an ealdorman of Mierce and I shall take you into my household. The first thing we'll do is give you a decent meal. I promise you, though it will take a while, I will avenge the loss of your family."

The men and the boy, casting lengthening shadows, set off toward the encampment. As they walked, Coelwald said, "There were no bodies."

"I buried them, Lord."

"What all of them?"

"Ay, I finished yesterday."

"All of them, on your own?"

The youngster nodded.

"No wonder you're all skin and bones!"

"It was a good thing you did, Ordric," Aethelbald said, then an idea came to him, "Tell me, did the men who did this carry a banner?"

"Ay, lord, they did."

"Well?"

"I saw it! A white bird with two heads, green behind it. Wings spread out."

"Coelred!" Meriet and Coelwald cried as one.

ELEVEN

Wealisc border, autumn 704 AD

Aethelbald knelt and peered at the hole punched by the spearhead in the close knit mail shirt.

"Unriveted," he murmured, "else the point had never penetrated."

Useless conjecture. He shrugged and stood to face Coelwald, "Another of our best thegns. Winter draws nigh and it's a mercy. We cannot sustain these losses much longer. Gwylog ap Beli outthinks us…he foresees our every move."

"Or his spies are the best in the world," his comrade sighed.

"A mystery," Aethelbald concluded before turning to Meriet to issue orders, gesturing to the scattered corpses, "See they bury them all except the Wealisc, deep enough to deter scavengers…and you," he called to a warrior admiring the dead thegn's axe, "lay that along the body. No offence to Christ but it won't harm to placate Woden. Who ever heard of a warrior turning up at the doors of Waelheal without a weapon?" He sneered and muttered to Coelwald, "Got no time for priests. What sense is there in a life without killing, fucking and wassailing?" He nodded towards the body, "Good man he was, and who's to say our forefathers were wrong? Best to give him every chance."

"You're more than half pagan, friend!" the aetheling chuckled then wondered whether his comment had substance.

The two men remounted and Aethelbald indicated the rocky defile, "We suffered twice their men killed. No surprise," he looked up the side of the deep cleft, "This is the perfect place to set a trap. How did they know we'd come this way?"

In the encampment after the usual meeting with the thegns, the puzzle tormented him until he fell into restless slumber.

In a nearby tent, young Ordric dared not close his eyes, as with every night, lest he relive the horrors of the rape and butchering of his loved ones. As a rule, what sleep he managed came with exhaustion. Now, silent and careful not to disturb the other youths, he slipped out into the night. A generous moon and the dying campfires provided him with wan light enough to pick his way to the edge of the camp where he found the lookout. As usual, when challenged, he explained his night prowling. No different from the other guardians on previous nights, the watchman welcomed another pair of eyes and a chance to while away time in company.

Deep into the night, Ordric excused himself and wandered down to the river protecting one flank of the encampment. There, although there was nobody around and the darkness shrouded him, out of innate bashfulness, he found a bush where he could relieve himself. As he did so, he stared up at a wondrous sight: the haloed moon, almost full, and the throng of stars marching past it like an endless and irrepressible horde. His awestruck contemplation was interrupted – by a sound! What was it? Motionless and rigid, he strained to catch the slightest noise. No mistake! In the weak moonlight, he made out a crouching figure moving with stealth along the river bank. Level with the bush, but six paces away from the trembling Ordric, the man squatted on his haunches: a Briton! A man of Powys! A moment later...*kee-wick*...the warrior mimicked the querulous call of a tawny owl. No more than three of Ordric's thudding heartbeats passed, then...*kee-wick*... came the answering notes. Afraid the pounding in his breast might alert the enemy, the youth did well not to gasp when a face he recognised appeared: one that haunted his nightmares. The dark form drew close to the other and a long, low exchange ensued.

Less than a leap and a bound away from him lurked the monster who had slaughtered his infant brother and raped his mother. Seething for vengeance but compelled to bide his time, Ordric's rage smouldered. Certain death lay ahead if he moved a muscle. Ay, he must wait!

At last, the Briton and the Miercian clasped hands and the former, crouching once more, hastened back the way he had come. Arms folded, the betrayer watched him vanish into the night. Behind the flimsy veil of leaves, Ordric stiffened when the warrior peered around in the gloom. Satisfied he was alone, he crept towards the encampment. Scared and quaking, but driven on by irrepressible hatred, Ordric drew the seax from his belt and followed. Light on his feet, in moments, the youth closed the distance between them without a sound. The long blond locks, tied back in a tail and a sign of rank, meant the doom of Ordric's quarry. A grasp of the hair and a violent downward tug offered no chance of resistance. The sharp blade, dragged with pent-up fury, sliced deep into the thegn's neck. Never having slit a throat, not even of a ewe, the young man did not expect the bellowing struggle of his victim nor such a mess of blood. Clinging to the blond mane with all his might, he plunged the seax down inside the collar bone and dragged it to one side. The warrior sank choking to his knees, clasping his throat with a glare, baleful and devoid of hope, at his attacker. After a moment, he toppled to the ground and lay twitching.

Ordric, trembling, burst into bitter tears and running to the body, kicked it over and over again until, rage spent, he retrieved his seax, and wiped the sticky haft on the man's tunic. This attempt, proving ineffective, he slid down the bank to the river and washed the weapon and his gory hands.

What to do next? Ordric had no wish to cause the lookout trouble but duty urged him to report what he had seen and done. Skirting the watchman's position, he returned to his tent, stood outside undecided for a while before sitting on the ground to await the dawn. Anyway, with the glazed stare of his victim in his mind and a head full of ghosts, how could he sleep?

Below the horizon, the first of the sun's rays tinted the sky a delicate greyish pink, when the flap of Coelwald's tent drew back. Ordric sprang to his feet, "Lord, forgive me, good morning! Lord–"

With a grin and a yawn, the aetheling rubbed his eyes and, amused at the awkwardness of the youth's greeting, demanded, "What rouses you before the larks?"

To Coelwald's growing surprise and consternation, Ordric related the account of the night's events. At a certain point, the nobleman stemmed the torrent of words. "Hold! All this you must tell again but this time to Lord Aethelbald."

"Lord, it weren't the watchman's fault, I swear!"

"Wait here!"

Grim-faced, Aethelbald placed a hand on the shoulder of Ordric when he had finished his tale, "Tonight you became a man and avenged your family. Fear not for yourself or for the night watchman. In truth, we are in your debt." Taking Coelwald by the arm, he said, "An end at last to Gwylog ap Beli forestalling our moves. The informer led the attack on Ordric's town—"

"A man of Coelred, then," the aetheling anticipated, "acting on his orders. Of course, my half-brother wants us to fail in Powys in order to strengthen his bid for the kingship of Mierce."

"Once again, as ever with Coelred: we have no proof. Had we caught the traitor alive, I'd have made him squeal till his heart burst. Come, Ordric take us to the body!"

Aethelbald stared down at the contorted, crow-pecked ravaged features. "Ay, the cur is one of Coelred's thegns. Took part in all our meetings—"

"Remember, he it was who suggested striking for Pengwern through that defile."

"May he rot in Hell!" Aethelbald drew his seax to cut away the thegn's clothing and expose his flesh. "Ravens and kites can pick at the dog of an informer. He deserves no better."

The last six weeks of the campaign brought but slight improvement in their fortunes since the Wealisc, as ever, proved valiant and obdurate adversaries. Torching deserted settlements served no purpose save to exact revenge for similar acts on Miercian soil. A dissatisfied Aethelbald led the men to the fortress of Bryn Alyn, organised winter provisions and forage before setting off with Coelwald to the royal palace at Tame Weorth.

The comrades approached the lofty, wide-gabled building and stabled their horses. Admitted into the hall with its high, gilded roof,

Aethelbald admired the splendour of the mead benches decked in gold. His hand closed over the pendant ring at his breast and his eyes roved up to the strong tie braces, *'One day, I swear, this magnificence will be mine.'*

He was brought back to earth by a greeting from King Cenred.

"Welcome to our table, cousins!" The restless pale-grey eyes shifted from one ealdorman to the other.

'He stares through us.'

"Take refreshment after your journey!"

The King clapped his hands. Serving maids brought a pitcher of mead and three drinking horns of dark-green glass worked with a vertical intertwined scroll design. The horns, struck by the weak sunlight from the high window, cast dapples the tints of lime leaf, fern, moss and pine. Following the curious gaze of the ealdorman and the aetheling, Cenred smiled, "I see the vessels please you, cousins. A gift from the Frankish court. They sent them in blue but I prefer the green. Come, let us drink!" He picked up a glass that a maid filled. Waiting until the newcomers were served and had supped a draught, the King commanded, "Tell me about the campaign on the border of Wealas."

While Aethelbald gathered his thoughts, Coelred leant close to the King to whisper in his ear. He moved away with a mocking smile.

'How venom spurts from the viper's fangs!'

"Lord, we penned Gwylog ap Beli within Powys. Attempts to push into the heartland to Pengwern were thwarted—"

"Wasteful losses of good Miercian warriors," Cenred interrupted, "these doleful reports fill us with sorrow."

'Here's the snakebite, by Thunor.'

Aethelbald glared at the smug amusement on the face of Coelred and clenched his fists.

"My King," said the aetheling in haste, knowing too well and fearing the likelihood of a rash outburst from his comrade, "may I speak?" At a slight tilt of the royal head, Coelwald began, "A high-placed betrayer in our midst informed the Wealisc of our every move. Hence, warned in advance, they set traps that cost us dear."

"And did you not lay bare and mete punishment on the traitor?"

Eyes narrowed, Coelred tensed.

"So we did, Lord, but the sly cur evaded our vigilance far too long. Six weeks before the campaign ended, a watchman caught him, deep in the night, consorting with the enemy and slew the dog on the spot."

"He did, by Christ!"

"Ay, Lord. Hence, we could not wrest from the snake whether he acted alone or on the orders of another."

The shoulders of Coelred relaxed, haughtiness restored.

The inexpressive eyes of the King shifted from the aetheling to Aethelbald and back again, "Cousin, you speak of a *high-placed* betrayer. Who was this man?"

"Lord, the truth behoves yet pains me to speak a name: Forwin," he pointed at Coelred, "a thegn of my half-brother."

Cenred turned to stare at his pale-faced, scornful cousin, who spluttered, "I know nought save Forwin was ever a loyal and trusted servant to our King, as am I. Let no man put it in doubt, lest he pay with his life."

"And yet," said Aethelbald, his wrath transformed into icy rancour, "we caught your thegn stealing away from the Britons. Your *trusted* servant lured his own folk – good Miercian warriors – to their doom."

Hostile, Coelred placed his hands flat on the table and leant forward, face irate, "As I do not doubt the truth of what you say, do not dare question my loyalty to our cousin. Now I think on, the mother of Forwin was a Briton, taken as a slave in the war with Gwent…"

'The slyness of the serpent!'

"Well that clears up the wherefore of his betrayal", said King Cenred. "A pity his death was swift and merciful. The pale-grey eyes slipped from Aethelbald to Coelwald, "It explains our heavy losses. And yet a heedful leader," he said, stroking his greased beard, "ought to have unmasked the deception sooner."

Coelwald, you will lead the next campaign. Aethelbald, you will remain here at Tame Weorth."

"But, Lord—"

"That is my decision," the King said.

The look of satisfaction on the face of Coelred did not escape

Aethelbald. Contemplating inactivity at Tame Weorth in the presence of this schemer gnawed at his spleen.

"Then Lord, I beg leave to return to Elmet to oversee the work on the defences—"

Even as he spoke, Coelred murmured contrary counsel close to the King's red-gold hair.

"You will remain here at Tame Weorth," the ruler repeated.

The ealdorman shrugged, "Coelwald will need more men at Bryn Alyn," he offered in support of his friend.

"Albeit not your concern," the emotionless eyes shifted around, "we shall raise more men in the spring. Now, "he clapped his hands, "recharge the horns and let us discuss more pressing matters."

'The weak fool cannot see past his nose. True, Coelred's convinced he has the upper hand. Thanks to him I lost my command but it might be no bad thing to keep the enemy close. Alert's the byword, lest the adder coils to strike again.'

TWELVE

Tame Weorth, 705 AD

"Lord, a further threescore men is not enough," Aethelbald said to his King in the first Moot of the spring.

"I beg to differ," Coelred said, "my half-brother has only to hold the border and prevent Wealisc incursions."

"As you well know, cousin, it's more than fifty leagues from the River Dee in the north to the Saefern in the south–"

The King, weary and of late, wearing a permanent worried expression, gazed from one speaker to the other before running both hands down the sides of his face.

"And," Coelred went on, "now we have a *competent* leader in Coelwald, I foresee no problems. Mierce needs its men for tilling and sowing," defiant, he challenged the gathering of noblemen, "I say sixty men suffice. A show of hands?"

Except for two of the West Miercian ealdormen, too close to Powys for comfort, the others, interested in keeping their men productive on the land, raised their hands.

"So be it!" declared King Cenred.

Other matters mooted, of little import to Aethelbald, ebbed around him like retreating tide about a rock. His mind wandered, torn between resentment for Coelred's smug insinuations and frustration at his own impotence.

'He outfoxes us all and rules in all but name.'

The meeting over, and missing Guthlac and Coelwald to confide in, Aethelbald roamed Tame Weorth with murder in his heart, heedless of his earlier resolution not to do so alone. The prospect of a year's enforced idleness threatened to unhinge his mind. Never had his dream of uniting the thrones under himself as *Bretwaldas* appeared more of a self-delusion.

'Look at me! Pursuing solace in a cup or in the arms of a whore: the reaction of a nithing.'

In fury, he kicked out at a frisking tail-wagging mongrel seeking his attention. The blow struck the stray in the ribs and it hurtled away whining. His ill-treatment of the dog served to make him opt for ale, given his foul mood, better not to abuse a wench. To his surprise, a servant of the King intercepted him before he entered a nearby tavern.

"Beggin' pardon, Lord, the King awaits and bids you come with all speed."

At a loss as to what the ruler wanted of him, Aethelbald's curiosity flared when the King led him out of the mead hall into an empty chamber. Although no other person occupied the room, the expressionless grey gaze darted around in search of...who...ghosts? The same eyes failed to meet the ealdorman's while the King spoke in an urgent whisper.

"I summoned you here, cousin, because I suspect things are not what they seem...*er*...it's hard to know where to begin..."

Cenred paced backwards and forwards wringing his hands. The silence lasted long enough for Aethelbald to frown and grow even more impatient with repetition of "...I summoned you here...*er*..." when the King blurted, "...because you are the only one of the witan *he* has not won over."

"Lord?"

"You pledged loyalty to me, just as *he* did. There is no-one else I can trust."

No doubt in the mind of Aethelbald to whom *he* referred, even so the ealdorman's restlessness increased at the other's failure to come to the point.

'Trust? I'd get rid of you quicker than Coelred would given half the chance!'

"You may trust me with your life. But what ails you?"

For a moment, their eyes met his, but at once shot to a dark corner of the chamber. Cenred half-whispered, half-hissed, "Coelred! He plots against me!"

'Ah! The sleeper wakes!'

"I am certain of it. For all his believable lies, *he* thwarted us in Powys."

The ruler, in what had become a habitual gesture, ran both hands down his cheeks as if to wipe away the perpetual expression of worry on his face.

"He wants the throne! And what better way to seize it than to discredit the King? Ensure the war in Wealas is lost. Undermine my position with the Church. Separate me from my dearest friends…"

"Lord?"

The King tugged at the point of his greased beard and sped up his agitated pacing.

"King Swaefred of the Estseaxna is closest to us. Why did he fail to send us warriors to swell the numbers of Coelwald? Why does the Bishop of Lunden defy my summons to Tame Weorth? Why are the southern underkings and nobles in turmoil?"

'Because you are a weakling and no-one respects you.'

"What is it you want of me? How may I be of service?"

At last, the King's gaze met and held Aethelbald's, "Cousin, I want you to travel to Lunden. Bring me back proof of Coelred's plotting. He is cunning and slippery. Pin him down and *I* regain the witan and *he* ends in exile."

"Why not simply slay the cur?" the ealdorman muttered but hastened to reassure the King, "Unwise, of course."

Cenred approached and laid a hand on his arm, "Aethelbald, I rely on you. Serve me well in this and I shall make you the second most powerful man in the kingdom."

'Why, who's the first? An interesting prospect, though!'

The ealdorman said, "I leave at once for Lunden."

The King did not remove his hand, but tightened his grip, "Move with the greatest of caution. Take six warriors. I shall put it about I've sent you to Elmet to ascertain the progress of our defences. Set off in that direction before doubling back. Not a word to your own men even when you are well on the way to the Kingdom of the Estseaxna."

Outside the hall, sliding his hand inside his tunic, he clasped Osthryth's ring, "By Thunor's hammer and anvil," he muttered, "what a turn of events! One minute, seeking a whore in desperation, the next, on the cusp of winning a throne!" Guilt all over his face, he looked around but the servant fifty yards away drawing water from the well did not possess the hearing of a long-eared owl.

An hour later, the ealdorman, uplifted by the reassuring presence of the stolid Meriet, rode with six of his best warriors through the North Gate of Tame Weorth. They cantered across a rickety bridge over the Trente and under the cover of woodland headed in the opposite direction to join a well-worn road to the south.

Easy riding and fine weather mellowed Aethelbald's mood, only for it to be darkened by the ever watchful, Meriet. The thegn leant over to his Lord, "I thought after the Trente, back i' the forest, we'd shaken off the cur."

"What are you—" the ealdorman turned to stare back down the road.

"No use lookin' now, Lord, he's too crafty, is that un. Wearin' a green cloak an' all, makes him hard to pick out. Been followin' us e'er since Tame Weorth. Seen him thrice now."

"Coelred!" Aethelbald snarled and his knuckles showed white around the reins. "He traps the King in his web and seeks to bind us in the same mesh."

Pointing ahead, down the road to a sharp curve, Meriet said, "Let me take one man into the trees beyond yon bend an' we'll pounce on the scout."

"Do it!"

The two warriors vanished into the woodland while Aethelbald and the others walked on their mounts at a steady pace. Unsure of the length of Meriet's absence but sensing too much time had passed, the ealdorman called a halt. A good place, he chose, where the road crossed a small stream in a dell. Little chance of an enemy taking them by surprise either, since they had an uninterrupted view in every direction. Distracted, the ealdorman observed the horses lap up the brook water swirling around their fetlocks. How to remain untroubled with no sign of his thegn and his companion?

What if there was more than one scout? A band of them? Every moment of eating, refilling flasks and watering the animals weighed on him until, to his relief, the two men appeared way down the road.

With a weary sigh Meriet threw himself down on the bank, "We waited for an age but he didn't come." He stroked his chin, "So when it became clear he'd given us the slip, we scoured the woods for any sign of him passin'." The thegn clicked his tongue and shook his head, "Not so much as a broken twig. This un's like a wraith – mingles wi' the air!"

They rode on southwards, camped overnight, travelled on and towards midday, one of the men pointed, "Up yonder, on the hill!"

A lone horse, easier to pick out than its rider in his green garb, stood motionless half a mile away on the crest above the valley. On being spotted, the horseman sped out of sight behind the rise.

"The swine-dog shadows our every move!" Aethelbald spat on the ground.

Apart from this occurrence, there were no further alarms or obstacles, nor were there on the following day. On the fourth morning out of Tame Weorth, they glimpsed their stalker *ahead* of them on the track. None of them, except Aethelbald, was destined ever to see him again.

A week after their departure, the small band entered the Kingdom of the Estseaxna. In woodland of small-leaved lime, in the upper valley of Weala-denu, two-score spearmen led by a long-haired, distinguished-looking man on horseback, sprang out on them.

"Aethelbald of Mierce," the nobleman declared, "command your men to dismount and surrender their weapons!"

"On whose authority?"

"On mine!"

"And you, who know my name," the ealdorman glowered at the Saxon, "might have the manners to state yours."

"It is for you to find out. I shall not ask thrice. Order your men to do as I demand!"

The odds stacked against them, with a sour expression, Aethelbald pursed his lips and nodded, gesturing for them to obey. Now on foot, his men buried their spearheads in the soft woodland earth, followed by their seaxes.

"Bind them, each one to a tree!" Sneering, his tormentor continued, "Now, Lord Aethelbald, off yon fine steed and give up your arms."

"I am on my way to meet King Swaefred at the behest of my King. Your Lord will not be pleased when he learns of this outrage."

The laugh of the nobleman was low and controlled, "You *were* on your way to encounter our King. Sad to say, it seems your plans are gone awry. Bind him!"

Dragged over to a lime tree, his wrists were pulled back and bound behind him around the trunk.

"Watch and learn, Aethelbald of Mierce, what happens to those who interfere in matters greater than themselves."

The lithe nobleman neared a stocky thegn and whispered in his ear. The warrior's pate shone as bald as that of a monk but from the nape fell blond hair tied in a ponytail. Vaunting a broken-toothed leer, the ill-favoured fellow nodded.

"Begin with the greybeard!"

Helpless, heart pounding, the ealdorman watched the cruel spearhead lower and the Saxon, with a rush, drove it into the thigh of the thegn Aethelbald loved as an elder brother. The Miercian did not scream but his face contorted in agony as the steel point was withdrawn and thrust again into the other leg.

The ealdorman struggled against his bonds and cried, "Meriet!" as, in horror, he saw the thegn's cream breeches stain crimson. The arms of the victim followed and only upon removal of the spike from the second, did the thegn utter a groan.

"Finish him!" came the callous command.

The pitiless spear plunged into the heart put an end to the thegn's suffering.

"A brave man," the Saxon leader conceded, "let's see if the others are made of the same stern stuff!"

One of the bound ceorls cried out, pleading for his life.

"Not the same mettle by any means," the nobleman tut-tutted, "begin with him!"

The screams rang around the glade with Aethelbald, forced to look upon the butchery until the final shriek of the last man was stifled by death.

"Shame! Our amusement ends there," the Saxon mocked. "Lesson learnt I hope, Aethelbald of Mierce."

The ealdorman glared at the executioner, "Amuse yourself some more, cur! Let me live and I swear I will hunt you down," he stared at the slumped bloodied corpses, "and their deaths will be gentle compared to what awaits you. I never forget a face."

"Bold words, friend – as befits a man of royal blood. But, for that exact reason, I cannot slay you, much as I'd like to. We do not seek war with Mierce – the inevitable result of such a deed. Who cares about a few ceorls?" He smirked at his men before looking back, "Tell King Cenred to keep his nose out of Estseaxnan affairs else the south will rise and slaughter the Miercians. Let the doom of these wretches vouch for it!"

The Saxon wandered over to Aethelbald's steed and inspected it, opening its mouth to check the teeth.

"A fine beast," he said before issuing orders, "thegns mount the horses and set five men on the others. Gather up the weapons!" He strolled over to Aethelbald's sword, tested its balance and grunted appreciation. To the latter's surprise, he approached and thrust the weapon into its sheath.

'Your first mistake, cur! And your second is you didn't take my purse.'

Drawing his seaxe, the nobleman sliced through the restraining bonds and left the ealdorman to untie his wrists. "A long walk awaits you, friend," he jeered as he mounted and wheeled away his horse, "Away!" he cried and the eight horsemen and the warriors on foot disappeared among the trees.

Aethelbald walked over to the bloodied body of Meriet sagging forward from the tree trunk and raised the head, staring into sightless eyes.

"Old comrade," he said through gritted teeth, "forgive me for leading you to this ignoble end. By God, I'll avenge you!"

He gazed around the glade, let the head drop on the chest and considered the situation.

'I will not leave you to scavengers. But alone, how can I bury you?'

Then a thought struck him. He rummaged thorough the clothing of his thegn and nodded in satisfaction. The next two hours, he worked like a mule, dragging logs into the clearing, piling them criss-cross fashion, interspersing them with twigs and smaller branches. At last, deciding the pyre was ready, he cut free the bodies and hauled them over, one by one, with difficulty scrambling the dead weights on the heap. When he had arranged the last body, he collapsed to the ground and lay chest heaving, until strength returned. Taking out Meriet's flint and small iron bar with its upturned curled ends, he struck the stone and sent sparks into the dry twigs. At first, he failed to start a flame, but after a few attempts and blowing on the glowing wood, the fire caught. Flames licked against the logs and, choosing a tree far from the earlier slaughter, he sat back to watch the blaze flare into greedy hellfire. There, he murmured a brief prayer for the souls of his men. Only with the first sickening stench of burning flesh, did he stand to set off out of the glade. If the fire spread to the surrounding woodland, he did not care.

'If it burns to the whole of fucking Estseaxna, so much the better!'

Dropping down into the valley, he looked back uphill to the forest. A dense black plume rose from amid the trees and he shuddered. A league ahead, down in the vale, less sinister smoke curled from the roofs of the houses of the settlement of Weala-denu. There, he hoped to do business and seek information.

Weary, rage smouldering within him, he accosted a tremulous woman washing garments at the stream and commanded her to take him to the town elder. She, a Briton like the other townsfolk, *'of course – Weala-denu, the valley of the Britons'* – led him to a broad-shouldered man with a straggly mane of red hair and an unkempt beard. Handy with an axe, the fellow split logs with the ease of one slicing through butter. At the woman's piping interruption, he broke off, wiped a hairy forearm across his brow and stared at Aethelbald with piercing blue eyes from under bristling eyebrows. The woman, task accomplished, hurried off back to her chores.

'By all the gods, he's hairier than Thunor's arse!'

The fellow leant on the haft of his axe, "Stranger, what brings you to these parts?"

The ealdorman took a gold coin from his purse, kindling immediate interest.

"I am Aethelbald, son of Alweo of North Mierce, Lord of Woercs-worth. What brings me is a need for something to eat and drink and, I hope, the chance to buy information and to do a little business."

"Well now, Lord, I am Flynn. So named for my red hair," he grinned, "and ealdorman to King Swaefred." He stuck out a huge hand and Aethelbald grasped it. "As for food and drink, no problem at all but information is never for sale. Either I'm glad to give it or I keep it close to my chest. As to business, well yon's the tricky one. Depends, it does, on what dealing a man has in mind."

The Briton raised his axe and buried it into the chopping block. "But come, you can tell me what you will, indoors over a platter."

He led the way into a spacious room with a central hearth over which an iron pot, its contents simmering, hung on a three-legged frame over the fire. A woman, sitting on a stool sewing under the window, laid down her work and rose to greet their guest. Introduced by her husband as Ineda, the dark-haired woman of pale complexion busied herself ladling eel stew into a wooden bowl. After a week of eating cold provisions outdoors, Aethelbald's mouth watered. The taste matched the tempting aroma. Young, hence sweet, eel in a stew of beans with wild garlic washed down with a beaker of ale soon had the Miercian feeling better.

The British ealdorman, not eating but sharing the beer with his guest, studied him as he chewed.

"Yon's the appetite of one who's been on the road too long. Am I right?"

Reluctant to pause but careful of his manners, Aethelbald laid down his spoon, "Ay, you have the right of it." Seeing the curiosity on the other's face, he put the question he burnt to ask.

"A Saxon nobleman in these parts...one who rides a white horse with a long mane...the harness boasts a round boss with a golden cross inside the–"

"Why would a Miercian Lord be wanting to know such a thing?"

'He's a Briton. There may be no love lost with the Saxons.'

"Did you see yon plume of dark smoke from the woods above the valley?"

"Hard to miss, I'd say."

Aethelbald fought to keep a rein on his temper and kept his voice flat, "Well, yon rose up from the pyre where I burnt the bodies of my dearest thegn and six of my warriors. Slaughtered," Ineda, at her sewing, gasped, "ay, murdered, in cold blood by yon swine-dog."

'Was it hatred I glimpsed for an instant? I have to trust him. I need his help.'

The Miercian's face hardened, "We were betrayed in our homeland. Sent on a mission to King Swaefred by King Cenred, our path stalked from the start, a score of them set upon us. we had no chance."

"And yet you live?"

Staring into the red-whiskered face, Aethelbald sensed the wonder behind the remark. Was it that this unknown nobleman's reputation tallied with the mercilessness shown in the forest?

"Ay, it suited his purpose to take my mount and let me survive."

"So that's your business."

"Eh?"

"You wish to buy a horse," the ealdorman grinned.

The astuteness of the Briton made him smile, "Ay, so it is."

"Well, yon gold coin you flashed earlier will do very well. I can let you have a three-year old bay. Wealisc bred, stands fourteen hands. Good stock. Steady beast. Does it suit?"

"It does."

"Finish yon stew before it gets cold. Then we'll see about the horse. You'll be wanting her to take you to Lunden, I suppose?"

Aethelbald halted his spoon mid-air, "How do you know?"

The Briton threw back his head and laughed, "You said you came to see King Swaefred. You don't strike me as one who'd slink back to Mierce, tail between his legs – anyhow, any foe of yon wicked bastard, Ealdorman Saelred, is a friend of mine."

THIRTEEN

(five years before)
Cruwland, end of October, 699 AD

"Push off, Brother Godric!" Bernulf called and he waved to the barefoot figure on the knoll dressed in skins. As they glided away from the island, he grumbled, "I can't scratch these bites while I'm rowing and the itching's driving me mad. I don't know how Guthlac can live amid swarms of bugs."

"Ay, and how he can stand the discomfort of otter pelts next to his skin is a wonder to me."

"At least there is a roof over his head now we finished the thatching."

"I must say, I'm grateful not to have to cart any more bales of reeds up yon hillock."

Bernulf scowled at the novice and scolded, "Your spirit of self-sacrifice needs to improve, Brother Godric. It is our privilege to assist and learn from a great teacher."

The boat cut through the placid waters of the fens causing the barest of ripples to sway the stems of the waterside plants. Among them, still as a marble statue, in a flash of white, an egret struck, emerging with a small rudd wriggling in its bill. The young monk nodded in approval of this silent killer of the marshland. He gloried at the marvels of Nature around him. In the month since Saint Bartholomew's Day, when they had arrived, unlike his companion, he had adapted well to his new surroundings. In a short time, he had become skilled with the oars on his twice weekly trips from Estdeping to the islet of Cruwland.

"Maybe so," the other retorted. "Whilst I'm grateful to the raiders of bygone times for not having to dig into the hillside, I'd never make *my* home in a burial mound. Yon tomb's full of dead heathen. And you know what Tatwine said. Accursed spirits dwell o'er yonder and come out at night. No man can withstand the horrors and fears, he says."

"Guthlac is not like other men," Bernulf said in awed tones. "Saint Antony sought out devils in the desert and in the same way our brother chose Cruwland for its demons. With the aid of the Holy Spirit, he will wrestle and resist them."

"Rather him than me!" Godric's face wore a puzzled expression, "but why go out of your way to seek out fiends?"

Bernulf sniffed, "Our Lady Abbess sent you with us because you have much to learn. By defeating the evil spirits, Guthlac will discomfort the Devil to the glory of God!"

"Ah!" the novice pretended to understand but the concept eluded him so he concentrated on trailing a hand in the water until the boat neared the landing stage at Estdeping.

"Of course, once he's quelled them, we shall go to live there. What greater honour than founding a community of brothers?"

"Well, I hope he does! I have no fancy to dwell among imps and trolls."

Lifting an oar aboard, Bernulf tossed him a rope, "Stop your childish prattle, make yourself useful and secure the boat!" At last, he was free to scratch at the irritating angry bites on his forearms.

Tatwine came out of his reed barn and hailed them, "Brothers, how is Guthlac? Did you give him the fishing net?"

Climbing out of the small craft on the landing stage, Bernulf replied, "Ay, we did. But he'll make no use of it. He insists he will eat nought but barley bread and drink but water, and that after sunset."

"A man can't live on so little! He'll fade away to skin an' bones."

"The Holy Spirit sustains him, friend Tatwine."

"That's as may be. But I'll put aside strips of dried fish an' meat and a couple o' bottles o' ale. Ye can take it to him next time ye go to him."

Bernulf gathered up an old sack and a trowel, saying, "Ay, in three days from now, but it's a waste of time, I know what he'll say." He turned to instruct Godric, "Let's get on with building our house. You carry on weaving the wattle and I'll go down to the clay bed Tatwine showed us. I'll fill this bag with buttery clay and hump it back here. One of us has to do the donkey work," he laughed and set off downstream whistling a merry tune.

Deep in the fens at Cruwland, in spite of the fortitude he displayed to his fellow monks, Guthlac sank into profound depression. Blaming Satan for troubling him over his choice of living alone, the truth was, he had too much time to think. The devilish arrow of despair pierced his spiritual armour as he began to dwell on his former sins and wickedness. As far as he could see, they were much greater than he might ever compensate for by holy practices and penitence. He rubbed his bare forearms and the flesh of his exposed calves. Insects tormented him as much as his bleak thoughts during the day and night.

In this state of mind, misery worsened by his headache and a chill running up and down his spine, Guthlac lay on his bed of reeds. Fatigued owing to his lack of sleep, sweating in spite of the coolness of the evening, he closed his eyes and mumbled a prayer *'…in tribulatione mea invocavi Dominum, et reliqua…'*

'Who is this at the foot of my bed? Why Saint Bartholomew in angelic beauty! What's that in your left hand? Oh my, the poor flayed skin of your martyrdom.'

The apostle raised his other hand and blessed Guthlac.

"I will support you in your tribulations, my son," said the martyr, "but for seven nights you must cleanse your sins by abstinence and fasting. In six days, the Almighty formed and adorned the beauty of the Earth and on the seventh rested. You must eat meat and rest the body on the seventh day."

At these words, uttered by a demon in the semblance of the saint, Guthlac sat up, his brow dripping beads of perspiration. Eyes blazing yet unseeing, he pointed a trembling finger at the false apostle, "Imposter!" he exclaimed, "Be gone! No flesh shall pass my lips – tell this to the Tempter who sent you!"

Bewailing, the fiend vanished in a cloud of acrid smoke. Further weakened by this ordeal, Guthlac slumped back on his bed and sought sleep in vain.

'Lord protect me! All these demons come to torment me. They fill my house. They swirl around my bed! Ah, huge vile heads and long necks! What horror! How lean they are of countenance! What filthy matted beards!'

The distorted visages with pointed hairy ears and fierce eyes made him cringe and cover his hearing at the foul obscene outpourings from their mouths. Through their horse-like teeth passed flame as they uttered grating speech or raucous shrieks. The small house resounded with terrible cries and Guthlac curled into a ball to protect himself.

Not to be denied, three of them, springing with crooked shanks, hopped on the bed cackling to bind him and to carry him out through the door.

'What are you doing? Where are you taking me?'

Down the hillock they charged to the moonlit waters lapping the islet.

'I beg you! In God's name let me go!'

There, by the reeds, they threw and sunk him in the muddy depths that closed in over his head.

'I must hold my breath else I'll choke and drown!'

Snatching him up so he might gasp for air, with hideous laughter they dragged him through thickets of brambles till torn and bleeding he begged for mercy.

'There are more of them! They have wings – the fiends! Iron whips in their hands. For Pity's sake, do not beat me!'

Pitiless, the demons thrashed him ignoring his screams until his flesh hung in bloody tatters. Blackness swept over him and he regained consciousness only when the devils flew him high up to the cold regions of the air. Thence they bore him down into the nethermost abyss.

'Aaaaagh! What is this? The souls of the damned! How the fiends plunge their bodies into cauldrons of molten metal! And there! Another hanging upside down on a spit and roasted over flames!'

The demons cackled and, in delight, speaking in British tongue, pointed out the intricacies of the evil torments one by one. They promised Guthlac because of his wicked past, he would sample them all throughout eternity. At the very moment when he thought he would lose his mind in the face of these hideous sights, the monk came to his senses.

'Woe to you, children of darkness, and seed of destruction!' he railed. *'Who granted you wretches, that you should have power over me? I am here awaiting my Lord's will; wherefore would you frighten me with your false threats?'*

Of a sudden, Guthlac found himself safe and free of wounds in his bed. The bright form of Saint Bartholomew appeared and the accursed spirits unable to abide the splendour of the holy apparition, fled wailing to hide in the darkness. The saint bent over him, concern on his benign face. With a damp cloth, he soothed the heated brow of the monk. Opening his eyes, Guthlac stared into the countenance of his comforter. The visage of the apostle, so kind and gentle, so troubled yet self-assured was also most familiar.

"Godric," said the well-known voice, "the ague is upon our poor brother. Prepare a potion of feverfew. Why he is all a-chilled. How he trembles! Such dark rings around his eyes! And his hair and clothes wet through with sweat."

"Saint Bartholomew, am I in Heaven?" Guthlac murmured.

"Dearest Guthlac, I am not Bartholomew. It is I, Bernulf! You are in your bed." The monk said to Godric, "The fever grips him. He is not himself. It is clear he does not recognise me. I ask myself, how long lies he here in this state? We cannot leave him until he is mended."

The novice stared, an expression of horror on his face, as if he, not Guthlac, had seen the torments of Hell.

"Brother, do not ask me to spend the night in this accursed place! I have not the strength to resist the wiles of the Evil One. Let's take him back to Estdeping in the boat. We can look after him better there."

"Silence! For shame, Godric! Can you not see our companion is in no fit state to travel on water? Now, for the last time, light a fire and prepare yon draught of feverfew. Must I do everything myself? Oh, and while you're at it, make a broth out of the dried fish Tatwine gave us. We need to build up Guthlac's strength."

The feverfew potion proved efficacious, either that or occurred the natural tendency of the marsh fever to subside after a bout of three days. Whatever, Guthlac woke with a beatific smile and Godric survived without a visitation from malign spirits.

"I spoke with the apostle Bartholomew," he told the young monks. "He will sustain me in my tribulations—"

Bernulf shot a meaningful glance at the novice. They had discussed how to react if the monk persisted in the delirium-induced delusion that Bernulf was Saint Bartholomew. Given the weakness of their mentor, they decided not to stress him by contradiction.

"How wonderful!" the young monk cried, "An apostle for spiritual sustenance and Tatwine for bodily nourishment. Come, now, you must build up your strength. Drink some broth Godric prepared for you from strips of dried duck meat—"

"I will not, Bernulf! After sunset, I will eat of the barley bread. Does not Proverbs instruct us, *'…put a knife to your throat if you are given to gluttony.'*?"

"Brother, you are anything but a glutton! Take a little broth to keep body and soul together. The Lord said, *'Man shall not live on bread alone…'*—"

The eyes of Guthlac flashed with a fervour that startled his young companion, "Do not presume to instruct me in the Gospel, Bernulf! *'not…on bread alone, but on every word that comes from the mouth of God.'* My loaf will do me very well. My Father in Heaven will give me the strength to fend off the demons who are sure to persist in their wicked desire to reclaim this place. They will not succeed for I shall chase them back to the bowels of Hell with the power of faith and the help of Christ to strengthen my spirit."

As Godric pushed the boat into the river, Bernulf settled his oars into the rowlocks and mused on what he had seen and heard. *'Either Brother Guthlac is a saint or he's a madman. His passion inspires me but what if it is mere folly?'*

FOURTEEN

Kingdom of the Estseaxna, May, 705 AD

The bay mare had a delightful temperament, she trusted and respected Aethelbald and he, not one to care overmuch for animals, began to grow fond of her. The gentle warming sun of spring burned away the cool morning mist and brought a sparkle to the tender leaves arching over his head as he rode towards Lunden. The beauty of Nature, as a rule, a matter of indifference to the ealdorman, eased the vile mood holding him in its vice-like grip since the death of Meriet. In midmorning, the air above the track reverberated to the buzzing of insects.

"*'A swarm of bees in May is worth a load of hay,'*" Aethelbald shared with his horse ceorlish wisdom he had once overheard. The splendid day worked its magic but he could not suspect every hoof beat took him nearer to one of three men he hated most in the world.

Thus, the welcome sight of curling wisps of smoke indicating a village and the chance to stock up on provisions turned sour. There he was, the evil bastard! Mounted on a horse, bald pate shining in the brightness of the morning. The ponytail falling from the nape and his stocky build left no doubt in the ealdorman's mind: the torturer of Meriet! Aethelbald drew his sword. At a shout from one of his men and a pointing finger, the thegn left off whatever unpleasant deed he was perpetrating in the settlement.

The nobleman surveyed the odds and his heart sank. However seasoned a warrior he was, his chance of overcoming six formidable mounted enemies looked bleak. Still, being outnumbered never daunted him in battle and the rage boiling in his veins sent the mare leaping forward. The blood pounding in his ears born of fury and the drumming hoofs meant he did not hear the thegn's cry:

"Take him alive! Unscathed!"

Only when his blade was met by an axe haft or parried by a sword did he understand. Unlike himself, the devils were not fighting to the death. They came at him from all sides so that from attack he was forced at once into frantic defence. Pain shot up his right arm. A mighty blow to his hand from the flat iron of an axe-head did the damage. By Thunor, they had him! His weapon fell from his numbed and useless grip. They pounced on him, hauling him from his horse. Knees pinned him to the ground, where rough hands pulled his arms behind his back to bind them. Hoisted to his feet, shoved forward, with great bitterness he watched the thegn dismount to thrust a leering face into his. The broken-toothed grin was too much to bear so he spat in the eye of his tormentor earning himself a split lip for his trouble.

The thegn bent to pick up Aethelbald's sword and slid it under his belt. "So, here we are again," he smirked. "Not a man to take good advice, eh? Up to me, I'd slice you limb from limb for the grief you cause." He scratched the side of his nose as if pondering some difficult decision. After a moment, he sneered, "Lucky for you, *I* follow orders." He turned and spoke to his men, "We'll take him back to Lord Saelred and let him decide his doom! Heave him up on his horse. No, back-to-front!" The mocking, humiliating laugh filled Aethelbald with a searing wrath that made his head swim.

'If I ever get my hands round his throat…'

Then, hopeless cold realism engulfed him in despair.

'What ill fate devised our paths should cross! I'm at their mercy and my mission's failed.'

One of the warriors took the mare's reins and they set off back in the direction from which Aethelbald had come. Not that he enjoyed the privilege of a different perspective. To his dismay, all he could see was the familiar view of the terrain where he had been headed diminishing in the distance.

His depression would have evaporated like the morning dew had he known the implications of his enemy's choice, in his arrogance, to take the quickest way to his master's land. This entailed passing through the valley of the Britons, shortening the journey by sixteen miles. In the vale, news travelled on the wind and before long, the breeze whispered in Weala-denu that Aethelbald had fallen helpless captive to the thegn of the detested Saelred.

The first Aethelbald realised his circumstances had changed came with the clamour of seaxes beaten on shields and piercing war cries. Twisting in his saddle, with difficulty, he strained to glance over his shoulder and his heart filled with hope. Two score Britons, he judged their number, fanned out around the Estseaxna, trapping them in a ring of steel.

The tall red-haired figure of Ealdorman Flynn grinned up at him, impervious to the venomous threats hurled by Saelred's infuriated thegn.

'By Thunor, am I glad to see you, you ugly brute!'

Firm hands lowered the Miercian from his horse before hacking through his bonds. Dragged from their mounts, the Britons relieved the captors-become-captives of their weapons. Flynn, testing the balance of Aethelbald's sword, handed it back to its rightful owner with a grunt of approval.

Throwing back his shoulders and folding his muscular arms across his chest, the Briton frowned at his fellow ealdorman. The effect of the pose was lost on Aethelbald. Too intent on probing the bruising of his sword hand, it needed the harsh words of his rescuer to gain his attention.

"What mire have you led us into, friend?"

"*Eh?*" came his distracted reply, having passed on to rubbing the life back into his numb and chafed wrists. He flexed his swollen hand. It would do. He could grip.

"We cannot let them live," Flynn jerked his head towards the captives. "If Saelred discovers we aided your escape, he'll bring fire and destruction to our vale. He's waiting for an excuse. Were it not for the protection of King Swaefred, he'd have done so before now." In ringing tones, he commanded, " Slay them like the swine they–"

"Hold!" cried Aethelbald, "I'll not stand aside whilst murder's committed!" He laid a hand on a hirsute arm, "These dogs are brave when they hunt in packs. Let's see their true mettle when the odds are even. I have a grudge to settle, most of all with yon," he pointed at the glowering thegn.

'Ay, let the hope shine in your eye in the place of terror. I'll snuff it out like a candle flame.'

A Briton handed the stocky warrior his sword. Weapon in hand, he sneered, "I need no pack to slaughter a tame goat, "the familiar leer returned to enhance his ugliness, "I ought to have slain you when I had the chance. Now's as good a time as any, I suppose!"

The Britons hastened to lead the horses to graze. Then they moved to form a wide circle around the adversaries, eager to witness a fight to the death. Wary in their movements, each combatant prowled waiting for the moment to attack. The Estseaxna lunged first and Aethelbald marvelled at the strength of arm of the other man as he parried the blow. They fought without shields, one driven by desperation in the knowledge he would never leave the vale alive, the other impelled by an all-consuming hatred.

A warrior of vast experience, thickset and powerful, vengeful and devious, the thegn launched a frantic attack. Aethelbald forced backward, grimaced as the shock of the blows striking sparks from his blade and sending waves of pain along his bruised and throbbing wrist. Oblivious to the cheering Britons battering their shields, his concentration never wavered. All his defensive skills came into play with a determination not to be blinded by the molten rage bubbling beneath the surface. His opponent was redoubtable but Aethelbald's practiced eye spotted one weakness. The sturdy thegn was not nimble. If he could allow the attack to last long enough, he would tire. All well and good, but his wrist felt as if he had the Devil gnawing at it. Would it resist? In the event, time was not important. His adversary made a double feint and the watchers gasped as the ealdorman saved himself at the last second, taking a nick to his upper arm. A slight gash, in truth, but it must have cut a vein, for the copious flow of blood made it look far worse.

The crimson river running down to his hand suggested to Aethelbald a ploy. Dropping his arm, as if useless, by his side and tottering as if sorely wounded, with satisfaction he saw the leer reappear on his enemy's confident face. He had fooled him. The Britons groaned. Incautious for the first time, the Estseaxna rushed in to strike the fatal blow. It came. But not from him. Lithe on his feet, Aethelbald sprang to one side, slicing down to sever the sinews behind the knee of his foe. The thegn, crying out in surprise and hurt, sank to the ground, supporting himself with his sword buried in the ground. The Britons cheered and hammered on their shields.

The suppressed hatred erupted. Aethelbald chopped downwards on the wrist grasping the hilt, lopping hand from arm. The warrior screamed and fell on his face. Pitiless, the Miercian wrenched him over with his free hand grinning down into the visage of his defeated foe. In triumph, he said:

"Remember what you did to my thegn in the forest? Now it's your turn."

He gazed on, unmoved, as his victim grasped the stump of his right arm in an attempt to staunch the bleeding.

"Look at my sword," he commanded and when the pain-wracked eyes did so, he plunged the blade into the warrior's left thigh to a rousing cheer from the bloodlusting onlookers.

"How does it feel? At least you aren't bound to a tree. You had a fighting chance." And the memory of that day enraged him further. He hewed an arm, then the other, into the right thigh slid the steel, each thrust delivered with a delay: with the slowness of calculated vengeance.

"And now, you go to Hell where you belong," Aethelbald pronounced, driving his sword deep into the chest of the Estseaxna, putting an end to his agony.

'For you Meriet. For you, my old friend.'

A red-haired arm clasped him around his shoulder, "'Twas well done!" said Flynn, "now, let us deal with the other—"

"No," he pulled himself free of the embrace and faced the ealdorman, "I'll fight them all. One by one."

"But there are five of them! You are sure to tire. Why risk your life?"

"Bah! I have a debt to repay and repay it, I will!"

A murmur went round the gathered Britons. Here was a tale to tell their grandchildren on a cold winter's night. The drumming on the shields began anew enough to unman the five captives.

"Who is brave enough to fight?" Aethelbald bellowed.

None of them moved.

"No blade of yours killed my friends. True enough. Yet they died because of you, bound helpless to a tree," he glared from one drawn face to another. "No more torture. I promise a clean death!" he shouted in the face of the biggest of the Estseaxna, hauling him by the tunic into the circle.

"I'm going to die anyway," mumbled the warrior, taking the proffered sword. Finding courage, he hissed, "but I'll take you with me!"

The threat proved in vain. In spite of his size, he was no match for the skill of the ealdorman, in a matter of three furious minutes of clashing steel and howls of glee from the gathering, the enemy lay at his feet. A gory pool formed, oozing from a clean gash across the throat.

Contrary to Flynn's prediction, Aethelbald did not tire. With each victim, he appeared to gain in strength. In the end, six sightless bodies stared at the indifferent clouds. But when he relaxed waves of fatigue overwhelmed the nobleman. With the cheers of the Britons ringing in his ears, he swayed on his feet. One of them thrust a water flask in his hand and grateful, he gulped down long refreshing draughts.

"Remind me not to make an enemy of you, Miercian," Flynn thumped him on the back.

Grinning, Aethelbald clasped the huge hand, "After what you did today, we are bound forever in friendship."

The Briton's expression grew grave. "In that case, heed my warning. You cannot just walk into the King's hall in Lunden." He moved close to the other's ear and whispered a name.

"Butcher's Lane?" Aethelbald muttered under his breath and frowned.

"Ask for him and he'll get you a secret audience with King Swaefred. That'll be better for your hide and for the well-being of the King." Once more, he clapped him on the back, "We'll get rid of these vermin. No-one will ever find a trace and Saelred will not be able to connect their disappearance with either of us."

Thus, three days later, Aethelbald, having found a stable for his mare, prowled the offal-strewn, slimy length of Butcher's Lane in

Lunden. The stench of the slaughter house, bestial shrieks, rivulets of blood and the sight of hewn carcasses had no effect on him. Worse had he seen on the battlefield where all these sights and sounds, gaping wounds and protruding bones of friend and foe alike, inured him to butchery. No, his problem was another. In spite of the press of customers, the presence of a warrior in this realm of buyers and traders provoked curious stares. Aware of the need to be discreet, for fear of thwarting his mission, he delayed seeking news of the name provided by Flynn.

Peering into each booth, he had eyes only for the merchant. One shouted what was his lordship's pleasure. Aethelbald ignored him and passed to the next stall pretending to be interested in joints of flesh. And so on, until he began to lose hope of finding his man. Before the last spark of faith died, there stood the red-haired Briton he sought: a cleaver in his grasp and a determined set to his jaw as he flipped over a piece of meat.

"Good fellow!" the ealdorman called, "This coin to buy a few words."

A frown creased the butcher's brow and his green eyes blazed suspicion. The small gold piece seemed not to interest him. Another customer tried to capture his attention but Aethelbald drew his hand seax and drove it into the counter.

'By Thunor's bulging muscles, you'll listen to me!'

The ealdorman sneered as he followed the butcher measuring the distance from his cleaver to his person. In haste, he said, "A friend sent me from…" he leant forward and amid the clamour of the busy lane lowered his voice so the trader strained to hear, "…Weala-denu." He hoped not to mention Flynn by name.

A marked change came over the Briton, his expression softening, he nodded and turned to a younger man at a bench behind him filleting meat, "Nephew, serve yon customer, like a good lad! I'll be back in a couple of minutes." He held his hand out for Aethelbald to drop the scillingas into his palm and grinned, "Follow me!" Pausing only to wrench free his hand-seax, the nobleman hurried after the leather-aproned figure between booths to a narrow and quiet alleyway.

Checking there were no others within hearing, Aethelbald said, "Ealdorman Flynn gave me your name."

"Oh, ay?"

"Hark, my men have been tortured and murdered in an attempt to stop me meeting with your King. It's a long tale but I'll tell you straight. Flynn told me you are the man to set me before King Swaefred without anyone knowing. Is he right?"

The butcher bit his cheek and shrugged, "Um, I dunno." He wrestled with doubt. At last, he came to a decision and met the Miercian's eye, "There might be a way, Lord. I serve the man you need. But who shall I say seeks our ruler?"

"Tell him Ealdorman Aethelbald of Mierce comes in the name of King Cenred."

The meat merchant's mouth fell open, "In that case, I can't take this. The gold coin reappeared to be held out to the nobleman.

For his part, Aethelbald closed the trader's fist around it. "Do this for me and there's ten more where that came from to show my gratitude." He hesitated, then made a decision. "Take this package from my King to *the man I need*. Guard it with your life. It must reach King Swaefred in person. Is that clear? Good. Now tell me of an inn for the night and when I can come for news."

"Ay, come on the morrow, but say nought. Even market stalls have ears!"

The next morning, the ealdorman went to the butcher's booth, where neither man uttered a word. Another kind of exchange took place. The trader pressed a small, square parchment sealed with common candle wax into the Miercian's hand. The warrior's heart sank. He needed to find someone who could read. How to wield an axe, a sword, and spear and to hurl a javelin was the extent of his learning.

'Guthlac ever insisted I must learn to read and write.'

Irritated, he handed over the ten scillingas promised.

Well away from Butcher's Lane, and reassuring himself no-one was following, curiosity led to him breaking open the seal. Relief at no writing on the parchment gave way after a moment to further irritation. The image of a beardless youth stared up from the page. In his right hand, he held a palm leaf and in his left, a sword.

'What is this? Some kind of saint? By Thunor, I'll have to find a priest to aid me with this!'

Where to find a cleric in Lundenburh? To avoid aimless

wandering in the maze of winding alleyways, he accosted a peddler with a basket containing bright ribbons, buttons, and threads. Who better than a street trader for directions? He purchased a green ribbon for a pittance, thinking he might use it to please a wench. It also bought him what he needed to know. The Church of All Hallows stood nearby, down by the River Temes.

The emptiness of the building frustrated him. A blessing he did not have to wait through a service, true, but where was the priest? Venting a sigh of frustration, far too loud for a place of worship, he sat on a bench to relieve his tired feet. A hand rested on his shoulder making him start.

"What ails you, my son, that you groan so?"

'A priest, by Thunor!'

The ealdorman stood and pulled the parchment from his tunic. Even in the act of producing the image, his spirits sank. Before him stood an unkempt figure in unwashed ragged garb. Did the fellow hate water? Could such a one be of use to him? But what other choice did he have?

"Are you a priest?" he said, through clenched teeth, eyes narrowed with a menace in his voice.

"I try my best to serve the Almighty," in contrast to his appearance the voice was that of an educated man, "how can I help you, my son?"

'Son, he says but I'll not call him father.'

Aethelbald unfolded the parchment and passed it to the clergyman, "Does this mean anything to you, priest?"

The cleric laughed, "Of course," he said, "this is Saint Pancras, a youth of but fourteen springs, beheaded by a Roman emperor for refusing to worship their false gods. There is a church built not long ago and dedicated to Pancras outside the burh."

The ealdorman beamed at the priest and, in his new-found mellowness, said, "*Father*, you do me a great service. Now, tell me, how distant is the church and how can I find it?"

The priest marvelled at the change in one who moments before was overwrought. Judging by his long hair and fine speech a nobleman stood before him and he rejoiced in the chance to aid such a person. A smile and a shrewd, appraising look, the priest said, "On foot, over an hour, but you will have a horse. Out of the church, follow the river to your right until you come to a smaller one flowing into it. Yon is the Fleta. Less than a league along its course will bring you to the Church of Saint Pancras." He made the sign of the cross in front of the ealdorman's face, "Go in peace, my son and may God bless you!"

Aethelbald felt in his purse and took out a scillingas. "Take this, father, buy some candles for the altar. Many thanks to you for your help."

An hour searching for the stable and half an hour to find the church anew restored the almost permanent rancour characterising him after the death of Meriet. The small river swirling and eddying into the vast breadth of the Temes brought a grunt of satisfaction and before long the mare cantered up to a settlement. Dominating the score of turf-roofed houses stood a squat square-shaped structure with two low wings. Surprised the village seemed deserted but for the protests of untended geese, hens and goats, Aethelbald dismounted in front of the Church of Saint Pancras.

Inside, the reason for the lack of people became apparent. Here the womenfolk and children were chanting prayers with the priest. The men, he guessed, must be about their toil. Given the sun high in the sky, this ought to be the service of Sext. The ealdorman joined the congregation and even though his knowledge of liturgy was rudimentary, Sext, he remembered with satisfaction, was the shortest of the services. Yet, the grip of this cleric on the villagers was something quite out of the ordinary.

The church emptied and the reason became clear. Tall, broad-shouldered, himself with a notable presence, Aethelbald stood face to face with one no less imposing. The priest of Saint Pancras gazed at the Miercian with unusual piercing eyes the violet hue of the wood vetch flower.

"Come," said he with no ado, "I expected you sooner."

Taken aback, the ealdorman followed on the heels of the clergyman who led him into a vestibule.

In little more than a whisper, he said, "Come into this room on the morrow, at the same hour, straight after Sext. Do not be late. Make sure no-one stalks you. I need not warn you, not a word to a soul about the meeting.

"And King Swaefred will be here?"

"Why else are you come?" the cleric reproved him. Like the other priest, this one made the sign of the cross and blessed Aethelbald.

'With all these blessings, what can go amiss?'

Women and children filed out of church the next midday, noisy as a field-full of startled crows. None of them noticed Aethelbald leaning against a tree in the graveyard. When they had gone to set about their workday tasks, the ealdorman hurried into the building. He made straight for the vestibule. Raising the door latch, he slipped inside. At a table sat a cowled figure, his face indistinguishable in the dimness of the tiny room, lit only by a shaft of light from the small arched window.

"Welcome to Estseax, Aethelbald, son of Alweo!"

'Why does he cover his head?'

As if in response to the Miercian's thought, the seated man threw back his hood and gestured to an empty chair facing him. The ealdorman sat and scrutinised the man across the table: fine-featured, long nose over a neat moustache, yellow hair cascading from a central parting either side of the bearded countenance. The blue eyes, alive with intelligence, studied him with the same intensity.

"Forgive me, but since we have never met, how do I know you are the person I seek?" The gloomy, suffocating surroundings and the odd circumstances of the meeting left Aethelbald uneasy. "And why so many precautions to exchange a few words?"

The man smiled and stretched a hand, palm down, across the unpolished oak surface. Without a word, he tapped the table with his middle finger. There, a heavy ring bore a flat disc where, in relief, the letter O resembling entwined cord contained three seaxes.

"Who might bear this jewel?"

"King Swaefred," Aethelbald conceded, "Well met, Lord."

A gracious tilt of the head and the King added, "As to the strangeness of our encounter, I am surprised you ask. Little happens in my kingdom unbeknown to me. Sad to relate, this is true also for at least one other who opposes my will." The ruler frowned and bit his lower lip, "It is with sorrow I learnt of the death of your thegn and men."

Silence hung like the drifting motes in the beam of light slicing across the pinched space of the vestibule. Aethelbald interpreted three different emotions crossing the visage opposite him: confusion, anxiety and, the last, determination. The window did not admit much air and the ealdorman's head began to spin. He longed to be outdoors – and if he might choose, far away in Mierce. At last, Swaefred spoke, "I read the message from Cenred, seeking proof of Coelred's plotting." The King shook his head and with a sorrowful glance at the ealdorman said, "I fear he misreads the situation. Let me explain."

Once more the stillness of the confined surroundings became oppressive as the ruler summoned his thoughts. But then his words came in a torrent. "Cenred and I are in similar circumstances. In Estseax, Saelred, who you had the misfortune to encounter, schemes against me. His strength grows daily. Unless something is done soon, he will usurp the throne. I believe he works hand in glove with Coelred." The King clenched his fist and the knuckles showed white, "I have no proof of this. But it is as clear as daylight…"

'The daylight I yearn for.'

"…you are my last hope."

Aethelbald started from his musing, straightened in his seat, "I?"

The King reached and took his hand in an unexpected gesture of intimacy, "Ay, Aethelbald, son of Alweo. Ride hard for Mierce. Carry this message to Tame Weorth. Tell Cenred, Swaefred is ever his loyal servant but has need of his overlord. At a sign from him, I can raise an army of those still faithful but I cannot defeat my enemies alone." He squeezed the ealdorman's hand, "Ask him to march on Saelred in Grantebrycge. Crush the cur and the rest will beg for mercy. Once Cenred is on the march from Mierce, I will lead my men from Lunden in a pincer movement. Make haste, Ealdorman, my throne depends upon it!"

FIFTEEN

Licidfelth, late spring 705 AD

"Cenred is a good man," Aethelbald told Coelwald, summoned from the war-wracked borders of Powys, "but he's too feeble for his kingship to last. Look how he failed to aid Swaefred. Lucky for the Estseaxna King he's made of sterner mettle and he's got some staunch ealdormen. Here, Coelred grows stronger every day."

"A church council!" the aetheling spat out the words, "What timing! How can ecclesiastical matters be more important than keeping the Wealisc from plundering our villages? Just when the weather's right for another offensive, damn it!"

"I've no idea what it's about," the ealdorman confessed. "What I do know is the way of the world means if a king fails to rank the Church behind him, he might as well set sail for Thule."

"Thule?"

"No-one knows where it is. Some say it's an island far off to the north."

"Ah."

Aethelbald drew his friend deeper into the shadows cast by the cathedral consecrated but five years before and lowered his voice to little more than a whisper. "Coelred's strutting around aloof as a cockerel ruling the roost. It's my guess he's turning the Church against the King and if he succeeds we ought to beware!" He grimaced, "As things stand, what words he deigns me at the moot are heavy with masked threats. What better occasion than this to demonstrate our king is unworthy to reign?"

"And to turn more nobles and clerics against him," Coelwald said.

The council assembled the next morning in the cathedral nave. For the purpose of the event, a large table placed in front of the altar accommodated the King. On his right, sat Haedde, Bishop of Licidfelth (hence of Mierce) and Lindissi, and on his left stood an empty chair. All the other nobles and clerics grouped together according to their status and roles. With so many present, those at the back ranged farther than halfway down the body of the church. Most eyes fixed on the bevy of nuns near the front of the throng or a taut-faced woman and her family glaring at them. The collective murmurings made for a clamour reverberating from the rafters such that the King battered the hilt of a gem-encrusted hand-seax on the table and called for silence.

"Bishop Haedde, pray proceed," said Cenred.

The bishop rose amid the expectant hush. This man ruled over the Church from the borders of Wealas to the Wash and from Elmet in the north to the Akeman Street in the south. And he looked the part. Tall and ascetic, his silver hair glinting in a beam of light from a window high in the wall. He cleared his throat and began an explanation.

"We are gathered here to attempt to reconcile the widow Aelfthryth with her kinswoman the Abbess of Medeshamstede. The dispute is over land where a church stands at Wockingas. The Mother Superior wishes to free the building of all obligations due to the King and the bishop…" he hesitated and nodded in apology to Cenred, "…thus with no obligation except to Saint Peter and the Abbey. *Er*, however, I do not see how we can proceed–"

"Why not?" Cenred frowned, a high-pitched edge to his voice.

"Because," said Haedde "the Bishop of Lunden refuses to come to Licidfelth."

"He *refuses!*" an ironic voice came from a clutch of nobles.

Aethelbald nudged Coelwald, "Coelred!" he whispered.

"How can this be? May a bishop *defy* his Lord, the King?" continued the nobleman.

Bishop Haedde tugged at his beard and glanced at Cenred, "You use a strong word, my Lord–"

"And yet, he did not come…"

Bishop Haedde spread his hands wide, "Bishop Waldhere writes he cannot come for he is ignorant of the position of Archbishop Berhtwald of Cantwaraburh on the matter–"

"Who then rules the Land? The Church?" Coelred stepped forward from his group of supporters, their expressions feigning wisdom and conviction. "My King," he said, his tone wheedling but outraged, "This cannot be. Allow this Waldhere to flout your authority and before long all the churchmen in these isles will do as they please."

A growl of assent came not only from those standing closest to the nobleman.

'How the silken-tongued cur sways them!'

"Give the command, Lord, and I will go and bind the wretch and bring him grovelling at your feet."

The Bishop of Licidfelth, flushed, pointed at Coelred, "Take a hold on your tongue, Lord Coelred, lest it strays into sacrilege! This matter can be resolved without force."

King Cenred ran his hands down both sides of his face and bowed his head.

"And how, exactly, *Bishop*? Do you mean to give the right of it to the widow? Where is the impartial sustainment of the Church for the Lady Abbess? Nay, I repeat, my King, let me dig out the priest from his burrow in Lunden–"

'The dog is sure those of the south no longer recognise Cenred's overlordship. He aims to prove it to all and sundry.'

Haedde leant closer to the King, "I beg you, Lord, act not in haste. I will write to Berhtwald that Waldhere–"

"*Write*, Bishop! But it seems *words* did not bring the priest of Lunden to this council." Coelred smirked at his followers who laughed and nodded in agreement.

The throng of people looked to the King. How would he react? What decision would he make? But he did not raise his head, leaving Haedde to struggle on.

"I will write this very morn. We cannot settle the dispute without the correct authorities present."

The family of the widow protested but no-one took the part of the most vulnerable of the parties. The abbess and the nuns turned away and left the building in studied silence, it being in the Mother Superior's best interest to do so. Coelred struck again, "And if the Bishop of Lunden defies you once more, Lord…"

"By Thunor," Aethelbald murmured in the aetheling's ear, "the mangy hound twists everything to his own gain."

"…a word from you and I will haul him before you."

"Thank you cousin, you bear my interests close to your heart."

So saying, Cenred stared at the body of his people in the nave but his gaze was blank.

'Poor fool!'

(four years later).
Woercs-worth, 709 AD

"Lord Aethelbald! Lord Aethelbald!"

The ealdorman put his head out of the smithy where he was engaged in whetting the edges of his weapons. The sight of the elderly thegn, Wulfric, red in the face and panting towards the forge at a pace that did violence to his aged body, roused his curiosity.

"Slow down, Wulfric, before your heart bursts!"

Having returned from a campaign in Powys to take over his lands upon his father's death the year before, Aethelbald had grown fond of Alweo's trusted thegns. What was the shepherd doing down in the farmstead? And why was he so alarmed?

"What ails you, old man?"

Behind him, Enulf, the smith, a head and shoulders taller than even his lofty lord, blinked peering against the daylight, bright after the dark of his workshop. Driven by the oddity of the event, he too gaped at the thegn, hands on knees, drawing huge breaths into his starved lungs.

"Lord Aethelbald," he wheezed, "a horseman, lord…he rode up to me…" he gulped in air, straightened and his words came in a rush. "on his way to Lord Coelwald in Wealas, he said. To warn him like."

"Warn him?"

"Ay. The King's gone!"

Aethelbald looked at the blacksmith who shrugged. They both stared at Wulfric in confusion.

"What yon said, Lord, was the King's been forced off the throne – though they don't say *forced*, right enough, says yon. Gone to be a monk they say. All in agreement wi' yon other king."

"Monk? What other king?" Aethelbald's jaw tightened. "By Thunor's red-hot iron, Wulfric! How did my father put up with you all those years?" He tapped his fingers against his thigh, "try to make sense, man!"

"Well, it's what he said, Lord. King Offer or something like that, an' our King Cenred, them's gone off to see the Pope in Home or something like that, yon said."

"*Rome!* with King *Offa*, Swaefred's successor. He didn't last long!" The ealdorman cursed and wished he had Coelwald or Guthlac to discuss this with, instead of a simple sheep thegn and a blacksmith. "It's been coming these last few years," he muttered, "Cenred's proved himself incapable of taking decisions – too weak." he shook himself out of his musings. "Wulfric! You said the rider was off to advise the aetheling. What did he say? Now, come on! Word for word."

An apologetic look came over the weather-beaten face of the countryman, "Lord, yon said to tell you, Coelred's made King. The nobles in Tame Weorth, they all decided like. Says he drove his horse the thirteen leagues thence in just this one morning to get here. That be real good goin', Lord!" The thegn hesitated and lowered his head, "Says yon be Lord Coelwald's thegn an' he got word that the new King plans to murder his master an'… an'… you, an' all, Lord. Says, to flee, at once, Lord!"

"I did well to whet my blades, this last hour," Aethelbald said, his tone grim. "Enulf, take off your apron. Take my horse and warn my thegns. I want them in the hall before sunset. Tell them to bring the men who fought with me in Powys. Off with you!" The ealdorman turned to Wulfric, "Faithful friend, while we are away, attend to the land, what men remain, and the women and children. Should King Coelred's warriors come to threaten you, swear you and all my folk stay loyal to the King. Tell the truth and that is Lord Aethelbald marched off to Lindissi." A sour laugh escaped him, "They'll lose themselves amid the fens if they dare follow us."

In itself, that bold statement might have been true. But Aethelbald and his band of two-score men received a rude shock. Setting off at dawn on the first day, they travelled but twelve miles, since most of the men were on foot and carrying weapons and a pack. On the second afternoon, with three more leagues behind them, they neared the village of Hludoham. Somewhere close to the horizon ran the Trente and in between it and themselves, they spotted metal glistening in the sunlight. No trees impeded the view since the land had been cleared by three scattered settlements. Alerted, Aethelbald ordered his men to slip their packs to the ground and to unsling their shields.

"How could they march thus far from Tame Weorth, so soon, Lord?" asked Allwald, in the absence of Wulfric, the eldest of his thegns.

The ealdorman scowled, "Do not underestimate Coelred. I reckon he sent out roving bands to cut me off in the event I chose to flee my homestead. Like the wind today, they come from the south-west." He peered at the approaching body of men still half a mile off. "They covered twice the distance we travelled but they had two days start on us. The new King is aware I love him not. Never forget," he said with pride, "I too am an aetheling, not of Penda's line like Coelwald but of his brother Eowa's. While Coelwald and I are alive, Coelred will not rest easy." He peered into the distance. "How many of them?"

"Hard to say. At a guess, their numbers are the same as ours."

"Form the shieldwall!" Aethelbald bellowed, tying the reins of his horse to a bush.

Three ceorls in the gap between the two forces dropped their harrows and fled for the safety of the village. The King's warriors halted and linked their own shields in a tight line.

"We have ten men less, Lord," said Enulf, undaunted, the tallest and strongest warrior on either side.

Only half-listening, Aethelbald studied his adversaries. Relieved they carried no spears, like his men, for ease of travelling, he looked for and found no weakness.

A figure emerged from the opposite ranks, "Lord Aethelbald," he boomed, "send your men home and come with us at the King's command."

The grin of the Lord of Woercs-worth spread wolf-like. The helm with a face plate covered a head he knew. Before him stood an ealdorman from Suth Mierce, a toad of Coelred's – whose name escaped him and which he did not care to remember.

Aethelbald advanced three paces, "I own no King," he cried, "mine is away to Rome. Know you, I am of mighty kin and the witan met without two aethelings present." A murmur of accord rose even from among the ranks of his adversaries. A usurper sent you from Tame Weorth. For this reason, I bid you turn back your men and we shall be on our way."

If the warrior's laugh had been the measure of his strength, Aethelbald might have trembled. But he knew the wretch was no match for himself. His ten-man advantage made him confident.

"Would you spill good Miercian blood? The king has no quarrel with your men. It is you alone who must come with us."

"Do not heed him, Lord," called Allwald to his back.

"No, Lord," hissed Enulf loud as his forge bellows.

"No!" joined in others of his men.

The wolf-like grin grew wider. Aethelbald had expected this persuasion from his foe.

"I, like you, wish not to shed your men's blood." He waited for his words to take effect until he could nigh on feel the relief in the other. Then he added, "Come forward and we will fight it out the two of us. Whoever dies has the wrong of it and everyone else goes on his way. What do you say?"

The silence hung as heavy as the late spring air between the two warriors while the Suth Miercian set the disgrace of being declared a *nithing* against his probable doom. His own men began to drum their seaxes against their shields. In glee, the men of Woercs-worth copied them until the noise could be heard in the village. The Suth Mierce ealdorman raised his hand and the beating stopped in an instant.

"So be it!" he cried, but with a flat voice.

A rousing cheer from both sides greeted these words. The men understood a preference to end life with a warlike death to living in shame. Thus began the wary advance of the combatants, each raising his shield, wielding axes and studying the other. The rhythmic battering on the shields started again in accompaniment.

Aethelbald took the first shuddering blow on his shield and using his great strength pushed the axe-arm of his opponent upwards to send him lurching backwards. Quick reactions fended off a flurry of violent hacks from Aethelbald. To the other man's dismay, such was the force of the insistent strikes that the alder planks under the leather coat of the shield began to cede.

'Cur-dog's toad! Go to hell!'

Noticing the state of his enemy's guard, a kind of madness gripped the ealdorman. Redoubling his efforts, likely seeing the face of Coelred before him, he parried, hewed and chopped till the shield hung useless and his axe-head bit into flesh, not wood. Using his greater weight to fall on his foe to cramp him, he hauled the wounded man to the ground. In a terrible frenzy, he destroyed his enemy's helm but the sudden silence from the shieldwalls brought him to his senses and the pointless blows to a halt.

When he staggered to his feet and in a daze looked around, then, only then, did a raucous cheer rise up. In surprise, he saw the foe cheering with his own men. A warrior stepped out of the enemy ranks.

'What, does he too come to the slaughter?'

The man removed his helm, revealing grey hair.

'A thegn, is it?'

His speech was not coarse, confirming Aethelbald's impression, "Lord, as the oldest of the thegns here, I am the voice of the men. A fair fight, it was, and as God decrees – you have the right of it! Neither have we love for Coelred. Men speak ill of him. We cannot go back for he is full of spite and will have his revenge on us. Take us with you, Lord. Unite our wyrd to yours!"

"Ay!" came the voices behind the thegn in a swelling tide of voices. "take us with you!"

SIXTEEN

Cruwland, 709 AD

Guthlac strolled towards the hollow on the north side of the isle where the visitors' shelter stood. The mid-morning sun cast a silver cloak over the water-world surrounding him and he breathed deeply of the sweet air, rejoicing in the glory of God's creation. The refuge for guests rose not far from the cluster of huts built to accommodate Bernulf and those few monks who had chosen to live and pray in the wilderness. All the buildings stood as distant as possible from Guthlac's mound since the anchorite for the most part eschewed human contact.

This sparkling morn, he knew not why he felt a compulsion to call upon the brother who had blown the horn at the jetty the day before. On the orders of his abbot, the man had travelled for weeks from an isle far to the north. The sole purpose of this laborious journey was to report to him on the hermit whose fame had spread beyond the borders of Lindissi.

A gentle knock on the stranger's gained him admittance but, hunched over a parchment, the monk did not break his fierce concentration to acknowledge the arrival.

"One moment, Brother," and there followed a flourish of his quill. Rubbing the loaded point against the rim of a pot of ochre ink, the artist proceeded to tint an empty square. "I'll be with you in a minute. Let me just complete this part of my work."

Curious, Guthlac stole across to peer over the man's shoulder. Luke, it must be, standing in a doorway and holding a paper in strange elongated fingers. Wavy blond hair falling to his shoulders, the square face of the barefoot saint bore an enigmatic smile.

The monk laid his pen to one side of the table and looked up. "Oh, forgive me, Brother Guthlac! I had no idea—"

"You depict Saint Luke, do you not? A labour of love to the glory of the Father."

"Indeed I do! Weeks of heedfulness not to overcharge the quill with ink and, oh, the strain on my poor eyes! But as you say…" The visitor picked up the parchment letting the sunlight release a formidable blaze of colour. "It is nigh on finished. Another coiled serpent in this oblong, just like the one on the other side…"

The hermit frowned and pursed his lips, "Without doubt, it is an object of great beauty and fit to take its place in a volume. Thus, turning the pages our looking is perfected – but we see less and less each day." The anchorite placed an arm around the shoulder of the monk. "Come, the day is splendid, walk with me a while to rest your eyes and wonder at a cloud or a bush."

The guest set down his work and followed Guthlac, leaving the door ajar. They exchanged thoughts about the life and gospel of Saint Luke, breaking off to marvel at a shoal of spine loaches scattered in the shallows by a marauding otter. The predator emerged with a fish in its mouth and plunged towards the bank and the safety of its den.

"O, my soul! O, what's to be done! All my work!"

The monk moved from one foot to the other and raised clenched fists to the sky. Startled by this behaviour, the hermit spotted the cause of his guest's agitation. A low-flying bird – the black thief – bore off the parchment in its beak.

Be not grieved, Brother! Make haste to the boat! When the raven flies up through the fens row after him, so shall you recover the page."

Face wet with tears of anguish and frustration, the brother set off on the water in the direction the winged pilferer had taken. Having rowed through the fenland, he came to a mere, not so far from the island. In the midst of this pool lay a bed of reeds. There hung the paper on the bur-reeds, unspoilt, as though the man himself had placed it there with care.

When he stepped on the jetty, overjoyed and clutching the parchment as though his life depended on it, the monk saw a peculiar sight. Guthlac sat, his back resting on a boulder half-buried in the earth. Twittering swallows perched on his drawn up knees and on his shoulders. At his approach, they swooped away.

Open-mouthed, the brother remembered his manners. "Thank you, Brother Guthlac, you had the right of it! I found my precious work."

"Thank me not, friend. It is the effect of God's mercy. Two ravens have settled on our island. They are greedy for whatever they can seize."

"How do you endure this, their greediness?"

Guthlac laughed, "Why drive away two poor birds when they serve to give men an example of the virtue of patience?"

"But how is it, Brother, "the visitor asked, "that you knew I should find the parchment? And how come the timid birds of the waste sit fearless upon you?"

"Our Heavenly Father granted me the gift of foresight and as for the creatures, he who leads his life after God's will, the wild beasts become more intimate with him. When a man passes his life apart from worldly men, to him the angels approach nearer. Now, friend, be gone and to each of us his labours." Thus, Guthlac dismissed the monk. The latter, astounded at what he had heard, watched the hermit retreat to his cell.

(the same day, to the south of Lindcolne)

In the uncertainty surrounding King Aldfrith's attitude to Coelred, Aethelbald gave Lindcolne a wide berth. His men emerged from forested land on the easier going of the limestone ridgeway known as the Lindcolne Cliffe three leagues to the south of the Withma gap. They skirted a settlement on the spring-line overlooking the river valley without alerting the villagers: no mean feat with a band of two score and fifty warriors. Their caution proved in vain.

Blocking the track ahead, shieldwall ready, a force as strong as their own awaited.

"This is familiar," Enulf muttered.

"The circumstances are the same," Aethelbald said to Allwald. "Thank Thunor for the men we gained two days ago! It appears Coelred spares no effort to rid himself of us. Form a wall!" he bellowed.

The situation differed as he discovered when he advanced alone and shouted, "Let's settle this in single combat. Who will fight me to save shedding Miercian blood?"

A helmed figure broke from the ranked men facing him to give an answer.

"Aethelbald of Woercs-worth, my King commands me to bring you to him as captive else to slay you and any who follow your cause. Send your men home and come with me, otherwise, we fight."

"Nought to be done, Lord. Let's have at 'em!" Allwald said.

"Ay," Enulf nodded and started to beat his seax on his shield, an act copied by all his comrades till the sound rolled like thunder.

In reply, the enemy began their steady advance.

"Hold!" Aethelbald caught and dragged back his smith. "Wait until I give the order and we'll rush them."

Ever closer came the foe. Beside him, Aethelbald could feel Enulf coiled like an adder poised to strike, so too Allwald and the others. Still, he kept silent. Their opponents neared until they could see the fine hairs on their tensed muscled arms. Five…four…three paces separated them when Aethelbald, at last, barked, "Now!"

The pent-up force of the forward spring and a hail of overwhelming blows knocked the advancing men off balance. Lucid, even as he hacked and hewed, Aethelbald reasoned these were not seasoned campaigners wilting under the assault but ceorls and retainers gathered in haste. How many such bands had Coelred sent out the length and breadth of the land to chase him down? By Thunor, lucky that Coelwald in Powys had a host of battle-scarred warriors at his back! The slaughter did not last long. As he stood, chest heaving, he gazed with regret at the gory corpses littering the track. What chance had they against his trained men? Why had their stubborn leader not fought alone when challenged? But he knew why. The nithing had been scared. Surveying his men, at a rough estimate, they had not sustained many losses and the few dead among his numbers, apart from Allwald, were the recent recruits.

With a shock, he saw Allwald amongst the bodies. He cursed and damned Coelred to Hell. The blood of his father's old thegn soaking into the Lindissi soil carried away with it better and nobler times – so he convinced himself.

He spoke with Enulf, who in unspoken accord, had become his right hand. They discussed the time needed to bury the dead and the risk it might entail. They could not be sure how many of Coelred's bands roamed the countryside in search of them. In the end, they agreed to lift Allwald's body on the back of the ealdorman's horse for a decent burial in a less exposed spot. They also decided henceforth to train their new followers for an hour a day in fighting skills.

"We must drop down to the valley and find a place to cross the Withma," Aethelbald said to his men. "This limestone ridge is easy underfoot but too open to sight. Once we reach the fenlands, we'll find a guide who knows the wastes. There we'll be safe from Coelred and there we'll build up our strength."

(later that day, Cruwland)

A boat nosed up to the landing place at Cruwland. The oldest of the men leapt ashore. He helped his wife on the jetty while two strapping youths battled to restrain their struggling, spitting brother. At the last instant, the first man out of the small craft managed to save the fifth passenger, a priest, from falling into the river from the rocking vessel. By sheer brute force, the brothers heaved their paroxysmic sibling to firm ground. Relieved to be more stable, the father seized the cow's horn dangling from a cord attached to a pole and blew a sharp note.

Moments later, a strange figure clothed in otter skins but clean-shaven and kempt descended from a hut half-buried in the side of a mound. The priest, realising that this must be the famed Brother Guthlac, strode to meet him.

"I was expecting you, Father," the anchorite said in a matter-of-fact voice.

"But...but...we told no-one of our journey—"

Shouting from the jetty cut short the exchange. Three young men, in a violent struggle, were rolling on the planks in peril of falling into the river. Next to them, a man clung on to a weeping woman. Amid a flurry of blows and obscene language, two youths managed to pin down the other.

"It is Hwaetred," said the priest, "he is in the grip of madness. When he does not hurt himself with iron or with his teeth, he inflicts harm on others. I have tried to exorcise the devil that possesses him but to no avail." the clergyman sighed, "The family is poor but they had to sell their animals to pay wergild for the unlawful wounding Hwaetred meted on his victims. One man lost an eye, another three fingers..."

"I know."

"How can you *know*?" the cleric asked, exasperated, "We come from the land of the Middle Angles and no-one—"

"I know!"

The anchorite laid a hand on the priest's arm and gave a beatific smile, "And, I *know* that Hwaetred will leave here sound in body and mind. But first, we need to bring him to the church. Come!"

The nearer the afflicted youth came to the place of worship, the more violent became the struggling and the more obscene the oaths. Dragged along the nave, writhing and vomiting, of a sudden, as they approached the altar, he slumped in their arms.

"The devil is intimidated in the presence of the Lord," explained the hermit. "You will stay three days in prayer and fasting before the altar. Only water shall pass your lips."

"Three days!" protested one of the brothers as the possessed youth dropped in a heap to the floor.

"If you wish for your brother to return to health. I will fetch cups and water."

When the sun rose on the third day, Guthlac wandered over to the church. There, the figure remained curled on the paving stones while the priest and the brothers knelt in prayer. The woman was drinking water and her husband, in spite of any good intentions, sat asleep against a pillar. The hermit brought with him holy water and used it to bathe the face of the youth who at once began to thrash and wail. Undeterred by the violence of the gnashing teeth, Guthlac pushed his face close and blew gently on Hwaetred's. At once, a thin grey wisp like smoke issued from the youth's mouth. Where before the eyes had been wild and unseeing, now they stared in surprise and recognition at his family. As if awoken from a deep slumber, Hwaetred sat up and asked, "Where is this place?"

"The accursed devil is gone!" Guthlac stood and called over his shoulder, "Also, I must go to give thanks and praise in private prayer."

"The man is a saint!" gasped the priest. "Come let us all rejoice and thank the Lord, for, in His mercy, He has snatched Hwaetred from Satan's grasp."

An hour later, gliding along the Withma, their joy-filled boat passed another bound for the island. A fierce-looking warrior sitting in the bows and rowed by the huge figure of a tall muscular man greeted them.

"He has the tongue of a Miercian," said the priest.

Aethelbald leapt on the landing platform, grasped the horn and blew a shrill note. His heart beat quicker at the thought of seeing Guthlac again after ten years. He did not expect the curious figure clothed in otter skins descending from a nearby mound.

"Guthlac! is that you? what garb is this and what became of your beard?"

The hermit laughed and hastened to greet his erstwhile comrade.

"Welcome, I was expecting you."

It was Aethelbald's turn to laugh, "Impossible!"

"And this is your smith."

The ealdorman started and his brow creased, "Why then, you have spies everywhere! Ay, this is Enulf."

The blacksmith nodded a greeting but a strange unease seized him before the piercing gaze of the anchorite. But more unsettling were his words.

"You will betray him, one day."

"Pah!" spat the warrior, turning away from the weird figure to make his way back to the boat. There, he sat in disgust to brood and await one to whom he could never be disloyal. Rather, he would die. "The monk's lost his reason in this forsaken place," he murmured.

Guthlac led his friend inside the hut where visitors never set foot. They talked about past events and Aethelbald's present exile. The sun sank low in the sky and the reluctant ealdorman understood he must leave if they were to return before nightfall. He rose to depart. The hermit seized his arm and looked him in the eye.

"God grants me the gift of foresight. Coelred hunts you hither and thither and he will not cease. O, my friend, I have full knowledge of your conflicts and your troubles, for this cause I took pity on you."

Rapt by these words, Aethelbald sank back on his haunches. The monk continued, "I prayed that He support you and He has heard my prayer, He will give you kingdom and rule over your people." Startled, the ealdorman unknowingly placed a hand on his chest and touched Osthryth's ring through his tunic. Noticing the gesture, Guthlac gave a taut smile, "You still carry it."

Aethelbald nodded but the monk, staring into space, carried on as if he had not interrupted.

"They shall flee before you who hate you and your sword will destroy all your adversaries, for the Lord is your crutch. But be patient for you shall not get the kingdom by means of worldly things, but with the Lord's aid, you will get it. Now go before night comes and makes it hard to row back. Embrace me, for we will never meet again.

Aethelbald started to protest but before the certainty in the unswerving gaze, it died on his lips. He hugged his friend and tears sprang to his eyes at the frailty of the once fearsome build of the warrior.

'What made him do this? and yet, there's something about him...'

In spite of the fading light, the ealdorman walked down the mound and back to the boat with deliberate slowness. All the way, fingering the ring under his clothing, he pondered on the anchorite's words.

He stepped into the craft to a grunt from Enulf, "You spent long enough with the madman."

"Shut up and row!" the venom in his voice and the menace in his eyes cowed the giant smith who deemed it wiser to row in silence.

'The Kingdom will be mine!'

The ealdorman threw back his head and guffawed sending coot scuttling into the reeds while Enulf marvelled at the madness the island induced.

SEVENTEEN

Dummoc, Est Anglia, winter, 710 AD

The biting wind howled around the timber church on the clifftop overlooking the mouth of the River Deope. The sombreness of the abbots and priests contrasted with the exuberance of the four score slaves assembled at the back of the cathedral. Separating the two groups, the rest of the congregation of mourners filled the place of worship. Under the veil of solemnity on the faces of the clergymen lay a curiosity, evident in their eyes all trained on the back of one man. Bishop Haedde of Mierce and Lindissi knelt before the coffin of Ascwulf, oblivious of the staring clerics.

In truth, the long journey undertaken by Haedde from Licidfelth to be at the deathbed of Ascwulf had elicited more than a little surprise. Heaven alone knew the Bishop of Dummoc and hence primate of the Est Angles deserved not only such an eminent presence but also that of the absent King Aldwulf. Dispute with the Church over *trimoda necessitas* – taxes for the bridge-bote, burgh-bote, and fyrd-bote – souring the requiem mass of the worthy prelate was a matter of considerable regret among the clergy. Those close to the deceased bishop, flattered by the offer of Haedde to conduct the funeral, were the most intrigued. To their knowledge, relations between the two prelates had been nothing more than formal and polite. Why therefore endure a tedious and wearisome journey? Why set aside the pressing demands of his extensive see?

The censers swung and cloying incense greyed the air. The curiosity of the clergymen would not be sated for some time as the monks began to chant the introit. *'Requiem aeternam dona eis, Domine'* – "Grant them eternal rest, O Lord".

Through the long service, the high spirits of the slaves continued to soar. From time to time, one or another had to be hushed. At last, the final chanted notes of *in paradisum* died away and the Mass ended. To general bewilderment, Bishop Haedde came forward arms raised. In his right hand, he bore a rolled, sealed parchment.

"As you are aware, every prelate and abbot attending the funeral of our beloved Brother in Christ is required to free three slaves. Three scillingas to each, he must give for the good of the deceased's soul and in honour of his memory. And this shall be done." An irreverent cheer from the rear of the cathedral greeted these words. The Bishop brandished the vellum. "This is signed and sealed by my own King Aldfrith of Lindissi. By its provisions, I am empowered to grant one hide of land in his kingdom to any man freed this day who chooses thereof to avail himself."

Gasps and murmurs, made louder by the height of the roof, caused many to stare at the agitated group behind them who could scarce credit their luck. "Moreover," the Bishop continued, "each among you who accepts this offer will receive from the King's purse a further three scillingas for the purchase of livestock." The prelate, forced to raise his hands once more to subdue the clamour of voices, added, "Be forewarned, the land lies on isles in the fenlands, a six-day journey hence. The Lord made the soil fertile to provide food in plenty. The customary obligations to your lord will apply. Any man who agrees to accompany me to Lindissi must give his name to my clerks outside the cathedral. I declare the Mass ended."

The Bishop made the sign of the cross and blessed the congregation which was too animated to notice the benediction.

(Seven days later)
Holbece, Fenlands.

The fenlander helped his distinguished passenger into one of the dozen boats moored at the landing place. They set off, driven forward by the strong practised strokes of the oarsman. Bishop Haedde had insisted on their being alone. From Estdeping along narrow reaches of brown glassy water between bare alders and the beige reeds, they passed into a broad lagoon where white wavelets scurried across the water. At two miles from the coast, the winter wind swept from the sea colder than at Dummoc, causing Haedde to shiver and draw his cloak tighter.

At last, the boatman-guide moored at a slippery wooden jetty and pointed out what he hoped was the comfort of a house. It stood the largest among a cluster of huts. Pitiless, he ordered the boatman to wait in the chill of the landing place for his return. The fellow, impassive, pulled a hood over his head and folded his arms. Hurrying to the reed-thatched building, the Bishop knocked. Inside, and seated, far from enjoying any anticipated comfort, an icy draught whistling under the door made him move his chair closer to the hearth. But bodily discomfort did not distract him from attempting to reassure his suspicious host.

"King Aldfrith has eyes and ears throughout his kingdom but as far as Coelred is concerned, he is clueless as to your whereabouts. I can assure you of this. These islands are as remote as you could wish. Nowhere could be safer. Indeed, the fact I found you is a blessing. I bear documents endowing the isles of Holbece and Lutton, making you their rightful lord."

"What does your King want in exchange?"

Unused to such bluntness of speech, Haedde looked Aethelbald in the eye and to his credit, his gaze did not waver before the ealdorman's piercing stare. "He requests you accompany me to Lindcolne as a matter of urgency."

"Is that all?"

"The details you can discuss with him in person. But I brought a token of goodwill. At Estdeping four score freedmen await your word to settle on these isles as your sworn men. This parchment sealed by Aldfrith attests to it. Est Anglian slaves, freed on the death of Bishop Ascwulf as custom decrees, now they are your ceorls. Warriors, many of them, defeated in battle, others debtors, thieves and a few enslaved for violence." The prelate smiled at the other's raised eyebrow. "For the present, they can create vills here on the two isles, plough the earth and in the spring buy young animals to rear. They are provided with coin. Take my advice and appoint a reeve to oversee the land division. On the isle of Lutton, there is a vill settled of yore by the pool. The folk there enjoy grazing rights established over time out of mind and they must be respected."

"It would seem, Bishop, you and your King give much thought to my circumstances."

The prelate laughed but his expression became serious, "We – you, my King and I – have interests in common. I shall leave for Lindcolne at once but arrange for the newcomers to be ferried across. Select a strong man–"

"I have such a one."

"Capable of taking charge in your absence?"

"Ay."

"Entrust him with land division and house building. Those are the most pressing tasks. As soon as you can, but no later than a fortnight, come to King Aldfrith."

Aethelbald stared at the door as it closed behind the clergyman.

'What can be so important to bring a bishop into the wilderness in the depths of winter? Eighty men to populate the isles. A handsome gift. What does Aldfrith want of me?'

He pulled on a heavy sheepskin cloak and slipped across to Enulf's hut.

'With all the new settlers, I'll have enough labourers to build a hall fit for an ealdorman. By Thunor, I didn't plan on staying in this wasteland overlong!'

A communal building was one of the many ideas he and his new reeve discussed well into the night. Another was how to get to Lindcolne without encountering Coelred's men, still seeking him the length and breadth of Mierce and its subject territories. Aethelbald decided to find a local man in Estdeping, if possible one who knew the kingdom of Lindissi as well as the shape of his own hand. Apart from the main trackways, he knew no other ways and Lindissi, different from other neighbouring kingdoms, lacked the cover granted by woodland.

(A fortnight later)
Lindcolne.

Thirteen years had passed since Aethelbald had stood before the King of the Lindisfarona. The intelligence in no way had diminished in the lively green eyes but they now studied him from a fuller, more careworn countenance.

This meeting, more auspicious than the previous one, began well, judging by the fleeting gratification in the King's expression.

"Lord, how can I thank you for your handsome gift of four-score ceorls?"... *'Let's see what you want in exchange.'*

A whimsical smile played on King Aldfrith's lips, doing nothing to set the ealdorman's mind at rest. "A self-interested bestowal, my friend."

"How so, Lord?"

"You will train them to fight. Together with the fifty men you settled in my kingdom, without a by your leave, I might add..."

'By Thunor! He knows everything about me.'

"...they will make a force to reckoned with." The ruler turned to the prelate by his side and said, "The time has come to take the Ealdorman into our confidence."

Bishop Haedde limited himself to an almost imperceptible nod.

"The death of King Aethelred ended a stable period when the power of Mierce stretched south to the borders of Kent and those of the Suth, and West Seax. Aethelred proved a decisive king and the Lindisfarona ask for nothing more. No-one in Lindsey forgets the harshness of Northanhymbrian overlordship or wishes to experience it again."

The King clicked his fingers and waved a hand to call for refreshment. Servants hurried to set small cups of fine pot, no taller than a man's thumb, before the three men.

'What drink is this in women's thimbles?'

A squat rounded vessel in blue glass contained a dark liquid. A maid filled the three beakers and stood back from the table. Aldfrith took a delicate sip as did Haedde but the unsuspecting Aethelbald, as was his wont, threw back the drink. He spluttered, coughed and his eyes watered.

"By Thunor's ear wax!" he bellowed, "How it burns the throat."

King and Bishop roared with laughter.

The ealdorman wiped his eyes and looked rueful, "And yet it lingers on the tongue in a most pleasing way. What is this wet fire?"

Aldfrith took the smallest draught, lowered his cup and grinned, "The Bishop mows down more men with this brew than my bodyguards in battle. Best let him explain."

"Willingly, Lord. But first, the ealdorman must promise to refrain from pagan oaths."

"Ay, but it is a treacherous potion: it sears the unwary throat."

When the Bishop had finished chortling, he began, "There is a monk at the Abbey of Beardan of late returned from the Holy Land. There he met an Arab physician who taught him how to make this potent beor."

"Beor?"

The prelate pointed to Aethelbald's vessel and the maid, trying to mask her smile, filled it.

"Take it steady," the bishop admonished, "it is strong. Made from fermented fruit, damson here. The Moors, for the most part, use grape or so the brother who supplies us tells me. He keeps the process well guarded. A secret – but a fine one, you'll agree?"

"By Thu– ... ay! Drink this before battle and I'd lead the kingdom to ruin."

The ealdorman sipped and smacked his lips in appreciation.

"Well," said the King, "As I was saying, a stable Mierce is our best hope to fend off the Northanhymbrians. King Cenred made vacillation the mark of his reign. Five years of indecision. He paid the price. Coelred drove him into a monastery."

"King Cenred went to Rome, Lord," Haedde protested.

"Same thing. There is a worse King on the Miercian throne. Cenred's successor is a coward as warped as unseasoned timber. The kingdom chafes under his yoke. Hwicca, Suthanhymbra, Est Seax, Est Anglia and my own land fret through his demands. Cenred lost sway over the southern lords owing to weakness while Coelred tests his supposed strength on loyal friends. The appetite to pay for his debauchery is excessive."

The King paused for breath and to control his mounting wrath. He sipped at the beor and rolled it around on his tongue as he stared into the distance, savouring the taste. Aethelbald did likewise.

"The vile wretch drove you into exile, Ealdorman, and still seeks you. The nithing fears to move against Coelwald for his half-brother leads a battle-hardened host in Powys who would follow him into Hell itself."

'What does he want of me?'

"Then there is the problem of the Church. Bishop?"

Haedde sighed and spread his hands palms upward in a gesture of hopelessness.

"Heedless of the exhortations of his clergy, the King commits the sins listed by the apostle in Galatians, chapter 5. There it is written, *'...sexual immorality, moral impurity, promiscuity, idolatry, sorcery, hatreds, strife, jealousy, outbursts of anger, selfish ambitions, dissensions, factions, envy, drunkenness, carousing, and anything similar.'* He oppresses the monasteries. Like a beekeeper removes all the honey from a hive, Coelred extorts coin from God's servants. He perverts justice, overturning wills and bequests. He stands accused of violating a nun. These heinous offences must not continue."

King Aldfrith slammed a fist on the table making the empty cups jump and roll. The maid scampered to set them upright.

"All this is why we have brought you here, Ealdorman…"

'By Thunor, we come to it, at last!'

"…on the throne of the West Seax sits one who is wise and rules well: King Ine. One of his first achievements was to settle a dispute with Kent to then work together with their king…"

'Why is he telling me this?'

"…introducing a law code, issued as an act of prestige to re-establish authority after a period of disruption – one like Mierce is suffering now. One year later, King Wihtred of Kent imposed a similar body of rules. Both kings reign for over twenty years…"

Aethelbald shuffled in his seat and sighed.

The King frowned, "Be patient, Ealdorman, I'm coming to the point. But first, let me give you a practical example you can use on the islands with your ceorls. It is reported that one law states common land might be enclosed by several ceorls. Any ceorl who fails to fence his share and allows cattle to stray into someone else's field is to be held liable for any damage caused."

Aldfrith stared at his guest and the ealdorman had the sensation the King was assessing him.

'There's more to this than meets the eye.'

A long pause followed as the ruler of Lindissi gathered his thoughts. The Bishop waved the maid to pour another round of drinks.

"Lord Aethelbald, Coelred must be removed from the throne. Then a fair body of law to safeguard the rights of all men introduced. There are two men whose birthright sets them above others – yourself and Coelwald, both aethelings. Coelwald is a good man but does he have the mettle of a ruler? I think not."

'By Thunor!'

This time Aldfrith sighed, "But the time is not yet ripe. The Wealisc cause endless problems. Hwicca is riven with internal strife and Coelred is enthroned for little more than a year. There are still ealdormen willing to give him the benefit of the doubt–"

"The church harbours no doubts," Haedde cut in.

"Indeed, *'the fine day is seen by the dawn'* as the old saw goes," said Aldfrith. "But, I fear things must worsen under Coelred before we can act. We must use the time well, Lord Aethelbald. In the Spring, leave for Wessex. There, study the law codes of the land. The knowledge will serve you well when you take the throne. Above all, turn Ine's mind to the benefits of moving his borders north into Hwicca beyond the Saefern. His forefathers once held that territory…"

"But it belongs to our allies," Aethelbald said.

"When you are King and Ine is gone, you can take it back," Aldfrith laughed. "Well, what do you think? Will you go along with our plan? Or must we approach Coelwald?"

Aethelbald raised his cup, "I have never doubted one day I would rule over Mierce. Let us drink to our friendship – an alliance set in stone."

"I will provide you with a letter of introduction to Bishop Daniel of Wintan-ceastre," said Haedde, "he is close to King Ine and will smooth your entry into his court. You will also go in the vestments of *King* Aethelbald."

"How so?"

Aldfrith reached for another parchment scroll, heavy with wax seals.

"This document, signed by my hand, and endorsed by the ealdormen of Lindissi and the Church, nominates you as King of the Fens – underking to myself and in consequence, to the King of Mierce."

"By Thunor!"

On the journey back to the Fens, thanks to his guide, by the most hidden and devious tracks, Aethelbald had much to think about. Often, his hand strayed to Osthryth's ring. What kind of man was this Ine? Would he befriend a Miercian exile? Even one with an exalted title? Could he be manipulated as Aldfrith suggested? If their plan to overthrow Coelred succeeded – and the cur must not be underestimated – what then of Coelwald?

One pressing matter concerned him. He and Enulf must train their ceorls to be more fearsome warriors than the men of Coelred. The smith, his reeve, must build a forge and supply his men with seaxes and spearheads.

His mare crunched over the frosty ground and Aethelbald's breath swirled in the crisp wintry air. With nobody to hear him he spoke his thoughts aloud: "By Thunor's iron bones! The wyrd is weaving, I am *King* and I shall be *Bretwaldas* after all."

EIGHTEEN

Estdeping, early spring, 710 AD

Aethelbald and his six warriors left the landing place of bobbing boats to walk to a hidden hollow outside the village. Merging into the surroundings stood a low construction, built the previous autumn, stabling ten horses. The men chosen to remain in the small fenland settlement were all among the ealdorman's most loyal followers. Each ceorl, like the horse-thegn and his two stable hands, fulfilled the task entrusted to him. Above all, they were essential lookouts wary of Coelred's roving bands. They ensured nobody in Estdeping, on pain of death, might betray the whereabouts of their lord. Plans to mislead the enemy were in place should they ever attempt to row towards the islands of Holbece and Lutton.

Avoidance of that foe on the long road to Wessex lay forefront in the mind of Aethelbald. The fenland landscape provided no cover proof against probing eyes. Seven horsemen on an open thoroughfare made for the easiest of sightings, meaning they had to count on luck.

"Lord!" one of his warriors pointed down the track, "A score of riders. Six furlongs, I'd say."

"A pox on Coelred!" Aethelbald thundered, "Back to Estdeping."

"Is that wise, Lord? Ought we not to lead them astray?"

The ealdorman wheeled his horse and galloped away, leaving his men no choice but to obey. They rode straight back to the stable and left their mounts.

"To the river!" Aethelbald roared. They ran, lungs fit to burst and piled into two rowing boats as the din of a score of horses' hooves drew nearer.

"Pull, hard!" the ealdorman cried, "Harder!" as a javelin splashed into the water between the craft. "Row for Holbece."

Confused, the oarsmen frowned. Over the last few months, it had been drummed into them that the whereabouts of the isle should remain secret. Why then did Lord Aethelbald, of a sudden, wish to lead the foe to their hiding place? With no question of disagreement, they pulled with all their might. As if they needed urging, another dart fell less than a boat length behind them. From that direction, a shout drifted on the breeze, "Quick into the boats, follow them!"

"Lord, it may be a trap," they heard a warrior protest.

"What trap? We'll never have a better chance to snare the renegade. Move!"

None of the three men in Aethelbald's boat failed to notice the fleeting smile of satisfaction appear on their leader's face. So, it was a ploy, but could they keep out of the way of the iron-tipped missiles? Muscles on fire, they sped into the rougher water of the mere and in consequence noted with dismay the six pursuing boats close the distance. A javelin thudded into the stern of the rearmost of their two vessels.

'By Thunor's whiskers, another yard and we'd lost a rower!'

"Up the rate!" the ealdorman yelled. He wanted to take an oar along with the other passenger to give his men a rest but they could not afford the loss of way it would entail. The enemy boats sliced into the lagoon, their oarsmen unprepared for the choppier water, for a few moments, needed to adjust their strokes. The brief respite served to restore the gap between the boats and Aethelbald seized the chance to relieve the rowers. At the same time, he called to his comrades in the other craft to do the same.

Fresh arms lengthened the space beyond throwing distance but they could not relent the pace. Holbece lay half an hour away and they needed to row past it, without being overhauled, for his plan to succeed.

Many a battle had Aethelbald fought, wielding a heavy shield, an axe or a sword for an hour or more of slaughter but his muscles never had ached so much. Stubborn and proud, he rowed beyond his limits and only when he judged the gap to be closing between themselves and the pursuers did he shout to their companions, "Change oarsmen!" This manoeuvre cost them headway and encouraged, their foe launched two more javelins. One fell short but the other found its mark. A throw so accurate, the passenger at the stern of their companion boat, did not cry out but on the instant, slumped forward dead. Spurred on by this success, lethal darts dropped like hail from the sky. Most missed their target by little but a dart bit deep into the seat beside the thigh of Aethelbald.

"Pull, pull, damn you!" he screamed at his oarsmen. They had to get out of range, but how many throwing weapons did they have left?

'We can't afford to lose another man but every javelin that misses plays into my hands.'

And this conviction grew stronger as Holbece came into sight.

"We're not landing," Aethelbald called to the other boat. "Keep straight on for Lutton."

As they passed the isle, the ealdorman unhooked the horn from his belt and blew one long shrill note. He looked back, worried at the effect the sound might have on their stalkers.

'Fools, they come on regardless. But, in their shoes, would I turn back?'

The ealdorman shook his head. Of course, he would not, with success within his grasp. The man they had killed was enough to drive them on.

'I am too fine a prize to let escape. Those men are Miercian warriors and know no fear.'

"Change oarsmen," he shouted, but as his words left his lips, he regretted them. But three men were there aboard the other boat. Where was relief with one man dead? There was no time to worry. He seized an oar as did his rested comrade. Yet more javelins splashed into the river too close for his liking but one, to a scream of pain, pierced the shoulder of an oarsman in the other vessel. To his sorrow, Aethelbald watched the wounded man's companion grasp the oar and strive to retrieve the situation. Too late. Coelred's men were closing and the slaughter was fast and merciless.

'They'll pay for that! By Thunor, they will!'

They rowed past the isle of Lutton and with bitter satisfaction, Aethelbald blew another prolonged note. A swift command and their boat changed course as he pulled her bows around the island. This was the crucial moment because they were rowing upstream now, against the current. Although the distance between the two small craft had shortened, no missiles flew overhead.

'They've none left to throw!'

The ealdorman's grin widened at the sight of a score of warriors with javelins running on the isle toward him. Three boats crammed with armed men pulled out from the Lutton landing place. They were not needed, nor were the boats full of fighters hastening downstream from Holbece. Death rained down from the isle on the pursuing vessels in the form of a swarm of cruel-tipped darts till not one man remained alive. The whereabouts of their refuge would be unknown to King Coelred.

The next morn, Aethelbald, with three warriors replacing those he had lost, set off for Wessex once more. No-one hindered their progress out of Lindissi, suggesting to the ealdorman the patrol they had slaughtered had been the only one in the area. The other potential danger, bands of thieves infesting the countryside, kept away from seven warriors with spears, axes, swords, and shields.

In the Est Seax valley of the Britons, he renewed an old acquaintance. Flynn's hospitality compensated for the squalor of the Est Anglian taverns they endured on the way. After two days rest, they resumed their journey and allowing two breaks of a single day to rest their horses, after eight incident-free days, they came within sight of Witan-caestre.

The sun sparkled on the flint rubble set in the pink-buff mortar of the turreted walls. To Aethelbald's military eye, they stood at least four yards high. Builders of long ago, not the Seax, had erected these defences. They crossed a bridge over the river to enter the town through the east gate. Studying the defences, the ealdorman hoped never to make an enemy of the West Seax. He had noted the walls erected on an elevated bank, making them higher, and the ditch running ten feet in front of the bank.

'Tougher to crack than a walnut between a maid's teeth.'

Horses stabled, an inn found followed by a reasonable night's sleep, in the morning, Aethelbald invited his men to enjoy the town. In their place, he knew what he would do. Instead, he had the serious matter of presenting himself with his document to Bishop Daniel.

Haedde had told Aethelbald that the Bishop of Witan-caestre was responsible for a huge diocese stretching from the south coast to the River Temes. Astonishing, then, to find the cathedral naught more than a small cross-shaped wooden church. An obliging priest agreed to take him the short distance to the prelate's house. Haedde had also informed the ealdorman of Daniel's erudition. Upon being admitted to his presence by a young cleric, it came as no surprise therefore to find the prelate scratching at a parchment. To Aethelbald's annoyance, the letter took precedence over himself. Only when the clergyman had sprinkled ground ash on the inked document did he deign to consider his visitor. His expression conveyed resentment at being disturbed.

"I am Aethelbald, son of Alweo of North Mierce and I bear a letter of introduction from Bishop Haedde of Licidfelth."

Without a word, Daniel rose, took the document and began to read with an ease the ealdorman envied.

The austere features of the prelate, framed by the first signs of greying at the temples, relaxed into something approaching welcome.

"From what my Brother in Christ writes, your presence, Lord Aethelbald, is of vital importance to the Church in Mierce. So...you wish to read the *Leges Inae* –"

"Forgive me if I interrupt. There is a problem. I am more suited to the seax than to the quill..."

"Ah, of course, you will have had no occasion to learn Latin," the clergyman's smile was diplomatic. "I shall provide you with a cleric to translate the many laws. As to a meeting with the King, it may be hard to arrange at this particular time."

"How so?"

"Did you not notice the number of warriors in the town?"

"Ay, but I thought it normal."

"Not so. King Ine has summoned his fyrdmen. In two days, they will march against Dumnonia. The Britons' incursions, alas, have rendered war inevitable."

"Your king might find seven Miercian warriors to his liking."

"And you would lend your arms to the West Seax cause?"

"Ay, were it to make of King Ine a friend."

The Bishop smiled for the first time. "Risk your life for a friendship?"

The ealdorman nodded.

"The meeting you crave ought not to be so difficult to contrive."

The invitation to dine came in the afternoon. Where the cathedral failed to impress Aethelbald, the King's hall blazed in magnificence. In awe, he gazed at the splendid wall hangings with the recurring emblem of a golden dragon. The carved and painted upright beams, alive and bright with writhing beasts outshone the Frankish glass twinkling in the torchlight.

At the centre of the table sat King Ine, not the mighty warrior the ealdorman expected. Wiry of build, the grey hair denoting his two-score-and-more years, but the high forehead and the alert deep-set eyes suggested shrewd intelligence.

"Welcome, Lord Aethelbald. To impress Bishop Daniel is a notable achievement," Ine smiled, "he cannot be with us as he prefers to stand all night long in a stream to cool his passions than to enjoy a good feast. What say you, shall we make up for the good bishop's lack of appetite? Come, sit by me."

Over a mouth-watering hare stew with barley, seasoned with bay leaf and sage, Aethelbald discovered the depth of Ine's character. A simple compliment for the Frankish glassware led to a discussion about the importance of trade.

"West Seax had no emporium, so was excluded from the Norðsae-Channel network of trading centres," Ine explained. "Near the coast, on the west bank of the River Itchen, lies my vill of Hampton and from the surrounding countryside, I moved the people to the new port. We call it Hamwic. The gravel and building materials, I shipped to the site, at my own expense," the King laughed and took a draught of wine. Setting down his glass, he went on, "Money well spent, my friend, apart from the benefits from minting our own coin, we trade hides, cloth and ironware for quernstones, whetstones, pottery and vessels such as these," he said, turning his cup to admire the play of light upon the vitreous surface. "Of course, I have to feed and house the population and the merchants need my protection…"

"How big is Hamwic?" Aethelbald asked.

"It has doubled in five years. My reeve calculated close to five thousand souls. Kingship brings a lot of responsibility, my friend…"

In that moment, Aethelbald realised the conversation was not small talk. Bishop Haedde's letter must have spoken of plans to replace Coelred with himself. This wise King had reigned for over twenty years. The ealdorman grasped the need to learn whatever he could from him.

The evening grew long and toward the end, Ine said, "Lord Aethelbald, my Bishop tells me you intend to fight by our side in the days ahead, is it so?"

"It is, Lord."

"This afternoon, a rider reached Witan-caestre. King Nothhelm of the Suth Seax ought to enter the town on the morrow. He unites his strength to ours." The expression on the face of the ruler hardened, "We cannot tolerate further incursions by Geraint of Dumnonia. Last month, he razed Hlydanford to the ground, enslaving the surviving men and violating the womenfolk. Now he is threatening Tantun. We must drive them back beyond the Tamur."

"I have but six warriors with me but any help–"

"You will fight by my side, Ealdorman," the King raised his glass and they drank to friendship.

(a week later)
Langeberga, Sumorsaete

Scouts and spies reported to Ine in the presence of Nothhelm and Aethelbald. The gist was the enemy had gathered men from Lyskerryt and Lyswythal – places with strange names that the ealdorman had never heard of – promising two acres to each landless man. The enemy host, estimated at three thousand warriors on foot and one thousand horsemen meant more to him. Geraint had chosen to encamp in an ancient hill fort near Langeberga.

"On no account ought we to try to attack that position," Aethelbald said, forgetting for a moment his role as a guest. "We cannot afford to give away the high ground."

"I agree," King Nothhelm frowned, "remember, one of the Britons' ploys is to roll carts filled with blazing tinder downhill at the shieldwall."

"Tell me about the shape of the land this side of the river," King Ine ordered a scout.

"The Perryt is tidal, Lord and on this, the eastern side, a long slope runs from its bank to a steep ridge. The incline provides some cover with hazels, withies and stunted oaks. Marshland lies below the southern slopes of the spur, where a shallow combe leads to the low crest. To the north, instead, there is a narrow valley—"

"How narrow?" the King of the West Seax interrupted.

"At any one time, no more than a score…or at most, a score and ten…horses may attack. The valley is approached through miry sedge-land and runs up to a ridge stretching north from the spur."

"This is what we shall do," King Ine's tone was decisive, "the main body of the West Seax host will defend the central ridge. We shall await the assault of the Britons for as long as it takes Geraint to make up his mind. To the south, my brother," Ine used the term of endearment to Nothhelm, "the Suth Seaxa will repulse any attempt to charge up the combe. Split your men, conceal some groups in the sedges and rushes to surprise the advancing foe. Aethelbald, my friend, you will lead the remainder of my men to seal the valley to the north. Is there anything wrong or to add to this plan?"

"It's a good scheme, Aethelbald said, "our men, Lord, ought to plant their spears in the ground at an angle, like this," he tilted his hand out in front of him, "on the crest of the ridge, so the enemy horses may not break the ranks. We should do the same," he said to Nothhelm.

"Let us move into position before nightfall," Ine said.

The next morning, a broad white band lay in the sky above the horizon turning to a dull grey overhead. A light drizzle driven by a breeze from the Saefern Sea to the north completed the gloomy scene. The occasional mewing gull, foraging inland, added to the dolefulness of the day.

Midmorning brought movement, at last. Over the ebbing river, three distinct groups of horsemen each led a host of men on foot. Aethelbald, at the head of the valley, peered at the banners fluttering among the riders. Those approaching his position displayed an emblem with a gold cross on a green background. Black flags with white crosses dominated the other two groups. Had the ealdorman understood the difference, at that moment, he would have been more excited.

Once across the river, the going was easy, but uphill, for the main central attack. Javelins flew down on the Britons and the screams of horses and dying men reached Aethelbald as they waited to act. The swampy terrain full of sedge to the north slowed the horsemen's approach. Aethelbald took advantage to make it quite clear to the men entrusted to him that they must not launch their javelins until he gave the command. On no account should they lose their nerve, but wait, for the order would be delayed to the last possible instant, he explained.

The ploy to hide the men amid the rushes and tall marsh-grass to the south brought devastating losses to the British horsemen. When the surviving riders swept up the narrow valley, they were funnelled against the fierce opposition of the shieldwall reinforced by the angled spears. There, the slaughter was relentless. The battle raged in the centre around the golden dragon of the West Seax and their King.

Still, the men to the north waited, but the charge up the combe, when it came, was fast.

"Hold, hold!" Aethelbald insisted, his words nigh on lost under the drumming hooves of the horses, the iron plates protecting their chests making them look more formidable. Yet the discipline the ealdorman yearned for held. "Now!" he bellowed and many a West Seaxa hurled his javelin with as much relief as fury. They could not miss their target from such close range and the riderless horses driven by panic ran onto the spears wedged in the ground. In many cases, the breastplates turned the iron spearheads but the cruel points finished in the flanks of the maddened rearing creatures. their thrashing brought down those behind them as the second wave of darts took their toll.

"Charge!" boomed Aethelbald and his warriors plunged down among the riders in disarray, hacking at thighs and plunging blades into the belly of the horses. The ealdorman hewed his way toward the green banner and came face to face with a grey-haired rider in leather breeches with shining buffed steel covering his breast. Reasoning this was the leader of the enemy's northern flank, he leapt forward. A swift blow of his axe to the horse's throat and the wounded beast reared, its throat spraying blood. With surprising agility for an older man, the rider sprang clear of the dying animal. His huge round shield protected him from Aethelbald's savage blows. But the warrior could not anticipate the ealdorman's next move. With a ferocious sweep of his arm, he flung the axe downwards sending the blade slicing into the ankle of his opponent. As the agonised man lost his balance, out came Aethelbald's sword and the point entered under the armpit of the falling adversary. The strike proved fatal. His own shield saved him at the last instant from a British sword, but the cry of *'King Geraint is dead! Retreat! Retreat!'* was taken up in British all around him.

In the heat of battle, the foreign tongue meaningless to him, the ealdorman with his handful of Miercians and hundreds of West Seaxa plunged down the valley. Hard in pursuit, they remained unaware of the devastating blow delivered to the enemy by that single sword thrust.

King Nothhelm to the south, battle over, brought the might of the Suth Seax host to strengthen King Ine in the centre. They had no time to be decisive, for word reached the Britons there of the death of their King. Their resolve broke and they too plunged down toward the river. The water level, lower now with the tide in full ebb, still proved an obstacle to the fleeing Dumnonians. The number of dead attained terrible proportions and although Aethelbald was not to know it, the Britons would never again prove a threat to the West Seax beyond the Tamur.

The battle over, the victors returned to their baggage carts and encamped for the night. They fetched Aethelbald into the splendour of the King's huge tent.

"Friend, Aethelbald," said King Ine, clicking his fingers, to bring a servant scampering with a folded green cloth, "hand it to its rightful owner," he ordered the man, with a smile.

The ealdorman took the bundle and, baffled, stared at the King of the West Seax.

"Shake it open," grinned the ruler.

Aethelbald obeyed and, from his hands, hung down the golden cross on a green background.

"The emblem of King Geraint son of Erbin, the man you slew to turn the battle in our favour."

"I slew?"

"Ay, so my men tell me. Did you not know?"

A bewildered frown was Aethelbald's reply.

"Aethelbald of North Mierce, we are in your debt. The West Seaxa will not forget what you did for them this day."

NINETEEN

Witan-caestre, summer, 710 AD

"Repeat after me," intoned brother Tidwulf, who began to chant, "*mensa, mensa, mensam, mensae, mensae* – nominative, vocative, accusative, genitive, dative—"

"Pah!" roared Aethelbald, "Why would I need to address a table? *'O, Table!'*"

A chuckle from behind a pillar made both men start. Each was convinced that they were alone in the basement of the bishop's home. But, the laugh emanated from Bishop Daniel himself, whose ascetic-looking face now appeared around the column.

"Good question, ealdorman... the very same that earned me a clip around the ear from my *magister* when I was an impudent youth!"

"*Ego sum placuit ego hic consentit,*" Aethelbald replied, showing off his new learning and earning plaudits for his assiduity from the prelate not only for himself but for the gratified monk. Brother Tidwulf went on to translate from the *Leges Inae* without difficulty or hesitation.

"If a ceorl and his wife have a child, and the ceorl dies, the mother shall keep her child and bring it up. She shall be given 6 scillingas [a year] for its care—a cow in summer and an ox in winter.

The relatives shall keep the homestead until the child has grown up."

Bishop Daniel clapped his hands in obvious approval of the worthy brother's effort.

"What a wise and kind man is King Ine!" Aethelbald exclaimed, his admiration sincere.

"You flatter me, Lord of the Fens," a deep voice came from behind the same pillar that had obscured Daniel moments before. "to be sure, a wise ruler ought to attend to the needs of everyone – men women, children alike, the old, the rich, the poor, the able, the mutilated." The slight frame of King Ine, incongruous with his baritone voice appeared.

"*Salvē!*"

"See how our guest makes progress," Daniel did not contrive to keep the pride from his voice. "Let us hope that he will make the same advances in Mierce for there the Church is sorely tried under the wickedness of Coelred. I received reports only yesterday of a monastery devastated by the king's forces on his direct orders and this follows the constant extortion he practises."

"What can be done to end this sorrowful state of affairs?" Ine asked.

The ascetic countenance brightened, "An alliance, Sire. We must overthrow Coelred and enthrone Aethelbald."

"*Haec est mea spes...*" said the Latin scholar.

He looked hurt and confused when the three men laughed in unison.

"In theory, that is the answer," Ine acknowledged, "but in practice, matters are more complicated."

"How so?" Daniel asked.

"First, we must settle the matter of the Britons. The death of Geraint will not pass without rancour. Already the king of Gwynneth swears to avenge his kinsman. As for Dumnonia we must press home our advantage." Ine frowned and his expression grew graver, "But what vexes me, is the thought of leaving West Seax open to an attack from the north-west. We would find ourselves between the hammer and the anvil. Thus, I settled upon a scheme to erect a massive earthen castle at Tantun. This will seal entry from that direction and thwart any onslaught of Rhodri the Bald and Grey."

"Who?" laughed Aethelbald.

"Rhodri Molwynog, King of Gwynneth. I sent orders to begin construction, but it is a vast enterprise and building the stronghold will take more than a year. We can use the time well. You, in your studies, and I, to seek an excuse to move against Coelred."

Aethelbald pricked his ears, so, at last, it was in the open: King Ine meant to aid him to take the throne of Mierce.

"An excuse?"

"Ay, a Christian king may not attack another without good reason. Else what will become of civilisation?"

"But, Sire," said Daniel, "with the moral authority of the Church behind you…"

"Ay, moral authority. there's the point. A *moral* attack it must be with good motive and I have one."

Aethelbald's ears pricked. Of the men in the room, as the only Miercian, he was the most interested. "Which is?" he said.

"I pretend the return to the West Seaxa of the brine springs at Salwic. From time immemorial they belonged to my folk until they were seized by Mierce."

"I know naught of Salwic, except that it is deep within Hwicca and as such, Miercian. How can a war be fought over something as trivial as salt?"

"*Trivial*, you say?" Ine almost spat the word. "Know you, my salter asks who fills his storeroom without his craft. All the butter and cheese in my realm would be lost without salt. How can you preserve meat and fish without it? Mierce alone takes ten tons of salt a year to sate its need.

Bishop Daniel's voice took on a didactic tone as he explained as if to a small child. "Brine rises naturally at three sites along the river Salwarpe and is extracted from pits by bucket for boiling. The largest and deepest is at Upwic where the buckets sink to thirty feet."

"Ay," said Ine, "and it is of the highest quality. It renders 2.69 pounds of salt per gallon of brine. Instead, our efforts with seawater produce slightly less than a pound per gallon and marine salt is of lower quality."

"I begin to grasp the importance, " Aethelbald admitted, "but Lord, much as I crave your aid for my cause, I cannot persuade myself to fight against my own people."

"Of course not, friend," Ine said with a warm smile, "you mistake my intentions. The idea is to strike at Coelred with our excuse at the most suitable time to help you. A king ought not to combat against his own folk. It is evident."

"Then how shall we proceed?" Aethelbald needed to feel, almost to taste, progress.

"I need time to secure my borders. The threat from Gwynneth is real. The Church needs time to weave its web in the court of the Northanhymbrians. *You* need it to prepare for kingship. Coelred needs it to offend Mierce beyond what he has now achieved."

"Then I must skulk away here in West Seax until all is ready?"

"You may stay as an honoured guest for as long as you wish," Ine shook his head. "But I believe your time can be better spent in the Fens, raising and training men against the maturing of our plans."

"*…et ex doctrina Latina?*"

"*Certe potest Episcopus Haedde parceret magistro…*" Daniel replied, and Aethelbald nodded, for Bishop Haedde, he was sure, could call upon any number of priests or monks to teach him Latin.

"Bishop," King Ine caught the prelate's attention at once with his commanding tone, "set this brother with ten more to transcribe the *Leges Inae*."

"But, Lord, it is a huge task. It will take eleven men at least a year."

"Let it be so! Begin at once!"

The Bishop bowed to the imperious command.

"In Lindissi, you will start to enact the laws, those that you see fit." Ine nudged Aethelbald, "Men will understand your worthiness for kingship and compare you with Coelred and his injustices."

"When the transcription is complete, return to the Fens. By then, you will be well advanced with Latin. Bishop, I implore you to concede this monk - whose name I know not…"

"Tidwulf, Sire," he said, bowing to his King.

"…Brother Tidwulf… as our personal messenger between West Seax and the Fens. A simple monk ought to travel unmolested and unhindered betwixt the two kingdoms," the King placed his hand upon his arm in a reassuring gesture of familiarity, "Tidwulf, you will leave with our friend, Aethelbald, when he departs Witancaestre, so that you can learn the way to Lindissi."

"Willingly, Sire."

The King looked to Bishop Daniel, who nodded his consent.

"Then it is agreed," the King strode over to Aethelbald and held out a hand, which the former ealdorman clasped, his expression one of curiosity. "I love you as a brother and assure you of my support in your attempt to take the throne of Mierce, to which you have an undoubted legitimate claim."

Aethelbald gazed into he eyes of the King and there saw sincerity and friendship. It warmed his heart and his mind began to race with certainties, no longer vague possibilities.

"Forgive me, I must leave you now," Ine said, "the crown weighs heavy, as you will learn. The most precious God-given gift is time and we must not squander it." The ruler turned on his heel and left the room.

Aethelbald wished to be alone with his thoughts but although Daniel too departed, he did so calling over his shoulder, "Tidwulf, continue with the *Leges Inae*… I shall find some of your brothers to begin transcription. I'll arrange for tables to be brought down here that they may work under my supervision. Carry on!"

"If a thief is captured, let him suffer death or redeem his life through payment of his wergeld…" Tidwulf translated without apparent effort, *…By "thieves" we mean men up to the number seven; by "a band" from seven to thirty-five ; by "an army" above thirty-five. One accused of belonging to such a band shall clear himself through an oath worth 120 hides or pay an equal amount as compensation."*

But Aethelbald could not concentrate on Ine's Laws; instead, his hand fiddled with Osthryth's ring and his mind raced ahead to a future where he led a host against Coelred. With Ine's support assured, how could he fail?

A year later, when Aethelbald arrived in Holbece, he was not fluent in Latin but he could read and understand the language quite well. Enough to please Tidwulf and to impress Bishop Haedde, who visited him from Lindcolne. This new conquest made him feel more complete, indeed, genteel and for sure, different from the rest of the warrior class with whom he still identified.

The Bishop sat with a document in his hand and read out

aloud... *'I, Aethelbald, by the grace of God King of the Fenlands, with the advice and instruction of Alweo, my father, of Haedde, my Bishop, together with all my ealdormen, the most distinguished witan among my people, and also a great assembly of God's servants, have taken counsel concerning the welfare of our souls and the state of our realm, in order that just laws and just royal laws should be established and assured to all our people, and so that no alderman or subject of ours should henceforth pervert these our dooms.'*

"These are indeed fine intentions, my son," the prelate smiled and, leaning nearer to the candle better to distinguish the writing, added, "let's study the laws in more detail. Mmm, what's this? He started to read:

'If someone captures a thief or is given a captured thief to guard, and then lets the thief go or conceals the theft, he shall pay the thief's wergeld as compensation. If he is an ealdorman, he shall lose his shire, unless the king will pardon him.

If a ceorl has often been accused of theft, and is finally proved guilty, either through the cauldron or through being caught in the act, his hand or his foot shall be cut off.'

The clergyman lowered the parchment and sat back in his chair to give Aethelbald an appraising look.

"You have been busy, I see. These laws cover all from the lowest to the highest in the land. If you enforce them, I believe that you will have little rest—"

"Rest is not my aim. In fact, I expect to fight to establish these principles. They are bound to bring me into conflict with the powerful – bishops included." He noted the pursing of the prelate's lips – but it is the price to be paid for a well-ordered society." Aethelbald pointed to the bundle of parchment tied together with a ribbon, "You may keep that copy and if it suits you, show it to King Aldfrith, who as my overlord, remains the highest authority in the land."

The sour expression on the face of the bishop relaxed into a half-smile.

"Your intentions are of the finest and exceed the expectations which accompanied you to Witan-caestre. What saddens me, Aethelbald, is that all this needs time to implement and it is time that Coelred ill-uses to oppress the Church."

"Ay, but the time is not ripe. I must build up my strength and my friends are not yet ready to come to my aid. My hope is that as word spreads, beyond the fens, of fertile land and a just community, men will come of their free will to join us."

"But then," said Haedde, his narrow face of a sudden, shrewd, "he will be breaking your own law," he fumbled at the bundle, "Ah, here it is! And he cited: *'If anyone leaves his lord without permission or steals away into another shire, and if he is then discovered, he must go back to where he was before and pay his lord 60s.'* The Bishop nodded and lent the gesture gravity, "Prepare your men for battle. I foresee turbulent times ahead."

TWENTY

Easter 714 AD, Cruwland

Aethelbald gazed up at the iridescent sky, "It's quite like the inside of this oyster shell," before pouring the shellfish down his throat and handing it to Haedde, who transferred his astonished eye from the one to the other.

"And so it is!" he confirmed.

An air of melancholy reigned over the forbidding marshes, compounded by the sorrowful nature of their mission. The news had issued from the wilderness of the death of Guthlac, hence this pilgrimage into the solitude.

On the familiar landing stage of Cruwland, Aethelbald spied a strange sight. A tall, slender woman stood beside what looked from his boat to be a stone coffin. The woman proved to be Pege, the deceased warrior-monk's sister, although Aethelbald knew her not since the siblings did not, in life, spend time together. Guthlac enforced the separate hermitage of Pege after a demon took on her form to tempt him to break fast before sunset. The coffin, she informed them was a gift from the daughter of the king of Est Anglia, the venerable abbess, Ecgburgh. It was lined with beaten lead and contained a winding sheet.

"This donation comes with a curious tale," Pege told them with irrepressible enthusiasm. "The abbess sent with it a question – who should be the keeper of the place after him?"

"And did he give a reply?" asked Haedde.

"He did. He said the man was of heathen race, not yet baptised; nonetheless, he should soon come and should receive the rites of baptism."

"A heathen?" Haedde could not contain his indignation, "it is unacceptable if not impossible."

"And yet my brother received from God the gift of foresight."

"Ay, he did that," Aethelbald, who had a vested interest, confirmed. "Come! we must go, seek out the body of my beloved friend and find how he met his untimely end."

"Then, search for a Brother Beccel, who was with him when his soul departed this world," Pege said.

The monk in question proved most forthcoming. "The saint was in church at prayers when, of a sudden, he was struck down with illness. He lay a week afflicted with the malady and certain of the outcome: I mean of his impending death. I found him praying on the Wednesday before Easter, clinging to the altar and when I cried at the sight of his suffering, Guthlac comforted me with these words, *'It is no sorrow that I am going to the Lord my God.'* The eyes of the monk filled once more with tears at the thought. Giving them a hasty wipe with his sleeve, he went on, "Then, on the first day of Easter in spite of his illness, he insisted on singing mass and offering communion. Such was the spirit of the saint. After the service, he gave orders to be wrapped in a linen winding sheet and laid in a coffin."

"But the coffin and cloth are on the landing place," Aethelbald objected.

"Ay, for it is mighty heavy and we used a coffin to hand in the crypt."

"I beg you to take us there. I would stand near him and pray."

Chastened, never so aware of his own mortality, Aethelbald emerged from the crypt. Turning to Bishop Haedde, he said, "We must build a shrine to the memory of this holy man. As soon as I return to Holbece, I shall make arrangements. Now, I wish to rest."

"Follow me, Lord," said Brother Beccel, hurrying towards one of the several scattered cells that prefigured the later monastery that Aethelbald had in mind to found.

With difficulty, Aethelbald squeezed his sturdy, iron-muscled frame through the low, narrow entry to the cell indicated by the monk. A simple bed with a straw mattress almost filled the interior. Grateful, he laid down on the bed and began to pray for the intercession of his dead friend. As he prayed, the small room lit up with a silvery light and in the corner, smiling at him as if in life, stood Guthlac robed in angelic splendour.

"God is with you, brother," said the familiar voice and Aethelbald's heart began to race with a mixture of joy and fear.

"How is this possible?" he exclaimed, "You are *dead*, my friend!"

The well-known laugh belied the sorrowful expression on the face of the saint. "Dead? Nay, I'm setting out upon life eternal. Worry not, brother, for the Lord decrees you will be King of Mierce within little more than a year. But, hark! Try to live a life befitting of one so blessed."

As these words died away, Aethelbald watched in awe as the vision of his friend also faded. He leapt to his feet and groped around at the air, his hands encountered naught but the rough stone walls. Nor had he expected any sign of a corporeal presence in the restricted space. He swore as he grazed his knuckles and sucking at the blood, he noticed the smell of the sweetest flowers in the room. Lying on the bed once more, he pulled the ring of Osthryth from under his tunic and brought it close to his eye. *'God wills I shall be King soon. And I vow in His name to build a shrine on this spot in honour of you, dear friend.'*

In the evening, their boat nearing the landing place at Estdeping, a commotion ashore caught Aethelbald and Haedde's attention. a group of mounted men formed a ring around a wretched trembling individual. The King of the fenlands leapt on the wooden stage and, approaching the grouped men, demanded an explanation.

"Who is in charge here?"

"I." the voice from under a helm came, muffled, but familiar. The steel cap was overlaid with a band of bronze across the eyes and worked with ornate scrolls, without doubt, the owner possessed considerable wealth.

"Pray tell me, what passes, here?"

"This slave," said the recognisable voice, "was caught stealing a goose from a neighbour's land. In the absence of his lord, away at

Lindcolne, he must find the wergild, but cannot, so he will pay with his hide, as custom demands. We are about to set up a neck-catch. In fact, this pole will serve, my man will drive it into the ground and split it at the top. There, he will be flogged."

Driven deep into the earth, the post stood as tall as the cringing slave. With a swift blow of his axe, the man responsible for creating the neck catch, split the stake a good foot from the top and prised the two halves apart. Two other men hauled the slave over and forced his neck in the split. The man holding the two halves apart released his grasp on the wood so that the gap closed and trapped the fellow's neck in a suffocating grip. Helpless, the prisoner could move neither forward nor backward. A warrior stepped up, swinging a scourge in his right hand, while the two who had hauled the captive to the neck-catch dragged his tunic to his waist, exposing his bare back.

The whip was composed of a handle some eighteen inches long, with three thongs of the same length, at the end of each of which was a hard knot, the size of a cherry.

"Wait!" Aethelbald cried, "What is the sum of the wergild?"

"Sixty scillingas," said the leader of the band, "but what is to you?"

"I shall pay the wergild till the man's lord comes to claim him."

"It is a sizeable amount to find for a scoundrel."

"Yet, I may have a use for him. But hold, I know your voice."

"And I yours, Aethelbald of North Mierce," said King Aldfrith removing his helm.

"Lord, forgive me if I recognised naught but your voice."

Aldfrith smiled, and explained, "I came to seek you, friend. This miserable creature was thrust upon us by an aggrieved ceorl as we passed by. But, stay, would you pay his wergild, and to what purpose?"

"This fellow is well made and with a little training might make a decent warrior. I am occupied building up a small army."

"It is of this I came to speak with you." Aldfrith dismounted. "Come, there is a reed-cutter's barn o'er yonder. Let us talk in private."

Curious to know what the King wanted of him, Aethelbald waited for the other man to talk.

"Further down this river, there is a crossing place, a stone ford, from which a walled burh takes its name – Stanford. The settlement is easy to defend. Now, you spoke of building your army. Good. I speak with the King of the Est Seaxa and I have heard from Coelwald. Both men wish to unite to your cause but the difficulty of reaching Holbece with many men is a significant drawback. Were you to make your base at Stanford, it would not be hard to reach nor exposed too much to Coelred and his rage. What say you?"

"Let me take this wretch without payment. I will need the money to pay for food at Stanford."

Aldfrith laughed, "You drive a hard bargain, friend. So be it!"

"I cannot move until the summer is advanced. There is much to be concluded hereabouts."

"Very well. but when you decide to act, send a messenger to me at Lindcolne." Aldfrith laid a hand upon Aethelbald's shoulder and gazed straight into the ealdorman's eyes. "Time presses. A monk in the Magonsaetan royal monastery of Much Wenlock had a vision of the terrible punishments that await Coelred on his death. The Abbess, Mildburh, the king's cousin, has done her utmost to spread word of this prodigy."

"This, of course, will make it easier for me to take his place– if the folk feel the King is not conducting himself in an appropriate manner."

"Indeed. The throne trembles. It may need just one final push to topple it once and for all. This strong shoulder might give it the necessary shove."

"I am in contact with King Ine. The *'shove'* might come thence."

"See that it does, my friend."

Screams from outdoors cut across their conversation.

"Let's put an end to the thrashing," Aldfrith said with distaste.

"Hold!" he shouted as he emerged from the barn and the warrior with the scourge stayed his whipping. "King Aethelbald will pay the wergild. Release the prisoner! There are more important matters to be dealt with. Bishop, will you return with us to Lindcolne?"

Bishop Haedde turned to Aethelbald and sketched a benediction over him in the air, "See to the shrine you spoke of and may God be with you, son."

"Amen. Remember to send me a mason from the town."

Back in Holbece, some weeks later, Aethelbald stood poring over sketches for the shrine.

"This one pleases me," he said to the bearer of the plans, indicating a plan containing a twelve-line acrostic, BEATUS GUDLAC down the left lintel and BARTHOLOMEUS up the right. What about the stone?"

"Lord, the local rock is perfect for our purpose and there is a quarry but ten leagues from Estdeping. It will be easy to carry the blocks by ox cart. If anything, the problem will be to float them to Cruwland."

"Ay, our small boats are not fit for the task."

The builder shook his head and sighed, "Have your men hew down trees, Lord. The trunks will make a raft strong enough to bear considerable weight and it can be towed to the isle."

"It shall be done. Will you make arrangements at the quarry?" Aethelbald asked, dropping a pouch of coins on the table.

A calloused hand snatched up the bag, "If the raft is ready before next Sunnendaeg, I'll drive the cart from the quarry down to the river. We need to send word to my master in Lindcolne, for I can lay the foundations and build the walls, but he alone can do the carving as in the design, wherein lies the beauty of the shrine."

The following Saeterdaeg, Aethelbald oversaw the unloading of the logs. He was pleased to see that they were sawn to the same length and this would save time in the construction of the barge. Shouting orders, he had the trunks laid out on the ground next to each other, where he ordered them to be lashed together with cord. When it was ready, it needed a score of strong men to heave the platform down the bank where it slid into the water which swept it away downstream.

"Make haste!" called Aethelbald, "into the boats, hurry, else soon the raft will be at the Nordsae!"

The difficulty of hauling the vessel back with three rowing boats bothered Aethelbald. If they had trouble towing it unloaded, what would it be like when burdened with limestone blocks?

The answer came the next day. The first obstacle was loading. The master mason had arrived and a long discussion began about the opportuneness of building a wooden crane to swing the blocks on the raft. At first, arguing against the time lost in its construction, Aethelbald, at last, acquiesced before the expertise of the craftsman.

By evening, the crane, a simple tripod structure with a jib, was ready and the first of the blocks, each of three hundredweights, settled on the raft to a collective release of breath from the gathered onlookers. Many of the men wondered if the raft would sink under the mass of stone as twenty-three more blocks joined the first. They need not have worried: all was well. But, it was clear to one and all more than three boats would be required to tow the load to Cruwland. In prevision of arrival, the mason ordered the crane to be dismantled and laid on top of the stones. It would be needed at the Cruwland landing stage to hoist the blocks ashore.

Aethelbald, following the slow procession of ten boats and the raft in his own rowing boat, had no regrets about this venture. Guthlac had been a true friend and, to his astonishment, the carousing, irrepressible warrior had turned into a saint. He deserved this monument and more, if for nothing else, by interceding with God on his behalf that he should become King of Mierce. Unable to caress Osthryth's ring since he was rowing, these thoughts whirling in his head, Aethelbald, nonetheless, felt the band pressing against his skin. Had it been red hot and searing, he could not have been more aware of it.

(three months later)

The master mason laid down his mallet and licking his lips, spat out stone dust. He had put the finishing touches to a roundel depicting Saint Bartholomew wrestling with two demons in the presence of Guthlac.

"That's it, lad," he told his apprentice, "we can say we're finished here, and a finer job than this'll be hard to come by, I'll tell ye."

He spoke true, for to Aethelbald's delight, the shrine was a work of art, well worth the gold he handed over with a good will. Pilgrims, he knew, would come in droves to pray at the tomb of Guthlac and his own prestige would grow by association. As Coelred was living proof, what worth had a King without the approval of the Church?

Aethelbald clapped the stone carver on the back, "A fine effort, fellow! The King of Mierce will make a rich man of you, in years to come."

"I do hope so, Lord," said the mason, weighing the pouch of coins in his hand. "But from what I hear, the King of Mierce spends all his gold on whores and wine."

"Do not worry on that score," Aethelbald said darkly, "kings come and go, by the grace of God, this one won't reign much longer."

TWENTY-ONE

Stanford, early June 715 AD

Brother Tidwulf, travel-weary and dust in the hair around his tonsure, blurted out his message,

"My Lord, King Ine is gathering his *fyrdmen* and wishes you to know that within the next moon, he will march on Salwic."

"Is that the whole missive, brother? asked Aethelbald."

The monk shook his head, "Nay, Lord, my king asks that you appraise Coelred of his intentions."

Aethelbald paced to and fro, with a wrathful face, "And how does he suppose I can do that without risking my hide?"

"I could go in your stead," Tidwulf proffered.

The monk did not expect the grating laugh his suggestion produced and raised a quizzical eyebrow.

"You have no idea, brother, of what Coelred is capable. He will not hesitate to wring my whereabouts from you, by the foulest and wickedest methods. I value our friendship too much to allow such a sacrifice." The would-be King resumed his pacing, "I have a far better notion for delivery of the message."

Aethelbald clapped his hands and a servant hurried over.

"The man I saved from a flogging, bring him to me."

He hastened away and a few minutes later returned with the

flustered slave in tow. In spite of his nerves, the fellow looked a sight better than when Aethelbald first set eyes on him.

"Hark," he addressed the anxious man, "Would you say you owe me a favour for sparing you a thrashing?"

The troubled eyes shifted backward and forward till, at last, a strangled "Ay," accompanied by a nod, indicated cautious assent.

"Then; my friend, I wish you to bear a communication to King Coelred in Tame Weorth. This Brother will act as scribe to draft a note for you to consign – *personally*. I will seal it. Can you do this?"

"Ay, my Lord."

"Heed me well, on no account will you betray my whereabouts to Coelred or any of his men: on pain of death."

"I will not, Lord."

"Do you know the route to Tame Weorth?"

"I do."

"Now come with me to my horse thegn. The journey will be easier on horseback. Can you ride?"

"When I was captured, I was in the Northanhymbrian cavalry, Lord."

"Then I was right to think you had the build of a warrior."

A mute nod by way of reply.

"Succeed and the horse will be my gift to you. Now, we go to choose the one you like best. Brother, prepare to draft a letter to King Coelred with Ine's message. follow me, I will show you the way to a scriptorium."

Wrinkling his nose at the strong odours of the stable, Aethelbald glared at his horse thegn for his words. "But this is our finest stallion, of Frisian stock. He stands thirteen hands. How can we give him to a *slave?*"

When Aethelbald's hand hovered over his sword, the horse thegn swallowed his indignation and proceeded to saddle up the restive beast.

"Every man knows his trade, Gerbert," said Aethelbald in a placatory tone, "this *slave* was a rider in the Northanhymbrian host. I think it no coincidence he chose well."

the thegn feigned agreement but a "Harrumph!" escaped him.

Aethelbald tuned to the cavalryman, "Wait here, someone will bring my sealed letter for Coelred. once delivered, return here and make sure nobody trails you, clear?"

Another mute nod.

Back in the scriptorium, pressing his ring into the sealing wax, Aethelbald enquired, "The contents, tell me, what did you inform Coelred?"

Brother Tidwulf blinked and smiled, "What King Ine instructed, namely, the West Seax reclaim Salwic and to make good this claim will take it by force within the next moon."

Aethelbald ground the heel of his boot on the paving. "I will not fight against Miercians but I will not miss the battle, for conflict is certain. Coelred is too proud and too foolhardy to accept any such slight."

"We shall await confirmation of delivery of this missive and then make our way to Salwic. *Quid dicis fratris Tidwulf?*"

"*I parere, dominus* – I obey, Lord."

"Please take this letter to the stable and hand it to the man who was with us before."

The monk bowed and hurried out of the scriptorium while Aethelbald sought a map of the area of central Hwicca. An obliging brother withdrew a scroll from a compartment and handed it to the imposing visitor.

"The route is easy enough, passing through Couentre…" he murmured to himself, "…which lies but a score of leagues to the west. The going is not hard along the river valleys. We shall aim towards the setting sun…"

Time passed and the endless wait for the return of the cavalryman as the moon waxed, gnawed at Aethelbald's patience. He imagined the worst possible outcome – the slave's torture and death and betrayal of his own whereabouts. So his relief was huge when after ten days, the fellow presented himself with an explanation.

"King Coelred received me, Lord, and read your message. He flew into a rage and I trembled for my life. He will fight King Ine and calls upon you to bring as many warriors as possible to Tame Weorth to swell his host–"

"Of course, I would if he hadn't spent so much time trying to murder me. What else?"

"I took great care that I wasn't followed. To be certain, I stayed two nights at Estdeping."

"That accounts for your late arrival."

"There's no cover out of Estdeping, so I was certain no spy followed me here,"

"You have done well. If your lord does not come to claim you within six moons, I shall keep you and make you a free man. Meanwhile, the horse is my gift."

"Bless you, Lord! Alcmund is your faithful servant."

"Well, Alcmund, your first duty with your horse is to accompany me and Brother Tidwulf to Salwic. But first, we must find you a spear."

"A slave cannot carry a spear, Lord."

"As well I know."

(four days later)

The town of Salwic, when Aethelbald and his band of a dozen men arrived, bore an air of abandon. The only noise capturing attention was the constant beating of a smith's hammer.

"Enulf," Aethelbald addressed his own smith, "get you in the forge. Smiths understand each other. Find out what's going on around here."

To his intense satisfaction, the steady ringing of steel hammering on steel came to an end and Enulf emerged beaming a few minutes later.

"Well?"

"Coelred and his host passed through the town three days ago. They returned north," Enulf pointed a muscular arm. "Yon smith says they retreated on account of the West Seaxa following 'em yesterday. He says he had to struggle to stay in his smithy, bein' as Coelred took the menfolk with him to fight. Seems they're headed for high ground. He says there's a hill fort at Wodensbeorg, eight leagues to the north-east and it's to that high ground Coelred is heading. There he means to make a stand."

"Where they lead, we follow," Aethelbald said. "Onward!"

The view from Knap Hill where Aethelbald's band arrived in the early evening sunlight, was spectacular. Off to their right, in the distance, rose the fortress of Wodensbeorg with its triple crown of turf ramparts. In spite of the long shadows cast by the declining sun, they could distinguish the dark form of massed men along the ramparts. Below and facing the fortress, ranked the men of West Seax. A grey mass, in their ringed steel shirts, they looked for all the world like a huge pack of wolves.

"Coelred has chosen well," Enulf muttered, "they'll never take the fortress yonder," the unmistakable tinge of Miercian pride coloured his tone.

Staring back up at the imposing height of the hill, topped with a long barrow known as Adam's Grave, Aethelbald's heart sank. He needed king Ine to inflict a crushing defeat on Coelred. But he feared this might prove ground not only for Adam's grave but also for the graves of many men from the West Country.

His musing was cut short by the sound of seaxes clashing on shields as the advance of the West Seaxa began. On the light breeze, war cries drifted to his ears and on the same wind, the emblem of a golden dragon so familiar to him, unfurled and fluttered.

Aethelbald and his men dismounted and let their horses graze on the lush grass of the hillside. Some took advantage of the soft turf, lying prone to watch the engagement. The figures, small in the distance, nonetheless, were easy to distinguish, backlit by the low sun. Each man on Knap Hill, in his innermost bosom, thanked God he was not advancing to face the certain hail of wicked steel points launched from above. They did not have long to wait to witness the screams and falling men as the storm of javelins found their mark.

'By Thunor, they've wreaked great losses upon Ine's men!'

And yet with exemplary courage, the West Seaxa continued unperturbed up the steep scarp, fending off another wave of javelins with their shields. Holding them above their heads when they reached the first turf rampart, they swarmed like ants over the defenders, hacking and hewing with all their might.

Of a sudden, hope sprang in the chest of Aethelbald as the attackers clambered up to the second ring of defence and overwhelmed the defenders. Another half hour, as the sky began to suffuse with pink-tinted clouds, what seemed impossible not long before now occurred. The West Seaxa clambered over the third and final rampart and soon, before Aethelbald's unbelieving eyes, they followed the fleeing Miercians up the hill to its summit and disappeared over the crest in pursuit.

Hidden from his view, the battle raged on but the outcome proved indecisive though tending to the West Seaxa. Twilight was upon them, the mantle of pale pink became a dusky purple pierced here and there by the silver pinpricks of stars.

"Come!" said Aethelbald, "To the horses! Down to the valley, we must find a place to lay our heads."

(Stanford, a week later)

"Brother Tidwulf, you bring excellent news," Aethelbald beamed at his friend and tutor. "So the West Seaxa have taken Salwic and Coelwald retired to Tame Weorth. Splendid! What more?"

"Ay, Lord, my King says the time is ripe. Hasten to Tame Weorth and claim the throne."

Aethelbald placed a hand flat at the top of his chest as if to physically steady his racing heart.

'Can it be, the time has really come? I do not feel ready.'

A pleasant surprise, later in the day eased his doubts and introduced a new one.

The smith, Enulf, sought him with a wide smile and an air of excitement.

"Lord, Coelwald has arrived, with hundreds of warriors.

"Coelwald? Is it possible? He ought to be in Powys. Can he be here in Stanford?"

"Ay, Lord, an' he begs to meet with you."

"Where is he?"

"Encamped by the river. I come directly from his tent. He sent a man to fetch me and ordered me to seek you out with his greetings."

"Will you take me to him?"

"I will, Lord."

The delight he felt at the sight of so many tents pitched on the floodplain of the Weolud eased his doubts but introduced another nagging one.

'Coelwald is an aetheling too. His claim is as strong as mine but backed by a seasoned and mighty force.'

He hurried to address these fears face to face with the interested party himself.

The warmth of his kinsman's embrace went some way to allay his worries.

"Good to see you, cousin. I am here because I have received messages from kings and ealdormen that you will move against the tyrant, Coelred, at any moment. I am here to lend you my strength. Coelred must be removed for the wellbeing of the land and the Church—"

"But you are his half-brother and as such have a strong pretence to the throne in your own right."

"It's true, but I have no will to fight you, whom I consider a friend and the right man for the crown. But hark, if the witan chooses me, I will not stand aside. If they opt for you I will serve you with all my heart."

"I echo your words. Let it be so: the witan will be free to decide."

They clasped hands and Aethelbald invited his cousin to evening meal. For the moment they were allies with the mission to overthrow Coelred.

This intention became more practicable the next day when Ealdwulf, King of the Est Angles, strode into Aethelbald's hall and offered the two hundred men now encamped opposite Coelwald's host. It stirred Aethelbald to issue a proclamation to arms to his own fyrdmen. *At last, the time was ripe.*

TWENTY-TWO

North Mierce, spring 716 AD

Coelred spread his spies throughout the land, so he was well-informed regarding the movement of troops. His foul mood contrasted with Aethelbald's joy when each man learnt of the mobilisation of the Lindisfarona. The so-called King of the Fenlands now headed an irresistible host and bore down on Tame Weorth. Coelred, instead, showed all the signs of a ruler backed into a corner.

Even by his opulent standards, the banquet he organised in a show of defiance, was prodigal. Wine flowed and the rich meats ranged from delicate fowl in sauces to the strong, dark flesh of deer – the venison so beloved of the King. As the meal went on, Coelred's visage grew increasingly incarnadine. The talk at the table, of course, concerned the impending revolt. Those within earshot of the King were wise enough to couch their language behind a tactful veil, none of which served to calm the extreme reactions of the unstable monarch. He was liable to fly into a rage at the slightest provocation and woe to whomever his rancour settled upon.

An unguarded comment by a Hwiccan nobleman referring to the seizure of Salwic by the West Seaxa led to a flurry of insults from the King aimed at all things Hwiccan. It went on till his exaggeration caused the retiring from the table of the unfortunate man. This event cast a pall of reticence over the meal. Everyone knew that an ealdorman could not retire from the King's presence without his leave and suffer no consequences. The malignant expression on the King's face boded ill. It required much wine to restore the convivial atmosphere but when tongues loosened, a voice was heard, "The Lindisfarona have united with the Est Angles and with Coelwald and Aethelbald. A moot is needed to decide how best to contrast this great host."

As occurs when the most inopportune speech is uttered, it is pronounced in unusual silence, so that every word rings clear and unmistakable. The quietness deepened as one and all awaited the King's reaction. When it came, it shocked them all. Coelred's complexion passed from flushed red to an unhealthy livid colour. He leapt to his feet and staggered, his face contorting around the mouth, his words, nothing but gibberish, had no sense. Some swore afterward that he cursed priests and spoke with demons. Coelred fell heavily to the floor and lay there convulsing.

"The King is thunderstruck!" shouted one of the ealdormen.

"Fetch a healer!" cried another.

"It is God's wrath," remarked another, to anyone prepared to listen. "It is said a visionary at Much Wenlock declared angels surrounding Coelred removed their protective shield and abandoned him to demons because of his many crimes. Sure enough, it has come to pass."

An ealdorman bending over the monarch withdrew his hand from the ruler's throat and shook his head, "The King is dead," he said, "there is no pulse."

"Dead," the word spread around the hall like wildfire, amid speculation as to who should be the next King of Mierce.

Heardberht, the brother of Aethelbald kept his head and spoke with a calm and authoritative voice, sufficient to hush the excited chatter. "Our first task is to bear the body of the King to Licidfelth, Bishop Haedde will know what procedures to undertake for the royal burial. After which, we ought to decide on a date for the witan to meet. Since my brother is marching as is Coelwald and both are aethelings, they, with the underkings at their side must be invited to the meeting.

The indisputable good sense of his words met with general approbation. Two ealdormen, sitting next to each other, volunteered to lead a small delegation to Aethelbald with the news.

When they met with the advancing host near to Snotingham, their information was greeted with astonishment and relief, for it meant slender likelihood of battle.

Once more, the word spread at an impressive rate through the army. To Aethelbald's dismay, the men of Coelwald began to beat on their shields and shout, "Long live King Coelwald!" The counter-cry of "Long live King Aethelbald!" arose from another quarter. Insults began to fly to and from the opposing factions. Urgent action was needed and Aethelbald took it.

Looking around, he saw the stump of a felled oak and, leaping on it, began to deliver a speech in a ringing voice. "Men of Mierce, Est Anglia and Lindissi, Coelred was stroked by God's hand. The new King will be elected by the witan as custom demands. Let no man go against that decision, whatever his heart says. If Coelwald is chosen by the witan, I shall be the first to bend the knee and all others ought to follow my lead."

"AY!" a great bellow of united voices arose, not only from Coelwald's men but also from many others. The situation was in hand. It only remained to march on Tame Weorth.

Tame Weorth, spring 716 AD

In the sumptuous palace of Tame Weorth, three days later, servants placed tables in the centre of the hall, ready for the members of the witan to take their places.

Another four nights passed before Aethelbald and the other high-ranking men of Mierce and its satellite kingdoms entered the hall and took seats according to friendship rather than rank.

The meeting commenced with a general condemnation of the ills of the previous reign and the collective determination to avoid another error in their choice of ruler. The church, in the form of several bishops, led by the vocal and esteemed Bishop Haedde had as great an interest as their secular colleagues, if not greater.

"I do not wish to speak ill of the dead," Haedde declared, then proceeded to do so, iterating the series of reprehensible acts carried out by the recently buried monarch. This was a deliberate lead into a plan concocted by the Bishop himself and King Aldfrith to put Aethelbald on the throne. "It is clear to everyone, we have two prime aspirants for he kingship with an equal and legitimate claim: namely, Aethelbald and Coelwald, both aethelings and men of unblemished character. How then, do we choose between them?"

Everyone started shouting at once for his personal favourite.

Haedde stood and demanded order.

"To avoid another mistake, I think we ought to do more than a straightforward vote," he said, enacting the plan agreed with Aldfrith.

"Before arriving at a show of hands, I propose we put it to the two candidates how they would decide on serious issues that might confront them daily."

This proposal met with general acclaim.

"Well then," continued the prelate, "let me ask each of you," he looked with deliberation from Aethelbald to Coelwald.

"How you would deal with this situation… a man is brought before you accused of murder. How do you react?"

Coelwald spoke first, "Why, according to custom. His kin is expected to support him with oaths."

"Is that all?" the bishop asked the perplexed aetheling, whose handsome face creased into a frown of confusion, "Ay," was all he said.

"And you, Aethelbald?"

"Well Bishop, I would refer to the law I introduced in the fenlands and intend to do so throughout Mierce, should the witan decide to offer me the throne."

"In this particular case, what does the code say?"

"May I send for it?"

Dissatisfied at this reply, nonetheless, the Bishop acquiesced and Aethelbald sent for Brother Tidwulf. Feeling acute awareness of the need for a response, Aethelbald spoke. While we await the arrival of the code, I wish to reply from memory… er…" his brow creased with the effort of concentration. "…In this particular case, I would require at least one high-ranking person among his"oath-helpers".

The oath-helper would swear an oath on behalf of the accused man, to clear him of suspicion of the crime. My requirement implies that I do not trust an oath sworn only by ceorls."

"Is that all?" the bishop repeated his earlier question.

Aethelbald shook his head, and added, "Nay, if the oath-helper is a communicant, then his oath will carry more weight than that of a non-Christian."

"Well said!" Haedde clapped his hands in obvious approval.

At that moment, Brother Tidwulf entered and handed a heavy, leather-bound volume to Aethelbald.

"Let me find and read you the relevant law—"

"But it is in *Latin*, Sire," Tidwulf said in a timorous voice.

"What of it?" Aethelbald growled, "I shall translate it for the witan.

A murmur of astonishment passed like a wave around the assembly, not only was Aethelbald skilled in the martial arts but he was also learned.

He browsed through the tome until he came to the relevant law, confirmed by the quavering finger of Tidwulf pointing it out.

Aethelbald read one sentence at a time in Latin and then translated it into English. To his relief, he had remembered the law to perfection. When he had finished, Haedde gave him further encouragement.

"Can you give us other examples of everyday laws you intend to introduce?"

Indeed, he could. The question was, how much patience had his fellow ealdormen to listen? Conscious that he must not overtax their patience, he selected a few laws that concerned noblemen. "For instance, the fine for neglecting fyrd, the obligation to do military service for the king, is set at 120 shillings for a nobleman, and 30 shillings for a ceorl."

This caused another discussion in the hall, but Aethelbald was pleased to see that the reaction, on the whole, was favourable. He chose another law and then one more, before closing the book with satisfaction.

"There!" said Haedde as though he had achieved a victory, which in fact, he had. "In my humble opinion, we have witnessed great kingship, today. I propose we vote for one or other of the aspirants, please raise a hand if your choice is for Coelwald, son of Aethelred. There followed a moment of embarrassment as each man looked to his neighbour. No words were spoken but Haedde noted with satisfaction a head shaken, here and there. After hesitation, one or two hands were raised and these belonged to close kinsmen of the aetheling or to his dearest associates.

"Now please show hands if Aethelbald is your choice."

In the general rustling of garments, the majority of hands shot up.

"The decision of the witan is made!" Haedde announced, "By the grace of God, I declare Aethelbald, King of Mierce. Long live the King!"

Heart beating fit to burst, Aethelbald stood and bowed around the room, voicing unheard thanks, under the clamour of the repeated four words, taken up by the assembly, even by Coelwald and his supporters.

"Long live King Aethelbald!"

To a cheer from all and sundry, Aethelbald strode across to Coelwald and embraced him. He whispered in his kinsman's ear, "Friend, worry not, I have an important role for you…very important."

Haedde clapped for silence and then spoke, "First, we must finish mourning King Coelred. I deem it correct that coronation of our new King take place after the next moon. King Aethelbald ought to be crowned in the cathedral at Licidfelth, in the manner of the Frankish kings, with the full and explicit blessing of the Church."

"Ay," added the new King, "there will be time thus to organise a great feast for the occasion."

This, his first real utterance as King, brought a rousing cheer from the assembled noblemen, many of whom now began to rise and extend their heartfelt congratulations. Aethelbald, for his part, remembered who were among the first to do so. He had serious plans to consolidate the heartland of Mierce and knew how best to reward loyalty.

TWENTY-THREE

Tame Weorth, late-April 716 AD

"Are you so fond of the military life that you need to burrow down on this damp plain?" said Aethelbald to Coelwald as he pushed into his tent. "Why not bring what serves you and take a bed in the palace?"

"And leave the discomfort to my men?" the aetheling shook his head.

"Prepare to move on. In any case, for I have plans for you."

"So you said, and what are these plans?"

"You will admit Mierce has lost its grip on its neighbours under Coelred?"

"It sorrows me to agree."

"Well, my first aim as king is to consolidate the heartland of Mierce. To the west, Wreoca, Magon, and Hwicca must lose their position. They will become Miercian *scirs*. With Northanhymbria torn with internal problems or struggling to keep the Picts at bay, our main threats come from the Wealisc or from the West Seax."

"What has this to do with me?"

"Everything. I am away to prepare the documents that will make you King of the Hwicca – underking to me, of course."

"I'm flattered and overjoyed, but King Ethelward of Hwicca might not be best pleased with your scheme."

"I will make him an offer he cannot refuse. He will become Ealdorman of Hwicca and I shall grant him Castra Weogernensis, as his in perpetuity…"

"A handsome gift."

"Ay, and one that would buy the co-operation of any man. Fear not, you too shall have grants befitting your status. I have until my coronation to …prepare the charters…" Aethelbald laid a hand on his cousin's shoulder to fix his attention, "…who better to have in Hwicca? Nobody has a more thorough knowledge of the wiles of the Wealisc than you. Your first task will be to re-take Salwic from the West Seax."

"Go to war with Ine?"

"Hold! Did I say that?" Aethelbald shook his head, "It will not come to that. We will concede a yearly amount of salt to the West Seaxa. The amount can be agreed in a spirit of friendship."

"You seem sure of what you say."

"I am. Now I must leave you, there is much to do. Have I your consent to my plans?"

"You have, my King."

Back in the palace, Aethelbald sent for his brother.

Heardberht was the only man in Tame Weorth who stood as tall as himself, he mused or was he deluded. But as he looked at his brother, it occurred to him what an effect his own physique must have on others. The fierce leonine features they shared, the tall, muscular frame…

'I would not care to engage Heardberht in combat.'

"Brother," he said and was gratified that before he could complete his thought, he was wrapped in a crushing embrace.

"Brother…" he took up, "I have plans for you. But, of course, they depend upon your own will."

"What plans?"

"You will admit Mierce has lost its grip on its neighbours under Coelred?"

This approach had worked with Coelwald, so he saw no reason to change. The answer was the same.

"It pains me to say *'ay'*.

"My first aim as king is to consolidate the heartland of Mierce. I have made progress with the western borders but now I pass to the north. There lies Elmet. Brother, I would not send you into danger even though I believe you are more than capable of facing any troubles." Once more, he appraised the sturdiness of his younger brother. "The defences of Elmet are secure. I made sure of that when I was there," he made no effort to hide the pride in his voice. My plan is to make you King of Elmet…underking to me, of course. I shall grant you lands in keeping with your rank."

Heardberht's face betrayed his emotions. Aethelbald was pleased to see that his gratitude outshone that of Coelwald.

"Of course, any future threat may come from Northanhymbria – a thorn in the side of our forefathers. Your task will be to strengthen the borders against any such danger. What say you?"

"My King, brother, I know not how to express my thanks."

"Not necessary, all I want is you assent and all I need is your loyalty."

"That is unquestioned."

"I have until my coronation to prepare the charters. But there is much to do and no time to be lost."

'By Thunor, things are falling into place!'

Aethelbald reflected on the concept of coronation. It was not quite unknown to the Anglo-Saxons in England, but almost. However, he could see how the ceremony tallied with his ambition to become Bretwaldas. he would spare no expense. The people must come from far and wide and they must be entertained. Therefore, he gave orders for a generous sum to be spent from the royal coffers and the Church seemed as eager to spend on the occasion for its part.

Talking of the Church, the guards admitted Bishop Haedde into his presence. He came leading a portly man dangling a cloth measure from one hand.

"Bishop, what is it? There is so much still to be done."

The Bishop bowed, "Lord, we have to take the measurement for your crown."

"*Crown?*" Aethelbald spoke the word as if it were of a foreign tongue. "I have no need of one.

"I fear, Sire, there can be no coronation without one."

"I suppose not."

The rotund man, in an evident state of trepidation, said, "B-beggin' your pardon, Sire, please to be seated, else I'll need a ladder to measure around your brow."

Aethelbald and Heardberht roared with laughter in unison while the craftsman trembled. The King waved to a servant, who hurried to fetch a chair for the operation.

The band of cloth passed around the monarch's brow, the fellow muttered 'inches' and withdrew, satisfied.

"The Church will pay for a gold crown worthy of a powerful Kingdom such as Mierce. A few gemstones, I think," Haedde said.

"The Church ought not to spend too much," said Aethelbald, "for an object to be worn but once."

"*Once!*" cried Haedde, "What is it you are saying? What then of the important services of Christ's Mass, Easter and Whitsun. The King must honour them and appear in splendour…not to mention the moots of state. It is the visible manifestation of your authority."

"And I thought that was my sword!"

Heardberht suppressed a snort, transforming it into a cough.

Haedde gave Aethelbald a reproving look. "One other thing before I take my leave. At the coronation, you will be required to take an oath in the presence of all and sundry but in particular before God."

"What would you have me swear?"

"*…ut promittat et iuramento firmet se obseruatturum iura episcoporum et ecclesiarum sicut debet regem in regno facere…*"

Heardberht shrugged and looked angry, "Speak in English, priest!" he hissed.

Aethelbald laughed, "It is not hard to swear and promise to observe the rights of bishops and churches as should a king in his kingdom etc. but mark my words, Bishop, I will not be a *slave* to the church in exchange for a coronation."

"First, let me congratulate you on your knowledge of Latin, Sire. All rulers ought to speak it. It is the universal language. But what an idea! The Church does not want you, King Aethelbald, as a *slave*. What the Church *wants* is a protector and supporter. Never ought there to be a return to the dark days of Coelred, who to be sure, now burns in Hell."

"Have no fear, Bishop. As King, I intend to rule respecting the rights of the meanest in the land. The Church, I consider a true friend, as we have seen in my accession."

"You will swear the oath? The Frankish kings do so without hesitation."

"Then, so shall I."

"By your leave, Sire. We must be away. There is so much to do."

The King agreed with all his heart. In truth, the days to the coronation passed swiftly for Aethelbald, taken up by meetings with counsellors to draft charters, the issuing of proclamations, the fitting of garments and the magnificent crown for the coronation. He was thankful that the arrangements for the cathedral at Licidfelth were not his responsibility. Soon, the moon would be full.

(Full moon 11 May 716 AD)

The ceremony was fixed for midday on the stipulated date. Licidfelth lay three leagues to the north-west of Tame Weorth, so the King rose early on the morning of the eleventh. After admiring the beauty of the countryside from the vantage point of his bedchamber, he ordered his servants to prepare for the short journey. He calculated a seven o'clock departure would be right for a comfortable arrival.

The throng of cheering folk throwing spring blossom at him while lining the road into Licidfelth exceeded his expectations. In great, high humour, conscious of the unfamiliar crown circling his brow, he dismounted before the imposing cathedral, waving to the gathered onlookers. Ringing cheers followed him up the steps into the nave, where he passed under the crossed spears bearing the embroidered emblem of Mierce: the golden dragon rampant on a blue ground.

'My dragon!' he told himself as he stooped under the alley of spears, he emerged to stand before a throne placed in front of an altar in the centre of the nave. Bishop Haedde was the only known face among a huddle of mitred bishops all in their finest regalia.

'By Thunor, what a gaggle of priests! They mean to do this well.'

The prelates urged the king to sit and the Mass began. It was some way into the familiar service, after the celebration of the Eucharist that the rites of coronation began. as if Haedde and the others could not wait, he commenced with the oath-swearing. Once Aethelbald, to their surprise uttered the oath in Latin, he had practised for days with Tidwulf, Haedde passed to unction, oil and chrism on the crown of his head, marking him as the heavenly-approved King of Mierce.

Even at his coronation, Aethelbald's hand strayed to Osthryth's ring that, although under his robes, he felt with difficulty.

'This is but the first step to becoming Bretwaldas.'

At the same moment, the cathedral resonated to cheers and the cry of *'Long live King Aethelbald!'* as if in approbation of his ambition. A wide grin spread across the careworn features of the King. His days of skulking in the fens were well and truly over.

EPILOGUE

Cruwland, July 716

Reflecting on the importance of his coronation for the legitimation of his reign, as he lay in reverie, Aethelbald, remembering his vow taken at Cruwland, came to an important decision. Many of his recent predecessors, above all, in other kingdoms, but also in Mierce had associated themselves with a saint. Aethelred with the martyr king Oswald, by founding the abbey at Beardan – and after all, Oswald had been the enemy of Mierce. Others came to his restless mind. He sighed, in truth, he had a real association with a saint – Guthlac, once his best friend. Moreover, he owed a debt to the saint, who sheltered him from the wrath and spite of Coelred and furthered his cause with the Church.

'By Thunor, what better idea than to grant lands to the monks at Cruwland and to found a monastery of my own? They will need an abbot of course. I shall set this in motion on the morrow.'

With this comforting thought, Aethelbald slipped into a deep sleep.

He rose with his head full of this deliberation, and to enact it, he sent for Haedde, whose advice he sought.

After explaining his intentions to the delighted prelate, he addressed the reason for his summons.

"Who is worthy of taking the position of abbot at the monastery of Cruwland?"

The prelate's brow furrowed, "At present, the monk of greatest repute is a certain Kenulph at Evesham."

"Then, summon him to our presence, I would speak with this Kenulph."

"It shall be done, Sire," said Haedde, hurrying to do this bidding, more certain than ever of the goodness of his choice of ruler.

Evesham, the king was informed, lay south of Tame Weorth at thirteen leagues. It was no surprise that Kenulph did not present himself at court for a week. But when, at last, he bowed before his king, Aethelbald was impressed by the open, gentle features of the monk and his meek manner. Taking an instant liking to the monk, Aethelbald did not find it necessary to impose conditions on the brother, satisfied with a simple account of the sanctity of Guthlac's life and how his memory should be honoured by the exemplary conduct that had been the mark of Kenulph's monastic life.

"I mean," said Aethelbald, to grant the abbey the whole island of Cruwland. The boundaries will have to be drawn with care to avoid disputes. You," he said, turning to Kenulph, "will be the first Abbot and I will give the abbey a grant of three hundred pounds in gold and one hundred pounds a year for ten years towards the construction of the monastic buildings."

Haedde clapped his hands in ill-concealed glee.

"There are serious problems to be overcome. You, Bishop, who have been to Cruwland many times, will concur that building in stone presents grave drawbacks, owing to the marshy nature of the land. Hence, I have issued orders for the felling of oaks and alders near Upland, whence the trunks will be transported by boat to be driven into the ground as piles. Thereafter, fresh, dry earth will follow in boats to fill up the swamp so that building may begin. All this is arranged. The wooden oratory of Guthlac will be replaced by one of stone. do you have any questions?"

"Ay," Haedde said, "I believe there are four hermits, a certain Cissa, Bettelin, Egbert and Tatwin whose cells are near the oratory. What will become of them, Abbot Kenulph?"

"I see no reason not to suffer them to pass the remainder of their days as they are."

"So be it!" said Aethelbald, much pleased by this response.

When Kenulph arrived in Cruwland some weeks later, he was met by another saint, Guthlac's sister, Pege, who presented him with her brother's psalter and the scourge given to the anchorite by Saint Bartholomew. She then retired to her cell eight miles from her brother's oratory, where she stayed for two further years and three months before going to Rome, where she died.

Aethelbald remained in Tame Weorth, overseeing the consolidation of his kingdom, installing friends and kinsmen in key positions. In the third year of his reign he promulgated the *'Statutum Ethelbaldi'*, by which all monasteries and churches in his kingdom were relieved from all secular service, except for the repair of castles and bridges.

He impressed his seal into the red wax, closing the document and he reflected, *'Matters are well in hand, my people love and respect me. All dangers have been quelled. By Thunor, all I need is a buxom wench!*

And he set about finding himself the first of many from among the serving maids.

- # -

MIXED BLESSINGS

SAINTS AND SINNERS BOOK 2

Special thanks go to my dear friend, John Bentley, for his steadfast and indefatigable support. His content checking and suggestions have made an invaluable contribution to Mixed Blessings.

'A man's worth is no greater than the worth of his ambitions.'
Marcus Aurelius – *Meditations*

ONE

Tame Weorth, 720 AD

When ambition is overweening and fails to consider the needs of others, he who is consumed by it performs wicked deeds.

Heardberht strode into the king's hall, wondering about the charter he was supposed to witness. To be truthful, he resented having to make the journey from Elmet to Tame Weorth just to place a signature on a document. He was too wise, however, to voice any such reservations.

"Heardberht! What in Thunor's name are you doing in Tame Weorth? You idle oaf! You ought to be building up Miercian defences in Elmet."

The offended party stared at King Æthelbald, his brother, prowling towards him, between the tables laid out for dining, with the mien of a hungry lion preparing to spring on its helpless prey.

"Brother, my king, have you forgotten? You summoned me here to ratify a charter. I know not to what it refers."

"By Thunor, you have the right of it!"

Beneath the shaggy beard, a disconcerting toothy smile appeared.

"Pay no heed to my harsh words. You are ever welcome in Tame Weorth, Heardberht," roared Æthelbald, King of Mierce, his booming voice befitting of his leonine aspect. "Forgive me," he said, clapping his hands for a servant, who hastened to draw near to his king.

"Sire?"

"A pitcher of cool ale. Pray be seated, brother. My mind is overwrought with problems, and I tend to forget matters of importance. But stay! We shall discuss why you are here and my problems over a beaker of ale."

"You look well, in spite of your troubles."

"Appearances can deceive. Ah! Here is our drink. And what is this? Smells good!"

A second servant laid down a platter of food. "Oatcakes, lord. Fresh from the oven, if you care for them, sire."

"Will you try them, Heardberht?"

"With all my heart, brother. I had to make do with vile food on the journey here. I could eat a wild boar whole!"

"Ha-ha! Do you hear, fellow? Take my order to the cook. This evening, roast boar at my table… and plenty of it."

"Sire." The first servant bowed and hurried away to do his king's bidding. Æthelbald dismissed the other with a wave of the hand, so the maid wended over to stand by the wall, ready to react to any need her lord may have of her.

"What problems beset you, my king?" Heardberht asked as he wiped foam off his whiskers with the back of his hand. "That's bitter and strong, just as I like it."

"Twice brewed from barley."

Æthelbald sighed and frowned, adding ten years to his countenance beyond the two-score springs he had lived. Heardberht dared not press him, but it pained him to see his elder brother careworn and distracted.

"All my plans, my ambitions," Æthelbald said in a flat monotone, "in the south of the land are frustrated by two old men."

"How so?"

"In Kent, Wihtred rules and has done so for twenty-five years while the West Seaxa are led by Ine for as long. After being independent for such a time, they will not cede precedence to a new king."

"But is Ine not a friend? Did he not aid you in your time of need?"

"True, but he remains an obstacle to Miercian growth. As for Wihtred, his envious eyes alight upon Lunden and along all the valley of the Temese."

"Mierce will never part with Lundenwic, it is the fount of our wealth."

Æthelbald gave his brother a pitying look as though dealing with a child who had stated the obvious.

"Not only Lunden interests me, brother, but the whole of the south. Have another drink." He gained time to think by pouring ale for them both before adding, "And not just the south. How's it going in Elmet?"

"We have taken Loidis and now press to hold the land as far as the river Weorf. As you well know, my king, across the river is the kingdom of Northanhymbre."

"Good. One day, we will bring that land to our dependency, mark my words!"

"What then of this charter?"

"Pah! A land grant to a priory near Loidis. That's why you are here. The monks will be reassured to know the most powerful man in Elmet is signatory to the deed."

"And do you care so much for the church?"

"Remember, brother, without the blessing of the church, we are nothing."

"Our forefathers managed well enough."

"Different times. In those days, there were no great kingdoms. There were other gods too. Now, the church watches over everyone, myself included, more's the pity."

The regal countenance clouded, and it seemed to Heardberht that his brother's blue-grey eyes had grown darker in an instant. He recoiled from the fierce gaze, failing to meet it.

"So, the church is bothersome?" he said, guessing it to be the root of the matter.

Æthelbald poured another drink and waved to the maid for her to fetch another pitcher. As she hastened away, Æthelbald smirked, "Pretty creature, don't you think?"

He waited for his brother's reply.

"Ay, but a king can do better."

The reaction this observation elicited shocked the underking of Elmet.

"Don't you start, brother! You're as bad as all the rest, church included. The wench is pretty enough for me, in fact, she warms my bed on many an occasion."

"I meant no offence, brother. Only, I thought you might wish to take a noblewoman for a queen."

"May Thunor blast your breeches!"

The object of the dispute reappeared with a ewer brim-full of ale. She set it on the table with a pretty smile to her king and then to Heardberht, oblivious of the tension between the brothers.

"I concede she is a comely wench," said the younger man, reaching for his refilled beaker and admiring the retreating figure.

"All the noble families of Mierce wish me to marry. To hell with them! I have no wish to take a queen."

He lowered his voice, for it had taken on a vehement, hectoring tone.

"We have seen, in recent times, how queens put their families first and their husbands second. I will not run this risk. Of course, these busybodies call upon the church for help. They send priests to batter my ears with verses from the Holy Book, condemning my way of life. See, brother, if I take not a wife and choose to live in abstinence then the bishop is happy, otherwise, I'm a *'fornicator'*, leading my people into perdition by bad example! But, see here, I'm no monk."

"You are granting land to the church to keep the bishops sweet, is that it?"

"Ah, I believe you are following the drift of my words. I should tell you, it's not just within Mierce. There are those in other kingdoms who would foist their daughters on me."

"An alliance of kingdoms. Is that such a bad thing?

"HEARDBERHT!" Æthelbald bellowed the name, slamming a fist on the table. Servants positioned around the hall exchanged glances and two guards stepped forward. "Thank God I sent you to Elmet, out of harm's way. Here, you would side with those accursed counsellors who would have me wed. By marrying a daughter of another kingdom I'd unpick my plans. It'd open the way for a rival to bend Mierce to his will. My plan foresees the opposite. Is that clear now?" These last words he enunciated one by one as if addressing an oaf.

A grudging apologetic smile served as a reply. In spite of the mellowing effects of the ale, Heardberht was on edge. Familiar with the volatile nature of his sibling, he dared not risk provoking his wrath further.

"Anyway," said Æthelbald, "worry not. I have a new plan to thwart the lot of them. I will not live like a monk – to the Devil with their *abstinence*! Neither will I wed a queen. There's more than one way to skin a wolf, Heardberht."

"What will you do, my king?"

Æthelbald, sniggered, "To begin with, I'll stop bedding the Tame Weorth wenches. I must aim higher, as you so wisely pointed out. After all, the religious houses are full of noblewomen, and most of them were forced into a nunnery against their will by their powerful fathers."

"You can't seduce *nuns*! You'll set the church against you."

"I can and I will! Think of the benefits. In this way, I can ease my way into more than one important family. Now, I'm off to tend to other matters." Æthelbald rose and seized his bother in a crushing embrace. "Good to have you here, Heardberht! You will sit next to me at dinner – roast boar!" With that, he turned and walked away, his mind racing.

'*I ought to have asked Guthlac if I'd become Bretwalda. I missed that chance.*'

His visage clouded with sorrow at the thought. What he would give to have his dearest friend by his side now, but Guthlac had died six years before, venerated as a saint in Cruwland in the Fens. His brother was one thing, but family seldom understands a man's dreams.

TWO

Tame Weorth, 720 AD

The delicate nature of his mission and weak position left the visitor anxious before the intimidating figure of the king. At last, he mustered the courage to begin, "Sire, my brother, Ealdorman Mensige, is sick and could not survive the journey from Ledecestre. Alas, his heart betrays him, not for the first time."

The cold grey-blue eyes of Æthelbald appraised the stand-in and were not impressed. One swat of his arm and the fellow would fly across the hall. What did this nonentity want of him?

"Mensige has a daughter of great beauty, Saeflaed, whom he has hidden away these six years. Now, in his ill health, he has decided she ought to wed. Hence, I stand here before you, my king."

"What have I to do with this decision?"

"As I said, sire, the allure of my niece is exceptional."

These fools wish me to marry an unknown maid!

Æthelbald stared at his visitor, much as a hunter might look at a fine stag grazing unawares within range of his arrow.

I can turn this to my advantage.

"Friend, tell your brother to prepare his kitchen for a royal visit. We shall come with a score of retainers a week from now to look upon your niece. You may leave us now."

The supplicant bowed his way out through the huge wooden door, the entrance to the hall. Æthelbald waited until it closed behind him before calling over a servant.

"Find my sword sharpener and bring him here, make haste!"

Gratified by the youth running to the heavy door and wasting no time on opening it the merest crack to slip through, Æthelbald thought over his scheme, searching for weaknesses.

In a very short time, the young servant returned. In his wake came Æthelbald's father's smith, Enulf. The office of sword sharpener, Æthelbald had created to keep his loyal friend close by. Now he had much greater plans for him.

"Good to see you, Enulf! Come, follow me. There is something I must show you, and we should talk in private."

To the surprise of the blacksmith, the king led him to his bedchamber. As far as the sword sharpener knew, only servants were allowed in there – comely wenches at that. Inside, Æthelbald alarmed him by staring at him as if sizing him up.

"Ha!" he cried. "I knew it! We are of much the same stature."

With that, he hurried over to open a huge carved chest at the foot of the bed. Rummaging within, the king emerged, clutching a pale blue tunic. He held it in front of himself as if measuring it for size. The garment dropped down to mid-calf length, revealing a bronze-coloured zigzag border above the hem.

"Off with that jerkin and tunic!"

"What, here, now?"

"Unless you wish to strip out in the yard!" Æthelbald roared.

Perplexed, Enulf tossed his jerkin, with an anxious glance at the king, onto the immaculate white sheepskin covering the bed. His eye continued beyond to the carved oak bed head where two gaping wolves' heads served to scare away evil spirits. The rest of the chamber displayed the luxury befitting a king. Enulf, at home amid the grime and soot of his forge, would have felt uneasy even had he not been standing in his undergarments.

"Here, pull this on," Æthelbald commanded, throwing the tunic to his smith who wriggled into the unfamiliar clothing. "Ha! Perfect! I was right. Eat little and drink less and it will be as though it were sewn for you."

"But why, Lord?"

There was no reply because the king again dug into the enormous box and reappeared with a belt whose gold buckle glimmered, even in the dimness of the room.

"Fasten this!" came the brusque command.

"I cannot, sire, there is no suitable eye for the prong."

"I told you – either lose weight or find a way to make a hole."

"Every smith has a punch to make holes in leather."

"Then do so, for this is a gift."

"But, my king, it's worth a fortune."

"It is the least of what I have in mind for you, and a man must look the part he has to play."

Enulf gaped at his king. What had the ruler in mind?

"Back into your own clothes, I will send for you when I have need," Æthelbald smirked. He enjoyed the power of keeping Enulf curious.

* * *

On the way to Ledecestre, a week later

"It is time I revealed my plan to you, Lord Enulf." The king edged his mount closer to the smith's.

"*Lord* Enulf?"

"Ay, did you not know I have ceded my estates of Snotingham to you?"

"My king, what can I say? What can I do to repay your generosity?"

"Well, there is something."

"Name it, sire."

"You can make me a sword befitting of a king."

"You shall have a sword to rival the best of Frankish craftsmanship, my word on it."

"Good, there is another thing. I wish for you to take a wife."

"But there is no maid in my life."

"Do you not like maids, Enulf?"

The smith ground his teeth. Was the king doubting his manliness?

"Ay, of course." He kept his tone polite, "It's just difficult to wed when there is no betrothed."

"But I have found you one, Lord Enulf."

The blacksmith glanced at his monarch. What was happening here?

It seems my plan is working wondrous well. Unite Snotingham to Ledecestre and Enulf will be the most powerful man in the East of Mierce. A truer or more loyal follower than my father's smith I cannot boast.

The sallow complexion and shortness of breath of their host, the Ealdorman of Ledecestre bespoke of the illness to which his brother had referred. After the niceties of welcoming, Lord Mensige broached the subject of the royal visit.

"I defy any man to show me a fairer maid in the whole of Mierce than my Saeflaed. The time has come for her to wed. Her beauty alone is worth more than all my estates."

"How old is your daughter?" Æthelbald asked.

The ealdorman hesitated, to gain a moment to think, "Two-score and two springs have passed since her birth, he spoke with a rasping wheeze.

"When may we gaze upon this embodiment of womanly charms?"

"Sire, I'll send for Saeflaed at once – prepare to lose your heart."

The fool truly believes I shall wed the filly.

"Saeflaed!" their host croaked, and a maidservant ran, skirt swishing, to find her mistress.

In moments, she returned, accompanied by a young woman of exceeding beauty. Copper-coloured hair framed an oval face, enlivened by deep violet eyes under arching eyebrows. The elfin smile charmed all the men in the room as she strode among them in a pale green silken dress to curtsey before the king.

"Come… Saeflaed… meet… your betrothed," her father said in joyous gasps.

"Ay," said Æthelbald, "meet him. Step forward, Lord Enulf."

The former blacksmith bowed to his intended bride, who, with admiration, eyed his muscular arms emerging from the short-sleeved tunic, given to him by the king.

"W-what—?"

The countenance of Mensige flushed the colour of ripe damsons, and beads of sweat appeared at the brow.

"This is Lord Enulf, Ealdorman of Snotingham, who will betroth Lady Saeflaed," Æthelbald declaimed.

"Trickery!... Snotingham is the king's burh... it's well known," Mensige rasped and wheezed. A hand flew to his sword, but before he could draw it, he gasped and croaked, clutching at his throat and chest. Shocked into immobility, nobody except Saeflaed moved as the ealdorman's knees buckled and he crashed to the floor. There he lay, sweating profusely and fighting for breath, his face a livid mask. His daughter knelt by him, her beauteous face wet with tears. "Father! Not today, on this happiest of days. Fetch water, girl! Don't stand there gawping!"

The words had barely left her lips when there came a deep rasping in the throat and Mensige's eyes glazed, staring sightlessly up to the rafters.

"No!" the damsel screamed and covered the dead Mensige's forehead with kisses.

Enulf stepped forward and raised the maid to fold her into his arms. She pressed closer to him and buried her head in his chest for comfort while the new ealdorman stroked her coppery hair and whispered into her ear.

Æthelbald sought the deceased's brother in the hall and, finding him, ordered a priest brought.

"Sire, the bishop's house is nearby. He was my brother's confessor."

"Better still, send for the bishop!" Æthelbald said with the distracted air of one whose thoughts are intruded upon by events.

How Doom springs from the darkest corner, crumbling lives in a shorter time than it takes darkness to obscure the sunset.

When the prelate arrived, the king finalised his plan, interrupted by the cruel fate of Mensige. "My Lord Bishop," he said, "we rely on you to arrange the funeral of our beloved servant, Mensige, and to establish a decent period of mourning before the wedding of Lord Enulf and Lady Saeflaed."

"Sire, with your leave, I will be proud to conduct both masses."

"Excellent. So be it. Now, poor Mensige had no male heir," he turned to the brother. "Some might argue that the lands go to you, good fellow, but I need Ledecestre and Snotingham to be united for greater strength. Enulf will be Ealdorman of Ledecestre. You, my friend, who are a worthy man, will come with me to Tame Weorth, where your loyalty will be well rewarded."

Glancing around the room at the expectant faces awaiting his reply, the impoverished nobleman bowed before his king.

"Sire, your wish is my command. I want only for my niece to be happy."

The lady in question broke away from her new love and flung herself into her uncle's arms.

All's well. A fine end to my scheming. Shame about the wretch lying on the floor.

THREE

Ledecestre, Enulf's Estates, 720 AD

Established in his new hall and feeling the most blessed man in the world, Enulf gathered his thegns to get to know them better but also to understand the management of his lands. With this in mind, he ordered them to saddle horses and to lead him around the boundaries of the important settlements.

The high, fleecy clouds in a blue sky did little to obscure the sun, which cast deep shadows emphasising the contours of the land. The horsemen came to a field where men were working the earth with adzes and hoes.

Enulf reined in his horse, bringing his companions to a halt.

"What's this?" he cried.

"A barley field, Lord."

"I mean why are they turning the soil by hand? Where is the plough?"

The thegn laughed but changed it to a discreet cough, better not antagonise his new master.

"Lord, these men are too poor to own a plough, let alone oxen. They barely scratch out a living."

"Then they contribute little to my coffers or my granary?"

"It is so, Lord."

"And the other villages hereabouts are they in the same condition?"

"They are, Lord."

In that moment, Enulf took a providential decision that would not only change the fate of the local ceorls, but also of the destiny of the kingdom.

"Take me to a smithy! The nearest to the hall."

They rode back to Ledecestre where the unmistakable sounds of his former trade brought a smile to the face of the new ealdorman. The metallic clash of hammering, the wheeze of bellows and the pungent smoke of the forge took him back in time to a past life.

The smith, together with all his fellow townsfolk, knew of the arrival of the king's man and like them, knew nothing of his past. As he stopped his battering on a red-hot bar, he understood that a finely dressed stranger had entered the forge, by appearances, a nobleman with the build of a warrior.

"Master Herrig at your service, Lord. How can I be of use?"

"What are you working on, master?"

"Makin' a spade, Lord. Just beatin' yon bar out to fold it."

"Ay, to strengthen the steel."

The smith shot the visitor a shrewd glance. This stranger knew a thing or two about his craft.

"Have you ever made a ploughshare, Master Herrig?"

The blacksmith wiped a hairy forearm across his brow and shook his head.

"Can't say I have. No call for 'em hereabouts, 'fraid."

"Would you know how to make them if I ordered some?"

The smith sighed and shot a desperate glance toward the forge where a boy of four-and-ten winters worked the bellows. The stranger's eyes followed the smith's gaze and the latter, noticing said, "My lad. Wi' his help we get by. I have a daughter and wife to feed too, Lord. But it's not as if I run a *thriving* forge, like."

"Do you know who I am, master?"

"No idea, Lord. Beggin' your pardon."

"I am the Ealdorman of Ledecestre and Snotingham. Your lord, who has decided things must change in these parts."

The blacksmith, thunderstruck, bowed his head and in a

wheedling tone said, "Welcome to my poor workplace, Lord," and repeated, "how can I be of service?"

"If I send you detailed drawings, will you make me the ploughshares I need? The piled steel must be good and hard but not brittle, especially the coulters, understood?"

The smith, sweating, running his forearm across his brow yet again, looked troubled."

"What is it?"

"Forgive me, Lord, I'm a poor man, an' as you can see…" he swept a massive hand toward the depths of the forge, "…I don't have many bars. An' the iron's not the best quality. Nowt to be done, 'fraid."

"I see," Enulf frowned, his expression too fierce to reassure the smith. "I will bring you the drawings at noon tomorrow. We shall speak of this again. Good day to you, Master Herrig."

The smith touched his forelock but looked uncomfortable. He had never exchanged words with a lord before, and judging by this one's ferocious demeanour, he preferred it that way. On the morrow at midday, he would be forced to do it again. He spat on the ground and seizing a pair of tongs in his huge hand, carried the cooled bar back to the forge.

"What you gawpin' at lad? Get pumpin' them damned bellows!"

Late the next morning, Herrig nailed the spade he had finished to a haft, and when Enulf arrived, he found the smith wielding the tool as if he were a ceorl in a field.

"Let me see," the ealdorman held out his hand and took the implement. Turning it upside down, he knocked on the metal with a ringed finger. The sound of the spade pleased him. "You work well, Master Herrig."

"Thank you, Lord."

Suspicion filled the visage of the craftsman, but where was the harm in a compliment?

Enulf handed back the spade and pulled a rolled parchment from under his cloak.

"This design is one quarter of the real size. You must make them four times bigger, right?"

Enulf spread the parchment open as Herrig hurried to clear space on the workbench, snatching up tools and nails and tossing them aside. "This is the share, but you must make a sharp chisel to run along the bottom edge.

"The frame… holds the share and the coulter, like so," he ran a finger down over the inked lines, "…it's a knife for cutting through the soil and must be strong. The mouldboard has to be rounded, just so… ay, so it turns the earth, see?"

"It's clear, Lord, but there's still the problem of the iron."

"Who supplies your iron?"

"There's a bloomer who comes from the forest with his ox-cart every few months. It's a while since he passed by. He offers different qualities of bar…"

"Where can I find this fellow?"

"All I know, Lord, is what he told me. He works near Hwita's Farm in the forest under the outcrop of white rock. Three leagues to the north-west, he said, Lord, an' if you pass Bardon Hill on the right, you ought to get there, no bother."

"Right! Master Herrig, you study my drawing, and you'll see how you need to work and shape the form. Leave it to me, and with necessary the time, I shall supply the iron."

"An' how many will you be needing, Lord?"

"That will depend on how much iron I can find."

The smith scratched his lank hair and, relieved, bade his lord farewell. This commission did not seem beyond his capabilities. He hoped his master would find good quality iron, otherwise, the plough would be useless. Herrig sighed, he was a strong man, but the ealdorman intimidated him for a reason he could not determine. Putting his worries out of his mind, he decided to get on with the scythe the nunnery of Saint Editha had ordered three days before.

The forest trail, at last, brought Enulf and his men into a clearing. Glancing around, he found a dwelling and next to it, logs in a neat stack. In the middle of the glade, like some ancient dolmen, stood a slag pit furnace, four feet high and three across. The ealdorman dismounted and rapped on the door of the hut with the pommel of his hand-seax.

A muffled voice, the words incomprehensible, came from inside. A few seconds later, the door opened a crack and anxious, fear-filled eyes peered out at him.

"Be not afraid, friend," Enulf said, pushing the door back and hauling the bloomer out by his filthy ragged tunic, "I am here on business."

The man gaped at the finely dressed intruder and at his armed men and trembled.

"Herrig the blacksmith directed us here."

At the familiar name, the ceorl began to nod his head vigorously.

"I am in need of good quality iron bars. Can you supply them?"

"Depends."

"On what?" Enulf snapped.

"On how much you be needin' an' what quality an' all."

"Show me what you have."

"Lord, beggin' pardon. I ain't got none. Just finished my rounds." He waved a hand in a vague circle.

"Who supplies the ore?"

"I gets it from Lindissi. It's found in the limestone there. I deal with a fellow who has a clamp."

"A clamp?"

"Ay, a great wood pile covered with soil and turf. It serves to roast the ore, gets rid of moisture and the stuff that's no good. Then they break the ore down, like, into small pieces." He held his finger and thumb about two inches apart.

"Hark!" Enulf said, "I will need enough bars to cover the planks on the bottom of that cart," he pointed over to the ceorl's ox-cart.

"Lord, what a problem! I ain't got the money for that much iron."

"Problem solved!" Enulf took out a gold coin and held it in front of the fellow's gaping face. "There's one of these for you too when you deliver the bars to Herrig's forge. But mark my words, the quality must be the best or you'll lose a hand and never smelt again, clear?"

Once again, the vigorous nodding, followed by, "But…"

"What?"

"Lord, this is going to take time. There's the journey to Lindissi an' back, The roastin' once there and then the smeltin' here. Me an' my men will need time."

"Your men?"

"Ay, I use six men to take turns on the bellows. They must never stop blowin' or the work's ruined. First, we need to make the charcoal, he pointed to a blackened stack. We'll be needin' ten pounds of charcoal for every pound of iron, Lord."

"Well, so be it! I see you know what you're about… can you deliver to Herrig after three moons?"

"Ay, Lord, if the weather don't spoil."

Enulf whipped out his hand-seax and held the blade to the fellow's throat.

"Don't fail me, Master Bloomer, or it will be the worse for you! Please me and a gold piece awaits you at my hall in Ledecestre."

On his return to the town, Enulf stopped at the smithy. There, he gathered, Herrig was rowing with his wife for his having chastised their lad with too much zeal. The woman, with a round face and striking flashing hazel eyes, framed by her olive complexion, might have been thought attractive ten years before. Named Goda, she set about her husband with a broom. The spirited woman ceased her assault when the ealdorman entered the forge.

"My wife, Goda, Lord. Woman, fetch some ale for our master."

With a bob and a smile, the smith's wife turned away to disappear through a door in the back of the forge.

"Your directions were sound, Master Herrig. After three moons, the bloomer will bring you the bars for the ploughshares." He paused when the woman returned with a tray and profuse apologies for the weakness of the ale.

"We are simple folk, Lord, with simple pleasures. We cannot afford twice-brewed ale."

The ealdorman smiled, "Simple? Like beating your man with a broom?"

Goda flushed and hung her head.

"Goodwife, I'm sure he deserved his beating," the ealdorman laughed, "and as to the ale, it will slake my thirst most well." He took the offered cup and swallowed a long draught. "Serve me well, Master Herrig, and you will be drinking the best ale in Ledecestre. Now, did you look at my drawings?"

The smith nodded, and there followed an exchange satisfactory to both men. The smith's suspicion the ealdorman knew a great deal about his trade was proved beyond doubt, and Enulf's hope that the smith was capable of skilled work resulted well founded.

Taking his leave, Enulf called from the doorway, as an

afterthought, "Ah, when the bloomer arrives with the iron, come to the hall together. I wish to inspect the metal before you begin work."

The tradesman touched his forelock and bowed before shouting for his son in a menacing voice.

The ealdorman smiled as he mounted his horse. Now, there remained the matter of buying oxen. As he rode up the hill toward the hall, he mulled over great plans to make his lands the most prosperous in Mierce.

FOUR

Tame Weorth, 721 AD

The king of the West Seax, Ine, an old acquaintance of Æthelbald, had occupied the throne for thirty-three years. His powerful presence, allied to that of Wihtred of Kent, whose reign was of similar longevity, was a source of frustration for Æthelbald's ambitions for the south. A debt of gratitude had curbed the King of Mierce's aggressive impulses towards the West Seaxa on more than one occasion. Years before, when Æthelbald was a harried exile, Ine had lent his assistance against his tormentor and predecessor, King Coelred.

Standing before him now, a messenger from that southern land entreated his aid on behalf of the aetheling, Cynewulf, *against* King Ine. Sedition and rebellion! As he stared into the face of the message-bearer, an eager expression betrayed the wolf-like expectancy of a pack leader ready to pounce on a lame fawn. Many thoughts vied in the head of the king at that moment, principal among them a desire to gain time.

"We will give you our reply in the morning." Æthelbald watched the disappointment creep over the messenger's face like a cloud obscuring the sun. The king clapped his hands and commanded a servant to provide a room, a platter of meats and cheeses and a pitcher of wine for his guest.

"Come to me early in the morn," uttered in a dismissive tone, gave no inkling to the West Seaxa of the likely outcome of his mission. He would have to be patient.

We aren't ready to take on the might of the West Seaxa. But we cannot send begging such an opportunity.

This was the first of many meditations, culminating with: *I will not wait for something to happen. One could wait a lifetime and end up with nothing. I will make something happen*, before waving a hand to beckon a servant and issuing further orders.

So, soon afterwards, before him stood Mensige's brother. Æthelbald greeted him with a ferocious expression and was gratified to see the fellow could not meet his gaze.

"Leofwig, how are you settling in Tame Weorth?"

"Well enough, my king, I thank you."

But his bearing and eyes gainsaid him, and the ruler was swift to seize upon it.

"I sense that all is not as it seems, am I right?"

"Sire, I do not wish to appear ungrateful, as my king's kindness knows no bounds, but…"

"Speak freely, friend."

"Sire, my life has no purpose, and the days meld into dull uneventfulness."

"Ha!" cried the monarch, causing the erstwhile nobleman to start. "It is right I have called you to me. Leofwig, can you vouch for loyalty to your king?"

"Sire, does the sun not rise in the east? My faithfulness is just as sure."

"Good man! I knew I could count on you."

And if I can't, four horses will tear you limb from limb!

"What passes between us here must never reach the ears of anyone. To succeed, ambition must be cloaked. Do I make myself clear?"

The man from Ledecestre gulped and nodded, "Ay, my king."

"You are to travel to the court of King Ine in Wintancaestre in my name. I will give you a token to present to the king. Your *supposed*… task will be to advocate an alliance with our kingdom and his." As though he had not stressed the word enough, Æthelbald repeated, "*Supposed*', understand? You will propose my wedding to one of the West Seaxa of blood royal. I have no intention of taking a wife, but you must seem sincere."

"What then, will be my true purpose, Lord?"

"Rebellion is in the offing. The aetheling, Cynewulf, moves to overthrow his king. I charge you with a perilous mission. A word whispered here and there in the right ear: *'Æthelbald of Mierce can be a powerful friend and a deadly foe.'* But hark! Trust no man, else your life will be as safe as that of a suckling pig on the eve of a feast. Try to draw the mighty of that realm to the cause of Cynewulf. If you succeed in this, Leofwig, I shall find you a bride of noble birth here in Mierce and endow you with lands befitting such a wedding."

The gleam of greed and ambition in the Ledecestre man's eyes did not escape the king.

"Come here in the morning, ready to depart. You will have a companion as far as Wintancaestre. Do you have a strong horse? Good! I will send ten warriors with you to ensure your safety on the journey. Remember, naught of this to a living soul."

Æthelbald watched the figure retreat out of his hall.

If this works in my favour, the game changes!

Leofwig arrived in the hall before the king who, at last, appeared with a sealed document. Handing it over, he gave clear instructions. The paper must not fall into the wrong hands and should only be consigned to King Ine in person.

Soon, they were joined by the messenger of the West Seaxa. After formal pleasantries, Æthelbald came to the point.

"Friend, we shall aid your cause. This is Ealdorman Leofwig, who will travel with you to the West Seax. His presence there will be under the pretence of arranging a bride for me with Ine. Only you two shall know that this is a ruse to cover his real purpose. Tell Lord Cynewulf to make sure my man has the ear of waverers."

Æthelbald glowered at the two men before him and his words also were pronounced with a menacing tone, "Do either of you have questions or concerns?"

"Sire, how shall I inform you of my progress?" Leofwig found the courage to ask.

"Outside, your escort is waiting: warriors who can become ten messengers as needed. Now, go! Farewell, and may God smile on your mission."

* * *

The fresh green of the uppermost leaves in the woodlands began to turn to gold, yellow and russet when, at last, the leader of the escort rode back into Tame Weorth. Five months had passed without word from Leofwig.

The king stretched out a hand, "Give me the message!"

"Sire, Ealdorman Leofwig knows not how to write. Nor would he entrust the task to another."

Æthelbald frowned but murmured, "Wise. What then is your news?"

"Lord, the aetheling, Cynewulf, is dead."

"Dead! How can this be?"

"Struck down by Ine's own hand."

"Our plans are ruined?"

"Leofwig impressed upon me to say – and he sets great store by it – he has the confidence of Ine's queen, Æthelburh. It appears that husband and wife are at each other's throats."

I can turn this to my advantage.

"Leofwig serves us well. By Thunor, he has the right of it! Is there more?"

"Ay, my king, the ealdorman says that there is much unrest on the borders with Dumnonia."

"Is there, indeed?"

Æthelbald smiled, "Hard times for Ine. Hark! You are tired after a long journey." The king reached into his tunic and produced a purse. He shook out four silver coins and gave them to the warrior. "Take two days rest, then come to me again for instructions. This is a gift, for you have pleased us well."

Effusive thanks and bows, in general, meant nothing to Æthelbald, but on this occasion, his mood was so buoyant, he rewarded them with a gracious smile.

In the sleepless hours before the warrior presented himself to the king, the latter spent time pondering on West Seax, to be prepared for their meeting, soon after dawn.

"Leofwig must find the rebel aetheling Ealdbert. He has a strong claim to the throne and much support. Also, the followers of Cynewulf will seek to avenge his death. By finding a means of strengthening Ealdbert's position and playing off King Ine against Queen Æthelburh, West Seax will plunge into chaos." The king turned a glass in his hand before quaffing the cool water he had called for. The drink seemed to refresh his thinking too. He grinned and added, "Tell Leofwig to rouse the folk of Dumnonia against Ine and to destroy the fortress of Tantun. Without that bulwark, the way will be open into the heart of West Seax, enabling the Britons of Wealas to aid their cousins."

Satisfied with these instructions, Æthelbald sent the messenger on his way. If his plans bore fruit, he would have hewn out a road as direct and broad as the one with which Fate had hitherto obstructed his progress. In his mind, this thoroughfare would be rutted and pitted, but when had his journeying ever been smooth?

* * *

West Seax, three weeks later

Leofwig found Ealdbert a companionable young man, but if he were to succeed with his plans, he could not let himself befriend the aetheling. The message received from Æthelbald needed all his inventive skills. What he was asking was too much for the efforts of one person. However demanding the king could be, he was equally generous. This comforting thought spurred Leofwig's creativity as he waited for Ealdbert's reaction to a suggestion he had just made. The delay proved to be positive since it provided time for inspiration to goad his thinking. Why not combine all the elements of Æthelbald's request into one master plan? Ay, that was it!

The ealdorman smiled at the hesitant aetheling and said, "I see you do not like my suggestion and, in truth, after further consideration, I too can see its faults."

"What am I to do?" the young pretender sighed. "Ine is gathering men to him as we sit here in futile discussions."

"Futile? Nay, the best ideas are like a good ale, the product of fermentation! My thoughts go on apace. What about taking your warriors to the fortress of Tantun? I was there a while ago, and to my eye, it is nigh on unassailable. Think on this. That stout stronghold stands near the southern borders of Mierce. It is a small step for King Æthelbald to make to unite his forces with yours."

The aetheling stared at Leofwig with a troubled expression.

"Do you really think King Æthelbald will come to my aid? Why would he do that?"

"I have told you. The king is tired of King Ine thwarting progress in the south. He wishes for new blood. An energetic ally, with whom he can work in harmony. He has great hopes of you, Lord Ealdbert."

"I shall take my men to Tantun without delay. Will you come with us, friend Leofwig?"

"Not at once. I will join you as soon as I can. But first, I have tasks to complete in Wintancaestre to confound and weaken Ine."

Leofwig rose from his seat and held out a hand that the aetheling clasped with ardour. The Ealdorman of Grantebrycge bestowed his most charming smile upon the muscular figure, so different from his own.

Who knows, I might be dealing with the next king of the West Seaxa?

It was possible, but in his callous heart, he doubted such an outcome. Grasping this hand, he felt like Iscariot upon receiving his silver. If his plans matured to perfection, Ealdbert was disposable.

Within the week, he stood before Queen Æthelburh. The flowing gown, embroidered in gold thread, did not conceal the lithe muscularity of the lady. So, the tales that reached him of her prowess as a warrior might be true, after all. He had also heard tell of the shield-maidens of the far northern lands over the seas. The amber-flecked hazel eyes stared at him with disconcerting intensity. He must not let himself be distracted by her charms.

"My king urged me to lend any help that Mierce can provide to you and your husband, the king. Hence, I came with information of the plotting of the rebel Ealdbert as soon as it came into my possession."

"And we thank you, Ealdorman. What is it you have for us?"

"It is not a casual choice that Ealdbert is holed up in Tantun."

"I told Ine that fortress would bring trouble. It is too distant to control," she hissed.

"My informants tell me that Ealdbert is in contact with Dumnonia that seeks revenge for recent defeats," he lied without so much as a blink. "Emissaries have crossed the Saefern to enlist the aid of Gwent. It is but two steps from Gwent to Tantun. They are sure to come to assist their British cousins. I fear a trap like a vice." His voice was as smooth as honey.

The queen swallowed the untruth as a hungry carp takes a baited hook.

"Not if we move with all haste," she clapped her hands and a servant hurried to her side.

"Tell the workshops to distil as much resin of the pine as they can, by the morrow!"

A thrill coursed through Leofwig. If the queen had ordered turpentine, it meant she intended to burn Tantun to the ground. His plan, in that case, had worked beyond every possible imagining. King Æthelbald would be gladdened and that meant glory for Leofwig.

One week later, he stood in the shadow of the fortress of Tantun. Twelve years before, King Ine had overseen the construction of earthworks, now the ramparts above them. Queen Æthelburh studied the solid palisade looming above, built of tree trunks brought from the Selwood.

She turned to Leofwig, "What do you say, Ealdorman. How can it be breached?"

"Not the walls, my lady. It must be the gates."

The queen concurred. To his surprise, she ended the conversation before it had begun. Turning to a warrior beside her, "The gates, we must burn them down. Have the men drag wood, branches and straw up to them. Soak them in the liquid we brought and set them alight. Shields above their heads, mind." she added, but the warning was gratuitous.

The defenders hurled weapons, rocks and insults on the attackers but could not impede the assault. Within half an hour, the conflagration had begun. The turpentine ensured a raging blaze and although the solid wooden gates were slow to catch fire, they succumbed in the end. Ealdbert's force was no match for the might of the queen's army. The slaughter was merciless and Leofwig, not a warrior by nature, contented himself with defending his person by cowering behind a shield. He let the eddy of battle sweep him into backwaters where blows were not being exchanged. From his vantage point, he was able to admire the lady of the West Seax, whose ferocity matched that of her most warlike warriors. He watched her dispatch two foes with her flashing sword and noted how she inspired the men around her to redouble their striving.

Leofwig stayed in the fortress to observe the destruction of the palisade and the buildings within the walls. Choking black smoke filled the air for three days until there remained nothing standing of the stronghold. Queen Æthelburh, however, allowed her temper to show when she discovered that the body of Ealdbert was nowhere to be found. He had escaped her wrath through a small postern door and fled to safety in the forest to the south. She need not have worried, for although she could not know it, his wyrd would lead him to his death at the hands of her husband. This would take place in the lands of the Suth Seaxa, but this event was in the future.

As for Leofwig, he hoped to enter further into the good graces of the warrior queen. But his first task was to send his report to his own king.

* * *

Tame Weorth, 722 AD

The news when it came, was gratifying. It exceeded Æthelbald's fondest hopes. King Ine's attempt to take over Dumnonia had ended in defeat in three successive battles. The monarch's glee, at hearing this, reached new heights on learning of the destruction of the fortress at Tantun. This Leofwig was a miracle worker. Æthelbald smirked; not so much as a hint of a possible West Seaxa bride, to mar his day either.

For the first time in several days, Æthelbald's good humour dissipated through an association of thoughts. The lack of a spouse from West Seax made him reflect on female charms and their absence at this moment, thanks to interference from the church. His habit of warming his bed with a compliant serving girl had come to an ostentatious end.

But I cannot live like a hermit. By Thunor, I'm King of Mierce! I can have any wench I choose.

The king leapt to his feet, upsetting a drinking horn in front of him. A servant hurried to mop up the pool forming and threatening to spill over the edge of the table.

It's time to start the hunt. What sport! Noble wenches instead of wild boar.

FIVE

Tame Weorth, 723 AD

Æthelbald postponed his travel plans until the winter weather gave way to freshness and the firmer roads of spring. It meant he had time aplenty to agonise over which nunnery to "raid". In truth, this decision eluded him, partly because there was so wide a choice, also for fear of the consequences of his actions. It would not do to offend a nearby abbey. Proximity, for sure, meant added complications. In the end, he decided to leave the selection to what he called "Providence".

It came in the form of his scir-reeve, an ealdorman charged with surveying the royal income. This official's report, on the whole, was satisfactory, for he was a scrupulous man. His attention to detail, however, exposed a few important cases of remissness. One, in particular, attracted Æthelbald's notice for sundry reasons: that of Glevcaestre, a port on the River Saefern. The king, in the six years of his reign, had never visited the burh. It lay just within the confines of the kingdom. He knew that Mierce had taken it from Hwicca, and it boasted a castle, a royal residence. The town, the ealdorman informed him, was governed by a port-reeve, whose duties included the yearly payment of taxes to the monarch. These had been unforthcoming for the past three years: an unacceptable state of affairs. Glevcaestre was also home to a mixed abbey. Founded by King Æthelred more than a half-century before, its abbess previous to the current incumbent, Cyneburh, who died in 680, was now revered as a saint. Pilgrims, no doubt, swelled the coffers of the present mother superior, Eadburh. Providence, Æthelbald convinced himself, had provided him with the answer to his predicament. Not only would he scare the port-reeve out of his wits, he would also "raid" the Abbey of Glevcaestre.

The main road into Glevcaestre towards the east was carried across three branches of the Saefern and low-lying meadowland by a series of bridges and a causeway. The royal party, a formidable sight, with many retainers, oxen-drawn baggage carts, emblems and armed outriders, approached without haste. King Æthelbald gazed with approval at the walls, built of grey stone blocks, punctured by the gate. To reach it, they would have to cross the bridge over the eastern branch of the river. As soon as the first rider set his mount's hoof on it, he unslung a horn and blew a commanding blast. The long shrill note cut the breeze off the water; the stone walls, echoing, replied. Thus, the gatekeepers were warned not to impede royal progress into the burh. Through the gate, Æthelbald was surprised to see that they also enclosed agricultural land. Ceorls tilled the soil of narrow strips, as it would not be long before the season of sowing would be upon them.

A warrior addressed one of the gathering onlookers, curious to see the king, "Fellow, which way to the castle?"

The question, not a difficult one, provoked discussion and consternation. The reason became clear with the man's reply.

"The castle is straight down this road, but know you, it stands in ruin for longer than any man can recall."

"What? Then there is no royal palace?"

"Ay, but you must turn back, leave the town and head north to Kingsholm, less than a mile away. Will the king not visit the shrine of our saint now he is upon it?"

Having overheard the conversation, Æthelbald dismounted and, accompanied by two warriors, made for the tomb of Saint Cyneburh near the Roman ruins of the south gate. The tall king forced his frame through the low opening to the tomb. Remembrance of his old friend, Guthlac, whose shrine he had provided for, lay behind this improvised visit. How he wished their lives had not grown apart. Would Cyneburh bring him the good fortune Guthlac had? His luck seemed to be guttering, like an overused candle. He needed a new impetus for his aspirations to be fulfilled. Thus, he found himself kneeling beside a ragged-looking monk before the sarcophagus of the former abbess.

"Lord," said the brother, who recognised rank, although he knew not he knelt next to his king, "place your hand inside the tomb and withdraw some dust. It will bring countless blessings upon you."

Inside the tomb? Ugh! Countless blessings, well, well!

Overcoming his reluctance and disgust, Æthelbald slid his hand through the opening and recoiled when it touched cloth. The winding sheet? In haste, he withdrew his fingers.

"Make the sign of the cross on your brow," whispered the monk.

What's to be lost?

He obeyed, gripping the brother's shoulder and patting his back in farewell as he rose, keen to leave the dank, dim shrine as soon as he could. He hoped the sainted Cyneburh might make this experience worthwhile as he breathed deeply of the fresh riverside air.

Content to be back in the saddle, Æthelbald gave the command to set the royal procession on its way back out of the burh. Was it only a foolish fancy or did his brow feel different? A sensation of a third eye, fighting to give him greater insight and wisdom? He laughed aloud at himself for his foolish fancy and looked around in haste to see whether this strange effusion had been noted. It appeared not. The hooves of his horse clattered across the bridge, the noise bringing him back to more pressing concerns. Foremost among them, he must find this palace and settle into comfortable accommodation. Laughing aloud once more at the thought of having tried to dwell in an ancient ruin, he wondered in what state would be this edifice – he hoped somewhat better than the one they had avoided.

He need not have worried. Before him, stood a large wooden hall, where a well-dressed man ordered a cluster of servants into two lines of reception. The official strode over to the king's horse, welcoming him to Kingsholm and declaring himself the steward. Flustered, the official made profuse apologies for being unprepared for a royal visit.

That such a hall, complete with steward, existed, made up part of the vast body of information about his kingship unknown to Æthelbald. Still, he reasoned, it came as a pleasant surprise, for his comfort hereabouts was ensured.

The steward led him to the royal bedchamber, where his mouth twisted into a wry grin when he saw the size of the bed.

Shame, it could hold me and three maids!

Throwing off his cloak, he lay down, ordered a pitcher of ale and summoned the leader of his warriors. When he arrived, he delegated the setting up of an encampment and the organising of watchmen and guards. The steward would arrange their meals in the Great Hall. Recovered from his initial panic, the man was eager to please and revealed that the last King of Mierce to reside in the palace was Æthelred, when that king oversaw a campaign in Powys. At that time, he explained, his father was steward and himself, a stripling.

Æthelbald dismissed them and settled down to quaff ale and plan his next moves. For sure, they would be delayed until the morrow. Resting confirmed the weariness in his bones after the journey. Replete with beer and relaxed, he slipped into welcome sleep. He awoke with a clear mind and a certainty of what his strategy would be. Had tiredness clouded his thinking or, less likely, had Cyneburh endowed him with wisdom? Either way, he could now see beyond the morrow, along a path that would lead him to rule over all the Anglo-Saxon kingdoms. At this thought – a lifetime ambition – his fingers sought the ring of Osthryth, his former queen. Always carried on a chain around his neck, in material form, it symbolised his aspirations, and from it, he drew inspiration.

An excellent night's sleep, after a bounteous meal, left Æthelbald reinvigorated in the morning. On awakening, for a moment, he knew not where he was, but a glance around the room cleared his sleep-befuddled mind. Bounding from his bed, he pulled on his tunic and cursed when he did not find his belt but remembered he had hung it from a nail on the wall. As well he had found it, he reflected, he might need his sword later that morning.

Leaving his retainers in the encampment, Æthelbald rode with a score of warriors to the south-west, which brought them to the bridge crossing the central branch of the Saefern. They clattered over it, past a bevy of fishmongers shouting their offers. A little farther, their mounts carried them to the Roman quayside wall. Maybe because of the river, the western walls of the burh were missing, but this was the limit of the town. The steward, back at Kingsholm, had been clear that here they would find a small stone-built construction, which served as the offices of the port-reeve. The king's roving eyes soon located it some fifty yards farther down the river, and he noted the number of vessels moored up between him and the building. There was little doubt in his mind that Glevcaestre was a thriving port, hence the port fees must account for a sizeable sum.

"Sire," the port-reeve, a stocky man whose beard showed signs of greying, displayed the onset of terror, "I can explain…"

"Then do so, and make haste," Æthelbald barked, "for my patience wears thin."

"The last few years have been full of unforeseen problems. Three years ago, we needed to drain a stretch of the river to remove a sunken boat, sire, else goods could not arrive at the wharf. We used the occasion to repair the quay. I believe it had never been made good since the days of its construction. All this required money to pay the labourers…"

"Why was I not informed of this?"

"My king, I thought you had more pressing matters."

Æthelbald struck with the speed of a striking adder. He leapt forward with a thrust of his sword, whose point smashed straight into the teeth of the shocked port-reeve.

"Learn from this not to lie to and steal from your king."

Blood trickled from the sides of the man's mouth that he spat on the floor.

His protests came, unintelligible as he wiped his mouth with a sleeve.

"My scir-reeve will stay here as long as necessary to examine your dealings. If he finds you have stolen from me, you will face my wrath and punishment."

Æthelbald strode out of the port-reeve's office and remounted, his mind elsewhere, on the future.

They rode back into the burh through the east gate once more and the king dismissed his escort until an hour before sunset. He sought the Abbey of St Peter and found it confining the northern wall of the burh. The abbey was a mixed house, for both monks and nuns, and Æthelbald, on admittance, demanded to be taken to Abbess Eadburh. The lady was of royal descent, but as far as he knew, no relation. Instead, his excuse for this visit based itself upon another relationship. Æthelbald knew that the monastery housed a distant cousin, Winflaed, some ten years younger than he. Not that he mentioned his purpose, under the stern gaze of the abbess, until she had listed the requirements of her poor house, most of which pertained to royal coinage. Granting gifts for repairs and construction proved an agreeable way of softening the severity of this mother superior.

When he explained his wish to meet with Winflaed alone – a matter of the greatest impropriety – he found her sternness unbending until he hinted at retracting his generosity. The king could resist any number of pursed lips and shaken heads, he, who, resolute, had stood against howling, axe-wielding enemies, flushed with bloodlust.

Hence, the irreprehensible Eadburh conducted him to Winflaed's cell, where the young nun knelt alone in prayer.

"You have a special visitor, my child. Greet your king! Since it is our God-appointed ruler, the rules of the abbey are waived on this occasion. *However*," she lingered on the word, "I ought not need to remind you, God sees and judges our every action." With this admonishment uttered in her severest tones, she turned with a swirl of her gown, shutting the door behind her.

To Æthelbald's surprise, Winflaed overcame her obvious amazement at a visit from the king and giggled in a most unreligious manner then imitated the harsh voice, "...*judges our every action*." The king could not help but unite his chortle to the nun's giggling.

With a complicit grin, Æthelbald shrugged off his cloak and bundled it on the nun's mattress.

"We are cousins, did you know that?"

Winflaed shook her head, and her expression told him she was surprised.

"Ay, albeit distant, on your mother's side. I knew her when she was young. She was beautiful, like you."

Her eyes brimmed with tears, "What's the use of a pretty face in a place like this?"

The bitterness in her voice made him think. "Hush, do not weep." Æthelbald strode across to her and stroked her cheek with a gentle hand and stared into her green eyes, two deep liquid pools that gazed back into his own grey-blue.

By Thunor, she is a pretty maid right enough.

The curvaceous softness of her excited him, compelling him to risk one kiss. At the least, he would discover how she reacted. His lips sought hers but no resistance came, instead there was a fierce, hungry response. Æthelbald ran his hand down the hollow of her back and felt a quiver of delight in her body. She stroked his cheek and tangled her fingers in his shaggy beard.

"We ought to leave, to free you of this abbey," Æthelbald said, doubtful of his own powers of resistance to her charms.

"They will never let me out of here," Winflaed moaned.

"You forget, my dear, you have the King of Mierce by your side. Now, come! Is there ought you need to bring?"

All of a sudden, her countenance cleared of gloom and became cloudless as the sky in the radiance of the rising sun.

"We are allowed no possessions in this horrid place." Her voice retained the previous mood.

"Then wrap my cloak around you, it's cold by the river."

An attempt was made at the abbey gate to prevent Winflaed from absconding. The fierce expression on the king's countenance and a brief dalliance with his sword hilt proved enough to see them out. Æthelbald led the way to his horse and lifted Winflaed into the saddle, surprised at her lightness. He heaved himself up behind her and once more wrapped an arm around her tiny waist. His other hand gathered the reins, and they were away. Sunset was a long way off, but the king did not wish to ride forth unescorted. It was easy enough to imagine what a warrior does with a free day, so he began a tour of the town's taverns. Before too long, he found a group of his men sitting around an outdoor table, heedless of the cool air their king was suffering through the lack of a cloak. Commanded to make haste, they gulped down their ale and hurried away to fetch their horses. Soon afterwards, the remainder of the escort rode up to join with the others, and the party set off for the royal palace. The king allowed himself a secret smile.

Soon be there, and we'll try out that big empty bed!

At the thought, Æthelbald tightened his embrace around the nun's waist. The pleasure and sense of security the strength of the muscular arm provided made her wriggle back in the saddle to press closer.

Inside his bedchamber, rich with wall hangings and luxurious in colourful paintwork, Æthelbald, removed the cloak from the maid and hung it where his belt had been in the morning.

"Thank you," she sighed.

"I hope you are not cold," the king murmured with a wicked smile.

"I think you will find me warm enough, Lord," she teased, but her flirtatious smile gave way to a look of despair.

"What is it?"

"Is it not a sin to be here alone?"

"More a sin to keep a lovely creature locked away against her will."

"Indeed, I never wanted to enter the abbey… my father—"

Her eyes filled with tears once again.

"Hush!" He placed a finger to her lips and was pleased when they puckered into a kiss. "Forget it! It is all in the past. You are here with me now."

I wish it were so simple! There are bound to be consequences. Pah!

The king stroked the maid's hair, cut short in the fashion of nuns, but of a delightful golden colour. His hand, slow and deliberate passed down her neck to her shoulder and round to her chest. Thence, it slipped down to her breast, which he cupped, at the same time, spurred on by her tremble, he closed in to press his lips against her. Again, with deliberation, he helped her undress and soon they were lying together under the heavy covers, naked and sated.

She nestled contentedly under his loving hands.

By Thunor, she's a virgin!

He would have gloated, but his sentiments were mixed. This, he appreciated, was a huge commitment for Winflaed. The last time he had deflowered a maid had ended in tragedy. His mind turned back many years to the beautiful, tragic Faryn, to friendship impaired with Guthlac and Coelwald, and filled with nostalgia, he frowned and sighed.

"My lord, my love, have I displeased you?" Again the eyes brimmed with tears.

"Why no, of course not, i-it's – *er* – that I knew not you had never lain with a man."

"Did it please you?"

He reached to pull her closer, "Wondrously so."

"God will *not* forgive us," she said, and the tears flowed down her cheeks.

"But He is the God of Love, is he not? What harm can there be in gentle loving?"

"B-but I am a bride of Christ."

"He has enough brides, one more, one less…"

"How can you speak so?"

"Because I am God's anointed, and nothing so sweet can be wrong. Be at peace, my treasure."

She snuggled closer to him and he kissed her brow, her wet cheeks, her throat, and his lips closed around a nipple.

"You will not send me back to the abbey?" Her words came as a pleading whine giving way to a groan of pleasure.

"Never! On my oath. Your future lies elsewhere."

But he would not speak of it for the moment, he had more imminent matters on his mind as his hand wandered up the silky smoothness of her inner thigh. He decided not to move Winflaed into the royal palace at Tame Weorth, since that would set countless tongues wagging. Instead, he would take her to Leofwig's house, after all, he had no use of it while he was in West Seax. There, exercising discretion, he could call on her whenever he liked.

"Lord," she sighed as she moved with voluptuous ease under him, "what troubles you?"

"Naught. I was thinking you must buy clothes in Tame Weorth, and I was making other arrangements for your well-being."

"My king is gentle and loving," she kissed him.

* * *

Tame Weorth, a week later

The king received the most unexpected and agreeable visit on his return to Tame Weorth. The tall figure of the Ealdorman of Snotingham and Ledecestre knelt before him, a long bundle wrapped in cloth balanced on both arms. Three years had passed since the promise of a sword fit for a king. In truth, Æthelbald had thought no more about it.

"Forgive me, sire, it has been a long time in the making, for I had much to learn from the Frankish masters. I pray that it meets your approval." So saying, still on his knees, Enulf whipped away the cloth concealing the weapon. There it lay, with its smooth tapered blade, ending in a rounded tip. Its shallow fuller caught the light, enhancing elaborate bands of pattern welding within the central portion. Enulf had exceeded his expectations.

"Enulf, it is a magnificent sword! Worthy of a king! Now stand and let me wield it."

The erstwhile smith stood, beaming, took the blade between huge finger and thumb and handed the weapon, hilt first, to his lord.

Æthelbald grunted his approval at the perfect balance of the sword.

"It's a wonder!" he said. "But the greatest marvel is how my father found a smith of such worth on his estates in the first place."

"Lord, it is still not fit for a king."

"What are you saying?"

"It is unfinished, sire. I am a poor smith, not a worker of jewels… the hilt… see, the pommel is simple steel. A king must have gold with jewels. I know not one who might put the finishing touches…"

"I will find him! Your work is done and done well. What of the Lady Saeflaed?"

"Well, sire, I thank you. She has borne me a fine son. We called him Alweo, after your father, my old lord."

"Did you so? Faithful Enulf! You have my deepest love."

* * *

In high fine humour, Æthelbald strode later in the day, head well covered, to the building where he had installed his mistress.

"How do you like your new home, Winflaed?"

"Sire, I like it well, but it is full of men's belongings."

"I told you, it is a friend's dwelling, but you can make it a home to your taste. He will not be coming back to Tame Weorth… anytime soon."

Winflaed blinked her long eyelashes and bestowed on her king a pretty smile, "Did you come only to ask about my comfort, Lord?" She half-turned, drawing her gown tighter to reveal the beauty of her curves.

The ruler of Mierce needed no further invitation, in two strides, he had her in his arms, guiding her into the bedchamber. Their lovemaking was more relaxed, familiar and exciting. But when they lay in quietude afterward, Winflaed breathed, "How can we make amends before God?"

"What do you mean?"

"It is a grave sin. We are fornicating in the eyes of the Lord."

"So, what is to be done?"

"Do you love me, my king?"

"Of course."

"You do not sound so sure…"

"It is that I have known you but ten days. Is it not hasty to speak of love?"

"The church will hold that to set this to rights, we must wed."

"Winflaed! Winflaed! I cannot take a queen on a whim."

"A whim, is that all I am to you?"

"Enough, woman! Be content I have freed you from the life you so hated. Or do you wish to return to the abbey?"

She gasped and put a leg over his, clinging to the sturdy body she loved so well.

"Never! I will not return to a monastery as long as I live. But I wish… I wish…"

"Hush!"

Æthelbald rose and dressed, "Have you ale? I have a mighty thirst."

"There is wine and mead, Lord, but no beer. Did your friend not drink it?"

"Wine would be good." He studied her pert breasts and slender waist as she slipped into her dress. A beautiful creature, but wed her?

In a moment of silent appreciation of Leofwig's wine, conscious of the piercing green eyes never leaving his face, he reflected once more:

What makes men want sons? Is it not they hope they will achieve the things they were not strong enough to attain themselves? Nay, to wed would be to invite the turmoil within my kingdom that I wish to create outside its borders.

SIX

Ledecestre, 720 AD

The ox-cart creaked and groaned under the weight of the iron bars up to the doorway of the smithy. Three days remained till the third full moon since the bloomer took on the commission.

"Mornin' to you, Master Herrig!" he called into the forge.

Out came the blacksmith with the usual cheerful smile he reserved for his supplier.

"You got it then, Master Bloomer?"

"I have, ay. An' you'll not find better bars in the whole of Mierce! Now give me a hand to unload."

"Can't do that, my friend. Not yet, leastways. Bring the cart round the back of the forge. Lord Enulf wants us both up at the hall first."

The bloomer's eyes lit up. The gold coin had made his task easy. In Lindissi, the cooperation and attention to detail were such as he'd never had at the clamp before. Back in his forest clearing, his companions had toiled without complaint for the little extra pay he had given them. The result was here for all to see – the finest quality iron bars.

Enulf, delighted his deadline had been met, hastened to the smithy with the metal workers in tow. Reaching into the cart, he heaved out an iron bar and to the surprise of both men, scraped its end against the stone wall of the smithy. That done, he examined the mark on the wall, grunted, replaced the bar on the cart, dug into his purse and pulled out a gold coin.

"You have done well, my friend." He handed the coin to the bloomer, "You have pleased me."

Every coin has two sides, reflected the forest dweller. *Glad I'm on your good side. Wouldn't like to be on the wrong side of you!*

The tone of his lord's next words confirmed his astute assessment.

"Well, you pair of idlebacks, what are you waiting for? Get on with unloading the iron! I want work started on the first ploughshare this morning, not tonight!"

The oxen plodded off with the empty cart and Enulf turned to the smith.

"Now, remember, when a sixteen-inch share is finished, the point, from the joint of the share to the extreme end of the point, should be twelve inches, not longer. The point acts as a lever on the plough, and if it is too long, the plough will not work well, and it is liable to break. Understood?"

Herrig scowled at the floor. Who was this lord to tell him his own trade as if he knew it better than he did? Still, better keep him contented. He had seen the gold coin, but he had also seen his irascibility.

"I want the first ploughshare ready for my inspection in a fortnight, is that clear? Here, take this…" he shook out a number of small silver coins, "…to be going on with, for your labours. There's a gold coin for you too when all the shares are finished."

The smith's huge hand closed over the coins with mixed feelings. He was not work-shy, but *two* weeks meant long twelve-hour days in the forge. He strode to the door for a breath of air but also to ensure Lord Enulf was out of earshot.

"Goda! Where are you, woman?"

He found her preparing vegetables in the kitchen. With a swagger, he handed over the money Enulf had given him.

"Damn his eyes!" he swore, "He tried to tell me how to do my job. What does a fine lord know about forging metal?"

"What do you care what he knows and what he don't? So long as he pays you…" Goda ran a tender hand over her husband's bulging arm muscles. "I'm off to the butcher's. We can buy *meat* with this. I'll make a stew."

"When I've done, he said he'd give me a gold coin, Goda. I seen him give one to Master Bloomer. A *gold* coin! what do you say to that?"

"Bless the day Lord Enulf came to Ledecestre. At last, someone appreciates your skill."

"Well, I hope you're right. Now, where's yon layabout! I need him to pump the bellows and fetch an' carry for me. I only got one pair of hands."

"Cwen!" Goda called, and a pretty, slight girl in a grubby shift came into the kitchen.

"Cwen, is your brother up yet? Be a good girl and rouse him. Tell him father needs him in the forge straightaway!"

"I will, ma, but won't Edwy need to break his fast, first?"

"More likely I'll break his nose if he don't get into yon forge damned fast!" Herrig still managed a sweet smile for the joy of his life. "Off with you, pet! Shake him out of bed!"

In spite of his father's castigation, Edwy lent a willing hand in the smithy. Catching his parent's mood of serious intent, he set about pumping the bellows with vigour and soon the forge reached welding temperature. The smithy rang to Herrig's zealous blows as he welded and refolded the metal into piled steel. He quenched the plate he created and reheated it but this time, over a gentle flame to temper it. Satisfied, he began to shape the plate into a share by beating around the horn of his anvil. The care he took to follow Enulf's design, although he did not wish to admit as much to himself, was born of double fear. The first, fear of angering his irritable lord; the second, fear of losing the gold coin.

Goda's meat stew, a rare treat, fired his determination not to lose the chance of a better life. By hard work and application, already on the first day, the basic share was finished. Over the next ten days, the chisel was ready, ground to a dangerous, sharp edge and fitted to the share. The coulter followed, a lethal weapon if put to incorrect use. The frame, which he had assumed to be the easiest part, cost him a day. He needed to start over, because the distance between coulter and share point was too large. How had he misjudged the angle of the frame bend? How glad he was, in spite of his string of oaths, that Lord Enulf had not witnessed his error. The next day, he got it right. The ploughshare was finished with three days to spare. Proud of his efforts, he hurried to the hall but was turned away until the afternoon because the lord was away "on business".

As it turned out, by surprise, it was Enulf who came to him in the afternoon. Informed of the smith's visit to the hall, he imagined either the work was finished or Herrig had hit a problem. The ealdorman's curiosity brought him in haste to the smithy.

Relieved the better of the two possibilities proved to be the case, Enulf inspected the ploughshare with expert eye and a series of grunts of appreciation. Herrig stood, twisting a rag in his enormous hands. To be honest, Enulf admitted to himself, for he did not wish to reveal his former life, he could not have done a better job. To the smith's surprise and delight, the ealdorman in one swift stride reached him and patted him heartily on the back.

"A fine piece of work, Master Herrig! My trust is well placed."

"Thank you, Lord."

"Well, keep up the good work! When you finish the bars, I will keep my promise," he smiled and clasped the huge grimy hand in his own powerful grip. "I will send men to collect the share so it can be fitted to a plough."

Leaving the smithy at a brisk pace, the ealdorman smiled and considered the progress of his scheme with satisfaction. This fertile part of the kingdom would repay his efforts with superb harvests. It was too late this year to reap his rewards… but next… For the present, the oxen were bought and grazing, the carpenter ready to fit the ploughshares…

A swallow winged towards him along the street, an inch above the ground. Straight toward him it flew, like an arrow, swooping upwards at the last second to avoid impact. The ealdorman shrank away involuntarily, then laughed at his lack of faith in the bird's aerial ability. His exuberant enjoyment of life touched new heights.

Three weeks had gone by and Herrig had finished two more ploughshares when his cousin, Heremod strolled into the smithy, whistling a merry tune.

"Lovely day, kinsman!"

"Heremod! it's an age since I last clapped eyes on you. What brings you here?"

"Truth be told, I need you to grind this hoe. Either it's getting too old to till the earth or *I* am!"

"Give it here, cousin." The smith inspected the adze head, appeared as by magic from his kinsman's tunic. He grunted in disapprobation. The cutting edge, pitted and blunt made the implement fit only for smashing clods.

"Hey! what's this?" Heremod gaped in awe at a ploughshare lying on a workbench. "I could use one of these!"

"You couldn't afford one, any case, you ain't got an ox."

"I know! I know! But my neighbour has a brute of a horse. If we got together we could work both our fields with one of them."

"Forget it cousin! You can't afford one of these. Best quality iron that is! Paid for by Lord Enulf."

"How much would one cost?"

"More than you two are worth – the pair of you together! Forget it!"

Disconsolate, Heremod stared at the adze head in his cousin's hand.

"Oh ay, there's this!" The smith walked over to a grindstone and began to work the treadle, setting the stone spinning. In a matter of moments, a shower of sparks from the iron fell to the floor. A few minutes later, the grim-faced blacksmith took a file and passed it over the cutting edge of the tool. When he had finished, he looked up and said, "I suppose you'll be wanting me to nail it to a new haft?"

"Can you do that, for me?"

"Of course."

"I can't pay you, mind. Else I won't have the coin for the ribbon our Osythe asked me to get from the market."

"How is she?"

"As well as can be expected in her state."

"What do you mean?"

"Did you not know? Osythe carries our child."

The blacksmith strode over to his cousin and drew him into a bear-like embrace.

"Go steady, Herrig! I only got one set o' ribs you know!"

"When's it due?"

"If she counted right, ought to be around Michaelmas."

"End of September, then?"

"Ay."

"Come on through, then. We have to tell Goda the news. An' drink a beaker or two to the mother's good health and safe delivery of the babe. Come on, what you waitin' for?"

As Goda gushed over her kinsman and pressed him for news of Osythe, an idea began to nag at Herrig with insistence. He felt sorry for his cousin, scratching a living from the unrelenting earth by the strength of his muscles alone. Now, with a family in the making, life would be even harder. How would Lord Enulf know how many ploughshares could be made from that quantity of iron bars? It would need an experienced eye beyond the competence of a nobleman. Ay, he would give one of them to Heremod so he and his neighbour could come to an agreement.

He was eager to make his decision known to his cousin but he dared not moot it in front of Goda. She would never consent to thievery – for that was what it was.

Back in the forge, he drew Heremod close to him and whispered his idea. It had to be done in the evening so that his cousin could smuggle the ploughshare away under the cover of darkness. There followed a heated discussion since Heremod was an honest man and feared the lord's reprisal. But Herrig's persuasive reassurances wore down his resistance.

Two nights later, Heremod arrived at the forge with another man and a horse and cart. As twilight turned to night, they loaded the ploughshare onto the cart and covered it with empty sacks. A shiver ran up and down the blacksmith's spine as the patient horse clopped down the hill out of town. Yet, he was quite sure no one had seen them.

"Who was that?" Goda appeared in the forge.

"Oh, just a horse needed shoeing," he smiled. "Five minutes and I'll be through. Just need to get things in order in here."

"Supper's ready," she shot him a loving glance. "Don't tarry!"

* * *

The anticipation of gold put a spring in Herrig's step as he strode up to Lord Enulf's Hall. The ploughshares were ready for inspection. Admitted into the great man's presence, the blacksmith's keenness to conclude his business was rewarded by the ealdorman's willingness to come at once to the smithy.

No sooner were they inside than the nobleman began to inspect the ploughshares. His pleasure at the craftsmanship became evident in his exclamations and comments. But, like a summer squall, all of a sudden, his mood changed.

"How many bars remain unused?" he said, his tone threatening.

"Just these, Lord." Herrig pointed to four bars lying on a side bench.

"Four, mmm." The ealdorman walked along the ploughshares lined up in a row and started to count them. Herrig began to sweat.

"So what have you done with the other ten bars?"

"Lord? I don't understand."

"Do not take me for a fool, Master Smith. There ought to be another ploughshare here or at least another ten bars!"

"Lord, I swear—"

"Enough! Either tell me what you have done with my iron or I will slit you like a suckling pig!"

The ealdorman drew his sword, "I'm no clot. So speak!"

At this point, Herrig made a mistake. He seized his long-handled hammer and raised it above his shoulder.

"I used all the bars and made this number of ploughshares."

"Liar!" the ealdorman shouted.

Incensed by the villain's effrontery and by his daring to raise a weapon against his lord, Enulf lunged forward as if in battle. The smith dodged the blow and swung his hammer, parried with skilful disdain.

"Out with the truth, idiot!" Enulf bellowed.

The blacksmith wheeled the heavy hammer with murderous intent, but before he could strike, a scream came from the door behind him. Goda, brought by the commotion to the scene, screeched, "Stop it! The pair of you! Have you taken leave of your senses? Herrig, put that hammer down!"

The good sense of the woman did not prevail. For reasons known only in Herrig's head, he delivered a mighty blow aimed at the ealdorman's face. With the agility of a trained warrior, Enulf skipped aside and brought his sword down across the neck of the smith. The strike proved fatal as blood gushed and pumped onto the smithy floor.

"*No!*" Goda wailed and hurried to kneel beside her dying husband. She turned her tear-streaked face up toward the ealdorman who stood, aghast at this turn of events.

"Why? Why did you do this?" the woman sobbed.

"I will not be cheated and attacked by a ceorl!"

"Cheated?"

"Ay, he stole my iron."

"But the ploughshares?"

She pointed a trembling finger at the row of implements.

"One short, at least."

The ealdorman sheathed his sword. He drew out his purse, never taking his eyes off the poor trembling woman.

"Here, I mean to keep my word. I promised a gold coin for the work, and here is another to help with the funeral."

He tossed two bright coins to the ground in front of her.

"Do you have family, you can go to, woman? I want this forge empty for a new smith as soon as possible."

"*Ha!*" she spat. "So not only do you slay my man, you turn me and my children out of my home too? She rose to her feet, "I curse the day you came to Ledecestre, Lord Enulf! You have not heard the end of this."

"If you know what's good for you, woman, you'll be gone from here as quickly as possible. Do not make matters worse than they already are."

Without a backwards glance, he left the smithy and headed for the hall in a much different mood from when he had come down to the forge. What had promised to be a marvellous day for him had turned sour. It remained a day of momentous importance, but Enulf could not possibly know this.

SEVEN

Tame Weorth, 725 AD

The still melancholy of autumn wrapped summer in a shroud before shedding it to the iron earth of winter and so on – ever on – year after year. Futile the labourer's lot to eke a dignified living from the grudging soil. Worse, the pain of childbirth and loss of infants for the half-starved womenfolk. To the poor and oppressed, the attractions offered by the monasteries appeared irresistible. But also the nobles, including kings and queens, induced by the numerous privileges of the monastic orders flocked to take the vows. The nuns wove and made clothes, worked the splendid vestments of the priests and bishops for mass and magnificent tapestries that adorned the churches. In the case of King Æthelbald, the passing seasons increased his boredom to intolerable levels. In Mierce, his rule was absolute and smooth, but beyond the boundaries of his kingdom, his aspirations were, for the moment, thwarted, leaving him frustrated.

In April, the death of King Wihtred of Kent brightened Æthelbald's mood. One of the twin pillars of resistance to his ambitions in the south was thus removed. His world-weariness diminished further at the news that Kent was divided between Wihtred's sons, Æthelberht, Eadberht and Aelfric, and their followers ruled jointly: a circumstance Æthelbald could exploit. Nothing easier than to play them one against the other.

This distraction was what he needed, for his everyday duties, tedious to him now, increased his listlessness. Sure he could turn the situation in Kent to advantage, he shrugged off his gloom. Elsewhere in his life, the excitement he experienced at the beginning of his relationship with Winflaed had settled into mundane routine.

"My king, if only we could lead our lives together in the open."

Æthelbald glared at her, this was typical of the hinting and nagging that were souring his feelings for her.

"Winflaed! You know that is not possible. How many times need we have this conversation?"

"I feel sure the church will fall in line if you insist."

"What I insist on is your ending this foolish pretence. I shall leave you now, as important and urgent matters require my attention."

The king did not deign her with his usual farewell kiss but strode out, slamming the door, determined to end this relationship, but to his gain.

The decision could not have been more timely, as he discovered back at his palace. Waiting for him, in a truculent mood, was Bishop Haedde.

"Sire," he barked the word like an angry mastiff, "I have been apprised by Abbess Eadburh you abused her hospitality by absconding with a young nun in her care. This is a grave accusation. One, I should add, that if true, will bar you from inheriting the Kingdom of God."

The king gave the bishop a look fit to make even an enraged hound cower.

"*If true*, you say well. I did no more than aid a poor kinswoman to cast off the shackles of a life to which she was not suited as, weeping, she confided to me."

"Then, you did not seduce and lie with her?"

A dangerous light blazed in the king's eye, causing the bishop to quail until his spiritual strength gained the upper hand, and he stared unflinchingly into the fearsome countenance.

"The maid confessed she was a virgin," the king steered close to the truth, "and as far as I know, she still is," he lied.

"Well, that is a blessing," Haedde said. "And they tell me you no longer sin with serving maids."

"Whoever *they* are, they speak true, though I know not what business it is of theirs."

"Sire, your glory and renown is the concern of all your subjects. Chaste abstinence adds lustre to your reputation."

"Well, priest, does not your own love of God mean you have more pressing matters to attend to? Be off, follow your calling!"

"One last thing…"

"What!" snapped Æthelbald.

"The nun, what became of her?"

"We parted here in Tame Weorth, and I have received no news of her in two years."

The lie came so smooth and without hesitation that the bishop believed it.

Haedde murmured to the effect he could now quieten the troublesome abbess, and with effusive apologies, left the king to reflect on the perils of keeping Winflaed in Tame Weorth. He began to ponder on being rid of her in a way that would benefit both of them.

But first, he reflected on his own situation. When he was young, his father had pointed out the black tufts on the ears of a lynx.

"Them tufts tell you it's a lynx, boy. It's how you know it's not just any common wildcat. It changes the colour of its coat in the winter, but it doesn't change its nature – yon's one of the deadliest killers in the woodlands."

The church wanted him, Æthelbald, to change his nature, but he too was a predator, and he neither would nor could change to suit priests. What he could do, he smirked, was to deceive them through lies and trickery, in the guise of generosity.

The first thing to do was set his scheme for Winflaed in motion, the first step being to recall Leofwig from West Seax. A fortnight later, Æthelbald welcomed the returning emissary in his palace at Tame Weorth with unaccustomed warmth. After heartfelt thanks, the king outlined his plan to the nobleman. But, before he could proceed, he called for a document to be brought. Unrolling the parchment, Æthelbald stabbed a finger and let it rest on a name – Grantebrycge. "This town has of late lost its ealdorman, Saelred, an old foe of mine. He met a most unlucky end," the king feigned a sorrowful expression, without success. "A dispute with Britons over a land claim led to bloodshed, but I resolved the matter by paying the wergild on behalf of my friend Ealdorman Flynn."

Leofwig, at this point, shrewd as ever, wondered whether the king's involvement in the death of this Saelred had really come only after the event, as he seemed to imply. Æthelbald cut across these musings by adding, "Flynn will make a stout neighbour and worthy friend to the new ealdorman," he grinned into the face of Leofwig – you!"

"Me Lord?"

"Ay, I need a loyal servant to hold the lands bordering on Est Anglia. Who better? You have proved your worth to me in the south. I honour my debts. This is the first half of my promise to you, the second will be eased by the first. Lowering his voice and handing the charter to Leofwig, he proceeded to outline the rest of his plan. The ealdorman expressed his willingness but mooted timid doubts.

"Walk in as if you own the place, which you do, and it will all come about as I foresee."

So, Leofwig walked straight into his home. Winflaed, preparing food in the kitchen, on hearing the intrusion, seized a long-bladed knife and, brandishing it, moved into the next room where she came face to face with Leofwig.

"Do not be scared, lady, I mean you harm."

"What are you doing uninvited in my house?"

"*My* house, fair maid. My name is Leofwig, Ealdorman of Grantebrycge." This, he said with a pompous tone, hoping to impress the woman with his new title.

"The owner of this house is in West Seax. I have this on sound authority," she said, on the defensive.

"*Was* there, lady. I travelled here these last two weeks. And who, may I be so bold, are you?"

"My name is Winflaed, a cousin of the king, who installed me here as I had no dwelling in Tame Weorth. I trust you will find your home well used... but oh, what is to become of me now?" Her eyes filled with tears.

Leofwig seized the chance to be munificent, so continued, "Why, what ought to become of you, lady?" He gave her his most charming smile, which Winflaed liked. She studied the man before her: not a warrior with the strong build of the king, she considered, but good-looking in a roguish sort of way. "The place is big enough for the two of us until I finish my business in Tame Weorth."

This recaptured all her attention, but on seeing her worried expression, he hastened to add, "I can use the spare bedroom if it is still a bedchamber."

"It is," she nodded, wondering if she could trust him. She had little or no knowledge of men, her father, a younger brother and Æthelbald the extent of it. She liked the householder's face and his manners, but whence might she draw reassurance?

As if he could read her thoughts, he said, "Fear not, Lady," drawing a cross from under the neck of his tunic. "I swear on the cross that no harm will come to you while I am here. I assure you of my respect."

Had Winflaed been able to penetrate his thoughts or been privy to the king's scheme, she would not have said, "Sir, the arrangement is more than kind on your part. I was preparing lunch, you must be hungry after your journey. It is but an eel stew, if it suits."

"Most considerate. On the road, decent food is hard to find."

Eating together, her confidence in him grew since he discounted the king's advice to seduce the woman, preferring to converse in a natural manner as if to a friend. Indeed, she now began to consider herself such. To undermine this progress, Æthelbald appeared over the threshold and at once stated his purpose.

"My dear Winflaed, do you not find Lord Leofwig the perfect match for you?"

He looked in amazement from one to the other at the clear distress his words had provoked.

The nobleman was the first to recover, "Sire, I think this delicate matter is best left to run its course."

Winflaed, instead, faced the dawning realisation the king was behind a plot to foist her on another.

"Leofwig, what *you* think is of little interest to your king. What I wish is that you wed this woman as soon as the formalities can be arranged—"

"Has the lady no choice in the matter?"

"None whatever," growled the monarch. "Winflaed, can you not see the benefits of wedding the Ealdorman of Grantebrycge? Or maybe you'd prefer us to send you to an abbey? There you could devote your soul to the Lord."

Mustering what courage she could, Winflaed glared at her king.

"This, then, is the choice you set before me?"

"Ay."

"Then I shall marry the ealdorman."

Leofwig gasped and started forward, "Are you sure this is what you want, my lady?"

"I will not become a nun," she said and noted the dismay in the nobleman's face. "Besides," she added in haste, "I am growing to like you, Ealdorman."

"I would not take you for wife against your will."

"I *would*!" the king snarled.

"Sire, what about my family?" Winflaed looked worried.

"What about them? It's better to organise a quick and simple wedding. No questions, no objections."

The king's meaning was clear to her, and she nodded. It would not do for their guilty secret to come out at this stage.

"Good, then I shall give away the bride," King Æthelbald said, "I'll find a priest and attend to the church and its needs."

"I'll find a seamstress for my wedding gown," Winflaed said, her enthusiasm kindled.

"When all the arrangements are in place, I will come here again," Æthelbald said. Winflaed did not miss the relief in his voice and glared at him again. It was wasted on him, more concerned as he was to hurry away to start proceedings.

When the door shut behind him, Leofwig turned to face Winflaed, "Why do I have the feeling that we are being used?"

This was dangerous ground and she wanted to steer him away from it.

"The king has my well-being at heart. I told you, Leofwig, knowing my distress at being forced into a nunnery by my father, he settled me here in your house. Now, he is determined, as a good cousin, to see me wed as befitting my station. His manner is somewhat rough, but he means well."

"You may be right, my lady, but will you be happy?"

Winflaed gazed at her betrothed and realised with this kind man, she would be. The least she could do was to show him affection.

Stepping over to him, she stood close and raised her face to his.

For his part, Leofwig had no hesitation or doubts. The woman the king proposed for him was beautiful and of noble blood. His lips pressed to hers, and he took her in her arms.

"We will grow to love each other," he murmured, "and keep the king as a friend."

What Winflaed felt about King Æthelbald, she kept well and truly locked away in her heart.

Back in his palace, the object of these feelings was faced with a welcome distraction. At last, after a long search and tedious discussions, a goldsmith stood before him: this was not just any practitioner of this craft but the finest in the land, he had been assured by his servants. Experience would not be a problem, judging by the man's white hair and wrinkled face.

"I will send for the weapon, Master – *er* – what name do you go by?"

"Forwin, sire."

"Ay, Master Forwin," Æthelbald clapped his hands and issued instructions to a servant whoreturned quickly, bearing a magnificent sword.

"See how the smith has left a detachable pommel in plain steel' What I want is a pommel, and hilt, for that matter, fit for a king. What suggestions do you have, master?"

"Sire, the fashion is for gold pommels with filigree interlace ornament. Here are some sketches I brought." With a shaky hand, he pulled out a roll of parchment with crude sketches of pommels. "This one is the beaded type with small circles… or," he hesitated and added in a croaky voice, "…if it does not suit, the pommel can be longer and flatter with inscriptions of your choice or with niello work…"

"Let fashion go hang, master! I prefer the old ways: red garnet and gold…"

"Ah!" the old man's face lit up, "I done many o' them, sire, in my time! Garnet be the symbol of Christ – what better for a king? Leave it with me. As for the hilt, maybe in ivory with an inlay of gold and rubies?" A shrewd expression came into the watery eyes, "It'll cost a fair amount, mind."

"Make sure it *is* fair, Master Forwin… and above all, make it the best work you have ever done. There is no hurry, but the sword, when finished, must shout to the world, 'I belong to a *great* king!' "

EIGHT

Tame Weorth, 726 AD

The self-satisfaction of Æthelbald reached new heights after giving away and ridding himself of the importunate Winflaed. At the same time, he had placed a faithful servant, Leofwig, at the strategic meeting point of the borders of Est Anglia, Est Seax and Outer Mierce. This complacency lasted no longer than the time it took to watch the groom and a dozen warriors disappear from his sight. They flanked the bride, travelling in a rolling, swaying canvas-covered cart, pulled by two horses.

Æthelbald still had not learned that harsh lesson of life: happiness begins where ambition ends. As a result, he turned away with a heavy sigh, comparing himself to a man standing on a clifftop unable to see the distant shore. Had he but known, the New Year would bring a fresh perspective, but the immediate future was more in line with his pessimistic mood.

Two days later, he awoke to find Bishop Haedde, in accusatory vein, awaiting him.

"Did you not give away, in wedlock, the nun with whom you absconded from the abbey in Glevcaestre?"

"Ay, and what of it?"

"Do you imagine you can wilfully set yourself above God's laws?"

"Priest, what ails you? The maid is saved from a cloistered life ill-befitting her and now is an honest and happy bride."

"Beware, lest you believe yourself greater than the Almighty and His providence, for He who raised you up and granted you every blessing may with ease cast you down."

"Which, among other reasons, Bishop, is why we are meeting this morning to consider your petition on behalf of… let me see, how did you word it?… ah… *er*… 'the Servant of God', Baegia."

The bishop's eyes shone, "Then, my king, you are minded to receive, with favour, our humble supplication?"

"First, reflect on how you misjudge me, priest. Set aside, for once, your blighted judgement, for we have decided to grant six hides of land at Daylesford that Baegia should found there a minster."

Astonished pleasure replaced the stern censure on the visage of the prelate.

Æthelbald studied the transformation with well-concealed satisfaction. He understood well, keeping the church from meddling in his designs depended upon its thankfulness for his munificence.

After witnessing the charter for the concession, Bishop Haedde went away, little suspecting the vindictive thoughts passing through the mind of King Æthelbald. If he could limit church interference in his affairs, he would. In any case, no one would stand between him and his ambitions, nor, for that matter, would they govern his lust. The land was filled with monasteries, in turn, teeming with young noblewomen. The king determined it was time for another "raid" on an abbey. Not that the vices of the king would trouble Haedde for much longer.

A few weeks after the signing of the Daylesford Charter, the good bishop died. Æthelbald hoped for a less troublesome incumbent, but he deemed ecclesiastical matters out of his sphere of influence. The elected successor, Aldwine, proved to be a man of strong character. Before this sad event, although the news arrived later, the political landscape around Æthelbald changed with another occurrence.

"What! How can it be? Are you sure?" The king's stare at the messenger was as intimidating as he intended.

"S-Sire, I had it from Bishop Daniel's own mouth."

"Ine has given up the throne and gone to Rome on pilgrimage? What makes a king do such a thing?"

"I know not, Lord."

"Did the bishop say who will now lead the West Seax?"

"Ay, his wife-brother, Æthelheard, but a cousin disputes the succession, says Bishop Daniel, one, by name, Oswald."

At last, West Seax is weakened. I can turn this to my advantage.

Before turning his attention to the distant realm of West Seax, the logical move was to break up the journey by stopping in Lunden. Lundenwic, after all, the greatest trading emporium in the land, was close to his heart and closer still to his coffers. The chaotic situation in Kent provided an opportunity as tempting as that of West Seax. Control of Kent would guarantee the security of Lunden. Also, it would provide a base for a push on the Suth Seaxa and subsequently on the West Seaxa.

The weather was mild and conducive to travelling. So, having considered all his possibilities and discussed matters with his counsellors, the royal party set off for the busy town on the Temese. Æthelbald chose not to stay in Lunden, despite its appeal, but to press on into Kent. This decision he took for a twofold reason. First, he intended to exploit forthwith, to his advantage, the dynastic struggle; second, his confessor, as they approached the kingdom, piqued his interest with tales of the minster at Thanet.

On that isle, the priest told him, a widowed noblewoman, Saint Domneva had founded an abbey, having been granted as much land as a hind could run over in a day. Her daughter, Mildryth was renowned, apart from her own saintliness, for wisdom accumulated in the Frankish lands where she was educated at the royal abbey of Chelles. It was this formidable woman, the daughter of an under-king of Mierce, whom Æthelbald resolved to visit. In truth, there was nothing holy underlying this decision but rather, the king pandering to his twin vices of ambition and lust. The former, Mildryth might be able to promote through her sage advice, and for the latter, the abbey, for sure, containing many young noblewomen, ought to provide an outlet.

Thus, Æthelbald, having crossed the flat meadows of rivers, farms and marshes under an endless sky where nothing intervened with what his eye perceived, presented himself unannounced at the gates of the abbey. Admittance to the sanctified presence of the abbess, King Æthelbald, unwavering before the penetrative gaze of the lady, revealed the purpose behind his arrival.

"We have come to assure ourselves of your well-being, my lady."

"My well-being? What makes you think it is in any way threatened?"

"What with the turmoil in the kingdom after the passing of the noble Wihtred."

The dark brown eyes of the mother superior showed no sign of ceasing their disconcerting probing.

In a dry, almost dismissive voice, she said, "The sons of Wihtred carry out the tasks conducted by their late much-lamented father. The eldest, Æthelbert, is in command, and although the brothers share their duties on the basis of old tribal alignments, they maintain peace and stability in the kingdom." The abbess waited. If possible, her stare became more challenging and penetrating. "What is it you really want with this visit?"

Unperturbed by this sudden change of tone, Æthelbald replied, "Advice. Word has it you are endowed with great wisdom, and I wish, under the circumstances, to avail myself of it."

A thin smile greeted his words, "If I am blessed with sagacity, such repute is undeserving of praise, as it comes direct from the Holy Spirit in response to prayer. What circumstances do you refer to, King Æthelbald?"

"The unrest and instability that from Kent passes through Suth Seax to the farthest reaches of West Seax. These are unsettled and dangerous times."

Impatient, the abbess, tapped the floor with her tiny shoe of red leather.

"Kings, even the best of them, come and go, like other men: either because the Lord gathers them to his bosom, as in the case of Wihtred or He calls them to his apostle in Rome as with King Ine. Life goes on. But you came for advice, and I shall do what I can to give it."

Æthelbald's eyes brightened.

"There is no doubt," she continued, "a strong king, ruling in fear and awe of God, provides for his people the example and security they need. Strength alone is no warranty. We spoke of well-being. Your predecessor, Æthelred, brought destruction to this diocese in my lifetime and ten years later, the king of the West Seax, Caedwalla, wreaked greater havoc. Folk still scare their infants with talk of it. My counsel is to be the strong king but to bend those to your will, not by force of arms but by promoting the common good. You must work *with*, not against the church. Choose a godly priest you know well and install him as archbishop, the next ruler of the church, in Cantwaraburh. People speak of your generosity to the church. May this continue," she said with a self-satisfied smile.

At least, that was Æthelbald's interpretation of the fleeting expression.

The lady has designs on my purse. It could work for my profit!

In an elegant, self-possessed manner, the abbess dismissed the king, who made for the cloister to reflect on the remarkable woman and her words of counsel. The sheltered well-tended quadrangle provided the perfect haven for undisturbed reflection.

All they said about Mildryth is true and more besides. I'd better tread carefully though, she seems to be able to know my thoughts before they issue from my mouth. Her advice is sound. It confirms me in what I was doing to make these underkings subservient. The best suggestion she made was to install my own man to the see of Cantwaraburh. The fact is, Berhtwald's health shows no sign of failing, and he's been a thorn in my side for a score and ten years. Yet, he is old and cannot live forever.

The twisted smile accompanying this last consideration made him look up out of guilt. Sitting on the low wall of the cloister, some six yards further forward, was a young nun whose eyes were fixed on his face. She was twirling a lock of blonde hair she had teased from under her wimple around her finger. Her tunic clung to her body, trapped artfully under her thigh, emphasising her curves in the most un-nunlike manner.

By Thunor, the wench is sending silent signals.

The king did the same, and with forefinger and middle finger united, he gestured for her to approach. With an unseemly lack of hesitation, the nun arose and walked over to him.

From the man's dress, she could see he was no common visitor.

"I watched you for some time, Lord. You were deep in thought. I trust you are not distressed."

"Only by the thought I know not one so fair of face."

The nun blushed and Æthelbald's pulse raced.

"It is easy to remedy, Lord. I am Ælfgiva, third daughter of Ealdorman Eomer of Burford and the most miserable of creatures."

"How so? What can lead to misery in so peaceful a spot?"

"Therein lies the response. My heart sighs to be free of this place where I am trapped like a songbird in a cage. How my soul aches to be out in the world to soar unbounded."

"You are enclosed here against your will?"

"My father paid the *fader-fiod* for my elder sisters, but when it came to finding such a dowry for me, his coffers were empty, so he sent me here."

A sigh that would have moved the stoniest heart stirred the king to react. He took her hand and noted with pleasure she did not pull it away but returned the gentle pressure he exerted.

"Do not be sorrowful, Ælfgiva. There is sure to be a way to redress this circumstance. On the morrow, I shall speak for you with the abbess."

"She will not hear of me leaving these walls. Not even the king himself could persuade her."

"Ah, but which king? Maybe *this* king can bend her will."

"Not hers! But *king?*"

"Ay, I am Æthelbald of Mierce."

The amazement on the young woman's face made him laugh.

"Sire, forgive my boldness," and now she snatched her hand away, "I did not know."

"That much is clear."

For the first time, Æthelbald came to his senses. He was in a compromising situation and carefree. He looked around the cloister, guilt writ large on his face. The nun, as if emerging from a dream did likewise.

"I must go," she whispered, "before tongues start wagging." One graceful movement and she skipped down on the flagstones.

"Hold!" Æthelbald hissed. "You have my word, in the morning, I shall speak on your behalf with the abbess."

Before she turned away, Ælfgiva's delightful smile, followed by a suggestive lick of her lips, set his pulses racing. A hesitant wave of her hand, and she went tripping out of the cloister.

By Thunor, the maid pleases me. The matter needs careful thought.

The next morning, after a restless night on an uncomfortable mattress, Æthelbald sought and obtained an audience with the mother superior. Without hesitation, he set out his case for the release of Ælfgiva from her vows. It flowed from his tongue, since he had practised this speech in his head repeatedly during his sleepless night.

Whereas he expected a rounded condemnation of the nun and a hardening of the abbess' severity, he was relieved at an unexpected reasonableness – or anyway, what he considered such.

The abbess fixed the king with a steely gaze, "A stainlessness of virginity must be accompanied by a chastity of the spirit to be a bride of Christ. Alas! This is not the case in Ælfgiva. It has been apparent to me for many months, she succumbs to the untamed impulses of bodily wantonness and this is manifest in her choice of garments. I fear they are designed to attract notice…" she paused and weighed up the king's reaction, before adding, "…how shall I put it?… to fan the flames of sexual attraction. I suppose you, sire, must have noticed as much…?"

The king bit his lower lip and looked at his feet: he might just as well have admitted the truth.

The abbess sighed, "Ay, well, you are not to blame. This would not have occurred were Ælfgiva of a chaste and modest mind."

"She is then not suited to her calling and you are minded to release her?"

The curious smile of the previous day appeared and vanished. The abbess nodded, "I am sure we can come to an arrangement. My poor house can ill afford to lose the considerations Ælfgiva's father makes each year."

"But I am sure the King of Mierce's *'considerations'* can surpass those of an ealdorman."

"One would imagine so, sire."

The enigmatic smile returned and illuminated the woman's countenance for a moment.

"The fact is, I am a long way from Tame Weorth. Here, there

are matters to resolve before we can bestow our beneficence upon your house. My word will have to suffice."

"Sire, I doubt not your word, as it will be in given the House of God. But I wonder as to what form it will take."

Ha! I have her!

"I had thought to grant the remission of toll on one ship a year in the port of Lundenwic. What say you?"

"Sire, it is a generous gift. but I worry for your soul, should our accord be sealed."

"How so?"

"You must not engage in depraved acts with this woman Ælfgiva. I release her on this one condition."

Depraved acts? What has she in mind?

Æthelbald shuffled in discomfort, "Lady," he said, "there is so much to be done here in the south. I doubt there will be time for acts, depraved or otherwise."

"Well then, I find we have an agreement. When you leave, you may take Ælfgiva with you. I caution against unwise, unrestrained behaviour before the eyes of your subjects. I must speak with her before you depart."

The king understood the subtle dismissal.

Outside, he breathed in the early morning air and chuckled to himself.

I spoke the truth to the abbess. There is little time for ought other than taking control of the south.

NINE

Near the River Saefern, 726 AD

The king surveyed the bustling arrangements of camp pitching with little enthusiasm. His bones ached from the permanent jostling of travel in the saddle. Resentment for other matters enforced on him worsened his mood. Principal among them, the constraint of heading for Powys at the behest of his old friend Coelwald. How could he refuse him in such a moment of peril? Since crossing the borders of Mierce, Æthelbald issued proclamations that brought warriors hastening to swell the ranks of his company, so the mass of men before his eyes elicited a grunt of satisfaction. His entourage had taken on the aspect of a small army, and given they would pass through Magon, there was every prospect of increasing his numbers to form a sizeable host.

Another issue preoccupying Æthelbald was the news out of West Seax. Their new king, Æthelheard, had fought for the throne with his wife-brother Oswald and defeated him – at least for the moment. Æthelheard, knowing Æthelbald to be present in the south, appealed to him for support. This was an opportunity for the king of the Miercians but also a nuisance. His reply, urging the king of the West Seax to meet him here by the Saefern, obtained a positive response, but the problem was one of time. Æthelbald would not abandon Coelwald, but the time consumed awaiting the arrival of Æthelheard was ill-afforded. He would never forgive himself if the Wealisc overcame his friend and forced their way into Mierce. The messenger from Wintancaestre, where the king of the West Seax resided, had taken almost five days to complete the journey. When pressed, he gave his opinion that should his king leave at once, it would take a week to reach them here in Bricstow.

When Æthelheard came, Æthelbald intended to persuade him, by any means necessary, to add his signature to a charter granting lands in Berrucscir. By complying, the king of the West Seax, to all intents and purposes, would acknowledge his subservience to Æthelbald.

Until this king arrived, the lot of the Miercian leader was to pace back and forth in fretful preoccupation. Weary of this, his lustful gaze swept over the canvas-covered cart provided to transport Ælfgiva. So far, on the journey, he had kept away from her. Whether this decision was conscious or one determined by deep-buried respect for the remarkable Abbess Mildryth, arisen when his priest told him of the miracle of Chelles, he was unsure. While his stare lingered on the cart containing Ælfgiva, Æthelbald reflected on the miraculous event once more. Mildryth's mother sent her to be educated at Chelles in France, where many young English ladies were trained for a saintly life. A nobleman, related to the Abbess of Chelles, implored her to arrange that he might marry this English princess. The mother superior tried to persuade her, but Mildryth said her mother had sent her there to be taught, not to be married. All the abbess's advice, threats and blows failed to prevail on her to accept the alliance offered.

At last, the abbess cast her into an oven where she had made a great fire. After three hours, when the abbess expected to find not only Mildred's flesh but her very bones burnt to ashes, the young woman came out unscathed and radiant with joy and beauty.

Although this tale made a profound impression on Æthelbald, he was not one to allow himself to be conditioned by religious sentiment unless it were to his profit. In any case, tales of miracles often left him incredulous. Enough days since the telling of this one had passed for the effect to wear off. Mildryth was in Minster and he was by the Saefern, far enough away to do what he pleased without censure.

Sweeping aside the canvas opening, Æthelbald peered inside the cart to discern Ælfgiva brushing her long blonde hair over her bare shoulder. His request to enter the wagon was not rebuffed by chaste protests, so, clambering into the soft luxury of the vehicle, his senses were assailed by the heady scent of lavender. The softness of the mattress, and the body pressed close to his, acted as a balm in his troubled state.

The arrival of King Æthelheard, three days later, removed the most pressing of his anxieties. A warm welcome from Æthelbald inside the king's splendid tent soon gave way to more intriguing ploys. Seizing the initiative, Æthelbald placed his visitor on the defensive at once by ascertaining that Æthelheard was not descended from Cynric by blood. This implied that Oswald had a better claim since the kings of West Seax gained authority by descent from this bloodline. The leverage obtained by hinting at throwing his support behind his rival's claim made Æthelheard malleable to Æthelbald's request for a signature on his charter.

Unrolling the document, the King of Mierce began to read to the assembled dignitaries.

"Æthelbald, King, to Saint Mary's Minster, Æbbandun in confirmation of lands and grant of twenty-seven hides at Watchfeld and ten by Grange Brook, Berrucscir, with further confirmation by Æthelheard, King of West Seax. Also signed by Bishops Walcstod, Folhere, Wor and Daniel." He paused and sighed from the effort of translating from Latin for the benefit of Æthelheard, who, he presumed spoke no other language but his own. Leaning over the signatories, he watched with pleasure as the last of the bishops inscribed under the other signatures. "*Ego Daniel plebi Dei famulus canonica subscriptione manu propria + firmani.*" This sensation was naught compared to the satisfaction of seeing Æthelheard add his name. The nature of their relationship was now clear to everyone present in this tent but most of all to the king of the West Seaxa himself. In the bosom of the man from the west must be entrapped the bitter awareness of subservience.

Over an otherwise pleasant evening meal, what was implicit in the signature was made explicit in words by Æthelbald. Support for

Æthelheard would be unconditional as long as he complied with all requests from Mierce. They drank to this accord, and amidst laughter and song, something approaching a friendship was forged. In exchange, Æthelbald made it clear to anyone listening that he would never tolerate the upstart Oswald on the throne of West Seax.

Thus it was, Æthelheard departed the next morning for West Seax chastened and yet contented. Æthelbald disentangled himself from Ælfgiva's embrace to bid farewell to his guest and to organise their own departure for Glevcaestre, three days away at the pace they travelled. A return there had a twofold benefit – the comfort of the royal palace (where he could once more enjoy the bed) and the size of the town. With the surrounding area, it ought to provide him with a sunstantial number of warriors.

The response to the call to arms in Glevcaestre was better than he had hoped. In part, he put it down to his presence among them and in greater part, to the plight of their own King Coelwald. The Hwicca had taken well to the appointment of an underking in the stead of an ealdorman. The nobility of Coelwald and his light approach to kingship had ensured their unswerving fealty.

Rejoicing in the strength of his host and content to be heading into battle once more, Æthelbald, a man of action, enjoined Ælfgiva to remain in the palace of Glevcaestre. The pretence of thoughtfulness for her safety and comfort overcame what small resistance she put up. Distractions of this type ought to be avoided on campaign, as the king knew full well. So off he rode in high spirits at the head of his host, banners fluttering in the breeze stiff enough to fleck the surface of the Saefern with wavelets.

The last message received from Coelwald was received from an encampment under the ancient fortress of Dinieithon. This hill fort lay in the area of Maelienydd between the Saefern and the Wye – distant five days' hard march.

On arrival, no sooner had Coelwald crushed his old friend Æthelbald in a warm embrace than he reproved him for the long time taken to react to his plea for aid.

"Count your blessings, Coelwald! We have pressing matters other than the persistent forays of the Wealisc."

"Wait till you see their strength." The underking pointed to the hill, standing like a man-made mound, which it was not, "Knowing the worth of their scouts, I am amazed they did not attack us before your arrival. You will see, their leader has amassed a huge host to rival even the one you stand at the head of."

Æthelbald squinted uphill against the low evening sunlight but detected no sign of movement.

"So much the better. I love a good fight."

"This is one we must win, my king, for the Wealisc destroyed Scrobbesburh with the pretence it was their old capital and they wished its restitution. Of course, I refused. All my lifetime, it has been held by Mierce. Before my time, I know not."

"Scrobbesburh is too well-positioned to surrender to the Wealisc. In their hands, it would open the way to our heartland, and the troublesome Britons, we know well, are never content with their own crops, herds and flocks. You were right to chase them back from our borders."

"Ay, but since our last clash, they have strengthened."

"Are you afraid, Coelwald?"

"Not now you have arrived, but the King of Powys holds the high ground."

"Then we must use our wiles."

"Do you have a plan, my king?"

"Not yet, Coelwald. Give me time."

Æthelbald sent for men well used to scouting and ordered a report by nightfall on the enemy's position and strength. More important, he demanded an attentive survey of the land surrounding the stronghold. Once more, he peered up the hill and noted, with satisfaction, that no ramparts were to be seen, not even ancient earthworks.

Having placed lookouts, the king ordered the main force to set about erecting an encampment.

The most enterprising of his scouts reported thus, "Sire, I reached the crown of the hill where a guard challenged me. I overcame him and spied the enemy encampment. Over the crest lies a deep, vast hollow, in which the Wealisc host is gathered."

"What is their strength?"

"Sire, they match our numbers, I would say."

The king's eyes blazed with a fierce light and the scout

wondered for a moment whether he had enraged the king with his words. Not so, the ruler couched his next question in a normal voice.

"What can you tell me about the land, good fellow?"

"That is a problem. The approach to the hilltop is barred by a rock wall the height of four men."

"A direct assault is to be excluded?"

"Ay, my king."

"How did you reach the brow of the hill?"

"There is a way around the side of the cliff, but it is steep," the scout intoned, full of doubt.

As it turned out, as the sun cast its first rays upon the wakening world, the idea of a Miercian attack on the stronghold vanished because the men of Powys were pouring in silence down the hillside toward the dozing encampment.

But for the artful placing of watchmen, the Miercians, many of them still asleep, would have been taken by surprise. Instead, the blaring of warning horns awoke the lightest sleepers who, in turn, with rough shakes or kicks roused their sleeping companions. After the shrill notes, although the Miercians needed no further proof of imminent danger, the war cries of the onrushing enemy assailed their ears.

Æthelbald strapped on his sword, rammed his regal helm on his head and, snatching up his battleaxe, pushed out of his tent. The sight before him was enough to weaken the knees of a lesser man. The foe poured over the foot of the hill, their faces daubed with blue paint, screaming and waving weapons above their heads. With every onrushing stride, in a sea of bodies rising and falling like the endless waves of the ocean, they advanced, reaching the first of the sleepy defenders.

A worse preparation for a battle, Æthelbald could not imagine. There was no time nor space to create a shield wall – his usual experience of warfare. As a seasoned campaigner, he soon sized up the situation, which he recognised as all to Miercian disadvantage. The only consolation was the scattered nature of the battlefield, since the ground was disrupted by pitched tents.

"To me, to me!" shrieked Æthelbald to the nearest Miercian warriors. They must create some semblance of a united force. In his heart, he knew that the day would be won by strength of sinew and, above all, the will to win.

Set the example.

The king charged forward leading the small band he had gathered, continuing to call men to him. He spotted a strong group of Wealisc setting about them with long swords. Seizing a shield from the ground, he hoisted it in front of him and thrust in among them without a trace of fear. His axe rained blows in all directions, wreaking a trail of destruction. Heartened, his warriors plunged into the enemy ranks, and others, disorientated and leaderless, hastened over to join them. To his relief, Æthelbald saw Coelwald rallying warriors to him. Not that there was time to relish the sight, for the slightest distraction on the field of battle meant instant death.

The fighting raged on until the weak sun, losing its own fight against relentless clouds, smiled timidly straight overhead. At this time, the momentum changed. The ferocity of the Miercian warriors turned the day in their favour, and at last, the Wealisc horns sounded the retreat.

Exhausted, like his fellow warriors, the king ordered his men not to pursue the fleeing men of Powys. Convinced enough damage had been inflicted on the Wealisc to prevent further attacks in the foreseeable future, he oversaw the creation of funeral pyres while his priest chanted a requiem for the dead.

The dense black smoke, swept by the incessant breeze in the direction of the hill fort, brought back sorrowful memories to Æthelbald. It seemed a lifetime ago when he had to burn the body of his faithful thegn Meriet near the settlement of Weala-denu.

Æthelbald said his farewells to Coelwald, recommending, as though necessary, vigilance on the frontier with Powys. It made sense to leave the warriors collected under the banners of Hwicca to Coelwald. He departed for Glevcaestre and the comforting embraces of Ælfgiva with only his small retinue.

Late to rise on the third morning after the battle, Æthelbald was in the sweet enfolding clasp of his mistress when a messenger arrived from Tame Weorth.

Upon receiving him, Æthelbald learnt of unrest in Northanhymbre.

"Ay, Lord, King Osric is ill and has named his successor – Ceolwulf, the brother of the king before him, Coenred—"

"I *know* who his predecessor was," snapped Æthelbald.

The messenger did his best to look apologetic, "There are whisperings of murder and betrayal in the offing, sire."

"Now that's more interesting," the king murmured.

The south is under my control. Time to turn my attention to the north.

TEN

Tame Weorth and Northanhymbre, 729-731 AD

At the beginning of May 729, King Osric died. The opportunity brought about by the circumstances of the treacherously and chaotically contested kingship in Northanhymbre proved too tempting for Æthelbald to resist. To exploit the situation to the full, however, he had to solve the question of who to employ. Since acceding to the throne, his policy of installing trustees in delicate areas disputed between Mierce and its neighbouring kingdoms had paid off.

The impediment was that there was not the infinite supply of men who combined trustworthiness with the clever cunning he needed to further his ambitions. This accounted for Æthelbald's restless pacing within the confines of the palace in Tame Weorth.

"You will go to Loidis with all haste," Æthelbald towered over the messenger he had summoned. Having, at last, overcome his scruples for the safety of his sibling, he went on, "There, proceed to the hall of my brother, Heardberht, and deliver this message. He is to venture into Northanhymbre, where he will meet with the powerful lords who oppose King Ceolwulf. At the moment, they are naught but an unconnected, grudge-bearing scattering of families. Tell Lord Heardberht to organise them, to stir them into rebellion. He can begin with the aetheling and king's cousin, Lord Eadberht."

The leonine appearance of Æthelbald took on a ferocious aspect, causing the slightly built messenger to cringe before him. "These instructions must be spoken in private only to my brother, do you understand? No one must ever connect them to me – on pain of death." The last words, he uttered with a malevolence that impressed even himself. In gentler tones and laying a reassuring hand on the messenger's shoulder, he said, "Bring back his reply with all speed, and I'll reward you well." This, he followed with an incongruous smile that unsettled the messenger more than his earlier venom. "Also," the king continued, "tell him he should find a way to *humiliate* Ceolwulf in the eyes of his people. Is that clear? And last but not least, make sure he understands the dangers of his mission. Say King Æthelbald warns against recklessness. Success is obtained by care and stealth."

The King of Mierce seated the messenger and made him repeat his communication until it was word perfect. Satisfied, he dismissed him with recommendations of the utmost speed.

Alone, he resumed his pacing, worrying about the peril his younger brother would face in the mission he had given him.

Heardberht is no fool, nor is he a weakling. I have faith in no one else. If ought happens to him I'll raze Northanhymbre to the ground.

* * *

Northanhymbre, five weeks later

Suspicion dripped in the air like the early morning dew from fronds of fern. Heardberht expected nothing less from folk, who, when not busy murdering their own, were the enduring enemies of Mierce. Looking around the group of noblemen assembled in haste and led by Eadberht, cousin to Ceolwulf, Heardberht, not weak of resolve, wavered in the conviction he could overcome their wariness. Hostile, mistrusting and brutal men, honed in merciless slaying across their borders stared at him with venomous hatred. But the Miercian had prepared well over the last month. Otherwise, one such as he did not arrive at the secret enclave of Eadberht. The time had come to convince them.

Conscious of eyes boring into his face, he attempted to make his expression as plausible as possible. He wondered whether to begin his speech addressing them as "Friends" but dismissed this idea as presumptuous, if not downright false. So he began, "Lords of Northanhymbre, I am come from my brother, Æthelbald, King of Mierce, in friendship, to promote and sustain the righteous claim of Lord Eadberht to the throne."

Now his month of subtle questioning ought to be put to the test. He hoped it would pay off. As expected, his words provoked a buzz of murmured approval around the gathering.

"What does a Miercian know about rightful or wrongful claims to *our* throne?"

The question, more a statement, came from a greybeard standing at the back of the aetheling Eadberht's chair.

No preparation had provided him with the names of Eadberht's household. At a disadvantage, knowing not with whom he was dealing, Heardberht drew himself up to his full imposing height, gained courage from the gesture and in a deep voice replied.

"My brother knows well that Lord Eadberht is son of Eata, son of Leodwold. Ceolwulf is son of Cutha, son of Cuthwine, son of the same Leodwold: thus Lord Eadberht's claim to the throne is stronger."

There followed grunts of approbation and nodding of heads, but nothing said so far, lightened the menacing atmosphere in the hall as the greybeard's next words demonstrated.

"And how is this of any interest to the King of Mierce?"

Heardberht expected this but forced himself not to blurt out a response. Better to let them think his answers were well meditated, not glib. He frowned, looked up at the tie beams and, clearing his throat, spoke.

"Our king fears Ceolwulf is weak and suspects the British and Pictish neighbours of Northanhymbre await only the right moment to attack. Mierce and your people have spent long years in conflict, but still, we are of the same stock and must not squander the conquests of our forefathers in animosity."

Crestfallen, Heardberht saw that his speech, meant to seduce the assembly, had elicited little effect.

Whoever the greybeard was, the Miercian understood *he*, not

Eadberht was the man to convince. The Northanhymbrian's next words came like a thrust to the gut from a seax.

"It would come as no surprise if, as we speak, the treacherous Æthelbald is in discussions with the Picts to form an alliance against us. Does not the King of Mierce hold sway over the whole of the south? Who knows where his ambitions will end?" He glared around the others to garner their support. Not that it was necessary, so deep-seated was the rivalry between the two kingdoms.

Insulted, Heardberht struggled to keep an edge from his voice but knew his face was flushed with resentment, and about that, there was nothing he could do.

"Why then, if Æthelbald were not in good faith, would he send his brother into the lion's den?" He continued, "Of course, he prefers a stable Northanhymbre on his borders with a strong king." At these last words, he looked straight at Eadberht and was gratified to see the slightest flicker of a smile. Inspired, he added, "So much the better if the two kingdoms are ruled by kings who understand and respect each other."

"What warranty have we for this?" the same harsh voice demanded.

The sincerity of the reply began to make inroads into the resistance of the rough noblemen.

"For the moment, none. That is why I come alone among you. Æthelbald wishes to make it clear he will sustain the claim of Lord Eadberht above that of any other. If called upon, he can supply arms, warriors, anything my Lord Eadberht might require." He bowed toward the aetheling, "Most importantly, his active support can be made known to anyone opposed to Ceolwulf, that the opposition to the king is organised—"

"Into rebellion – is that what you want, Miercian?"

There was no doubting the antipathy and menace in the voice.

"My lord," Heardberht addressed the greybeard, "I beg you to set aside your ill feelings for Mierce. my brother and I do not suggest bloodshed…only when all else has failed—"

"Enough, Berwyn!" Eadberht turned in his seat and looked up at the grizzled counsellor, "Have we not talked of rebellion and bloodshed among ourselves? We must think over and consider this offer from Mierce."

"But, my lord—"

Æthelbald had chosen well, Eadberht was no weakling, Heardberht understood from what followed.

"An end to it!" He cut across the Northanhymbrian lord, his elder. "My decision is made, we will discuss this offer from our neighbour."

Following the guidance of Eadberht, who had resolved to take the direction described by Æthelbald, Heardberht made his way into the stronghold of another leading family of the northern kingdom. He had never ventured so far north, and everything had a strangeness to it, from the language – the accent caused him difficulties – to the wild, rugged landscape. The grey skies and howling wind that swept across the moorland made him long for home. To increase his unease, the suspicion he met in Eadberht's hall was more intense here among the latter's kinsmen. The emotions were rawer, and the task of persuading these savages not to attack the royal palace and murder King Ceolwulf fell to him. Contrasting them without losing his own life tested all his new-found diplomatic skills.

He stared into the broad, flat visage of Calunoth, cousin of Eadberht, leader of this moorland tribe and as wild and ferocious as the weather of the land he occupied.

"My brother is right. Kill Ceolwulf and wounds will open that will not heal for generations."

This he knew to be true. The solution proposed, humiliating the king before his people, might work. But Heardberht was not as cunning as his sibling. How could he persuade these blood-lusting wildlings to a scheme that he knew not how to bring about?

It was easy enough to rally support for Eadberht, such was the general dislike of Ceolwulf, but a full year passed by without Heardberht getting any closer to conceiving a ploy to mortify the king. Indeed, his frustration and weariness led him to vacillate when confronted with Eadberht's rage at the lack of progress. It was the catalyst making him accept the aetheling's invitation to go with him to the court at Eoforwic. This pleased Heardberht, because of the name of the settlement – meaning *"wild boar town"* – given his liking for the flesh of that beast. Dwelling on this fact gave him, at last, an inkling of an idea for how to demean the king. Now he was also within striking distance of the ruler.

As an anonymous member of the public at the council meeting, Heardberht put together the last piece of his plot.

His attention was taken by a sneering comment from one of the lords directed at the king.

"You, with your feeble nature are more suited to running a cloister than a kingdom."

Heardberht imagined how Æthelbald might react to such a remark from one of his counsellors and had visions of bloody entrails strewn across the flagstones. Still, it provided the solution. Now all that remained was for Eadberht to play his part. He could not wait to tell the aetheling and enlist his aid.

Drinking ale and in the company of Eadberht's most trusted advisers, Heardberht outlined his plan. It depended upon the aetheling being able to persuade Ceolwulf to hunt for boar. One condition was overriding for the scheme to succeed – Ceolwulf must not be harmed. The assembled group liked the idea and suggested it would be easy to convince the king to go on a chase, since it was one of his preferred pastimes. Once stipulated that Eadwulf must appear innocent and ignorant of the outrage, the final details were debated. It would be Heardberht, whom the king did not know, to carry out the affront in person. Everyone agreed to the scheme, amid considerable mirth and banter. It remained only to await a fine day suitable for the hunt.

In the mild spring of 731, it was not long in coming. Even so, it would be summer before the sun was strong enough to dry out the muddy woodland tracks. Riding at the back of the hunting party, his face covered by a linen scarf, Heardberht rode along with four men entrusted to him by Lord Eadberht. In the depths of the forest, on the trail of the boar or any other appetising four-legged creature that had the misfortune of crossing their paths, the riders decided to rest and refresh their mounts by a rivulet. This was the prearranged moment for Heardberht and his cronies to carry out the ambush.

Creeping up behind the king, distracted in artful manner by Eadberht, two of the four burly brutes seized Ceolwulf, pinning his arms to his side. Meanwhile, Eadberht pretended to protest, drawing his sword and feigning a fight with another of the rogues. Amid shouting and scuffling, Heardberht set to with a pair of shears, cropping the locks of the king – the sign of his nobility –

until a yellow heap lay on the ground. The next stage was the razor. Scraping it across the crown of the struggling king's head, he could not avoid nicking the skin and drawing blood.

"Hold him still!" Heardberht cried.

The two men managed, in spite of the frantic resistance of the ruler, sufficiently for Heardberht to complete the tonsure.

"Put up your weapons," Heardberht bellowed at the sham fighters, "else I'll slit his throat!"

The fear in the eyes of the king moved him to pity. Safe in the knowledge that no harm would come to the monarch, as soon as the clash of steel ended, Heardberht's booming voice mocked him in the sudden silence.

"Would you slay each other for the sake of this *nithing*? One who is fit only to rule over a cloister? See how the tonsure becomes and befits him! Our work here is done. Now we must away."

"Seize them!" the king shouted.

"Nay, let them go!" Eadberht exclaimed. "The hair will grow anew. No harm is done."

In the confusion of the moment, Heardberht and his four accomplices made good their escape. On the road to Eoforwic, they separated and Heardberht began the long journey to Tame Weorth. As far as he was concerned, he had fulfilled his mission. There was no doubt about the contempt in which the tonsured king would be held by his own people. Æthelbald would be delighted with the outcome. What puzzled Heardberht was the subtlety of the plan. Why not do what the rough Calunoth wanted – slay Ceolwulf and install Eadberht on the throne? True, it might lead to generations of turmoil and murderous infighting, but was not that more or less what the King of Mierce benefitted from elsewhere? Heardberht shrugged and rode on, feeling sure his brother knew best.

ELEVEN

Cantwaraburh, 731 AD

The sainted Berhtwald, ninth Archbishop of Cantwaraburh, died in his eighties. On hearing the news, Æthelbald made all haste to Kent to appoint a successor. Once arrived, he discovered a conclave of the cathedral canons and southern bishops meeting in the cathedral to elect one of their number. This, he announced, was unacceptable.

Bursting unheralded into a room annexed to the body of the church, Æthelbald boomed, "What is going on in here?"

Tired and irritated, armed in spite of being in a sacred edifice, his voice and appearance terrified the clergymen.

"Sire, we are come together to elect the most worthy among us to succeed the late, lamented Berhtwald."

"It cannot be," Æthelbald raged, glowering at the dismayed gathering. He let his words hang without any desire to break their effect with further speech.

One brave bishop rose from his seat.

"King Æthelbald, what do you mean by this interruption?"

"I have come to inform you this meeting is improper."

"How so?"

"I have installed the new Archbishop of Cantwaraburh."

"This is irregular! I object!"

The king's hand strayed to the hilt of his sword.

"Object all you like, Bishop – while there is still breath in your body to protest with."

An eternity passed, it seemed, before the prelate's buttocks finally reached his seat.

A collective sigh occurred when the King of Mierce released his grip on the weapon.

Wary in his tone, another prelate asked, "Lord, King, may we ask whom you have chosen?"

Given he had spent two days informing himself of the most suitable candidate with Bishop Aldwine back in Licidfelth, the monarch felt on sure ground.

"You may!" he barked. "He is a Benedictine monk, abbot at the Abbey of Briudun. His name is Tatwine, a blameless, holy man and a scholar, grammarian and maker of riddles – so no man can object to my choice."

The last words were added with spite and a venomous glare at the bishop, target of his earlier wrath.

The prelate, however, was not without backbone.

"This is most irregular! A *Miercian* occupying the cathedra of Cantwaraburh – is unheard of!"

There was a general murmur of assent.

"Silence!" bellowed King Æthelbald.

"We shall protest to the Holy Father in Rome and overturn this outrageous imposition!"

"The pope is my friend," Æthelbald puffed out his chest. "He knows full well how many generous favours I have bestowed on the church in these isles. If you continue with your objections to a saintly man, I shall remove the archbishopric from Cantwaraburh. There are many who feel the church should be governed from the centre of the land."

These words had the desired effect on the score of seated men in the room. Not least, on the truculent bishop, who in the gentlest of tones, said, "Sire, it may well be that God has guided your choice. His will be done!"

"Amen," intoned Æthelbald. With that, he turned on his heel and left the room in a rank bad mood, in spite of his victory. Churchmen irritated him beyond all measure. They were always trying to curtail his power.

King Æthelbald stayed for the swearing-in ceremony of Tatwine. The cathedral, built on a Roman road, was entered through a narthex, used to congregate penitents and for housing the font as a reminder of their own baptism to the passing faithful. Augustine had had this edifice constructed, Æthelbald reminded himself as the Gospel of Saint Augustine was handed to Tatwine to swear on. This magnificent Bible of two hundred and sixty-five leaves, sent to the saint by Pope Gregory the Great was considered the oldest book in Britain. After the swearing in, the pallium was presented to him, and the recipient rose and blessed the congregation.

By Thunor, it is done! My power is increased!

Æthelbald winced at the unspoken and recurrent pagan oath in his thoughts, and for shame, here in this, the most important of God's houses in the land. Kneeling, he silently sought to make amends in Christian prayer.

* * *

South of England, 732 AD

Autumn surrendered to winter before the welcome arrival of spring and the weather made travelling long distances practicable. The cold months, Æthelbald spent in administrating the southern lands, tightening his indirect hold over them. With a reasonable dry spell in April, he decided to return to his heartland.

Back in Tame Weorth, he received his brother with affection, who had arrived in his absence.

"All reports from Northanhymbre are encouraging," he told Heardberht.

"How can that be, brother? Ceolwulf is still king."

Æthelbald laughed at his sibling's honest, perplexed expression. "You did a perfect job on him," he said, clapping the younger man on his back. "His people are disaffected, leaving him king in name only. Eadberht holds the reins of power and casts a wary and obedient eye south, to where *real* authority resides."

"Then your plan succeeded?"

"Did you doubt it?"

"Not for a moment, but I do not grasp these things."

"Ha-ha! Can you grasp a beaker of mead?"

"Right willingly." Heardberht relaxed.

Laden with gifts and charged with instructions for pushing the Elmet border into Northanhymbrian territory, Heardberht left Tame Weorth in a cheerful frame of mind.

Æthelbald, instead, armed with another charter, signed also by Heardberht, set off at the beginning of autumn for the abbey at Intanbeorgan near Weorgoran caestre. There, he had to settle a dispute for the abbess over some hides of land granted to the convent by King Æthelred. In effect, he had already decided in her favour, as testified by the charter, prepared in advance and packed with care into his travelling chest. For appearance's sake, he had to hear both parties before making his 'decision'. In truth, it was in the territory of the Hwicca, but Coelwald was away fighting in Powys, and the abbess had implored him for help on more than one occasion. Since he had other designs in that general direction, this time, Æthelbald acceded to her request.

The royal party covered the fifteen leagues to Intanbeorgan, at ox pace in three days. Not a long journey, but pleased to rest in the abbey, Æthelbald consented at once to a conversation with the abbess. A dignified, long-faced woman in her fifties, she launched into an explanation of the land dispute. Æthelbald heard her out and promised to preside over the hearing the next morning. His interest grew by significant degrees when, in response to his questions about the welfare of the house, the abbess began a litany of complaints. Her main objection, among more serious problems, was to the perceived lack of vocation of some of the young noblewomen foisted upon her.

"Indeed, I had one followed by a... *er*... spy at the end of harvest time, last year. On the heathen festival of Samhain, my servant caught her joining in pagan rites."

"What!" Æthelbald cried. "I will not have pagans in my kingdom!"

The abbess gave him a thin smile and frowned.

"Ancient customs die hard, sire. Especially those associated with fertility."

"Did you punish the miscreant nun?"

"Ay, but she shows little sign of a real vocation and encourages a small gaggle of wretched girls who prefer to wear unsuitable silks and rings. I know not what to do lest the canker spreads. My poor house suffers in its reputation and donations are dwindling. People will not leave their riches to a blighted house."

"I see. How many are the offenders?"

"The worst are but four or five. They are quite lacking in a calling."

"This is easier to solve than you may think, Mother."

"How so?"

"When I depart these hallowed walls, I will take them with me and, with God's grace, find suitable husbands for them."

Æthelbald tried to keep any deceit from his eyes, adding, although he had no intention, "A king can find a good dowry where an impoverished father cannot."

"I will talk with the women concerned. It will be one less problem for me in the running of this house," said the mother superior. "But come, let us off to the refectory, you and your lords must be ready for a meal."

The king bowed graciously. The abbess, whether witting or unconscious in her actions, was tending to his various bodily needs.

The next day, refreshed, the king rose to chiming bells and, after attending Lauds, ordained he would hear the land dispute as soon as the parties could be assembled. Before witnesses, the abbess produced a sealed charter from the reign of King Æthelred. After careful scrutiny and finding nothing irregular, Æthelbald called the landowner contesting the grant.

"Sire, it is a forgery!"

Æthelbald stared at the plaintiff, a weaselly wretch, with distaste.

"Are you accusing the Lady Abbess of the crime of falsification?"

The slender frame of the landowner trembled, "Nay, sire, I mean not to slander the mother superior. This document dates from before her time. The land I refer to is on the western slopes, sire, with views of Bredon Hill. It has been held by my forefathers for generations. That is, till it was granted by King Æthelred, in error."

"To criticise the former King of Mierce… is to criticise me,"

Æthelbald glared at the claimant with an expression he knew intimidated all who challenged him.

This fellow was no match and began bowing and muttering, "So be it!" repeatedly.

"I declare the document binding," Æthelbald smiled at the abbess. "This session is closed."

Sometime later, Æthelbald received a message from the mother superior to go to her quarters.

Upon entering, he was struck by the presence of five young nuns each wide-eyed at seeing the King of Mierce among them. Their eyes met his, causing them to blush. This coyness, for him, added to their charms.

The abbess cleared her throat and began in a stern tone, "I have explained the situation, sire, to these young women. I made it clear no one is removing them from the abbey by force. Their free will is of the utmost importance. I begged them to consider their calling…" she paused and looked from one to another of the nuns as if for reassurance. One nodded, so the abbess continued, "If they are not stirred by love of the Lord to remain, they may seek a new life under the guidance of the king."

"Well then," said Æthelbald, keeping the longing out of his voice, "be clear nobody will force you to do anything you do not wish. If you agree to come with me, you will begin a new life at my court." He hesitated and coughed to compose himself, "Who among you will come away from Intanbeorgan?"

"I, sire," said the one who had nodded earlier.

"I, too," the others said one at a time, stepping forward.

"Then, it is settled," the abbess said in a strange voice, a mixture of relief and censure. "At least take away with you something you have learned in your days here and never forget to pray morning and night. Try to set aside foolish fancies and become good wives and mothers."

The young women exchanged glances and the boldest of them giggled.

"Out!" cried the mother superior, exasperated, but calmed at once to add, "May you go with God!"

The five nuns curtseyed and hastened out of the room, engrossed in unseemly chatter.

The distraught woman standing before her king wrung her hands, "What is the world coming to?" she moaned. "These are girls from excellent families, King Æthelbald, at least one is more important than my own. Yet they behave like common alehouse sluts."

"Once at court, in spite of the lightness of heart befitting their youth, they will change," Æthelbald said, hiding behind a mantle of feigned wisdom.

Another heavy sigh came from the good woman, "I can pray it will go as you say and for the good of their souls. I am grateful, for now, to be rid of them. Rotten fruit must be removed from the basket before it spoils the sound flesh."

A few pleasantries exchanged and guarantees given by the king, the abbess blessed him and he withdrew. His thoughts raced as he proceeded to organise the departure.

I will not force myself upon the maidens, but I will keep them in the light of day as my mistresses if they are willing. Who is there to stop me? I control the church through Archbishop Tatwine. My power is unchallenged!

To further strengthen his grasp was the objective of his departure. Twenty-four leagues separated him from Bricstow, where he was due to meet with Coelwald and his army. At least the tracks hereabouts were dry – a small miracle this late in the year. The journey perforce must go at ox pace, more so, now that another two carts were adapted to carrying the five nuns he had acquired. The slowness displeased him, but he did not wish to leave the oxen and the transport behind. He did not intend to return this way.

The procession passed through the eastern part of Bricstow to the royal estate either side of the River Beydd. Once across the shallow river, little more than a stream after the dry summer, the travellers headed straight for the palace. It was nothing grander than a spacious hall. By rights, it belonged to the kings of Hwicce. For this reason, Æthelbald had granted it to Coelwald and hence had informed him of his intention of stopping there. A steward, prepared for the arrival of the regal guest, bustled about making arrangements with the retinue for cooking and the organising of servants to ready the royal chamber.

Soon, the king had the room to himself, where he began to scheme. Opening a small treasure chest, he selected a delicate jewel. A pendant, it consisted of a garnet stone enclosed in a gold frame and clasped by small serrated teeth, dangling from a fine chain of the same metal. The king admired the trinket, one of many arrived in his coffers, and turned it in his hand. The flames of two candles reflected in the smooth red gem. This would be the first of his gifts. Slipping the splendid bauble inside his tunic, he called for a servant and sent for the nuns.

"We shall stay here until King Coelwald and his men arrive," he told them. "Since this may involve some delay, I must see that you are provided with comfortable quarters."

The steward was given the task of settling the five women into suitable accommodation, but as he started off to lead them to their lodgings, the king spoke.

"Not you!" he said to the nun who he had discovered had been reprimanded for taking part in a pagan festival and who seemed the most vivacious of the group. "Wait, for I must speak with you."

Once the others had gone, Æthelbald turned back to the woman and raised the matter of the heathen rites she had attended. In his position, he could not afford to have a practising pagan in his household.

"It may have been a foolish act, lord." She made her eyes bigger and pleading, "I was desperate, so when God didn't respond to my prayers, I turned to the old gods and, lo! They granted my wish!"

"How so?"

"I prayed to be rescued from the abbey and given a fresh start, and here I am!"

"They did not answer you for more than a year! What is your name, child?"

The king studied the lascivious smile on the wanton's face and knew he was not mistaken about her nature.

"Merwenna, sire."

"What fate did the abbess tell awaited you and your companions once outside her walls?"

"That you would care for our futures, sire."

"Ay, and that I will, Merwenna," he said with feeling. "So, what is it you would wish your king would do for you?"

"I am in your hands, Lord," she said with a toss of her head and a wicked smile.

Æthelbald reached inside his tunic and pulled out the pendant.

In two steps, he was over to her and clasping the jewel around her lovely neck.

"This is my gift to you," he smiled. "It becomes your beauty."

She took the gem from her breast and raised it before her eyes in wonderment. The same eyes passed to the face of her benefactor and held his with a quizzical expression. Not that there was much room for doubt.

"You said you were in my hands," he said in a husky voice. "Would that you were."

One of rebellious nature and the desperation of her father from an early age, she needed no further encouragement but strode into his waiting arms and before long, his bed.

After their lovemaking, the king found out as much about his new mistress as he could and, above all, explained to her what her role in his life would be. He made it clear she might not be his only mistress. Indeed, he expressed the hope the other four might also be in his hands. The opportunist in her reacted, she had an eye for more splendid gifts. Might she not persuade her friends of the king's desires and of his generosity? Æthelbald was quick to seize on her offer and understanding her as well as she understood herself, promised her she would be his favourite, with all that it implied. So it was, his wait for the arrival of Coelwald was spent in the arms of one or another of the five nuns. Otherwise, in moments alone, it passed in preparation for increasing his sway over the country.

A messenger arrived from Coelwald. The underking could not come to Bricstow. His spies had informed him the Wealisc were plotting to unite the men of Dyfed to those of Powys. This, Æthelbald knew, made for a threat to Mierce itself and must be snuffed out. He could not risk losing Coelwald, his friend and staunchest ally. Thus, he told the messenger, Coelwald must find a safe retreat for the time being and hold the position against all comers until his king arrived with an army. Once Coelwald's refuge was known, he was to send another messenger to Bricstow to divulge its location.

Æthelbald saw this as another opportunity to increase his power in the south-west. After all, he was here for this reason, not to idle away his time in lechery. With this in mind, he sent a messenger to King Æthelheard of the West Seaxa, outlining the situation. He made sure to stress a Powys-Dyfed alliance would also threaten West Seax – the more so if it defeated Hwicce.

The King of Mierce expected his request to be satisfied and three weeks later, was gratified when his scouts reported back that a "great host" was advancing from the south. The warrior in him thrilled at the prospect of battle but the ruler in him, even more, at having prevailed over Æthelheard. They would march under joint banners, but under his sole command, to the rescue of Coelwald and to the confounding of the Wealisc.

TWELVE

Pen-y-crug, Powys, spring 733 AD

Coelwald drew his cloak closer to his chest to shield him from the biting westerly wind sweeping over the summit of the hill known to his scouts as the Crug. This fortress dated from the dawn of time. Where once stood stone ramparts, he imagined, with wooden palisades, rose five grassy banks interspersed with ditches. They presented a formidable barrier to any enemy wishing to struggle up the steep slope from the land, nine hundred feet below, where the River Usk twinkled in the sunlight.

    The primitive builders had contrived to build one entry to the south-east and Coelwald had placed men to guard it well. From the highest vantage point, his eyes scanned the surrounding terrain, not for the Wealisc enemy, encamped in the flood valley, but for the arrival of friends. His heart felt as bleak as this windswept stronghold. Why did they not come? His food could not last forever. Two moons past, he sent a messenger with details of his location. Still, they waited, likely because the March weather proved more ferocious than usual. The earth-pounding rains would have washed away the smaller stones in runnels, turning the hard, dry roads of summer into clagging mud.

    Strange notions passed through the underking's mind. Why

might his old friend, Æthelbald, abandon him to the might of the Wealisc? Try as he may, he could think of no advantage for his king in such a decision. No, it had to be a question of travel difficulties, squelching through sludge. How long could their supplies hold out? He had placed his men on half-rations. Before the arrival of the Wealisc, he had been prudent and provided for many water casks to be carried up to the fort. Thirsty, hungry warriors made for weaklings. His last foraging party had met death, overwhelmed by the men of Powys. Sooner, rather than later, he would have to make a move.

Coelwald blew out his cheeks in relief when he spotted a golden cross on a blue ground next to a golden dragon rampant on red, fluttering over a dark mass of men approaching from the south! The emblems of Mierce and West Seax were drawing near. Æthelbald must have called on King Æthelheard for support, knowing Dyfed and Powys had united. Coelwald rubbed his chilled hands together, cupped them and breathed warm air into them before shouting for one of his thegns. He tasked him with bringing the advancing army into their stronghold. The warrior hastened to do his lord's bidding, and Coelwald was sure he saw the same reassurance he felt in the eyes of his man.

The underking of Hwicce took up his position once more. As if to verify he had not imagined the approaching host, he stared out to the south. A wry grin twisted his mouth when he spotted a lone rider on a Wealisc pony galloping towards the enemy encampment. Soon, the foe would know of the arrival of a mighty army to reinforce the men of Hwicce.

"Æthelbald, my friend! My king!" Coelwald made to kneel before his old friend but found himself hauled into a crushing embrace. The king had lost none of his famed strength.

"Come, Lord, from over here, you can see the Wealisc down in the valley."

The king whistled between his teeth. "You chose your position well! But not only for defence; we can fall on them like wolves upon a flock. We attack at dawn. What say you, Æthelheard?" Making an effort to remove the sullenness from his face because he felt excluded, the King of West Seax peered down to the valley, "A noteworthy advantage. I will give orders to whet our blades."

Coelwald, aware the food no longer needed hoarding, ordered cooks to make free with the supplies. So, it was a well-fed, cheerful army preparing to face the forthcoming battle. Many of the men gave in to their curiosity and approached the vantage point to spy the foe before daylight faded. Those who had not bothered to peek over the ramparts were left in no doubt, by the more curious among them, that a mighty force awaited below.

Before first light, Æthelbald rose and dressed, tucking two throwing axes into his belt, hefted his battleaxe and smiled at its familiar weight in his grip. The rush of excitement he felt before a battle was now upon him. Would the sun never raise its head to smile over the horizon?

As the sky tinged with pinks, violets and greys, the sound of voices drifted up from the valley. Was it possible the Wealisc had decided to seize the initiative? Æthelbald hurried to the earth rampart and stared down. The men of Powys were indeed riding up the hill on ponies. Not the enemy host! Only ten men under a white banner were coming up the slope. Mixed sensations stirred within the King of Mierce. He called for King Æthelheard and for Coelwald. When they arrived, he put into words these conflicting emotions: "It seems we are to be denied a victory. By Thunor, the Wealisc are suing for peace unless I'm mistaken! Do we give it to them? *Eh?*"

Coelwald looked glum.

"If we do, what's to stop them resuming their raids when we've gone?"

"I say we hear them," Æthelheard muttered.

"Right, gather ten of our best warriors, and we'll meet them halfway under our own white flag," Æthelbald said.

He removed the axes from his belt and ordered his horse to be saddled: he did not intend to encounter mounted foes on foot.

At the head of the Wealisc rode a splendid figure bearing a crown of twisted gold links; at his arms and ankles, gold circlets too, the signs of sovereignty. This was Elisedd ap Gwylog. Æthelbald hoped the King of Powys knew not that he, Æthelbald, had slain his father in battle. Astride the pony next to Elisedd sat another king.

"Rhain ap Cadwgan," indicated Elisedd, "King of Dyfed."

Æthelbald replicated the formalities on his part before waiting for the Wealisc to explain themselves.

"King of Mierce," the strong accent grated but, unlike his late friend, Guthlac, Æthelbald, speaking no Brittonic, was grateful for at least understanding the gist, "why settle with blood when words can suffice?"

"But do you have *the words*, King Elisedd?"

"Our peoples are at war only because my kingdom is overrun by Angles and I seek to restore and maintain my borders."

Coelwald tossed his head and tut-tutted, "If that is the case, why then did we fight at the gates of Scrobbesburh?"

The grin of the enemy king transformed into a snarl, "Because only by raiding in your land can we bring an end to your incursions."

Æthelbald, distracted, asked, "What is your argument with Mierce, King Rhain?"

The King of Dyfed spoke no English, but hearing he had been addressed by name, asked Elisedd to translate.

That done, a stream of guttural and incomprehensible sounds issued from his mouth.

Æthelbald looked from Rhain to Elisedd.

"The king says today, you raid into Powys then tomorrow, into Dyfed. Britons must aid each other for the well-being of one and all."

Æthelbald made to wheel his horse around, saying, "King Elisedd, you still have not found the words to prevent war."

"Wait! Will you not hear my proposal?"

"Let's hear it then!"

"Powys and Dyfed propose a truce. The borders of Powys will go back to what they were eight winters past, when I took the throne."

"This is very well, King of Powys, but what warranty have we you will keep your word?"

"I will supply a hostage."

"Nay, king Elisedd. King Rhain will provide the hostage. Thus, you will not dare break your word."

On hearing his name, Rhain looked to Elisedd for explanation. After a rapid exchange, Rhain stared at Æthelbald, the respect clear in his face. He nodded and said a few words that the King of Powys translated.

"King Rhain offers you his son, Tewdwr ap Rhain but in return wants the King of West Seax to supply a hostage. Good faith thus can be maintained on both sides and with the same reasoning."

Æthelbald turned to Æthelheard and raised an eyebrow.

King Æthelheard concurred, "They can take the aetheling, Sigeberht, for my part... and good riddance," he murmured under his breath.

"Aetheling?"

"Ay, what you call a 'prince'."

Both parties nodded at each other in conclusion of the pact and rode off to fetch the respective people pledged.

The Wealisc returned with a handsome youth, his face smeared after a poor attempt at removing blue warpaint. They departed with the aetheling, whose pouting expression revealed the resentment burning inside him. Æthelbald chuckled, Æthelheard had made another dangerous enemy. He did not trouble himself over this, rather thinking he, in the King of West Seax's stead, would have had no one to offer as a pledge. Then again, kings did not make sons so they had ready-made hostages. For that matter, he did not care about a successor.

I intend to reign to a ripe old age. First, all of Angle-land must be mine!

This happy thought aside, he began to organise departure from this wild outpost, content that bloodshed had been avoided. He glanced over at King Æthelheard and wondered if he, Æthelbald, had achieved enough by extracting this promise of aid. At this, a germ of an idea infected his mind. First, though, he had to see Æthelheard on his way back to West Seax. Their directions were different, Æthelheard heading south and Æthelbald and Coelwald, east. Thus, they separated, Æthelbald with false oaths of lasting friendship to the King of West Seax.

Back in the welcoming arms of his mistresses, Æthelbald delayed enacting his scheme. He wanted Æthelheard back, without doubt, in distant Wintancaestre.

On 27 May, to the shock and horror of the populace, the daylight disappeared with the sky becoming mysteriously overcast.

Coelwald hurried to find his friend to express his dismay at this ill portent.

"Nonsense!" Æthelbald laughed, "It is an augury that the time is right for action."

"What action?"

"I want you to lead your men down to Somerton and take it in my name."

"Somerton? Is it not a royal burh of the West Seax?"

"Ay, what of it?"

"Will it not provoke Æthelheard into war?"

"It might, and it might not. In either case, it will be interesting."

"But Lord, what of the strange darkening of the sky? Is it not a bad sign?"

"Pah! Coelwald, do not talk like an old woman!"

"And what of the useful alliance between Mierce and West Seax?"

"Somerton holds the passage to the south-west. It is more important than friendship. I hope Æthelheard does not feel the same way. Listen, will you do this or not?"

The dangerous tone of Æthelbald's voice left Coelwald little choice. Also, holding Somerton would be strategic for the defence of his own kingdom. With no further prevarication, he replied, meeting the king's eye, "I will, my lord."

"Good man! I knew I could count on you. If need be, starve them into opening the gates. Here, take this," he held out a bag of coin. "It takes money to feed and keep an army. I heard your men were grumbling about pay, up in that godforsaken Crug." Embracing Coelwald, he stoked his ambition, "Friend, we go back a long way. Serve me well, and who knows, your lands may not be limited to Hwicce. Leave on the morrow. Best not to set off on the day of an untoward sky– not that *I* believe in tales of the kind!"

In mid-July, Æthelbald received news to transform his mood to match the splendid weather: Coelwald had taken Somerton. In effect, his borders, reckoning Hwicce as Mierce, had advanced almost twenty leagues to the south. Life was glorious! The dry month allowed him to indulge in hunting and hawking, his frontiers were expanding in all directions but without excessive tribulations, and he rejoiced in his night-time activities. These, of course, sooner or later, had to bear fruit, the king being in fine fettle and virile. Still, it came as a surprise to him when Merwenna informed him her flow had interrupted and to prepare himself for the birth of a child. Æthelbald did not know how to react. He looked at his mistress' belly and found it impossible to imagine a human being gestating therein. It was an intellectual concept with complicated implications. Would he legitimise the child? He pushed the thought of scandal to the back of his mind for the moment and gave priority to embracing and kissing the future mother of his first offspring.

To lessen his zest for life and kingship, a messenger arrived from Wintancaestre to protest against the seizure of Somerton.

"Sire," said the emissary, "my king bids me explain the difficulties in which the taking of the royal burh places him." The tall, dignified figure drew himself up, took a deep breath and continued choosing his words with care. "In West Seax, there are those who claim the throne and… seek little excuse to… weaken my lord's position—"

"And they press for war with Mierce to avenge the loss of Somerton?" Æthelbald intervened.

"Indeed, sire."

There was a moment's silence, but the messenger added, "My king, of course, values your alliance and does not wish to break it with a call to arms."

"Of course."

"But he begs you, sire, to understand his position. The taking of Somerton must be balanced by an act of goodwill."

"*Goodwill?*"

"Ay."

Æthelbald stood.

"Come, friend, we must partake of drink to raise our spirits, and you will explain to me at table who dares oppose Æthelheard in West Seax."

The conversation was long and detailed, but by the end, having followed it with inordinate interest, Æthelbald sighed and, thoughtful, tugged at his beard.

"What it comes down to," he said, "is those who claim descent from Cutha and, thence Cynric, believe King Æthelheard to be a usurper. They will not rest till one of their own takes the throne. Is that it?"

"Ay, Lord, it is so. Hence the king's need for an act of goodwill."

"Which he shall have, my friend, upon my oath. Give me time to decide what it will be."

The King of Mierce sent the messenger back to Wintancaestre with his solemn word but no concrete detail to provide for his master. In his own mind, he was clear about the nature of this act of goodwill, which was why he summoned his own rider, a reliable thegn, to dispatch to Somerton.

In the fine July riding conditions, the horseman covered the fifty leagues in eight days. Thus, Coelwald was charged by King Æthelbald to enter West Seax to seek out and slay Eafa, aetheling, son of Eoppa and descendant of Cutha. Æthelbald promised Coelwald a reward beyond his imaginings for this service on behalf of King Æthelheard. This was the essence of the message.

Coelwald received it with disdain. He was a warrior, as such he feared no man, but he was not a murderer. On the other hand, he was too wise to cross Æthelbald, knowing only too well the unforgiving volatile nature of his king. He often thought that Æthelbald, had he not been so gifted, would have been nothing more than a tyrant, but his king's character was tempered by generosity.

Patience was not one of the king's virtues, so the weeks seemed interminable as they ran together while he waited for news from Coelwald. When the messenger arrived from his friend, his forbearance was tested again because the message was not what he expected, nor what he hoped for. Coelwald had disobeyed orders, refusing to slay Eafa. Instead, he had delivered him into the hands of Æthelheard. Doubtless, Coelwald considered, this amounted to the same thing. To be sure, it fulfilled Æthelbald's promise to his fellow king. The King of Mierce decided not to punish his under-king for disobedience, but he would not honour his incentive of more lands, either. Æthelbald never did find out what fate befell Eafa, nor did he care.

THIRTEEN

Tame Weorth, spring 734 AD

Whether or not Æthelbald believed in the portentous nature of sky formations, how was he to explain away the malign effect of the moon appearing as if covered in blood? Not long after this disturbing spectacle alarmed the populace of Tame Weorth, the news arrived of the death of Archbishop Tatwine. The two events, the king failed to separate in his mind, also because having his own nominee as Archbishop of Cantwaraburh had proved an astute move. Now, after little more than three years in office, came his death.

Bishop Aldwine hurried from Licidfelth in response to his king's urgent summons.

"Sire," began the prelate of notable character, "if the rumours of the seduction of nuns and flouting of concubines are true, you have incurred the awesome wrath of God!"

"Bishop, what is *true* is that I cannot harm that wagging tongue of yours, out of respect for the church. It is also true I can send you among the Wealisc to draw them nearer to the Church of Rome."

The prelate blanched and stammered, "L-Lord, as your pastor, I am c-concerned for your spiritual welfare."

"For that, I have my confessor, Lord Bishop… and my

conscience. Pay no heed to vile rumours."

"But sire, there are no waves without wind. A ruler must set the example of a blameless life."

Restless at the tiresome discussion, Æthelbald treated Bishop Aldwine to the sharp edge of his tongue, "Had I wished for a blameless life, I'd have entered the church. Now onto more important issues…"

The king challenged the prelate with a long and ferocious stare which ended only when the churchman found the good sense to say, "My king?" in the meekest voice.

"Are you aware that the Archbishop of Cantwaraburh departed this life ten days ago?"

The Bishop of Licidfelth crossed himself and muttered something in Latin the king failed to catch.

"God rest his soul. He was a charismatic man, an inspiration to everyone."

"Where do we find another such, Bishop? I seek your counsel – it is the reason I called you away from your manifold duties. The new incumbent ought to be chosen as a matter of extreme urgency, and he must be a Miercian."

"We might pray for guidance, sire."

"Come then, let us repair to the chapel."

Kneeling beside his bishop, deep in prayer, Æthelbald's mind fluttered like a butterfly from one pressing issue to another until the bishop whispered, "I have a name, sire."

Æthelbald started from the depths of his thoughts.

"*Eh?*"

"Might I suggest a name, sire?"

"That is why we are here, Bishop."

"You need to look no further than among your own counsellors, Lord."

"Who?"

"Among them is the arch-priest of the cathedral of St Paul in Lunden."

"Nothhelm? But I know little of him."

"A man beyond reproach, but above all, in close correspondence with our Holy Father, Gregory."

"*Close*, you say."

"Ay, he visited Rome and researched the history of Kent in the papal library: all through the good graces of the pope."

Instinct told Æthelbald he had found his man. Nothhelm fulfilled all his prerequisites, a Miercian but also one involved with Kent. This would keep the canons of Cantwaraburh on their leashes. Nothhelm it would be!

"Bishop, I cannot argue with your God-inspired suggestion. We must leave for Lunden, collect the priest and take him to Cantwaraburh for his appointment."

While in Lunden, Æthelbald granted a number of toll remissions on ships to the Bishops of Lunden and Hrofæscæstre, nor did he forget his obligation to the abbess of Minster-in-Thanet. In Cantwaraburh, as foreseen, the canons greeted his choice of Nothhelm with suitable approval. The land of the Middle Saxons was his to dispose of as he wished. So confident did he feel of his authority there, after giving a sumptuous feast for the lords of the area, he returned at once to pressing business in Mierce.

One of the most pressing, although he knew it not upon his departure, was the imminent birth of his child. Merwenna's waters brokeearly in the tenth moon. The king paced backwards and forwards outside the birth chamber until he heard the cough and wailing of the babe. He pushed into the room, and his first emotion was relief to see the mother and child both in health. Tears welled in his eyes, and for no discernable reason, he felt proud and protective. The infant lay on her breast but turned its head, squashed, deformed for the moment by the birth, towards his father. Æthelbald stepped over and lifted the babe into his arms, holding him close to his chest. With his finger, he stroked the palm of the perfect little hand, whose tiny fingers curled around it. The king laughed, and a tear of joy coursed down his cheek.

"The child will be named Æthelstan. Ay, Æthelstan," he said, savouring the sound of the name, "Here, Æthelstan, go to your mother," he handed the child back to his adoring mistress. The change in Æthelbald, quite perceptible to those close to him, centred on his attitude to life, altered by those deep blue eyes staring unfocused into his face.

* * *

The most urgent issue awaiting Æthelbald was unexpected. In his hall stood the wiry, long-limbed figure of a man from the far north beyond the confines of Angle-land. His long reddish hair fell either side of a broad face covered in tattoos, as was the rest of his exposed skin. The flowing, curvilinear designs, tinted from iron, added to the ferocious appearance of the warrior, the custom gave his people also their name "Picti" – "*the painted ones*". This Pict presented himself to Æthelbald.

"King Æthelbald of Mierce, my name is Oengus-mac-Fergusa, king of the Picts these past two winters. I come in peace to speak with the greatest king in the whole of Angle-land."

Understanding the strong accent with difficulty, Æthelbald yet managed to glean the sense of the compliment and nodded his pleasure.

"What is it you seek here in Mierce, King Oengus?"

"A pact. As you know, friend, my people and yours have a common enemy: Northanhymbre. The fact is, we are at war with the Scoti. I mean to drive them out of our land, but I cannot do so if the Northanhymbrians move against me. What I propose is a pact where if either one of us is attacked by Northanhymbre, the one intervenes to aid the other. What say you?"

Æthelbald stepped down from his throne and seized the hand of Oengus-mac-Fergusa in a warm clasp. He recognised an indomitable fellow warrior, and while for the moment, he had not excogitated the advantage to himself in such an arrangement, he followed his instinct to proceed. Oengus, delighted at a swift and satisfactory conclusion, drew a gold torque over his wrist and held it out to Æthelbald. The magnificent twisted band, each twist interspersed with a narrow dotted cord of the same precious metal, ended in two fine bull's heads. The unfeigned pleasure on the Miercian's face, as he pulled it over his hand, provoked Oengus into hauling the monarch into a fierce embrace. Startled and emotional, King Æthelbald patted the broad back of his new ally, who released him and grinned up into the visage of the Miercian.

"Let us drink to our friendship!" Æthelbald roared for ale.

Over twice-brewed ale, Oengus explained how the Scoti, formidable sailors, came from and went to the large isle to the west: Eire. There, the idea of a high king meant that covetous eyes were cast across the sea to the land held by the Picti. The moment was ripe, Oengus explained, to put an end to any designs on his territory by driving the Scoti into the sea. His numbers, he pointed out with glee, were far greater. Indeed, five years before, in a terrible battle, he defeated and slew with his own hands, Drust, the king of the Scoti. He expressed no doubt of his future success unless, of course, the Northanhymbrians allied with the Scoti. He worried about this because of late, under Eadberht, the signs were they were pushing into the British-held territory of Rheged, confining with Pictish lands.

"Worry not, friend Oengus, I keep Eadberht under my sway. I will send a messenger to warn him against any attack on your people for it will invoke the fury of Mierce."

So saying, Æthelbald sent for a rider and, in front of Oengus-mac-Fergusa, made him repeat back, word perfect, the said communication before sending him off.

That night, after a feast in honour of his guest, the King of Mierce could not sleep. His overactive mind and the effect on his digestion of the heavy meal kept him awake. By habit, he fingered the ring of Osthryth that lay on his chest as he pondered the possible consequences of his latest alliance. It came to him that honouring his word to Oengus might not be such a bad thing in view of his lifelong ambition to become Bretwaldas – not just king of the south but of *all* of Angle-land. Only a week or so ago, he signed a charter with the appellation *Rex Britannicus*. This would sound less hollow if his rule extended also over Northanhymbre.

The next day, he was saddened to see Oengus depart: in him, he identified a kindred spirit. Every effort he made, to convince him to extend his stay. The king of the Picti explained he had been away three weeks, although only two days of them had been spent with Æthelbald. His journey back through Elmet and Rheged, more than a hundred leagues over difficult terrain, albeit on horseback, would take him ten and eight days. This, he considered too long to leave his son, Brude, alone to face possible aggression in his absence, on the part of the wily Scoti.

No sooner had Oengus departed than another unexpected visitor arrived. He announced himself as Forthhere, Master Goldsmith, the son of Forwin.

"Eight years!" Æthelbald growled, "Seven winters gone by without my sword. It is true I told Forwin to take his time, but I never meant to do without it for so long."

"Sire, my father died these five winters past and until not long ago, I knew naught of this commission."

"I sorrow to hear it, for Master Forwin pleased me. But tell me, how came you to discover the work?"

"Father would disappear into his workshop and bear no disturbance. Last winter, I decided to explore in there when I found the sword. Tied to the hilt was a parchment, and upon unrolling it, I found the design. With a little searching, I found the pommel completed as in the drawing. Then I studied the haft and across the scroll on the cross guard, the words '*Æthelbaldus Rex*'. That was when I understood the work was for you, sire. Father never spoke to me of it, and each toiled in his own workshop… so, I took it upon myself to finish the piece he had started, hence the long delay, for which I beseech your gracious pardon, Lord."

"And where is the sword?"

"At the door, sire, the guard forbade me to bring it into your presence."

"Guard!" the king's bellow nigh rent the eardrums of the cowering goldsmith.

The guard hurried in with his own sword at the ready and another wrapped in a cloth, just as Enulf, long ago, had presented it. The guard halted, looking from his king to the craftsman with suspicion writ plain across his face.

"Hand it to Master Forthhere, fellow!"

The guard obeyed but did not resist a menacing scowl at the king's guest before retreating to his post.

With care, Forthhere unwrapped the roll of cloth before his sovereign's greedy stare. What emerged from the bundle was a sparkling red and gold object of breathtaking beauty.

"Father soldered thick ribbons of gold to the base of the sunken area, sire, which he then filled to make the compartments for the garnets. This is all offset by the ivory haft, reinforced with twisted gold wire wound around and inlaid so it will never break or betray in battle. I set in the rubies myself, according to father's design, God rest his soul."

"Amen."

"What say you, sire? Does the sword please you? Is there anything to add to it?"

It did, and there was not. For once, Æthelbald stood speechless – this was what he had hoped for and more besides. What an exquisite figure would the King of Mierce make as he strode among his people or encountered other kings.

"Might I be bold and make a suggestion, Lord?"

"*Eh?*"

The goldsmith's words shook Æthelbald out of his fond reverie.

"Ay, go on!"

The craftsman gave a light cough, "Such a weapon, sire, ought to have a befitting sheath so that hanging by your side, it will dazzle all who behold it."

"Have you designs for me to consider?"

The goldsmith shook his head, "...I would not presume... but, my king, I can prepare them overnight that you may choose... only—"

"What?"

"—the cost, Lord. It is high already without the scabbard."

The king took the sword from the master craftsman's hands and, wielding it, made it sigh through the air in a dazzling flash of red and gold.

Enamoured of the masterpiece, Æthelbald did not care about the price. The royal coffers overflowed. Now, for the first time, his outward appearance would match his ambitions.

"Master Forthhere," he said, "come, and I will settle the debt incurred thus far. This, I suppose will enable you to proceed with the sheath?"

Agreement on price reached, the king waited expectantly to pore over a choice of designs the next morning.

So it was, three weeks after that day, King Æthelbald buckled the gem-studded belt bearing the tooled leather scabbard, where dazzling jewels flashed at his slightest movement. Over the sheath, the ivory and gold hilt presided, its rubies competing for attention with the garnet and gold pommel. A magnificent monarch, and no one else was meet for such a wondrous display – which was what Æthelbald had intended all along.

FOURTEEN

Countryside near Ledecestre, thirteen years before, 721 AD

The sense of guilt tormenting Heremod for the death of his cousin led him to make enquiries about the king's court. What he learned about it at Tame Weorth gave him hope for justice. It must be true that the king defended the poor and oppressed, if this was the opinion held by everyone he had spoken with at market. In that case, he must convince Goda to appeal to Æthelbald.

Heremod's common sense told him their situation was unsustainable. Scraping a living for himself and Osythe was hard and with a babe on the way... now, the widow and her two children were a burden beyond his strength and means. For the moment, the woman was paying her way, but the money could not last forever.

Steeling himself for a difficult conversation, he raised the subject at the table.

"Goda, people I spoke with at the market told me the king will hold court next month at Tame Weorth for any grievances his people wish to settle. They say the king is favourable to the poor and the oppressed."

"Cousin, how can I take my grievance to the king? A feeble widow against a mighty lord?"

"Well, that is a case of oppression if ever there was one!"

"Ay," Goda's eyes filled with tears, "but there weren't any witnesses to the slaying of my Herrig. It's my word against that of an ealdorman. Who do you think the king will believe?"

"Goda, you should trust in God. You are in the right. I will accompany you to Tame Weorth."

His words made Goda feel guilty, aware she had concealed some facts. She prayed God would understand and forgive her enough to not let her be found out one day.

"And what of Osythe? What if her waters break while you are away?"

"It's next month, Goda! Too soon for that to happen. Anyway, her mother can look after my wife. Look, you must think of your children and what awaits them. If the king finds for you, you will secure their future. If not, it's going to be hard to manage. I blame myself for all this. It's the devil's work. I ought never to have given in to temptation."

"You did it for Osythe and the babe. Don't trouble yourself." She reached across the table and squeezed Heremod's hand.

"Ah, Goda. you are a good woman! Wait and see how much soil we can till in the spring with the plough. I never used one in my life, but they say it's not so hard to keep a straight furrow. But for the moment, will you come to Tame Weorth to plead your case?"

Goda's brow wrinkled, and she looked suddenly older than her years. She bit her lower lip, on the verge of shaking her head, when the waiflike figure of Cwen slipped into her line of sight. A tear rolled down Goda's cheek and either the wetness or the fire of determination made her eyes flash.

"I will!" she said in a strong voice.

"Good! I'll go and tell Osythe of our plan an' then I'll walk over to my wife-mother's to let her know."

"I can't believe I'll get to see the king in person. Oh, Heremod! Do you think it's possible?"

"Ay, why not? You ain't done wrong. But hark, Goda! No one must ever find out about yon ploughshare else the ealdorman will slay me too."

"You needn't worry 'bout that Heremod. I won't have it my Herrig died in vain."

* * *

Tame Weorth, two weeks later

The king's scrivener, a young monk with a narrow visage that appeared all eyes and thick lips, gazed at the round-faced woman seated in front of him. Judging her to be of pleasant but timid disposition, he treated her to a reassuring smile and urged her to tell her tale.

"Be not afraid, mistress. What is it you wish our king, God save him, to hear?"

"It's like this. I'm from Ledecestre where my poor husband had a smithy. One day, the ealdorman came and charged Herrig, my man, the smith, to make ploughshares from iron bars he bought and caused to be delivered."

"Who bought the bars?" the scribe said, distracted by his effort to keep his writing abreast of the woman's deposition.

"The ealdorman."

The monk scratched a further entry with his quill.

"Go on."

"All seemed to be going well because Herrig did good work. The ealdorman said as much. But when Herrig finished the shares, the ealdorman accused him of stealing iron. Like, he made out that there weren't enough ploughshares from the iron he supplied."

"And was it true? Remember, woman, God sees and judges everything. The king represents His justice here in Mierce."

"Of course it wasn't true," her voice little more than a whisper.

"Speak up!"

"It wasn't true," she cried, outraged.

The quill scratched on. "Well?"

"Then I heard shouting, and I left off preparing vegetables and hastened into the smithy. There… there…" her eyes filled with tears, and her lower lip trembled, "…I saw Ealdorman Enulf strike my husband across the throat with his sword. Poor Herrig died on the spot."

Goda began to sob, and the monk rose to stand behind her and lay a comforting hand on her shoulder.

"What's done is done," he whispered. "Tears won't bring him back. But find strength in God's mercy and finish your tale."

"Ay," Goda nodded, wiping her eyes.

The scribe sat again and took up his quill, dipping it in ink. When he was ready, Goda continued. "To be fair, the ealdorman paid a gold coin for the ploughshares Herrig made," she sniffed, swallowing hard, going on with brave determination, "and, another for the funeral. But what's so unfair is he turned me out of my home and took the smithy. Now I own nothing." Her lip quavered again, but taking a deep breath, she ended, "…I'm here for my two children, Cwen, she's nine and Edwy, he's seen ten and four winters. How are we going to live? The ealdorman's taken everything from *me*!"

The last word came out as a protracted wail.

"Woman, take comfort, the king will hear your case on the morrow. Now, do you swear all you have told me is the truth?"

"I do!"

The scrivener made a note of this and insisted on reading what he had written back to her.

She heard him out, nodding occasionally.

He ended… "*and the widow, Goda, swears that everything herein noted is the whole truth.*"

She tilted her head again, and hid the guilt that lay heavy on her heart.

"Good, then," he said, turning the parchment toward her and handing her the quill.

Goda looked at the feather as if it were a dangerous weapon.

"It needs your signature," the monk said in a gentle voice.

"But I can't write."

"Make any mark you like, it will suffice."

She scrawled a vague shape that looked like a rosebud.

"Perfect," said the scribe, taking back the quill and adding next to it, "*the widow, Goda – her mark*". "Now, remember, rise early tomorrow and come to the king's hall. Yours is not the only case to be heard. You will wait until you hear your name called. Be prepared to give honest answers to the king's questions."

A weak smile and she took her leave. The scrivener watched her go with a feeling of pity for the wretched woman. He waved the parchment in the air to dry the last of the wet ink. Satisfied, he rolled it up and tied a green ribbon around it before placing it in a basket with four similar scrolls, each a deposition for the morrow.

The next morning, Goda, accompanied by Heremod, Cwen and Edwy – with hair, for once, combed and neat – stood among a crowd of people in the hall. The hubbub of voices died down as everyone rose on the tips of their toes to glimpse the king, seating himself on a throne at the front of the hall.

Goda gasped as the full weight of realisation bore down on her. She would soon argue her case with King Æthelbald, the crowned figure everyone bowed down to. Surrounding him were important men, and among them, her startled, frightened eyes picked out a countenance she had hoped never to see again. There was no mistake! It was Ealdorman Enulf. Of course he would be here. The king was holding court, and for sure, he needed to meet with the high and mighty. Her head filled with wild thoughts. *"What if...?"* She knew she had lied over one important detail, but God willing, it would never come out. What was a bit of iron to help a poor family against the theft of a home and a smithy? So, she justified herself but was terrified of facing the king and hoped her case might be the last, or was it not better to get it over first?

It was a vain hope, for a man dressed in black, standing near the king, called out Master Andhun against Master Wulflead, to step forward. The case, presented by Andhun, was read out in a loud voice by the same man in dark clothing. Although she didn't catch every word, Goda understood that Wulflead stood accused of having lain with the other's serving maid. Witnesses were called, including a trembling young woman. In the end, the king rose and in a resounding voice declared, according to his laws, Wulflead should pay six scillingas compensation to Andhun.

Goda, distracted by the thought that witnesses had been summoned and that she did not have any, failed to hear her name called. The tugging at her sleeve and nudge from Heremod, "Widow Goda, that's you, go on!"

She moved to the front of the hall to bow before her king in a mechanical action that had naught to do with her brain. It was awhirl with uncontrollable fears and sensations. How would she be able to express herself in front of her monarch?

The official began to read out her case. Only in that moment did she become aware that a pace behind her, to her left, stood the Ealdorman of Ledecestre and Snotingham, the hated Enulf. When the flow of words drew to an end, amid murmurings from the gathering at her back, the king gestured for her to draw nearer.

"Widow Goda," the king's tone was gentle and not intimidating, "these are grave accusations you make against one of my most trusted counsellors. Are you quite sure of what you claim?"

"I am, sire."

"And, this is very important, are there any witnesses to the slaying of your husband?"

"Only I was in the smithy, sire, when…" her eyes brimmed with tears, "…when…"

The king looked into the round, pleasant face of the widow, and he was moved to pity.

"Catch your breath, Mistress Goda," he said.

She gave her king a mute nod and a weak smile of gratitude and with all her courage added, "…when the ealdorman…" she couldn't bring herself to pronounce his name, "…slew my husband with one blow of his sword, there was no one else present." The last words came in such a low voice that none in the hall heard it but for the king to whom it was addressed.

"No witnesses!" Æthelbald exclaimed.

The official leant over and breathed something into his king's ear.

The ruler nodded and sat back on his throne, "Fetch it!" he commanded.

The man who had read out the scroll and just spoken to the king, hurried out of the room. Goda, worrying about her lack of witnesses, did not notice how many minutes passed. Nor did she hear any of the low voices discussing her case, nor yet observe the king scrutinising her face and its emotions as she considered her position.

The black-dressed fellow returned carrying a square-shaped box with a cross surmounting it.

"This is an altar," he said, "in the absence of witnesses, Widow Goda, you must swear before the Almighty that your deposition is the truth."

She nodded and said, laying her hand on the altar, "I swear what I have said is the truth."

The king smiled and waved away the receptacle. He did not speak to her but addressed the ealdorman.

"Lord Enulf, you heard the sacred oath of the Widow Goda. Do you deny slaying her husband?"

"I do not, sire…" There came a collective gasp in the hall. "…but the smith cheated me of my iron and when I confronted him, he came at me with a hammer."

"A hammer?" The king laughed, "But you are a warrior, tested in battle. It was no even match. It is enough, and I will pass judgement, but first, Lord Enulf, I will say this. I raised you up to rule over my scirs as a just man. It is not in your place to slay a man no better nor worse than yourself. Need I remind you that you were my father's blacksmith? I, who raised you, can dash you down just as easily."

Goda started and gazed in astonishment at the ealdorman who glared back at her. This humiliation in front of the crowded hall was one he resented to the core of his being.

"You, Lord Enulf, ought to have accused the smith of theft if you were sure of your facts. You may not take the law into your own hands. The smith would have been tried as you are tried today. No man is above my law. In fact," the king smiled at the widow, "the law states if a man slays a free man, he shall pay fifty scillingas to the king for the infraction of his rights. This you will pay, Lord Enulf, within twenty-four hours. For a smith, this wergild is doubled to one hundred scillingas." The ealdorman, seethed inside that his old friend should belittle him in front of the gathering. But he was too wise to let his emotions show. He would not forget this day for the rest of his life.

The king stood and in a thunderous voice, declared the case closed. Turning to Enulf, he said, "I hope you know I will not tolerate another such outrage from you, Lord Enulf." In truth, he was angered by what he felt a breach in the faith he had put in the ealdorman. He believed he deserved even more loyalty from the fellow than Enulf had given to Æthelbald's father.

The nobleman bowed, glowered at the widow and regained his place behind the king, who now spoke to her.

"Mistress Goda, you find yourself without a home and with two children to support. You will come to this hall tomorrow and speak with me again. Now, there are other cases to hear. A good day to you, mistress."

"And to you, sire," she curtseyed and sought Heremod.

"What did King Æthelbald say to you?" her late husband's cousin pressed her, and her children drew close to hear.

"He is a kind man," Goda said, "but I did not receive justice. Lord Enulf must pay the king one hundred scillingas for his crime. Am I to get *nothing*?" She started to cry into a kerchief.

"Is that it?" Heremod was aghast. "Are we to go back home with naught?"

"The king wishes to see me on the morrow," she said in a voice muffled by the cloth.

The voice of the king's official ordered two more people into the king's presence.

"Let's go and find something to eat and drink," Heremod suggested. "My throat is on fire, there's no air in this place."

At a table in a tavern, they discussed the morning's proceedings.

Cwen made them laugh by saying, in her piping voice, "Did you see how handsome is the king. I wonder why he has no queen?"

"Maybe because he's waiting for you to grow up!" Edwy teased her.

"Ma, did you see his crown? It must be heavy on his head!"

"Children, your mother and I have important things to discuss," Heremod's strict voice quelled their chatter. "You said the king wants to see you tomorrow, Goda?"

"Ay, so he said."

"You know what that means?"

"I do not."

"I reckon Æthelbald seeks to settle the matter in private. It may be he did not wish to make his final decision in front of all the people. In any case, he passed judgement on Lord Enulf."

"Ay, but that sum is naught to one as rich as he."

Heremod stifled his reply since the innkeeper arrived with a platter of cold meat slices and a bowl of onions in vinegar. When the man went off to fetch their drinks, he said, "The real punishment for one such as he, is to be in the king's bad graces."

"Did you hear the king say Enulf was his father's blacksmith?"

"I did."

"That's how he knew there was iron missing," she whispered.

"Ay. Keep it to yourself, Goda."

The drinks arrived and they speculated on what the king might do the next day.

The wait, in the chamber giving onto the great hall, the next morning was hard to bear for Goda. She had left the children in the care of Heremod, whose intention was to take advantage of the fine weather and to stroll around the town. The suggestive glances she received from the guard on the door to the hall cheered her a little. It had been a while since a man had shown any interest in her.

A servant appeared, after an age, to lead her into the presence of King Æthelbald.

"Be seated, Mistress Goda," the king gestured to a bench before sitting opposite her. His encouraging smile captivated her.

"I asked you here today because the manner of your treatment by my ealdorman dismays me but at the same time puts me in a difficult position. I shall not make an attempt to explain, except to command you to keep what passes between us here in the utmost secrecy."

"Of course, sire."

"The wergild paid to me by Enulf is yours." The king tossed a sizeable bag of coins on the table. "It will help you start life anew. You are still an attractive woman. Find a man to protect you and your children. But I have thought about the loss of your home. Tell me, mistress, is there no man you can rely upon?"

Goda's smile was puzzled. Where were the king's words leading her? When she set out this morning, she did not expect this kind of intimate discussion with a man whom she thought of as a godlike, unapproachable being.

"Sire, for the moment, I am staying with my husband's cousin. His wife is with child," she hastened to add to prevent misunderstanding.

"There is a small farm, mistress, on royal lands to the east of Glevcaestre. The ceorl who managed it died three months ago. It comes with good fertile land. I would prefer to give it to you, thus righting the wrong committed by my ealdorman." The king paused, and his eyes fixed those of the widow. Was it the pleasant gentleness of her face that made him behave so or the desire to make amends for Enulf's misdeed? He knew not. "How old is your son, mistress?"

"Four and ten, sire."

"Too young to manage a farm, but not for long. A scheme begins to form in my mind. What say you if I send a man with experience to train the boy? Three years ought to be enough. Does all this please you, Mistress Goda?"

"Sire, I do not command the words to thank you for your kindness. It pleases me beyond my wildest imaginings. How can I ever repay you?"

"Keep me in your prayers, mistress."

By Thunor, if she knew how much they serve to offset my sins!

"I will, sire."

"Return to the hall a week from today. In the meantime, I will make arrangements for men to keep your family safe on the journey. I will also find the farm manager. A good day to you, Mistress Goda."

The king watched her leave the hall and smiled. When he became king of all Angle-land, he wished to be loved by his subjects and known as a protector of widows and the poor. This was one small step in the right direction. But he knew in no small measure he had done it because Enulf had betrayed his trust.

Imparting her news to Heremod and her children, Goda could scarcely contain her joy. The king, in his wisdom, had provided for the future of Edwy. For the present, she had money to spend. Here in town, she might be able to find clothes for the new babe. Heremod was right to persuade her to appeal to the king. None of this seemed real to her, but then, she knew little of divine providence. King Æthelbald knew even less.

One week later, Goda, Cwen and Edwy bade a safe journey home to Heremod. Goda slipped him a small bag of coins she had prepared for him and promised to come and visit to see the child when she could. Inside the hall, she found a servant and told him of her appointment. He disappeared and on his return gave her instructions to go to the south gate of the town where she would find a man called Trygil waiting for her.

The king had chosen well. The ceorl, a well-built man in his late twenties, together with presentable looks, lacked nothing in intelligence. Spotting a woman with a girl and a youth, he reached the conclusion this was the family he had been commanded to accompany to Northleach.

Introducing himself, he was pleased with the charming round-faced woman whose enforced company he would have for the next three years. She too, delighted by her first impressions, was quick to ask, "What of the escort promised us, Master Trygil?"

"Supping ale, I reckon. In the tavern by the gate." He pointed to an inn. "I'll step along and fetch the wastrels."

He soon returned with a florid-faced warrior. This man touched his forelock and said, "The others will be here in a moment, mistress. I sent them to bring the horses and the cart." He saw her reaction, "Ay, we'll need them. It is a journey of nigh on forty leagues, mistress."

They set off before noon and Goda cast a mournful glance back at Tame Weorth from her position at the back of the cart, drawn by two horses. The town, she realised, was important to her. Never had she dreamt as a young woman that she would go there, let alone speak with the king. The regret was she had not been able to say farewell to King Æthelbald. Now, she would never see him again. Or so she thought, knowing naught of divine providence.

FIFTEEN

Tame Weorth, 735 AD

To go to war, Æthelbald needed to convene his council so that his ealdormen might summon the fyrd to arms. The news out of Northanhymbre put him in belligerent mood. A mixture of aggression and irritation best described his frame of mind as he glared around the assembled lords and bishops.

"I am not the least troubled that Eadberht has used his influence to install his brother Ecgbert to the bishopric of Eoforwic. What annoys me is he managed to persuade the Holy Father to elevate the city to an archbishopric. This cannot pass unpunished. I intend to march on Eoforwic…" With a flourish, he drew his jewel-encrusted sword in a dazzling arc of red and gold to emphasise his words, "…and raze it to the ground."

There followed a huddle of heads and murmuring around the hall. At last, Bishop Aldwine rose and asked to speak. Speech granted, he said, "Sire, the appointment of an archbishop in Northanhymbre has a certain logic. The land stretches from the River Hymbre as far as the territory of the Picti. The church needs a central see to control and coordinate the others over so vast an area."

"Northanhymbre need not suppose receiving the pallium increases its standing in Angle-land," Æthelbald snarled.

"Why, not at all," Aldwine gave what he hoped was a reassuring smile to his king, and his tone was mellifluous. "The Church of Rome is strong on tradition. Cantwaraburh is where Saint Augustine founded the church in these lands, and it is *there* ecclesiastical authority resides."

"Well," King Æthelbald, with some ostentation, sheathed his sword, "in that case, I shall stay my hand as far as Northanhymbre is concerned."

Unless Eadberht provokes me!

"Now, there is another matter," he continued. "As you will know, King Aethelheard in West Seax is not enjoying good health. His lady, the admirable Queen Frithugyth, is struggling to keep some factions among the West Seaxa under control. I am informed of elements hostile to Mierce, and since we took Somerton, our confines are further south and west than before. I mean to move on Sumersaet, take the scir with its natural borders, where the sprawling Selwood and the high hills provide the protection I crave. We will march as soon as I have assembled the men here at Tame Weorth." His eyes sought out a friendly face and settled on the Ealdorman of Ledecestre. "Lord Enulf, how many warriors can you supply for this venture?"

Enulf creased his brow and tugged at his beard, "Three-score and ten at least, sire, more if you need them."

"Splendid! And you King Coelwald?"

The underking of Hwicce, like Enulf, hesitated a little. "My fyrdmen are stood by, sire. A good two-score and ten are garrisoned at Somerton. Also, I can call on those who served with me in Powys – as many as you need."

"There may be rewards for any other who wishes to join us," the king looked around the room.

A familiar face grinned back at him, "Count on me, my king. I can fetch up to four-score warriors."

"I thank you, Lord Leofwig," Æthelbald smiled. "That concludes our business today."

Three months later, the host led by Æthelbald took Sumersaet without undue resistance. The scir pleased the king, who seized a royal hunting lodge at Ceodor and made it his own for the whole summer. The fertile land of the Gorge proved both scenic and bounteous. Whatever pressing matters awaited him in Tame Weorth, Æthelbald put off while he enjoyed the sport provided by the excellent hunting. West Seax smarted at this affront, but secure, the King of Mierce sat behind his new boundaries. His army waited, ready to repel those meagre forces the West Seaxa might raise. Queen Frithugyth remained in control of her noblemen and Æthelbald won her goodwill by granting land to her sister's abbey near the south-eastern borders of the territory he had seized.

The king met with Coelwald and made arrangements for the garrisoning of fortresses through the winter months. The majority of his army returned to Tame Weorth where they were paid off and dismissed for service on the land. This was an urgent matter with the harvest to be gathered before the inclement weather closed in.

* * *

Tame Weorth, six months later, 736 AD

The following year brought a significant change to Northanhymbre. King Ceolwulf, for so long derided over the episode of his forced tonsuring, caused momentary wonder by demanding to be tonsured of his own free will. This, he accompanied with a request to resign his throne. Whether it was also his unforced decision, Æthelbald doubted. Whatever the case, Ceolwulf upped and retired to the island monastery of Lindisfarne. Less than the time it took the moon to pass the Dog Star twice and Eadberht declared himself Lord of Northanhymbre. This did not concern Æthelbald, who had tolerated his kingship in all but name for long enough. The rival factions within the land showed no sign of abating their efforts to seize power from Eadberht. In this insecurity, Æthelbald always prospered. So it came as a surprise when the new king raised an army and marched it into the Brittonic territory of Rheged. Ferocious fighting followed, but Eadberht prevailed and declared the territory a part of Northanhymbre.

The conquest of inhospitable moorland, lakes and turbulent brooks bothered Æthelbald not a whit. What concerned him rather more was the mentality underlying the expansion. What did Eadberht have in mind next? Elmet? Where his brother held the northern confines of Mierce safely at his back? Or Galloway, controlled by the Picti?

King Æthelbald considered these possibilities, and neither pleased him. He needed to deal with Eadberht. Above all, his pact with Oengus nagged away in the forefront of his mind.

By good fortune, the south was calm. Although her husband was not in the best of health, Queen Frithugyth felt secure enough of her husband's power in West Seax to embark on a pilgrimage to Rome.

Æthelbald decided to meet with Eadberht. The encounter was to take place in Loidis, where his brother, Heardberht, as underking of Elmet, had his hall. A messenger rode to Eoforwic to summon Eadberht to the moot.

***

"Why does the King of Northanhymbre not come?"

Æthelbald paced to and fro in the enclosure in front of the hall. How many times had he asked the question? He smashed a fist into the palm of his other hand to vent his frustration. He would give Eadberht two more days. If he defied him any longer, he would send a dozen riders to different parts of Mierce to raise the host and then – ah, then – he would devastate the natural enemy of the Miercians.

The arrival of Eadberht the next day allayed Æthelbald's ire but not the sharpness of his tongue.

"You kept me waiting and tested my patience, King Eadberht – never a wise choice."

"Then you have not heard?"

"What?"

"I could not come, for the Picti broke an agreement we signed seven years ago and made a treacherous attack on us from the fortress of Dunadd."

"It is of the Picti I wish to speak."

King Æthelbald studied the reactions of his fellow king. The two men were physical opposites, Æthelbald, tall and lean with the muscular attributes of a warrior. Eadberht, plump and mellow in appearance, had not risen to power through intimidation. This reflection prompted Æthelbald to thrust his leonine visage into that of the Northanhymbrian.

"By seizing Rheged, you provoked my friend, Oengus-mac-Fergusa."

Eadberht countered, "In doing so, I put an end to the thieving of our beasts across the confines."

"I am here to warn you, Eadberht, Mierce will not tolerate any aggression against the Picti."

"But they attacked us, in breach of our settlement. What am I supposed to do? Ignore their violence?"

Eadberht's voice had taken on a whining tone, which roused Æthelbald's temper.

"Be warned, if you dare invade Dàl Riata, you will have me to reckon with, since Oengus is a friend to Mierce."

"What care you for the Picti? They are too distant from Mierce to be a threat. Northanhymbre, instead, lies on your northern borders. Is it not better to befriend us than the Picti?"

"A friend is a friend, not to be cast aside like an old shoe."

"I propose a peace treaty with Mierce."

"So you can do what you like in the far north? It is out of the question. You have been warned."

In spite of the niceties of the next two days, hunting and feasting, Æthelbald proved inflexible. Every attempt by Eadberht to persuade him of the benefits of an alliance between their kingdoms met with a rebuff.

The warning must have had an effect, since two years of relative tranquillity followed. But this did not last as the decade wore on. Eadberht contented himself exerting control over Rheged while he cast an anxious eye over his northern borders, where Oengus resumed his hostilities against the Scoti. Before long, Oengus carried the war overseas to Ireland. Meanwhile, Mierce prospered as never before.

* * *

Tame Weorth, 740 AD

In Ireland, Oengus inflicted defeat on the Scoti at about the time the news broke in Tame Weorth of the death of King Æthelheard. Under other circumstances, Æthelbald would have become involved in the appointment of his successor but Eadberht of Northanhymbre made his move against the Picti and distracted him. The aggression of the Northanhymbrians came as a result of Oengus's second victory – a massacre of the Scoti – in Ireland. There, he, in person, beheaded the Scottish king the following winter of 741. It meant that Oengus now had undisputed control of all the land to the north of Northanhymbre. As such, he was a constant menace to the disputed lowlands between the two countries. Much bloodshed had occurred in the past, not to be expunged overnight by peaceable words. Eadberht decided to act before Oengus could regroup. He mobilised an army and headed north, hoping Æthelbald might be occupied with the death of the King of West Seax.

For his part, Æthelbald felt strong enough in the south and was more concerned about exerting his power over Eadberht. Thus, Cuthred became king of the West Seax without interference from Mierce. Æthelbald summoned a meeting of his council.

"Lords and bishops," he began, "King Eadberht defies the authority of Mierce and must be punished. As I speak, he dares to wage war against our ally, the king of the Picti. This cannot be!"

His calculated discourse stirred the ancient hatred of the Miercians for Northanhymbre. Not a man in the hall opposed the king's words, layman or otherwise. The bishops, aware of Northanhymbrian opposition to the will of Rome over the years, harboured rancorous thoughts. Above all, they were grateful to their king for his cooperation with Archbishop Nothhelm, who oversaw the reorganisation of the Miercian dioceses in 737. The archbishop consecrated Witta as Bishop of Licidfelth and Totta as Bishop of Ledecestre. This latter action established the diocese of Ledecestre where earlier attempts had failed. Unsurprising, therefore, none of the "men of peace" opposed the king's warlike intentions.

"I mean to lead a host into Northanhymbre to make him pay for his arrogant disobedience."

"Ay!" roared the ealdormen, and the bishops nodded wisely. King Æthelbald had the unanimous assent he sought from his council with no need for arguments or persuasion.

Æthelbald decided to gather his army in Elmet for practical reasons. Principal among them, he would constrain his brother to muster his fyrdmen. So, each ealdorman agreed to raise the fyrd and head to Loidis, whence under the banner of Mierce and led by the king, they would march on Eoforwic.

A month later, the great host assembled in Loidis and departed into Northanhymbre where foraging began at once to feed the hundreds of warriors. The resulting devastation of the farmsteads met with no restraint from Æthelbald, but with his approbation; thus would Eadberht learn not to resist his will. The seven leagues to Eoforwic over soft ground could be covered in a day and a half of steady marching. However, Æthelbald rested his men with frequent stops and more punitive expeditions into the surrounding area than an advancing force would conduct in other circumstances. Thus, on the third day, farther along the river valley, they caught their first glimpse of the town.

The approach proved complicated, owing to large pools formed by the flooding of the tidal river Ouse where it met the Weorf. Their advance, up the south bank of the Ouse, of necessity, was slow. It gave Æthelbald time to study the layout of the town. As far as he could determine, the centre of the settlement lay near the river crossing on the slopes of two low hills on this, the south bank. Across on the north, rose the stone fortress, built long ago by the Romans. The king called his army to a halt. The numbers were too great, he decided, to be deployed in a sensible manner among the buildings. He issued orders for scouts to find suitable land for encampment elsewhere, since the waterlogged ground thereabouts proved unsuitable.

Drawing Heardberht aside, he instructed his brother to separate his men from the host and to prepare them to slay anyone they found in the town. The place should be plundered of its wealth, churches and their contents excepted. Priests and nuns were to be spared the slaughter. The dwellings, he said, must be torched. This established, he set them about their task.

The scouts indicated a suitable knoll to the south-east of the town. Æthelbald ordered encampment there. From this vantage point, he watched the first smoke swept away over the river by the brisk wind. Reliable Heardberht! The king's smile broadened when his brother returned. Behind him, four men staggered up the soft ground, dragging a cart containing some weight wrapped in a filthy blanket. Heardberht raised a hand and the men stopped, setting their burden down with relief. There it stood, propped on its shafts, the dream of every plunderer – gold! Turning back the cover, it glinted before the unbelieving eyes of King Æthelbald. He could find nothing less pointless to exclaim than, "What's this?"

"Gold, sire. We found Eadberht's mint. Look!"

He opened the fingers of his closed fist. In his palm lay three gold coins. Æthelbald took one and studied it, his heart beating quicker. The piece bore a cross on one side and on the other, what looked like a city gate – maybe the old Roman entry.

"We followed your orders and torched the mint, but it seemed a pity to leave this behind," his hand swept through the air toward the cart.

"Well done, brother!" Indifferent, Æthelbald glanced at the dense black pall hanging over the town. "Half shall go to you and your men. The other half will pay the fyrdmen gathered here today. Thus, Eadberht will render a high price for his disobedience!"

The king's words, heard by the warriors standing closest, passed from man to man until the general exuberance caused a din. It was difficult for Æthelbald to give his orders but at last, Heardberht understood. Men were sent into the countryside to find two oxen and a yoke. The raid on Northanhymbre was all but over. Whatever else they achieved in this land would not be worth the effort. Much better to head back home with the treasure secure and Eadberht's capital reduced to ashes.

Eadberht's hatred of Æthelbald reached new heights when he had to break off his engagement with the Picti upon learning of the burning of York. He would exact retribution for this effrontery. If only his position within and without his kingdom were more secure. For the moment, he admitted sorrowfully, the outrage must go unavenged. But the time would come when Æthelbald paid for his misdeeds.

SIXTEEN

Northleach Farmstead, Gleawcesterscir, 721 AD

The alarm calls of birds in the shrubbery along the woodland trail alerted the captain of Goda's escort. He drew his sword and deployed his men around the horse-drawn cart. Caution had ever been his watchword. Everyone knew that forestland sheltered not only wild beasts but, sad to relate, also cut-throat robbers. Well, let them come if they dare. He was ready!

The rustling in the undergrowth continued, followed by the snapping of a dry branch underfoot.

"Show yourselves!" bellowed the warrior, certain of human presence. Nor was he wrong, for out of the tangle of bracken and buckthorn stepped a ragged figure carrying a wicker basket, its bottom lined with mushrooms.

"I ain't done nothing, Lord!"

"An' I ain't no lord!" the leader of the escort replied. "Are you alone, fellow?"

"I am that."

"Well, maybe you can help us, after all. We seek an empty farmstead in the valley of the Leach. Is this not the said vale? It lies to the north of the river."

With his free hand, the ceorl scratched his lank hair.

"It's hereabouts right enough, an' the river's o'er yonder." He jerked a thumb to his left. "Might it be the owd mill farm ye be seeking?" He screwed up his face, the wrinkles making him look like a wizened old man. "Nah!" he shook his head, "no one's lived there for many winters. Used to be something of a farm did yon." He pointed along the trail, "Keep goin' another two miles an' then the track forks. Bear left, it drops down, steep-like but it'll take ye to Mill Farm. Mind ye, they say it be the king's property."

"An' so it was," said the warrior, sheathing his sword. "Thank you for the information, farewell, fellow."

The directions proved sound. The way dropped down to the valley bottom, and the trees surrendered to land, now tangled with weeds and briar but that once must have been cultivated. By the time the riders reached the middle of the former field, they were up to their saddle-girth in meadowsweet, the feathery whorls pressing together after the broken passage of the horses. Once across, they passed a pond and came to an enclosure incorporating two barns. One barn formed one side of a walled yard; a stone-built house stood opposite. The yard was entered through a double-leaved gateway, each leaf hanging from a large pier supporting a pitched timber roof.

Goda stared, amazed at her new home; it was beyond her wildest expectations. Jumping down from the wagon and rubbing life back into her jarred and cramped limbs, she hurried over to inspect the gable-roofed house. The roof looked to be in good condition, even if the farmstead had not been lived in and worked for the "many winters" of the ceorl they had met. It had to be at least two-score winters, judging by its appearance. The edifice had a central door separating what were essentially two square structures overlapping. She pushed the door open to begin her exploration. One glance told her it was big enough for her family and... a thrill passed through her at the thought... and for Trygil. Her face flushed with shame. She had known him for the time of their journey here, but the more she spoke with him, the more she liked him. Could it be that she was falling in love? Again? At her age? She began to sing as she skipped through the rooms. Cwen joined her as she trilled like a linnet.

"Where is Edwy... and... Master Trygil?"

"Gone to check on the outbuildings, Ma."

"We need to gather wood for a fire, Cwen. The place is so cold. No one's lived here for many winters. Be a good girl and lend a hand."

They left the building, Goda in search of short branches, Cwen gathered twigs for kindling. After three trips backwards and forwards, as far as the trees, Goda decided it was enough for now. Soon, a fire blazed in the kitchen hearth, and the widow began to worry about practical problems such as cleaning and preparing food. She was muttering about the need for water when Trygil strolled in, his face alight with a wide grin.

"The farm has everything!" his enthusiasm cheered her at once.

"I must have water to scrub this place," she pointed to the dusty, filthy table, complete with mouse droppings.

"Then there's the problem of lunch for more than a dozen people," her eyes filled with tears. She felt overwhelmed and helpless.

"Nay, mistress, don't take on so."

Trygil strode over and embraced her, patting her back in gentle reassurance. "The men have gone."

"Gone?"

"Ay, the captain said Glevcaestre is but seven leagues to the west. It's there he's headed."

"Thank the Lord," Goda breathed, disentangling herself with reluctance from the strong arms of Trygil.

"As for water, there's a well just outside the yard. The stonework's fine but the wooden structure will need repairs. It's been covered to keep the water pure and there is a bucket and rope in the barn. I'll see to drawing the water right away."

He strode away, whistling a cheerful tune.

"Don't just stand there Edwy, see if Master Trygil needs a hand."

"Ma, there's a mill over yonder!"

The youth could not contain his excitement. He might be just a lad, but one day he'd show his mother he could make up for the loss of his father. Oh ay, he'd be a miller, all right!

Goda watched him dash out of the house calling Trygil's name, and for the first time since the death of Herrig, her spirits soared.

They rose even more when she sipped the well water. It was sweet and clean. What few pots and pans she had been able to salvage from the house in Ledecestre were now arranged in fresh-scrubbed cupboards. When they sat at the table to eat, like a real family, her happiness knew no bounds. Edwy hung on Trygil's every word. The boy hero-worshipped the fellow, that much was clear. It boded well, since Edwy and his father had had a more troubled relationship; Herrig had never been satisfied with the boy's efforts. Little Cwen, no less than her brother, was eager to fetch and carry for Trygil. But what pleased Goda above all else was when he helped her to air the mattresses in front of the blazing fire.

"No point in preparing one for me, mistress," he whispered with a roguish grin, "we can keep each other warm."

"Hush!" she scolded. "Don't let the children hear or see anything untoward. Their father's been gone fewer than two months."

"Forgive me," he said, "but you must know we are drawn one to the other."

"It's too soon, Master Trygil. I don't deny it! Give me time, and fetch your bedding to warm."

He looked glum but obeyed.

"At least give me hope," he murmured.

"There is every hope," she sighed. "We ought to get to know each other, that's all. Be patient!"

In contrast to her cautious words, her heart sang.

The days passed in the hard work of cleaning and repairs. Edwy spoke of nothing else but the mill and how he meant to become a miller.

Goda succumbed to his insistent persuasion to inspect the building. She knew nothing of milling, but the structure stood in good condition, as far as her inexperienced eye could judge. Trygil agreed that it was in working order and pointed out all its features. The upper part of the driving mechanism was fitted to the underside of a beam running across the interior at a height Trygil could pass under. The grindstones were turned by two men pushing a bar, and they set it in motion for her to see. Two men could turn the huge stone at some seven revolutions a minute. She could see where the grain would be introduced and where it would be shed as flour into a trough under the edge of the grindstone. There was just one problem and it was they had no grain. This, she pointed out. Trygil sat down on the stone.

"It's a day or two I've been wanting to talk to you, Goda. Just that it seems like I'm sticking my nose into your business. But if we are going to make a go of this farm, we have to take the cart to town, to the market. I don't know how much money you got, mistress, but you have to spend some. We need a cow for milking and an ox to pull the plough that's in the barn: the one with the white-plastered walls. And we can buy some chicks for fresh eggs."

"How much does a cow cost?"

"At Ledecestre market you can get one for eighty-eight scillingas."

"Well, I can afford that."

"And chicks?"

"Fifteen a penny."

"But you know, what we need most of all is not an animal."

"I do not take your meaning, Trygil."

"Two men."

"Men? You cannot buy men."

"…Maybe you can."

"Slaves?"

"We must get more hands. There's so much to do, and it's a sizeable farm."

There was no gainsaying his reasoning, but when she was alone, Goda counted her money. She had spared some for her husband's cousin. But the gold piece used for the funeral of Herrig still left her with plenty of scillingas, and she also had the coins the king had given her. If necessary, she could buy three or four cows. She would not do that right away – one would serve their needs but she fancied buying pigs. There were brick-built sties behind the white barn standing empty. But slaves? The idea made sense, yet at the same time, repelled her.

Glevcaestre proved to be a bigger town than she imagined. It had a castle, a port and a large market. The latter was the reason for the being of the settlement. Goods arrived along the Saefern, so a bewildering array of stalls bore all manner of things. Furniture, pans, glassware, metalwork and tools were pointed out by the bawling tradesmen. The stalls with country produce competed for attention. Then there were pens with animals for sale. Fishmongers and butchers swatted away flies from their produce. In short, everything people might need could be found at Glevcaestre market. Trygil, an experienced farm labourer, chose what the seller insisted was his best cow. He knocked the man down from eighty-seven scillingas to eighty since he was prepared to pay the same sum for a sturdy ox. The deal settled, the children led the two animals back to the wagon, where the horse was drinking from a stone water trough. They bought three piglets that Trygil carried squealing in a wicker cage to the cart. "They are little, I know," he said, "but these will grow to be huge beasts by Christ's Mass, next year."

He persuaded Goda to buy a virgin swarm of bees. It cost her sixteen scillingas, but that included the hive. The trader swore that the queen had mated and showed Trygil the mixed brood, with some capped. It meant, he insisted that she had laid at least nine days ago. Satisfied, he concluded the transaction, and Goda paid. The idea of producing her own honey pleased her. They carried the hive with great care back to the wagon.

It was Edwy who reminded them of the seed they needed to grow barley and oats. It was this trader Trygil asked about slaves.

"There is no slave market in Glevcaestre," the man answered. "I heard tell that if a man is prepared to pay to set slaves free, and swears to their freedom before the abbot, it can be arranged."

"What use are freed slaves?" Goda asked as they carried the two sacks of seed back to the children.

"They get their food and accommodation free and are paid a low wage. Most of all, they are free."

"But will they stay and work?"

"Where else would they go? They wouldn't risk being enslaved or leading a life as outlaws."

"I like the idea of freeing slaves," Goda said.

"Let's go to the abbey and see if it can be done."

The abbot, a kind, white-haired man named Ælfsige, agreed that there had been other cases in recent years. The abbey had a number of British slaves, most of them donated to the religious house on the death of their owners. Ælfsige, shrewd and practical, not prepared to tolerate timewasters, came out with, "The cost of freeing a slave is sixty scillingas."

Had he seen their laden cart, he might not have been so sceptical.

Goda, desperate for extra hands around the farm, considering she had paid little more for a cow, agreed at once.

"We need help on the land, Father Abbot. The price is not a problem."

"Well then, I will send for the slaves to be gathered in front of the church, so that when you have chosen, we may proceed to the swearing ceremony.

The assortment of slaves, assembled before Trygil and Goda, varied in age and physique. Given they needed labourers, they naturally concentrated their attentions on the tallest and most muscular.

"Him and him," Trygil suggested to the widow, who gave her assent.

The abbot called the two slaves to step forward and explained the purpose of the convocation.

He concluded by asking, "Are you in agreement?" He would have been astonished had the slaves turned down the chance of emancipation. The relief and joy was so clear on their faces that Goda felt a surge of elation.

"Come," said the abbot to Goda, we must complete the transaction." He led her to a small side room of the church, full of vestments. "One hundred and twenty scillingas is the agreed sum."

"It is," Goda concurred, counting out the coins and handing them to the abbot.

"Do you realise that as emancipator, you will take the freedmen's heritage and wergeld and guardianship of his household, wherever the freedman might be? And this solemn duty you will sear before God at the altar?"

"I do."

"Very well, bring the slaves into the church."

The abbot waited for them at the far end of the nave before the altar and ordered them to kneel. He began by reciting the *Pater Noster* in Latin. Then he spoke to the red-haired Britons, "You will be freed. Until otherwise agreed, you will live with these people and you must abide by the same laws binding them. You must not work on Sundays, else you will pay sixty scillingas as a fine or return to slavery. Obey the rest of the church's laws and those of the king, and nothing will befall you."

He turned to Goda, "This is a pious act you undertake, mistress. Our Lord said, '*Inasmuch as ye have done it to one of the least of these, my brethren, ye have done it unto me.*'" A warm smile followed these words before he began to speak in Latin, which none of them could understand. He ended with, "*Non in servitutis tristitia sed in libertatis... laetitia.*'" Seeing their troubled faces, he translated, "Not in the sadness of servitude, but in the joy of freedom... well, there remains your solemn oath on the altar to abide by the conditions we agreed. Step forward, all three, and place your right hand upon the altar and swear."

At last, the cart creaked and groaned into the farmyard. Trygil lost no time in setting everyone to work. He had discovered names and skills on the journey. "Faelan, take the pigs and settle them in the sties, behind the white barn. Drustan careful with the hive! Take it to the most suitable place you can find. Face it to the south-east in a sheltered position. Cwen, take the chicks to the old henhouse. Put some fresh straw inside for them."

"What about me, Trygil?" Edwy asked.

"Take the cow and the ox over to the pen. Check all the stakes are sound in the fencing. If you find any loose or rotten, call me, all right?"

So began the revival of Mill Farm. As far as Edwy was concerned, the best news arrived in the following days, when Drustan revealed he was an experienced ploughman. Leastways, he had farmed before his capture fighting against Coelwald of Hwicce. The youth told the Briton of his plans to grow barley and oats and to become a miller.

"But first, I need two fields, Drustan."

"We'd best get started, clearing yon field of weeds and brambles," he said in his strange sing-song accent. "But without the right tools..."

"What?"

"Scythes, picks and hoes and... a plough."

"Well, we have them *all*! In the white barn." Edwy could not contain his enthusiasm. He was running ahead of Drustan. His patience was tested. First, he learned that nothing can be rushed if it is to be done "*As the Lord God commands*" was how Drustan put it. Uprooting tenacious briars there was the hardest work he had ever undertaken. Also, there was a season for tilling, another for sowing and one for harrowing. But the golden corn swaying in the breeze in the autumn made it all worthwhile.

A year to the day passed from the death of Herrig before the church would allow the widow to remarry. To the delight of Edwy and Cwen, Goda chose to wed Trygil in Glevcaestre. They were a family once more and Mill Farm showed signs of returning to its former productivity – with grain in the granary, it was no longer only a *buying* farm. Soon their produce would go to market.

SEVENTEEN

Tame Weorth, 740–741 AD

The keeping of his word and sharing of the gold plundered from Eoforwic with his brother did not weigh on Æthelbald. As usual, he did not allow any opportunity to pass him by. Aware that Heardberht viewed him with the reverential eyes of a younger sibling, he profited from this moment of generosity by broaching a new possibility.

Blue-grey eyes similar to his own stared back with earnest reassurance, "Whatever it is you wish, my king, just command."

"It is a dangerous mission, but who else can I trust to see it through?"

"I thrive on danger," Heardberht puffed out his chest. "Am I to sit around and become an old maid?"

Æthelbald laughed.

"Hard to imagine you in a skirt and bodice! Still, I think I will change my mind. I cannot risk losing the last of my family. Will you not marry?"

"Will you not?"

The king glowered, and his voice carried the ire of the glare.

"Why would I? I have bed-warmers enough! Comely and

winsome, at that. But *you* might give wedlock some thought. We get older, and Mierce will need young blood one day."

Far in the future, I hope!

He stared at his king. He had not heard him talk this way before. For the moment, he, Heardberht, did not wish to seek a wife.

"My king, I beg you, change your mind. The more the risk, the more it suits."

A wave of the hand, a servant dispatched for a pitcher of mead, Æthelbald locked eyes with his brother and hesitated. He waited till the golden liquid in its fine glass beakers twinkled in the beam of sunlight striking the table. Reaching for the vessel, he raised it before Heardberht's face.

"Let's drink to the success of your mission!"

"To success! Wherever and whenever it comes!"

"As to that," Æthelbald said, "as soon as possible, within the month and far in the north. You must seek out the former King of Northanhymbre, Eadwulf. He is exiled, and my spies tell me he can be found near the great fjord, what Oengus calls the Foirthe. You'd better travel through Rheged from Elmet. The direct route is too perilous, especially after our recent venture into Deira."

"What is it you want of Eadwulf?"

"They tell me he sustains the followers of the late Bishop Wilfrith at Inhrypum. He was a learned prelate and supporter of the Church of Rome who sought to impose their rules upon the king's brother, who then was the Bishop of Eoforwic. Wilfrith claimed metropolitan authority over the northern part of England. This, Eadberht and his brother would never have accepted. Instead, *I* see great promise in such an imposition – along with the return from exile of Eadwulf."

Heardberht, never slow on the uptake, grinned at his king, "Two plovers with one stone, eh? In this way, you rid Northanhymbre of its king and its archbishop!"

"Was there ever a better moment?"

"What shall I tell Eadwulf when I find him?"

"All you need tell him is to continue the vision of Wilfrith, for in this way, Æthelbald of Mierce is to be his sworn friend upon whom he may call whenever he wishes."

Heardberht leapt to his feet, "I am on my way!"

Thus, before his departure, Heardberht benefitted from the unscrupulous scheming of Æthelbald. Satisfied he had his brother well prepared for any eventuality, he let him leave but not without feeling qualmish.

The best-laid schemes, even those of Æthelbald, sometimes throw up unexpected outcomes, as in this case. Heardberht carried out his commission with such verve, it provoked a short civil war, ending with the siege of Bebbanburgh and the defeat of Eadwulf by Ealdorman Berhtfrith. The latter, on the instructions of King Eadberht, murdered Eadwulf's son, Earnwine.

When the news of these events reached Æthelbald, heedless of his own contribution, he prayed for the soul of Earnwine. This unforeseen death, although it saddened him, paled into insignificance at his joy at the opposition he had stirred up against Eadberht among rival families. Northanhymbre emerged from the war weakened, but Æthelbald underestimated the fortitude of Eadberht. His abilities, step by step, began to restore the kingdom to its former wealth and glory. This stuck in Æthelbald's craw: he would do everything in his power to prevent it from continuing undisturbed.

For the present, however, there were other matters on his mind. King Mildfrith of Magon died. The subkingdom could not be allowed to drift into the wrong hands, so Æthelbald, swift and determined, enthroned one of his trusted ealdormen.

* * *

Miercian–West Seaxa border, spring, 742 AD

A year later, Cuthred of the West Seax tested the waters of his independence from Æthelbald in Berrucscir, by granting lands. The King of Mierce considered the scir his domain and lost no time in mustering a force to retake control of the county. To enforce his authority, he summoned Cuthred to a moot while leading his host to the confines of the Miercian–West Seaxa border. In the face of this aggressive display of power, Cuthred succumbed at once and presented himself before his warlike neighbour.

"Why did you call me to your presence?" Cuthred wasted no

time on pleasantries, and this lack of respect hardened Æthelbald's resolve.

"Be under no illusions *King* Cuthred, without my tacit support, your reign cannot last. I will not tolerate interference in *my* lands."

"To which lands do you refer, *King* Æthelbald?"

Cuthred matched Æthelbald, sneer for sneer.

The face of the King of Mierce darkened, "To Berrucscir, of course."

"Correct me if I err, but that county belonged to the West Seax."

"You err not, friend Cuthbert... *'belonged'*... is the right word. Now the scir belongs to Mierce. Do not forget this simple fact. I am right in counting you as a friend, am I not?"

Hesitation did not help Cuthred's situation. At last, he dredged forth a reluctant, "Of course."

"That is as well," Æthelbald's tone was stern. "My informants warn of meetings between Gwent and Powys. They are set to attack West Seax at the instigation of your neighbour, the restless Dumnonia."

These words had an evident effect on the King of West Seax, whose countenance, swarthy from exposure to the ocean air, paled before his gaze.

"Ay, these bothersome Britons are no respecters of truces." He went on, "Your predecessor, the late, lamented Æthelheard, and I sealed a pact that they would not raid Angle-land. Of course, their treachery is renowned—"

"Why does a Wealisc strike on West Seax interest you, King Æthelbald?"

"Because I am a man of my word. A British assault on West Seax is an attack on *me*."

Cuthred looked at the King of Mierce with renewed respect.

"Do you mean to support me as you would have supported Æthelheard?"

"I do. Unless..."

"Unless?"

"You give me a reason not to be your friend any longer. It would, believe me, pain me beyond mere words."

"I shall give you no such motive, King Æthelbald."

The visage of the West Seax king, he did not trust, but the moment was too propitious to waste. On impulse, he stretched out his hand – again the hesitation – how could he rely on such a man? But, Cuthred, after the unfortunate delay, clasped his hand in friendship.

"Well, I am glad I called this meeting, we understand each other, *friend* Cuthred. The Wealisc, to attack you by land, must perforce invade Mierce. I will hold my warriors ready for any such misdemeanour and will expect you to hasten to our aid. On the other hand, they may invade West Seax direct across the Saefern from Gwent…" Æthelbald paused for effect before adding, "…in which case, we will speed to your aid."

King Cuthred nodded, and as there was nothing else to be added, he excused himself by indicating he needed to depart to see to pressing matters.

"One such issue ought to be to raise your levies," Æthelbald admonished.

Another curt nod and Cuthred pushed his way out of the canvas doorway of the royal tent.

"Good riddance!" Æthelbald hissed between clenched teeth, glaring at the flap.

Why, I almost hope the Wealisc threat is unfounded.

The king sat on his bed and pondered on the meeting.

If Gwent and Powys force my hand, it makes keeping Cuthred under control easier, but it will grieve me to aid the cur!

* * *

Tame Weorth, two months later, 742 AD

A rider galloped, in a cloud of dust, to the palace at Tame Weorth. In his haste to dismount, he almost fell, alerting the guard at the ornate doorway, who drew his seax.

"I have an urgent message from Lord Coelwald for the king, my good man."

"Wait there!"

"The communication will not wait!"

"I have my orders!"

The guard brandished his seax.

"And so do I! Will you let me pass?"

The rider reached for his own seax and parried the scything blow aimed at his head.

Using his strength, for which in part he had been chosen, the messenger thrust the guard off balance so, as he lay flailing on the ground, he darted inside. He had not taken more than six steps before guards, hurrying from all directions, overcame him.

"An urgent message from Lord Coelwald for King Æthelbald!" he bellowed.

A voice louder still rang out, one with a tone of command no man dared gainsay.

"Dolts! Let the fellow be!"

Rough hands released him with the same vigour with which he had been seized. Thus, the messenger, propelled from behind, staggered toward King Æthelbald.

"What is so urgent?" the king asked.

"Sire, my Lord Coelwald sends notice the Wealisc are over the border into Magon and press on south-east into Hwicce." The messenger hesitated, struggling to recall the exact words of his communication, "*Er…*"

"Well?" the word boomed, echoing from the rafters.

"*Er…*" he said, "er… he's tracking them and avoiding engagement thus far… and to implore you to come with all speed, sire… for… at his reckoning… the enemy host numbers more than four hundred. It is all."

"Good man!"

The king dismissed the rider, "Mmm!" he murmured, "Coelwald has an experienced eye. If he judges four hundred, then so it is!"

This consideration made him take action, summoning messengers with orders to his ealdormen to raise the levies once more.

Within an amazingly short time, the march to the south-west began. Æthelbald headed a host of three hundred men under the golden cross of Mierce. The horsemen rode sixteen abreast wherever the roads permitted, which was seldom and only where the verges had been cleared to make it impossible for outlaws to lurk. The majority of his army, however, was made up of men on foot, carrying javelins and shields. When conditions were firm underfoot, they managed no fewer than eight leagues a day. In five days, they reached Bricstow, which by any standards was exceptional, considering they also picked up men on their way down the country. Another hundred added to his army made Æthelbald feel more secure.

He knew Coelwald must lead a hundred men, at least. Over and above their joint forces, he ought to add the West Seaxa, renowned fighters and the object of the enemy attack. He supposed the Dumnonians would already be crossing the Tamur. They, undoubtedly, were another factor to be given serious consideration when calculating their relative strength. But his reflections stopped there, the more pressing circumstance being to join with Coelwald without stumbling upon the Wealisc.

In truth, he had made the speed his friend, the underking, had pleaded for. In return, he hoped Coelwald's scouts would find him. Still, he sent out his own spies on horseback, as a precaution, spreading his net wide. Even so, it was still a surprise when one of them returned in but an hour, trailing another rider he did not recognise.

"Sire," the scout dismounted and bowed. "I came across this fellow," he jerked a thumb over his shoulder without taking his eyes off his king. "He claims to be a scout of Lord Coelwald."

The other rider sprang down and knelt before Æthelbald.

"My king," he said, gazing at the figure towering above him, "I am glad to find you. My lord, Coelwald, ordered us to find your host as soon as possible and to… with your consent, of course, lead you to him…"

"Stand, my fine fellow! How far away is the force of Lord Coelwald?"

The scout rose and rubbed his breeches at the knee.

"Sire, I left at first light and rode north-west until I met your man."

"An hour ago, sire," Æthelbald's scout cut in.

"Are they encamped?" the king asked.

"Nay, Lord Coelwald sets traps for the Wealisc spies and thus far has stayed out of sight under cover of woodland. It slows us down, and we too lose scouts to the enemy. We are still on their tails."

"Excellent! How long to reach Coelwald?"

"Three hours if we move fast, unless—"

"Ay?"

"…unless we chance upon the Wealisc first."

"It is your task to safeguard against such a mischance."

The scout caught the menace in his king's voice.

"Ay, Lord. It is my bounden duty."

Æthelbald deigned Coelwald's outrider with a grim smile and chose six horsemen.

"Follow this man, in relays, one hundred and fifty yards apart. It will speed up the journey. Off with you, fellow!"

The scout leapt on his horse, and in an impressive display of agility, in one movement, wheeled it away at a canter. The first of the six watched him increase the distance to one hundred and fifty yards and then kicked his mount off at the same pace. The king waited until the other five chosen men had done the same before ordering his men off when the same gap had formed for the last time.

At this rate, we'll join Coelwald within the three hours.

An outrider, rearguard of Coelwald's force, challenged the first scout after two hours. The fellow reined in to explain the situation, and as he did so, his shadow, the second horseman, reached them. Without further hesitation and with relief on his face, the covering guard set off, leading the others along a woodland trail. Soon, Æthelbald waved his men to follow into the trees. At last, they came to a dell where a stream trickled between the slopes, and horses were up to their hocks, drinking their fill. Either side of the narrow brook, tents, pitched at the strangest angles, leaned down the wooded declivity. King Æthelbald halted his army among the trees before heading for a large tent, over which fluttered the banner of Hwicce with its white leaping stag on a green ground.

Before he entered the tent, Coelwald came out, a wide grin on his face.

"My king," he made to kneel, but Æthelbald was having none of it, hauling his friend upright and into the usual rib-challenging embrace. "Are we glad to see you!" He lowered his voice as if the enemy might hear him from here, in spite of the racket their joint forces were making. "The Wealisc are the other side of the woodland," he continued. "They know we are here, but I doubt they are aware of your arrival, sire. We have been here since a little after dawn."

"What are the movements of the Waelsic?"

"The last scout back, an hour since, reported they proceed south-west along the ancient Britayne Street leading to Escancaestre."

Æthelbald clasped his hands together and moved them backwards and forwards in front of his chest.

"If they keep on that road, they must come to Somerton, am I right?"

"Quite right, my king."

The eyes of Æthelbald took on a ferocious light, designed to intimidate his friend.

"Did you follow my instructions and leave a garrison there?"

"I did, Lord."

The fierce stare gave way to a savage embrace.

"How many?"

"Four-score."

"We have them, my friend! Order your men to break camp with all haste!"

EIGHTEEN

Somerton, two days later, 742 AD

Once more, events did not transpire as Æthelbald supposed, imagining, as he did, a crushing defeat of the Wealisc, trapped between hammer and anvil. Instead, a white flag greeted his advancing host. Elisedd sought to parley with him. This concession granted, the ruler of Powys introduced Ithel-ap-Morgan, King of Gwent.

The latter spoke first, "King Æthelbald, we have no quarrel with you. We are marching to the aid of our cousins in Dumnonia who are at war with the West Seax. We cannot ignore a plea from our kinsmen."

Æthelbald used his most intimidating expression to reply, his face and eyes as hard as steel.

"How well I, a ruler, understand you. Do you suppose I can turn my back on an entreaty from one of my underkings? Such is Cuthred. You," he glared at Elisedd, "have broken your word and crossed into Mierce."

"We do not command enough ships to transport my warriors across the Saefern… come, Lord Æthelbald, we do not wish, either of us, to spill blood in a useless battle for folk far away from our homes."

"In spite of our agreement, Powys continues to annoy my people. There have been reports from our borderlands of raiding parties burning crops, seizing cattle and anything they can carry—"

"What can I do?" Elisedd shrugged. "They are as likely to raid in such a way into Gwynneth or Gwent, against our own people. These young men do this as a necessity! A way of proving themselves."

"Your blithe talk leaves me hot with anger while you sit trapped between my host and the fortress of Somerton, full of my men. Show me a way to avoid slaughtering your army. But hark! You need to offer me something I cannot refuse. I do not wish to lose face over this."

"Well, since you object so much to the incursions into Mierce from Powys, I propose the construction of a boundary between our two lands – a barrier where Nature falls short."

Intrigued, Æthelbald admitted, "I do not follow you."

"I can supply a workforce of slaves to dig a dyke and bank it up along a set route determined by both parties. Let's say we begin in the south at the marshland where the Morda Brook joins the River Vyrnwy. Raiders cannot cross the marsh. Thence we start the construction and proceed north until we reach the estuary of the Dee."

"But that's a good thirteen leagues!" Æthelbald stared at the King of Powys as he might at a simpleton and yet the scheme began to appeal to him. "There would be steep valleys and rivers to deal with," he said, giving the matter serious consideration. "And what about you?" he fixed a hostile glare on Ithel-ap-Morgan.

"I repeat, Gwent has no argument with Mierce. If you settle with my kinsman," he nodded at Elisedd, "then I will withdraw my men to Gwent."

"And what of Dumnonia?"

"They must fight their own battle. It is already a great service to them if we avoid the might of Mierce from joining with the West Seax."

"I'm going to be honest," Æthelbald growled. "If I accept the madcap proposal of King Elisedd, I will withdraw the bulk of my army. But I must honour my word to Cuthred and send a small force to his aid."

"King Æthelbald, you will not, therefore, object if a harrying party sails across the Saefern from Gwent to the succour of our cousins?"

"What I do not see cannot provoke me! Back to this construction. I shall provide the engineers and you the slaves, King Elisedd. One moon hence, meet me at the Morda Brook with your men armed with spades and picks." He thrust out a hand to seal the agreement. The King of Powys clasped it, content in the knowledge his brilliant scheme had saved the Wealisc from a likely massacre.

The more Æthelbald considered the idea, the more it appealed to him. Of course, he needed to summon the most practical men in Mierce to see if it could be achieved. His own common sense told him it could, and in doing so, he would create a marvel worthy of his own greatness.

Pity I cannot slaughter the Wealisc, but this is the excuse I need to save face.

These thoughts passed through his mind as he shook hands with Ithel-ap-Morgan.

Gwent, I will leave to the not-so-tender care of the West Seaxa.

As the Wealisc returned to their army, Æthelbald shouted for Coelwald. The underking of Hwicce rode up and with quizzical eye stared at the retreating white flag.

"We attack, Lord?"

"We do *not*!" Æthelbald explained.

"A thirteen-league dyke! It is madness!"

The fierce, wild glower the king gave him, made Coelwald eat his words.

"Then again, perhaps not. If the Wealisc slaves create the ditch… the barrier will give our people time to raise the hue and cry in the case of assault."

"My exact thought. I see you understand the worth of *my* idea."

"I never question your wisdom for more than a moment of confusion, sire."

"Good, then you should know, dear Coelwald, I have a task for you. You wished to attack the Wealisc and – so you shall! Take your men into West Seax, join with King Cuthred and defeat them on his soil. May God be with you, my friend. When you return to Tame Weorth, I hope the great dyke will be complete."

Coelwald tilted his head and rode back to his men, content his force would not be denied the battle they craved. As he cantered back, he could not help shaking his head at the foolish scheme his king had adopted in exchange for not annihilating the foe when he had the chance. He hoped he would not regret his choice. The young Æthelbald, whose memory he cherished, would never have let such an occasion slip through his fingers like finely ground salt.

For his part, Æthelbald summoned his ealdormen and thegns and described his scheme in detail, for by now, in his mind, it became *his* plan. He was relieved to see – differently from Coelwald, no doubt – only amazement in the receptive eyes of his chief supporters. This assured him of the wisdom of his decision. It occurred to him that Hwicce was much further south than where he meant to start construction. This might explain the diffidence of Coelwald and the enthusiasm of his Miercians.

It only goes to confirm the goodness of my choice.

* * *

Morda Brook, a month later

From his hilltop vantage point, Æthelbald surveyed the sinuous brook as it wound its way into the River Vyrnwy. The air over the marshland shimmered in the morning sun as its rays released a haze. In his fanciful imagination, the king compared the light to a hunter, casting a silver net over the water...

"A raiding party would lose its life down there, sire." The master mason expressed his own more practical thoughts in words and in doing so, brought the king back to earth.

"Ay, but now we ought to move on and see where the ground becomes firm enough to begin the trenching."

The group of a score of warriors, five masons, two architects and King Æthelbald urged their horses northward until the king halted them after half an hour's canter and pointed across the river Vyrnwy. In the distance, a large mass of men waited, and at their head, he made out a solitary rider. Was it Elisedd?

"We must ride over there to meet them," Æthelbald said. In silence, he hoped for no betrayal. He had twenty armed men. A rough guess told him there were at least a hundred Wealisc slaves awaiting them. His lively stallion trotted across the soft turf toward the mounted figure, who indeed proved to be Elisedd.

"King Æthelbald," he greeted. "Welcome. See how we have honoured our word."

A quick glance told Æthelbald the men at the disposal of Powys were indeed armed with picks and shovels and kept in order by a score of surly warriors.

"We too, King Elisedd," he said. "I have brought the experts, he gestured to bring forward the masons and the architects.

"This is level ground," he said, sweeping his hand in an arc. "My men tell me in such soil, a ditch eleven yards wide and two yards deep will suffice."

"Excellent," Elisedd waved an imperious hand to the north, and a stout, stocky figure came forward. "*Un ar ddeg llath o led a dwy llath yn ddwfn,*" he commanded in a strange, guttural language.

"*Le, sire!*" the man nodded and called over a group of men, each holding a rock.

"*Ei roi yno ac yna iard ar wahân.*"

"What is he saying?" Æthelbald asked.

"To place the stone there and the others a yard apart." Elisedd translated, "They will follow the line at the suggested depth and width."

At these words, the plump fellow began to pace out the width and drew a mark in the turf with the heel of his shoe. Satisfied, he waved at a man with a hammer, stakes and cord, who hammered a stake into the ground, tied the string and started to uncoil it, following the line of stones until he had left them all behind and the rotund overseer called him to a halt. There, he drove in another marker and knotted off the string before cutting the ball of cord free. With surprising alacrity, the overseer hurried up to him and paced out eleven steps eastwards before pointing to the ground. At the exact spot, the man fixed another peg and tied the string before unwinding it in the wake of the overseer. He, by some miracle, kept his route back unswerving to stop opposite the first stake. Again, he pointed to the ground, for another stake to be driven, with more tying off and cutting.

"Divide the men into gangs," King Elisedd ordered the overseer, who had already begun to do so, sending a dozen men to the far end then an equal number within ten paces of them and so on until he had deployed all the diggers.

"*Dechreuwch!*" the monarch cried, and the labourers set to cutting into the turf and flinging it just over the eastern length of string.

"Sire!" one of Æthelbald's masons hissed with urgency, "The bank must be at least five yards high if it is to serve."

"Five yards?" incredulous, came the king's reply.

"I mean from the bottom of the ditch."

"Ah, then, three yards of bank?" Æthelbald said, reassured.

"Forgive me. It is what I meant. It will create a real obstacle to raiders. But we must have them save the turf to make a revetting wall to the front above the ditch."

Æthelbald urged his horse near to Elisedd's and passed on the request.

Once more in the alien tongue, the Wealisc ruler called out, and men were sent to retrieve the turf for use as revetment.

"We cannot sit here all day watching them toil," King Elisedd said. "Come to my hall and we'll eat and drink together. In the morning, we'll check on progress. What do you say?"

"Gladly. One moment though." Æthelbald rode over to his head mason.

"You and the others, ride north and study the route the dyke must take. See if there are natural obstacles that can be incorporated."

The man knuckled his forehead and bowed.

Æthelbald trotted his horse back to Elisedd, "You will forgive me if I bring my warriors with me?"

The King of Powys laughed, "Bring them, but rest assured, a score of men will not serve against the might of Powys. But know you we honour our guests, and hospitality is sacred among my people."

"Mine too," Æthelbald concurred. "But not all folk are the same. For instance, I would not trust a Northanhymbrian's word."

They rode on in companionable discussion about neighbouring peoples. Thus, Æthelbald learned of Powys's distrust of Gwynneth – something he wondered might be useful to know in the future. He felt a little ashamed of this thought, but Elisedd had not proved to be as trustworthy as he would have hoped. Again, at this consideration, a shiver ran down his spine. Here he was, riding into the enemy heartland, innocent as a babe. If they slit his throat, it would be no consolation to know a bloody war between their peoples would result.

The day passed in a pleasant blur of food and drink, and Æthelbald had no regrets when he slipped into a comfortable bed, covered with soft fleece. He did not spare a thought for the guards he had placed at his door or for his masons out in the windswept marshland.

A little before noon, Æthelbald and Elisedd rode with their respective guards to the site of the dyke. Considerable progress had been made. The King of Mierce surveyed the trench running north for more than a hundred yards and nodded his satisfaction. He nudged his horse to the edge of the ditch and did not need to haul on the reins, the animal stopping and whinnying, tossing its head. Æthelbald peered into the depths of the excavation, and his eyes followed the turf bank upwards. For sure, a man on a pony could not pass. On foot, he would have a devilish job to clamber down and up the other side to surmount the obstacle. He grunted his approval, turned his horse and sought out his head mason.

He found the fellow supervising the revetment at the end of the dyke at the extreme point where the diggers had arrived. Æthelbald called him to his side.

"Did you survey the land as I bade you?" his eyes flashed.

"Ay, sire, seven leagues of this level ground will take us to a river the local folk call the Ceiriog. It is a fine stream running north-south for many miles. We can use it as a continuation – a natural barrier."

"Is it deep enough to fulfil its purpose?"

"Ay, Lord, we plumbed it and at its shallowest, it is two yards deep. The current is sufficient for the river to be full of trout."

"It will save a lot of work. How long do you think before the slaves reach the river?"

"The ground is easy to work here. At this rate, I'd say six weeks or two months."

"As long as that?"

"Sire, they are but men!"

The king grunted. "And if I deliver a hundred slaves from Mierce?"

"That would speed it up – twice the men, half the time."

"It will take time to send them here, but I have decided."

"What is the form of the land beyond the river?"

"Lord it runs into the Dee, a great stream which does not oblige us with its course. There, we must cross over and continue the dyke."

"So be it!"

Æthelbald, his decision set on fetching slaves from Mierce, rode back to gather his guards. He also needed to bid farewell to Elisedd and to urge him to press on with the work in his absence.

From Tame Weorth, he sent out bands of warriors to round up slaves from the surrounding farmsteads, heedless of the hardship the loss of labour might cause. His priority was the dyke. What was a little privation compared to having one's farm and crops burnt by raiders from Powys? The dyke would put a stop to that! And he would be remembered as the visionary who made it possible.

He spent the next few weeks catching up on all the administration he had neglected on his jaunt to Wealas. In the evenings, he caught up on bedroom activities. If there was a more satisfied monarch in the world, Æthelbald could not imagine it! He did not know he had reached the peak of his glory, and whereas he could sign his charters '*Rex Britanniae*' for a few more years yet, the end was beginning.

The spring gave way to summer, and persuaded by the favourable weather, Æthelbald decided to ride to Powys to check on the progress of his dyke. The work had gone beyond the Dee, thanks to the doubling of the slaves. Once there, the king spoke with his master mason.

"Sire, this stretch runs from the Dee to another river, the Alyn. The challenge is different there because we have hills and valleys to contend with."

"How will you do that?"

"We must make use of the lie of the land by following the natural contours."

Æthelbald, always swift to understand, said, "So, the dyke will no longer run straight?"

"A sinuous course it must take, Lord. Then again, the valley of the Alyn is steep, so we must alter our approach to the building."

"In what way?"

"By scarping back and constructing a counterscarp from the spoil."

"I see, and is that difficult?"

The mason tut-tutted, "If anything, Lord, it is easier. Another thing, there is a series of small streams we can use to reduce the digging needed."

"What lies beyond the Alyn?"

"At that point, the dyke nears its completion by cutting across to the estuary of the Dee at Basingwerk."

"How long before the work is finished?"

"We must stop for the winter rains, sire, but I think we can finish in the spring of next year."

This reply pleased Æthelbald. Northanhymbre was in chaos, West Seax distracted by Dumnonia and Powys quiet for the moment and in all likelihood also in the future – thanks to his dyke. His greatness was assured forever!

NINETEEN

Saxony, twenty years before, 722AD

The missionary, having ventured this far into pagan Saxony, was not prepared for the savagery he was about to witness. His arrival had been greeted with a mixture of suspicion and the customary hospitality of these people. They equated him with their own sorcerer, and for this reason, he was treated with respect, except, of course, by the pagan priest himself. His evil eye transmitted all of his loathing to the alien-god worshipper.

An early riser, Boniface was at his morning prayers when shouting and wailing from outside his hut disturbed him. Jumping to his feet, he pushed his way past the rickety door, hanging askew on worn leather hinges. Hastening outside, he sought the cause of the commotion: the enactment of a punishment. The men of the village loitered in doorways or against the walls of the houses since the main participants appeared to be elderly matrons. They set about ripping and cutting away a young woman's garments to the girdle. The older women began to slash and prick the younger woman's unblemished back with their knives, before also attacking her arms and breasts.

Boniface hurried to the nearest bystander and asked, "Why are they wounding the woman?"

The fellow did not wish to be distracted and did not answer at once as he craned his neck over Boniface's shoulder so as not to miss a moment of the spectacle. The matrons pushed the wailing bloodied wretch toward a house, where another angry woman waited, knife in hand, eager to inflict further harm on their victim.

"That's the wife!" The fellow explained, and Boniface struggled to understand the strange guttural dialect.

"The wife?"

"Yon slept with her husband, see?"

Other tormentors joined the women, and Boniface covered his eyes. A miracle was needed to save the once pretty woman, now bloodied and scarcely alive. The missionary began to pray for divine intervention but then stopped to reflect. Who was he to condemn this heathen behaviour? Might these rude people not have the right of it? But what about the man? Was he not guilty too? Boniface's own god forbade adultery in the Ten Commandments, and here he was, witnessing a zeal for modesty the like of which he had never seen before. Sickened by the cruel scene, he turned back into his hut to pray for enlightenment to descend, not only on himself but also on this savage populace.

* * *

Tame Weorth, twenty years later, 742 AD

King Æthelbald stared from the messenger, Coela, to the three raptors on his arm.

"A most welcome and appreciated gift." The monarch waved to a servant to relieve the traveller of the birds of prey. "Read me the letter!" he ordered the gift bearer.

The man cleared his throat in a show of self-importance and began to read:

"*To his revered and beloved lord, Æthelbald, king of the Miercians, greetings of deepest affection from Boniface, servant of the servants of God.*

"*We pray thy highness' mercy, deign to comfort and aid this, my messenger, by name, Ceola, the bearer of this letter, on this journey and on any occasion when he is in need. And may God reward you because you did give every assistance to my messengers who came to you last year, as they brought back word. Meanwhile, we have sent to you, as a sign of true love and devoted friendship, a hawk and two falcons, two shields and two lances. These small gifts, unworthy though they are, we ask you to accept with our love and blessing. Let us all hear the conclusion of the whole matter: Fear God and keep His commandments.*

"*We beg also that if any written words of ours come to your presence by another messenger, you shouldst deign to lend your ear and harken to them carefully. Farewell in Christ.*"

Having listened to this missive from the eminent missionary, beloved of the Holy Father and responsible for the organisation of Christianity in Germania, King Æthelbald wondered what underlay the gifts.

* * *

Tame Weorth, three years later, 745 AD

King Æthelbald had reached the height of his splendour and Mierce, the peak of its wealth and stability. All around the kingdom, chaos afflicted other lands less fortunate. In Est Seax, followers of Swithred murdered the elderly King Selered and installed their man on the throne. This fate was common enough doom for anyone considered a poor king. Northanhymbre, torn by internal dissent, also faced the threat of the Picti on its borders, word being that war might break out from one day to the next. The south of the land still remained under Æthelbald's sway, but in Angle-land, kingship did not offer the assurance of longevity.

King Æthelbald, secure in his power, had begun to abuse it. Among his misdeeds, the stealing of ecclesiastical revenue, violation of church privileges, imposing of forced labour on the clergy and fornicating with nuns, could not go unheeded. Not by a church establishing its hegemony in Western Europe – Æthelbald might have been wise to temper his behaviour.

The letter received from Boniface three years earlier ought to have alerted him to the church's attention, although suspicious of the gifts, he did not mend his ways. Boniface, as ever, moved with intelligence and caution. He and seven other bishops penned a letter of reproach. Unwilling to act on hearsay, the venerable missionary sent it first to Ecgberht, Archbishop of Eoforwic, asking him to correct any inaccuracies and to reinforce whatever was right. Also, he requested that a priest, Herefrith, one whom Æthelbald had listened to in the past, should read and explain it to the king in person.

Thus, the courageous priest sat across a table from Æthelbald in the king's private chambers, far from indiscreet ears, and began to read.

"*To the dear lord, King Æthelbald, in the love of Christ to be put before all other kings, Boniface, archbishop, legate in Germany of the Roman Church, and Wera and Burghard and Werberht and Abel and Wilbalth, fellow bishops, send greetings of undying love in Christ…*" They went on to praise Æthelbald's faith and almsgiving at length… which Herefrith read with confidence and under the king's approving gaze, but then the mood changed…

"*But among these reports, one rumour of evil character concerning your highness' life has come to our hearing; we were cast down by it, and wish that it were not true. From many sources, we have learned that you have never taken a wife in lawful marriage. But marriage was established by God from the very beginning of the world and has been enjoined anew by the apostle, Paul, who teaches: 'Nevertheless, to avoid fornication, let every man have his own wife, and let every woman have her own husband.' If you have determined to act thus because of chastity and abstinence, that you may abstain from intercourse with a wife for the love and fear of God and have shown this to be something truly accomplished for God's sake, we rejoice thereat; such a course deserves not blame, but praise. If, however, as many say – God forbid – you have never taken a lawful wife nor preserved a chaste abstinence for God's sake but, under the sway of lust, you have destroyed by licence and adultery your glory and renown before God and men, we are greatly grieved: such conduct must be regarded as criminal in the sight of God and destructive of your reputation before men.*

"*And what is worse, those who tell us this, add that this crime of deepest ignominy has been committed in convents with holy nuns and virgins consecrated to God. There can be no doubt that this is a twofold sin. How guilty, for instance, is the slave in the master's house who violates the master's wife! How much more guilty is he who has stained a spouse of Christ, the creator of heaven and earth, with the defilement of his lust! As says the apostle, Paul: 'What! know ye not that your body is the temple of the Holy Ghost?' and elsewhere: 'Know ye not that ye are the temple of God and that the Spirit of God dwelleth in you? If any man defile the temple of God, him shall God destroy: for the temple of God is holy, which temple ye are.' And again when he mentions and enumerates the sins, he joins adultery and fornication to the slavery of idolatry: 'Know ye not that the unrighteous shall not inherit the Kingdom of God? Be not deceived; neither fornicators nor adulterers, nor effeminate, nor abusers of themselves with mankind, nor thieves, nor covetous, nor drunkards, nor revilers, nor extortioners shall inherit the Kingdom of God.' And elsewhere it is written, 'Men do not despise a thief if he steal to satisfy his soul when he is hungry: but if he is found, he shall restore sevenfold: he shall give all the substance of his house. But whoso committeth adultery with a woman, lacketh understanding: he that doeth it, destroyeth his own soul."*

Herefrith paused for breath and studied the king. Unless he was mistaken, the ruler appeared paler, with his face drawn and anxious.

"Is everything quite clear, sire?"

Æthelbald nodded before asking, "Is that the end of the letter?"

The priest shook his head, swallowed and continued, "*It would take too long to enumerate how many spiritual physicians denounced the dreaded poison of this sin and laid a terrible ban upon it. Fornication is more grave and repellent than almost any other sin and can verily be called a noose of death and a pit of hell and an abyss of perdition.*"

The letter went on at length to invite the king to repent and mend his ways. Æthelbald struggled to pay attention until Herefrith read about other lands.

"*Not only by Christians but even by pagans is this sin reckoned a disgrace and a shame. The very pagans, who are ignorant of the true God, in this matter observe by instinct what is lawful and what God ordained from the beginning, because, while they preserve faithfully the tie of matrimony for their own wives, they punish fornicators and adulterers. In ancient Saxony, if a virgin defiles her father's house by adultery, or if a married woman, breaking the marriage tie, commits adultery, at times they force the woman to hang herself by her own hand and so to end her life; and above the pyre on which she has been burned and cremated, they hang her defiler. Or at times, a multitude of women gathers, and the matrons lead the guilty woman, bound, through the village, beating her with sticks and cutting away her garments to the girdle; they cut and prick her whole body with their knives and send her from house to house, bloody and torn by the many wounds; new tormentors are always joining the band out of zeal for modesty and leave her dead or barely alive, so that others may have fear of adultery and wantonness.*" The priest read on, the letter explaining how

Christian kings set an example to their people, and if the example was bad, the nation would become as depraved and degenerate as their leader. What was sure to happen was the Omnipotent Judge would allow avenging punishment to come and destroy them. He went on to cite the terrible deaths of King Coelred of Mierce and King Osred, king of the Deirans and Bernicians. "*...they were cast down from their royal thrones in this life and surprised by an early and terrible death; deprived of the light eternal, they were plunged into the depths of hell and the bottom of the abyss.*"

With further warnings not to lose his immortal soul and to avoid the hellfire of the pit, the letter continued for more pages until Herefrith declared it ended.

As if King Æthelbald had not heard enough recommendations and censure, the priest stood and added his own warning, out of kindness and a sense of duty.

"Sire, forgive me, but in the interests of your soul, I would ask you to remember how fugitive is this present life. Moreover, how short and momentary is the delight of the impure flesh, and how ignominious it is for a man with his brief life to leave an evil example to posterity."

Æthelbald rose from the table and accompanied the cleric out of the chamber. He felt a tightness in his chest, and his breathing became laboured. Had this letter, from men so beloved of the pope, the Vicar of Christ on Earth, the power to send him to hell if he ignored it? For the first time since he had taken the throne, he was unsure of himself. He feared no man, but God was a different matter.

TWENTY

Tame Weorth, 747 AD

Æthelbald lay on his back in a darkened chamber and stared at the rafters. Beyond the reassuring solidity of the roof, he imagined the immense sky and farther still, the celestial dome, where, all-seeing, the Heavenly Father looked upon the meanest of his creatures. The eye of the Almighty Judge, therefore, must pay particular attention to the kings who reigned over the poorest. No act, good or wicked, of Æthelbald's, would have escaped His observation. Thus pondered the ruler of Mierce, chastened by the words of Archbishop Boniface, a man venerated throughout the world.

I must repent to save my immortal soul. What am I to do?

With these unaccustomed sentiments to the forefront of his mind, Æthelbald wrote for advice to his appointee, Cuthbert, Archbishop of Cantwaraburh. The prelate responded by reminding his king of the resolution, ignored, made at the Council of Clofeshoch, five years before, to hold an annual church council there. In the light of the king's letter, the venerable Cuthbert informed the pope of Æthelbald's intention to call dignitaries from the various provinces of Angle-land to a second council.

Æthelbald blasphemed when he received this letter.

May Thunor blast the old dodderer with a bolt from Waelheal!

When he had recovered from confrontation with this accomplished fact, the king sat and dwelt on the possible benefits. For sure, the church would drag forth the matter of the abuses of power of which Boniface accused him. This, of course, were he to concede, would diminish the flow into the royal coffers, but the whole purpose of seeking advice had nothing to do with worldly wealth. Spiritual well-being was what he needed at this stage of his life. If it meant sacrifices to obtain it, so be it. The king rolled his signet into the wax, sealing his letter of acceptance. In doing so, he acceded to the convocation of the prelates, aethelings, underkings and chiefs to Clofeshoch.

* * *

Clofeshoch, August, 747 AD

Gathered in the Great Hall, the most important dignitaries of Angle-land led by King Æthelbald, sat awaiting Archbishop Cuthbert to begin proceedings. The elderly prelate proceeded to translate a letter from Pope Zachary, containing a fervent admonition to amendment of life, addressed to the English people of every rank and condition. The Holy Father required those who condemned these warnings and remained obstinate in their malice to be punished by the sentence of excommunication.

The severity of the condemnation left not a single person, not least the king, in any doubt about the intentions of the church. The day dragged on as thirty-one canons were drawn up. Many dealt with ecclesiastical discipline and liturgy, but others made Æthelbald blanch, for he was well aware he must sign a document protecting the monasteries from his future rapine. He would have to issue a charter stating the churches exempt from all public taxation and clergymen free of all works and burdens except the repair of bridges and fortifications.

The king, whose coffers were in rude health, for the moment, was not too upset by these resolutions. It troubled him to put his signature to a clause forbidding the legitimation of children of concubines. His son by Merwenna, now a sturdy fellow of thirteen, had not received official recognition and now never would. Æthelbald had never given importance to an heir of his own, else he would have wed. Still, he loved his boy and had begun to take him hawking and other pastimes enjoyed between father and son. The consolation that sprang to mind while signing was the realisation that the life of his child, unable to claim succession, was safer.

Back in Tame Weorth, whatever way Æthelbald looked at the outcome of the church council, he could see no solution other than to mend his ways. Excommunication for him equated to a death sentence. For this reason, Æthelbald began a period of discreet behaviour and respect for the rights of the church.

* * *

Tame Weorth, 749 AD

Two years of stability, along with the continued wealth of Mierce, served to endorse Æthelbald's conviction that God observed his every action. After all, had not his sainted friend Guthlac told him, when it appeared least likely, that God would raise him to kingship? The death of King Ælfwald of Est Anglia came as sorrowful news to Æthelbald and plunged him into deeper reflection. His neighbour had been a reliable ally and had led a saintly life, founding many monasteries. His reign of thirty-six years proved that longevity of rule was no protection against the machinations of powerful pretenders; nor was virtuous conduct. Now Est Anglia was divided between three new rulers. Æthelbald ground his teeth. He was especially fond of Ælfwald since he was responsible, as the patron of the learned monk, Felix, for the writing of the *Life of Saint Guthlac*.

These considerations revealed to his own blighted soul the extent of his sufferance of the church's yoke on his back. The moment he decided as a consequence to shake off his restraints was the beginning of a downward spiral.

He had behaved with restraint, not flaunting his mistresses, had borne in mind accusations of tyranny and ignored the hate-filled stares of some of his chieftains. Above all, he had kept his promise and not oppressed the monasteries. As king, he was no longer of an age to wield a battleaxe, and of late, he had organised some of his most faithful lords to form a bodyguard. After years of doing as he pleased, this circumspection chafed. The leader of the pack might lose its fur but it does not shed its instincts. The combination of the king's character defects and outside events, for the first time in his reign, led him into situations beyond his control.

As a final act of subservience to the church, Æthelbald ratified the resolutions of Clofeshoch at a synod in Gutmundesleah – Godmund's Clearing. Having bent the knee to the church, the king began his private rebellion. Grown tired of his mistresses, he sought a new adventure and to satisfy his lust, he travelled to the abbey at Glevcaestre. A passing comment by one of his counsellors that his niece had entered the convent, with reluctance, set his pulse racing. Fully aware of the risks, he ran with his obstinacy in vice; in moments of solitude, his heart bore the weight of self-loathing. Yet, his desires proved stronger than his remorse.

Once again, using the prestige of his kingship, he prevailed upon the abbess to allow an encounter with the novice. Skilled in seduction, he convinced the young woman to abscond and meet him outside the walls of the religious house. Flattered by a king's interest and thrilled to flee her unwanted destiny, the maid confided in a close friend and this proved their undoing. The confidante succumbed to the mother superior's interrogation and revealed the truth. The abbess, a kinswoman of the girl's father, contacted him at once and he, in a spasm of rage, mounted a horse and galloped away in search of the king.

Knowing the royal palace at Kingsholm stood nearby, the irate father chose to ride there as a first, likely retreat. Gripped by anger, the nobleman did not consider how he might confront the mightiest man in Angle-land. His only thought was to rescue his daughter's virtue and restore her to her vocation.

In a paroxysm of wrath, he overcame the two guards at the door of the palace. Alerted by the clash of steel, the king seized his sword and dashed from the bedchamber toward the entrance of the hall. He did not reach it before he was confronted by a sword-wielding madman. His wild flashing eyes made Æthelbald regret, in the interests of secrecy, leaving his bodyguard in Tame Weorth. For this same motive, he had brought with him too small a number of armed men.

"King Æthelbald," roared the deranged fellow, "you will restore to me my daughter!"

"Who are you to be giving orders to your king? *I* command this land."

"You do not rule over God! Do you think you can abscond with a bride of Christ, ravish and defile her without punishment?"

"Do not test my patience, fool! Out of my sight before it is too late!"

Driven by rightful fury, the incensed father leapt at the king with weapon raised.

Æthelbald, at last, gratified to be able to use his bejewelled sword, parried the blow with ease. After warding off a number of similar assaults, Æthelbald, tiring of the sport, with precision, smote his adversary on the sword arm. The strike caused the man to howl and drop his weapon, while at the same time, a shrill cry came from the bedchamber door.

"Father!" the young woman exclaimed in anguish. "Do not slay him, sire!" she begged the king, the point of whose sword now pressed against the throat of the defenceless man.

"Get you hence!" Æthelbald hissed. "No man attacks his king and lives… but in this exceptional case… you must thank your daughter."

"This is not the end of the matter, King Æthelbald! You cannot behave like a tyrant and survive!"

"My patience is worn thin! Get out!"

Considering his wound and the fame of the king as a warrior, Lord Maldred retreated, swearing revenge as he left. Two considerations filled his head. First, he must alert his kinswoman, the mother superior to these events. She would know how to alert the church. Second, he needed to ride to Tame Weorth to recount all to his brother, Lord Beornred, one of the king's trusted counsellors. The oppressor must be brought down.

The king returned with his new mistress to the palace in Tame Weorth. In spite of the king's rational fears, there came no immediate censure from the church. Neither did it mean the outraged uncle made no move. On the contrary, he trod with the utmost care, invoking the support of prelates and fellow noblemen. Finding much dissatisfaction with the king gladdened his heart. However, the king remained a powerful and well-sustained ruler. Any attempt to overthrow him required more favourable conditions. The wise head of Beornred counselled caution for the moment. One bishop advised that prayer might bring about a change in Æthelbald's behaviour or, indeed, his fortunes. Æthelbald had never lost a battle in his long reign. Where was the enemy to challenge him?

Beornred suspected, without real evidence, that outside Mierce there were rulers who would be glad to see the back of the monarch who had subjugated them for so long. He could not see strong leaders in these kingdoms, only chaos. But there was one exception, and soon this king would make his move.

Northanhymbre, fresh from victory in the north against the Picti and the seizure of the plains of Kyle, slipped into internal feuding. Offa, the son of Aldfrith, tried to snatch the throne from Eadberht but was forced to take refuge at the relics of Saint Cuthbert at Lindisfarne. Thence he was dragged from sanctuary, half-starved and cruelly slain. Eadberht, displeased with the Bishop of Lindisfarne for sheltering him, imprisoned the prelate.

The political situation appeared to favour Æthelbald, but it turned out only to be an impression. In West Seax, King Cuthred had strengthened his position, but his ascendancy was not accepted by some. In particular, Æthelhun, a Miercian ealdorman of arrogant disposition – owning lands in West Seax, owing to pressure from Æthelbald – organised an uprising against the king. Cuthred raised an army and marched against the rebels, crushing his adversary and slaying Æthelhun. Fortified by victory, he set his sights on regaining West Seax territory lost to Æthelbald.

His manoeuvres could not be left unchecked, so Æthelbald summoned the fyrd and headed south to engage the upstart.

TWENTY-ONE

Beorhford, Oxnafordscir, 750 AD

The Miercian army, led by its standard bearers, crossed the River Wenrush and halted before the hill where the settlement of Beorhford loomed over them. Æthelbald stared up, perplexed. Based on the information provided by his scouts, the West Seax force ought to be lined up on the crest of the hill. Instead, it appeared the enemy had abandoned the heights. With due caution, the king ordered a steady advance to the village and beyond, as far as the top of the ridge. Thence, he gazed down on the plain where the West Seaxa deployed their host. It troubled him they had forsaken the heights. It was a tactic *he* would never use. Could it be the West Seax, and Cuthred in particular, were inept in battle? His experienced warrior's eye swept over the enemy formation below, at once identifying a weakness.

Calling over his battle-hardened thegns, he invited their opinion without expressing his own.

"Sire, their right flank is weak, we ought to attack them there in great numbers."

The others added their voices in assent and Æthelbald agreed. They gave him the confirmation he sought.

Of late, Cuthred had fought many battles with the Britons and was not the novice Æthelbald took him for. In fact, the King of Mierce fell straight into his trap. The West Seax held back their reserve, at this moment, on a forced march to arrive in time, even as the Miercians sent a heavy force pouring down the hill, thus overextending themselves. The ploy proved successful, since the West Seaxa right flank, though outnumbered, contributed to the scheme by fighting a desperate battle to hold its ground. Certain now the Mercians were committed, seeing his reserve force appear, Cuthred struck. His troops charged up the hill and smashed the Miercian centre on the heights with a vicious assault. Meanwhile, his reserves, as ordered, curled around the isolated Miercian left flank. The West Seaxa swept through both Miercian flanks and sent them fleeing in chaos, slaughtering or capturing hundreds of prisoners. Æthelbald, unused to defeat, could not contemplate capture and humiliation. Outwitted by Cuthred, he accepted the reverse and fled with other lords on horseback as soon as his standard-bearer fell, breast impaled by a lance.

Across the ford in the Wenrush, with no sign of enemy pursuit, Æthelbald reined in and consulted his thegns. The best decision, they agreed, was to head westward to Glevcaestre, where Coelwald had strengthened the royal burh with a sizeable garrison. It lay a day's ride hence, but although they would not arrive before nightfall, their formidable appearance would deter outlaws.

With no time to waste, they set off along the ridgeway towards the sun. On the journey, as the shadows lengthened, a sudden inspiration came to Æthelbald. It occurred to him that there was no need to set up camp for the night after all. A much more welcoming hearth awaited them in the vicinity.

The ten armed riders, led by King Æthelbald, reined in their horses before the double-leaved gate of a farmstead. The gates were closed at this hour as the remaining daylight faded into dusk. One of the thegns fumbled at his belt and unhooked a horn. A long blast warned the residents of their arrival, so after a few moments, a red-haired man opened the gate no more than a crack to peer through. Appalled at the sight of armed men, the fellow slammed the gate shut again.

"Who goes there? What do you want?"

The accent made it clear a Briton stood behind the solid wooden barrier.

"Tell your master that King Æthelbald wishes entry. We mean you no harm."

The horsemen waited for a reply, but none came until the gate swung open, revealing a sturdy man in his early forties who bowed low.

"Welcome to Mill Farm, sire."

The group of riders cantered into the yard and dismounted.

In the doorway of the house stood a woman, judging by her grey hair, some sixty years old. Going by her demeanour, she was agitated at the arrival of such exalted visitors.

Satisfied at seeing the horses led to a stone trough, the king strode over to the woman. Age had dignified the rounded features of Goda's face, and the wrinkles could not detract from the gentle mellowness of the woman.

"Time has treated you well, Mistress Goda."

"Thanks to your gift, sire. As you see, Mill Farm is thriving. It is a great surprise and honour to welcome you into my home."

She stepped aside to let him enter, and only then was she dismayed as his eyes swept around the kitchen. Everything was clean and tidy but not of the quality fit for a king.

Goda bustled around, fussing to determine what the king needed. Food? Drink?

Both of these she supplied to the hungry men. But first, she provided hot water and soap so they could remove the fearsome signs of battle they bore, spattered on their skin.

That they had come from a momentous event soon became clear from their talk. A defeat? It was unthinkable. Defeated? What, the king, who was famed for being the most powerful in the whole of Angle-land?

Settled at the table, the king questioned Goda about the farm and her life. She summoned two men to approach them. One, he who had opened the gates, she introduced as her son, Edwy. Proud of him, she explained how from the first day on the farm, the boy wanted to be a miller and how now, in middle age, he supplied flour as far afield as Glevcaestre. All the food and drink, she chirped, was produce of the farm. The king and his men ate with good heart, quick to acknowledge the wholesome goodness of the fare. The second man, Trygil, the king remembered him, was now her husband, and she had borne him two children.

"So you see, sire, how you saved a poor widow and made her the happiest woman in the kingdom. Not a day goes by without me remembering you in my prayers."

"And yet, today, God forsook me," the king's tone was bitter.

"Tomorrow is another day, Lord."

Goda's sage reply heartened him. Indeed it was! Every day, for that matter, is a new beginning.

In the morning, he rose to admire the red-flecked streaks of the dawn in a grey and orange sky, contrasting with the black outlines of the treetops beyond the gates of the farmstead. determined on early departure, the king greeted its owner from his saddle.

"Mistress, farewell. Our thanks for your hospitality. Go on praying for me, I beseech you."

She watched the man to whom she owed everything ride away, defeated but unbowed, and blessed him.

A week later, Æthelbald arrived in Tame Weorth, where in the light of defeat, he was obliged to call a council meeting. The gathering of lords, thegns and bishops presented faces longer than he feared. The hostile air hanging over the moot, not experienced in his long reign, was reminiscent of the later councils of the unlamented Coelred.

Earl Beornred set the tone of a dismal meeting for Æthelbald, demanding wergild for the wounding of his brother at Kingsholm. There was little the king could do. His own laws established the compensation for unlawful wounding. The ensuing heated discussion brought up matters he would have preferred to let lie.

A bishop rose to take the word, "King Æthelbald, you have reneged on your promise to lead a reformed life in the service of God and your people. Your unbridled lust led you to defile a virgin voted to Christ and to do so, attempt the murder of her father! These are grave charges against anyone, the more so against a king! How do you respond?"

Æthelbald glared at the prelate and stared in defiance at the assembly.

"I deny striving to slay the maid's father. Indeed, I pardoned him for his wilful and unjustified attack upon his king. The fellow is lucky to be alive. Had I so desired, he would have paid with his life. Now you have the gall ask me to compensate for the wound he sustained when I defended myself. Have you taken leave of your senses?"

"Sire," said Beornred, "the fact remains that you absconded from the abbey with my niece and ravished her."

"There is no proof of that!" Æthelbald roared. "The young woman had no desire to remain enclosed in a convent, as you well know. I did no more than rescue her from her enforced servitude."

"Then, you deny having lain with her?"

"Do you wish to besmirch the reputation of your niece and that of your king? For shame! Hark! I am prepared to overlook the assault on my person by your brother and willing to pay the wergild demanded, however unjust. I will also compensate him for the taking of one of his slaves. For such is how he treated his daughter. Does this satisfy you, Ealdorman?"

"How will you pay, *sire*? In debased Miercian coin or in the fine silver coinage of Est Anglia?"

Ay, Est Anglia. I'm weakened today without my stout friend Ælfwald to support me.

By drawing coinage into the argument, the ealdorman tapped into another source of discontent. Right from the beginning of his reign, Æthelbald had to face the doubts and hostility of some factions, since he was not a direct descendant of Penda. In spite of the opposition, he had provided them with a stable and powerful kingdom. Now, in the face of his first reverse, the old antipathies had not tarried in surfacing. The angry faces around him, true, not belonging to all the present company, though too many for comfort, made the atmosphere heavy with unveiled menace. His darting eyes picked out the whisperings and beginnings of silent pacts aimed against his person.

"What do you mean to do about West Seax, Lord?" asked Ealdorman Enulf, one of his most loyal subjects.

The king stared at his former blacksmith, and his forced smile conveyed nothing more than his unease.

"Nothing."

"Sire?" Enulf insisted. "Nothing? But King Cuthred must pay for his effrontery."

There came a general murmur of agreement in the hall. Dissent filled the air. If the faithful Enulf questioned him, Æthelbald's position remained anything but healthy.

"Nothing, *for the moment!* Cuthred gained a little independence. It will not last. How can you fail to notice how the power of Mierce has grown, year by year, during my reign? Place a little faith in your king! The West Seaxa are at war with the Britons. It is true they won a victory over us – but at a price. Dumnonia will seize the initiative and cross the borders into Cuthred's lands, mark my words! In addition, Est Anglia, our closest ally, needs time to settle. I must wait to make of their King Beonna the kind of friend I boasted in his predecessor. When the moment is right, I will make West Seax pay."

There were enough of his supporters in the hall to ensure this speech was greeted with a buzz of approval. Æthelbald's words bought him respite.

After a few weeks, the news of war in West Seax going awry against the Britons reached Mierce, proving Æthelbald right. The king's speech, however, did not assuage the fears and resentment of all the powerful men of Mierce.

Lord Beornred sought out Ealdorman Enulf, one of the most influential landowners in the kingdom. Alerted by the unexpected intervention of the said nobleman in the council meeting, Beornred hoped to draw a man famed for his unswerving loyalty to Æthelbald to his cause.

He caught up with Enulf outside the royal stables.

"Wait, friend Enulf! I would exchange a few words."

Surprised to be addressed in a friendly manner by a man whom he ever viewed with diffidence, Enulf halted and rubbed a hand across his brow.

"Well?"

A furtive glance around, Beornred lowered his voice before saying, "Am I mistaken, my lord, or are you disappointed in the state of the kingdom?"

"Are we not *all* downcast by the defeat at Beorhford?"

"Indeed. But worthy as our king has proved over the years, there are more problems than the West Seaxa that need addressing."

"What is it you want of me, Beornred?"

"I cannot make a move to improve matters without your support, Lord Enulf."

"How so?"

"Can you not feel it? Change is in the air. Maybe it is right to act now."

This time, it was Enulf who looked about him to ensure no one was taking an interest in the unlikely confidants. How could he betray the man who had given him everything? Yet Beornred had a point; was Æthelbald losing his grip on Mierce through unnecessary distractions? And hadn't he vowed never to forget how the king had humiliated him at the court hearing? Everyone remembered the evil, dark days of the previous reign, and no one wanted the kingdom to slip back into tyranny. This thought, perhaps unwisely, led him into a deeper discussion with Beornred. They reached an eventual agreement to meet with other like-minded individuals at a hunting lodge at Mannesfeld in the vast forest of Bilhaugh. The secluded retreat, located between the lands of both men, was situated away from prying eyes and suited Enulf well.

The meeting, as often happened in those days, degenerated into a convivial drinking bout. The outcome, in part, satisfied Beornred because, under the influence of drink, Enulf's tongue loosened, as far as to confess his anxieties about his beloved king's fitness to rule. All the would-be conspirators agreed that action should be delayed since the king still enjoyed the support of the church. Æthelbald, no fool, had ridden the scandal of Beornred's niece by leading an overtly blameless life since the last council meeting and by making further endowments to various monasteries. The sole agreement obtained in the lodge was that should Æthelbald make another false step, they would act as one and remove him from the throne. Enulf came under close scrutiny at this juncture, but his fellow drinkers noted he did not baulk at the possibility.

TWENTY-TWO

Tame Weorth, 755 AD

A combination of circumstances saved Æthelbald from the plotters. Weeks slipped into months and into years, bringing with them external events of significance. In 754, Boniface suffered martyrdom in Frisia. Æthelbald would receive no more condemnatory letters from that source. More important to his position in Mierce, the following year, Cuthred died, putting an end, after just five years, to the independence of West Seax. Never one to spurn an opportunity, Æthelbald studied the situation in the south-west. Who could he turn to in an attempt to bring that kingdom once more under his control? Who, if not the "miracle worker", Leofwig? A messenger sent to summon the Lord of Grantebrycge, Æthelbald spent his time waiting for the ealdorman to arrive by plotting how best to use his undoubted abilities.

Greeting the slightly built figure of the ealdorman with unfeigned pleasure, Æthelbald asked himself, not for the first time, how such an unimposing presence could manipulate a rabble of bloodthirsty warlords. The king was under no illusion about the difficulty of the task he was about to entrust to his loyal servant.

"Did you know, Leofwig, that King Cuthbert is dead?"

"In Grantebrycge, news is slow to arrive, sire. I knew it not."

"Well, he is, and it would be false of me to say I regret his passing. I do not! Indeed, it is of the greatest comfort, and Mierce must profit by it. Hence, I have called you to me. I need your precious aid in these delicate circumstances."

"How may I serve you, Lord?"

King Æthelbald, to the ealdorman's dismay, looked confounded and lost for a moment but was quick to regain his certainty.

"From here in Tame Weorth, it is hard to know what is happening in Wintancaestre. Events move there apace, but the latest particulars we gleaned is that a distant relative of Cuthred, Sigeberht, took the throne but not to universal acclaim. In fact – and here we may profit – a group of West Seax lords, led by a certain Cynewulf, another of that name, who pretends to have a stronger claim by bloodline, are engaged in an attempt to overthrow Sigeberht. That is where you can be of service to Mierce."

"By helping to unite any opponents to this Sigeberht and assuring them of the support of our king."

"Well said, Leofwig! I see you have lost none of your quickness of wit."

"I thank you, sire."

"I have no need to warn you of the perils of such a mission. Move with feet of lead, my friend."

"Ay, sire, I will!"

The king laughed, and his words were ironic. "What advice do I give? I mean for you to depart without delay and travel with the wind! There is no time to be lost."

"I will leave at once, Lord."

"We will provide an escort that you may arrive in safety at Wintancaestre."

* * *

Wintancaestre, nine days later

The journey, as often the case with a well-armed escort, proved uneventful and also uncomfortable. But, Leofwig rode into a town that had changed little since his last visit, in the days of King Ine's wise rule, nigh on a score and ten years before.

Discreet enquiries – they were what he needed to make – where better to make them than in a tavern? With the willing compliance of his men, they found a hostelry close to the royal palace. With plenty of silver coins at his disposal, it was not difficult once he separated from his Miercian guards. The natural suspicion of the West Seaxa, he overcame with his smiling generosity. The assertion that he was from Est Seax rather than Mierce, also helped combat any reticence.

Thus, Leofwig engaged in conversation with a tin merchant who confessed he traded with the old enemy, Dumnonia. "Sometimes you have to fight back the bile if you want to do business…" he explained, "…I run a ship to and fro from the estuary at Plymentun to Hamwic. Thence, we unload the smelted tin and bring it in carts overland to Wintancaestre for the joy of the tinkers. There's a workshop across the road from here. Don't know if you saw it when you came in?"

Leofwig shook his head and steered the conversation away from the subject of tin pans.

"Have another drink, my friend? I heard the sad news of the death of King Cuthred."

The trader breathed in, "It was a sorrowful day. We have a new king now, Sigeberht," he sighed again and shook his head, "but the least said about him the better." This, he said, casting a wary eye at the next table.

"King Cuthred was much loved then?"

"I'd not go as far as to say that," the trader pursed his lips. "That he brought respect back to West Seax, there's no gainsaying, but for a man who pursues my trade, he wasn't the best king."

"Are you talking about the wars with Dumnonia?"

"Ay, I thought I'd go out of business at one point, but the folk of Plymentun can be obliging when there's coin to be had!"

The ealdorman shared a conspiratorial laugh, "And, of course, Cuthred defeated the Miercians at the famous battle of Beorhford…"

"He did. There's that to be said for him, but the days of King Ine are long gone, more's the pity."

"You don't seem keen on this new king."

The merchant shrugged and darted a cautious glance around

once more. The sight of Leofwig pouring him another beaker of ale urged him to confide.

"Fact is, my friend, they say King Sigeberht is responsible for *unrighteous deeds.*"

The ealdorman frowned, struggling to grasp the meaning. It rang of religious censure to his ears.

"Do you mean he's at odds with the church?"

"That too, I'd guess. But the real problem is between the high and mighty. Those who command the rest of us, if you follow my drift." He looked warily at Leofwig who, by his dress and manner, might well be one of them.

"I think I take your meaning. For those who wish to be rid of the king, an excuse is found wherever the church is upset. Am I right?"

"Hush, hush! Loose talk can get a man a seax between the ribs in these dire times. But I'd say you more than caught my meaning." He shot a shrewd appreciative glance at his companion.

"So you don't think this king will rest easy?"

The trader sat back in his seat and stared hard at Leofwig, "Mind if I ask you a question, friend?"

The ealdorman was prepared for this. "Ask what you will."

"What brings you to Wintancaestre? Are you here for business?"

The ealdorman laughed, "Of sorts, but I am not free to divulge its nature. Forgive me. Let's say that I am an emissary who needs to settle a matter with the king of the West Seax. A peaceable matter," he hastened to add.

"I thought you might have some authority, by your way of speaking. Begging your pardon if I offer a little advice."

"Pray do."

"If you wish to deal with the king, move with good speed."

"Why"

"You asked me if the king might rest easy. Well, if what I hear is right, it's a matter of days before there's likely to be an attempt to unseat him."

"A revolt?"

"Another trader, a friend of mine who deals in cloth, warned me to leave the town on the morrow."

"Really? As bad as that?"

"He says the king is busy raising men to fight for him."

"A war among themselves, then?"

"I fear so, and I'm away at first light. I counsel you not to linger in this place."

Leofwig could almost smell the dread of the merchant. He lowered his voice, leant forward and said, "One last question, friend. Do you have the name of he who will lead the rebels?"

Terrified, the man shook his head, "I cannot say, it's too great a risk."

"Just give me a sign if I'm right." Never taking his eyes off the tin trader, Leofwig whispered, "Lord Cynewulf."

The merchant's eyes widened, and the ealdorman picked up an almost imperceptible nod.

"Worry not, dear fellow. We have never spoken of such matters. So, do you leave the town in the morning?"

"I do. I'm headed back to Hamwic. In a couple of days, we'll sail over to Wiht and sell tin there. There's always a need for pots and pans."

"I suppose." Leofwig was bored and tired now. He had discovered what he needed to know. It was time to retire for the night. Making his farewells, he left the trader to mull over the strangeness of the encounter. He had not revealed who he was and why he was here. So much the better. He had no reason not to sleep well.

Ealdorman Leofwig spent three days trying to find a way to make contact with Lord Cynewulf, but all his attempts brought him up against a wall of suspicion and fear. Despairing of attaining his objective, he awoke on the fourth morning to the clash of steel and the anguished screams of wounded men. Recognising full well the noise of battle, he dressed in a hurry and strapped on his sword. From the window of the tavern, on an upper floor, he spied men and women running, some shouting and waving their arms in agitated supplication. But from his position, he could hear but not see the engagement of weapons. The first thing to do was to gather his escort for his own safety. With this in mind, he hurried to the dormitory along the corridor, where his ten men lodged. He found them in various states of undress, except for the leader of the men, who, ready for action, strode over to him.

"Lord, what passes?"

"It has begun, Captain. The king fights to save his throne from the rebels."

"What are your orders, Lord?"

"To stay out of trouble. It is not our fight. Should we be called upon, I will let you know. For the moment, be prepared only to defend your own persons and mine, of course. I suggest we search for food downstairs."

The men grinned and laced up their shoes.

Below, the innkeeper had barred the door and closed the shutters. He was only too willing to earn some more money, providing he did not have to open to the public.

Leofwig listened to the sound of clanging weapons diminish. The tavern was close to the royal palace, which likely accounted for the early clamour. The best thing to do, Leofwig decided, was to stay in the safety of the inn until they were quite sure the battle was over. This proved to be a solid enough plan, after all, food and drink were assured, and as the afternoon wore on, relative silence reached them from outside. The barking of a dog and the occasional raised voice, the trundling creaking of a cart but nothing untoward. Before dusk, Leofwig persuaded the innkeeper to open his door to allow him and his escort to venture outdoors.

They strolled the short distance to the palace, where a guard on the door refused to admit anyone. Still, he informed them the king had fled, pursued by his own lord and others, all led by the new king.

"And who may he be, good fellow?"

"King Cynewulf, Lord."

"Very well. You keep your eyes open, and we'll leave you in peace."

Leofwig believed his mission was proceeding to perfection without him having to make a move of any sort. Had he been able to follow the course of events, he would have been even more reassured.

* * *

The Andred Weald, the next day

Cynewulf surveyed the bodies strewn among the trees. The dead men were, for the most part, the rearguard of Sigeberht's force, fleeing to the south-east.

"Burn the dead!" Cynewulf's tone was dispassionate, but in reality, in spite of his success in overthrowing the usurper, he was saddened by the loss of West Seaxa lives. A usurper was how he considered Sigeberht, for his own claim to the throne as a direct descendant of Cerdic, was unquestionable. There was no doubt in his own mind that West Seax was now his. He had the support of the most important families. The only cloud in the sky was that Sigeberht had escaped into the depths of the weald, likely he would head for the estates of Cumbra in Hamtunscir. This was an irritation rather than a problem. Cynewulf, sure that Sigeberht was no longer a threat, needed to establish his position in Wintancaestre and beyond the borders of West Seax. Among his first priorities was to assure the goodwill of King Æthelbald of Mierce, the strongest of his neighbours.

Convinced that divine providence favoured him when he received an emissary from that king into his new palace, Cynewulf greeted Ealdorman Leofwig with good grace. In truth, he had little time for Miercians and one day, he intended to regain Berrucscir and maybe even Lunden from the old enemy. These thoughts he kept to himself; for the moment he needed to keep king Æthelbald on his side. This, by the grace of God, was the gist of the message from Tame Weorth, delivered in the person of the likeable ealdorman from Grantebrycge. Pleased that Leofwig was in no hurry to return to Mierce, Cynewulf spent more and more timewith him. They rode out hunting and hawking and, in general, enjoyed each other's company. This suited Leofwig. Already, he rejoiced in the friendship of one mighty king, to befriend another was beyond his wildest imaginings. Only benefits could come of it, so he thought.

Thus it was that Leofwig was in King Cynewulf's presence when a messenger arrived from the south-east.

"Sire, I am to inform you that Ki – *er* – Sigeberht is dead."

"How so?" Cynewulf could not keep the glee out of his voice

and countenance.

"Murdered, sire, by a swineherd in the forest."

"A swineherd! What are you saying?"

"Sire, it is true! The ceorl was a bondsman of Ealdorman Cumbra, he who fought beside Sigeberht."

"I *know* who he is!"

The messenger swallowed hard, "Of course, sire, I did not mean... but the ealdorman is dead too."

"This is all mighty confused, fellow," Cynewulf hissed with some menace. "Tell it straight!"

"Ay, Lord, begging your pardon. It is that Ealdorman Cumbra and Sigeberht had a falling out... over you, sire. Cumbra wished to make his peace with you, and in a fit of rage, Sigeberht slew him in his own hall."

"Sigeberht was ever an ungrateful cur! What of this swineherd?"

"Seems he loved his master, and hearing of the treacherous act, he awaited his chance. It came when the ki— when... Sigeberht rode into the forest. By a brook, when the traitor was watering his horse, he crept up on him and slit his throat!"

"It was well done!" Cynewulf crowed. "I must send a gift to this swineherd... two more problems solved," he murmured, thinking of the death of his opponent Cumbra.

A few more pleasant weeks passed in Wintancaestre when a messenger for Leofwig arrived from Tame Weorth. He brought another task for the ealdorman.

"King Æthelbald wishes you to persuade King Cynewulf to come to Tame Weorth to witness a charter."

Leofwig understood the implications underlying the request and was sure that Cynewulf would too. So it was with some trepidation that he raised the matter with his friend.

"We shall travel together to Mierce," Cynewulf decided after hearing the proposal. To Leofwig's surprise, he made no other remarks. There was something about the depth of Cynewulf's character that suggested to Leofwig that Æthelbald should not underestimate him. For the present, he could relax in the knowledge of another mission accomplished. Æthelbald, too, would be able to demonstrate to the dissident Miercians that he still had a grasp over the south. But for how long?

TWENTY-THREE

Tame Weorth, 757 AD

"You can't make someone a falconer. You either are one or you aren't," King Æthelbald said, looking fondly at his strapping twenty-one-year-old son, Æthelstan. "Is it not so, Master Falconer?"

"Ay, sire, but Lord Æthelstan's a born falconer, if I may say so."

"And yet, he has never captured and trained his own hawk."

"For lack of opportunity!" Æthelstan's indignation flashed in his blue-grey eyes. "I would trap a gyrfalcon if I had the chance."

The king's smile was indulgent. His sense of guilt at not legitimising this fine image of himself from bygone days drove him to shower the young man with favours.

"Where's the nearest place the gyrfalcon breeds?" he asked the expert.

"Among the crags of the fells to the north-east, sire."

"Can you teach Lord Æthelstan to snare a falcon? And take him there to do it?"

"Ay, the season is right."

"Then do it, Master Falconer."

"Thank you, father." The young lord's eyes shone with pleasure. "I shall have my very own hawk!"

* * *

Deorbyscir Fells, one week later

The falconer and the lordling spent a tedious morning staring into the skies, but the expert eye of the thegn found a gyrfalcon.

"She's nesting up yonder, Lord. Likely she's taken over a raven's nest... er... even if ravens are scarce enough in these parts."

This particular hawk did not serve their purpose since a juvenile was preferable for training. But where there was a mature female, the likelihood of finding a juvenile was high, the falconer assured him. Sure enough, the keen eye of the thegn spotted the ideal raptor in the afternoon, little more than half a mile away from the first sighting.

"Put into practice what I taught you, Lord Æthelstan."

The lordling called for the box of mice they had brought and emptied them into a wire-domed cage. Striding away from the group of accompanying companions, he approached the foot of the craggy outcrop. Choosing his spot with care, he satisfied himself that the bait was scuttling around and visible in the trap. He removed himself five yards away to crouch behind a rock. A glance assured him his assistants had taken to lying out of sight in silence amid the gorse. Patient anticipation was needed now. The grey and white mottled hawk did not disappoint him. Within twenty minutes, his anxious wait was over when the gyrfalcon alighted on the trap for its meal. Its feet snagged in the small nooses as planned. Æthelstan leapt up to release the protesting raptor. This he did with gentleness, copying the manipulation the falconer had shown him in practice. Taking advantage of the state of shock of the bird, he enfolded her in his hands. Resisting the temptation to run back to his companions, he strode over, making sure he did not trip on the uneven ground and lose his captive.

Back with the falconer, delighted, he displayed his prize for inspection.

"She's a fine 'un all right, master."

The thegn was a man of few words, and his approval meant a lot to Æthelstan.

Back in Tame Weorth, in days spent "manning" the hawk,

getting her used to human presence, installing a relationship of reciprocal benefit, Æthelstan did not encounter his father. He could not wait to show off his bird. Impressing the king with his achievements meant a great deal to him, since the fact of his birth rankled and smarted. As a boy, he endured the deep cuts of the cruel barbs of other children. It explained why his prowess in the fighting arts was peerless. He knew his father observed him at sword practice from the shadows, making him redouble his efforts.

When, at last, the king sought him out at the falconry, he found him with Cille settled on his arm. The name chosen after a pretty maid he had admired in the town.

"It is a fine hawk," the king conceded. "Did you capture her, or is this the work of my falconer?" The king's eyes sparkled with humour at the outraged reaction of his son.

"*I* set the trap and I trained her *myself*. Yesterday, I flushed out a grouse and she… she swooped down and snatched her. Oh, father… the sheer speed and grace of her!"

"Well, as soon as I settle a few urgent matters, we'll ride out together to see how your *fledgling* fares against my falcon. Consider the challenge launched." The king laughed, squeezing his son's cheek between thumb and forefinger. Æthelstan felt irritated but at the same time, pleased by the gesture. He watched his father walk away and shook his head. He understood why he did not enjoy a family life like other boys, but understanding did not make it easier to accept.

As for King Æthelbald, the seed of an idea germinated in his mind. Proud of his son, the bitterness of regret tormented his waking hours. How could he go back on the charter signed at Gutmundesleah? By now, his dearest wish was to legitimise Æthelstan. Soon, he might have to prove his strength in battle, but no doubt, the lad was as redoubtable as he, Æthelbald, had been at the same age.

With this project in mind, the king called a council meeting. Getting the normal administrative business out of the way with no hint of opposition and emboldened, Æthelbald plunged into the thorny issue. "My lords, bishops and thegns," he began. "As you well know, I signed a document at Gutmundesleah, accepting that a child by a concubine cannot be legitimised. Everyone here knows full well

I have such a son. My desire is to legitimise Æthelstan." He paused amid gasps in the hall, looked around and found it difficult to discover a single look of approval. "Ay," he continued, "but what worth has the word of a king if it is set aside when it suits? I will not go back on my signed oath." The exchange of puzzled glances quickened his desire to reveal his decision. "No, I will not, but nowhere is it written that I cannot legitimise the child of my lawful wedded wife. My lords, I intend to marry Æthelstan's mother. As a matter of undisputed fact, the boy then becomes my legitimate son. I shall wed Merwenna, who will become your queen before Lammas and the trees shed their leaves."

Some faces displayed relief, others, angry frowns, but Æthelbald expected no less and rejoiced that years of careful planning meant he still enjoyed the faithful support of at least some loyal friends.

Outside the hall, in the relative secrecy of a narrow lane, Beornred caught Enulf, whom he had followed this far, by the arm.

"Friend, this cannot be! It is one thing to be saddled with a doddering king, but to have his bastard foisted on us is quite another."

Enulf shook off the hand, "Æthelstan is a fine young fellow. What are you suggesting?"

"I mean no harm to Æthelstan. But this wedding cannot go ahead."

"How can you prevent it?"

"Alone, I cannot. It is why I need *you*."

"Me?"

"You are in charge of the king's bodyguard, are you not? If Æthelbald is to be removed, it needs to be done with the least commotion possible. Mierce requires a strong king from the right bloodline, not an unproven callow youth. Nor yet an old king whose tyranny increases with every passing moon."

"Who would this new king be?" Enulf had no doubts but wanted it from Beornred's mouth.

The ealdorman glanced around to make sure there were no spies.

"I have the support I need for such a claim."

"You are asking me to betray the man who has given me everything," Enulf said through clenched teeth. "Why should I not slay you, here and now?" And yet the humiliation of his appearance in court still rankled.

"Because here stands another who will give you even more. What say you to the lordship of the *whole* of Eastern Mierce?"

Experienced in negotiating, Beornred caught the wavering acceptance, albeit fleeting, in the countenance of Enulf.

Seizing the moment, he clasped the Ealdorman of Snotingham and Ledecestre's hand.

"My friend, we have an understanding," he said, real warmth in his voice.

"How is it to be done?"

"I leave it to you, but be sure there is no sign of violence – no blood."

Enulf nodded and departed, the weight of the world on his broad shoulders. Strange to relate, the memory of Saint Guthlac's words that he would betray Æthelbald did not dismay him. Instead, they allowed him to convince himself it was the will of God. How could he rail against that? Thus, Enulf comforted himself. The thought that his beloved Mierce might emerge stronger for the act further strengthened his resolve. Also, he had to admit, the whole of Eastern Mierce was worth a fortune.

Determined to strike at once, Enulf hastened to the Nunnery of Saint Editha that stood not far from the royal palace. Admitted on a pretext, he asked to be taken to the infirmary where he spoke to an elderly, robust and benign nun. The woman fussed over him when he told her he needed a potion to help him sleep. Mission accomplished, he left the building with a small phial, wrapped in a piece of cloth. It contained the gall of a barrow swine. The sister swore that three spoonfuls would leave a man unconscious to the extent that he could be cut open and not awake. Enulf planned to slip it into the ale he would give to the guard at the king's bedchamber that evening. This, he would be able to do, but not in Tame Weorth, as hewould have preferred, because Lord Beornred had invited the king to his hall in nearby Seckington. In his role in charge of the bodyguards, Enulf rode the short distance to Seckington in the king's retinue.

With the trumped-up excuse he needed to check on the hall's locks and bolts, he arrived early enough to commandeer a flagon of ale and mix the potion into it. Assured the king had retired, he chatted to the sentry, leaving the leather container and a wooden cup.

The infirmarian had assured him the effects of the drug were nigh on instant. Taking no chance, Enulf waited until he had counted to a hundred, ten times. For a big man, he moved with surprising silence and agility, in spite of having to carry a candle. The guard lay senseless with his shoulders propped against the wall. Enulf hissed next to his ear but the man's regular, deep breathing did not falter. Satisfied, he turned the ring handle of the royal bedchamber and, pleased the hinges were well greased, stole inside the room. By the feeble light of the taper, he made out the form of the sleeping king. With relief, he saw that the huge bed contained no other person. The possibility of finding a woman there had worried him all evening. Enulf set the candle down with care and considered the situation. The king's breathing, deep and regular, assured him the monarch would not wake at the sound of small movements. The ealdorman reached for a goose-down pillow and fluffed it up in his hands.

There was no time to change his mind – *now or never* – he bent over the prone figure. Over Æthelbald's face, covering nose and mouth, he pushed the cushion. Pressing down with all his might, Enulf swung his legs on the bed and knelt with one each side of the king, thereby stopping him, imprisoned by bedcovers, from thrashing about. The strength of the king, now past his sixtieth year, could not resist the might of the younger former blacksmith.

By Thunor, murder! I cannot breathe!

Thus, Æthelbald died in the forty-first year of his reign, slain by the commander of his own bodyguard. Certain of the deed, Enulf removed the pillow and stared down at the shadowy features of his king. He checked for any signs of an unnatural death but could see none.

"You were a great king," he murmured. "You had the desire for success, but it did not burn so strongly in you that you were prepared to overcome your character to attain it. Had you married, as many of us wished, it would not have come to this. After a lifetime alone, why wed now? Fool!"

The ealdorman wiped a tear from his eye and tossed the pillow to the far side of the bed. Taking up the candle, he left the chamber and spared a glance at the slumbering guard. To make sure no one would suspect foul play, he gathered up the bottle and cup and removed them to the guardroom. There, he disposed of the contents of the flagon before burning it and the cup on the fire. The last remaining chore was to hoist the sentry over his shoulder and sit the fellow in a chair in the guardroom. When he awoke, slumped over the table, he would have no memory of getting there.

In the morning, he would tell the sentry he had fallen sick on duty and been replaced. It would be he, Enulf, who would announce the sorrowful news of the peaceful passing during the night of their beloved King Æthelbald and the accession of a new ruler in Mierce.

EPILOGUE
MILL FARM, 757 AD

The priest from the small wooden church of St Mary's in Thormarton, the hill village to the north-east of Mill Farm, took his seat opposite Goda.

"You don't know the news, I'll wager."

"What?" asked Trygil.

"I'm back from Glevcaestre and the town's full of it."

"Are you going to share it with us, Father Esegar, or is it a riddle?" Cwen smiled.

"Cwen! You keep a civil tongue in yon head!" Trygil admonished.

"The king is dead."

"King Æthelbald? But that's—" Edwy wanted to say "impossible" but bit off the word not wishing to offend the priest, "…so unexpected," he said in haste.

"Ay, the king was here in person not long ago," Trygil frowned. "I wonder how he died? And who's to be king now?"

"They say he was a guest in a hall near Tame Weorth. He died in his sleep. God is merciful. There's talk of a King Beornred, but no one in Glevcaestre knows much about him, at least, not the traders I spoke with. One of the king's counsellors, they say."

Goda, who had sat silent and pale while the others spoke, offered in a strained voice, "May God give his soul rest. Æthelbald was a good king."

"Well, that's a moot point," the priest murmured with muted truculence.

"I'll not hear a word spoken against him, Father, we owe him all we have," she swung a vague hand around the room. "He cared for the weak and downtrodden."

"Like any other man, he will answer to God." The priest was taking a neutral stance in the face of the woman's vehement defence of the late king.

"One thing I'll say," Trygil joined the discussion, "the king made Mierce strong, like in the old days. He settled the problems outside the borders. They say the folk along the confines to the west bless the king every day. The Wealisc no longer raid their farmsteads."

"There's truth in all of that," said Father Esegar, "but the church had its difficulties with him, although, in recent times, he helped change the monasteries for the better."

"Ay, and I know for a fact, he founded a good many religious houses," Edwy contributed. "But it's also true," he shot a wary eye at his mother, "at the market you get more for your money if you use Est Anglian or Northanhymbrian coins. Folk say King Æthelbald's coin has less silver than the others."

"All told, I've been luckier than other clergymen," the priest murmured. "I never suffered forced labour on the king's property, but others did. All in all, I'd say King Æthelbald's reign was one of mixed blessings."

"It must be so, Father Esegar," Mistress Goda said with her usual calmness. "If we four in this room have different feelings about the king, then it must truly be a case of mixed blessings."

"They say the king is buried in the abbey of Hreapandune. They built a *shrine* to him," the priest shook his head, full of doubts. He knew of tales of fornication with nuns. But this was something he might never raise. Not in *this* house.

* * *

A few months elapsed, in fact, it was after Lammas, that Edwy the miller brought news back to the farm of the death of the new king.

He had not sat a year on the throne. Beornred's rule was short and, by all accounts, unhappy. The man who dethroned him was named Offa – a cousin of Æthelbald and a descendant of Penda's brother, Eowa.

It was natural enough that the residents of Mill Farm should dwell on Offa's lineage and hence on the past. They were not to know by following the template laid down by Æthelbald, Offa would become the greatest King of Mierce. His determination to raise the moral tone of his kingdom and to imitate the grandeur of Charlemagne, emperor of the Franks, meant that his reign, at least, would not be one of mixed blessings.

The End

GLOSSARY

Anglo-Saxon names and their modern equivalents:

Æbbandun: Abingdon, Oxon
Bebbanburgh: Bamburgh, Northumbria
Beorhford: Burford, Oxon
Berrucscir: Berkshire
Bricstow: Bristol, Gloucs
Britayne Street: Bartholomew Street, Roman road
Briudun: Breedon-on-the-Hill, Leics
Cantwaraburh: Canterbury, Kent
Ceodor: Cheddar, Somerset
Clofeshoch: location unknown, possibly in Oxfordshire
Cruwland: Crowland, Lincs
Dàl Riata: Gaelic kingdom on west coast of modern Scotland and northern coast of Ireland
Deira: Anglo-Saxon kingdom from the Humber to the Tees
Dinieithon: Cefnylls Castle, Ranorshire, Powys
Dumnonia Brittonic: West Country
Dyfed: south-western Welsh kingdom
Elmet: Brittonic kingdom, modern Peak District and parts of Yorkshire
Eoforwic: York
Escancaestre: Exeter, Devon
Est Seax: kingdom of Essex
Foirthe fjord: Firth of Forth
Glevcaestre: Gloucester, Gloucs
Grantebrycge: Cambridge
Gutmundesleah: Gumley, Leics
Hamwic: Southampton, Hants
Hreapandune: Repton, Derbys
Hrofæscæstre: Rochester, Kent
Hwicce: Anglo-Saxon kingdom, south-west Midlands
Inhrypum: Ripon, cathedral city, North Yorks
Intanbeorgan: Inkberrow, Worcs
Kingsholm: Royal Palace near Gloucester, gloucs
Ledecestre: Leicester, Leics
Licidfelth: Lichfield, Staffs
Loidis: Leeds, Yorks
Lunden: London
Lundenwic: port of London
Maelienydd: east central Wales
Magon: Anglo-Saxon kingdom on Welsh border
Mannesfeld: Mansfield, Notts

Mierce: Mercia, Anglo-Saxon kingdom centring on the Trent Valley (Midlands of England)
Miercian: Mercian
Northanhymbre: Northumbria
Outer Mierce: south-east Midlands
Oxnaforscir: Oxfordshire
Powys: Welsh kingdom
Rheged: Brithonic kingdom in north-west England
River Beydd: ancient name of River Malago, Bristol, Gloucs
Saefern: River Severn
Scrobbesburh: Shrewsbury Salop
Snotingham: Nottingham
Suth Seax: Sussex
Sumersaet: Somerset
Tame Weorth: Tamworth, Staffs
Tantun: Taunton, Somerset
Temese: River Thames
Vyrnwy: River in N. Powys, Wales
Weala-denu: Saffron Walden, Cambs
Wealas: Wales
Wealisc: the Welsh
Wenrush: River Windrush, Gloucs
Weorf River: River Wharfe, Yorks
Weorgoran caestre: Worcester
West Seax: Wessex
West Seaxa: Folk of Wessex
Wintancaestre: Winchester, Hants

OFFA - REX MERCIORUM

SAINTS AND SINNERS BOOK 3

JOHN BROUGHTON PREMISE

As a premise to this novel, I would like to cite the renowned Anglo-Saxon scholar, Sir Frank Stenton:

"The re-establishment of Mercian supremacy by Offa is the central fact in English history in the second half of the eighth century. But the stages by which it was brought about cannot now be reconstructed. No Mercian chronicle has survived from this period, and charters alone give any definite impression of Offa's place among English kings."

Therefore, the kind reader will understand that this novel, written to follow the reign of King Offa after that of Æthelbald in *Mixed Blessings* as the third book of a trilogy, is by *force majeure* a mixture of researched history and literary fantasy. My sincere hope is that the reader will enjoy my novel and turn a blind eye to any small historical discrepancies that I have managed to conjure from the shadows of the dark and dim past.

Thank you for your indulgence,
John Broughton

PREFACE

AD 747, Kingdom of Mierce

The doom-mongers were proved correct: the eclipse of the sun and the earth tremors had presaged the king's murder, the civil war, and the pestilence that had befallen the Kingdom of Mierce. Superstition and traditional beliefs accounted for many strongly-held views, but there were also spiritually-minded soothsayers swelling their ranks, who had predicted the unleashing of God's wrath on the kingdom as punishment for King Æthelbald's wanton ways.

Some years previously, whilst continuing his invaluable work as a missionary in Germania, dismayed and well-meaning voices alerted the venerable Boniface to the sorry situation in Mierce. Since there had been no papal legate to the British Isles since the days of Saint Augustine, Boniface unofficially took on the role of pastoral care for the nation of his origin. Never one to act on mere hearsay, the missionary drew up accusations listing abuses of power by Æthelbald, whose misdeeds included the stealing of ecclesiastical revenue, violation of Church privileges, imposing forced labour on the clergy, and fornicating with nuns—all of which were serious and none could go unheeded. This was especially true at a time when Christian men and women daily risked their lives among the heathen to spread the faith that must be seen to be unblemished at the highest levels.

Since Boniface had heard tell of Æthelbald's faith and generous almsgiving, he wished to give the king the benefit of the doubt and the possibility of denying the charges. He, therefore, sent the list of misdeeds first to Ecgberht, Archbishop of Eoforwic, asking him to correct any inaccuracies and to reinforce whatever was right. Also, he requested that a priest, Herefrith, one whom Æthelbald had listened to in the past, should read and explain it to the King in person.

Herefrith sat opposite the glowering king and courageously read Boniface's skilfully-worded letter, first praising Æthelbald, which earned him an approving smile, but then proceeding to address the vexed problem of Æthelbald's never having taken a wife, just as quickly producing a sharp change of mood. Slowly, weighing every word, Herefrith read Boniface's lengthy preamble about the virtues of matrimony, then, in an accusatory tone continued: *If, however, as many say — God forbid — you have never taken a lawful wife nor preserved a chaste abstinence for God's sake, but, under the sway of lust, you have destroyed by licentiousness and adultery your glory and renown before God and men, we are greatly grieved: such conduct must be regarded as criminal in the sight of God and destructive of your reputation before men.*

Æthelbald slammed his fist down hard on the table and, about to have the priest thrown out on his ear, thought better of it. He knew that the charges against him were all true and easily proved. Kings had been dethroned for less and he knew down to every last enemy, who wanted to unseat him. So, he bit his tongue and waved the trembling priest to continue: *And what is worse, those who tell us this, add that this crime of deepest ignominy has been committed in convents with holy nuns and virgins consecrated to God. There can be no doubt that this is a twofold sin. How guilty, for instance, is the slave in the master's house who violates the master's wife! How much more guilty is he who has stained a spouse of Christ, the Creator of heaven and earth, with the defilement of his lust? As says the apostle Paul: "What! Know ye not that your body is the temple of the Holy Ghost?"*

The elderly priest's voice grew in strength and conviction as he saw the king slump on his throne as if resigned to the awful burden his conscience carried. In the unerring manner of learned priests, the holy man cited several other condemnatory passages from the Holy Book.

Herefrith paused for breath and studied the King. Unless he was mistaken, the ruler appeared paler with his face drawn and anxious.

"Is everything quite clear, Sire?"

Æthelbald nodded before asking, "Is that the end of the letter?"

The priest shook his head, swallowed, and continued, at length to invite the King to repent and mend his ways. Æthelbald struggled to pay attention until Herefrith read Boniface's account about other lands, thus providing a greater weight of authority to his words. He chose examples closer to home: Christian kings set an example to their people and if the example was bad, the nation would become as depraved and degenerate as their leader. What was sure to happen was the Omnipotent Judge would allow avenging punishment to come and destroy them. He went on to cite the terrible deaths of King Coelred of Mierce and King Osred of the Deirans and Bernicians. Æthelbald knew these cases only too well and a groan escaped him when he heard: *'They were cast down from their royal thrones in this life, and surprised by an early and horrid death; deprived of the light eternal they were plunged into the depths of hell and the bottom of the abyss.'*

With further warnings not to lose his immortal soul and to avoid the hellfire of the pit, the letter continued for more pages until Herefrith declared it ended.

As if King Æthelbald had not heard enough recommendations and censure, the priest stood and added his own warning out of kindness and a sense of duty.

"Sire, forgive me, but in the interests of your soul, I would ask you to remember how fugitive this present life is. Moreover, how short and momentary is the delight of the impure flesh, and how ignominious it is for a man with his brief life to leave an evil example to posterity."

Æthelbald rose from the table and accompanied the cleric out of the chamber. He felt a tightness in his chest and his breathing became laboured. Had this letter, from men so beloved of the Pope, the Vicar of Christ on Earth, the power to send him to Hell if he ignored it? For the first time since he had taken the throne, he was unsure of himself. He feared no man, but God was a different matter.

He would try to lead a better life and would have a scribe send a long letter expressing his profound penitence to Boniface. Could Æthelbald have hoped to convince men like Archbishop Boniface and Pope Zachary, skilled at dealing with the worst of reprobates? Were they ever likely to leave Angle-land in the hands of one so unworthy? Of course, there was a price to be paid. The price on this occasion was a Church Synod to be held at Clofeshoch, in August 747 AD.

Gathered in the Great Hall, the most important dignitaries of Angle-land, led by King Æthelbald, sat awaiting Archbishop Cuthbert to begin proceedings. The elderly prelate proceeded to translate a letter from Pope Zachary, containing a fervent admonition to amendment of life, addressed to the English people of every rank and condition. The Holy Father required those who condemned these warnings and remained obstinate in their malice to be punished by the sentence of excommunication.

The severity of the condemnation left not a single person, not least the King, in any doubt about the intentions of the Church. The day dragged on as thirty-one canons were drawn up. Many dealt with ecclesiastical discipline and liturgy, but others made Æthelbald blanch, for he was well aware he must sign a document protecting the monasteries from his future rapine. He would have to issue a charter stating the churches were exempt from all public taxation and clergymen free of all works and burdens except the repair of bridges and fortifications.

The King of Mierce, after years of abuse, knew that his coffers were bulging. It was fair to say that his turn had come to pay for the upkeep of public works.

The clause forbidding the legitimation of children of concubines, which would require his signature, distressed him. *Damn the Church!* He was on the brink of legitimising his thirteen-year-old son, a strapping youth by Merwenna. Only recently had he begun to love him like a father, taking the boy hawking and hunting. Now, it was too late; the Church would not allow him to rectify the status of a concubine's child. The king had given no importance to having an heir. After all, in Mierce, he had seized power by the strength of his arm and will, not thanks, certainly, to anything his father had done for him. The consolation that sprang to mind while signing was the realisation that the life of his child, unable to claim succession, was safer.

Whatever way Æthelbald looked at the outcome of the Church Council, he could see no solution other than to mend his ways. Excommunication for him equated to a death sentence. For this reason, the king began a decade of discreet behaviour and respect for the rights of the Church.

(Ten years later – AD 757)

Æthelbald's reluctance to wed, paradoxically, had kept him on the fringes of factional quarrels in Mierce as powerful magnates could not find stronger contenders than the king to sweep him aside. Not even an alliance between two powerful families could risk the combined fury of Æthelbald and a coalition of leading families. Undoubtedly, without pressure from the Church and the looming threat of excommunication if he could not bridle his lust, he would not have considered matrimony. Now, however, given his irrepressible yearnings and certain material advantages, including an admirable ready-made son, the concept of a wedding had gained in appeal. Its greatest benefit would be to please the Church and remove the threat of excommunication that so perturbed him, once and for all.

On the other hand, as Æthelbald could well imagine, there were those who found the idea far less congenial. In a secluded corridor of the royal palace at Thame Weorth, Ealdorman Beornred met with the ealdorman in charge of the royal bodyguard.

Ealdorman Enulf of Snotingham and Ledecestre shook off the avuncular hand. "Æthelstan is a fine young fellow. What are you suggesting?"

"I mean no harm to Æthelstan. But this wedding cannot go ahead."

"How can you prevent it?"

"Alone, I cannot. That is why I need *you*."

"Me?"

"You are in charge of the King's bodyguard, are you not? If

Æthelbald is to be removed, it needs to be done with the utmost discretion and the least commotion possible. Mierce requires a strong king with the interests of its people at heart. Æthelbald would foist onto us an unproven callow youth. We need one such no more than we need an old king whose tyranny increases with every passing moon."

Beornred lowered his voice, which had risen with the strength of his feelings, and glanced around cautiously. Enulf asked quietly, "Who would this new king be?" He had no doubt what the reply would be, but he wanted it from Beornred's own mouth before deciding how to react. The ealdorman also glanced around to make sure there were no spies.

"I have the support I need for such a claim."

"You are asking me to betray the man who has given me everything," Enulf said through clenched teeth. "Why should I not slay you, here and now?"

"Because here stands another who will give you even more. What say you to the lordship of the *whole* of Eastern Mierce?"

Experienced in negotiating, Beornred caught the wavering acceptance, albeit fleeting, in Enulf's countenance. Seizing the moment, he clasped the Ealdorman of Snotingham and Ledecestre's hand.

"My friend, we have an understanding," he said, real warmth in his voice.

"How is it to be done?"

"I leave the details to you, but be sure there is no sign of violence – no blood. Also, until the deed is done, it will be well that we are not seen together in public."

They nodded at each other and went their separate ways.

At once, Enulf hastened to the Nunnery of Saint Editha, not far from the Royal Palace. Under the pretext of needing medical assistance, he asked to be taken to the infirmary, where he spoke to an elderly, robust, and benign nun. The woman fussed over him when he told her he needed a potion to help him sleep. Having accomplished this mission, he left the building with a small phial wrapped in a piece of cloth. It contained the gall of a barrow swine. The sister swore that three spoonfuls would leave a man unconscious to the extent that he could be cut open and not wake. Enulf planned to slip it into the ale he would give to the guard of the King's bedchamber that evening. However, he would not do this in Tame Weorth, as he supposed, because Lord Beornred had invited the King to his hall in nearby Seckington. In his role in charge of the bodyguards, Enulf rode the short distance to Seckington with the rest of the King's retinue.

With the genuine excuse that he needed to check on the hall's locks and bolts, a standard part of his duties, he arrived early enough to commandeer a flagon of ale and mix the potion into it. Once assured the King had retired, he chatted to the sentry, leaving the leather container and a wooden cup.

The infirmarian had assured him the effects of the drug were almost instant. Taking no chances, Enulf waited until he had counted slowly to a hundred. For a big man, Enulf moved with surprising silence and agility, despite having to carry a taper. In the flickering light cast by the candle flame, the ealdorman discerned the guard lying senseless, his shoulders propped against the wall. Enulf hissed next to his ear, but the man's regular deep breathing did not falter. Satisfied, he rearranged the man into a more natural sleeping pose, with his head nestled in the crook of an arm, before turning the ring handle of the royal bedchamber and, pleased to find the hinges well-greased, stole silently into the room.

By the feeble light of the taper, he made out the form of the sleeping king. With relief, he saw that the huge bed contained no other person. The possibility of finding a woman there had worried him all evening. Enulf set the candle down with care and considered the situation. The king's breathing, deep and regular, assured him the monarch would not wake if he moved without making a noise. The ealdorman reached for a goose-down pillow and fluffed it up in his hands.

There was no time to change his mind – *now or never, any moment one of my patrols might arrive* – he bent over the prone figure. He pushed the cushion over Æthelbald's face, covering his nose and mouth. Pressing down with all his might, Enulf swung his legs onto the bed and knelt, one on each side of the king, thereby stopping him, imprisoned by bedcovers, from thrashing about. The strength of the king, now past his sixtieth year, could not resist the might of the younger former blacksmith.

'By Thunor, murder! I cannot breathe!' was the king's last conscious thought before his body went limp. Thus, Æthelbald died in the forty-first year of his reign, slain by the commander of his own bodyguard. Certain of the deed, Enulf removed the pillow and stared down at the shadowy features of his king. He checked for any signs of an unnatural death but could see none.

Even as he tiptoed across the room, glancing back regretfully at the still figure, "You were a great king," he murmured, almost as if to justify his atrocious action to the monarch's soul, trapped in limbo. "You had the desire for success, but it did not burn so strongly in you that you were prepared to overcome your character to attain it. Had you married, as many of us wished, it would not have come to this. After a lifetime alone, why wed right now? Fool!"

The ealdorman wiped a tear from his eye and placed the pillow to the far side of the bed, far enough out of reach to make it look innocuous. Taking up the candle, he sneaked out of the chamber and spared a glance at the slumbering guard. To ensure no one would suspect foul play, he gathered up the wooden bottle and cup and removed them to the guardroom. There, he disposed of the contents of the flagon down a drain before burning it and the cup on the fire. The last remaining chore was to hoist the sentry over his shoulder and sit the fellow in a chair in the guardroom. When he awoke, slumped over the table, he would have no memory of arriving there.

In the morning, he would tell the sentry he had fallen sick on duty and been replaced. It would be he, Enulf, who would announce the sorrowful news of the peaceful passing during the night of their beloved King Æthelbald and the accession of a new ruler in Mierce. Truth be told, the ealdorman reflected sorrowfully, few men would have had the force of personality to make himself the Bretwalda, but having achieved so much, what a shame that the nobility of his character did not match the nobility of his birth that he so flaunted. Enulf recognised that he was no replacement for King Æthelbald and sincerely doubted that Ealdorman Beornred, for all his ambition and promises, was the man to lead Mierce out of the inevitable chaos of civil war, or the equal of Æthelbald capable of once more uniting Angle-land under one Bretwalda. Was there such a man lurking in the shadows of Mierce, waiting for his moment to arrive?

ONE

Tame Weorth, AD 757

Lady Cynethryth stood, her fine cornflower-blue dress, despite the terrible mugginess of a summer's day in the heart of Mierce, draping around her, the soft rustling of the expensive fabric pleasant to the ear. The colour suited her as it brought out the flush of her rosy cheeks and the lightness of her long, tightly braided blonde hair. She was not a tall woman, but there was something about her posture that made her imposing, even terrifying to some. Her bearing was born of confidence, an awareness of her attractiveness and nobility. Not for nothing had she chosen her consort with care and calculation.

Cynethryth had a dream, an unconfined vision, which depended upon her spouse, Offa, for its realisation, although he did not know it yet. Now was the time to act! The king's murder had thrown Mierce into disarray—civil war was the inevitable result of the power struggle that had left Æthelbald bloodied and dead after a long and successful reign. Offa, a distant relative of Æthelbald, was descended from Eowa, the brother of the greatest Miercian king, the pagan Penda. His lineage entitled, nay, obliged him to seize the moment. She would urge him to act against the pretender, Beornred, whose only virtue was his resolve. He had declared himself King of Mierce, but that crown would be Offa's, and she would be Queen—not just of Mierce but of the Englisc! Now, to share her vision with Offa!

She glided rather than walked across the great hall, conscious, as ever, of all eyes on her regal presence, and indeed, although she did not like to boast about it, she, too, was descended from former royalty, in direct line from Penda's wife, Cynewise, and her daughter, Cyneburh—did not her name reflect this lineage?

"Husband, I need to speak with you in a quiet place."

He gave her a curious look, shrugged, and linked arms, steering her outdoors into the shade cast by the building and away from indiscreet ears. "Well, what is it? Are you with child?"

She looked miserable, "Nay, but not from want of trying!" She smiled coyly and pressed closely to him. "I want you to go away for a while, my dearest man."

"Go away?" He looked shocked.

"Aye, gather your warriors and ride east towards Bedeford. There you will encounter the force of Beornred. He is rightly unpopular and not fit to be King of Mierce. *You*, instead, were born to rule this land with me by your side. Hark! I have spoken with Ealdormen Heardberht, Bercol, and Sigebed, and all three agree that you are of the right age and have the attributes for kingship. They are prepared to bring their warriors if you agree to lead them."

"By God, woman! I have but a score and seven years. You have been busy and you almost put me to shame. But I have not been idle, I have spoken with Ealdormen Ealdwulf and Eadbald, and they wish me to lead them, more so now, I imagine, thanks to your good work!" He kissed her fiercely and declared, "Messengers! I will send to all of them and we shall gather in the Tame valley at the rising of the moon, ready to march on Bedeford at dawn."

Offa surveyed the well-armed black mass of men with satisfaction; they were little more than shades in the faint light of the breaking day, but importantly, enough to challenge Beornred and, if God so willed, conquer him.

After an eastwards march, Offa's army camped overnight in a meadow near Bruna's homestead, ready to react to the scouts' reports at first light. At dawn, Offa listened to his spies attentively and decided to lead his force along the Great Ouse valley until he saw the enemy. He grinned contentedly, for he would never have chosen Beornred's position, so vulnerable with their backs to the wide river. He summoned his ealdormen and found them equally astonished at the folly of their foe. They all agreed that an outflanking manoeuvre in a wide arc would place Beornred's army in an impossible position. An archer brought down an enemy scout galloping to warn his king about the imminent danger. His elimination was enough to gain the advantage that surprise brought, for as Offa's main force marched, banners swirling in the wind, defiantly towards the facing enemy ranks, Heardberht's men burst from the woodland upon their flank while Ealdorman Sigebed's force struck from the rear.

Offa had little time to reflect as he strove to defend himself in the van of his army, but at the sight of what should have been friendly banners fluttering over Beornred's army, sorrow at slaying fellow Miercians overwhelmed him. Was there anything worse than civil war? He swore that when he was king, as surely, he would be, Mercian arms would only be wielded against external enemies. The time for hesitation was over as he hewed and hacked at arms as strong as his. Encouraged by the steady advance of his men, he redoubled his efforts. Offa had fought against the Wealisc under King Æthelbald, so he was unmoved by the spattering blood and the screams of dying men, except that this time, Miercians were falling on the sodden turf. Suddenly, under pressure from all sides, with retreat impossible, the enemy laid down their arms, most likely inspired by the same thought that they were fighting their brothers and aware that their leader had taken flight into the nearby woodland. Offa sent a small band of men to search for the fugitive king, but despite their efforts, he made good his escape. When he turned around, it was to see his men and the 'enemy' working in unison to tend the wounded.

The same spirit of unity prevailed during the gathering and burning of corpses. An ealdorman, named Cyneberht, who had fought alongside Beornred, and with whom Offa had twice signed King Æthelbald's charters, came and knelt before him, swearing allegiance and offering his men. The blood-spattered warrior hoisted him to his feet and, embracing him, showed magnanimity.

"At the death of our late lamented King Æthelbald, you stepped into the breach filled by Beornred. I cannot blame you. The kingdom needs a strong leader and, give Beornred his due, he acted decisively, but now, brother, I need men like you by my side, for I must consolidate my hold on Mierce, else today's victory has been in vain."

Back in Tamworth, Offa approached his wife. Cynethryth wrinkled her nose in disapproval as he snatched the wooden beaker of water from her outstretched hand.

"At least, tell me you won the battle," she said, eyeing his disgusting state with distaste. He noticed the water, not her, swilling it into his parched mouth with a filth-encrusted hand. Dust stained his face, his clothes, and his weapons glistened with what she suspected was gore of the battlefield. And he stank of sweat and horses. She was staggered by the state of him.

"Of course, I won. I'm alive, am I not? I set Beornred to flight; my only regret is that he escaped."

She compressed her lips and summoned servants. "A hot bath for my husband and fresh clothes, if you please."

When he returned to her and noticed her smile of approbation, he said, "What did you expect after a battle, a scented meadow flower?"

She laughed and kissed him. "You know that the task is not even half-completed. Your hold over Mierce must be consolidated, and you must have the ealdormen declare you king."

"I know all that and more! I shall summon the lords here on the morrow. First, we all deserve a good rest and strong drink." He clapped his hands and ordered twice-brewed ale.

She sat beside him and quaffed the ale as well as any man. It gave her the courage to speak her mind.

"I have no intention of being merely the *controller of the household*. Alcuin! Where are you, you miserable wretch?"

A cleric stepped forward, "My Lady?" he bowed.

"Husband, this is Alcuin, a scholar and teacher. I have instructed him to teach you Franconian and Latin."

"Woman, who are you to decide such things? Let me remind you that *I* wield the sword in this household."

She glared at him, "Who am I? I am soon to be the Queen of

Mierce and you will learn from Alcuin how to become a ruler like King Charlemagne, for he regularly travels between Mierce and Frankia. One day, you will stand before Charlemagne on equal terms and impress him with your knowledge of his language. Now, I will leave you two men together to make your arrangements." She swigged down the rest of her ale and swanned away with a smug smile, aware that she too could win battles, but her weapon of choice was her mind.

Offa was happy to do his beautiful wife's bidding, especially when her demands coincided with his desires. For this reason, the next two days saw the steady influx of ealdormen through his door. Among them arrived a figure carrying a sack, whose appearance resembled that of Offa himself when he had arrived straight after the Battle of Bedeford. Offa thought he recognised the fellow as one of the warriors who had fought beside Ealdorman Sigebed on that fateful day. He summoned him over with a gesture.

"Young fellow, don't I know you? You look as if you have come straight from the battlefield."

"Ay, lord, you know me. I am Sigeberht, son of Ealdorman Sigebed and, in a manner of speaking, I have come fresh from an engagement."

These words pricked Offa's interest, "How so?"

The young man reached into his sack and, grasping a handful of hair, hauled forth a severed head. Offa recognised it at once. "Beornred!" he gasped, "What is this?" The same question that the now silent, awestruck assembly asked themselves.

"After the battle, lord, I pursued him into the nearby woodland. It took me more than a day to catch up with him, but when I did, we fought to the death. My axe put an end to your foe, lord. I brought his head as proof of my words. The wild beasts will feed on his body."

"I am your debtor, Sigeberht and I never forget my debts. Sigebed!" he roared.

The young man's father hurried across the room to stand beside his son.

"You can be proud of your boy," Offa growled, "Look what a present he has bestowed on me! Heaven knows, I was happy to drive him into exile, but this is a better solution!"

Sigeberht held up the gory, ashen head for his father and the whole gathering to see better.

"When I am elected king, in the next few days, I will make over Beornred's estates to your son and create him an ealdorman. I will need such loyal and trusted men by my side." Offa caught the glint of pride and appreciation in the ealdorman's eyes and knew that he had gained two certain votes at the forthcoming Great Council.

Before losing the advantage gained by Sigeberht's revelation, Offa summoned a warrior to his side—he meant to make the most of the attention he had gained.

"Take the head, mount it on a stake and display it over the town gate. Let's show the world the fate of Offa's enemies!" He glared around the hall and noticed with satisfaction that nobody held and challenged his gaze.

He spoke quietly with two or three of the leading ealdormen and relied on them to spread the word of a Great Council Meeting in the royal palace, until recently the seat of King Æthelbald. In this way, he reasoned, the powerful lords would not feel commanded to attend but have the sensation of a groundswell of sentiment to elect a new king. Thus, the meeting was called for two days hence at noon. It was clear to all parties involved that Mierce could not drift along without a steady hand on the steer-board.

Cynethryth waited until Offa was almost asleep at night, a technique she had developed to get her own way because his desire to sleep outweighed any inclination to discussion. She prepared him for the meeting, imagining herself in his position and drawing upon her intimate knowledge of the nobility's mentality. She pictured how her father would feel on hearing of the pretensions of a twenty-seven-year-old warrior.

"My sweet," she murmured, caressing his inner thigh, "capture their imaginations. Æthelbald succeeded in becoming Bretwalda, ruling over the whole of the south, tell them you will do the same. There is no reason why Miercian power should be confined within man-made borders drawn up by its enemies in the past. We are in the here-and-now and intend to show the other Englisc kingdoms the unrestrained might of Miercian arms under your leadership. Point to the imperial expansion of Charlemagne in Frankia. He too, was a young and energetic leader with ambitions." She felt his body responding to her ministrations and pressed closer to him, her lips seeking his mouth. No more convincing was needed. He showed her how much he loved her.

She was not disappointed because he returned from the Council Meeting and ordered her to arrange the transfer into the royal palace. "Your *king* commands you to organise the servants to move the barrels, the dried, salted meat and the furnishings you retain necessary to the royal abode, *my queen*. Ay, you are the Queen of Mierce and I am your king! By the way, the ealdormen and thegns took little convincing when I expounded our vision of the future.

TWO

Tame Weorth, Mierce, Hereford and Kent AD 760-764

During the early years of their marriage, Cynethryth grew used to her husband's periodic outbursts of rage; at times directed against insubordinate thegns, at others, against incursions along Mierce's various borders. She was gratified to make it her business to aid and support his decisions because she observed how much importance he gave to her opinion.

As she never tired of telling him, "My love, it is early days. You have been king for only three years. Do you suppose that King Æthelbald could style himself *rex Britanniae* after so short a time?"

His shoulders sagged as her words struck home. Of course, she was right. If he were ever to pronounce himself Bretwalda as Æthelbald had done, he would have to move successively in all directions. But it was not simply a question of military matters. The financial aspect was of prime importance, too. "Look," he took a silver piece from his purse and handed it to Cynethryth, who studied it carefully. On one side she read, CARo/LUs and on the other, the location of the mint—Liège Leo/DICo. Then she handed it back.

Offa continued, "I can see how that reinforces his image and authority on a daily basis. I also shall have coins minted with the inscription *Rex Merciorum* for all to read. You will be the first queen to have her head on a coin, my love. Some of Charlemagne's coins, like this one, only have writing, others have a temple, a gateway, or his portrait. We'll change the word rex to *regina* for you."

"Are you serious?"

"Never more so. It will enforce the Christian value of matrimony and please the pope. We shall make our system the same as Charlemagne's: he uses a pound of silver to make 240 denari or twenty solidi. I will call them pounds and shillings."

Cynethryth wrinkled her brow. "Will you not risk Charlemagne's wrath by introducing a rival coinage?"

"You'd think so! But there's the beauty of it—it will not be a *rival*. Charlemagne's father, Pippin, closed the mints of other magnates and established minting rights as an exclusively royal privilege—and that is what we shall do. As we speak, a certain Ethilwald, a Lunden engraver with the necessary skills to mint our coins, is on his way to Winchester. I shall instruct him to make our coinage exactly the same weight and measure as the Frankish coins, so there will be no dispute when people trade or exchange them."

"Ah, that's clever, Offa!"

"I shall want my portrait in the style of a Roman emperor, with a diadem in my hair."

Cynethryth snorted and shot him an ambiguous smile. He did not notice because he had returned to reflecting on military matters.

To the west, the Wealisc forever caused Mierce problems, especially the powerful kingdoms of Powys and Gwynedd, which were a match for Mierce. For some time, Northumbria had not been a problem, not even for his predecessor, because internal strife had led to its isolation so that, as Cynethryth had pointed out, Æthelbald when defining himself *rex Britanniae* in a charter of 736 that the studious Cynethryth had discovered in a strongbox in the library, unfurled and read, referred to what he called *all my provinces south of the Humber*. His wife, as ambitious as he—if not more so—had immediately drawn it to his attention. "What was Æthelbald's is also yours by right, husband. It is a question of *assertion*. You must assert your strength over areas that have become the subject of debate and false claims. Look, for instance, to the country either side of the middle and upper Thames. It's true that Wessex has a more ancient claim, but Æthelbald regarded Lunden and its port as his town. If you are to be taken seriously, Offa, you must ensure that everyone sees that rich city as yours."

"Wessex! Pah! I'll deal with the West Saxons in due course. As for them, I owe a debt of thanks to my predecessor. The day he took Somerton over thirty winters past, my love, it made Mierce the direct ruler of areas of Wessex beyond the great Selwood. Now, I don't expect you to be a military strategist as well as my counsellor," he said patronisingly, "but Somerton is of immense value to Mierce and Æthelbald realised it when he drove a hard bargain with King Aethelheard, in exchange for allowing him to marry his ward Frithugyth. Ay, that is the weakness of Wessex. Since King Ine abdicated, they have had a succession of weak kings—five in all, of uncertain lineage—and it is an ongoing situation in my favour. Wessex is nothing more than a large outlying Miercian province, and I intend to keep it that way."

"There you are, then, my sweet, why the bad mood?"

"You haven't heard, then?"

She looked at him anxiously, judging by his thunderous expression, something was seriously amiss. "What is it that I should have heard?"

"The Wealisc devils have crossed the borders and pillaged several villages on the fertile plain across the Wye near Hereford." His fist thumped down on the old oak table, a gesture she had seen several times, used only when he was enraged and determined. "I have mustered all my vassal ealdormen to raise the fyrds. They are happy to oblige, my Queen, because as Ealdorman Sigeberht's villages are enveloped in smoke, so could theirs be if we do not defend Miercian territory as a united force. I march with my houseguards from Tame Weorth at first light. We shall teach Powys a lesson he'll never forget."

In an involuntary gesture, Cynethryth placed her hands flat and protectively over her lower belly, above the groin area. Offa noticed at once and raised an eyebrow.

"Ay, I have missed the monthly bleed, husband, and suffer the morning sickness."

"So," he said gleefully, "my darling, you are with child!"

"Ay, it would seem so."

"Fear not, I will lead my men, but I'll not leave my son without a father!"

"You men are all the same! Does it not cross your mind that the babe may be a girl. What then, will you not love her as your own?"

Offa strode forward and took his wife of the trembling lip and tearful eye in his strong arms.

"Of course, I'll love my daughter, when she comes, but this child is a boy, I *know* it!" He gave her an intimidatory glare to accompany his reassuring squeeze as if challenging her both to defy his words and his imprisoning embrace. She felt all resistance course out of her willing body and instead, pressed her lips to his in a lingering kiss. Then, she gazed into his eyes, "I want nothing to happen to you. I'll pray for your safety tonight."

"Feel the strength in these arms, God willing, they will smite the Wealisc and secure our borders."

In the first three years of his reign, Offa did not need to prove himself as a military strategist since his fighting was limited to quelling the odd rebellious thegn and his armed presence was enough to win the day.

The king would have been the first to admit that his knowledge of strategy and tactics was limited despite his notable intelligence, while his ealdormen, although experienced warriors, were not convincing leaders. The lesson that Offa learnt the hard way from the Hereford engagement was not to take anything at face value on the battlefield.

Offa's instinctive shrewdness warned him not to be drawn too close to the river Wye, but as the dawn broke in the east, the sight of the enemy camp with a few fires burning below in the river valley and several figures moving about their early-morning tasks proved irresistible. Offa ordered the charge into the enemy camp, where the dozen sacrificial lures were easily overwhelmed. But Offa and his ealdormen had overlooked the dense woodland falling down to the river to their left. Even as they jubilantly slew the brave decoys, the Wealisc warriors poured out from their hiding place in the trees and, whooping, fell upon them, forcing the Miercians back to the river. Offa and his army had fallen into a well-conceived trap. Outraged by the memory of the smouldering villages on their territory that they had passed, torched by the enemy, the

Miercians fought for survival and vengeance. This combination meant that the ferocious Wealisc assault, whilst devastating, did not succeed in its intent to drive the Miercians to a watery grave in the Wye.

The men of Powys actually lost more warriors than the Miercians, whose losses were considerable. Offa's ealdormen were impressed with the king's improvised tactics in the heat of battle. Whenever the enemy overcommitted in attack, he organised a punitive assault on their weakened point, understanding the ebb and flow of battle as easily as if reading a document. They were impressed by his courage, too, seeing him always at the head of each new manoeuvre. It was noticeable how the enemy wilted at the sight of the oncoming bloodied Mercian king—a daunting figure.

When Offa returned home, he grinned at Cynethryth, who, as ever, was commanding her small army of servants to prepare his bath and clothes. She insisted on soaping his weary shoulders herself, and as he relaxed, she asked, "Did you win a decisive victory over the Wealisc?"

"When it comes to warfare, I have much to learn. We lost too many good men. But, ay, I reckon it was a momentous battle. Powys lost more than we did, so they will not raid into our lands lightheartedly for a long time. That was my purpose, after all. Besides, from this battle, others will learn that Offa protects his people whatever the cost."

"Well said, husband!" She poured warm water over his matted hair and recoiled at the red liquid that ran between his shoulder blades as he tilted his head back. She picked up a bar of soap and worked suds into his wavy locks until she was quite sure that the last of the enemy blood was washed away. Cynethryth did not regret soaping her husband's hair instead of leaving it to a servant, although she felt better not dwelling on the provenance of the crimson in the rinse.

Offa concluded, "We cannot call today's battle a victory, but neither is it a defeat, and Mierce has learnt much from the clash: not least that the Wealisc are cunning enemies to be respected," his hands gripped the sides of the iron bath so that his muscular forearms knotted, "but nobody will harm my people and destroy their homes whilst I am king," he hissed.

The Queen massaged his shoulders and whispered, "Relax, my

love, you will be the greatest king Mierce has ever had." She had not witnessed the battle, but instinctively, she knew she was right.

In the following days, Offa drew conclusions from the Battle of Hereford and its wider significance. His men had paid a high price; therefore, the impetus of the outcome must not be lost. First, he must ensure that the western borders were secure against Wealisc raids before turning his attention to the rebellious province of Kent.

As if it were not enough that they contested his kingship, they even found cause to object to his coinage. A case had come to his attention that had occurred in the port of Deal. Two traders had come to blows over his silver shilling. One had agreed on the price of a length of cloth for a shilling. The cloth merchant refused to accept the coin because it showed a woman's head: the portrait of Queen Cynethryth by Pendraed the moneyer, the finest die cutter in Lunden.

"And I tell you it's a fake!" the cloth merchant snatched back the neatly tied parcel of cloth that he had wrapped and tossed the debatable coin onto a bale of damask. "Who's ever heard of a coin with a woman's head on it? Nay, you'll pay me with the king's coin or nought else!"

"But I don't have a coin with the king's head on it. It's the queen or a Frankish coin, that's all I've got in my money pouch."

"I don't want that Frankish rubbish, either, it's worth less than good Mercian money."

"Until last year, you were eager to get your grubby hands on Frankish deniers."

"Ay, but that was then, now is now!"

"Set that parcel aside. I'll see if I can get one of the other traders to exchange the queen's shilling for that of the king." His attempt led to another argument, the drawing of a dagger, and a wound that came to the attention of the local reeve. Soon, the tale was on everyone's tongue, and it needed the reeve to threaten punishment to anyone refusing to accept the queen's shilling.

Offa noticed that Cynethryth lay awake next to him, smiling fondly at his thoughtful face, and decided not to upset her with the question of her silver shilling, but instead, changed to another subject bothering him. "I shall never forget or forgive what happened at Hereford only three years into my reign. I'll summon the lords whose estates are at risk."

From the lords who lived on the border with Wales, Offa learned that there were no incursions where his predecessor had built an insurmountable dyke, a linear earthwork running through the northern Wealisc Marches from Basingwerk Abbey on the River Dee estuary, passing east of Oswestry and on to Maesbury in Shropshire. "The problem is that King Æthelbald was on good terms with Gwent and did not extend the works to the south. That is where the incursions now occur. Hence our defeat at Hereford," one lord dared to recall.

"It was not precisely a defeat, but we will avenge our losses when it suits me," Offa growled with a thunderous expression clouding his handsome features. "On the other hand, I do not wish for all-out war with Powys or Gwent just now. Whom among you knows of the engineer who constructed King Æthelbald's dyke?"

"Sire, I know of one of them, but he is an old man. Would you like me to go to him?"

"Nay, we'll all go. I wish to speak with him in person to understand better this construction."

Offa gently raised the trembling white-haired builder to his feet. "Cast your mind back to when you worked on the late king's dyke. I wish to know all about its construction and whether it can be extended southwards."

"Ay, Sire, so it can," the elderly engineer said confidently. "King Æthelbald had a pact with the King of Gwent at the time, so the dyke was never continued down to the Saefern, but it can be done as far as the river Wye. Then we can use the river for some miles before renewing building from the Wye to the Saefern. It will require many men to dig it, though."

The king of Mierce followed the old man's directions and rode out to survey the trench running north, nodding his satisfaction. He nudged his horse to the edge of the ditch and did not need to haul on the reins, the animal stopping and whinnying, tossing its head. Offa peered into the depths of the ditch and his eyes followed the turf bank upwards. For sure, a man on a pony could not pass. On foot, he would have a devilish job to clamber down and up the other side to surmount the obstacle, not to mention the wooden palisade, still manned in turns by local patrols. He grunted his approval, turned his horse and sought out the mason again.

"The bank must be at least five yards high if it is to serve," said the head mason whom he had brought along to the borderlands.

"Five yards?" came the incredulous reply from the King.

"I mean from the bottom of the ditch."

"Ah, then, three yards of bank?" Offa said, reassured.

"Forgive me. It is what I meant. It will continue southwards to create a real obstacle to raiders. But we must have them save the turf to make a revetting wall to the front above the ditch. Sire, the dyke built by the late king runs north, incorporating natural obstacles as far as the Dee estuary. We can do the same, southwards as far as the Saefern. But what of the labourers, Sire?"

"I shall employ the corvée system, requiring my vassals to build certain lengths of the earthworks in addition to performing their normal services to me. Slaves will complete my workforce. The Wealisc are the reason we need this work, so we'll bring an army, ravage the region, and enslave the menfolk. They will be forced to dig to the tune of the lash across their backs. We'll begin next week, for there are several months before the weather turns this land into marshland," he surveyed the landscape thoughtfully. "Next week, I'll lead the men of Mierce to yonder village," he pointed to houses in the distance, where grey smoke coiled towards a greyer sky.

The first foray proved almost bloodless as the overwhelming Miercian force seized the fleeing Wealisc and bound them together, driving them with their cattle as far as the dyke where they were supplied with spades and forced to dig along the line of a taut rope. Another force galloped forth to raid another village and return with men and beasts.

Offa calculated that he would need to pillage a further dozen villages to have enough slaves but considered the likelihood of King Morgan's retaliation to be extremely high, so he sent for the Hereford fyrd. With this display of force, he was able to convene a parley with Gwent. He wished to avoid outright war, but if there was to be a battle, this time, he intended to win it.

Talks with the Wealisc king were productive. Wary of the strength of the Miercians, King Morgan insisted only that no more villages were pillaged and managed to negotiate that the fertile slopes on the Long Mountain near Trelystan remained in the hands of the Wealisc. Although it would mean the dyke veering to the east, King Offa conceded it for the greater gain of concluding his defensive construction. He also had to compromise further; near Rhiwabon, the route was designed to ensure that Cadell ap Brochwel retained possession of the Fortress of Penygadden. And, for Gwent, Offa had the dyke built on the eastern crest of the gorge, clearly with the intention of recognizing that the river Wye and its traffic belonged to the kingdom of Gwent.

Offa smiled at the thought that from Cynethryth he had learnt the art of diplomacy. A man needed patience, first because it would take years to finish the construction and, secondly, his skill at compromise guaranteed that the work would proceed without raids delaying or impeding progress. Rather than slaughter the Wealisc, his workforce would construct Offa's Dyke, as he fondly named it. Would posterity look at the whole length and consider it all his work? How he would like that!

THREE

Offa's Dyke at Montgomery and below Chepstow, AD 764-771

In the two years that followed Offa's decision to complete the dyke, he was rarely present at his court in Tame Weorth. The execution of the work required the constant presence of the king and his personal guards. Offa was well aware that no delegate could have enforced compliance with the surrender of territory according to his agreement with the Wealisc.

Seven months after work had begun, a messenger arrived to the south of Montgomery, where Offa's surveyors had determined the continuation of Æthelbald's dyke. The rider displayed the urgency of his communication by fairly throwing himself off his panting beast and kneeling at his monarch's feet. "Sire, I bear joyous tidings from Tame Weorth: you have a son!"

"I told her it would be a boy! I'll name him Ecgfrith." He called for a cask of ale and had foaming beakers handed to everyone on the site before calling for his horse and guards and galloping off to see his newborn child.

He burst into the queen's bedchamber to the screech of handmaidens as he pushed them out of his way. The babe was suckling at his wet nurse's breast as Cynethryth lay back on her down pillows, tired and happy.

"You came at once, my love," she said weakly.

"How are you, my darling wife?"

"All right, now! No thanks to that little monster! He was reluctant to come into this world."

"Don't call Ecgfrith a pest! I wish to hold him." Without anyone's consent, he took the babe in his arms and was rewarded with a milky belch, which made him howl with laughter. "Like his father after too much ale," he jested, handing the babe to his mother, who cradled him lovingly to her swollen breasts.

"I cannot stay, but I'll return in a matter of days for another brief visit." He bent over his wife, stroked her blonde hair away from her forehead and kissed it, noting the beads of sweat. "Are you well, my sweet?" he asked anxiously.

"Ay, just weary after bearing our child."

With that, Offa kissed her and the babe and hurried away. His presence was needed at his dyke, where he would not risk the failure of his engineering feat for the selfishness of a powerful nobleman.

Prescient this thought, for on one occasion, eighteen months later, in the area below Chepstow, where the ditch struck away from the river Wye to head for the margin of the Bristol Channel, Ealdorman Sigeberht, hitherto one of his most faithful vassals, confronted him, his nostrils flaring and eyes bulging. The warrior pointed westwards over the fertile land of the plain, below the course of the dyke, "Yonder land is my territory, Sire, granted to me by King Æthelbald—I have the charter to prove it—and you mean to surrender it to those savages who burnt my villages." The ealdorman clenched and unclenched his right fist.

"Ay, about that, good Sigeberht, who came to your aid, losing many a fine warrior? Who is to say that but for our intervention you would not have lost all of your land to the King of Powys?"

"I might not have charged into the Wealisc trap."

"Are you accusing me? Do you defy me?" A large vein throbbed at Offa's neck, and his face became dangerously red with rage; his stare fixed the ealdorman's eyes, and his hand dropped to his sword hilt.

Sigeberht detached his gaze and dropped his head but summoned the courage to mutter, "Who is to say that when this vallum is completed, the cunning Wealisc will not find a way to circumvent it and burn my villages again?"

Offa steadily quelled his fury. It would gain him nothing by striking off the head of one of his most powerful ealdormen, except an unwanted reputation for being a tyrant. Nay, he would have to use reason. He lowered his voice and said calmly, "It's true that in the heavily wooded area of the middle Wye, I have had my engineers attempt nothing more than the construction of short lengths of ditch and bank across the open valleys or where there are trackways. But don't you see, my old friend, what an advantage these works give us? Wherever you stand on the banks, you command a westward view so that no movement can be made without our knowledge. Thus far, this has not been the case for your lands. Let's say the Wealisc try to come through the almost impenetrable woodlands—what then? Would they commit the folly of having dense woodland, rivers, or our dyke at their backs? It would be they who walked into a trap! Did you think we would go to all this trouble to build a worthless construction?" The king did not give the ealdorman a chance to answer but took his hand from his sword hilt and, smiling, said gently, "I promise you will lose no more land; also, dear friend, you have my word that if by some strange doom the Wealisc manage to set foot on your estates, we shall come to your aid at once and slaughter them. Hereford was a harsh lesson we have no wish to repeat."

Ealdorman Sigeberht sank to his knees, bowed his head, and mumbled, "Forgive me for my rash words, Sire. It stuck in my craw to see productive land go to those who had defiled my estates."

Offa looked around and noticed with pleasure that among the onlookers were several other ealdormen. He did not raise Sigeberht to his feet, but laid his hand on the grey hair of his vassal as a father might bless his child, "You are a loyal friend, just like the others here. The safeguarding of our borders, whatever the cost, is for the common weal." At last, he removed his hand and raised the ealdorman to his feet, embracing him as a brother, certain that he had imparted a lesson that nobody present would easily forget.

Back in Tame Weorth, Offa requested to be left alone for a few minutes with Ecgfrith, a request that even Cynethryth respected with pleasure. As soon as they were alone, Offa began to speak to the babe as if he were an adult, even though logically he couldn't understand or do anything other than widen his blue eyes and gurgle happily.

"Little Ecgfrith, I'll tell you a secret that I haven't shared even with your mother," he said quietly. "I have a plan. Within ten years, I intend to rule over the south as *rex Merciorum*." He remembered the Latin lessons of Alcuin and added, "or better still, *rex totius Anglorum patriae*." He grinned into the babe's gurgling face and gently wiped the side of his mouth with a clean linen kerchief. "You are my heir, Ecgfrith, and I mean to leave you a great inheritance. I'll achieve it by vigorously suppressing those who prefer to think of a king as ruler over a people rather than a country. I'll show them, my boy! *Rex Merciorum* will one day become *rex Anglorum*." He beamed at his kicking son, "There, my boy, I have shared my undisclosed dream. Cynethryth!" he would have bellowed the name, but stifled it to a mere call, so as not to terrify the babe. She heard him and entered in a rustling of sage-green silk that offset her corn-coloured, braided hair to perfection.

"My son and I have had a lovely conversation," Offa beamed.

"Silly, the babe cannot yet speak!"

"Nay, but he listens very well, just like his mother."

They grinned at each other; he would share his words with her when he needed her counsel.

Now that the Wealisc border was as good as sealed, Offa felt that his presence was no longer needed there on a daily basis, so he could stay at home to enjoy his family, which he did only too well, as Cynethryth soon declared herself to be expecting their second child. "This time, I'm certain it will be a daughter," she told him triumphantly, and, to please her, he agreed that a girl would be a gift from God to them both.

With the Wealisc border sealed, Offa could divert his attention to other parts of his realm. In reality, he was given no choice. Strangely, the threat to his overlordship came from the South Saxons. Sussex, which was divided among a number of kings, was an area that had given him no problems in the early years of his reign when he confirmed grants of lands made by two individuals, each of whom bore the royal title in that country. They belonged to the western and central districts, however, and Offa had gained no power in Sussex east of Pevensey until this year—771.

Offa was drunkenly celebrating the birth of his daughter, Eadburh, when a message from Sussex sobered him. The men of Hastings had risen in revolt. They had been troublesome for some time since they considered themselves a people separate from the South Saxons and more akin to the men of Kent, with whom they shared similar customs and the same dialect. The flashpoint was over the payment of tribute. Instead of sending the annual tribute to Offa, they sent insults in Kentish dialect. Enraged, Offa consulted Cynethryth.

"Take enough men to fight the whole of Kent if necessary. In that way, you are sure to conquer Hastings, which, in any case, will give you control of the south from Hampshire to the Kent border in the east. I doubt whether Kent has the strength to take you on, my dearest husband."

As usual, she had found the words to fire his resolve.

"War it is!" He made an announcement, "We'll gather men as we march eastwards. Be ready to set off at first light!" Thus, the king brought an end to the celebrations for the birth of his daughter.

Outside the Hastings town gate, King Offa sent a message to the leaders of the Hastinglas, "Lay down your arms and King Offa will spare the population. Fail to do this and all your menfolk will be slaughtered."

Offa turned to the ealdorman at his flank to explain. "Whatever happens today, I have decided to make an example of Hastings that will deter others from open revolt."

The leader of the Hastinglas heard the message and curled his lip, "Tell your King Offa that Hastings does not recognise either Mierce or Sussex as its overlord and will only bend the knee to Egbert, King of Kent. Warn him that it is *his* men who will be slaughtered."

As Ealdorman Sigeberht pointed out: "This revolt had been a long time in the planning, for see how well-armed they are." It was true, not only did the enemy all carry a spear and a shield, but each man also wore a helm and a mail shirt. They formed into serried ranks before the town walls, their mass of men sprouting spikes—a giant hedgehog to set upon. Attack they must, Offa sighed, but it was far from a sigh of resignation, more one of frustration at the inevitable losses that would occur thanks to the foe's obdurate leadership. He thanked his foresight in bringing so many men to Hastings as the enemy was better prepared than he could have imagined.

Lined up with their backs to the town wall, the enemy presumed that the Miercians would attack frontally. Offa waited and stared up at the sky, his breath pluming white in the crisp seaside air. Ever, the gulls circled and wheeled, circled and wheeled, their mewing cries floating back to the earth like the haunting lament of lost souls. He was no fool, a frontal attack would be costly as there they would encounter the most spears. He summoned Sigeberht, who nodded his grey head sagely, going off to detach his men and divide the army into two. Offa led the other half to the enemy's left flank, where a side attack would expose them to only three spears. They moved rapidly to give the foe little time to react. Sigeberht did the same at the right flank and, although the well-armed Hastinglas defended ferociously, the sheer weight of the Miercian attack told. After an hour's bloody battle, the enemy buckled. Hampered by their dense, tightly-packed ranks that, at first glance, had seemed such an advantage, spears and shields had become unwieldy, but the Miercians had no such drawback to contend with, striking at the serried foe at will. Offa's shouted order to spare not a single foe passed from man to man, reaching Sigeberht on the opposite flank, who, meanwhile, was making the same inroads. As the Hastinglas warriors tried to break out of the central part of the vice they found themselves in, Offa reacted quickly, leading the counter-move himself, cutting down the bold leader and causing doubt and confusion to spread through the enemy.

Another hour, and the blood-soaked ground was littered with the Hastings dead. They had fought bravely but were outnumbered four-to-one. A wiser course of leadership would have been to surrender as requested.

"Into the town," Offa commanded, "I want every woman and child taken alive." He explained to his impressed ealdormen, "I shall transfer them to Bexhill, where I will grant the land to the bishop of Selsey. He will add these souls to his flock in exchange for my generosity. When the town is completely empty of people and animals, torch the buildings. Whoever comes to Hastings must see what it means to cross King Offa. I do not wish to see a habitable building left in the town."

Unrestrained destruction is in the nature of warriors fresh from combat. Lucky for the women of Hastings that these valorous fighters could vent their rage on the buildings and not on carnal satisfaction. Besides, King Offa had ordered them not to harm the women and children, so the operation went smoothly, except for the sobs, wails, and backwards glances as the leaping flames, driven by the stiff sea breeze, consumed their homes. On this day, the rebellion had cost them husbands, brothers, and nephews as well as all their possessions. None of the sobbing women realised, at that moment, that a new life lay ahead in the town of Bexhill. Many would remarry and have children there. Offa felt sure that his act of mercy would be less noticed than his ruthless extermination of the rebels.

He repeated Cynethryth's words to himself. A king must be loved in the same proportion as he is feared and respected. His lovely wife was his wisest counsellor. If she had been born a man, he would have a fearsome enemy to conquer.

FOUR

Tame Weorth and Bexhill, East Sussex, and Ottansford, Kent AD 771-76

Just two leagues to the west of Hastings lay the village of Bexhill, which King Offa intended to give to Oswald, Bishop of Selsey. So, the uprooting of the Hastingas women was not such a severe detachment from their birthplace as it at first appeared. On the short march, one warrior chose an unattached and attractive young woman to befriend. A romance blossomed, and although he dared not approach King Offa, he spoke to his ealdorman, who then referred his request to the king. Offa was delighted to allow the warrior to stay in Bexhill and to construct a house to share with the woman. Perplexed by the whirlwind speed of the betrothal, the king was secretly pleased because there was an advantage to be gained from his consent—he would ensure at least one loyal supporter in East Sussex. Out of the most banal circumstances, profit could be gained, he told himself.

Offa organised a building programme of simple houses for the women and children, so that the warrior's romance was not the only one; some of the builders found a widow to console, and several weddings were conducted by the local priest, albeit without a bride price.

The king summoned Bishop Oswald and told him of his plans for Bexhill. "You will have an influx of souls in your see, Bishop. As things are developing rapidly, I foretell a great expansion in Bexhill," he chortled. "I shall bring my scribe and summon witnesses for the signing of the charter in the New Year. First, I must spend Yuletide with my family."

Spending more time with Cynethryth enabled him to gain more useful counsel.

"As you have discovered, you can turn the simplest situation to your advantage, husband. As I said before, consider politics as a game of chess."

"Speak your mind, my dear."

"We all know that undersigning charters is a tacit admission of subservience. You should call those magnates you feel are less inclined to obedience and force them to witness Bishop Oswald's charter. After the Hastings affair, nobody will dare defy you."

"I should hope not! Ah, you've given me an excellent idea!" He knew exactly how to put her words into practice.

Offa waited until Yuletide had ended before taking a sizeable force, for intimidatory purposes, to Bexhill. The weather at the year's end had been unseasonably mild and dry, so he was delighted to see a large cluster of new houses, each with smoke swirling from its roof.

Bishop Oswald greeted him with a wide smile; overhead, the inevitable gulls dipped and soared as the ruddy-faced prelate took the king's hand in both of his and bent an arthritic knee unathletically. *Goodness knows how he kneels before the altar!* Offa thought, hauling him upwards almost off his feet. "No need for that, Bishop," he roared, "Have the witnesses arrived? And where will the signing be conducted?"

"The Hall is small, Sire, but the table is sturdy and will seat all our guests. Ay, they await your pleasure, there. Egbert, king of Kent is there, as is Cynewulf, king of Wessex—"

"The charter is prepared," Offa said. "The order is clear, I will sign first, then under my signature, Cynewulf's, and under his, Egbert's. Then you, Bishop." He addressed his scribe, saying, "Bring your bag and the vellum, good fellow."

"My goodness!"

"What ails you, Oswald?"

"Well, my name above the four magnates of Sussex you summoned."

"Indeed! Trust me, I shall make my purpose clear."

Everything went smoothly according to Offa's plan until the first of the magnates signed, as he had done in the past, *Aldulf rex*.

"Nay, that will not be acceptable!" Offa bellowed. "Scribe! Scratch out the r and the e of rex and he can change them to a d and a u."

The scribe rummaged in his bag and took out his scribe's knife with its sharp, curved blade. "Sire, we'll have to wait a few minutes for the ink to dry."

"You're the expert. We'll wait!"

"Dux! The former king's expression became apoplectic. "B-but I have ever signed *rex!*" he stammered.

"Not anymore! Scribe, you will not substitute the scratched-out letters; prepare a quill and hand it to *Dux* Aldulf, who will make the change himself, *if he knows what's good for him!*" he hissed in a low voice. He would not have it said that Aldulf had not signed on his own behalf. The scribe gently scratched out the two letters, then rummaged in his bag, for he knew that he had not brought any powdered pumice to make the change undetectable, but he should have a dog tooth burnisher, which would suffice. His fingers closed around the wooden handle, or perhaps he would carefully use the back of his thumbnail to buff the change. His monarch watched the neatly-done operation through narrowed eyes, as the scribe sought perfection and tutted in concentration.

At last, the operation completed, under Offa's approving gaze, the scribe slid the vellum document to the magnate and handed him a lightly charged quill. The trembling former king, now demoted to local leader or dux, had to wait an unconscionably long time to achieve an unshaking hand to make the required changes, as laboriously, where it had read rex, now it became *dux*. Not even the most critical eye would detect the change effected.

"Excellent! Osmund, you will do the same." The other former king of Sussex glared but did not hesitate, signing *Osmund dux* with a flourish.

To add insult to injury, Offa called on two other magnates, who had never claimed the title *rex*, saying, "You two *duces* sign below Dux Osmund. At a stroke of the pen, he had granted equivalence to these two men with the former kings—all now *duces*. Henceforth, he would know whose loyalty he could count on in Sussex. He blessed Cynethryth for having planted the seed of this idea. It was a masterstroke because it transformed former local rulers effectively into the ministers of a sovereign whose authority they acknowledged as permanent. They did not lose local power, that was the beauty of it, but they had publicly accepted his overlordship. What he had just done in Sussex, he would be sure to attain in Kent, where the magnates were more rebellious by nature. He had a feeling that Kent would be the next province to cause him problems. So, he was gladder than ever for his unbridled demonstration of power over Hastings. It had certainly cowed the witnesses of his Bexhill grant.

Several weeks went by before Offa's premonition proved correct. Although Offa treated King Egbert of Kent as a mere dependant, he retained his title with determination, and although this did not disturb Offa, the Mercian king took it amiss when he had to revoke a grant by Egbert on the ground, in his own words, that *it was not right for a man to grant away land which his lord had given him, without his lord's assent.* Offa then studiously dealt at his own pleasure with land in Kent and in 774 granted two important estates to the Archbishop of Cantwaraburh, deliberately not making reference to any local ruler.

Despite his munificence, Offa was to find out the hard way how deeply sentiments ran in Kent. His actions were seen as the highhanded interference of a foreign king, and they provoked a rebellious reaction among the Kentish nobles, who gathered around Egbert as their leader.

Offa could not accept this challenge to his authority, so marched his Mercian army through Sussex; indeed, adding to his force many men from that province. He marched to a plain to the south-east of Lundenwic, where a small chapel stood. It was called *Seouenaca*, the name given to a small chapel near seven oak trees. King Offa, who had brought a priest, summoned him, "Father, conduct a short service of benediction for myself and my ealdormen, since a battle is inevitable."

Just one hour's march due north brought the Miercians within sight of the Jutish force. The Jutes were renowned warriors, hence Offa's desire for benediction. He knew his limitations as a general, not having won decisive victories in battles in the past. He recognised that sometimes not losing a battle was as important as winning. This proved to be the case at Ottansford. It was no coincidence that the Kentish Jutes had chosen Ottansford to make a stand against Offa, for the Mercian king had given the place to the church at Cantwaraburh.

About half a mile from the enemy army, Offa called over his ealdormen and pointed at the Jutish position, on a rise beyond the River Darent.

"The Jutes want to lure us across Ottansford, where they will strike whilst our army funnels across the ford, but we shall not fall into their trap. What is your counsel, Sigebed?"

"Sire, we should use their plan against them, march to the river and not cross, but wait until they descend from their favourable position. If they wish to fight, it is they who must cross the ford."

Offa laughed, "Your plan has a glaring weakness, my friend. Why should the Jutes descend and cross the river?"

"Because you will provoke them, Sire, saying you will retire and spare them if they hand over the disobedient Dux Egbert. The Jutes are a proud race and their rage will be their undoing. I'm willing to wager they will not resist!"

Offa frowned and considered. Following this advice would cost him nothing, as there was no advantage in his present position. Yet, if Sigebed was right, the balance might just tilt in his favour. "Who is the brave man who will take this provocative message?"

"I, Sire," it was Sigeberht, son of Sigebed, whom Offa had raised to ealdorman years before.

"Nay, Lord, I beg you, it is my plan," Sigebed said, "Let it not be said that I sent my son to his death."

"Not even the Jutes would slay a messenger," Offa said, "but friend Sigebed, I hear you. I can think of no-one more provocative than you! Make sure you sting the Jutes to the quick!"

"Sire, I beg you! I can be more offensive than the old man," Sigeberht pleaded.

"Enough!" Offa growled, "I have decided, it is Sigebed's scheme and he will bring it to fruition. You, Sigeberht will lead our attack on the Jutes as they wade the ford. Javelins, I think, but wait until the foe is midstream."

"Ay, Sire, it shall be so! God speed, father."

Sigebed urged his reluctant horse across the ford, but the beast, realising that the water only reached its mid-pastern and that the riverbed was solid, plunged forward onto the far bank. The Miercians studied the water depth with interest and calculated their chance of victory. Much depended upon Sigebed's affected arrogance.

The ealdorman approached slowly with his right hand raised in a gesture of parley. He quickly identified the regal figure of Egbert, whom he had known from a peaceful previous encounter.

"Men of Kent! *Dux* Egbert," he began provocatively, "King Offa will retire his army and give you pardon for your rebellious actions. He would let it be known that he does not desire to spill Kentish blood for the sake of one misguided wretch!" He pointed at Egbert. "Consign this reprobate to King Offa and avert the war. What say you, brave men of Kent?"

"Go, worm! Tell Offa that he can return to his pigsty in Mierce," a Jutish ealdorman shouted, a vein throbbing at his forehead.

Sigebed improvised, "Very well, but let it be known that King Offa reclaims the land across the river from the Church. He rescinds his grant. The river Darent and its ford are now his!"

With this spontaneous stroke of genius uttered, Sigebed turned his horse and rode slowly away, ignoring the insults and oaths directed at him. He smiled grimly, aware that he had stung the Jutes into a desire to reclaim the ford and the land beyond it. As soon as he was sufficiently distant, he kicked his steed into a gallop and slowed to wade it across the ford.

"Prepare your ranks, Sire. Oh, they will come!" He referred his ploy to Offa, who could not contain his joy, but dragged Sigebed in his saddle towards him, kissing him on the brow. This act of friendship and gratitude done, he called to Sigeberht. "Make as if to create a shield wall this side of the ford, but hide your javelin throwers behind it, so the enemy cannot see their weapons. Each man must have three javelins each, but will not hurl them until they hear my command."

Sigeberht glanced across the river and, sure enough, the Jutes advanced downhill. He needed to act quickly and shouted orders so that a long shield wall lined up parallel to the river. The spearmen lined up behind them.

"The foe must not see your javelins; keep them well hidden. You will hurl them on the Jutes only at King Offa's command, not before. Do not waste your weapons; aim well at the men in the water! May the Lord of Hosts guide their flight!"

Unaware of the javelins hidden from sight, the Jutish vanguard strode into the water. Offa waited, then, suddenly bellowed "Javelins!" The Jutes, caught with their shields in carrying position, had no time to raise them and fell, transfixed, or tripped over a body as a javelin thudded into unprotected flesh. The deadly hail continued until the men of Kent halted their advance to gaze in horror at the ford that had become a bridge of bloodied corpses. But they made no further attempt to cross. Offa stared, his lip curling in disdain before realising that his ealdorman was addressing him. "Eh?" he asked distractedly.

Sigebed said, "I enquired whether we should cross to engage the enemy?"

"What on earth for?" Offa snapped.

"We have not captured that wretched Egbert. So, we cannot count it a victory."

"Oh, ay, we can! I have asserted my authority, retaken this land and the ford, and slain all those Jutes. Would you call that a defeat, Sigebed?"

"Nay, Sire, but will the Jutes not crow victory?"

"What, when they dare not even cross a ford? We'll wait to see what they do."

Offa did not have long to wait. Leaving their dead like the worst of pagans, the men of Kent turned and marched away, shoulders drooping and heads hanging.

Yet, Ealdorman Sigebed was not wrong. This was no victory. Indeed, the next few years proved him partially right as his king was on the worst of terms with the Kentish people. The enmity he felt towards them would lead, not to war, but to a diplomatic crisis with the Archbishop of Cantwaraburh. Until this occurred, Offa prepared no more charters and grants in the province of Kent as silent hostility seethed between the two peoples. Violence might erupt from one day to the next between an assertive sovereign and a rebellious province.

FIVE

Tame Weorth, Mierce, The Lateran Palace, Rome, AD 784

During the early years of their marriage, Cynethryth grew used to her husband's periodic outbursts of rage; at times directed against insubordinate provinces, at others, against incursions along Mierce's various borders. Never had his wrath been aimed, as on this occasion, at the Church and this worried her.

"Let it go, husband, this is one battle you cannot win. Imagine you are playing chess with me. Do you not deliberate your moves at great length?"

"Ay, I have to ponder them carefully, otherwise, you beat me."

"It is the same with the Church. You should not think about winning, but rather, about not losing."

Exasperated, Offa snapped, "Speak clearly, woman! Enough of your riddles!"

"How do you suppose you can take up arms against the Archbishop of Cantwaraburh? Would defying Rome not serve to invite your enemies across the confines to ally against you? Don't you have sufficient enmity with Kent? Worse still, look overseas, can you not see the might of the Frankish Empire? Charlemagne is a close friend of the pope. He would surely sail forth from his shores in aid of the Holy Father, who gives him divine authority to rule. You should follow his example—use the brains God has granted you in abundance."

Offa protested, "Archbishop Jaenberht has broken the law and seized a wealthy manor near Lundenwic. I signed Æthelbald's charter ceding Ethelred's Hythe to Mierce myself, as did several Miercian bishops."

"Æthelbald is dead, Offa, and *you* rule over Mierce. You must beat Jaenberht at his own game."

"How do you suppose I can do that?"

"Send two of your most trusted bishops on a pilgrimage to Rome. Have them bear sumptuous gifts to Pope Hadrian and allow them to build a case with him against the Archbishop of Cantwaraburh. If you like, I will go with them and do it myself."

"Are you mad? In your condition? I will not permit you to undertake so arduous a journey and risk losing my son."

Cynethryth smiled adoringly at him and placed her hands flat on her belly, protectively. "Again! And if it's a girl?"

"I will not risk losing our *child*. But, by all the stars, you are a clever creature! I shall do as you suggest. After all, Bishop Hygebert of Licidfelth was one of the signatories of that charter. He will put our case to Pope Hadrian. By the way, look at this, I had it made in Lunden by Ethilwald." He withdrew a scintillating gold coin bearing the name OFFA and the year 774. "It's a gold dinar copied from a coin of the Abbasid caliph, al-Mansur. It's my present to the pope. I think I will send him 365 such pieces every year to keep him on my side in disputes." Cynethryth gasped and turned the precious object in her hand. She, no more than Offa, could interpret the Arabic words on the coin, which ironically, given its destination, stated *there is no God but Allah alone.*

Together with the Bishop of Shelborne and accompanied by an escort of burly bodyguards to a waiting ship in the port of Glevcaestre, Hygebert carried with his baggage a portable coffer crammed with gems, and gold coins from Frankia: Offa's gift to the pope. The Bishop of Licidfelth boarded the ship with Offa's words still ringing in his ears, "Impress upon the Holy Father how Jaenberht has overreached his role. He has stolen the manor of Ethelred's Hythe from Mierce, disguising the theft as an ecclesiastic matter. The manor is an important trading station. The kingdom of

Kent is rife with such docks! I demand its return to its legitimate owner. Remember Hygebert, you were one of King Æthelbald's signatories to that charter. Emphasise to Pope Hadrian that I have no wish to overthrow his archbishop, but if the matter is not resolved in our favour, Mierce will take up arms to retrieve its rightful property." Just thinking of these words, Hygebert broke into a cold sweat. Undoubtedly, the generous coffer in his custody would help promote his case. The bishop was not a worldly man, but he understood the importance of the Lundenwic manors that had been taken by Mierce at the cost of lives and blood. Legally, he knew, Offa was in the right. It was true that he, Hygebert, had signed the charter openly without constraint in the presence of the present king and his predecessor. Surely, Pope Hadrian would understand the importance of a powerful, Christian kingdom in the south of the Englisc lands and recognise the value of a reliable ally such as Offa. Obtaining that recognition was the task entrusted to him and his fellow bishop, Herewald.

He was delighted with his travelling companion, a man whose spirituality was etched in the open, if somewhat pallid, countenance with its ready smile. They conversed in Latin and Hygebert was enthralled by his colleague's grasp of St Paul's letters, something he felt was lacking in his own preparation, having given precedence in his studies to the gospels. So, the hours passed pleasantly, although he needed to act the nursemaid to Herewald, whose stomach was not suited to the open sea. Fasting was obligatory for him under the circumstances, but Hygebert's attempts to have him eat plain rye bread and a piece of cheese were in vain. The Bishop of Licidfelth fasted only in the Lenten period and was a man of frugal habits, but partial to the red communion wine. He knew that Italian wine was renowned and looked forward to partaking of it on their pilgrimage.

After the rough seas in the Atlantic, the calmer waters of the Mediterranean came as a relief and a fair wind accompanied them past, what they were told was the isle of Sardinia.

Emboldened by the intimidating presence of the Mercian bodyguard, Hygebert persuaded the captain to accompany him and Herewald into one of the several taverns in the dubious dockland area of Ostia, the port of Rome. On dry land, terra firma, Herewald's appetite returned and the landlord, impressed by Hygebert's ready silver coins, produced a superior red wine from under the counter, reserved for quality guests, not the vinegary concoction he served to the locals.

Enjoying his episcopal role, he blessed the innkeeper and his wife, in return, receiving smiles and a linen-wrapped truckle of sheep's cheese, the *pecorino*, for the production of which the Roman area was rightly famed.

At the Lateran Palace, to enter the *Sancta Sanctorum*, the two bishops and the captain, bearing the precious coffer, climbed the twenty-eight white marble steps, the *Scala Pilati*, on their knees, as was the accepted custom. As Herewald explained to Hygebert, according to Church tradition, the Holy Stairs were the steps leading up to the *praetorium* of Pontius Pilate, on which Jesus Christ stepped on his way to trial during His Passion. On hearing this, the bishop of Licidfelth stopped his laborious ascent, bent forward, and kissed the step in front of him, a gesture the spiritual Herewald was happy to copy. As he looked sideways, the Bishop of Shelborne huffed, "Did you know that these stairs were brought to Rome by Saint Helena hundreds of years ago?"

"I did not," Hygebert said and, visibly moved, bent to kiss the step again. But this emotion was nothing compared to the bishop's sensation when he reached the chapel and gazed upon the icon of *Santissimi Salvatore Acheiropoieton*, the icon of Christ Pantocrator, known as the *Uronica* supposedly begun by St Luke and finished by an angel. The eyes of the icon seemed to stare deep down into his soul, but surprisingly, Hygebert felt a sensation of peace and calmness pervade him, replacing the agitation he had felt on entering the building. This state of tranquillity enabled him to face the Holy Father with an equanimity he would never have imagined.

The Pontiff, a man with a full grey beard and matching curly hair, greeted the Mercian bishops with a smile that broadened and became astonished at the sight of the coffer's contents.

"Tell your generous king that the gems will be used to decorate the leather binding of my personal bible. The Lord Bless and keep King Offa!" He turned the gold dinar appreciatively in his hand, surreptitiously testing its weight to his satisfaction.

"Regarding that, my king has entrusted me with a – *ahem* – delicate mission, your Holiness." Hygebert went on to explain the recent actions of Archbishop Jaenberht. He watched, heart in mouth, as the pope's expression changed from smiling to a corrugated intimation of concern, followed by a mien of craftiness that unsettled both his guests.

"We must put Jaenberht in a position whereby he cannot bring disaster upon himself and Cantwaraburh," Hadrian said slyly. "My dear Bishop Hygebert, Herewald, you are fine servants of the Church. Come to me on the morrow, and I will have the solution to King Offa's problem. Why, I have it half-formulated already, but you will agree that a little private prayer is necessary to seek guidance." The pope cast his eyes towards the ceiling, depicted with angels of various ranks. Both bishops bent to kiss the Holy Father's outstretched hand, an elegant sign of dismissal.

The following day, Pope Hadrian, the son of a Roman nobleman and the first pope of his name, received them affably. "The solution is easy and bloodless," he said. "Step forward, Archbishop." The two bishops looked at each other in bafflement and the pope laughed, delighted at his joke. "I refer to the Archbishop of Licidfelth," he chuckled, handing the startled primate a white, embroidered pallium. "Wear it with distinction, Archbishop Hygebert." He clapped his hands and a clerk brought a parchment, which the pope handed to the astonished neo-archbishop. "This document, you will note, bears my seal and contains instructions to Cantwaraburh to restore the manor of Ethelred's Hythe to the see of Licidfelth. Please convey to Archbishop Jaenberht our displeasure at his high-handedness," the pope paused, then added with a smile, "and to King Offa and his Queen our blessing, we shall be in contact through you and recommend that you, my son, conduct the baptism of their third child. I believe the queen is in—*ahem*—a state of sweet waiting." Hygebert smiled at the pope's delicate and literal translation of *dolce attesa*, referring to the queen's pregnancy.

The two bishops had the privilege of attending a private Mass, conducted by the pope, and Hygebert had the opportunity to taste the best red communion wine of his life.

With the papal blessing ringing in his ears, Hygebert, who had been too overwhelmed to consider the implications of their visit, now had time to reflect. The first change he noted was the deference with which his travelling companion spoke to him.

"Nay, Bishop, our relationship must be as before. I am a humble man and nothing has changed."

"That cannot be, my lord Archbishop, because you are now my superior and the first priest of Mierce."

"I had not thought of it in that way, but my dear friend, you have my utmost love and respect."

"Thank you, my lord. See, there is a small church, let us enter and pray for a favourable wind and a safe journey."

Hygebert sighed contentedly, it would be undoubtedly safer without the jewels and coins of the outward journey. After all, his most precious possession now was a finely embroidered piece of cloth, which would mean nothing to the average thief. In any case, they had an escort, now on its knees behind them, all heads bowed just like the two prelates.

* * *

Back in Tame Weorth, King Offa stared at the embroidered accoutrement around Hygebert's neck and lying on his chest.

"What is that pretty article of clothing, Bishop?"

"It's my badge of office, Sire."

"Badge?"

"Ay, it's called the *pallium* and Pope Hadrian gave it to me."

"Speak plainly, Bishop."

"Archbishop, Sire. Mierce's first archbishop."

Offa looked thunderstruck. "What is the meaning of this?"

Queen Cynethryth smiled happily, "I'll tell you the meaning, husband. It means Mierce has its own archbishop and the Mercian church no longer needs to take its orders from Cantwaraburh."

Offa's mouth fell open. "It does?"

"Aye, Sire," Archbishop Hygebert ran his hand over the beautifully crafted stitching, the work of Roman nuns. "I also have this important document with Pope Hadrian's seal." He pulled it forth, unrolled the page, and read its contents.

"The pope must have appreciated my gift, then."

Cynethryth laughed. "I told you so, Offa. We sent two bishops to Rome, but a bishop and an archbishop have returned and with them your manor in Lundenwic. What need was there for arms? It's called diplomacy, my sweet."

"Excuse me, Sire, but my work is not yet finished," Hygebert said. "I beg the pleasure of delivering this document in person to Archbishop Jaenberht, for I wish to see his crestfallen face. He will not dare defy the Holy Father. Let me take a detachment of warriors to reclaim Ethelred's Hythe on my way to Cantwaraburh."

King Offa was quick to agree and soon arrangements were made. When the archbishop had gone from the royal presence, Offa turned to his wife and said, "We need to have a long talk, Cynethryth. This thing you call *diplomacy*— I need to understand it better. With it, I shall rule my kingdom more successfully."

SIX

The Manor of Ethelred's Hythe, Lundenwic and Cantwaraburh, Kent, AD 784

The Manor of Ethelred's Hythe was a large village on the river Thames with a quay where fishing vessels that plied the river as far as the North Sea came and went. If Archbishop Hygebert anticipated trouble, he was pleasantly surprised because his detachment of twenty-five Mercian warriors was more than enough to seize the one pocket of resistance, which was the manor house. There, the lord of the manor, named Cynric, directly appointed by Archbishop Jaenberht, justifiably argued his case for retaining his property. The several men at his disposal eyed the Mercian warriors warily, and for good reason, as Archbishop Hygebert nominated the captain, who had accompanied him to Rome, as the new lord of Ethelred's Hythe. The escort, therefore, was hand-picked, each man a formidable warrior. Wisely, Cynric's new vassals were not disposed to sacrifice themselves for him.

"But Excellency, I am a warrior in the service of King Offa," the captain protested.

"You still are, Leofhelm. You will better serve your king here, pay him his dues and keep the rest for yourself. I will be surprised if you are not called upon to fight for King Offa hereabouts in the future. I nominate you lord of Ethelred's Hythe by the authority of

King Offa. Upon my return from Cantwaraburh, I shall have the new charter drafted. Guards, arrest this man, we shall return him to Archbishop Jaenberht. Treat him kindly, for he has done no wrong." Cynric's shoulders sagged, but he did not resist as his position was hopeless. "Come, we shall ride to Cantwaraburh," said Hygebert, instinctively patting his tunic to ensure that the pope's invaluable document was still in place, "so that we arrive before nightfall." This timing was easily achievable from Ethelred's Hythe since it was early afternoon.

The small party rode into Cantwaraburh as dusk crept inevitably over the land. There was no question of seeing Jaenberht that evening, so Hygebert decided to seek lodgings for the night at St Augustine's Abbey since he knew that Jaenberht had been a monk there before his appearance the previous February at Offa's court, where he was appointed Archbishop of Cantwaraburh. At the time, Offa had taken a liking to him and, as overlord of the kingdom of Kent, had approved the enthronement.

The Abbot of St Augustine's welcomed his illustrious guest with warm salutations and provided a splendid meal. He was only too willing to talk about Jaenberht since he was proud that one of his former monks had been enthroned as the archbishop at Christ Church. As for Hygebert, he was also keen to discuss the archbishop, on the basis of 'know your enemy'.

"I always thought that Jaenberht was special," said the kindly father abbot. "You see, he was a very saintly person ever with a kindly word and a smile on his lips. He would go out of his way to perform even the most daunting charitable act." The abbot paused to gauge the effect of his words and grinned when Hygebert said, "Which would explain why King Offa was so eager to ratify his nomination to the see of Cantwaraburh."

"I would imagine that your king knew that Jaenberht comes from a prominent Kentish family. His kinsman is Eadhun, who is reeve to *our king*, Egbert." The archbishop of Licidfelth did not miss the emphasis on the possessive and the title and could understand that not all men of Kent were happy that Mierce had subjugated the kingdom of Kent. It seemed likely that the benign abbot was of this bent.

"Would you say that Archbishop Jaenberht's character has changed, Father Abbot, since he took office?"

The abbot's shrewd eyes detached their gaze from Hygebert's and he replied evasively, "Of course, we are not in contact on a daily basis, but I have found him unchanged and," he said thoughtfully, "I have only heard good things spoken about him."

Hygebert was not inclined to reveal the nature of his mission, so contented himself with, "I am enthusiastic to meet my fellow archbishop and brother in Christ."

He felt that there was little else to be learnt from the good-natured abbot, so determined to enjoy his stay and especially savour the superb Frankish red wine on offer. He had a quiet word with his captain, who would only take up his new role at Ethelred's Hythe on their return. "Leofhelm, circulate among the brothers and encourage them to reveal all they know about Jaenberht, see if you can find any fault or weaknesses in the man. The abbot seems to think he's something of a saint," he whispered. Leofhelm eyed the archbishop's beaker of wine regretfully and the prelate followed his gaze, "Ah, perhaps before you set about it, you'd like a beaker of wine?"

The captain accepted gladly as Hygebert summoned a hovering monk and requested a beaker. Leofhelm drained it in one long draught and, nodding his thanks, began to circulate in the refectory, almost immediately, to Hygebert's approbation, stopping to chat with one of the brothers. Out of the corner of his eye, the archbishop observed the captain speaking animatedly and at some length before clapping the monk on his upper arm and moving on to his next conversation.

The following morning, the small party, after a frugal breakfast, set off on foot across the city to Christ Church, to the accompaniment of bells ringing the faithful to services. The archbishop could not help but notice how Cantwaraburh, despite its many abbeys, nunneries and churches, seemed reluctant to abandon its rural nature, since the countryside intermingled with the various agricultural trades of the cartwrights, coopers and smiths. Here, although it was only late summer, Nature had sidled autumn into the hedgerows, bedecking them with red hips, haws and black sloes as Pope Gregory would adorn his leather-bound bible with Offa's gems, the archbishop smiled wryly at the thought. Wasn't Man's art but a poor imitation of the Great Creator's handiwork? Not even the solemn Gregorian chants that so stirred his soul every time he had the pleasure of hearing the choral singing could compete with the dawn chorus that at present delighted his ears. He closed his eyes as he walked, stumbling twice as he misplaced a foot while saying a rapid prayer of thanksgiving for bountiful Nature, but he could not help but insert a plea to the Lord to help him expedite his mission to the most satisfactory of conclusions.

He had to admit that he was anxious about his forthcoming encounter and, regarding this, Leofhelm walked beside him and mentioned the task entrusted to him the previous evening.

"Excellency, all the monks were united in praise for the goodly nature of the archbishop, except for the Provisioner, who provided me with a different insight. He said that he had little time for what he called Jaenberht's *politicking*. He was somewhat apologetic when he told me that Jaenberht resented us Miercians and our *sway* over Kent. It seems that Jaenberht on occasions comes close to sedition. The Provisioner was insistent that this politicking was at the expense of contemplation, and, as such, to be deplored." The captain frowned with the effort of trying to recall the exact words but said, "The good monk stated that he was not surprised when Jaenberht became archbishop, for it was a role, he suggested, that suited his political bent." Leofhelm shook his head, "I'm not sure the appointment bodes well for our king's vision of a united south, but these things are beyond me, Excellency, I am a mere soldier."

"Not any more, Lord of the Manor of Ethelred's Hythe, I fear that you, like many true servants of the Crown, will be caught up in a conflict with the Church if this Jaenberht is allowed to have his way. That is what we have travelled to counter," he muttered thoughtfully.

For a while, the two men walked in pensive silence until they came upon the large church and opposite it, the archbishop's palace. Hygebert ordered two of the guards to escort his prisoner to the door of Jaenberht's residence and asked the captain to come, too.

A servant opened to the visitors' imperious knock and delivered their message within. At once, the same servant showed them into a cavernous room, dimly lit by a high window and two candles burning on furniture against the wall, which cast elongated, flickering shadows.

"Cynric! What is the meaning of this?" Archbishop Jaenberht stared at the two guards, each clinging to the prisoner's arm.

"I am Archbishop Hygebert of Licidfelth and—"

"Licidfelth is only a bishopric," Jaenberht interrupted, his expression hostile.

"Not unless you wish to challenge the Holy Father's decree, Archbishop Jaenberht. Mierce has its own archbishopric now, and I have come to reclaim the property of that kingdom. Hence, we restore Lord Cynric to you, unharmed. Meet the new Lord of Ethelred's Hythe. Step forward, Lord Leofhelm!"

Leofhelm obeyed and bowed to the Kentish archbishop, who failed to meet his eyes or acknowledge him in any way.

"To be quite clear, I have this document from His Holiness, Pope Hadrian I, signed and sealed in my presence." Hygebert pulled forth the document but did not hand it to the startled prelate.

"Are you telling me that you have been to Rome?"

"Ay, with Leofhelm, who can testify to the Holy Father's displeasure with you for overreaching your duties and offending his dear ally, King Offa."

"Goodness knows what lies you subjected the Pontiff to!"

"Do not offend me. We are brothers in Christ. Show some respect!"

"Respect for Miercians? Only over their graves!"

"Enough! Read the document, and with it, consider this, Archbishop Jaenberht, you will make no further attempt to illegally sequestrate Miercian property, or my king will invade Kent and remove you from office. Also, all ecclesiastical matters within the borders of Mierce are under my jurisdiction, not yours."

"But Cantwaraburh has always dispensed canon law in the south—"

"No longer! Not now that Licidfelth has been raised to equal status—will you not read the papal document?"

Pallid-faced, his hands trembling with barely suppressed emotions, Jaenberht unrolled the scroll and read. His expression became increasingly angry, and colour flooded back into his countenance: an unhealthy puce.

To further enrage Jaenberht, the Archbishop of Licidfelth added, "Beware, Archbishop, my king is prepared to petition the pope to have the see of Cantwaraburh transferred to Lunden, dependent on your behaviour. There, you would be on Miercian territory and closely subject to his control."

Jaenberht's patience snapped. "Are we men of Kent not already under the yoke of the Miercian tyrant? I pray daily that the Lord will relieve us of this intolerable burden."

"Be careful, Archbishop, lest your words are referred to King Offa, who will not stand for treason."

"I respond to the pope, not to King Offa," growled the archbishop.

"You would do well to recall that in non-ecclesiastical matters, you are under the king's law, like any other citizen. I am sure that you do not wish for bloodshed in Kent, Excellency."

"I wish only that my friend, King Egbert, enjoyed the liberty of his forebears."

"King Egbert need only continue to underwrite Offa's charters and—"

In a spasm of fury, Jaenberht grasped a bronze candlestick and brandished it menacingly. At the same instant, Leofhelm whipped out his seax, and Cynric stepped forward, only to be hauled back by the two guards. Realising the gravity of his situation, Jaenberht set down the candlestick and glared at Hygebert, who said coolly, "Change the purport of your prayers, Brother. The sick and the infirm are worthier of your petitions than the status of King Egbert!"

"I shall pray that one day the Lord will punish your arrogance, Archbishop Hygebert."

"You might also consider improving your hospitality to match that of your former abbot, Brother Archbishop." With this stinging remark, Hygebert led his three men out of the room but caught Jaenberht's parting shot: "I shall obey only the pope's orders."

"Well, that would be a step forward," Hygebert muttered, more to himself.

The journey to Lundenwic was uneventful, and Ethelred's Hythe made a useful overnight stopping place for the archbishop and his escort, who were grateful to sample the fresh fish landed at

Leofhelm's quay that afternoon. The new lord of the manor expressed himself satisfied with his servants and the state of his buildings. He arranged for one of his men to show him around his estates the next morning when his guests departed.

The following day, Hygebert reported to King Offa. "Sire, I have installed your captain of the guards as lord of the Manor of Ethelred's Hythe. We shall have to keep a careful watch on the Archbishop of Cantwaraburh, for he is a patriotic man of Kent and faithful to King Egbert."

"I am in favour of loyalty to one's king," Offa chuckled, but Queen Cynethryth, who had listened intently, said unsmilingly, "Offa, send reliable spies to watch over this Jaenberht, lest he instigates insurrection. I feel that he cannot be trusted."

"Don't fret, my love, I have already decided to do so. Should the Archbishop of Cantwaraburh take another false step, I shall crush him in my iron fist. I will turn a blind eye this time for love of the pope and respect for the Church, eh, Archbishop?" The king bellowed a laugh, but slammed his iron fist down hard on the table before him, his countenance taut and serious.

SEVEN

Cantwaraburh, Kent, Tame Weorth AD 784-786

The monks of St Augustine's would have laughed in the face of anyone suggesting that Jaenberht was a violent man. Indeed, after his encounter with the Miercians, the archbishop spent much time on his knees, beating his breast and reflecting on the extreme folly of brandishing a candlestick that could have led to bloodshed—the blood undoubtedly would have been his. Yet, looking back on his momentary madness, Jaenberht realised he did not regret having demonstrated to the Miercian upstarts the reaction of a patriot to the arrogance of the invaders. However, if he wished to continue his attempts to throw off the yoke of the Miercian king, he could not resort to brute force but would have to be more subtle. Firstly, he must not appear to be the instigator as he had already offended Offa and his lackey, the so-called Archbishop of Licidfelth. Nay, he would have to rely on others.

So, several weeks passed until Jaenberht devised a scheme, and it came when the death of a Miercian landowner in the see of Rochester occurred. What better an opportunity could arise? Kent was ruled by two sub-kings, his friend Egbert, and King Sigered. Neither was, as with previous kings of Kent, descended from Oisc, the son of Hengest. This unfortunate circumstance could also be attributed to Mierce, and, in particular, to Æthelbald, Offa's predecessor, who had subjugated the three joint kings connected with the ancient line. How much easier had it been for him to gain ascendancy over men with a lesser claim to the throne of Kent, reducing them to mere puppets?

The estate in question comprised the lowest crossing point over the Medway, its important ancient bridge allowing the development of an important and lucrative weekly market. Jaenberht would urge the Bishop of Rochester to draw up a new charter superseding the previous one, as he had done with Ethelred's Hythe, and have King Sigered, not his favourite Egbert, brazenly seal the instalment of a Kentishman there.

Jaenberht went out of his way to suggest incorporating in the charter the most favourable terms for the See of Rochester to overcome Bishop Eardwulf's timidity. The bishop rightly feared Miercian reaction to the subtraction of one of the richest manors in the kingdom. Jaenberht might have been more concerned had he known that Offa's spies studied his every move after his attempt to purloin Etheldred's Hythe.

* * *

Offa summoned Hygebert from Licidfelth, and whilst awaiting his arrival in Tame Weorth, a distance of three leagues, easily ridden at a trot in an hour, spoke urgently with his queen. He valued Cynethryth's advice since she had the pleasing ability to clarify his thoughts. She happily gave her opinion: "Kent, like Hwicce, has more than one sub-king. This is Æthelbald's doing and makes little sense. It's a mere fob to the sensibilities of the more powerful men of those kingdoms. Hark, Offa! You should not consider Kent as a separate kingdom but as a *province* of Mierce. This is just the occasion you need. Your spies tell us that behind Sigered and the Bishop of Rochester's action are the machinations of Archbishop Jaenberht. If he continues to have his way, dear husband, he will start a conflagration that will spread from the North Sea to the Sussex border. Did you know that Sigered styles himself *rex Cantiae*? You must seize the opportunity to march on Kent. What is the sense of these sub-kings? Reduce them to ealdormen in your service."

Offa stared in admiration at his outspoken wife. Of course, she was right; he must follow her advice if ever he was to surpass Æthelbald's achievement and put the south under his hegemony.

She had not finished, but before she could speak, he hastened to say, "I shall punish Sigered in this way, but I'll need an excuse to dethrone my friend Egbert, who has given me no cause to turn against him."

Cynethryth pursed her lips and frowned, her tension evident in the white knuckles of her small hand grasping the arms of the throne. "That is just, Offa. You must not be seen as a tyrant, but if Egbert takes up arms on behalf of Sigered, you will have your excuse. When you have finished with Kent, why not turn your attention to Hwicce, where three brothers rule as underkings? What sense has that? Theirs is but a shadow of kingship. Make them all ealdormen by your dispensation as their overlord. Hwicce is too weak to resist you, Offa, and by doing so, you will make a clear statement of your authority way beyond your frontiers."

"Indeed, but I must first deal with Sigered in Kent and hear Hygebert's attitude to Jaenberht."

Hygebert came promptly and spoke with purpose. "This is an act of defiance, not only to you, Sire, but also to the Holy Father. I witnessed the most inappropriate behaviour in a priest when Jaenberht raised a heavy candlestick and threatened me with it in a moment of rage. Luckily, I had captain Leofhelm to protect me; otherwise, things may have gone very badly."

"Did he, by God? My spies are quite sure that Jaenberht is behind this move by King Sigered. So, what do you suggest, Archbishop?"

"Take an army into Kent, Lord, and rescind the land grant, by force if necessary. Place your chosen man as lord of the manor and threaten King Sigered with war if these abuses continue."

"And Archbishop Jaenberht?"

"Nothing, Sire. Mierce cannot risk offending the Pope, and I would suggest that you pacify Kent by showing goodwill to King Egbert if the opportunity arises."

King Offa marched into Kent and reversed the terms of the charter by appointing his own man to the manor. He summoned King Sigered to the bishop's palace in Rochester and commanded him to kneel before him and place a trembling hand on the bishop's personal bible to swear allegiance to the throne of Mierce.

"Ealdorman Sigered, ay, *ealdorman*, for you are no longer a king! Dare to break this oath, and I shall come to Kent, remove your head and display it over the city gate, just as I did with Beornred's." Offa laughed chillingly, without a trace of humour. "The crows feasted on *his* eyes."

"Forgive your humble servant, Sire. I am your sworn man; I give my word upon the good Book."

"I shall forgive, but time will tell. Bishop, you might make it clear to your archbishop that my patience is wearing thin. If it comes to war, which nobody wants," he stressed, "I shall be after his head, too! Now, I shall visit King Egbert to persuade him of our sincere friendship."

In the presence of Egbert, to ensure that these words were not simple posturing for the benefit of his captive audience, Offa conducted an act of statesmanship that would have made his astute queen proud of him. Taking aside Egbert, a distinguished-looking man dressed in Frankish-style finery, Offa whispered in his ear, noting the man used a perfume befitting of a maid. His lip curled, but he concentrated on his important communication.

"King Egbert, we can make a pact that will strengthen your authority and mine at one stroke. Do you own land within the walls of Rochester?"

"Ay, there is such land."

"I want you to make it over to the Bishop of Rochester in a charter that you will submit to me in Mierce and I will ratify it with a postscript giving the bishop power to alienate the land. Thus, we neuter Jaenberht, gain the bishop's gratitude and loyalty, and you will have my goodwill, friend Egbert."

"It is a masterstroke, Offa, and shall be done."

Within the month, Offa was visiting land in his kingdom at Medeshamstede when a messenger from Egbert brought the charter. He completed it with the postscript, signed and sealed it, and had it sent to Rochester. Offa smiled ruefully—if only he had the undisputed power of the king of the Franks—he considered Charlemagne's position and determined to speak to Cynethryth about it. He wanted to recreate the same uncontested uniform supremacy that the Frankish king enjoyed, but here, over the Englisc. He had suffered enough in his first seven years of rule; now, the time had come for him to re-establish Miercian supremacy in all directions beyond his borders.

He spoke to his queen, "What is it that has enabled the King of the Franks to achieve undisputed power? Whichever direction I look in, there is someone who wishes to challenge me. To the west, the Wealisc raid into my lands. I will put an end to their incursions once and for all! Kent is forever on the verge of rebellion; however, I have gained a friend in King Egbert. He is more than ever under my sway," he said this, but as he did so, felt an unease he could not explain. With some gusto, he explained his latest diplomatic move for his queen's approval.

"You have been wise not to attack Kent like an enraged bull. Charlemagne has built his strength on his splendid relationship with Rome," she purred, "and you must do the same. He also minted his coinage. 'Look,' she took a gold piece from her purse and handed it to Offa, who studied Charlemagne's profile and read the Latin inscription around its edge. Then he handed it back. "I can see how that reinforces his image and authority on a daily basis. I also shall have coins minted with the inscription *Rex Merciorum* for all to read. You will be the first queen to have her head on a coin, my love. We'll change the word *rex* to *regina*."

"Are you serious?"

"Never more so. It will enforce the Christian value of matrimony and please the Pope."

"Talking about matrimony, Charlemagne has strengthened his position by astutely marrying his children to powerful neighbours—"

"We'll do the same, but—"

"But Eadburgh is only an infant," she chuckled, "we'll have to wait more than ten years to wed her off," Cynethryth concluded, "but it's the way to go," she smiled whimsically.

"There's time to do all these things, God willing, for we are still young," Offa said. When he said, "We'll do the same," without specifying which neighbour he had in mind, he was thinking particularly of Wessex, for whilst King Cynewulf was sovereign there, he had regained most of the territory lost to King Æthelbald and Offa had been unable to acquire any influence over that kingdom. Cynewulf was recognised as king in Berkshire and north Wiltshire as well as in Hampshire and Wessex beyond Selwood. For a while, he was master of a stretch of territory north of the Thames. Not only that, he was also beginning to irritate Mierce by disputing ownership of lands on the other side of the Thames, so Offa decided to settle the matter by summoning his warriors and marching towards Oxfordshire.

EIGHT

Bensington, Oxon and Tame Weorth, AD 779 - 786

Before the battle, which to Offa's seasoned eyes seemed unavoidable given the West Saxons' well-equipped warriors and the strength of their numbers, he nonetheless attempted to reason with King Cynewulf. The latter, buoyed by arrogance founded on a long and successful reign, refused to negotiate the question of Mercian overlordship in the Thames area with a provocative reply: "If anything, it is Offa who will bend the knee to Cynewulf." The Mercian king skilfully made use of this reply by passing it on to his ealdormen, whom, he knew, would refer it to their thegns so that the humblest of his warriors would grind his teeth in anger and give the last ounce of energy in their king's cause.

The battle was the hardest fought that Offa had experienced. Strategy and tactics were not the order of the day, but the willpower and strength to match the well-drilled West Saxons blow for blow left both sides sapped and reeling. Offa would no more call a halt to proceedings than Cynewulf. The two men eyed each other from a distance and, unless Offa was much mistaken, Cynewulf nodded respectfully towards him, a gesture the king of Mierce reciprocated.

There was little fight left in either side as the evening sky dulled into twilight. That was when Offa took a decision, sending a messenger with a white flag to Cynewulf.

"Sire, my Lord, King Offa, says that night falls. He means to take the town of Bensington and reclaim his ancient overlordship over the Thames territories. If Wessex will accept these terms, my king declares an honourable truce and makes no further claim to King Cynewulf's territories."

"Tell King Offa that he has my respect and that as of now, Wessex and Mierce are at peace."

The messenger bowed his way out of Cynewulf's presence and gladly delivered the reply to Offa.

"Ha! The fool should have accepted my terms before the battle, and we would not have both lost so many good men. But, there again, he is not such a fool; he also has my respect. Come! We march to take the town."

Luckily, for the Mercian warriors swaying with weariness, the tidings that the Midlanders had won a great victory over Wessex was enough to gain admittance without resistance. Mercian authority was restored in the region and peace with Wessex held for seven years until, suddenly, Cynewulf was murdered.

Offa received the tidings that arrived from Winchester in 786 with mixed feelings. Gone was an obdurate old adversary, but the manner of his death bothered him. King Cynewulf was suddenly attacked by Cyneard, brother of Sigeberht, who had ruled in Wessex before being deposed by Cynewulf thirty years before. Both Cynewulf and Cyneard were killed in the course of a struggle, which was referred unclearly to King Offa by a West Saxon messenger whom he sought to intimidate into clarification. The browbeaten wretch's account became even more garbled due to his anxiety. So, Offa decided, at this point, to send his own Ealdorman Sigeberht to discover the truth of the matter because if there was a regicide at large, Offa considered it his kingly duty to make an example of him.

Sigeberht's confusion increased on hearing gossip and speculation in wayside taverns and from local priests. He realised that only by reaching Winchester might he discover the truth of what had happened to the king of the West Saxons. His source would have to be authoritative to satisfy the wrathful Offa, and thus ward off his likely outburst of anger.

For this reason, Sigeberht requested and obtained an audience with the Bishop of Winchester, Dudd. The prelate was an amiable individual with a ready, but weak, smile. His pallid face was deeply scored with lines that suggested suffering so that Ealdorman Sigeberht would not have wagered a sceat on the bishop's longevity. Still, the kindly man listened to Offa's concern that there was an unpunished murderer at large.

"Nay, it was a complex affair," the bishop explained. "But hark! Here at Winchester, the monks keep a canonical chronicle, which traces events year by year as far back as the Roman invasion by Julius Caesar. I shall have a monk transcribe the entry for this year for your king so that he can read the authorised version of events for himself."

Bishop Dudd summoned a scribe.

"Brother, transcribe faithfully the entry from our Chronicle for this year of Our Lord, 784. Be sure not to err or blot, for your copy is for a king to read!" The monk bowed and muttered his obedience to the bishop's command. The prelate entertained the ealdorman with honey cake and mead, but Sigeberht noticed that a sparrow would have eaten and drunk more than the bishop. Not that this observation curbed his own appetite after his strenuous journey.

At last, the monk brought a neatly copied parchment and handed it to his bishop, who, after casting a critical eye over the contents, commended the beaming brother for his precise calligraphy.

"Here, Ealdorman, I will attach my seal of approval for your king." He dripped red sealing wax under the careful handwriting, blew on it, and impressed his signet of two parallel keys intersected by a sword.

Ealdorman Sigeberht rode back through the Selwood in high spirits because he could think of no better outcome than the sealed manuscript to assuage Offa's wrath.

To his dismay, when he arrived, the king was in no mood to strain his eyesight and commanded him to read the parchment. The ealdorman cleared his throat and began to read hesitantly. Reading was not his strong point.

"A.D. 784. This year Cyneard slew King Cynewulf," "Come on, man, get on with it!" Offa barked irascibly. "Ahem, and was slain himself, and eighty-four men with him. Then Beorhtric undertook the government of the West Saxons, and reigned." The document went on to be more specific, and Sigeberht's confidence grew:

"This year Cynewulf, with the consent of the West Saxon council, deprived Sebright, his relative, for unrighteous deeds, of his kingdom, except Hampshire; which he retained, until he slew the ealdorman," he paused and said slowly by way of explanation, "I think he means by the ealdorman, Cumbra, here, Sire," "who remained the longest with him. Then Cynewulf drove him," "ahem, the ealdorman looked embarrassed, "I believe he refers to Sebright, here," "Ay, ay, go on!" Offa said grumpily, "to the forest of Andred, where he remained, until a swain stabbed him at Privett, and revenged the ealdorman, Cumbra. The same Cynewulf fought many hard battles with the Wealisc; and, about one and thirty winters after he had the kingdom, he was desirous of expelling a prince called Cyneard, who was the brother of Sebright. But he, having understood that the king was gone, thinly attended, on a visit to a lady at Merton, rode after him, and beset him therein; surrounding the town without, ere the attendants of the king were aware of him. When the king found this, he went out of doors, and defended himself with courage; till, having looked on the ætheling, he rushed out upon him, and wounded him severely." "Ay, Cynewulf was a fine warrior," Offa muttered. "Then were they all fighting against the king, until they had slain him." Offa's face fell. "As soon as the king's thanes in the lady's bower heard the tumult, they ran to the spot, whoever was then ready. The ætheling immediately offered them life and rewards; which none of them would accept, but continued fighting together against him, till they all lay dead, except one British hostage, and he was severely wounded." "That is what I would expect of my loyal retainers," Offa observed. Sigeberht ignored the interruption and continued, "When the king's thanes that were behind heard in the morning that the king was slain, they rode to the spot, Osric his ealdorman, and Wiverth his thane, and the men that he had left behind; and they met the ætheling at the town, where the king lay slain. The gates, however, were locked against them, which they attempted to force; but he promised them their own choice of money and land, if they would grant him the kingdom; reminding them that their relatives were already with him, who would never desert him. To which they answered, that no relative could be dearer to them than their lord, and that they would never follow his murderer. Then they besought their relatives to depart from him, safe and sound. They replied, that the same request was made to their comrades that were formerly with the king; 'And we are as regardless of the result,' they rejoined, 'as our comrades who with the king were slain.' Then they continued fighting at the gates, till they rushed in, and slew the ætheling and all the men that were with him; except one, who was the godson of the ealdorman, and whose life he spared, though he was often wounded. This same Cynewulf reigned one and thirty winters. His body lies at Winchester, and that of the ætheling at Axminster. Their paternal pedigree goeth in a direct line to Cerdric."

The ealdorman paused, out of breath.

"Is that it, Sigeberht?"

"It is, Sire."

"And do you believe this monk's garbled tale?"

"Sire, I believe he was not such a learned monk, but a truthful one! And the copyist has been faithful to his account."

"In that case, I need not interfere in the matter, since Cynewulf does not need avenging by my justice. But this is the opportunity I have waited for to put Wessex under my jurisdiction. The new king is Beorhtric. I must speak with my queen. Good work, Sigeberht."

The ealdorman bowed and absented himself to respect the king's wishes, relieved that the king had not treated him to one of his occasional outbursts.

"Cynethryth! Where are you, my sweet?" Offa's mood had improved dramatically after hearing the monk's miserable account. If he moved his pieces carefully, to adopt his wife's chess metaphor, he would at last have Wessex in his grasp. However, he now needed his wife's co-operation.

She came, as usual, in a rustle of silk, this time cornflower blue, and a waft of perfume, likely sandalwood, although he was no judge of such niceties.

"My sweet, we have four daughters and a son."

She winced dramatically, "As if I didn't labour to bring them to your attention!"

He laughed, to please her. "Of course, you know this! But my point is, they are all unmarried."

"What are you plotting, husband?" Her interest was pricked.

"Do not berate me, but I forget who is the eldest of the girls?"

"Fair enough! Eadburh! A score and three years have passed since her birth!"

"So many? Then, Eadburh is no longer my little girl that I dandled on my knee. She's a woman!"

"Oh Offa! You are always so busy with kingship. Is it possible you have not noticed what an attractive creature you have as a daughter? Shall I send for her?"

"Not yet, I want your opinion, first."

"You wish to wed her off, do you not?"

"Are you a witch? Can you read my mind?"

She ignored him. "I think you'd better speak your mind, don't you, Offa?"

"Ay, to put it plainly, Cynewulf of Wessex is dead and his successor is a young ætheling by name, Beorhtric. He is a direct descendant of Cerdric, so his lineage is not open to discussion. By wedding our daughter, his position will go unchallenged and in return, we'll control Wessex! Is it not a good plan?"

"Superb! I'll talk with Eadburh and make her see the advantages she'll enjoy as Queen of Wessex."

Cynethryth took her daughter into a private chamber and shared her thoughts on queenship with her. "The art is to let your husband think that he is making the important decisions whilst all the while you are steering him like a good captain directs his ship. Your counsel will keep him out of danger and bestow power and wealth on your kingdom. Oh, and remember daughter, your father and I have given the Church no grounds to doubt our piety, unlike King Æthelbald, his predecessor. Indeed, Pope Hadrian named me as co-ruler with Offa."

"But what if this Beorhtric's aspect does not please me, mother?"

"It is true that I have not set eyes on him, but he is not much older than you, so I doubt that he is hairless and without teeth! If you agree to travel to meet him, your father will not insist on a wedding if you dislike him. *I'll* see to that! Besides, he must like you and the bride price must be established, but I think your father can cope with those details. How do you feel? Would you like to be queen of Wessex?"

"Ay, I think I shall be a queen like you, mother. I admire you so!"

Mother and daughter embraced before returning to the Great Hall where they informed the delighted Offa of Eadburh's decision.

NINE

Winchester, AD 786

Seemingly, every living soul in Winchester had assembled in the minster, which made Beorhtric's decision stranger. Cynethryth had to use all her powers of persuasion on her husband for two days to arrive at a compromise. The king of the West Saxons wanted a traditional wedding. "You mean a pagan affair! These people are still half-savages," Offa grumbled. "Nay, my daughter will be wed in a Christian ceremony, or nothing!" Offa was on the point of leaving, dragging his wife and daughter back to Tame Weorth when Cynethryth's gentle reasoning prevailed. "Husband, as you said yourself, once Eadburh is wed, Wessex is practically yours. Do not spoil everything now! I can persuade Beorhtric to have Bishop Dudd follow the hand-clasping with the Christian ceremony. Thus, our daughter will be wed in the faith before the population of Winchester and in the presence of the Lord at His altar."

"As ever, I have your good sense to thank, Cynethryth." King Offa was satisfied with this arrangement—what did it matter if he had to concede a sop to a half-pagan? *Not a jot, so long as I control him!*

When the bride arrived, the crowd fell silent. Feeling all eyes on her, she blushed and lowered her head. A waiflike form broke away from the throng and thrust a tightly-bound bundle of meadow flowers: poppies and daisies among others, into her hand. When in gratitude she bent to kiss the child, a cheer burst out.

Beorhtric, in a clean tunic, with no weapon or armour on his person, greeted her with a warm smile.

"My lady is comelier than her wild flowers!"

Cynethryth took her daughter's hand and placed it into the groom's. The hand-fast began the ceremony before the bride spoke her ritual words. "I take you Beorhtric," her voice firm and even, "to be my wedded husband, to have and to hold, from this day forward, for better for worse, for richer, for poorer, in sickness and health, to be bonny and buxom, in bed and at board, for fairer for fouler till death do us part."

The West Seaxe king made his solemn pledge in a deep assured tone and a mighty roar and clapping signalled the binding.

He fumbled in his clothing and pulled forth the arrha — the gold ring also necessary for the Christian rite.

"Let this band be an earnest to seal our love," he said and kissed her to further acclamation. He pushed the ring on her fourth finger, such was the usage.

When Eadburh nudged her, Cynethryth drew forth a gold object and passed it to her daughter.

"Let this ring be an earnest to seal our love," she repeated and craned up to kiss his mouth to the clamour and banter of the people. Never had such happiness existed, for political expediency apart, Eadburh was deeply attracted to her spouse. Distracted, she tried to slip the band on his fourth finger, but too small, it did not pass the first joint. This time, the surrounding throng shared their laughter when the nearest onlookers explained the reason for their mirth to those who did not understand. The bride slipped the gold band on the groom's little finger with a silent prayer he would never link it to betrothal with another, for that was not the case.

What happened next shocked her. Caedwalla reached into his tunic once more and pulled out one of her shoes. Before she blinked, he struck her on the head with it.

"Wha —?"

"A sign," he said, his voice loud for all to hear, "of your husband's authority." He handed it to Cynethryth, "Place it at the head of the bed. On my side. Now," he pulled an unhappy face, "let the Christian ceremony begin!"

To satisfy tradition, Eadburh flung the bundle of meadow flowers over her head and back into the gathering for a maid to catch.

Bishop Dudd stepped in front of the couple and ordered them to kneel, then in a deep, loud voice that betrayed his frail, cadaverous figure, enunciated Psalm 128, placing particular stress on:

Your wife will be like a fruitful vine
within your house;
your children will be like olive shoots
around your table.

His rheumy eyes seemed to bore into Beorhtric's as he intoned

Yes, this will be the blessing
for the man who fears the Lord.

From the minster choir came the unified voices of the monks, who continued the psalm to its hopeful ending:

May the Lord bless you from Zion;
may you see the prosperity of Jerusalem
all the days of your life.
May you live to see your children's children—
peace be *upon* Israel.

The crowd dispersed but well before dusk, the men made their way into the hall to the sound of the horn blast. A scop began to play the lyre and promised tales of past glorious victories over the Britons, in exchange for yarrow-flavoured ale. Some of the women looked after the children while in the kitchen the rest worked the fires and ovens. From the latter, wafted a mouth-watering aroma as they drew forth loaves half the size of cartwheels on wooden shovels. In clouds of steam, others drained vegetables while some sliced meat, dripping juices, or filled bowls with broth. Another used a willow switch to whip salivating dogs and prowling cats out of the room. Amid the bustle, the voices of the cook and Cynethryth issuing orders rang out over the din of clattering pots and light-hearted banter.

In the hall, the king's lady, Eadburh, hair raised in a crown of honour, bore a cup to her husband in the manner of her folk. An evening of serving him at table awaited her, but his high good temper and loving glances made her consider it worthwhile. She lost count of the trips the women made to the kitchen.

Bowls of bacon barley broth preceded the boiled goose eggs, baked pike fillet, roasted plover and smew, and grilled cow steaks with vegetables. These, they consigned to her and she set them before her lord. All this time, she filled the drinking horn with ale and wondered whether her man would survive the evening sober enough to fulfil his night-time duty. King Offa would not, judging by his red face and over-hearty laughter! Either the drink was weak or Beorhtric's resistance was stiffer than she had imagined for he showed no sign of the drunkenness she had witnessed with distaste at her father's hall—what seemed a lifetime ago. When he wiped his mouth with relish after consuming a griddle cake dribbling with honey, Beorhtric caught her by the arm, "Send for your maid when you are ready, wife."

In the calmness of her quarters, her servant bathed and dried Eadburh before seeking a vial of precious elderflower oil to scent her skin. "Best to dress in a linen slip, my lady," said the maid with surprising practicality for a young virgin. Down came her mistress' hair and she combed it into a blonde cascade to her waist.

"Go and inform the king of my readiness."

After a night of passion followed by a deep sleep, Beorhtric gently wakened Eadburh.

"Come! Time for your morning gift."

Not a calculating woman, she had forgotten this custom, so in surprise, she followed him. As they approached a stable, a youth dashed inside to reappear a moment later leading a grey foal with a white flash, reassuring the timid creature with soft words.

"What think you, wife? The filly has five moons and is weaned."

"Oh, she's a wonder! What's her name?"

"That is for you to decide."

Eadburh strode over to stroke the velvety muzzle and received a gratifying whinny and a toss of the head.

"I shall call her *Mistig* because she is as grey as a Holy Month mist." The holy month was so called after when religious festivals were held to celebrate a successful summer's crop, but it was also a time of mists and overripened fruit. Her dark blue eyes flashed love and gratitude for the generous bestowal. "Shall we ride out together, today, husband? You can show me the land around this, our city."

"I have promised to meet with your father to discuss affairs of state," Beorhtric said glumly. "But I promise, we shall do it on the morrow."

In the afternoon, Beorhtric fully realised, if he had not previously done so, what his relationship would be with his wife-father— one, if not of subjugation, of subordination.

"Hark, Beorhtric, on my return to Tame Weorth, I intend to take the quickest route, which means I will march through the centre of Hwicce."

"But won't that be a provocation to King Ealdred?"

"What king? I have styled him *Dux* in my charters. He has received land from me and signed for it in that manner. In any case, do you think he would have the nerve to challenge Offa and take on the might of Mierce?"

"Nay, I suppose not."

"You suppose, young man? This is not a time for suppositions. Can you think of no reason why I am telling you this?"

"Has it to do with my marriage to your daughter?"

"Of course! Now you are thinking! The alliance between Wessex and Mierce is formidable. You may rest assured, my son, that Mierce will come to your aid at once if the Britons dare to attack from Wealas or from Dumnonia."

"What is it you want from me, father?"

"Naught more than a display of strength, my boy. There will be no bloodshed. You have my word. I require ten-score Saxon warriors bearing the West Saxon emblems to escort me through Hwicce. That will give Ealdred and his co-rulers, Eanbehrt and Uhtred, pause for thought!" Offa laughed unpleasantly—something between a guffaw and a sneer.

"But did you not come with a large escort?"

Offa looked pityingly at the youthful monarch. He had much to learn. "I did! And I will return with the same in addition to your men. It will make an intimidating display of strength—a reminder, if one were needed, of the solid ties between our two kingdoms. One wonders what will be said if we accidentally lose our way and stray into Northumbrian territory on our return?" Offa repeated his earlier unpleasant chortle. "Don't look so shocked, young man! I have no intention of waging war on Northumbria; can you, of all people, not see that I believe in more peaceful methods of extending Mercian influence? After all, I have three more daughters! Nay, I just wish to keep young King Aethelred on his toes!"

"I have heard that he is younger than I and there's talk of him being deposed."

"Is there, indeed? Well, that does not please me. I shall send an emissary to the Northumbrian lords to make sure Aethelred sits firmly on his throne."

"Would you do the same for me, King Offa?"

"Ay, if necessary. Listen to Eadburh's counsel and your throne will be as solid as a rock."

Beorhtric scrutinised his wife-father's face and saw that he did not jest. He began to re-evaluate his spouse at that precise moment. He had heard that Queen Cynethryth was the driving force behind King Offa, although looking at the rugged, determined features of the king in front of him, he found it hard to believe. However, he thought, if Eadburh could help him to achieve similar power to Offa, he would be content. While Offa lived, he could not reasonably push his frontiers eastwards or northwards, but he might be able to persuade his new ally to help him drive westwards, but there was time aplenty for such plans.

Offa studied the distracted face of his daughter's husband and broke across his thoughts.

"So, do we have an agreement?"

"Eh?" Beorhtric berated himself silently; he must not daydream in the presence of this warrior-king, this almost, but not quite, overlord.

"I refer to your escort of two hundred men with the golden wyvern fluttering above them."

"But King Offa, how am I to explain to my ealdormen the need for such a massive escort?"

"A real king does not explain; he imposes!" Offa snapped; the lie made to sound convincing.

"Yes, well, I'll try to persuade them."

"Have them ready to accompany me at dawn the day after the morrow."

"I'll try, father."

"Be a strong king, Beorhtric. Together we shall do great things."

Ay, I'll tell them that—it should convince them! He kept the thought to himself, but found that when he used the concept at his council meeting, it worked wonders. The ealdormen were only too pleased to keep King Offa of Mierce as their ally. Besides, it was their king's first entreaty to them, and they wished to please the man who had shown the wisdom to make such a favourable marriage.

It had been many a long day since Winchester had seen such a massive gathering of warriors—the pride of the West Saxon army—beneath the fluttering red banners of the rampant golden wyvern. At their head, King Offa of Mierce dismounted, to embrace the new Queen of Wessex before remounting and leading the mighty mixed Miercian and West Saxon force. The Miercians marched under their blue emblem with its yellow cross and superimposed double-headed eagle.

Some of the grey-bearded Wessex ealdormen wondered privately at the purpose of such a force: was it just, as their king claimed, to create an impression on the neighbouring states? Time would tell. They preferred the comforting thought that the traditional enmity with Mierce had been settled by matrimony.

TEN

Derby, AD 786

Hwicce's populace cowered and sensibly did not raise a crest in the face of such a massive show of strength, so Offa proceeded into his kingdom, stately and proud at the head of the irrepressible force. He did not linger in Tame Weorth, staying just long enough to allow his queen to leave the journey, for he had other plans.

After bidding farewell to Cynethryth, the columns of armed men set off through the north gate of Tame Weorth and continued in that direction straight to the Miercian border with Northumbria. A few miles beyond lay the town of Derby, whose ealdorman, an influential noble in the court of Bernicia, as Offa well knew, received early tidings of the joint Miercian and West Saxon advance. Incredulous because of late, Mierce and Northumbria had been on peaceful terms, nonetheless, he set his garrison up defensively and hoped that King Offa did not have bellicose intentions.

That sovereign had no such resolve, wishing only to demonstrate the devastating potential of the joint kingdoms.

He did not need to act to display his might, "Ealdorman Oswig, I counsel you to convince your fellow lords to restore the youngster to his throne." He referred to King Aethelred, whom the Northumbrian nobility had imprisoned, taking advantage of his youthful inexperience to wield power, "for I have certain plans for him," Offa boomed and held Oswig's eyes with a fierce stare. It was true, but what Offa did not add was that he was in no hurry because he had more than one eligible daughter. The Northumbrians did not need to know that first, he planned a trip to Frankia to the court of the Franconian king. If he could wed Aelfflaed to Charlemagne's son, Charles the Younger, he would establish himself as the undisputed leader among Englisc kings. If anything, she was prettier than Eadburh, so he had high hopes. Either way, he would wed her off, either to Charles or to Aethelred, and his power would flourish.

Judging by the expression on the face of the ealdorman and the shifting of his eyes over the warriors under his command, ranked outside the town, Offa's warning message had been received. Therefore, there was no need to delay his return to Tame Weorth. On the one hand, he was pleased that he had delivered his message peacefully; on the other, he would have appreciated a brief crushing victory. It would have made for a splendid send-off to Frankia, but in truth, war with Northumbria was far from his thoughts.

Although the fame of the Franconian king preceded him, Offa did not know too much about Charlemagne, more about his success. That he was a charismatic figure had been relayed to him with the curious detail that the king was as tall as seven lengths of his foot. Offa had considered this fact so many times during the crossing that he had drawn his companions' attention to his constant staring at his feet. Offa's feet were normal for his build, so when he finally came face-to-face with the long-nosed blond giant, he was not surprised to see that he had large feet. He also had a ready smile and a pleasant personality, which certainly dominated the palatial chamber. Sitting to his right on a smaller throne was a young man of lively features, his hair too was blond and shoulder-length.

"This is my son, Charles," said the king, "and I presume, King Offa, that this delightful creature is your daughter."

"Ay, this is Aelfflaed. I am sorry that my wife Cynethryth could not travel with us, but she has caught a bad cold and we thought it best for her not to aggravate it by crossing the sea, although she is much better at this sort of thing than I."

"What sort of thing, my friend? What is it that you are up to?" The broad, pleasant countenance broke into a grin, but instinctively,

Offa did not trust it. There was something in the steady blue eyes that did not share the smile on the lips, but spoke of calculation and shrewdness. "Surely, the king of the Miercians as well as suggesting my daughter Bertha for his Ecgfrith, is not proposing to wed his daughter to the next king of the Franks?"

"Well—er—"

Charlemagne guffawed, and it was not a pleasant sound to Offa, who felt strangely uneasy in this dominant presence.

"I can see why Queen Cynethryth is better at this sort of thing. But do not worry, I'll deal with it myself." The king's blue eyes fixed on Aelfflaed, and a gentle smile played on his lips under the broad blond beard and moustache. "Draw nearer, young lady," Charlemagne gestured with his right hand.

Offa's chest swelled with pride as his daughter moved elegantly in her pastel spring-green silk gown, which her mother had fitted for this occasion, offsetting her corn-gold locks beautifully. She curtseyed elegantly before the great man and, although she smiled at him, managed to do so demurely under a bowed brow.

"My word, you are a delightful creature," Charlemagne said, "It is almost a shame to put you to the test, but I must do so. Look at my son carefully, then look at me."

She obeyed.

After a while, Charlemagne asked, "If you had to choose which of us to wed, me or my son, who would you choose?"

Aelfflaed blushed prettily, but looked the king straight in the eyes.

"Well?"

"Your son, Sire."

Charlemagne sat back in his throne and held her gaze. "And why is that?"

Aelfflaed looked confused, but spoke confidently, "Because he is younger and *unwed*, Sire."

The king of the Franks barked a laugh that did not please either Aelfflaed or her father.

"It's a pity, for if you had chosen me, I would have let you marry Charles, but as it is, your journey has been in vain."

"Come, Aelfflaed, we are wasting our time here," Offa said bitterly, glaring at Charlemagne. He knew he had much to gain by staying, and that Cynethryth would not approve of his reaction, but the king of the Franks had offended him. He took his daughter's hand, didn't give her time to bow a farewell, but tugged her away as he turned his back on the Franconian ruler and on all the possible commercial advantages a pact might have brought. Already his mind was working feverishly on Aelfflaed's future and it did not directly involve the Franks.

Offa had taken the slight to heart, but not so badly that he could not appreciate the elegance and luxury of the imperial court: the curtains, drapes, cushions, indoor plants, and finely wrought candlesticks. The bustling court did not contain one shabby person, but many dressed in velvets and satin. As they hurried to their awaiting ship, Offa asked Aelfflaed anxiously, "Did you see Charlemagne's wife?"

"Empress Hildegard? Ay, she is very pretty, but as old as my mother, I'd say. She kept quietly in the shade behind the thrones and listened to everything."

"So, you'll be able to describe her and her clothes to your mother," he said with relief, anticipating a torrid time with a disappointed Cynethryth. It suddenly occurred to him that his beloved daughter might be disappointed—but discovered it was not so.

"Nay, father, Charlemagne jested. He never intended for me to marry his son. He could not take me as his wife because in the eyes of the Church he is married to Hildegard. And I'd never be anyone's concubine!" she said this so fiercely that Offa had to smile and hug her. She continued, "I'm glad because I do not like Charles the Younger—he's got a long nose and his eyes are too close together. Lucky Eadburh, she has the handsome Beorhtric!"

"I still have plans for you, Aelfflaed. I cannot swear as to Aethelred's appearance, but we'll find out. Northumbria is a great kingdom with vast territory and a noble past. We'll go home first and see what your mother thinks about all this, for I'll do nothing without the approval of mother and daughter.

The North Sea, grey as ever, was in a benign mood, so it was easy for Offa to pick his way to the stern to speak with the steersman.

"I wish to return to Tame Weorth as quickly as possible, Master. Where shall we leave the ship?"

"We should sail into the Humber Estuary, Sire, and this ship is of the latest shallow-hulled design, so we can row down the River Trent as far as Snotingham. I will not risk going farther. Begging your pardon, Lord, but from there, you could march to Derby and thence, easily to Tame Weorth."

"Then, that is what we shall do."

King Offa stared at the coast as the ship approached and pointed out three kingdoms to his daughter. "Lindsey is yonder to the south of the Humber, but it is no longer a kingdom in its own right, I took it off Northumbria, so it belongs to Mierce. On the other side of the estuary, Northumbria stretches far north to the land of the Scots. It used to be two kingdoms: Deira and Bernicia—but fear not, King Aethelfrith united them in my father's sire's day. Way down yonder," he pointed, "out of sight is the kingdom of East Anglia and it is an annoyance to me. If you were Queen of Northumbria, I could move freely against that realm."

"I should like to be a queen, like my mother, to command servants and enjoy the riches of the kingdom—like honey and mead," she said, where he'd expected her to say gold and gems. He looked at her face, prettily reddened by the biting North Sea air. She was still little more than a child with simple desires! Charlemagne was a fool to turn her down, he considered, but then shook his head. The Frankish king was no fool. Perhaps he found me too loutish, Offa wondered, but shook his head a second time. *Nay, I gave him splendid gifts and offered him my pretty daughter. He must have other designs to the east. I have heard that our Englisc missionaries have to battle with pagan savages beyond Charlemagne's frontiers to bring them to the Lord. I will make a friend of him yet, for there is much to admire and learn.* I wonder what Cynethryth will have to say. She can't blame me for a failed mission. Perhaps he took offence when I suggested his daughter Bertha should marry Ecgfrith. That was the moment he became difficult, but I think Charlemagne had already decided.

Offa placed his hands well apart flat on the oak table in his hall in Tame Weorth and leant forward, now almost nose to nose with his seated queen. The more effective he could make his presence, the easier this dreaded conversation would be. He took her through the events in sequence, neither changing nor otherwise embellishing what had happened, although Cynethryth occasionally glanced at Aelfflaed for nodded confirmation.

"It was as if he had decided that my family and Mierce were not good enough for his almighty Frankia!"

"Nay, I doubt that my love, but I should have advised you against pressing for the hand of Bertha for Ecgfrith. Can you not see, it is all too much, too soon? That is something we could have worked towards more calmly after Aelfflaed's wedding to Charles. Are you disappointed, my sweet girl?"

"Nay, mother, for I liked him not with his long nose and almost crossed eyes!"

"Well, that's a relief!"

King Offa snorted. "So it is! Anyhow, we'll have nothing more to do with this Charlemagne and his superior ways."

For the first time, Cynethryth looked aggrieved. "Don't be foolish, husband, on the contrary. We must make Charlemagne sit up and take notice of us."

"And how am I supposed to do that? He has rebuffed and insulted me. Lucky for him the sea lies between our lands!"

"Keep to your original plan. Take Aelfflaed to Bebbanburh—she is of marriageable age and becoming the Queen of Northumbria is almost as exalted as becoming the Princess of Frankia. Offa, you already dominate the south; with the north in your grip, even Charlemagne will sit up and take notice. Once that is done, we shall begin to imitate Frankish modes to make Mierce the cultural centre of Britain. Then, he'll regret not having made a pact with your family." A faraway look entered her eyes. "You say that he has closed trade with British ports—pah! Anyone would think you had insulted him! You say you did not and I believe you, so, mark my words, it will be soon enough when we can buy wares from his kingdom to make our court as pretty as his." "I hope you are right. There's much to think about. I have a plan to make King Charlemagne change his mind soon enough. What if I make my coin incompatible with his? If you were a trader and suddenly found that Offa's coin was increased in size and weight, but still carried the same face value, whose coin would you choose?"

"Diabolical! It will work, for sure!"

How is your cold? Are you well enough to travel north? This time, I want nothing to go awry. I do not think I should summon the men of Wessex. Word will have spread from Derby of what I can do if necessary. This must come across as a peaceful mission, although I expect trouble from some Northumbrian magnates, who will not take kindly to me ruling through Aethelred…and his wife!" He beamed at Aelfflaed, who smiled happily at her father. She just hoped that Aethelred was as handsome as Beorhtric.

ELEVEN

Bebbanburh, Northumbria AD 792

On the long march north, the warriors tramping beneath them, the embroidered double-headed eagles glared balefully as the stiff breeze ruffled their heads. On his horse, Offa, when not conceding time to Cynethryth and Ælfflæd in their carriage, reflected cheerfully on his last words with his son, Ecgfrith.

The boy had wanted to accompany him at all costs, but Offa was adamant: his heir would stay in Tame Weorth. In the unlikely event of an invasion in his absence, Ecgfrith would fight shoulder to shoulder with Ealdorman Sigered.

"Nobody will dare set foot on our territory, father. But if they do, I'll summon Beorhtric from Wessex to aid me in slaying even more enemies than Sigered."

"*Ah! The recklessness of youth!*" Offa chuckled. "*I'd have said the same to my father.*" Occasionally a herd of wild moorland ponies caught his eye. These were hardy beasts that knew how to survive on little and endure the harsh moorland winters. He knew that the Britons captured and broke them in, and that man and beast had given his ancestors a hard time in battles between Mierce and Elmet. The proud Britons were absorbed into his kingdom and Northumbria, no longer causing trouble, but he knew that on

Northumbria's western borders, farther north, the Britons of Rheged still claimed the land among the lakes. Well. It was not his problem, unless lines of horsemen suddenly appeared against the skyline. He glanced uneasily into the distance, where a peak dominated the landscape. Luckily, they were now following an old Roman road, and he felt sure that he could cope with any adversary on the open road who came upon his three hundred warriors. He had felt it necessary to bring a full-scale army since he intended to liberate and sustain King Æthelred I. Without powerful enemies, the young king could not have been imprisoned in his own castle. Yet, events in Northumbria were so knotty that even Offa's best spies could not untangle them. He had a simple interpretation: however formidable Æthelred's foes, they would not be mighty enough to resist the combined strength of Mierce, Wessex, and—if it came to it—Sussex. Offa smiled smugly; he had not included Æthelred's supporters, who would come flocking once the lad was married to Offa's daughter. He watched a plunging lapwing and smiled; ay, his enemies would fall as swiftly as plovers before his might. He had calculated well. Also, the moment was right. He had systematically built up his strength, and Ælfflæd had developed breasts like yon proud lapwing's chest. The bird's crest was a good omen, too; it rose fiercely above its head like his Mercian emblems, and the bird and the banner were both black and white. As if to please the onlooking Mercian king, the bird put on a striking aerobatic display, including its famous flight call, *peewit*. Offa only cared for bird omens when he could adapt them to his needs. He called to a nearby ealdorman, "Look!" He pointed at the bird's antics. "A sure sign of a great triumph in Bebbanburh!"

"Ay, Sire, for it is not only a moorland bird but also a shoreland creature that wades into the sea."

"And Bebbanburh overlooks the waves!" Offa smiled smugly, craning his neck, but there were still many leagues before they reached the salt air. He had wisely broken the journey overnight so that they would reach Bebbanburh before nightfall. Besides, Offa enjoyed tales and songs recited around a campfire, and years had passed since the building of his dyke when he had revelled in the experience. True, he could sit by his hearth and enjoy a scop chanting ancient tales, but it was not the same atmosphere as being alert to danger under twinkling stars.

At mid-morning, Offa glimpsed the long sandy beaches of the north-eastern coast, where, to his immense pleasure, he spotted a lapwing mingling with the other waders—a sure sign of the success of his mission. When, at last, the imposing wooden structure of Bebbanburh castle loomed on its hill, Offa gazed critically at the walls. If he were ever to launch an attack, he would do it at this spot in the hollow, where the oak trunks were in sore need of replacement. How long had this castle stood here? He would wager that successive generations had neglected it. Yet, one could never be sure whether an assault would come from inland or overseas, or as in this case, from within those very walls. The heads that wear a crown sleep uneasily, Offa smiled wryly, which was why he spent so much time developing the thegns of his realm.

The rebel lords, largely out of respect for Æthelred's lineage, had treated him well in his imprisonment, ensuring regular good food, and no maltreatment. His only hardship was solitary confinement in a tower room. For he, who enjoyed a gallop along the strand, it was a severe punishment, but lo! what was it he spied approaching the castle? An army? His heart leapt in his chest from exultation, for surely his confinement was about to end, and also from fear. Had a foe come to definitively take away his birthright? He narrowed his eyes in an attempt to discern the emblem. The banners displayed no purple and yellow, so it was certain that this armed force was not from within the confines of Northumbrian territory, which was a relief. But hold! Was that not a double-headed eagle? Mierce then! He had spent pleasurable hours on his father's knee defining territories from their insignias. His favourite was the rampant golden wyvern of Wessex, so much more thrilling to a child than their own boring purple and yellow vertical stripes.

A simple change of chamber uplifted Æthelred when his gaoler, one of his long-time servants, apologetically led him down the spiral staircase, along a corridor, and into the familiar great hall. It seemed curious to him that everyone was bowing and smiling towards him after what certain lords had done to him. But who was this, standing before his throne?

"King Offa of Mierce, Sire," whispered his retainer. Æthelred gathered his sorely-tried wits and in a surprisingly ringing voice, declared, "King Offa! A warm welcome to the court of Northumbria! What brings you so far from home, Sire? Are you set to invade the land of the Picts?"

"Indeed not!" Offa smiled smugly. "Mierce has a much sweeter conquest in mind, but only with your majesty's agreement!"

Æthelred could not imagine what the Mercian was talking about, although he had noticed the queen and a princess a couple of paces behind the monarch. Now, Offa brought them to his attention. "This is my wife, Queen Cynethryth and our daughter, Ælfflæd."

After some pleasant exchanges, Æthelred showed his thoughtfulness by saying, "Ladies, you have had a long journey; perhaps you would like to bathe and rest before mealtime?" Without waiting for a reply, he gestured to a serving maid, who curtsied and received rapid instructions.

"As for you, Sire, who are of an entirely different mettle, I suggest a few beakers of ale or mead; which is your preference?"

"Ale for sure—it puts hairs on your chest!" he bellowed with laughter, making the king with his largely hairless chest, fortunately covered from sight, feel even more insecure— "and by the way, they say it has a way of loosening tongues, but I wish to speak frankly with you from the outset, King Æthelred."

The king looked concerned. Such a mighty warrior with a reputation for getting whatever he wanted would not have travelled so far without good reason. Æthelred was rightly worried. "I have had my monks study the events leading to your enthronement. Is it true that you were a mere child when you became king?" Offa asked.

"Ay, Sire, my uncle—" he paused, seemed to think again, "but now I have eight-and-twenty years behind me on this throne."

"So, you are not so young as I thought."

"Nay, I have survived a score and a dozen winters."

Offa calculated, "Mmm, thirty-two, that's a good age, then. Northumbria is a bloody mess!" Offa growled bluntly. "Let me speak clearly. Do you suppose that you would stand in front of me now, a free man if I had not decided to journey from Mierce?"

"The lords are divided among themselves and forever in ferment."

"And you and I shall put a stop to that, Æthelred. You need just one thing."

"What is that, King Offa?"

Offa sneered, "The one thing your *five* predecessors lacked—ay, five! —two abdications, two depositions, one exile, and one murder! One was deposed *and* exiled. What they lacked was power. It is power I bring you."

"You bring me?"

"Ay, naked power—or at least, she'll be dressed till you marry her!"

"Wed your daughter? That beauty you brought with you?"

"The very same—I'm glad you like Ælfflæd. Will you wed her then?"

"Fast as an arrow shot from yonder tower! But will she have *me?*"

"Mmm. I don't know. We'll have to ask her."

At that precise moment Ælfflæd was discussing the King of Northumbria with her mother.

"I think he's better looking than Beorhtric, although I would never brag about that to Eadburg."

"I should hope not! So, will you wed him, Ælfflæd?" asked Cynethryth.

"If he'll have me."

"Good Lord, girl! In his situation, his life might depend upon it."

"*B*-but, I want him to wed me because he desires me, not for political convenience."

"Then, I suggest that now we are more presentable, we should rejoin the men in the hall and you can decide for yourself. He made a good first impression on me…and I'm not talking about his looks," the queen added hastily. "He was concerned about our wellbeing. Most men are boors and do not think of such niceties. Let's go and see if his character is really so thoughtful. Remember, my dear daughter, we will not force you to marry a man you dislike."

"Like Charlemagne's son," Ælfflæd muttered so low that her mother did not hear her.

In their satin gowns, they approached the high table like two gliding swans and immediately caught Æthelred's attention. "Ladies, please join us. We are supping ale, but I suggest something a little more refined." He turned and said something to a serving maid in a low voice, who nodded, smiled, and failed to glide across the hall, her attempt making her look ungainly. Still, she returned poised enough, bearing a tray containing blue Frankish glassware, two glasses, and a tall silver-beaked decanter. King Æthelred gestured to the two ladies and the servant poured a dense red liquid from the contrasting blue glassware. He raised his drinking horn and proposed a toast of welcome to the Mercian royal family.

"Mmm. This is delicious," Cynethryth approved. "What is it, King Æthelred?"

"Freshly squeezed raspberries stirred into mead, Your Majesty. I hope you like it, Princess."

"Oh, ay, it's delightfully sweet and tasty—I don't think I'll ever find anything to better it!"

Æthelred smiled and said, "I shall make it a life's quest to surpass it for you."

"A life's task?" Ælfflæd queried mockingly.

"I can think of no better way than passing time with you, lady," he said with a winning smile. "Tell me, what other activities, other than drinking the juice of the raspberry, please you?"

"I like riding, but my mare is in Tame Weorth."

"We have long majestic beaches and it is a delight to ride along the strand and breathe the sea air. Only, my lady, the Northumbrian air is chillier than what you are used to in the Midlands, especially by the seaside. If you promise to wrap up well, I shall provide you with one of my favourite mares so that we can ride up the coast where the scenery is quite splendid…" he paused, "of course, only with your consent, Sire."

"Consent! Ha-ha-ha! I have travelled all this way to wed the maid to you, King Æthelred. See what a pretty creature she is and as pure as a nun!"

"Father! Do not speak so in front of everyone. Anyone would think I was a sack of turnips for sale!" Her blue eyes flashed angrily.

Before the discomfited monarch could reply, Æthelred intervened, "Nay, Lady, a turnip is not a thing of beauty. You should have said a posy of violets, but nay, even that is not enough, for if I had a violet for every moment I have thought of you since your arrival, why, I should require a meadow of violets and an entire summertime would not suffice to contemplate them all!"

Queen Cynethryth sighed happily. Such a romantic thought Offa had never addressed to *her*.

As enchanted as her mother, Ælfflæd declared, "In that case, my Lord, I believe we are betrothed. Will you not kiss me?"

He would and did, seeming never to want to release his embrace, but finally, he declared to the assembled lords and populace, "Behold, my betrothed, the fair Lady Ælfflæd! The room burst at once into prolonged applause. Even some of the former conspirators were placated by the thought of a union between Mierce and Northumbria: one that would grant peace and prosperity.

"I liked him the moment I set eyes on him," Ælfflæd whispered in her mother's ears, but his sweet words won my heart."

Cynethryth almost replied, "and mine!" but contented herself by squeezing her daughter's hand. It had been a wearisome journey and up here in Northumbria, her daughter would be too far away, but if Æthelred maintained his word, it would be worthwhile.

TWELVE

Cantwaraburh AD 785-792

Hesitantly, Brother Fulk stood with fist raised to pound on the archbishop's door but found himself paralysed by reluctance. Many years before, the provisioner had been a simple scribe in the service of this same man who, at the time, was a benign, even jocular, character. Archbishop Jaenberht, it was generally recognised, had changed. His morose countenance was achieved by a constant frown, compressed lips, and a pinched face. Rarely, if ever, did he smile. Undoubtedly, the demands of the see he ruled with an iron fist and his incompatibility with his secular overlord, King Offa of Mierce, caused the severity of his manner.

As the provisioner knew well, empathy should lead to compassion, but it is difficult to be virtuous in the face of an irascible, sour-faced prelate.

No sooner had the scribe entered the room than Jaenberht began railing against incompetence in general.

"I have called you here, Fulk, because I remember you as a competent scribe. I will not tolerate ineptitude! No crossing out, scuffing or imprecise spacing, for this letter is destined for the eyes of the Holy Father himself. Do you understand?"

Fulk murmured some set phrases.

"What? Stop mumbling, man, for Heaven's sake! To make matters perfectly clear, I will accept nothing less than perfection!" The querulous voice had become dangerously high. "Sit there, at that desk, come on, man, move! Now let me see…" he said, more to himself, adding for the scribe's benefit, "make sure you are comfortable and everything is laid out neatly. I'll tell you when I'm ready to begin dictation."

A few moments elapsed, in which the archbishop grunted and tutted at his own words impatiently.

"Ay, this will have to do. Take this down: _I, Archbishop Jaenberht of Cantwaraburh, beg and entreat Your Highness who bears the insignia of the supreme pontificate in the name of God the Father Almighty, of Jesus Christ, His Son, and of the Holy Ghost, by the Trinity and Unity of God, to cast his eyes upon these shores. In the name of his beloved predecessor Pope Gregory, who sent St Augustine to establish our mater ecclesia in this kingdom, to note the interminable undermining of its authority by King Offa of Mierce, first, by subtracting its supremacy of jurisdiction in favour of the illicit see of Licidfelth and then by summoning unapproved Church councils at Brentford, led inappropriately by the said Offa. I again beg and entreat Your *Holliness*—Stop! Imbecile!" the archbishop had stationed himself at the scribe's shoulder and observed every letter with a jaundiced eye as it flowed from the quill. "I explicitly ordered you not to make any errors or cancellations. Don't you know that the word 'holiness' has but one 'l'? Otherwise, it is a prickly bush with red berries! Foolish and worthless scribe! You will now copy everything except the mistake in your best hand, pah!" With a vicious swipe, the archbishop sent his ornamental candlestick crashing to the floor, causing the scribe to jump and blot the vellum —not that it mattered in any case because he had to fold it and place it in a litter container.

"I am relying on you, Brother Fulk," Jaenberht thrust his sour face aggressively into the monk's face, "No further mistakes. I'm warning you, or you'll be sorry!"

The provisioner, known for his kindliness and spirituality, hastily apologised and promised to do his best, inscribing the vellum with a splendid embellished curvilinear capital *I*, which elicited a grunt of appreciation from Jaenberht. The lip-biting, brow-furrowing time necessary to copy everything to perfection, including the word *Holiness*, left the archbishop and scribe ready to finish the document which politely requested the return of Licidfelth to its former status of bishopric and an embargo on Offa conducting Church councils.

Scrutinising Fulk's work before expressing himself satisfied, Jaenberht sent the monk away with the admonishment to be more careful in future and without a word of thanks. Alone in his room, Jaenberht re-read the letter and almost recalled the scribe to write it again with minor additions. Only from a desire to expedite the dispatch to Rome did he resist this urge and instead, sealed and placed the letter in a blue velvet pouch with certain other administrative documents for the Holy See's approval.

* * *

Not for the first time, King Offa berated his misfortune to have been born in this precise epoch. "Of course, I wouldn't have had you and our wonderful children, Cynethryth. My bad luck, on the contrary, is that King Charlemagne could not have been born later and Archbishop Jaenberht earlier—that's what I mean! These two wretches are doing their best to thwart me at every turn. The real problem is that Pope Hadrian believes, rightly, that I am a pious king and esteems me. I have no concubines and do not fornicate; I love and honour my wife and children; pay my dues to the Church and regularly attend the services. However, if I arrange to have Jaenberht murdered, can you not see that he would no longer acknowledge my piety?"

"Offa! Things cannot have come to such a pass!" his wife protested.

"Indeed, they have! My spies tell me that Jaenberht has conspired with Charlemagne to admit him into Cantwaraburh, should he invade Britain."

"Nay, Charlemagne would not risk the pope's goodwill by moving against a fellow Christian king."

"Would he not? But then, what do you say to Pope Hadrian's refusal to grant my request to transfer the see of Cantwaraburh to Lunden? I asked for that because Jaenberht had the audacity to request that Licidfelth be demoted to a bishopric."

"My opinion is that neither you nor Jaenberht will get anywhere trying to adjust Church matters to your own ends. Steer well clear of them, my love, for, as you say, the Holy Father believes you to be a pious king and will permit you to rule unhindered unless his interests are compromised."

"Would impaling Jaenberht's head on a stake be to compromise his interests?"

"Offa, for God's sake! Surely, you can think of various means that are not ecclesiastic to limit the archbishop's interferences."

"I have already decided to leave for Kent in the next few days, where I intend to create three new abbots. They will be the three æthelings! I shall depose King Egbert and his entire dynasty. It'll be no use that old goat, the archbishop bleating, because I have proof that he was fomenting rebellion in Kent. Egbert is his surest ally, so by removing him, the wretched priest's secular power will be more than halved."

"But you must not touch his canonical power, Offa."

"Oh, I'll see to that, too. Do you know what the loon has done? He has claimed lands that belong to the crown. I have the documents. Not even our dear friend Hadrian can do anything when I seize them back. And another thing, did you know that Jaenberht has minted his own coins in Cantwaraburh? Displaying his portrait—isn't that vainglorious for a priest?"

"Well, you can't just sweep up all the Church's silver, Offa!"

"What do you take me for, woman? I shall send out the reeves and have them make a fair exchange with our coins, which will involve replacing them until there are no more in circulation. Then, they will be returned to the mint, melted down and the dies confiscated and thrown into the Thames."

Cynethryth clapped her hands and grinned, "Wonderful! In that way, the church and our merchants do not lose a single shilling, and nobody, except Jaenberht, can go griping for redress."

"If he's not careful, I'll arrest him for treason. Then we'll see what his friend Charlemagne will do. The Frankish king need not think that the men of Kent will welcome him with open arms. It has been referred to me that they are happy with my control of the kingdom since the beginning of this year, 785, which is nigh on ending. Talking about coins, Charlemagne still hasn't unblocked his ports to our goods. I will retaliate! Ay! I shall prohibit the circulation of Carolingian money and other foreign coins in England so that only our currency will be valid. Again, there's nothing he can do about it, because I'll have his silver and gold melted down and re-minted. Ha-ha!" Offa's guffaw boomed down from the rafters.

Three days later, the impressive force that met at the gates of Winchester was as imposing for its number of heraldic devices as for the aggregate of its men. Banners from Northumbria swirled among those of Mierce and Hwicce and were joined by the fluttering emblems of Wessex. In turn, these mythical creatures and stripes would have the addition of the South Saxon motifs and, before arriving at their destination, probably those of loyal Kentish standards. The colourful pageantry was awe-inspiring and did not remotely suggest vulnerability. Indeed, it occurred to King Offa that he was taking a smith's lump hammer to open a walnut laid carefully on an anvil.

He proceeded to accomplish the scheme he had outlined to his queen, as the bewildered and impressed population watched on. First, he drove into the Medway valley, confiscating the rich red brick land of sand, pebbles, and clay and regranted them to a faithful thegn, sending the former proprietor packing to the archbishop of Cantwaraburh. Similar good land was confiscated in the Darent and Stour valleys, again, granted to trusted thegns.

King Egbert fled into exile without opposing any resistance, and Offa had his three sons conducted under armed escort to live out the rest of their natural lives in monasteries in Mierce.

In a matter of weeks, not a single Carolingian coin or one impressed with the head of Jaenberht could be found in Kent, unless buried in a farmyard or hidden elsewhere, where it was of no use, anyway.

* * *

In the court of Frankia, Charlemagne ordered a priest to read him a letter newly arrived from Pope Hadrian. The message was deferential, in which the pope went to great lengths to disclaim a belief in a rumour that his deposition and the election of a Frankish pope had been proposed to Charlemagne by Offa. As the wide-eyed priest reached the end of the page, Charlemagne threw back his head and howled with laughter. "The old fool! Is this the best the leading British churchman can do to stir up trouble for the King of Mierce?"

At the beginning of the New Year, Charlemagne learnt that Hadrian was about to send George, bishop of Ostia, and Theophylact, bishop of Todi as legates to England. The bishop of Ostia was an old man, of long experience in papal business, and his selection showed how much importance Hadrian attached to the mission. In the previous generation, the leaders of the Englisc church had looked to Boniface rather than the pope for guidance in maintaining ecclesiastic order. Indeed, no papal legate had visited England since the mission of Augustine. Charlemagne asked himself reasonably whether the recent rumours about Offa's hostility had revealed the dangers to the pope of allowing England to slip out of the range of the pope's direct influence.

Charlemagne was a wily politician and so, he smiled to himself, Offa had every reason to welcome a reassertion of papal authority over the Archbishop of Cantwaraburh! Also, the blockade on Englisc trade was hurting his own coffers, so the King of the Franks decided to use the legates to restore his former good relations with Offa. How the man had become an inscrutable force in international politics since the day Charlemagne had sent him packing from Paris with a failed marriage contract! The Franks would be happy to have their currency circulating once more in Kent and Lundenwic. Charlemagne was loath to admit as much, but he had met his match in King Offa of Mierce. Charlemagne laughed again at the thought of the one thing that Offa had failed to achieve. How he would have loved to have seen Jaenberht's face when he had learnt of the Mercian's attempt to have him transposed to Lundenwic from St Augustine's seat in Cantwaraburh.

Few men had used the authority of the church to the effect of Charlemagne, but the King of the Franks had little doubt that he could teach King Offa very much in that respect.

THIRTEEN

The Hereford countryside near Sutton Walls, AD 794

King Offa rarely let an idle moment pass without considering aggrandisement—either personal or of Mierce, which essentially amounted to the same thing. Recently, he had given thought to his remaining nubile daughter, Ælfthryth, wondering which might be the most advantageous marriage for her, or more precisely, his family.

He had come to the conclusion that his eyes would have to settle on an alliance beyond the shores of Britain, when he chanced upon his wife walking in the palace gardens. She took his hand and led him to a bench where they watched darting red squirrels shoot up and down the slender tree trunks.

"Offa, there's something I've been meaning to show you for several days, but it's so seldom that we find a few moments of peace together.

"Cynethryth, I can't believe you are the sort of woman who worrits over a few squirrels!"

The queen giggled, "Not the squirrels, silly, but you will admit that *this* is worthy of your attention!"

She produced a shiny, newly-minted coin from out of her dress pocket and pressed it into his palm. The king stared at the reverse of the coin, making no attempt to turn it. The silver piece showed a Roman she-wolf, suckling twin babes—presumably Romulus and Remus. Offa drew his own conclusions: "Jaenberht!" he exploded.

"Nay, husband, not this time!" Cynethryth smiled slyly and gently turned the coin to its obverse, where Offa read two names: one was most familiar to him as his moneyer—Lul— the other, that of his sub-king Æthelberht II of the East Angles. The little silver coin was indeed designed to flatter, not the King of Mierce, but rather the Pontiff of the Church of Rome.

"Blast his eyes!" Offa shouted, sending a temerarious red squirrel scuttling, which had encroached on the royal presence. "The man presumes too much! He assumes a greater degree of independence than I am prepared to tolerate, my dear!" He turned the coin over and pointed to the she-wolf. "I presume you know the full meaning of this, Cynethryth?"

She pursed her lips and drew the obvious conclusion, "It's the symbol of Rome and Æthelberht is trying to ingratiate himself with the Holy Father," she looked pleased with herself.

"Ay, well there is that," Offa said grudgingly, "but there's more! Æthelberht claims to be of the East Anglian ruling dynasty: the Wuffingas. The allusion is clear, hence the Roman she-wolf and the title REX on his coin." The ferocity of his glare would have made any other woman tremble, but she was safe in the depths of his love. "You know what this means, of course?"

"What?"

"War! I'll not rest till I've driven him into the North Sea!"

"Offa, do not allow your temper to cloud your judgment. I always think that war should be used as a last resort."

"Why, do you have a better idea?"

"At least three or four," she teased him.

"Let's hear them, then!"

"The first one should suffice with a few calculated changes. Instead of marching into the wolf's lair in East Anglia, where even you might risk defeat, why not bring him here to Mierce?"

"What makes you think he will accept such an invitation?"

"We shall need to tempt Æthelberht with an irresistible offer."

"Heavens, woman! Are you suggesting—" His wife had the knack of following his recent thoughts.

"Ay, we'll bring him here to wed Ælfthryth—he's young, but two-score winters and," she smiled, "strong and good-looking by all accounts. As her husband, he will be in your power. Or," he saw a strange light glow in her eye, one he had never seen before and that made him involuntarily recoil, "or, we'll slay him here in Mierce and he will trouble no one further."

"You know I am reluctant to slay my enemies. In any case, I'd much rather murder Archbishop Jaenberht if it came to a choice!" Offa growled.

"Ay, folly of follies! You cannot murder a Prince of the Church."

"But you suggest that I *can* kill an anointed king!"

"Nay, I don't want *you* slaying anyone, Offa."

"Who then?" He stared at her and the dull mist of incomprehension dissipated. "*You* will do the deed!"

"Not exactly! But promise you will leave the details to me, which is why you must invite Æthelberht to your royal vill at Sutton Walls. Do not bring him here to Tame Weorth and, most importantly, do not spread the word that the King of the East Angles is coming to visit Mierce." She looked smug and hissed, "It's one thing to bandy him about your capital and quite another to spirit him away into a remote vill in the Hereford countryside."

Offa gazed at his wife in undisguised admiration. "Just how long have you been plotting this scheme?"

"Do you remember me showing you that bale of golden damask from Italy a few days ago? I know you are not particularly bothered about linens and suchlike, still you wanted to know rather more about the weaving than I could tell you."

"I remember, right enough, for I had to send down to the ship for someone to explain the draw looms to me. They have them in Italy, or in the absence of such looms, we cannot make similar materials in Mierce." She tried not to show her boredom when he explained draw looms, which were looms with two harnesses that allow for the creation of patterns a standard loom cannot accommodate. "I might order one built here in Tame Weorth so that you can choose cloths fit for your costly tastes, my dear," he added glumly.

"But what has the cloth to do with your notion to bring Æthelberht to Mierce?"

She giggled contentedly, "There's always an explanation, Offa. Years ago, before you and Charlemagne had your disagreement, we used to bring special cloths from Frankia. Now, we trade directly with Venice. They send regular ships to Frankia, but I discovered that Venice trades with Gipeswic in East Anglia, taking back salt and wool to Italy."

"I must re-open commerce with Frankia. It's as much in their interests as ours." Offa's tone was grumpy. "I still don't see the connection with Æthelberht."

"The coin, it came among the change for the cloth. The she-wolf caught my eye. Then, I thought that you would not have appreciated the king of the East Angles minting coins that circulate in Frankia and beyond."

Offa eyed a red squirrel holding an acorn in its front paws and glared at it venomously as if the tiny creature were to blame for Æthelberht's audacity.

"I do not appreciate it, Cynethryth, but tell me, are you more set on wedding Ælfthryth to him or on—" he paused meaningfully and cleared his throat— "*eliminating* Æthelberht? Surely, if we take the latter course, East Anglia will be lost to us for good."

"Do you suppose I hadn't thought of that, there's always a risk that wedding negotiations go awry, whereas, blood ties rarely fail."

He looked at his wife musingly, "What is locked away in that corn-coloured head?"

"I'll give you your due, Offa, you have a much-vaunted lineage, but you do not harp on about it. Well, neither do I!"

His eyes seemed to glaze over, but only momentarily, for suddenly he sat up straight on their bench with the revelation. "That's it! On your father's side, you are a descendant of Penda like me—but on your mother's a Wuffingas! But will your brother, Eadwald have any truck with murder?"

"Of course not! What do you take him for? All that Eadwald needs to know, when the time comes, is that Aethelheard had met with an unfortunate accident and that in his stead, he has been elected the new king of the East Angles."

"But will the Angles accept that?"

"They will not dare to defy the great King Offa of Mierce, especially when the proposition is for them to have a new Wuffingas to replace the old," she chuckled delighted at her cunning. But she looked shrewdly at him, "You did promise to leave the details to me, Offa?"

"Did I?" he asked distractedly; he didn't remember making any such promise, but it seemed she had concocted the scheme to a satisfactory end. "I suppose I did promise. Just tell me what I need to do."

They sat, their heads touching as she outlined what he had to do next. It was easy enough except for one minor detail, which she now explained. "In normal circumstances, Æthelberht's retinue would be accompanied to Tame Weorth with all the pomp of your entourage, but on this occasion, it will just be the one messenger, who, in order not to arouse Æthelberht's suspicion, will explain that you are dealing with internal factions at Tame Weorth, who have set their eyes on Ælfthryth for a bride—"

"Brilliant!" He interrupted, "The competition will make him desire Ælfthryth even more!"

Her plan complete, Cynethryth left him in the garden whilst she went to choose a messenger and set him to his task. That accomplished, she moved on to the delicate part of the scheme.

Meanwhile, Offa kicked the heel of one boot against the toe of the other as he sat head bowed in reflection. There was much to think about. He was not enamoured of his wife's idea of regicide, but if it could be accomplished without too much fuss, he would rid himself at one stroke of a potentially over-ambitious rival and have the malleable and worthy Eadwald enthroned as his ally. By Thunor! How crafty was the little minx! He smiled fondly at the red squirrel, flicking another acorn with the toe of his boot. He grinned when the rodent sprang agilely to catch it in mid-air.

Five mornings later, Cynethryth intercepted him returning from Prime.

"Everything has proceeded smoothly, Offa. Take an escort, your falconers and Ecgfrith to the vill at Sutton Walls. Make it seem like an ordinary hunting trip. Above all, take Ælfthryth in a carriage, she must be dressed in finery, believing herself on her way to a betrothal. Nobody must suspect anything wrong," she pressed his hand. Her voice lowered to a whisper, "Thegn Grimbert, one of my oldest and most loyal retainers, has dealt with everything."

When King Offa arrived in a cheerful swirl of banners and sounded his horn beneath the gates of Sutton Walls, everything must have appeared to the East Anglian onlookers as entirely normal and innocent, especially when Princess Ælfthryth, wearing a fine pink satin gown, stepped out of her comfortable carriage and looked keenly around the East Anglian ranks for a glimpse of her beloved.

"Father, where is King Æthelberht?" she asked in a clear, bell-like voice.

King Offa strode over to a dignified-looking, grey-haired warrior to the fore among the East Anglians. "I take you to be a nobleman, Lord, where is your king?"

"I am Ealdorman Ælfwald, Sire," the nobleman looked embarrassed, "would that we knew King Æthelberht's whereabouts. He has vanished!"

"What nonsense is this? The king cannot simply vanish!"

"He was last seen coming out of terce yesterday morning. Our king is very pious and never misses a service, which makes his non-attendance at subsequent services the more remarkable."

"Did he confide in you, Ealdorman?"

"Ay, Sire," came the proud reply.

"Did the king express doubts about marrying my daughter?"

"Nay, King Offa, on the contrary, he was enthused to become—as he put it—*ahem*, part of your family. He was initially surprised not to be met by you and escorted to Tame Weorth, but Thegn Grimbert met us and delivered your personal message. King Æthelberht understood the delicacy of the situation."

"I am glad of it. Now Ealdorman, is there nobody at all who perhaps saw the king ride out the gates or exchanged a word with him?"

"Ay, there is, Sire, a boy—a groom, but the fact is, the lad is a simpleton, albeit an excellent groom."

"Take me to him. I will speak to the youth."

The halfwit made an awkward bow to King Offa and could not help gaping at the monarch.

"Close your mouth, boy, lest a bluebottle fly in and you swallow it!" Ealdorman Ælfwald said sternly.

The boy shuddered and obeyed.

"When did you last see King Æthelberht, lad?"

"Yesterday mornin', when them bells were a-clankin'."

"After Prime then?"

"Ay, if that's what they call it."

"What did the king want of you?"

"'Is 'orse. Asked if 'e'd been fed and drank."

"Did he say anything else?"

"Ay, he said 'e was pleased the 'orse was ready 'cause he was going to see the an-an," the boy looked upset because he couldn't say the word."

King Offa bent over him and said gently, "You are not in trouble, lad. If you want to help your king, try to remember the word—do your best!"

"An- an." Saliva dribbled from the side of the boy's mouth. He screwed up his face, which made him look idiotic, and he gulped before shouting "anthracite!". That's it, the boy crowed, "that's what the king said *anthracite!*

The king and nobleman exchanged astonished glances. "What would King Æthelberht want with coal?" Offa grumbled. "Are you sure that's what he said?"

"Ay, anthracite!"

Offa was not as sharp as Cynethryth, but he was quick-witted in his own right. King Æthelberht was pious and known to attend all services. He might not need anthracite, but might be interested in an anchorite!

"Listen carefully, young man," he said gently, ruffling the boy's hair, "is it possible that the king said *anchorite?*"

The gleam of recognition in the boy's eyes was sufficient for Offa without the frantic nodding of the tousled head.

"By all the saints!" Ealdorman Ælfwald cried, "That's it! If there's an anchorite hereabouts, you can be sure our king would seek them out."

"To find Æthelberht," Offa declared, "all we need to do is locate this hermit. But it is growing late to go riding off into the forest. If your lord has not returned by morning, we shall ride out in search of him."

Offa needed time on his own to reflect on events and to know how to react to others' comments so as not to betray his involvement in the disappearance of the East Anglian ruler. For this same reason, he had deliberately kept away from Thegn Grimbert, for he did not wish to be seen conversing in private too much with anyone, especially if that someone was later found responsible for the outrage.

The king, therefore, withdrew to his quarters and gave the guard strict orders to admit nobody, except Thegn Grimbert. He was sure the thegn would come, so used the time to order his thoughts. Piecing the facts together as he knew them, he concluded that the thegn, playing on the king's well-known religiosity, had lured him into the depths of the nearby forest to meet with the anchorite, renowned as a saint and prophet in the area. What more propitious time to consult an oracle than before one's betrothal? Offa chuckled into his beard. Grimbert would then have surprised Æthelberht and slaughtered him, disposing of the body in a place the Mercian king hoped was well-concealed from search parties.

That the king's reconstruction was precise was soon proved when a sharp rap on the door led to the admittance of Thegn Grimbert. The thegn was an old acquaintance, as he was a long-standing servant of Queen Cynethryth's father and a man upon whose devotion she could count blindly.

"Friend, I know your father well as he has served me faithfully as a counsellor."

The thegn dropped to his knees and with bent head begged, "Sire, there is no need for my father to know anything of this business. He could not bear the shame. I believe that I have fulfilled my task so well that nobody will ever solve the mystery, thus there will be no scandal."

"I promise your father will learn nought of it from me, Thegn. I shall make you wait for your reward so that folks will have forgotten and be unable to associate the matters. Discretion! That is why I have stayed far from you for two days; also, you will have a care not to linger near this chamber when you leave. But, hush! What about the body?"

"Have no fear, Sir, I dragged it into a bear's den. There were signs of the creature's most recent dwelling there. Nobody in his right mind will enter that low cavern."

"Excellent! Now, you are quite sure Æthelberht was dead?"

"Ay, Sire, unless a man without his head can roam the land!"

"How did you manage it?"

"I set off and arrived at the anchorite's cell before him. The king was following my directions. Sire, the terrible thing is that she knew my purpose and told me I would have to serve an archbishop's penance."

"Ah, that can be arranged!"

"She told me not to torment myself because it was God's providence, since He has other plans for Princess Ælfthryth."

"I shall order search parties out in the morning. You will lead one, Thegn, well away from where the body lies."

Alone at last, Offa flung himself on his bed and studiously avoided contemplating the crucifix hanging from a nail in the wall. *Thou shalt not kill*, he repeated softly to himself. Offa was learned in both the Old and the New Testaments. Especially in the Old, which detailed many examples of regicide. These were often justifiable because the victims were tyrants. By no stretch of his imagination could Offa convince himself that Æthelheard II was a tyrant. From what he had heard, the slain king was a youthful, devout and admirable monarch.

From the corner of his eye, Offa glimpsed the crucifix and his conscience caused him to groan. He remembered a passage from the second Book of Samuel and moaned more deeply. Was he, too, doomed?

Samuel told how Rekab and Baanah stabbed Ish-Bosheth in the stomach as he was resting from the heat of the day, then cut off his head. Offa groaned again. They took it to King David at Hebron and said to him: "Here is the head of Ish-Bosheth son of Saul, your enemy who tried to kill you." Samuel concluded, *"This day the LORD has avenged my lord the king against Saul and his offspring."*

Offa trembled, would the Lord avenge the East Angles against him and his offspring?

He lay in guilt for a long time, denied sleep, startled by the creaks and groans of the old timber structure. He thought of other biblical passages and found no consolation, but then remembered the words of the anchorite as reported by the assassin thegn: *it was God's providence, since He has other plans for Princess Ælfthryth.* If the hermit was a saint and a prophetess, surely, she had spoken the truth. In that case, it was God's fault, not Offa's, that Æthelberht lay headless in a bear's den. That was another fact in his favour. In the morning, drawing ever closer, the search parties would not find a body and without it, there was no proof of foul play.

King Offa acted his part well, showing deep concern for King Æthelberht's welfare. He created two search parties and ordered them to spread out well. The East Angles he placed under Ealdorman Ælfwald and the Miercians under Thegn Grimbert, having previously whispered to Grimbert to lead Ælfwald as far astray as possible from Æthelberht's corpse. However, to keep up his part, he openly suggested to Ælfwald that he should visit the anchorite. "As a prophetess, she might have an insight into what has happened to the king and where he may be found."

"Ay, good idea, Lord. That's where my search-party will start—with the anchoress."

Offa watched them trot downhill with anxious misgivings. Why did he always have to make suggestions instead of holding his tongue? What if the prophetess blurted out the truth to Ælfwald? In that case, war would already break out here in Hwicce.

The anchoress could not or would not help Ælfwald. First, she complimented him on being a devout servant of his God and King, then recommended he continue in righteousness by returning to the royal vill to attend Sext. After the service, she told him to return here, to accompany Princess Ælfthryth, for God wished for them to speak.

Ælfwald was just beginning to make out the features of the anchoress as the sun rose sufficiently to shine into the narrow slit where well-wishers passed food into the cell. He could see her grey matted hair, unkempt, which contrasted with her well-spoken noble voice, and he noted with approval the large, wide eyes either side of an aquiline nose. The firm chin-line also told him that he was dealing with a strong character, a patrician who had dedicated her life to abnegation and the service of the Lord.

"Hark!" she said suddenly, "Take your men back to the palace, for you will never see your king again. A grave misfortune has befallen him, yet, he is now seated beside our Saviour in Paradise. Ay, Saint Æthelberht will perform many miracles, but among them will not be his sudden reappearance. Your kingdom will have a new leader. Seek counsel from the king of this land, for the Lord has favoured him with great prodigies." The anchoress waved her hand at the ealdorman as if driving away an irritating insect. "Bring the Princess!" she ordered by way of closure.

Ælfwald returned slowly to his horse, astonished that anyone, never mind a noblewoman, could live in such a cramped, comfortless cell every day of her life. The ealdorman felt sure that she had not revealed all she knew about his king's disappearance. What had she said? A *grave misfortune*, but that implied ill-chance, an accident then, of some sort? He felt sure that had foul play been involved, the saintly woman would have told him. The anchoress had lived through constant tribulations, but her life of prayer provided her with certainties. She knew that the important matter was not Æthelberht's murder, but her forthcoming intermediacy between God and Ælfwald.

King Offa was dismayed to see the East Angles returning so soon—why, he had not yet heard the call to Sext. To his guilty mind, such an early return could only mean that they had found the king's headless corpse; yet, scan their approaching ranks as he might, he could not see a body draped over a horse.

"Ealdorman! Have you no tidings of King Aethelheard?"

"On the contrary, Sire, the anchoress informed me that he has gone to join our Redeemer in Paradise."

"What? Æthelberht is dead? Did she say how?" He almost choked over these last words.

"Ay, she said a grave misfortune came over him and that I should seek your counsel when nominating the next king of East Anglia, for you have been blessed, nay, hold! *Favoured* was the word she used, favoured by God."

Offa gasped and could feel the tension flowing out of his taut muscles. "Did she say that?"

"Ay, and she said she needed to speak urgently with Princess Ælfthryth. By your leave, I am to accompany the princess."

Offa grasped a handful of his green woollen cloak in his fist and clutched it so tightly that his knuckles turned white. "Did she say why she wanted to speak to my daughter?"

"Nay, Sire, I supposed it might be owing to the loss of her betrothed. Perhaps the Lord has some other purpose for Lady Ælfthryth."

"That might be the case," Offa said in a wavering voice, "you have my permission to accompany the Princess, Ealdorman. Let nothing untoward befall her."

He watched the East Anglian nobleman stride into the hall and worried again, "Was the recluse about to blurt out his darkest secret? But then, why would she have said he had been favoured by God? Why did she want to speak with his daughter? There was much more to this affair than met the eye. If only Cynethryth were here to advise him!

On the ride into the forest to the anchorite's cell, Princess Ælfthryth pressed the ealdorman for his opinion of what had happened to her husband-to-be.

"Perhaps we shall never know, my Lady, we are only men, after all. The holy woman who is in daily communication with God implied that he had met with an accident. I shall certainly try to have her tell me more."

"What kind of man was King Æthelberht?"

"A kindly man and a good king. For his good deeds, some held that he was a saint. I wouldn't go that far myself, my Lady. But he was surely a good man! He was looking forward to meeting you and making you his bride."

Ælfthryth's lower lip trembled, but she controlled her emotions. "You have no reason to believe there was," she hesitated and added in a tremulous voice, "foul play."

"Murder? Good Lord, no. Who would gain from it? None of the Angles. We brought only true and loyal fellows with us. Mierce? Nay, she had only to gain by marrying a king's daughter to the King of East Anglia. Nay, Lady, the more I think on it, the more I fear a terrible misfortune occurred, as the holy woman says."

"That's a relief, but these forest byways are so scary. Who knows what monsters lurk in the hidden depths? Oh, why did poor Æthelberht come here alone?"

"He was a brave warrior and feared no man, my Lady."

"But what if it was no man? Have you heard the tale of Grendel, Ealdorman?"

He snorted and said impatiently, "It is but a tale, Princess. But see, we have arrived. Permit me to go first so that I can press her for greater details."

"By all means."

Ealdorman Ælfwald was in a mood for answers and pressed the anchorite, "Ay, I have brought the princess here, but will not present her to you until you give me the answers I seek about my king's death."

"I cannot give them to you, but I can help you seek them, Ealdorman."

"Help me then, woman," Ælfwald growled.

"You seek who killed your king. So, you must seek in the night sky. Observe the sole star that never bathes in the ocean wave."

"Sister, I am no stargazer!"

"Then you must enlist the aid of one who appreciates the firmament. It is not a difficult riddle for a man from the eastern coast to solve. In return, you will do something for your king. Hark! More days will go by then, the saint's body will be found and his killer become clear. At once there will be miracles and wonderful events. So, you must take King Æthelberht's body to Hereford Cathedral, where you will ensure that a shrine is built to his memory."

"All this I will do. I will bring the Princess to you now and go to ponder the riddle you have given me."

"You will solve the riddle before night sets in, when you will be certain of it!"

Ealdorman Ælfwald strode back to the horses feeling no wiser, but strangely buoyed by the hermit's words. He would have the answer to the king's slayer before midnight.

The anchorite planned on telling the Princess nothing beyond what she had said to the ealdorman regarding the royal death and said as much. "Do not trouble yourself about the young king's murderer, Princess. Ealdorman Ælfwald will bring you the answer before midnight. It was a terrible misfortune!"

"And what of me, Sister? You wished to make known God's will for me. Will you not do so?"

"You must travel far across the land, leaving your home and

family and all worldly chattels to lead the same life as I lead. Except that you will have the proximity of a venerated saint—Saint Guthlac. Study his life before you leave to reach his shrine."

"Is it not in the Kingdom of Lindsey?"

"Ah, you *do* know! God is already preparing you."

"You ask a lot of me, sister, and I am but a child."

"*I* ask nothing of you, Princess; we are all children in God's eyes."

FOURTEEN

Sutton Walls and Hereford AD 794

The two riders, returning the short distance to Tame Weorth, were subdued and taciturn until Ælfwald said, "My Lady, do you study the night sky?"

The princess smiled and shook her head. "I fear that most nights I lie fast asleep, but why do you ask?"

"According to the holy woman, the secret to King Æthelberht's death can be found in the night sky. Alas, Lady, my knowledge of the heavens is very limited.

"Mine, too, but you are lucky."

"How so?"

"Look at the sky today, Ealdorman. It is gloriously cloud-free for this time of year. You'll see all the stars you need tonight."

"But it's just *one* I need," he grumbled, feeling overwhelmed by the task in hand.

The princess caught his mood but instead of sinking into gloom she sought a solution.

"Priests and monks are the best informed about celestial matters, Ealdorman. You should obtain aid from a religious sky gazer."

"But where will I find one such hereabouts?"

"The town of Hereford lies over yonder," she pointed. "It has no monastery, but I've heard that the bishop is a most learned man. The building of the cathedral is in its eighth year and although it is not finished, my mother tells me that the dean and chapter have inaugurated a splendid library here in Hwicce, beyond anything we have in Mierce."

"My Lady, I'm in your debt. I believe you have saved me in my ignorance. Look! Just beyond the curve in the road lies the trail up to the gateway of Sutton Walls. I will accompany you to the gate and then set off at once for Hereford, which, as I recall, is but four miles away. Kindly inform your father whither I am bound, but not my purpose. I do not wish to raise false hopes."

"Very well, Ealdorman, but I have faith in your investigative skills."

They separated at the gateway, Ælfthryth impressed with the East Angle's good manners and sighed deeply at the loss of the king she had never known. How then could he be a loss?

As she strolled into the great hall, Ælfthryth reached a decision. She would, for the moment, tell her father nothing about the vocation awaiting her. Instead, she would ride on the morrow to Tame Weorth and reveal everything to her mother.

To Offa, she explained why Ælfwald had gone to Hereford. "He needs some information there, father, from the priests. When he has that, the holy woman promised that the ealdorman would know the king's killer before Lauds."

"Did she, by heaven?"

King Offa wandered off to his room to brood. Before Lauds meant that in the early hours of the morning, Ealdorman Ælfwald and the East Angles would know the identity of the killer. And even if he had not bloodied his hands, Offa's conscience troubled him in a way that he had never known.

Hereford's Anglo-Saxon cathedral was a large imposing wooden building, which was also a hive of activity. At the great west doorway, beggars gathered, several wearing tattered rags, others lame and hobbling on crutches, crying out for alms. Monks moved among them, giving comfort and occasionally producing a bread roll snatched in desperation amid exclamations of joy and blessings.

Some clerics in black robes strode, glancing warily upwards, important-looking documents in hand, into the building under scaffolding rearing up above the doorway, ropes trailing downwards, as work continued on the construction of a tower.

In the cavernous gloom of the interior, daylight lost its battle to penetrate the ranks of small rounded-arched windows, totally inadequate for their purpose. Architects still hadn't solved the problem of enlarging the windows without weakening the structure. Ælfwald, who was not practically minded or particularly artistic, nonetheless felt sure that the day would come soon when such magnificent buildings would be lit more in keeping with the splendour of God's light.

As it was, the ealdorman's eyes were drawn the length of the nave to the distant altar where countless candle flames danced like daffodils in a breeze. The united flames produced a twofold effect: the surreal elongation of shadows and the bartering of light in exchange for smothering smoke. The gaily-painted walls behind the altar brought much-needed relief from the oppressive spirituality of the place.

Suddenly, Ælfwald was seized by a desire to pray for the soul of his king. After all, to know how the young monarch's life had been snatched away was the reason for his presence here. Ælfwald was about to kneel before the altar when a hand tugged at his shoulder, "Buy a candle, lord, so that your prayers will be carried upwards by its flame."

"Ay," Ælfwald groped in his purse for a silver coin. The chandler's eyes widened: a whole shilling was far more than the three-penny-candle was worth. In the gloom, teeth that hinted of yellowness flashed, "I have no change, lord. You can have four candles for that sum."

Ælfwald 's patience was exhausted, "Give me four then and leave me in peace!"

The man's fussing accompanied the transaction and Ælfwald, knowing he had been swindled, nevertheless was pleased to contribute to the cathedral's role of alms provision. Also, Æthelberht 's soul was well deserving of the four hefty candles which the ealdorman carefully lit, transferring the flames from one to another, standing them upright on the altar before stepping back, sinking to his knees, and meditating deeply on the man whose life had been snatched away, only days before, and who then had been his hale and hearty liege lord.

"There comes a time for every man when he must leave the crowd behind and meditate," said a gentle voice. Ælfwald looked up into a kindly smiling face.

"Are you a priest, then?"

"Ay, so I strive to be."

"Perhaps you could help me, Father," Ælfwald rose slowly and rubbed his knees, chilled by the stone paving.

"What is it, my son?"

Ælfwald explained his encounter with the holy hermit and the riddle she had given him.

"Alas, *culpa mea!*" The priest struck his chest with a fist, "My knowledge of the stars is minimal, but do not despair, we shall go to Bishop Utel's quarters. He's sure to have the answer you seek."

Bishop Utel was a stocky, bald character with an unpriestly bad temper, "Are you telling me that you don't know the answer to a question that the most unlearned of our novices would supply on the instant! Shame on you, wretch! Go and recite twenty Hail Marys. Shame on you, too, Ealdorman, to whom God has given honour and wealth, yet you spare no time to study His night sky."

"Before you reveal the riddle, Bishop, let me explain why it is important to me." The ealdorman explained the journey to Sutton Walls for the betrothal of King Æthelberht and Princess Ælfthryth and the subsequent disappearance of the king. He hinted at a suspicion of foul play and how he hoped to capture the murderer and bring him to justice.

The rubicund countenance of the bishop spread into a broad grin, "I should think that will be particularly difficult, Ealdorman. You are seeking the one star that never bathes in the ocean wave, you say? First, you must understand what that means, Ealdorman. For sure, you will have seen the sun at dawn rise out of the sea and the morning star do the same. The opposite at night, they sink into the waves. You need to find a star or group of stars, what we call a constellation, that never sinks below the horizon.

"And are there such stars, Bishop?"

"Indulge me, Ealdorman, I am still annoyed by yon shameful wretch, who could not reply to your question." He pointed at the kneeling figure reciting his Hail Mary penance. "I can answer your question, but come, let us find a novice, who will supply your answer and in so doing, assuage my wrath."

For such a stocky, bandy-legged figure, the bishop moved swiftly and Ælfwald hurried to keep pace. Outside the cathedral, where the bright sunlight lit the beads of perspiration on the bishop's bald pate, the cleric grasped the arm of a passing novice.

"Answer this riddle, my son—which is the one star that never bathes in the ocean wave?"

Intimidated and shy, the young priest replied hesitantly, "Ursa Major, Excellency?"

"Exactly! Well done! There's your killer, Ealdorman—the Great Bear!"

The ealdorman's brow wrinkled as he struggled to understand. "That must be it. Our king left the anchorite and, riding in the forest, came upon a bear, who slew him! Thank you, Excellency, I must be on my way."

"Wait! Was your king as pious and devout as you say?"

"At least the triple!"

"Then, find his body in a bear's den, bring it here and we'll build a shrine as the anchorite suggested. We are looking to consecrate the cathedral soon and need a dedication. The cathedral church of the Blessed Virgin Mary and Saint Æthelberht has a fine ring to it."

"I must take my leave, your Excellency."

Face-to-face with King Offa, Ealdorman Ælfwald revealed what he had discovered.

"A bear!" Offa roared, "There are too many wild beasts in our woodlands, he acted his part well, "but God moves in mysterious ways, that a bear should martyr the king of East Anglia is almost beyond my comprehension! *Let them believe this and I am free to proceed with my plans!* He thought quickly: *better to have proof!* "The sun will soon set, Ealdorman, but on the morrow, gather all the local woodsmen and have them lead you to every known bear den. You shall take the body to Hereford as the anchorite and the bishop suggest. I shall establish three new monasteries in Hwicce, each dedicated to Saint Æthelberht." *That should restore me into God's grace and if it's not enough, I'll found several more and go to Rome on pilgrimage.*

The following morning, King Offa had Thegn Grimbert organise every available woodsman to lead them to known bear dens. These were often no more than holes hollowed out of the undergrowth, filled with leaves and quite difficult to spot. Grimbert remembered, however, the place where he had hidden the king's body, at the base of a rockface in a low-roofed cavern.

He manipulated the situation so that they arrived there among the first dens. At all costs, he wished to avoid the loss of a life to an angered bear. They had brought a cart drawn by two horses with them. One of the woodsmen bent forward, holding a flaming torch in his right hand and a seax in his left.

"There's a body in here!" he bellowed. "No bear, neither! Come on, let's be getting it out." Two others hurried forward, grabbed a leg each and dragged the corpse out of the cavern, the blazing brand revealing the headless body to a collective groan. The first man ducked into the cave and, seax sheathed, returned with King Æthelberht's head, which he placed reverentially on the cart next to the body.

"I'll have none of that nonsense!" Thegn Grimbert shouted in response to murmured insinuations, "the bear took off the king's head—that's quite clear! Anyone who says otherwise will have me to deal with! Now turn the cart around and let's be getting back to the vill."

Before the horses were in position, a little girl, wearing a dark-green peplos held by only one brooch at her shoulder to indicate her young age, came into the clearing, leading a sightless man with a grey beard in ragged clothes by the hand.

"Alms, my lord, for this poor blind man and his daughter!" The girl, about eight years old, tugged her father near the well-dressed thegn on his horse. Grimbert was taking a couple of pennies from his tunic and bent to hand them to the girl just as the cart horses behaved erratically. Something in the undergrowth, most likely the returning bear, had unsettled them. They set off with such a jolt that the king's head rolled off the boards onto a bed of leaves. Only the girl saw this and, with remarkable bravery, dashed forward to retrieve it. She picked up the gruesome object and, about to place it back on the cart, instead responded to her father's desperate call, "Ethel!" The poor man felt alone and vulnerable in strange circumstances without the tiny hand to cling on to. So, she rushed to his side and said, "Father, I have a man's head!" The blind man reached out, ran his hands over the royal cranium and gasped. The thegn and his men were too busy advancing with spears into the undergrowth to scare away the bear or struggling to get the panicky horses under control to notice these occurrences.

"Ethel, I can see! It's a miracle! This must be a holy man's head. You are just as pretty as I imagined you."

The girl, with tears of joy streaming down her face, flung her arms around her father's waist and clung onto him like a barnacle to a rock.

"Hey, you! Put the king's head back on the cart!"

"It fell off during the commotion, lord. My girl gave it to me and it restored my sight, praise be to God!"

"What! You two will come with me to tell King Offa your tale."

When the slow procession reached Sutton Walls, Offa ordered the royal remains to be covered in sumptuous silk, largely because he wanted no further speculation about the decapitation. How could a bear's claws neatly behead a man? It made no sense and rumours would be quick to begin.

Ealdorman Ælfwald came hurrying to the cart and, turning to the king of the Miercians, said, "It is exactly as the holy woman foretold: the killer was a bear and a miracle has happened immediately. This blind man touched the king's head and his sight was restored! His daughter, Ethel, swears that since her birth, her father has been without sight. The child is beside herself with joy. Pardon me, Sire, but I think we should take the king's body to Hereford at once, where it can be sanctified and placed in a shrine.

Eager to rid himself of the proof of his misdeeds, Offa accepted readily, saying, "It is only right that the men of East Anglia accompany King Æthelberht to his final resting place."

At this juncture, Offa remembered his daughter. "Send for Princess Ælfthryth, she will want to bid farewell to her ill-starred betrothed."

Shortly, a servant came to Offa. "Sire, Princess Ælfthryth has ridden off to Tame Weorth with an escort on urgent business."

Urgent business? Pah! And without my leave! What can be so pressing?

In Hereford, Ethel's peplos pocket filled rapidly with small coins donated by exalting pilgrims, flocking to see the beneficiary of God's grace through his holy martyr. She could not recall a day of such great joy in her short life and would not let go of her father, who still needed to gain confidence in walking and not bumbling around in the dark. Before his affliction, Ethel's father, Bordan, was a craftsman, skilled at making glass items. His eye disease had put an end to his promising trade. He very much wished to discover whether a workshop in Hereford might be interested in his expertise but found instead that the faithful swarming into town, uplifted by his tale, gave him and Ethel no respite. Everyone wanted to hear for themselves, in the protagonists' own words, how touching the sacred head of King Æthelberht, martyr to a savage bear, had restored the glassblower's sight. Bordan would have to be patient, for more than a year would go by before the yearning of the pilgrims would ease enough for him to consider opening his own workshop in the town. The accumulation of coins donated and Ethel's careful management of the money made such an enterprise a real possibility. Bordan's glassware could compete with the finest from Frankia and the only expensive item would be the powders used to tint the glass. One or two sales would allow him to reinvest in materials and his business would flourish. That was his plan, but he had been blessed and people would still come to seek him out as his small workshop flourished. He received a surprising number of commissions for glass bear statuettes. Ethel never ceased to remind him how hard life had been when she had had to lead him by the hand from village to village begging for alms.

Now, she even had shoes to protect her feet from sharp stones and she could let him out of her sight as he worked, whilst she went to market to buy fish, cheese, and fruit. The stallholders knew her as the glassworker's daughter and everyone treated father and daughter as befitting those blessed by God. Even the King of Mierce had wanted to hear from her lips how her father's sight had been restored. This audience occurred a few days before Ethel had to recite the tale in public at the consecration of the cathedral in Hereford to an ardent congregation. In a remarkably strident voice for a nine-year-old, she delivered her tale, enhancing it with the mournful details of the monstrous bear lurking in the undergrowth, only scarcely repelled by the king's brave spearmen.

The Bishop of Hereford conducted the service of dedication so that henceforth the church would be known as the Cathedral of the Blessed Virgin Mary and Saint Æthelberht Martyr.

FIFTEEN

Tame Weorth AD 794

Cynethryth found it difficult to disguise her favouritism for her only son, Ecgfrith, but among the three daughters, her best-loved was Ælfthryth, the youngest. She was, therefore, delighted to see her riding along the river with a small escort towards the palace earlier than expected. Pleased as she was, this unexpected turn of events bothered her. Why alone, not with her father or her betrothed?

She knew far more than she was prepared to reveal about Æthelberht's doom, so decided to keep her darkest secret well hidden, especially from Ælfthryth, who must never know that she was the victim of her mother's machinations. Thus, to see the two women so wholeheartedly embracing might have misled the sincere onlooker.

"What brings you so soon to Tame Weorth, daughter?"

"Oh, mother," she pressed more closely into her parent's comforting breast, "King Æthelberht met a terrible end, slain by a bear in the forest."

Cynethryth feigned shocked horror and even managed to weep in her daughter's arms, bathing the soft skin of her cheeks with her tears. Her strangled words were even more convincing. "A bear? But why did the king ride into the forest, and was he alone?"

Ælfthryth took a deep breath; now came the difficult part for her. "Alone, ay, for he had ridden to seek out an anchorite. Although your tears are shed most worthily for my poor Æthelberht, you should be glad for him because he is a saint in Paradise. Already, he has performed miracles." She related everything she knew to her astounded parent. When she had finished talking about the forthcoming building of a shrine, the queen held her daughter by the shoulders and peered into her eyes.

"My poor girl, you must be distraught. We are talking about Æthelberht, who lost his life, but what will happen to you, who have lost her betrothed?"

"Do not worry about me, mother, for I spoke with the same anchorite, who revealed God's plan for me."

"Are you to marry some prince from across the seas?"

Ælfthryth's tinkling laughter contrasted strongly with their earlier sombre mood, "Ay, mother, I am to be a bride, but this time, a bride of Christ. I, too, will become an anchorite, dedicating my prayers day and night to those who need them."

"Never! I forbid it. No daughter of mine will be sealed in a living tomb."

Ælfthryth held her mother tightly again and murmured, "Dearest mother, I have grown up in complete obedience to your authority. It pains my heart even to consider defying you because you have always known what is best for me."

Moved by these words, Cynethryth's blue eyes again filled with tears. "My sweetest child, do not allow the ravings of a poor demented soul to influence you. Just ask the question: would anyone sealed away from the rest of the world be in her right mind? Come to my chamber; I wish to show you something." The queen took her daughter's hand and led her through the door at the end of the hall and thence into her bedchamber. Against the wall was an iron-bound chest fitted with three locks. Cynethryth took a ring of keys from her pocket and, selecting a key, opened the first lock, which sprang open. She performed the same operation twice more. Gently, she lifted the heavy lid back, resting it against the wall.

Ælfthryth listened to the clinking of coins slithering over each other as her mother sifted among them.

"Ha! Here it is!" she cried, holding up a silver penny featuring a bust portrait of herself. "I am the only Anglo-Saxon queen, consort and wife, to have coinage struck in her name alone, Ælfthryth. What do you think of that?"

Ælfthryth took the coin in her hand and studied the obverse with the queen wearing a peplos-style tunic fastened with round pins at the shoulders. Her hair swept away from her face in stylized curls, and she wore a simple round diadem on her head. The whole effect was similar to that of a Roman empress. Wasn't it Helena, the mother of Constantine, whose image she had seen in the Tame Weorth library? She noticed the carefully hammered lettering 'Cynethryth Regina' running around the edge of the circumference. The queen studied her daughter's reaction as carefully as the young woman inspected the image of the coin. She watched her flip it over to admire the reverse, featuring a barred Mercian M with pellets around and within. There was also the inscription, Eoba, the name of the Cantwaraburh moneyer.

"It is a very impressive piece, mother."

"Ay, in itself that is true, child, but its real value to me is what it conveys to the simple man who takes it in his hand during his daily business. What does he see? The affirmation of his queen's power and of her alignment to the Roman augustae. Isn't that what I want for my daughter?" She tossed the coin, which landed with a satisfying clink among the others, and explained as she closed and locked the chest. "Ælfthryth, if we steer you in the right direction, you can become an empress and have similar coins with your bust impressed thereon."

Cynethryth smiled sweetly at her daughter. *An anchorite indeed, what nonsense!* and waited for a reply.

"Mother, it would seem very difficult for me to become a powerful and respected queen like you. I have lost my chance to become Queen of East Anglia," she sniffed.

It's only natural the poor child is still suffering, but she added aloud, "Poor angel! Don't worry, we'll find you a different suitable husband. You are young, and your father's prestige grows by the day."

"It will be as you say, mother," she lied. "Now, I must go and bathe to wash away the traveller's dust and change into clean clothes."

Some time passed before the queen came across Ælfthryth's chambermaid, carrying clean linen, in a corridor.

"Has your mistress finished her ablutions?"

The startled maid looked at a loss. She had not seen Princess Ælfthryth since she left for the royal vill at Sutton Walls and told the queen as much.

Suspicion clouded Cynethryth's mind and with it her temper rose. *Has the wilful child disobeyed me? I must hasten to her chamber.* The queen found no sign of her daughter there and, on checking her attire, could find nothing removed or out of place. *How dare she? She needn't think she'll get away with this! An anchorite indeed! But where?*

It was pointless fretting, Cynethryth decided. She would have to wait for Offa's return and then, her husband could call upon all his resources to run the princess literally to ground. Ælfthryth must have taken the horse she had arrived on. After inquiries, the queen discovered that her daughter had ridden off without an escort. *What folly! She has placed her life in danger. May God protect her! After all, it's thanks to Him that she's behaving like this.*

The Queen retired to her chapel to pray for her daughter's welfare.

As she rode north-eastwards, the princess's mind was in turmoil. Even to herself, it wasn't clear where the boundaries of obedience lay. She had always been a devoted and dutiful daughter, but the anchorite had been explicit, relaying God's instructions: *Go to the island Guthlac trod.* If she believed in the higher authority of the Heavenly Father, this was also due to her parental education.

As she looked anxiously all around her, for she had never ridden out alone any great distance, she prayed that He would keep her safe from outlaws, ruffians, and rapists. Her only means of defence was a dagger she carried at her belt and the fact that she was an excellent rider. She had to thank her father's gift of a pony on her fourth birthday for that. As the years passed by, she became ever more proficient until she achieved the unmatched task of dominating her father's unmanageable black stallion that only he could ride. Dominating was the wrong word—persuading—for when she whispered gently in its ear, it became docile and to everyone's astonishment, and Offa's pride, allowed her to ride him.

So, now, as she approached Minsterton Monastery, regretting only that she had not set off earlier, for it would not be long until dusk, she knew that she could deal with the threat of another rider, but a band of ruffians was another matter. The closing of the day brought her increased anxiety and led her to urge on her steed to greater efforts. Minsterton was within sight and the abbot would not refuse accommodation to a princess royal! She would reach her destination, Crowland Abbey, easily during the following day. God willing, she would arrive at Minsterton before nightfall. It would be a close-run thing! She could have stayed at Tame Weorth, slept in her own bed, and left with the dawn in the morning.

She smiled at the thought, knowing that her mistrust of her mother's intentions for her was well-founded. Queen Cynethryth saw her daughter as a pawn in a game of chess to be best utilised as a sacrifice for her overall game plan. Her mother would have found a way to keep her at Tame Weorth until the most desirable marriage occasion arose. Luckily, she had no idea of her destination; it could be in Wealas for all she knew!

She hurt her tiny fist hammering on the monastery door and with some relief saw a panel draw back to reveal curious eyes peering at her. In an imperious voice, she said, "You should fit an iron knocker to the door. I have hurt my wrist; now, let me enter, I am Ælfthryth, daughter of King Offa." The manner of her words was potent and the door swung back on well-oiled hinges, admitting the princess, leading her steed by the reins.

"Brother, I have ridden the poor beast from Tame Weorth. Do you have a stable for him? As for me, I beg for your hospitality for just one night as at dawn I must travel on eastwards."

"My Lady, I am Prior Ceatta and as Abbot Earcon's deputy, I am authorised to welcome you to our humble house. Brother! Come here! Take the lady's horse to the stable. See that it drinks and feeds and brush him down."

The monk obeyed his prior, a charismatic, commanding, though skinny figure, and led the weary beast to the stables.

An equally fatigued Ælfthryth trudged behind the prior but was soon restored to high spirits by the generous offerings provided by the kitchen. The monks' oven gave her warm crusty bread to pour delicious honey on, provided by their hives. As she ate, she responded to the prior's gentle questioning and was glad that her replies were sincere when he provided her with a detailed route to Crowland Abbey, which she memorised to perfection.

The bare cell the brothers gave her lacked basic comforts, but even the hard pallet seemed a luxury to her tired bones, so that within moments she fell fast into a dreamless sleep.

* * *

Back in Tame Weorth the next morning, Offa stared incredulously at his wife, "What do you mean she's gone off to be an anchorite? How could you let our daughter live like a badger in a sett?" He glared at Cynethryth with the thunderous expression she knew meant that he was losing control of his reason.

"Like you, I was set against it, but the crafty maid tricked me. She sneaked away when my guard was down and who knows what will happen to her now, riding alone to goodness knows where?"

"I will send men out to find her."

Cynethryth's lip curled, "Hopeless, she might be anywhere, not even in Mierce perhaps. You need a definite indication and there's only one who can provide it."

Offa's expression changed from bleak despair to slim hope. He would attempt anything to bring his beloved youngest daughter home. "And who is this person?"

"The same who planted the seed in her head—the anchorite at Sutton Walls."

Offa called for a beaker of ale and for the first time since his return, relaxed.

"I don't think that I can go bowing and scraping to this hermit," Offa growled, "Wouldn't it be better if a monk or a priest got it out of her?"

"A simple monk will do as well as a bishop or a *king*," Cynethryth said calmly. "Such as *she* is impressed by only one Master."

Offa supped his ale and then made arrangements for Thegn Grimbert to accompany a monk to the anchorite's cell. He told the thegn to stay away from the seer and to bring the monk back with all haste as soon as their conversation was over.

The journey from the royal palace to the hermitage was short, so even allowing for the monk to wait his turn to speak with the anchoress, the two men returned to the king before sunset.

The monk scanned the royal countenance because his message

was complex and bore within it an authority that one could not lightly use to address a king. The more he delayed, the more set the sovereign's jaw appeared. He gathered his courage and said, "Sire, I know where the Princess may be found, but the holy woman accompanied her information with warnings." He stopped, daring not to utter them.

"Well?" boomed Offa, "A messenger is never to blame, however unwelcome his message."

"Forgive me, Sire, but the anchoress stated boldly that it is God's will that must be done, not King Offa's. She warned that further interference might, in her words, send the cart veering off the straight road on which it is travelling. She was very insistent on this point and stressed that Eadwald should replace Æthelberht, oh, and that people should believe in the bear, lest—*ahem*—the cart veer into a swamp. Sire, the holy woman speaks in riddles."

"Riddles, nay, Brother, I understand her only too well," he exchanged significant glances with Cynethryth, "and I will leave my daughter to follow her calling. But tell me please where she has gone to ground."

"Ay, Sire, she has gone to Crowland in the Kingdom of Lindsey, to continue the work of Saint Guthlac."

Offa dismissed the monk and thegn and, when he was out of their hearing, turned to his wife. His expression was strangely indecipherable, "You understand what's going on here, don't you? It's a *quid pro quo:* God strikes a deal with Offa! He retains the services of our daughter in exchange for your brother becoming King of East Anglia."

"Mmm, a favour for a favour!" Cynethryth's face crumpled and she sobbed at the thought of her daughter entombed for life.

Moved, Offa stepped over to her and pressed her corn-coloured tresses into his barrel chest. "This is what we shall do," he murmured gently. "I shall summon Eadwald here and we'll lead a strong force into East Anglia, where he will be enthroned. On the way back, we'll deviate to Crowland and you will speak with your daughter."

SIXTEEN

Crowland Abbey, Kingdom of Lindsey and Dunwich, East Anglia AD 794

King Æthelbald chose Abbot Kenulph, a former monk of Evesham, as abbot for his Benedictine monastery at Crowland, newly founded in memory of his friend, Saint Guthlac, because of Kenulph's apparent meekness and spirituality. Therefore, the abbot, when approached by the Princess Royal, seeking to convince him of a lifetime entombment as an anchoress in Guthlac's cell, brought all of his virtues into addressing her plea. The forbidding gravity of the request had to be weighed against the earnestness of the young woman and, by her own account, the circumstances leading to her arrival at Crowland.

Kenulph refused to accede to her request on the instant, instead gaining time by requiring her to keep an overnight vigil with him before the abbey's main altar. As he prayed for guidance, the abbot occasionally cast a sidelong glance at Ælfthryth, and was impressed by her wakeful prayerfulness. After all, the poor young woman must be wearied by her journey, yet her resolve was clear to him.

With the first crowing of a cockerel at dawn, the abbot reached his decision, gently raising the princess, swaying with fatigue, and leading her to a cell where she could rest and recover for a few hours. He promised to give her his decision before midday if she agreed to sleep. Her body, rather than her mind, consented and, almost before he had closed the door on her with a benevolent smile, she fell into a deep sleep.

The kindly abbot returned to the chapel and, head bowed, expressed his anxieties once more. *Beloved Lord, I sought your guidance and heeded your reply. Your will be done, but I beg you to harken to my weakness of spirit, your humble servant. How can I, in all conscience, entomb alive a fair and regal maiden? She wishes to follow in the steps of Guthlac to best serve you. Dear Lord, please send me a sign, so that I am sure to be doing your will.*

On his way into the chapel, the abbot had noticed that it was one of those patchy days with scudding clouds that tended to obliterate the sunshine and reduce it to momentary shafts of light that illuminated details in the surroundings, a momentary brilliance of a mass of yellow flowers or the reddish stonework around an abbey window. So, it was, suddenly, through that very window, a shaft of sunlight pierced the chapel gloom, to illuminate the face of the statue of Guthlac whose radiant visage gazed up to that of the Lord, whose hand he was holding. This was the sign that Kenulph ardently sought. A fleeting confirmation of the Saviour's will before a cloud obscured the shaft of light but not the abbot's certainty. He was now sure that Princess Ælfthryth should indeed become an anchoress, according to God's will.

* * *

During the two days it took for the abbot to fulfil Ælfthryth's request and seal her into Guthlac's cell, King Offa led an imposing force eastward to the coast of the South Folk, to Dunwich, the capital of East Anglia. There, in the royal palace, he summoned the kingdom's lords to proclaim their new king. When the assembly had hushed in anticipation of Offa's words, the Mercian king announced in a ringing voice, "Lords, we were deeply saddened by the death of King Æthelberht whilst on a visit of betrothal to my daughter Ælfthryth."

"And how did this sudden death occur?" a white-haired ealdorman named Ordgar asked in a challenging tone.

"Without prior warning, King Æthelberht rode into the forest alone and met his doom at the paws of a bear."

"Is it usual for your guests to ride out alone into the forest?" Ealdorman Edulf, a giant of a man, scoffed sarcastically. "It is too convenient for Mierce to rid itself of our beloved king."

"*My guests* are not given to slipping away into the forest without forewarning, Ealdorman, and beware, I do not care for your insinuations."

"Yet, here is the King of Mierce, with an army, I'll wager to install his favourite on our throne."

"Watch your tongue, Ealdorman! I am here to ensure the continuity of the Wuffingas dynasty, which is what you all wish, is it not?" This remark caused much confusion and murmuring in the hall.

Ealdorman Edulf sneered, "You refer to your wife-brother, Eadwald, who will be your puppet! I, for one, will not stand by and see East Anglians become the servants of Mierce!"

"Then come forth and fight me!" Offa reached for his sword hilt.

Edulf made a fateful mistake; in his desire to catch Offa by surprise, he rushed forward blindly, sword drawn, and did not see a small three-legged stool in his way. He stumbled over the obstacle and fell sprawling at Offa's feet.

Before the horror-stricken gathering, the king of Mierce mercilessly plunged his sword, double-handed, with all his might, downwards between the sprawling man's shoulder blades. A collective gasp greeted this deed and even as he pulled his blade free and wiped the blood on the dead man's clothing, Offa challenged, "Will anyone else defy my choice?"

Silence reigned until the elderly Ordgar cried, "God save King Eadwald!" Offa sheathed his sword and grinned; East Anglia was now effectively his.

Three days later, a bishop crowned Eadwald in public and Offa left with his army direct to Norwich, the capital of the North Folk, largely to ensure that there would be no resistance in that quarter to Eadwald, but also because it was on his way to Crowland. He camped for two days outside the town, having received courtesy visits from the most important men of the region and ensuring that there was a universal acceptance for a Wuffingas king. Then he set off for the Fens and Crowland Abbey, where he encouraged his wife to visit Saint Guthlac's hermitage.

Horrified, Queen Cynethryth stared through the stone slat into the comfortless stone cell, once the abode of Saint Guthlac and now the habitation of her daughter. The queen gasped, but not even that sound issuing in the total silence made the neo-anchoress move from her huddled position and turn to face the narrow opening in the wall. She knew that there was another presence and uncannily, without looking, who it was.

"Mother, there is always a price to be paid for a crime."

"Ælfthryth, my angel, I don't know what you mean."

"Ah, but you do! It was *you* who arranged for the death of my betrothed."

"Have you begun your ravings so soon? It's inevitable, I suppose, shut away from the world like this."

"Mother, Æthelberht came to me in a vision and told me what you had done. Now you will pay."

A shiver ran down Cynethryth's spine, for there was no natural way her daughter could know the truth.

"How am I to pay?" Cynethryth's tone was acid.

"When father dies, which will not be so many years hence, you will found an abbey, become the abbess, and bring many young women to Christ. You will then go on a pilgrimage to Rome, but you will not come here again. Only then will your sin be expiated." Cynethryth's breathed apology and loving words were futile as she could not elicit another sound from her daughter, so she walked away with a heavy heart and tears coursing down her cheeks.

Offa and Cynethryth discussed the matter of their daughter deep into the night. Slowly, Offa came to realise that there would be no purpose served by visiting the anchoress. He confessed to his wife that maybe they had made a mistake by having Æthelberht, a good man, killed. Yet, as Offa pointed out, his primary concern as king was to secure the succession of his own heirs, and to deny any other potential claims from adjacent royal bloodlines who might seek the throne. In this respect, what he had allowed Cynethryth to arrange on behalf of Eadwald was no different from what other Anglo-Saxon kings did by murdering family members and any blood relatives who could claim the right to rule through familial inheritance. "However," he concluded, "I feel particularly at fault over Æthelberht and need to seek repentance.

I have an idea, but it will have to wait until I'm back in Tame Weorth."

"So," concluded Offa, "I will not discuss these matters with our daughter, who has taken leave of her senses. I shall not visit her but will return to Tame Weorth, where I shall dedicate myself to ensuring Ecgfrith's succession. Let it be clear, my beloved wife, my door is forever open to my dearest daughter should she repent of her choice. Go and tell her this before we depart."

Ælfthryth ignored her mother, making her disapproval of her conduct evident by keeping her back turned to the access slat. Queen Cynethryth's return journey to Tame Weorth was characterised by silent reflection. She drew her conclusions: her husband was now effectively ruler from Dumnonia in the south-west to Scotia in the north and this was what they ardently desired; their daughters were happily married except for Ælfthryth, who, in any case, insisted that she was—to Christ; Ecgfrith's situation needed attention as did her conscience and that of her husband.

On the latter account, Offa was the first to move. As soon as he reached Tame Weorth, he summoned the scholar Alcuin and spoke at length about his desire to found a monastery in expiation of an unspecified sin. Thus, it came about that Alcuin related the martyrdom of Saint Alban. "Sire, we have an early Christian martyr as yet unrecognised in our land and I believe his end merits a foundation such as you have in mind."

"Tell me about this saint, Father."

"Alban lived in Verulamium, during the third century after our Lord's birth. At that time, Christians began to suffer cruel persecution. Alban met a Christian priest, Amphibalus, fleeing from persecutors, and sheltered him in his house for a number of days. He was so impressed with the priest's faith and piety that he soon converted to Christianity. Eventually, Roman soldiers came to seize the priest, but Alban put on his cloak and presented himself to the soldiers in place of his guest. Alban was brought before a judge and was sentenced to beheading. As he was led to execution, he came to the fast-flowing river Ver, crossed it, and went about 500 paces to a gently sloping hill overlooking a beautiful plain. When he reached the summit, he began to thirst and prayed that God would give him drink, whereupon water sprang up at his feet. It was at this place that his head was struck off. Alban's head rolled downhill and a well gushed up where it stopped. Sire," Alcuin paused and gazed at the impressed king's countenance, "It would be glorious to build the monastery at the site of Alban's martyrdom."

"And that is what I shall do!" Offa bellowed, full of piety and enthusiasm. He at once made arrangements in the scriptorium for a charter to be drawn up. In it, he specified the land grant at Holmhurst Hill, the execution site, and construction of a double abbey, to follow the Benedictine rule, at the place to be known henceforth as St Alban's.

On the suggestion of Alcuin, Offa invested the saintly monk Willegod as the first abbot of St Alban's Abbey. This act of munificence and piety removed the ghost of King Æthelberht from his nighttime torments.

Having dealt with one priority, Offa turned his attention to another—his firstborn child—Ecgfrith. For some time, he had contemplated Charlemagne and his activities regarding his son. The Frankish king had his sons Pippin and Louis anointed kings of Italy and Aquitaine respectively by Pope Hadrian in a grand ceremony in Rome; the eldest son, Charles the Younger, had to wait because Charlemagne intended to become emperor before passing on his kingship. Offa had kept himself well informed of these procedures and once again, had to admit that the Frankish king had acted admirably to secure his dynasty. Offa wanted to do the same for Ecgfrith and with this in mind, contacted an old antagonist, the Archbishop of Cantwaraburh, Jaenberht. When requesting Ecgfrith's anointment, Offa quoted Romans 13:1-8 and Wisdom 9:1-12 in which Solomon is chosen by God as king, requesting wisdom to rule justly and wisely.

Whether Jaenberht took exception to a king quoting him the Bible, or more likely refused to break with the Anglo-Saxon tradition of a king being selected by the lords of the land post mortem of the current monarch, or again, his Kentish resentment of all things Mercian, he flatly refused to anoint Ecgfrith as Offa's successor.

A virtual war of letters to the pope ensued, Offa demanding that the diocese of Cantwaraburh be divided into two sees, one based in Lundenwic, and Jaenberht retaliating by initiating a rumour accusing Offa of conspiring with Charlemagne to depose Hadrian as pope, which luckily, the pontiff refused to believe. However, Jaenberht did write to Charlemagne, offering him Cantwaraburh as a base if he decided to invade Britain. When Offa learned of this proposal, he flew into a rage and declared war on the archbishop, who had once again minted coins with his archbishop image in Cantwaraburh.

Well aware of the strength of support he had created in Kent by giving confiscated lands to his favoured thegns, Offa would have taken up arms against Jaenberht, against Cynethryth's urgent pleas not to do so, had it not been for divine providence, for on 12 August, the archbishop suddenly died, mourned by many and, indeed, elevated to sainthood by the Church, although Offa was not among the mourners, nor convinced of Jaenberht's saintliness.

SEVENTEEN

Crowland Abbey, Crowland Fens, AD 795

The anchoress hissed like an angry cat on the defensive. "Mother, I thought I told you never to come here again!"

"But you are my daughter, and people speak of you as a great prophetess—"

"Perhaps it is as well that you have come so that you can prepare for the future of Mierce without *him*."

"You have been in seclusion for almost two years, and yet you pretend to know the future of the kingdom?"

"I did not ask you to come here; as I remember, I forbade it!" the anchoress said bitterly.

"Who are you to forbid your mother and Queen anything?"

"I am but God's humble handmaiden, and, ay, it has been two years, but I shall be in here for forty years, contemplating long after your death, mother."

"*Forty* years? You are insane!"

"Nay, no one is saner of mind than I, Queen of Mierce. So, let me tell you what you and your husband have achieved and will achieve, and at what cost, if you have the courage to look into the mirror."

"I am ready for whatever you have to say, daughter. I have but one sin to expiate."

"Which is more than can be said of my father! Even as we speak, you know well that he is engaged in a battle with the Wealisc, who dared to attack the new frontier in Tegeingl. Fear not, Mother, for your husband will win a great battle at Rhuddlan Marsh. Just think," she began to moan, and a wild look came into her eyes as she rocked, haunches on heels,"

Cynethryth leapt back from the slat, momentarily awed, but returned at once to call, "What ails you, child?"

"Naught. I have looked far into the future and ha-ha!" her laugh was sardonic, "father will be remembered most for a ditch! The famous *Offa's Dyke!* But never forget, Mother, what is written in Ecclesiastes 1:14," her voice rose harsh and condemnatory as she cited the Old Testament: *"In a word, all these things together are but vanity; satisfaction is not to be had therein: I have seen all the works that are under the sun, and behold! all is vanity."* She paused and her voice became gentler and more considered, "And yet, it is the work of a statesman to grasp the notion of a negotiated frontier—no other king had managed it," she said with an unseemly pride for an anchoress. "God will weigh the balance, but posterity will make judgment right or wrong on him. That I am here is thanks to his—and your—sin."

An involuntary groan broke from Cynethryth's throat and as the minutes passed, it became increasingly clear to her that her daughter spoke with an authority greater than that of an earthly princess. She, therefore, listened attentively.

"Mother, prepare yourself for widowhood, for I will give you the exact date and place. Father will depart this world soon, very soon. It will be on the twenty-sixth day of July at a place called Offley in the scir of Hertford. They will take his body to the banks of the river Ouse and bury him in St Paul's chapel near Bedford." Her voice broke, and as a good daughter, she sobbed, but as a saintly virgin, she crossed her arms tightly across her breasts and regained control, realising that her father's earthly travails would be over. Cynethryth, instead, shocked by the sudden imminence of the event, wailed and flung herself to the ground, burying her head in her arms and sobbing all of her deep regrets.

Almost as if Ælfthryth could see her through the solid stone wall encasing her, the anchoress paused to gather her thoughts. How best could she explain to her mother? If she could succeed in giving her a fair and well-balanced insight into her joint reign, perhaps her mother would be able to offer her undoubted talents to God's service. So, she gathered her thoughts and fought back her own tears, better to be lucid. She prayed for help and guidance and waited until her intuition told her she should continue.

"Mother, may I continue?"

"My sweet angel, I now understand for the first time why you have enclosed yourself within those walls: God has blessed you, and I surrender my daughter willingly to him."

"Thank you, Mother. I wish to return to father's legacy, for it is ambiguous and goes well beyond his ditch! The coinage you and he are so proud of, with some reason, based on the silver penny, will continue for hundreds of years until the reign of a king whose name," she sighed heavily and concentrated, for it meant nothing to her, "will be Henry, the third of his name."

She groaned again, and Cynethryth watched as her daughter's body convulsed and shook, "I told you that Offa was a statesman, and not just for the frontiers, but also because he has been the first Englisc king to play an independent part in continental affairs. Others will follow where he led. True, he failed to marry my brother to the Frankish king's daughter, but it was for the best. Father also understood," she now tried hard to help her mother cope with her mounting grief, "it is the duty of a king to encourage foreign trade," she laughed, "and Mother, that is something you will continue, but not as a queen, as an *abbess*. I'll explain later." She paused and was wracked by a deep and worrisome cough. *It must be cold within those walls; I'll bring her a sheepskin to enfold around her frail shoulders,* Cynethryth thought.

"Forgive me, as I was saying, it is the duty of a king to encourage foreign trade, even with places as far away as the Caliphate. Do you remember how he had gold coins struck especially to trade with the caliph's people? There is a good side to him, for he promised to send 365 mancuses to Rome each year for the relief of the poor—but it's his bad side too—it was a thank-offering to Saint Peter in gratitude for the victories granted to his kingdom. Father knew very well how to use the papal authority over the English church for his own political advantage. To his shame, he hated the saintly Archbishop of Cantwaraburh."

"Nay, Ælfthryth, I must disagree there, Jaenberht was no saint, but far more grasping and ungodly than your father, who was right to quarrel with him."

"I will seek guidance on that issue, Mother. But hark, I have spoken kindly of Offa hitherto; now I must balance it with a harsh judgment, so that you shall understand and draw conclusions that will help your own future."

"I am listening, for I know my husband is no saint."

"Unlike my betrothed," Ælfthryth could not restrain her bitterness. She ordered her thoughts and said: "Nine years ago, father had my brother, hallowed in what was the first consecration of an Englisc king. He copied the Frankish custom and all this in vain!" Ælfthryth screamed, making Cynethryth gasp and clutch her throat. "What is it?"

"Hark, God punishes those who break His commandments. My most noble young brother will not die for his sins, but the vengeance for the blood shed by my father has reached his son. For you know how much blood Father shed to secure the kingdom upon his son?" Ælfthryth wailed, adding: "This was not a strengthening of the kingdom, but its ruin! Father was driven by power and personal ambition rather than any sense of nation building and was feared as a vigorous king who terrified all the neighbouring kings and provinces around him; oh, Mother, that is why poor Ecgfrith will reign but 141 days. He will be seized by a malady and leave us in December of this year." She sobbed wholeheartedly, and Cynethryth would have given all her wealth to enter the cell to embrace and comfort her daughter, but truth to tell, she, herself, also was greatly in need of comfort. Her daughter had permitted her to glimpse the future in all its unveiled horror.

When at last, Ælfthryth recovered enough to continue, she said, "Need I quote the same passage of Ecclesiastes? Is it not in vain that Ecgfrith will rule but for five moons? By the end of the year, Mierce will pass to a distant kinsman, Cenwulf, who, as you know, is not the worthiest or closest of our kinsfolk, whom father had murdered in secret. Did you not procure the poison for some of them, Mother?" Cynethryth gasped. Could her daughter read within the darkest recesses of her heart? "Is it not in vain then, that Kent will rebel just before father's death? True, Cenwulf will suppress it, for father leaves a strong Mierce, but he will hand Kent to his brother Cuthred, so the kingdom of Kent will be independent of Mierce once more—all in vain! Father and Beorhtric drove Egbert into exile. Beorhtric will not long outlive father, and Egbert will return as King of Wessex—all in vain! Aargh!" Her scream startled Cynethryth.

"What now?"

"Next month! Mercian influence in Northumbria will end with the murder of King Æthelred. Oh, poor Ælfflæd!"

"All in vain, indeed!" Cynethryth muttered. "My poor girl," she referred to her second daughter, "what will become of her?"

Either the hermit had not heard or had not sought the answer, but as yet she did not describe her sister's fate.

"Now, Mother, I wish to speak of your future. As I told you, it is bound up with the church. You will no longer be queen, but you will have influence as a respected abbess. Seven years hence, there will be a provincial council of the Church at a place called Clofesho and there, it will be decreed that no power in church or state shall diminish the honour of Augustine's see of Cantwaraburh…Eek! The anchoress' scream resounded in the tomblike silence. It made the hair at the nape of Cynethryth's neck stand on end. "What is it?"

"Oh, Mother, a terrible, terrible deed, many years, perhaps three hundred ahead, the saintly archbishop of Cantwaraburh will be slain by the king's hounds"—her voice broke and she wailed—" three knights will cut him down in his cathedral nave. Poor Saint Thomas, I see his kindly face smiling at me!"

"But if he hasn't yet been born!" Cynethryth ran the nails of both hands down her cheeks in awe at the mysticism of what she was seeing and hearing.

"Mother, I understand your anguish, but I am telling you these things in order to deepen your respect for the Church. When you are abbess and the position weighs heavily on you, you may come here to seek me out and I will offer my advice."

"Daughter, where will I be abbess?"

"At the beginning of next year, you will establish an abbey, a double house, monks and nuns together, near Reading, in a village named Cookham in Berkshire. It is a pleasant place near the Thames on the contested boundary between Mierce and Wessex. As such, it will be of strategic importance, also for commerce. Remember, I said you will need to use your political and commercial skills. Oh, and one very important detail…"

"Ay?"

"Be sure to construct the abbey on the gravel island so that it will rise above areas subjected to frequent flooding."

"I will be sure to do so."

"Also, you must settle disputes in favour of the Church and remember, the calling of an abbess is to approach young women to godliness. *I have already done this if you are truly to stay here for forty years, my child. Oh, God, You move in mysterious ways!* She kept this thought to herself but on saying farewell to her daughter, added, "Apart from the Abbey, I will also take charge of the church at Bedford, where they will inter my Offa." With this resolution, she brought to an end the story of the most powerful royal couple in Anglo-Saxon England.

As prophesied by her daughter, Ælfthryth, King Offa died suddenly on 26 July AD 796, whereas Cynethryth lived on as an esteemed abbess at Cookham. Her death date was not recorded, but she outlived Offa and was likely buried at Cookham. Even though Cynethryth was in retirement in a monastery and had lost her power, she never lost her dignity.

THE END

Cynethryth's Silver Penny

NOTE

Historians once saw Offa's reign as part of a process leading to a unified England, but this is no longer the majority view: in the words of historian Simon Keynes, "Offa was driven by a lust for power, not a vision of English unity; and what he left was a reputation, not a legacy." His son Ecgfrith succeeded him after his death, but reigned for less than five months before Coenwulf of Mierce became king.

POSTSCRIPT

I have written this postscript for two reasons: first, I believe my readers will be interested to learn of the fate of Eadburh after the death of her father, Offa. Second, it's a wonderful excuse to refer you to the writings of fellow historical novelist and blogger Susan Abernethy, who shares my love of Anglo-Saxon history, not to mention the other periods she deals with splendidly. I have deliberately left the hyperlink, so just click on her name (below after the date) to explore her writings. What follows is entirely Susan's research and I am indebted to her for allowing me to reproduce it here. Had she not been so kind, I would have had to paraphrase and undoubtedly would not have done such a good job. Please read on:

Eadburh, Queen of the West Saxons

October 11, 2013November 12, 2016 Susan Abernethy

Whether she deserved it or not, Eadburh of the West Saxons is infamous for being an evil queen. She was the daughter of the powerful eighth-century King Offa of Mercia, who may rightfully claim to be the first King of the English. Eadburh perhaps was an ardent student of her father's politics or her reputation for wickedness may have been part of a smear campaign by later chroniclers.

Eadburh was the daughter of King Offa of Mercia and Queen

Cynethryth. King Offa had come to the throne after the murder of King Aethelbald in 757. During a period of civil strife in Mercia, Offa gradually consolidated his power there and in Wessex and Kent, Hwicce, and Lindsey. There is a lack of dependable contemporary records for Offa's reign but based on records from his later years, he seems to have ruled with a combination of military strength and competent negotiating. His consolidation seems to have been at its high point by 760 when he turned his attention to fighting the Welsh.

Offa's control of Kent allowed him to establish a trade route out of London along the Thames and also put him in contact with Canterbury and beyond. The kings of Kent had an established relationship with the kings of Francia and Offa may have instituted his own connections with the Frankish court around this time. He made an alliance by marrying Cynethryth, possibly a Mercian princess. Cynethryth seems to have wielded considerable clout at the court of Offa. Her likeness appears on coins from Offa's reign, one of the earliest woman's images to appear on English coinage. Cynethryth was ambitious and wanted to marry her son Egfrith to one of Charlemagne's daughters, an offer that Charlemagne rejected. Cynethryth is also blamed, rightly or wrongly, for the scandalous murder of (Saint) King Aethelbert of East Anglia in 794.

Offa arranged to marry his daughter Eadburh to King Beorhtric of Wessex in 789. Beorhtric had become king in 787 and this was a mutually beneficial political alliance. Beorhtric needed help in fighting off a claim to his throne from Egbert, grandfather of King Alfred the Great, and Beorhtric's eventual successor. They did manage to drive Egbert into exile to the court of Charlemagne.

The story of Eadburh is now taken up by Bishop Asser in his "Life of King Alfred". Alfred supposedly told the tale to Asser so he could record it. After their marriage, Eadburh quickly came to dominate Beorhtric, becoming active in politics and asserting her own rights. Beorhtric retained his title as king but all charters were issued in Offa's name so it's possible Eadburh was acting in her father's interests as well. While her father was seeking to suppress a resurgent Kent, Eadburh may have been keeping Wessex from challenging Mercia.

Eadburh's dominance supposedly went so far that she began to loathe any men that Beorhtric liked or trusted. She would denounce these men in Beorhtric's presence. She was called a tyrant. If she couldn't get her way through the king, she resorted to poisoning the food or drink of the hated councillors and others. Eventually there was a young man who became a favourite of Beorhtric. Eadburh denounced him but Beorhtric wouldn't give in to her. She decided to poison the young man but Beorhtric took the poison by mistake. Both the king and the young man died at Wareham in 802.

The death of her husband forced Eadburh's life to take a completely different turn. Egbert was recalled and elected King of Wessex so Eadburh was unable to stay. Her father and her brother had died in 796 so she was unable to return to Mercia. Asser says she packed up countless treasures and fled to Francia and the court of Charlemagne. It is unclear if the treasure consisted of what she owned or was part of the royal cache.

The legend goes on to state that Eadburh was bearing gifts before Charlemagne as he sat on his throne. Charlemagne supposedly asks Eadburh if she would choose between him and his son who was standing next to him. She said she would choose the son as he was younger. Charlemagne smiles and tells her if she had chosen him, she could have had his son. But since she chose the son, she couldn't have either one of them. Charlemagne then gives her a large convent of nuns over which she would rule as abbess.

Unfortunately, just as she had lived recklessly in England, she lived recklessly in Francia. Eadburh was caught in an act of debauchery with an Anglo-Saxon man and ejected from the convent on the orders of Charlemagne. She would live a life of poverty and misery until her death. She was seen at the end of her days, wandering the streets of Pavia in northern Italy with a single slave boy, begging. Her tomb in Pavia was reportedly shown to passing English pilgrims. King Alfred himself may have seen the tomb on his visits to Rome as a young boy.

ABOUT THE AUTHOR

Award-winning author, John Broughton was born in Cleethorpes, Lincolnshire, UK, in 1948, just one of the post-war baby boomers. After attending grammar school and studying to the sound of Bob Dylan, he went to Nottingham University and studied Medieval and Modern History (Archaeology subsidiary). The subsidiary course led to one of his greatest academic achievements: tipping the soil content of a wheelbarrow from the summit of a spoil heap on an old lady hobbling past the dig. Fortunately, they subsequently became firm friends.

He did many different jobs while living in Radcliffe-on-Trent, Leamington, Glossop, the Scilly Isles, Puglia, and Calabria. They include teaching English and History, managing a Day-Care Centre, being a Director of a Trade Institute, and teaching university students English. He even tried being a fisherman and a flower-picker when he was on St. Agnes Island, Scilly. He has lived in Calabria since 1992, where he settled into a long-term job, for once, at the University of Calabria teaching English. No doubt, his "lovely Calabrian wife Maria stopped him from being restless.

His two children are grown up now, but he wrote books for them when they were little. Hamish Hamilton and then Thomas Nelson published six of these in England in the 1980s. They are now out of print. He's a grandfather and, happily, the parents wisely named his grandson Dylan. He decided to take up writing again late in his career. When you are teaching and working as a translator, you don't have time for writing. As soon as he stopped the translations, he resumed writing in 2014. The fruit of that decision was his first historical novel, *The Purple Thread*. The novel is set in his favourite Anglo-Saxon period. Subsequently, he has published eighteen novels set between 450 and 1066 AD, including three trilogies, with Next Chapter Publishers. They also published *Angenga*, a time-travel novel linking the ninth century to the twenty-first. This novel inspired John Broughton to write a series of novels about psychic investigator Jake Conley, whose retrocognition takes him back to Anglo-Saxon times.

In order to put his writing versatility to the test, he embarked on a series of detective mystery novels set in London with the Metropolitan Police, who have to deal with a criminally insane serial killer in *The Quasimodo Killings*, *The London Tram Murders*, and *The Thames Crossbow Murders*. The latter was voted among the best twenty-five independent books of 2022. Heartened by this venture, he completed a fourth mystery, *The Thames-Tigris Connection*. To widen his experience of genres, he decided to write an apocalyptic novel entitled *The Remnant*, a science fiction novel. However, he returned to his first love with a historical saga, *Expulsion*, about the expulsion of the Vikings from Dublin and the subsequent diaspora. *The Reversed Hermit* is his first novella. Newly committed to historical fiction, he embarked on *Rhodri's Furies*, which is Book 1 of an early medieval Welsh trilogy, *The Bretland Trilogy*, of which *Avenging Rhodri* is Book 2, and *Hywel the Good* is Book 3. *The Wyvern's End* is Book 3 of the Wyrd Trilogy.

* * *

To learn more about John Broughton and discover more Next Chapter authors, visit our website at www.nextchapter.pub.

Printed in Great Britain
by Amazon